**NEW YORK REVIEW BOOKS**
CLASSICS

**BOMARZO**

MANUEL MUJICA LAINEZ (1910–1984) was born in Buenos Aires, Argentina—a city that one of his ancestors had helped to found. It was also the city where he was raised, though with long periods away in Paris and London, where he studied French and English. Not long after returning to Argentina, he dropped out of law school to pursue a career as a writer. Several of his novels revolve around the history of Buenos Aires, though he is perhaps best remembered for a fantasy novel, *The Wandering Unicorn* (1965), and *Bomarzo* (1962), which was awarded the John F. Kennedy Prize.

GREGORY RABASSA (1922–2016) was born in Yonkers, New York. One of the most respected translators of his generation, he brought the work of many writers into English—among them Machado de Assis, Julio Cortázar, Gabriel García Márquez, Clarice Lispector, and Mario Vargas Llosa. He was the recipient of the PEN Translation Prize, the Gregory Kolovakos Award, and the first National Book Award in Translation.

ÁLVARO ENRIGUE has been a fellow in the Sistema Nacional de Creadores de México, the Cullman Center of the New York Public Library, and the program in Latin American studies at Princeton University. He is the author of ten books of fiction and nonfiction, among them *Sudden Death*, *Now I Surrender*, and *You Dreamed of Empires*. He teaches at Hofstra University.

# BOMARZO

**MANUEL MUJICA LAINEZ**

*Translated from the Spanish by*
**GREGORY RABASSA**

*Introduction by*
**ÁLVARO ENRIGUE**

NEW YORK REVIEW BOOKS

*New York*

THIS IS A NEW YORK REVIEW BOOK
PUBLISHED BY THE NEW YORK REVIEW OF BOOKS
207 East 32nd Street, New York, NY 10016
www.nyrb.com

Copyright © 1962 by the estate of Manuel Mujica Lainez
Translation copyright © 1969 by Gregory Rabassa
Introduction copyright © 2025 by Álvaro Enrigue
All rights reserved.

Library of Congress Cataloging-in-Publication Data
Names: Mujica Lainez, Manuel, 1910–1984, author. | Rabassa, Gregory, translator. | Enrigue, Álvaro, 1969– writer of introduction.
Title: Bomarzo / by Manuel Mujica Lainez; translated from the Spanish by Gregory Rabassa; introduction by Álvaro Enrigue.
Other titles: Bomarzo. English
Description: New York: New York Review Books, 2025. | Series: New York Review Books classics |
Identifiers: LCCN 2025003832 (print) | LCCN 2025003833 (ebook) | ISBN 9781681379418 (paperback) | ISBN 9781681379425 (ebook)
Subjects: LCSH: Orsini, Vicino, 1523–1585—Fiction. | Renaissance—Italy—Fiction. | Sacro bosco (Bomarzo, Italy)—Fiction. | LCGFT: Historical fiction. | Novels.
Classification: LCC PQ7797.M74 B613 2025 (print) | LCC PQ7797.M74 (ebook) | DDC 863/.64—dc23/eng/20250310
LC record available at https://lccn.loc.gov/2025003832
LC ebook record available at https://lccn.loc.gov/20250

ISBN 978-1-68137-941-8
Available as an electronic book; ISBN 978-1-68137-942-5

The authorized representative in the EU for product safety and compliance is eucomply OÜ, Pärnu mnt 139b-14, 11317 Tallinn, Estonia, hello@eucompliancepartner.com, +33 757690241.

Printed in the United States of America on acid-free paper.
10 9 8 7 6 5 4 3 2 1

# CONTENTS

Introduction · vii

1. The Horoscope · 7
2. The Uncertainties of Love · 84
3. The Appearance of Magic · 171
4. Giulia Farnese · 225
5. The Duke of the Cats · 281
6. The Portrait by Lorenzo Lotto · 321
7. A Wedding in Bomarzo · 358
8. Orazio Orsini · 425
9. The Accursed War · 502
10. The Sacred Wood of the Monsters · 563
11. My Lepanto · 623

# INTRODUCTION

IN JUNE 1962 Manuel Mujica Lainez—then fifty-two years old—might have been regarded as a writer past his prime in a country going through a period of brilliance like no other national literature in Latin America has ever seen. On a wet, cold, gray day that austral fall in Buenos Aires, one could see Jorge Luis Borges and Adolfo Bioy Casares having lunch in the Florida Garden restaurant. Two blocks down, at San Martín 689, Victoria Ocampo would be discussing the contents of the next issue of the magazine *Sur* with José Bianco. (In 1962, Graham Green, Jean-Paul Sartre, Malcolm Lowry, and Saint-John Perse were among the non-Spanish-speaking contributors.) In San Telmo, Ernesto Sábato would be having a glass of wine in the Bar Dorrego—maybe satisfied with the critical success of *On Heroes and Tombs*. Julio Cortázar was not in Buenos Aires in 1962, but in Paris he may well have been dining with Alejandra Pizarnik, as he and Aurora Bernárdez did frequently. Pizarnik had just published *Diana's Tree*, and Cortázar's *Hopscotch* was soon to roll off the presses. Antonio Di Benedetto, ignored by all because he lived in Mendoza, had already published *Zama* and was at work on *The Silentiary*.

In the midst of this experimental writing frenzy, Mujica Lainez must have seemed like a writer looking backward. Before the publication of *Bomarzo*, he'd been considered a Gallicized realist who'd transplanted the Proustian mode into roman à clef studies of the Argentine criollo elite. His cycle of novels about the children of local patrician families—*Los ídolos* (1953), *La casa* (1954), *Los viajeros* (1955), and *Invitados en El Paraíso* (1957)—reads today, as it surely did at the time, as a project closer in spirit to the decadence of Huysmans's *À Rebours* than the earnest vitalism that could be breathed in Argentina.

When *Bomarzo* appeared, Mujica Lainez had not published a book in more than five years. During that time the political map of Latin America, and the world, had taken a Copernican turn: Fidel Castro and his Argentine friend Ernesto "Che" Guevara had secured a previously unimaginable victory in Cuba, and readers were more interested in a new, revolutionary humanity than in the declining last survivors of the aristocracy that had founded, designed, and ruled Argentina—with some populist interruptions—since its independence in 1816.

Yet *Bomarzo* was a success. It came out under the very prestigious seal of Editorial Sudamericana, won the National Literature Prize of Argentina, and shared the Kennedy Prize with *Hopscotch*. Whereupon Cortázar fired off a telegram to Mujica Lainez from Paris proposing to make a book together named *Bomscotch*, maybe *Hoparzo*. (Not many writers could boast that Cortázar recognized them as equals.) Meanwhile, at a banquet in Buenos Aires, Borges gave a speech comparing *Bomarzo* to James Joyce's *Ulysses*. The book earned Mujica Lainez the Order of the Merit of the Italian Republic, and it was published in German and English (in Gregory Rabassa's vigorous translation, reprinted here) at a time when the circulation of Latin American literature in other languages was not at all common. In 1967 the novel was given a second life as an opera—by Alberto Ginastera, with the libretto written in verse by Mujica Lainez himself—which opened to critical acclaim in the Lisner Auditorium in Washington, DC.

*Bomarzo* has hardly ever been out of print in Spanish and today can be read in the canonical Colección Austral, as well as in a more recent edition brilliantly introduced by Mariana Enríquez, who sees the book as one of Latin America's contributions to the fantasy genre. The novel, after all, can be read today as an unknowing precursor to *Interview with a Vampire* or *The Rocky Horror Picture Show*. It is also a clear antecedent to the explosion of queer literature in the region. It would be hard to imagine the writing of masterpieces like Reinaldo Arenas's *Hallucinations*, Sergio Pitol's *El tañido de una flauta* (sadly untranslated), or Fernando Vallejo's *Our Lady of the Assassins* without the successful circulation of Mujica Lainez's novel.

\*

*Bomarzo* tells, in first person, the life story of Pier Francesco Orsini from the moment of his birth, when his horoscope predicts eternal life, to his last transit—or whatever it is that happens to those with the Draculaesque gift of immortality. The young Vicino (as his family called him) is second in line to inherit the title of Duke of Bomarzo, but he is the polar opposite of what is expected from a male of his lineage. The Orsini—and this is a historical fact—were a family of condottieri: commanders of private armies that, for a hefty fee, served princes, emperors, and popes. Mercenaries, but of the highest noble condition.

A "hunchback" whose body is ill-adapted to physical action, Vicino has a traumatic childhood. Mocked, bullied, and tormented, he becomes a ruthless politician. When he inherits his father's title, he uses it to wage war not against other armies but against all conventions, rebelling against everything from normative masculinity to Catholicism to the inevitability of death. The span of his years and the privilege of his parentage allow him to bear witness to such extraordinary events as the coronation of Charles V, the battle of Lepanto, the decadence of the Medici, the rise of the Farnese, and the most glorious hours of the Serene Republic of Venice. As he moves restlessly through Italy, Vicino comes into contact with Giorgio Vasari, Benvenuto Cellini, Lorenzo Lotto, the alchemist Paracelsus, Miguel de Cervantes, and a long lineup of cardinals, popes, and princes who gave us the gift of modern sensibility during those final, convulsive years of the Renaissance. In his retirement, Vicino oversees the design of the dreamlike gardens of Bomarzo—the Sacro Bosco—studded with mannerist sculptures.

Whatever Borges said at the banquet in Buenos Aires was never published, though parts of it seem to have ended up in a note he wrote later about Mujica Lainez's novel *The Wandering Unicorn*. Two people, nevertheless, did record their impressions. Bioy Casares, whose dislike for Mujica Lainez ran deep, noted in his journal that Borges's speech was brilliant. He does not make clear why but notes that the author of "The Aleph" spoke about the influence of Ludovico Ariosto's *Orlando Furioso* on modern novels. An anonymous note about the event also appeared in *La Nación*, written by a harried reporter unaware of the importance of what he saw then for future nerds like us. He tells us that Borges's comparison of *Bomarzo* to *Ulysses* had to do with dimension.

Not with the number of pages but with the effort to represent a complete universe in tireless detail, as the great epics do, from *The Odyssey* to *The Aeneid*, the Viking sagas and the Arthurian tales, and, of course, *Orlando Furioso*, which crops up again and again in *Bomarzo*. All of them are books that contain everything their authors knew about their subject matter—and life.

Mujica Lainez confirms what Borges sensed in a note written at the end of the manuscript of *Bomarzo*, completed on October 7, 1961. He says that, as empty as he feels at losing the company of Vicino Orsini, and knowing that he would always miss him, "to have finished the novel feels like an enormous relief." He also says that he will never again write "a novel as vast, as arduous, as demanding as *Bomarzo*."

The book was written by an author with a firm, steady hand. The manuscript (and it is truly a manuscript, handwritten from start to finish) begins as the printed novel does, with the horoscope of Pier Francesco Orsini and its strange promise of eternal life. The first attempt—one paragraph—is crossed out. Then come three more false starts, but by the fourth we find ourselves in the novel that would be published three years later. The manuscript fills three notebooks, 708 pages of meticulous longhand. There are crossed-out lines and insertions, but not many. In addition to the three notebooks that compose the novel itself, there are another seven (hundreds and hundreds of handwritten pages) filled with notes, chronologies, family trees, biographies of every historical character—no matter how small its incidence in the novel—and long critical meditations on the books he read in order to construct the consciousness of Vicino Orsini. The notes devoted to *Orlando Furioso* could be a short critical book in their own right. Also, of course, there is a handwritten encyclopedia of the influential personalities, noble families, and ruling cities as they existed during the sixteenth century.

*Bomarzo* is a book full of Italian Renaissance gossip in which most of the characters are who they were historically: popes who were thieves, bishops who fathered many children, princes who were assassins, poets and artists as skilled at their craft as they were at the more complicated art of surviving an era in which the infliction of pain and the desperate rush for power or pleasure had very few moral constraints.

The seventh notebook is composed of additions: sentences and paragraphs, organized by page, to be inserted in the manuscript when it was transcribed on the typewriter. And then there are the notes on the final architecture of the book, which sounds, sometimes, more like a cathedral than like a novel. These notes are the descriptions and personal—and only personal—interpretations of the nineteen sculptures and monuments of the Sacro Bosco of Bomarzo that are the organizing principle of the story, each piece a reference to a plot-changing event in the life of Vicino Orsini. After this narrative map of the Sacro Bosco that is also a map of the novel comes the list of the eleven titles of the book's eleven chapters.

Yet *Bomarzo*, though it seems to meet most of the requirements expected of heavily researched fiction set in the past, is not a historical novel but a fantastical one. It is another example of the delicious, if sometimes confusing, freedom that Latin American writers have taken with material from other traditions. It is less that Mujica Lainez had the experimental impulse of Boom writers like Carlos Fuentes, José Donoso, Juan Carlos Onetti, Gabriel García Márquez, and Julio Cortázar, and more, I think, that he was forced to deal with precarity and he did so splendidly.

When, in 1952, Mujica Lainez visited the Sacro Bosco of Bomarzo for the first time, the garden was in a state of abandonment that made it look more like the ruins of a monstrous, extinct civilization than the touristic Renaissance traipse it is today. There is a very accessible film in which Salvador Dalí visits the Park of the Monsters just a few years earlier and its state of abandonment is notorious. The same was true of the biography of the man who designed the garden: it was overgrown with vegetation, and almost nothing was known about him. Mujica Lainez was thus free to imagine a literary Duke of Bomarzo, incarnating the contradictions of his period. A tremendously powerful man who felt like a victim due to his physical disadvantages. A shy, sensitive noble of vulnerable sexuality, but also a cold-blooded murderer and rapist. A man of enormous ambition who could never get over his childhood. A luminous patron of the arts attracted to everything occult, dark, and demonic.

\*

It was after the publication of *Bomarzo* in Italian, and perhaps partly because of it, that the Sacro Bosco became a place of interest not only for tourists but for historians and scholars. Documents lost for almost half a millennium were found: birth and marriage certificates, legal and commercial affidavits, and a good number of letters written by, to, and about Pier Francesco, in the archives of Viterbo (the municipal seat, not far from Bomarzo), as well as in Rome (there were Orsini popes and bishops, and an Orsini palace in the Eternal City) and various academic institutions overseas. (One important collection of letters written by Pier Francesco was discovered in the custody of the University of California in Los Angeles.) We now know who he was: a very rich and successful condottiere with a taste for earthly pleasures; a man uninclined to the occult and, as far as it is possible to know, to queer practices. We even know how he looked: There is a medal with his portrait in the holdings of the British Museum, which Mujica Lainez never saw and which today anyone can access online. A number of serious critics and excellent readers still assert that he was the model for Lotto's *Portrait of a Young Man*, a whimsical touch that Mujica Lainez decided to add after a visit to the Accademia in Venice, where the painting is on display.

Mujica Lainez's sources were touchingly poor: an issue of *Quaderni dell'Istituto di Storia dell'Architettura* published in Rome in 1955, the autobiographies of Cellini and Vasari, and an edition of *Famiglie celebri italiane* published in Milan in 1918. In addition to these few publications, the author also mentioned, in an interview given two decades after the novel first appeared, a topographic study of the Sacro Bosco and a brochure written by the parish priest at the local church. In the same conversation, he confessed that he had visited Bomarzo only twice, and only for one day in both cases: first as a simple tourist in 1952 after reading a newspaper story about the Bosco, and again when he was already writing notes for the novel. On this second trip, thanks to the intercession of the Argentinean ambassador in Rome, he was permitted into the palace of Bomarzo—at the time closed to the public—and the chapel, where he saw the skeleton with a "crown of withered cloth roses" that would become essential to the novel's plot, one source of the trauma that would make Vicino a stranger to mercy.

INTRODUCTION · xiii

Mujica Lainez used to brag, and I find no reason to doubt him, that when the sculptures and paths of the Sacro Bosco were restored and became a frequent stop for visitors to Lazio, the local tourist guides described Pier Francesco Orsini as the bisexual alchemist tormented by an imperfect body that Mujica Lainez had invented in his book. If nothing else, the novel was effective: In his article about visiting Orsini's "deliberately discordant" gardens, published in *The New York Review of Books* in 1972, Edmund Wilson bought Mujica Lainez's version of the hunchback duke hook, line, and sinker.

The biggest influences on the novel, however, are literary. Reading Cellini's *Life* in the light of *Bomarzo*, one gets a bird's-eye view of Mujica Lainez's workshop. The naturalness and even lightness with which the Argentinean author describes the brutal life of a man of the cinquecento comes directly from Cellini, who narrates the siege of Rome as if it were a *calcio* match in which, now and then, some of the players were blown to bits by the enemy's cannons.

There are also more transparent borrowings. In Cellini's book, a courtesan named Pantasilea makes a passing appearance. Later, Cellini is invited to a dinner and shows up with a young man dressed as a woman; the courtesan, his lover at the time, is also at the dinner, which leads to an enormously violent scene. In Mujica Lainez's novel, Cellini tells the same story after dropping a quick, intriguing kiss on Vicino's young lips. As *Bomarzo* progresses, Pantasilea grows to monumental proportions, becoming an emblem of the duke's troubling relationship with sex and beauty. He makes her a grotesque allegory of decayed glamour—a monster—as he does with the stones of his garden, his lovers, and everything else he touches.

Something similar happens with the character of Giulia Farnese, the historical Duchess of Bomarzo. Not much is known about her except that her husband dedicated a temple to her in the Sacro Bosco. Mujica Lainez, nevertheless, appears to take biographical details about her famous great-aunt of the same name—a sister and lover of popes—to produce a magnificent portrait of a serene, resentful duchess in whom all the perversions and servitudes of an esteemed Renaissance lady are carved with believable detail.

This recycling of historical materials, multiplied by the dozens of characters developed in *Bomarzo*, produces a mimetic effect. The reader spends the days or weeks it takes to finish the novel submerged in an enormous fresco governed by a subtle design in which every major event in the life of the young and brilliant Pier Francesco Orsini finds a bizarre echo in the obscure years during which he constructs his garden. His wedding with Giulia Farnese repeats itself as comedy in the wedding of Pantasilea. The pitch-black moment in which he inherits his father's title after a series of horrid crimes and dark-arts plots is offset by the luminous coronation of Charles V. His father's Spartan court turns vaudeville when, in his later years, he becomes a patron of mediocre poets and artists who leech all his money. His second wife, rich and vulgar, is the polar opposite of the first duchess's distinction, just as Paracelsus's elegant opacity is a better version of the paltry resident magician and alchemist whom the duke can afford.

In "Odysseus' Scar," the imposing first essay of *Mimesis*, Erich Auerbach proposes that European realism issues from two sources: on the one hand, the very dry telling of biblical stories, in which nothing is visible—no landscapes, no descriptions of characters, no temporal frames—except the action of the main characters; on the other, the Greek epics, in which every detail of every scene and every feature of every character is visible under the zenithal light of Homer's style. It may have been this second filiation that made Borges think of *Bomarzo* and *Ulysses* as consummate examples of a modern epic. Mujica Lainez's imaginary Vicino Orsini could not be further removed from his true, historical character. But the historical character's adventures, whatever they were, could never be as revealing of the ambiguities and contradictions of the human condition as the mythical Vicino—no more than a historical Achilles could achieve the capricious pathos of Homer's creation. For all its darkness, Mujica Lainez's Duke of Bomarzo is a lantern that illuminates the place and period that brought us modernity and, as such, our tenebrous but also brilliant little lives.

—ÁLVARO ENRIGUE

**BOMARZO**

To
the painter Miguel Ocampo
and to the
poet Guillermo Whitelow,
with whom I was in Bomarzo,
for the first time,
July 13, 1958.

                        M.M.L.

Sappi ch'i' fui vestito del gran manto;
E veramente fui figliuol de l'orsa...

*Inferno*, XIX, 69–70

# 1. THE HOROSCOPE

*Niccolò Orsini's astrologer—My family—The hunchback—The imposed female masquerade—The skeleton—My father and Michelangelo's David—Etruscan Bomarzo—A meeting with Benvenuto Cellini—Exile to Florence—The two pages*

SANDRO Benedetto, physician and astrologer to my kinsman, the illustrious Niccolò Orsini, a condottiere who after his death was compared to the heroes of the *Iliad*, cast my horoscope on March 6, 1512, the day on which I was born, at two o'clock in the morning, in Rome. Thirty-seven years before, on the same March 6, but in 1475, also at two o'clock in the morning, Michelangelo Buonarroti saw the uncertain light of the world for the first time in an Etruscan village. The coincidence was nothing but a fortuitous accident of hour and date. In truth, the stars that presided over our respective appearances on life's chessboard had arranged their players for quite different matches. When Buonarroti was born, Mercury and Venus were in the ascendant, triumphant, naked, facing the throne of Jupiter. It was the dance of heaven, the mythological contradance that welcomes creators who touch divinity. Glory awaited the person who first opened his eyes underneath that splendor which transformed the firmament into a brightly lit salon, all candelabra, with the god floating among them in the transparent glow of the atmosphere, stately and dignified. When I was born, however, Sandro Benedetto pointed out important contradictions in the cartography of my existence. It is true that the Sun, in the sign of water and strengthened by my good position in respect to the Moon, conferred upon me occult powers and a vision of the beyond along with a vocation for astrology and metaphysics. It is true that Mars, the basic ruler, and Venus, the occasional one of House VIII,

Death, were located, according to what Benedetto strongly emphasized, in the House of Life and removed from death; and that fact, along with the favorable aspect of the Sun and the Moon, appeared to bestow a limitless life upon me—something which puzzled everyone who saw the ornate manuscript—and it is true that Venus, well situated opposite the luminaries, indicated a facility for subtle artistic invention. But it is also tremendously true that malevolent Saturn, aggressively located, foretold infinite misfortunes for me, unable to be neutralized by Jupiter, whom the ungrateful planetary arrangement had not seen fit to use. What particularly surprised the physician Benedetto and all others aware of these grave matters who saw the horoscope, was, as I have said, the resultant mystery of the lack of any end to life—my life—which was deduced from the removal of Venus and Mars from the logical necessity of death and, consequently, the supposed and absurd projection of my existence for a limitless period. I know that some experts criticized Benedetto's tedious study, the beautiful signs and figures of which I had had copied a half century later in a fresco in one of the main rooms of the castle of Bomarzo, and they judged that his sketch was impossible; but the author's wisdom, demonstrated so many times, kept their carping mouths shut.

My father, also a condottiere and a famous one, revered the memory of his uncle, the great Niccolò Orsini, who had fought equitably and indifferently according to the terms of the contracts he signed with various public governments in Italy, sometimes in favor of, sometimes against the Aragonese, sometimes in favor of, sometimes against the Venetians, and who, between one battle and another, when he should have been resting and taking the waters, had taken time to kill his stepmother Penelope and his bastard brother for intimate reasons too long to go into. That just and personal suppression of infamous relatives had contributed much to the respect in which my father held him, for also, as a man of the same calling, he had a professional admiration for the commercial and martial efficiency of his deeds. For that reason, although of a brusque and ill-tempered nature, my father, Gian Corrado Orsini, accepted with noble courtesy the horoscope of Sandro Benedetto, the astrologer whom Niccolò had always consulted. What was most obvious was that the horoscope did not interest him in the least. Nor did it interest him that I had been born on the same day as Michelangelo Buonarroti; that my horoscope was stranger than that of the master; stranger and richer too than those of the Emperor Augustus, Charles V, and the future Grand Duke Cosimo, who had the singular situation of Capricorn ascendant, much appreciated by specialists. He simulated a discreet urbanity and it did not go beyond that, because in such things he shared the ironical disbelief of Pico della Mirandola, whom he had known as a boy in the court of the Magnificent. Pico della Mirandola, author of the *Disputationes adversas astrologiam divinatricem*, had more faith in the prognostications of villagers with respect to the weather—villagers who would announce that a storm was coming because the flies were annoying an ass—than in the reports of official astrologers. My father too. Five years earlier my older brother, Girolamo, the one destined to succeed him as Duke of Bomarzo, had been born. In his case, that of the first-born, my father would have been interested indeed in Benedetto's work in spite of his skepticism, and he would have asked a hundred questions and would have turned the matter over in his mind a hundred times, but it was a question of me, Pier Francesco, and I represented very little for the family and for his proud paternal egotism. My mother, who like him belonged to the House of Orsini, but to the Monterotondo branch, died the following year, when Maerbale, the third and last of her offspring, was born, so that my father was widowed for a second time—he had been married for the first time to a daughter of the Count of Anguillara—and he did not remarry.

I came into the world during a time of violence. During that year of 1512, old Julius II, the terrible, tireless pope who, in spite of the Gallic ailment and the gout, which wrenched his body, would drag cardinals, princes, and leaders along on wild rides, and who lived among soldiers, the sheepskin he wore over his cuirass greasy with blood and mud, had swapped his warlike weapons for those of astuteness and pretended to be dead, using the trick of the fox who passes from stiffness to the bite, in order to attract to Rome those hostile prelates who, in line with foreign aims, had met in council in Pisa. When he had them in his power, he terrorized them and reduced them to obedience. During that year Pandolfo Petrucci, the tyrant of Siena, died, and no one wept over him, for his life had been full of crimes. After a long republican interregnum the Medicis returned to Florence, also during that year, with their two future popes and their two insipid and elegant dukes, the "Pensieroso" and his uncle, who contemplate each other for eternity on the tombs done by Michelangelo; and Machiavelli retired unwillingly to meditate on Livy's decades and plan his portrait of the Prince, the breviary of wise perfidy. That year the Sultan Selim I ascended the throne, the parricide poet who killed his entire family and lived only to make war. And Europe shuddered in panic. The most illustrious of the ancestors of poor Toulouse-Lautrec (who had inherited, if not his physique, his disdainful lordly audacity), Odet de Foix, Viscount of Lautrec, in whose ranks my father had fought, was gravely wounded in Ravenna that year. That year saw the death of Gaston de Foix, a young nephew of Louis XII, with fifteen wounds on his face, and the king lost Italy. All Italy was resounding and flashing with the clangor of armed clashes. And that year Alessandro Farnese began to show his claws, the one who was to be Paul III, who had received orders as deacon. But also during that year, six months after my birth, Michelangelo Buonarroti had taken down the scaffolding that encircled the paintings of the Sistine Chapel like protective wooden dikes; he descended, like a hermit prophet emerging from his long confinement, and the creation of the world was revealed, powerful, glorious, voluptuous, intimidating in an impassioned linking of agile and young muscles, to the stupefaction of the pontifical court who would go into battle shaken by the constant presence of death and rancor in the military camps, as they saw up there, up, up, over the twisted profiles, over the painful necks, over the panting of their breath, in all of its robust confusion, a multicolored sea of foam about to burst forth, shouting, roaring, free of the dikes and the broken-nosed magician who had immobilized it, over frenetic Italy, the orphan of God.

Paradoxically, while the peninsula was involved in struggles that were as bloody as they were useless, my warlike family was entering a period of rest. Pope Julius II had obtained in 1511 what his holy predecessors had not managed: the Pax Romana—as it was called—between the rival stocks of Orsini and Colonna, so entwined by numerous marriages, as he gave the hand of a niece of his to Gian Giordano Orsini, and that of another niece to a Colonna, and established the post of attendant to the throne, held in turn by a Colonna and by an Orsini, as the sole representatives of the nobility. A curious medal was struck at the time which bears the obvious allegory of a bear embracing a column. The bears of the Orsinis and the columns of the Colonnas were united at last. My maternal grandfather, Franciotto, the cardinal, was one of the signers of that memorable peace, immediately after which the tumultuous Roman patricians who used to pour into the chapels of the Vicar of Christ during the great ecclesiastical ceremonies, shouldering away with feudal pride the princes of the Church and trampling the purple robes under their iron heels, to occupy the most important places in the presbytery and from there, with their prayerful hands together and their disdainful lips tight, to cast haughty looks at the faithful, were required to retreat and group themselves behind a railing, because only an Orsini and a Colonna, alternately, could exhibit their martial arrogance in that privileged place. Satisfied in that way, the rivals calmed down, while the rest clenched their fists along with the ancient disputes that the Frangipanis, the Tebaldeschis, the Alberinis, and the Annibaldi della Molaras had carried on behind our flags; while the Colonna war cries led the Contis, the Cesarinis, the Marganis, the Corraduccis, the Porcaris, and the Capoccis, the disputes that had stained the streets of cities and the bluffs of the castles, and gave way miraculously now that the ancestral bear of the *editus ursae* and of the *filii ursae* (as we took pleasure in calling ourselves) embraced the heraldic column... perhaps, who could tell, repressing inner urges to knock it over, for it showed the same live-and-let-live enthusiasm with which Fabrizio Colonna and Giulio Orsini had embraced and publicly patted each other on the back and had left buried in the bonfires of the past the battles between Guelph and Ghibelline.

Two centuries earlier a similar agreement had been sought without success when Napoleone Orsini and Stefano Colonna, young and ardent, in the church of Santa Maria in Aracoeli, went through the strange rite, during the course of which twenty-eight noblemen prepared for them in the midst of the nave a bath sprinkled with rose petals and two perfumed beds on which the young knights rested the entire night, so that on the following morning the festivals and tourneys could begin which would lead the people to think that peace had been established between their wrathful chiefs. The hope had not lasted long that time, but now it had, and evidently the desired concord had been attained, and it took place during the moments I was arriving in the world, in Rome—and therefore the poet Betussi would later sing with courtly exaggeration, giving a great deal of pleasure to my hungry vanity, that the Tiber could boast that I had been born near its banks, near the church of Santa Maria in Traspontina, where I was baptized.

That church was a few steps away from our palace, a dark palace with rooms like dungeons, hung with somber tapestries on which one could barely make out the hieratic figures, and which no longer exists, because in 1527, when Rome was sacked by the Spaniards, many eminent families abandoned the city, taking refuge in their villas and castles (some of the Orsinis were settled in Viterbo at the time), and my family established themselves in Bomarzo. Bomarzo has always been my home. I do not recognize any other. Furthermore, the craggy neighborhood between the Castel Sant' Angelo and the Vatican, where our palace stood, was soon one of the poorest and least populated in Rome. Our dwelling—unlike the Torlonia palace, which belonged to Leo X, and that of the Knights of the Holy Sepulcher, the property of Cardinal della Rovere, which are still in the neighborhood—changed with the passage of time and lost all trace of grandeur, until its last anonymous remains disappeared in 1937 when Benito Mussolini ordered the opening of the Via della Conciliazione, which gave a clear view of Saint Peter's, demolishing between the Borgo Nuovo and the Borgo Vecchio the narrow Spina di Borgo. I would be guilty of a lie if I said that I lament that disappearance. My home, my marvelous home was Bomarzo. The memories that I still have of the palace in Rome are still limited to damp rooms which no fireplace, enormous and crackling as it might have been, could have hoped to warm; to some narrow windows through

## THE HOROSCOPE · 13

which the wind slipped in, making the tapestries quiver and animating the ghostly scenes for my superstitious anguish, as if it were really taking place there and those beings and monsters were the only living things in the great house; to some ancient armor and tattered banners hanging on the walls under which, in the glow of the logs on the fire, like another specter, the fearful shadow of my father passed back and forth; and to some icy corridors through which my brothers Girolamo and Maerbale, growling like wolves, would chase me and threaten me with pikes and rapiers that were yellow with rust.

There is one thing, however, that must have reconciled in me the fright of those memories which still intimidate me as I recall them today—and years and years and years have passed since I left those accursed quarters forever—and that is the memory of my grandmother.

My paternal grandmother was named Diana Orsini, and she was the widow of her uncle. Just as I do not recognize any other home but Bomarzo, I do not recognize in my veins any other blood except that of the Orsinis, except for the contribution of the Colonnas, who, battling tirelessly inside of me with their age-old rivals, must have contributed to my unbalance. Those Orsinis mixed with Colonnas, dueling in my body, which they twisted and tortured with invisible, remote hands, waged in the secret galleries of my insides, without anyone's being aware of it, with no one but me feeling and suffering from the violent battle, their atrocious fights. Sometimes I think that if I suffered because of the irregularities I brought into the world—it is difficult for me to use the word deformity—it is due to that mingling in which, with disproportionate insistence, there predominated the flow of one blood (that of my grandfather, Girolamo Orsini; that of my grandmother, Diana Orsini, daughter of Orso Orsini, Lord of Bomarzo; that of my grandfather, Cardinal Franciotto Orsini) as it coursed through my weak flesh, and I think that if my brothers were saved from the stigma it was because a cruel and wild fate, sensed by Sandro Benedetto when he cast my horoscope, had designated me, in spite of the victory of my incomparable future, to bring together and share destructive inheritances that were not distributed elsewhere. In any case, in spite of that minimal participation of the Colonnas, I have been a pure Orsini, too pure, and from being so, I brought with me the curse that lies in wait for lines whose Pharaonic vanity makes them feel themselves somewhat divine and which, with an illusory Olympian restlessness, somewhere between religious and fatuous, surrounds the descendants of the incest, which in reality they consider as the only form capable of their worthy perpetuation.

Had my grandmother Diana been different from what she was, I do not think that I would have survived my years of infancy. In the midst of my bitterness and resentment, her stupendous beauty which had not diminished with her great age, and the fervent love in which she wrapped me, illuminated and made my childhood glow. Nobody has loved me so much, nor has anyone given me such a deep proof of love as the one I shall describe later, and which, if it does show an unexpected aspect of harshness, a terrible coldness toward my brother Girolamo, whom she detested—as he detested her, as I detested him—affirms her solidarity with me and her unmovable zeal to sacrifice anyone, when the occasion arose, in favor of her grandson Pier Francesco Orsini.

I can see her, intact, luminous, transparent, over the immense distance of time, crossing the rooms of the Roman palace, conjuring up with her appearance the elves and vampires that inhabited it. I can see her leaning on the terraces of Bomarzo under a round parasol, or walking through the Italian garden of the villa amid the geometric stonework, so radiant that her blue eyes were brighter than the jewels she wore on her hands and on her breast, and her skin, glimpsed under the veil that protected her from the air, seemed to distribute a soft clarity as she passed, as if all of her were a lamp of glowing alabaster. When Benvenuto Cellini told me that when he came out of the prison of the Castel Sant' Angelo there had been a halo around his head and that he could show it to his friends at will, I immediately thought of my grandmother. Her image is inseparable from the idea of light, radiation. Her name was Diana, and like Diana she had a majestic bearing. She walked as if she were gliding along. She would go down the steps at Bomarzo accompanied by her ladies in waiting with an opulent rustling of the long gowns which reminded one of the archaic fashions of the times of Lorenzo the Magnificent, the family pearls trembling at her throat, and it was as if Diana

Artemis, she of the determined expression and the firm step—a very old and a very young Diana—were preparing to leave for a hunt among her excited nymphs. It was she who told me, during the evenings at Bomarzo, stories of my line; she who inculcated in me the pride of race, which stimulated me through vicissitudes; she, in truth—she and the inexorable secret that we shared—who made me Duke of Bomarzo; she who alleviated the affliction that my physical state caused me, and who gave me the courage to go forward along the path through the dark woods.

My Roman and country childhood and, after my return from Florence, the short time during which I enjoyed the affection and pity of my grandmother in the refuge of Bomarzo were peopled with the dynastic figures that she spoke of. At that time there was no archivist or historian as adept as my grandmother Diana in chronicling our family and in dedicating herself to pass it on to me, for I was very small, knightly deeds along with barbarous crimes, attempting in that way—that was what I came to realize when I was older—to shore up my weakness with the glorious and tragic models that would warm me like vintage wines and make me face up to the labyrinths of existence with the proper virile daring of my caste, efficiently infusing me, beyond morality and the conventionalisms that we revere, with an invulnerability that came from the certainty that whenever I undertook a magnificent deed or followed through with an obligatory violent crime, I would always be in the right, for it was enough for me to search my memory, the rich store of ancestral tales, to find some opportune antecedent that would corroborate and justify my attitude if I had need of such. An original pedagogical method like that molded my personality in a curious way. One must not forget, of course—I must vindicate my adored grandmother—that the bases of conduct in those days were quite different from those of today, and what is condemned today was not in the sixteenth century. Therefore, for example, my father, my grandfathers, and my great-grandfathers had all been condottieri. The condottieri commerced in war as others commerced in wheat. They feathered themselves like pheasants, they covered themselves with armor forged by fine goldsmiths, but what they were, nothing more or less, was efficient merchants of war who rented out their military merchandise to the highest bidder. No patriotic ideal guided them in their actions, and according to how the political balance moved with regard to supply and demand, they had no difficulty in switching allies in the middle of a campaign in accordance with their monetary interests. It should not be thought, however, that I am speaking this way out of hatred for my father; that was how things were and no one would have thought of changing them, even though numerous cities suffered the consequences of that uncertain system. Venice had found no better way for protection against treason than to contract the services of a number of condottieri, calculating that this would hinder deceit and desertion and facilitate, by means of denunciation, their discovery in ample time. I have already noted that Niccolò Orsini, Count of Pitigliano, had backed the Aragonese and the Venetians in turn. My father, Gian Corrado, had contracts with Brescia and the Friuli; he was with the Medicis in 1478 during the conspiracy of the Pazzi; he served Bartolommeo d'Alviano when he went to the aid of Pisa; he took part in the defeat inflicted by Bentivoglio; he guarded Monopoli in Puglia in 1528 alongside Lautrec under a contract from Venice. He was valiant and astute. He knew how to obtain his contracts. He would go hither and yon with his men shining of sweat and steel, black and heroic scarabs on the roads of Italy, abandoning the imperial highways to take twisting paths that would lead them suddenly and unexpectedly to the places under siege. That was why I saw so little of him. It was rare for him to be in Rome or Bomarzo. More than once, late at night, as the fog covered the feudal acropolis of Bomarzo, I would sit up in my bed and peep out of the half-open window toward the roads leading to Orte or Viterbo and watch his impressive return amid the disheveled flames of the torches, the noise of horses, harnesses and hoofs, and the husky voices of command that rang out in the quiet of the countryside over the murmur of the brooks; and out of the distance from the scattered houses fearful lights would creep in, announcing that the master had returned from the wars.

The stories of my grandmother Diana which fascinated me most were those that dealt with the origins of the clan. I was especially enchanted by those which, as they ascended the river of my blood, would finally reach in their long journey the magical instant of that primordial totem, the Mother Bear to whom we owe our name, the mythology where men and beasts were genealogically entwined, joining us to the legends of the gods and making us somehow in that initial alliance with the dark forces of nature gods too, blood brothers of the fabulous beasts who had reigned in the world when fragile man had hidden from the gigantic and implacable monsters, when only divinities had dared confront them. That was how my imagination, aroused by my reading of myths, interpreted the stories my grandmother told.

Our earliest ancestor, a Gothic chieftain, had a son who had been suckled by a bear and who was named Orsino. We were his descendants. The milk of the Bear nourished our blood. Or we descended from Caius Flavius Orsus, a general of the Emperor Constantius. It could be. But the Bear belongs to us. No one can take her from us. We have not incorporated her into our coat of arms—a shield with a rose and a serpent—but we have preserved her, multiplying her into the two bears that hold up our shield, the supports as they say in heraldry. We are *editus ursae*, those engendered by the Bear. The bears who hold up our shield serve as support for us too, like black allies linked to the Orsinis in an immemorial pact. In Bomarzo, when I could not sleep because doubt kept me awake and I would go out to stroll through the corridors that were dimly lit by dawn's hesitation, I would hear cushioned, silent footsteps, like those of one afraid of making noise and giving himself away, and they went along with me on my nocturnal walks. They were the bears, the guardian bears of the Orsinis, whose shaggy fur was disguised by the shadows of the galleries. They followed me softly, cautiously, enormous and mute. They watched over me. I never succeeded in seeing my secret escort. Once I thought I could make out the flash of teeth, of claws. I jumped over, but all I saw was dusty shadows. A few days ago I read a poem by Victoria Sackville-West which describes an identical feeling. In the castle of Knole, the leopards on the coat of arms walked behind her—"velvet footsteps"—just as the bears of our arms (the bears and not the serpent; the bears, the bears) walked behind me in Bomarzo. There is a form of other-worldly faithfulness that only the elect can perceive. I felt it. I enjoyed that strange privilege.

The Massimis claimed to descend from Q. Fabius Maximus; the Mutis from Mucius Scaevola; the Cornaros from the Corneliuses; the Antinoris from Antenor, a prince of Troy; Pope Pius II Piccolomini from the Juliuses perhaps; the Colonnas—always exaggerating—from Julius Caesar himself. It was the fashion of the time, the same fashion that led the patricians of those houses to have their busts made with the adornments of Roman emperors. They all wished to be descended from some illustrious, some most illustrious person, the mention of whom would help them tread firmly on the land across which their purported ancestors had trod in their togas and with their legions. We had our Caius Flavius Orsus, it was explained, a general of the Empire. But just as Romulus and Remus had their Wolf, we had our Bear. Bears are fearsome. I would not exchange our Bear for a double eagle even, or a phoenix, or a griffin. The Devil changed into a bear in order to kill Pope Benedict IX in the depth of the woods, and according to what we can see in primitive Christian art, the Devil's appearances as an animal are limited to four determined figures: the lion, the basilisk, the asp, and the dragon. It was necessary for him to change into a bear in order to murder a pope. The prophet Daniel mentioned a bear among the chosen beasts when his vision spoke of the four realms of the Earth. There are bears too, Ursa Major and Ursa Minor, in the heavens. I hope that my bearish pride will be forgiven, but I consider bears to be kinsmen and they are very important to me. After all, my pride can be forgiven, for it rests upon a special sort of snobbery which afflicted us (and exalted us) the same as everyone, great and small, during that time, and which has not lost its influence in the world as it continues to develop, even in Communist countries.

I remember coming across a phrase by Eugenio d'Ors somewhere in which, speaking of the Renaissance, he declares that it was a time of purely aristocratic vocation, and he points out that any artisan, goldsmith, forger, or printer would not rest until he had obtained a certificate of nobility from the authorities of his guild. It was asserted that the great Michelangelo was descended from the line of German emperors; my friend Benvenuto Cellini claimed to be descended from one of Julius Caesar's captains, the one for whom Florence is named; my friend Paracelsus—of whom I shall speak at length later on—the son of a modest physician of Einsiedeln, swore that the blood of a prince, of whom his father was the natural son, flowed in his veins; Girolamo Cardano, physicist, mathematician, and half-wizard, traced his origins to the proud family of the Castigliones; Ariosto to that of the Aristeis; Giuseppe Arcimboldo, a prestidigitator of painting, the inventor of "composed heads" and mannerist allegories, boasted that in his line there were at least three archbishops, reposing together in a marble tomb in the Duomo of Milan, and he would not give up until Rudolph II of Hapsburg made him a count of the Palatinate. Who would find it strange, therefore, that we Orsinis insist on our Caius Flavius Orsus, on our Mother Bear, and on our Gothic chieftain, the conqueror of the Vandals, with such confidence and ease? My grandmother told me those tales from the moment when my eyes of understanding were opened, along with many others concerning our Roman descent. They have meant for me—fulfilling in that way Diana Orsini's refreshing hopes—a protection that was necessary for my fateful life. The auxiliary bears, my invisible aides-de-camp, were always near me. They are still near me. Let me render here the tribute of my gratitude to my grandmother and to those immaterial and affectionate monsters. With her prideful insistence, which many readers will judge bold and demoralizing (primary school teachers particularly, if there are such among my readers), Diana Orsini furnished me with what nature had denied me: a security in myself, in my own strength, which, since it was lacking in me, I had to seek in other forces, real or fantastic, until I could afford myself a vigor and a faith that came, if not from me, from a mysterious cohort, as old as the history of my family, which gathered about my weak figure the breastplates of Constantius and Theodosius II, who had anointed us princes, along with the papal tiaras of Celestine III, Stephen III, and Paul I, the last two both saints, and Nicholas III, the one who dreamed of dividing Italy up among his Orsini nephews, and the mantles of the endless flow of queens from our house, queens of Poland, Naples, Hungary, Thessaly, Castile, and Empresses of the West, and swords brandished by the Orsini warriors who made Italy tremble with the brazen noise of their parades and skirmishes, tracing a wide, seven-colored frieze which encircled my timidity and my exhaustion, a frieze in which there stood out above the crowns, scepters, croziers, flags, and stiff-plumed helmets the swaying figures of the black bears as they rose up in their supreme and fearful majesty.

I think that the time has come to deal with the theme that I have avoided thus far and which, as one of the most important, I should have dealt with at the beginning of these memoirs. I refer to the theme of my physical appearance. I shall reveal it right off, all at once, with no roundabout expressions, even though it pains me, for it is a difficult thing for me to do. Here it is: When I was born, the family Aesculapius in charge of easing my entry into the world noted an anomaly on my back, one brought on by the curvature and deviation of my vertebral column toward the left side. Then, as my body grew and took shape, it was certain that there was a hump, a hunch, a protuberance, call it what you will—I said it, I said it—a deformation to which another was added in my right leg, obliging me to drag it slightly, something the Aesculapius in question had not noticed at first.

People who have written about me with aulic rhetoric have prudently kept quiet about those defects. If I detail them it is because they help to explain my character and because it is a matter most essential to me. What is certain is that in Sandro Benedetto's horoscope, where he sketches the promise of life with no fixed end, there is, on the other hand, no mention of the role that the stars may have played in the disorders of my malformed skeleton. Some artists have limited their praise to my soul—and on doing so they fell into an adulation as absurd as those that ludicrously extolled my body, but at least they did not contradict the obvious—and so Annibale Caro termed me a "good lord," and Betussi called me a "true friend of men and of God," while Francesco Sansovino spoke of my "honorable presence" and, going further, of my "regal appearance." Of course, without saying so openly, I must have influenced the last one. Sansovino understood my urge to be praised for my physique, my weakest point, and he proceeded with courtly eloquence. And there has not remained for the future a single trace of such obvious and pathetic irregularities; not even in the marvelous portrait of me by Lorenzo Lotto in the Academy of Venice, one of the most extraordinary effigies ever known, in which my back and my legs do not figure at all, where the brushes of Magister Laurentius, I was twenty years old at the time, emphasized the best I had—now that I have mentioned the bad, I must mention the good as well—my pale, thin face, sharply outlined by the edges of my cheekbones, my large, dark eyes and their melancholy expression, my thin, tremulous, sensitive hands, of admirable design, all of which leads a critic (who could not have imagined that the figure was the Duke of Bomarzo, as no one has suspected and which I publish here for the first time) to refer to me, wisely, sensing me with startling psychological penetration, as the "Despair of Love." That is how I see myself when I cast my eyes upon the reproduction of the portrait that hangs among the books in my study—the original is far away, alas, and can no longer ever belong to me, and no scholar would ever take my word that it is I, Pier Francesco Orsini—and I discover a romantic relationship between the image and the *Desdichado* of Gérard de Nerval, so much abused by the attention of literary commentators: *"le ténèbreux, le veuf, l'inconsolé, le prince d'Aquitaine à la tour abolie."* It enchants me, even today, to seek out similarities along those lines, possible affinities that I may have with mysterious and ill-fated heroes, with "interesting" people, because if not for purely physical reasons, the enumeration of which has been so painful to me, for others, more subtle—and ones also linked to definite aspects of my traits and my grace—I became aware from the time when I first began my journey through life that I should use this imponderable attraction to compensate for the disadvantages of my hump and my leg.

As I was quite small and obsessed with my congenital inferiority, I made an effort to disguise it by all possible means, rehearsing in front of the mirror the most favorable poses and angles. I would spy on myself in the mirror in my grandmother's room in Rome, and I would see myself floating, impaired, sickly in that greenish light that hovered about the rooms of that gloomy palace, the same color as the tapestries, the furniture, the portraits, and the canopies, an unreal haze that had been torn into transparent strips that were not of that time but something out of the Middle Ages, and it would remain there flickering in the bedrooms, where in the corners it would settle down and never escape from its glacial enclosure, and it would envelop us, old and young, and infect us with a strange glow. I would straighten up, raise my head, place my hand on my waist... On more than one occasion my brothers had caught me that way, and that cruel persecution of which they had made me the object would flare up again amid their mocking shouts. My horror of ugliness and my passion for beauty in human beings, in objects, in poetical games, had produced disappointment and bitterness in me, but it had given my life an exalted tone and a certain tormented grandeur: it came from a horror of myself and the resulting disgust caused in me by any teratological aberration. When my grandmother—whose beauty had worked upon me before I could grasp the value of her love—would speak to me of Elisabetta Gonzaga, the Duchess of Urbino, whom she loved and admired in a singular way, and she would tell me how much she had been amused by the dwarfs who had been part of her retinue and with whom she had romped in the famous library of the Montefeltros—those dwarfs for whom she had ordered built to size a chapel and six rooms—she thought she was amusing me and, yet, sitting in the shadows beside her bed, I would shudder with revulsion.

Among the feelings I am evoking I must trace the roots of the enthusiasm that I shared with so many of my contemporaries for evidences of classical antiquity. Those feelings too, as I shall clarify later on, are affirmed in the paradox of the Sacred Wood of Monsters that I put together in Bomarzo. My Renaissance contemporaries sought out the noble vestiges of previous cultures, moved by the Hellenic and imperial imitations that characterized the time; by the urge to learn about and set up the canons of the exact beauty that the Greeks and Romans had propagated; or simply by the aristocratic ambition of having unique and coveted works in their possession. I did it for more complex reasons. Perhaps I had hoped that the nearness of those harmonious survivors would be some kind of magical therapy for me; perhaps I had calculated that if I sank into a sea of beauty, surrounding myself with rhythmic marbles until I disappeared behind their intertwined appearances, in the midst of something motionless and fragmentary, where every item, the smoothness of a brow, the arc of an arm, the proportions of a chest, would arouse the emotions that joined poetry to mathematics, it would succeed in making me forget about myself.

The disdain which my father showed toward me, for he had become convinced of his inability to correct my malformed body, was as vehement as the love shown me by my grandmother. Gian Corrado Orsini could not resign himself to a hunchbacked son, and instead of helping me forget my imperfections, or at least have them less present and in my nightmares, he never ceased to remind me of them, pitilessly, with a grimace, with a rapid blink, with a distasteful shrug of his shoulders, when chance would bring us together in one of the great rooms in Bomarzo or in Rome. That was why I would avoid him, that was why I would be so happy when I heard in the courtyard of one of our houses the preparatory sounds that foretold his departure on some military expedition. Disappointed, irritated, that aggressive man about whom it was whispered in Bomarzo there hovered so many ferocities and injustices, constantly proclaimed that he had but two sons: Girolamo, the future duke, and Maerbale, whom he planned to give to the Church, with the help of his father-in-law the cardinal.


I should dedicate some special paragraphs to my grandfather Franciotto, who along with my grandmother Diana was the only direct blood relation I knew from that generation, for my other grandfather and grandmother had died before I had come into the world. Franciotto Orsini had been a condottiere like most of my forebears. He had grown up in Florence at the court of his uncle, Lorenzo the Magnificent, and his contact with that refined and esthetic milieu, even though it softened his ways and imbued him with a certain courtly dandyism which came to serve him well in the pontifical environment, did not penetrate the glacial regions of his soul. He was, like my father, his son-in-law and nephew, an insensitive person. In 1497 and 1503 Cesare Borgia had captured him and then given him back his freedom; in 1511 he had signed the Pax Romana with the Colonnas; in 1513 he fought against Bentivoglio. Twice widowed, he ended up by abandoning his armor for the purple, which his cousin Leo X awarded him in 1515. From then on he dreamed of becoming pope.

We Orsinis had not had one of our own on Peter's throne since the death of Nicholas III in the thirteenth century and our prestige demanded it. Our finances as well. My grandfather Franciotto thought that he was the one most indicated to make up for that serious lack, and he set about to crown his apostolic ambition with the same drive that he had put into his warlike ventures. He almost obtained the tiara in 1522, but they unexpectedly elected Adrian VI; the following year his arrogance of a great Roman nobleman received another affront when Clement VII ascended the throne. He was never able to console himself for those outrages. Passing him over, the son of Orso Orsini, called the Organtino, a captain who had shown his courage in favor of and against the Church, and the grandson of Giacomo Orsini, a condottiere of the Most Serene Republic and of Pope Eugenius IV! And passing him over with no sense of the worldly hierarchy or the prerogatives of blood for the benefit first of a ridiculous Fleming, whom everyone laughed at, and then to favor an illegitimate Medici, a bastard of that Giuliano de' Medici whom my father had almost saved from death during the conspiracy of the Pazzi! It was something that Cardinal Franciotto Orsini could not comprehend, because it went against the healthy logic of his set of values. His despair and disillusionment had been even greater at the elevation of Clement VII, because that time they had practically taken out of his mouth the sweet that he was preparing to savor. It was all the fault of Cardinal Pompeo Colonna, who vetoed his candidacy, putting the inflexible weight of its enormous influence in opposition. The Colonnas were always crossing our path. How my father and my grandfather spoke about the Colonnas that afternoon, how they cursed them!

"But," Cardinal Franciotto pointed out, lowering his voice, "don't think that things will go well with the one who snatched the tiara from me thanks to that infernal Colonna. Not for a minute. A ragged shepherd from Abruzzi is walking through the streets predicting the imminent extermination of Rome. And people say that he is a saint."

The miraculous breeze floated over them for a second. They did not dare to think that what they were seeing in their imagination—the city sacked, burned, the pontiff in flight—would soon be an atrocious reality. Then my grandfather picked up the thread of the story again. He wanted to poison Cardinal Pompeo, but he lacked the decisiveness. That was what he was like: a tiger on the field of battle, and in conclaves, a hare. They swamped him, they laughed at him. He would roar like a bull in the intimacy of our home and return to the pontifical court, where he took great pains to mend the torn fabric of his intrigues. After a time he would come back to us with fresh hopes that my father did not always share. They would argue until late in the night, and when my father had retired, half intoxicated, the old cardinal would smooth his disordered cape and hide hesitantly in the shelter of the fireplace, muttering confused words, and he would only grow calm as he caressed his victorious dream, which showed him in the red and golden licking of the fire the form of the tiara which was ascending like a church cupola covered with precious stones—the sapphire, which grows pale in the presence of the impure; the emerald, which crumbles in the sight of an illicit act; coral, which fortifies the heart; chrysolite, which cures melancholy; the diamond, which saves one from fear; and that sacred stone, blue and green, of the Egyptians, which has more supernatural power than any other—jewels that sparkled in the crackling fire, promising him with their bright winks that Nicholas III and the holy popes of our line who had preceded him would have in him, Pope Franciotto, an august successor for the House of Orsini.

The real reason for his resolve not to abandon his ambitions is that he felt himself predestined to realize the highest aspiration of Nicholas III Orsini and to divide Italy among his descendants, just as the Holy Father had planned to divide it among his nephews, ringing the Papal States in order to strengthen the peninsular and ecclesiastical power against foreign rapine, and also, with farsighted nepotism, in order to assure his own exclusive power. I do not know whether or not there was something for me in the division envisioned by my grandfather. I think not. Everything would have been for my father, for Girolamo and Maerbale; perhaps for the grandsons of the other branch: Francesco, the one who defended Siena, conquered Corsica, and married a woman who was so virtuous that she was considered a saint; Leone, the millionaire, the richest member of the family; and Arrigo, the condottiere, the bandit, who committed fierce excesses. But there would be nothing for me, nothing. I am sure of that. Nothing for Pier Francesco, nothing for the cripple, for the one who in his jerkin and tights, in spite of the distinction of his face and his hands and in spite of the fact that he towered in front of mirrors, looked like an Orsini jester, a kind of Rigoletto without a voice and without the credentials of a baritone.

Until my grandfather unwillingly gave in at last, for events were disillusioning him and repeating to him that this was not his destiny, and that it was easier to flourish a sword and roar in the midst of a battle, with banners and beards waving in the wind, than to speculate in the subtle secrecy of conclaves, and he transferred his intentions onto the shoulders and the mind of my younger brother, little Maerbale.

As before, my father and the cardinal would shut themselves up and argue for hours. I was so young at the time that I cannot remember, but I have heard the servants speak of it. Then they would go over to Maerbale, thin and delicate, and they would rock him in his cradle for an instant, almost with respect, as if instead of his infantile hair they were stroking the liturgical robes of the Vicar of Christ. But Maerbale would not be pope either, nor even a cardinal. It would be necessary to wait a long time, two centuries, until 1724, for an Orsini, Benedict XIII, to restore the supreme hierarchy of the Vatican to us. Of course, neither Franciotto nor Gian Corrado could have guessed it, and they conspired impatiently in the solitude of the house, surrounded by the coats of mail, the helmets, the breastplates, and the swords on which the fire was being reproduced with its heated brushes, all of which knew better than anyone of the ancient martial glory of the hand-to-hand combat that both had seen. As support for the success of their maneuvers they shuffled the names of the saints and the holy men of our tribe, from Bishop Orsino, the martyrs Giovanni and Paolo and the Patriarch Benedetto, up to Queen Batilde and Cardinal Latino, that son of Mabilia Orsini, who left for all times his composition of the dramatic *Dies irae, dies illa* of the response, adding to them as a bargain the names of the four popes who up to that time had figured on our genealogical parchments. They thought it was inadmissible that with antecedents like those being tirelessly listed one after the other, alternating wrathful outbursts with formulas of elegant irony that both had learned in the court of the Medicis, and with forebears such as cardinals, archbishops, senators, prefects, and gonfaloniers of Rome, constables of Sicily, and grand masters of the Templars and the Order of Saint John of Jerusalem, without neglecting our queens, of course, so decoratively gothic, that the tiara should not come flying through the air like a solid gold bird with bejeweled reflections to alight upon the weak and frivolous head of Maerbale, not mentioning that Franciotto himself, a cardinal deacon and vicar of Stimigliano, Vianello, and San Polo, had not succeeded in spite of his stubborn insistence and the kinship that had linked him to Leo X.

So that two factions had grown up in the family. On one side were my grandfather, my father, and my brothers; on the other my grandmother and I. It must be stated that the first was the stronger. In its favor were not only the resources of numbers but influence too. The harassment with which they encircled me ever since my childhood, no matter how much I turned the matter over in my mind, was something I was never able to understand at that time. What did I represent for the cardinal; for the condottiere; for Girolamo, athletic, handsome, muscular, petulant, obtuse, impudent, and despotic; for Maerbale, troublemaker, hypocrite, trickster, but also charming, resembling me very much in his eyes and the arrangement of his features? What did it matter to them? Why would they not leave me in peace, for I did not bother them, but on the contrary, I always avoided them, letting my lonely hatred ripen in solitude? Did not the future belong to those who were going to be a duke and a cardinal? Had my nullification not been taken into account; had it not been calculated that because of my fragile condition I would not live for long? And how mistaken, how fantastically mistaken were the four Orsinis in that matter, because who would ever suggest to them the extravagant and outlandish idea that someday (now) I would be writing about them, while they would be dead, quite dead, reduced to dust, covered by four centuries of death and oblivion and with no one to remember them! But that incredible distance in time which separates us allows me to probe with more clarity and experience into the dark dilemma and discern some explanations.

Basically, it is obvious, they were offended by my appearance, as it showed me to be an intruder, unworthy and shocking, in the divine race of the Orsinis, who were men born for the rhetorical grandeur of equestrian statues, for the pomp of theatrical sepulchers, and to inspire respect and submission with nothing but their regal bearing. There were no hunchbacks among the Orsinis. There was the scarcely mentioned and fleeting exception of my cousin, Carlotto Fausto, but he had stood out for his bravery in the militia. My father looked upon my twisted figure as a crime of lese majesty against the decorum and lordly position of the family. One day, hiding behind a tapestry, I heard him debating with my grandfather over the problem that my presence aroused at every moment. They were shouting like people possessed. Each blamed the respective branch of the Orsinis to which the other belonged for the decadent responsibility of my formation.

Gian Corrado mumbled, stroking his beard, "We've never brought offspring like that into the world. It must be the work of the Devil. Or foul infidelity. If it were not for the veneration that Clarice's memory deserves, I would have to think that Pier Francesco's mother was unfaithful to me, who can say with whom... with one of those damned Gonzagas, hunchbacked from father to son, frightening Mantua with the horror of their monsters."

And the altercation, as they became distracted and recalled remote princes, calmed down as they brought up details they had heard about the lords of Mantua. The hump that dominated them was the malignant legacy of Paola Malatesta. Her son Ludovico, the second marquis, had been hunchbacked. So were his brothers, Alessandro the mystic and Gian Lucido the poet; and then there were Ludovico's children, the nuns, the Countess of Gorizia, the third marquis, Federico, and the unfortunate and criticized Dorotea, the fiancée of Galeazzo Maria Sforza, but she never married him, because the Sforzas, who aspired to a better alliance, an alliance with kings, had decided to postpone the wedding for four years of humiliating alternatives, that only accentuated in Dorotea the deformity suffered by her brothers and father. Only in the next generation, that of Federico's offspring, was the grotesque tradition broken, as if the poison that had brought it on had run dry. Those references awoke in me an avid curiosity concerning those who had suffered before I was born from similar distress, and later on, when I was able to, I became interested in their unfortunate lives and I had copies made of the verses that Gian Lucido Gonzaga had written in honor of the Emperor Sigismund, and I even added to my collections, like exquisite small jewels, the delicate medals that Pisanello had struck bearing the effigies of the Gonzaga family. A phrase of Cardinal Cesarini's, inspired by the young deformed poet, "splendid, more than for his body, for his wit and manners—*ingenio magis cuam corpore lucens*," sang in my ears like celestial music, for it occurred to me that it had been meant for me in some premonitory way, out of the mist of the centuries. But that, as I have said, was much later, in the days when I was already Duke of Bomarzo. The day when I heard those names for the first time, they did not serve me as an alleviation. They rang out like insults, arousing ancient echoes in the green and yellow sorrow of our Roman palace. Cardinal Franciotto and the condottiere Gian Corrado were speaking about the princes of Mantua and their humps with exaggerated, violent expressions. I hid myself, O Lord, and I gnawed on my fists and wept.

In addition to my anomaly, what roused up my father and my brothers against me was the attitude shown toward me by my grandmother, a lady whose human qualities were unmistakable, evident in the high regard she enjoyed beyond Rome, in Milan, Rimini, Mantua, Ferrara, Urbino, Naples, where she enjoyed illustrious friendships. Their reaction—I refer specifically to Girolamo and Maerbale at this moment—was translated, if not into ungracious expressions in the presence of Diana Orsini, for they would not have dared so much, in a kind of mordant tolerance, as if they understood that the love that my grandmother showed me was the result of a rather aggravated form of pity. And little by little—if, as I have mentioned, they did not yet dare make it public—their feeling changed into something that resembled rancor and jealousy too, aroused by the noble lady who not only did not share their cruel attitudes, but had adopted an opposite position which was, because of her generous tenderness, one that corresponded to the situation, and they secretly hated her, they hated her as they knew how to hate, in an exemplary way.

Finally, to end this bitter analysis, I must note that it has occurred to me now that if my father, my grandfather, Girolamo, and Maerbale dealt with me with such extreme perversity, it was perhaps because they had grasped from the beginning that I was essentially different—different for stupid physical reasons, but also for others much more lofty, more complex and inaccessible—from the handsome and closed circle that they formed. Perhaps there was something surrounding me, an air, an aura, a vibration that cannot be touched or explained and which floats about the elect like a magical proclamation, and they sensed in perplexity but without realizing the origin of the vague unrest that they felt that I, Pier Francesco—Pier Francesco the clown child, the little Vicino, as my grandmother used to call me in memory of her great-grandfather Vicino Orsini, the first lord of Bomarzo—had been singled out and reserved by fate for an incomparable destiny, infinitely superior for its being unusual to that which governed their trivial lives of petty aristocrats. Because they did not understand that (and no one could have understood it), their anger must have been all the more embittered as it showed itself in harassment to which there may have been joined, despite their apparent brutal naturalness, a certain mysterious fear. Would that that secret ingredient—fear—had intervened in the daily battles that darkened my childhood. Would that it had been like that, because that would assure me, posthumously, that even then, even when my father despised me, Girolamo beat me, and Maerbale, the cynic, imitated my walk and my figure, sinking his head down on his chest and dragging one foot, I was the strongest of all, the enigmatic, splendid victor, if not for my body, for my wit, like the delightful son of Gian Francesco Gonzaga and Paola Malatesta, even more splendid than he, no doubt, because his fame depends upon the admiration of the Emperor Sigismund, the sage Vittorino da Feltre, and Cardinal Cesarini, while I am beyond the repeated human molds, I break them, and not even Pisanello would have been capable of designing a medal worthy of me, of my enormous victory and my enormous defeat, even if his uneven chisel could have repeated the allegories of stars and unicorns.

The most painful part of all this that I am showing as shameful and base matter is that I would have loved them, I would have adored Maerbale and Girolamo just as I adored my grandmother. I would have adored the cardinal and the condottiere. I needed them; I needed them terribly, just as I needed the invisible bears that protected me in Bomarzo during my nocturnal strolls. But they rejected me, they humiliated me. And the resentment grew inside of me like a black plant nourished by gall. Girolamo Cardano points out in the pages of *De subtilitate* that hunchbacks are the most sinful of men because that mistake of nature has enveloped their hearts. That is not true. They attacked me and I defended myself. They hated me and I hated back. But I yearned deliriously, to the point of tears, for them to love me.


I will eliminate the long tale of the miseries that went along with my childhood in the midst of which my grandmother shines like a beacon. There is, however, one episode about which I must not be silent, because the picture of it still gives me anguish today, as if I were living it again with all of its terror at this moment as I write in the quiet of my library, opposite the print of Lorenzo Lotto's portrait, and I can feel the blood burning on my cheeks the same as it did so many years ago, and my heart is beating anxiously as it did so madly that morning in Bomarzo when I had just turned eleven years old.

My brothers delighted in dressing up in disguises. In that, as in other respects, they were quite Italian. I also liked to do it, but I did not dare for fear of accentuating my ridiculous appearance. Girolamo had taken down some suits of armor from the trophy stands—gauntlets, a buckler, a helmet of the kind called burgonet, a sword, a gorget decorated with damascene work—and after putting them on and hitching them up, he took long strides and gave hoarse shouts as if he were a condottiere of our line, the condottiere that he aspired to be. His figure and his vigor, exceptional for his fifteen years, permitted him to strut like that, despite the weight of the metal. On the other hand, Maerbale, who was ten years old, had improvised a cardinal's cape out of a ragged piece of purple cloth; around his neck he had hung the Byzantine cross that our grandfather had given him, and with the gift of mimicry that characterized him, he was having fun imitating Cardinal Franciotto, and right and left he distributed exaggerated blessings, adding some macaronic phrases in Latin, quite different from those that our tutor, Messer Pandolfo, doggedly taught us.

They were in one of the attics of the castle of Bomarzo which, for lack of any other function, served as storerooms and which we entered only occasionally, so immense was the medieval building. They had forced open a window and a thin column of sunlight in which innumerable dust particles were dancing was slipping in, coming to rest diagonally in a corner of the room. I was passing through some rooms nearby, and when they spotted me, they called me over to admire their respective outfits. Such opulence required an audience and I was the only one who could supply it. I obeyed, thinking that it would be best to do it willingly or else they would make me.

I can remember the intense smell of dampness and a certain acrid odor of mice, of closed-up things, which impregnated the attic. I can remember perfectly the ray of sunlight which crossed it with its tremulous column, and scattered about on the floor or on the trunks there was a disorder of multicolored clothing. Those trunks held clothes that had belonged to my father's two wives, Lucrezia dell' Anguillara and Clarice Orsini, as well as some old dresses and adornments that belonged to our grandmother. Girolamo had torn the hinges from the rotting wood, sure of the impunity offered him by the certainty that no servant would enter the abandoned attic for some time. Slashed pieces of cloth with their insides bulging through the sleeve openings lay about among fabulous birettas, broken and drab feathers, bits of silk and velvet, and silver and gold brocades of the type that Italian merchants established in Nuremberg sold to the Germans. Pieces of cheap jewelry, pinned to cloth remnants, sparkled here and there among the tabards with their metal and stones, edging, embroidery with emblems, lace, wrinkled ruffs, coifs, and veils were all joined in anarchic disorder to the stiffened rigidity of the dresses. My esthetic pleasure, quite alert already, triumphed over the fear that was always aroused in me by my brothers' proximity, and for a few seconds I enjoyed the chimerical spectacle that was spread before me by that confusion of elements, to which the evidence of Venetian fashion added unforeseen Oriental touches, mingling reds, yellows, violets, and tones of lemon, mother-of-pearl, and olive, all crossed by flashing stripes of golden thread and which the filth of the attic and the wrath of time and the moths were converting into spectral adornments.

My pleasure did not last long. At once, imperiously, Girolamo brought me back to reality as he clapped his metal gauntlets together.

"You put on a costume too," he ordered. "You'll be the Orsini jester."

Maerbale let out a sharp laugh, stuck out his tongue, and gave me a blessing.

My resistance was in vain. Between the two of them, Girolamo weaving back and forth like a deep-sea diver, and Maerbale treading on his purple train as it hindered his leaps, they placed a flat bonnet with a dirty tassel on my head; over my shoulders they threw a bright-colored tabard, half-orange and half-blue, rubbing my back as they did it, despite my convulsions and hand-waving, and they curled my hand around a cane that was almost a staff.

"The Orsini jester," Girolamo decreed, "shall amuse the duke and the cardinal."

They sat down on a chest, accentuating the solemnity, and alone in the center of the room I hesitated, feeling myself terribly unprotected in my grotesque clothing. What could I do? Shout? No one would have heard me in the vastness of the castle. My grandmother was far away. I stood there motionless, waiting; they could kill me—I swore, without moving my lips, they could kill me—but I would not be the butt of my executioners' laughter. Girolamo was becoming impatient. He took off his helmet, gloves, the musty pieces of armor, which fell noisily about him, and then I noticed with surprise that he was almost naked, like an adolescent gladiator. Maerbale made the hysterical rattle of his laugh ring out gaily through the room. He traced a cross in the air with his right hand and recited in a twangy voice:

*Postquam prima quies epulis mensaeque remotae  
crateras magnos statuos et vina coronant.*

I recognized the lines from Virgil that Messer Pandolfo had made us translate the day before, and I was surprised that Maerbale had remembered them, but Girolamo did not give me any time to put my thoughts in order.

"Since you refuse to fulfill your duties as jester," he exclaimed, "you shall be the Duchess of Bomarzo."

I did not understand what he meant, and he in the meantime was tugging off the wild costumes that had been withering me and he quickly pulled over my head the first dress he found at hand, putting my arms through the sleeves, almost tearing them, covering my head with a veil, picking up a handful of jewels and fastening them onto the folds of the dress, which, too large for my slight figure, was spreading out in wrinkles on the floor.

Mute with terror, I waited. As if in a dream I could see the thin, quivering solar column, the clothing scattered about; I could hear Maerbale's childish laughter; and I could feel on my face my older brother's breath, an angry faun who was busying himself with brooches, necklaces, and bracelets. Then he stepped back, threw back his head, crossed his arms, and looked his work over.

"Now," he said slowly, "Cardinal Orsini shall marry us. I am going to marry Francesca, the hunchbacked girl."

Maerbale came forward, mumbling vague Latin phrases. He stretched out his arms, put his thumbs and index fingers together, and adopted a pose of ecclesiastical modesty. In the window opening a bird had stopped and had begun to sing, and when I heard it in the panic of my nightmare, it was as if the soft countryside of Bomarzo—the rolling land, the brooks, the valleys, the live-oak trees, the elms, the flocks of sheep and goats, the gray crags, all that was most mine in the world— had come magically into that dark attic of the castle to witness the humiliation of the condottiere's son, the cripple, the hunchback, who stood there petrified, dressed in female clothing, his eyes burning with tears under the haze of the veil between a naked boy who was clutching his hand and a child cardinal who was inventing liturgical gibberish in the center of a room whose wild disorder recalled the sacking that that same castle had suffered centuries before.

Then I did something untoward: I raised my fist and hit Girolamo full in the face with all my strength, that face of an ancient statue that my father used to contemplate so much. I was surprised at my own audacity. I had responded to a mad and most dangerous impulse, which I had not thought myself capable of, and my two brothers were looking at me in astonishment in the silence that was barely broken by the crystalline and weak notes of the bird. Maerbale laughed, but it was a nervous and artificial laugh; Girolamo raised his hand to his face as it started to turn red. He was trembling the same as I. He gave a short shout and then, clenching his teeth, his eyes flashing, very blue, like those of my grandmother, he pounced on me with the rage of a wounded animal. He threw me down on top of the pile of clothing and I could feel my back paining me horribly. He knelt on my chest and I thought that he was going to bite me, that it would not be enough for him, for as he held me pinned down and mistreated me, he searched about himself like a madman for something, something that he could use so that the punishment for such an offense would be even more barbaric, more definitive. Until he found it. On the floor there within reach was a pile of odd jewelry, broken, useless. His fingers closed over a long gold pin and, holding me inert with the weight of his body, with his hard knees, with his sharp elbows, he turned my head and sank the pin into the lobe of my left ear. His ferocious shout, mine, and Maerbale's joined together and echoed through the expanse of the garrets that crowned the great house. The blood wet my cheek and flowed down to my mouth.

"No, no!" Maerbale shrieked, and above Girolamo's angry face, in a flash I could see the lividness of his.

But that was not the end of it. Girolamo, like so many men whose insane wrath has blackened our family history with the whispered tales of their crimes and tortures, lost control of himself as the onset of wrath blinded him, and he had to sate himself in fury, go to the hungry root of the rage and feed it before it would go away. His drive, as he faced the despised Orsini who had dared to offend him, had still not reached its high point. He raked around, almost without looking, in the pile of jewels. His torso, bathed in sweat, was sparkling as if it had been anointed with oil. Finally he found what he was looking for, an earring, a part, perhaps, of a lost set of jewels, with an amethyst cameo which I will never forget, for during two vital seconds it was swinging back and forth in front of my eyes like something alive, as if it were breathing, as if it were some kind of strange insect with several legs of twisted gold and a purple body covered with unimaginable figures, and he put the hook into the hole that he had just opened in my bloody ear.

"No, no!" Maerbale shrieked again, scared to death.

Girolamo released his pressure. His anger had doubtless been pacified now and he too was frightened by his perversity. I took advantage of this to escape, and holding the earring with one hand, for I did not dare take it off, and using the other to lift up the skirts of the absurd dress, I began running through the hallways, downstairs toward my grandmother's rooms. The lobe was paining me as if it had been torn off, and in spite of that torture and the idea of my laughable appearance—a hunchback dressed as a woman with a long earring hanging from his left ear, fleeing, bloody, moaning, limping through the rooms of the old castle—what bothered me most was the idea that at any moment I might run into my father. My brothers, who had also reacted, were following me at a distance, wary of the consequences of their act. I turned in my flight and I could make them out, the older one naked, tall, thin; the smaller one still covered by the purple cape which he had not succeeded in taking off in the confusion. My grandmother's quarters were only a little way off. I was getting there now, I was getting to my refuge, my salvation, the place where I could be cared for, petted, and the calm I had lost would return relatively soon.

At that instant a door opened and my father appeared on the threshold. He stood there, stiff as a lordly portrait, framed in the carved wood. He made no comment; he allowed himself to raise his eyebrows slightly and then to frown. The look of disdainful disgust that I knew so well disfigured his patrician features. I would rather he had insulted me, shown me some interest, some curiosity, facing that second son who ran past his door weeping, his hands red with blood. But he stood there silently, as if he were a hallucination, because the presence of a personage of such knightly solemnity was impossible in the castle of Bomarzo, where the future descendants of the Orsinis ran about masked or naked, changed into witches and slaves, or as if I had been some abominable phantom, neither man nor woman, limping past in ridicule and mockery—so that when all was said and done, one could not tell who the real people were and who were the illusory ones in that brief and singular scene—and he stepped back, noiselessly closing the door and locking it.

My grandmother held me in her arms for a long time. With delicate tenderness, she took off the dangling cameo, washed me, bandaged my ear, helped me get out of the insulting clothes. Her arched hands, which she would sometimes compare to mine—if Girolamo had inherited her blue eyes, I had inherited her tapering fingers, graceful in shape, as if the refined relics of our house had been distributed among us—alighted softly on my cheeks, my temples, my hair during the unfolding of my tale, in which I omitted nothing, and during which my tears dampened her soothing queenly hands, while her eyes became clouded too, marvelously sad.

"I have something for you," she told me when I had finished, "something that they found today in the Grotto of the Paintings. Girolamo can only have the arms that he takes out of the trophy cases here; but these are something unique, intriguing, and they were here in Bomarzo when the place was called Polimartium after the temple of Mars near Lake Vadimone."

She led me behind her bed, and behind the curtains she showed me the arms that a villager had chanced to discover as he followed his plow near the Grotto of the Paintings. They were some greenish metal pieces which, after being cleaned, glowed as if they had been powdered with gold dust. A helmet, a shield, an iron sword, a pair of greaves, a bronze lance, and four knives had been placed on a kind of foreboding dummy that kept watch in the shadows like a warrior who had come from beyond time and its shadows to look after me.

Our peasants were used to making similar finds, but until then they had not dug up anything as complete or as disturbingly beautiful in its sober and orderly grandeur. One would have to wait several centuries, until 1845 (and the waiting lasted longer than that for an Orsini pope), for a piece of that importance to be unearthed in Bomarzo: the small vase that revealed in its design, for the eagerness and consternation of archeologists, the first Etruscan alphabet known up until then. All of Bomarzo, actually, and the area of craggy rocks around the height that served as the base of the castle, was an immense Etruscan necropolis, like the one near the lucumonies of Tarquinia, Piamiano, Piano della Colonna, and Monte Casuli, the localities around Castelluzzo, Rocchette, and Castello, and it abounded with evidence of the most undecipherable people of Europe. Sometimes I think that deep in my personality there are survivals of traits of that primitive race, so poetic, so melancholy, so sensuous and bloody, just as capable of making pacts with demons as of being mystics possessed with mad lyricism, because Bomarzo was saturated with their unknown and fascinating magic, and on moonlit nights, when as an adolescent I would ride out across the hilly realm, I could sense curling up along the paths forms that would burst forth out of the caverns, perhaps, like miasmas, enchanted vapors, furies, gorgons, harpies, Moiras, Graie with a single tooth and a single eye, who were born extremely old, orgiastic *pretidi*, satyrs, nymphs, titans panting in the darkness; the world of those woods, that of those sepulchers of ageless Tuscia which I first visited with my tutor, Messer Pandolfo, and later with a scholarly friend, afterward, much later, with colorless guides to see in the dancing light of torches or in the exact clarity of electric flashlights the silhouettes of the ocher warriors, the dancing girls, and the blue monsters lying in wait for Pirithoüs and Theseus, waving their terrifying crowns of vipers; the actors of the drama of love and death, of torture and concupiscence, laid out in the Plutonic frescoes that the dampness was eating away and which, for that very reason, were all the more disquieting; and to gather the objects that the Grand Duke Cosimo of Florence was so enthusiastic about, the vases, the instruments of war, the reliefs, the candelabra that had fallen about the sarcophagi, and their obsessing, indifferent figures as they smiled at the superstitious fearfulness of the peasants.

From that world, from the Polimartium founded by Tyrrhenus, King of Lydia, came the armor that my grandmother had given me. From there, so far away, she had brought me a prestigious ally who, like a static robot, would stand guard over my sleep. They moved it to my room and there it remained until I disappeared from Italy. Some time ago, in the Gregorian Etruscan Museum, I was overcome with strong emotion as I came upon my piece of armor. Although the public is told that it comes from Bomarzo, nothing in the Vatican collection indicates that that iron group had belonged to Duke Pier Francesco Orsini. The centuries have been merciless with the duke, wiping out his traces, as with the comments made about my portrait by Lorenzo Lotto, the "Young Man in His Study"; it represents—oh, wonderful irony!—a personage of the family of the counts of Rovero, because the likeness for a long time—I do not know why—was in their house in Treviso; nothing is known of what those Etruscan arms had meant for me during a painful moment of my life as symbols of solidarity and support.

## THE HOROSCOPE · 39

Things, which people say lack souls, are in possession of deep secrets that have been impressed on them and which give them a kind of soul, a very special kind. They overflow with secrets, messages, and since one cannot communicate with them except through the medium of chosen beings, they become, with the passage of time, strange, unreal, almost thoughtful. We speak of patina, polish, the tones of the centuries as we recall them, and it never occurs to us to speak of soul. The Bomarzo armor has a soul. And we recognized each other in the papal museum.

My father did not react immediately to the revulsion caused in him by the womanish disguise of his deformed offspring. But he took it very seriously, as if I were not a child and, especially, as if I were not a victim. He was no doubt conferring with Girolamo, who was giving him the version that most suited him in the matter and to whom he listened closely. That week I ran into the condottiere four or five times and I always avoided his look, but I could feel it weighing upon me, on my hesitant tracks, grim, accusing, until finally the wrath that he had been feeding exploded.

He was a man of tremendous rages. One day a delegation of magistrates from Bomarzo came to the castle, people who would gather there from time to time in order to establish the contributions, tributes, and homage that the fief required. They came to prostrate themselves before him to beg for his clemency, for they considered the taxes excessive. Gian Corrado Orsini listened to them in silence. He watched the bowed gray heads. And when the stammering and plaintive discourse was over, he ordered them jailed and had the tribute doubled. In 1503, when Bomarzo was freed by Bartolommeo d'Alviano, my father had fought valiantly beside him, and he could see that the village would never be able to pay him what they owed him for his valor and his lordly rule. He rigorously followed the code of Viterbo and used the rights granted him over young wives and all women of humble origin in Bomarzo, the *homagio mulierum*. Until the end of his life, and he died fighting at the age of seventy-four, his carnal appetite never diminished. Servant girls, my grandmother's ladies in waiting, peasant women of Bomarzo, and even the mistresses and maidens of castles and estates in the region, from the fortress of Bracciano, built by Napoleone Orsini, to Orte, Vitorchiano, and Bagnaia, feared his insatiable lust. I later learned that many of them really loved him, for he was capable of repeated sensual acts of prowess. At dusk he would ride off, his white beard sunken in his muffler, with no fear of highwaymen and with no defense except his sword and his dagger, rejecting the escort of his pages and squires, and he would return when the sun was up, quite pale, dark rings around his eyes, shouting for them to give him something to eat. When Girolamo turned fourteen, he took him along, proud of the elegance of his body. He initiated him simultaneously into the strategies of war and of voluptuousness. He wanted him to be a perfect Orsini. I spied on them many times, envying them as the horseshoes raised sparks on the stones of the courtyard and the stablemen hurried to take the old duke's reins as he dismounted with a leap, with the same gallant agility shown by his eldest son. It is easy to understand, therefore, that my father detested me because I represented exactly the opposite of his manly and princely elegance and his boastful attitude toward life, rattling his arms, flashing through bivouacs and sieges, jubilant in the scandal of orgies and rapes.

His menacing calm could not last long. On the fifth day, when I was already breathing easier, hopeful that he had forgotten the episode, he had a page summon me. One of the peculiarities of his character (borne out by what subsequently happened) was his inclination toward black humor, macabre diversions. He was basically a sadist, as was Girolamo, his favorite. That was why they understood each other so well.

More dead than alive, I entered the room where he was accustomed to receive his vassals and with a sour look go over the accounts of his farms and his tribute. He was in a terrible mood. In Rome they had elected Adrian VI pope, making his father-in-law Franciotto's chances evaporate, and he had totaled up so many sumptuous illusions that it doubtless added to his exasperation. That was an ominous year for us. The unpaid Swiss had mutinied against his illustrious friend Lautrec and they had suffered a defeat under his command at La Bicocca. The world was conspiring against the lord of Bomarzo. Since there was no one at hand more indicated than I upon whom to channel his rage, he remembered me. And he devised my punishment with that refined imagination and atrocity of a Renaissance man.

Since I have mentioned Odet de Foix, Viscount of Lautrec, once more, I must point out a fact that to my mind is quite interesting. Without doubt, Lautrec and my father, who were intimate friends, had discussed my case at some time. The Viscount had seen me in our palace in Rome through chance, when Gian Corrado Orsini had been unable to hide me. My father must have lamented, with confidential bitterness, the unlucky fate that had imposed a son like me on him. That was what he was accustomed to do. And the brave, audacious, and vain Lautrec, whose credentials as a warrior were shown by Brantôme in juxtaposition to his incapacity as a governor, must have consoled him in his way, using a frank military rudeness. Both considered themselves two demigods in their male potency, two living heroic statues, models of their respective lines. And the irony of the matter is that the glorious name of the Viscount of Lautrec, governor of the Milanese and Guyena, lieutenant general of Francis I in Italy, and brother of Madame de Chateaubriand, one of the king's beautiful favorites, was eclipsed in the passage of the centuries by the name of his descendant Henri Marie Raymond de Toulouse-Lautrec Monfa, a dwarf painter who frequented low places and was more deformed than I. No one, except those who study historical details, remembers the man who thought that he was the crowning Lautrec, the colossal bronze Lautrec who held his staff of authority over Italy; while no one with any culture is ignorant of the work and the details of the life of the monstrous genius who was his heir, an absurd gnome, a painter of cabaret posters and bored prostitutes, a man who, if the brave Captain Lautrec could have foreseen him, would have disgusted him as a human leech and an unhealthy dauber of intolerable colors. A similar thing will happen to my name if these memoirs are published someday, and it will inevitably take precedence not only over that of my father, but over those of the most renowned personages of my line, including saints; popes; Matteo Rosso, the thirteenth-century senator who originated the three great branches of the family; Napoleone, the one who bathed in roses in Santa Maria in Aracoeli; Romano, the friend of Saint Thomas Aquinas; Niccolò, the friend of Saint Brigid and Boccaccio; Raimondello, the one who left for the conquest of the Holy Sepulcher and whose widow married the King of Naples; Gian Paolo, commander of the Florentine troops in the battle of Anghiari, which inspired Leonardo da Vinci; Gentile Virginio, the possessor of such status that in a parade he took precedence over the sons of Alessandro Borgia, and in the coronation procession of Alfonso II over the princes of the House of Aragon; Gian Giordano, the central figure of the Pax Romana; the Count of Pitigliano, the Homeric one; my grandfather Franciotto; those who fought at Lepanto; Virginio, called "the greatest nobleman of Italy"; Paolo Giordano, the Duke of Bracciano, a man of letters, the ambassador to Elizabeth of England, whom Shakespeare placed in his *Twelfth Night*, by which the Orsinis—as was stressed—who had been sung of by Dante, were also sung of by the greatest of English poets; and so on down to the famous Princesse des Ursins, as the branches of our leafy genealogical tree spread out and on which tiaras, crowns, swords, and miters turn up everywhere like golden fruits sparkling in the complexity of the foliage. None of those famous names that were raised like banners over the cortege of the ancestral bears, none will shine like mine, Pier Francesco Orsini. Because I am unique in my broad heritage, I am the only one who can now write of his life of four centuries ago. And thus we have the caustic paradox that a dwarf and a hunchback far outweigh in merit the two triumphant warriors from whom they are descended, the Viscount of Lautrec and the Duke of Bomarzo, who, furthermore, adjudged their glory as plumed combatants as a supreme summit, and who, if they could have imagined what would happen later on, would have declared with bitter disdain that the world, surrendering to abominable aberrations, had gone mad. I suppose that all of this, so disturbing, so damaging to pre-established molds, is what the British call "poetic justice." A posthumous and extravagant form of revenge that makes Toulouse-Lautrec and me brothers in time.

It is obvious that on that morning when my father resolved to give free rein to his bad mood, to face me and punish me for something for which I was not to blame, I did not have at my disposal those elements that assure my superiority over him today and, quite the contrary, I was miserable and destitute, bewildered in the presence of the majesty of an omnipotent judge resolved to condemn me without a hearing.

For the moment, spitting into the burned-out fireplace from time to time, he gave me a sarcastic exordium. His Florentine upbringing had taught him that atrabilious and mordant piece of rhetoric. Florence was a nest of intriguers, given to gossip, implacable scoffers, and it was there that he had developed his style. He spoke openly of the opprobrium I had brought upon the family—I was only eleven years old!— he compared me to Girolamo and Maerbale, lowering me; he laughed at the armor that my grandmother had given me, the only kind worthy of me according to him, because it was unusable; he ridiculed the woman's costume in which he had seen me. As he went on his indignation grew. He had begun in a muttering and contemptuous tone, but since that tone was artificial and had been learned in the court of the Medicis, it did not match his bilious and impatient nature, whose brusque tartness was struggling to show itself; aggressive, deaf to any reason, he quickly changed his manner, turning to foul words and the energetic, brutal inflections he used to intimidate his soldiers. In the midst of his ranting he remembered Sandro Benedetto's horoscope, which I had never heard mentioned until then, and he vulgarly mocked the occult powers and the limitless life it had promised me. And while he went on about my hump and called me a jester and a clown, his insults were only brushing my surface, for the fantastic revelation of my fate, which, without meaning to do so—and he probably regretted it immediately—he had passed on to me, had distracted me with its astounding novelty, which I did not understand precisely and which seemed made to measure to impress my poetic spirit in all that was chimeric, magical, and different from routine material in its implications. But I soon had to abandon those thoughts, postponing them for a better occasion, because my father began to make concrete allusions to the woman's dress that Girolamo had put on me, shouting "son of Sodom" at me, a term that I did not understand at the time, but which kept ringing in my memory and I interpreted it years later, although I deduced at that moment from the fire that was reddening his eyes as his upset reached its height that he intended to put me through something particularly bad. He stood up, knocking over the chair from which he had been speaking to me, and he seized me.

"Now we have to lock you up," he said. "But never fear, you won't be alone."

He touched a spring that I had never noticed and a wooden panel in the wall slid back. There were many secret passageways and chambers in Bomarzo of whose existence even the owners were unaware, for the castle was very old, and in the twelfth and thirteenth centuries, for example, there had been more than a hundred owners, the descendants of the Frankish and Lombard nobles who had lived in it before, and because those lesser heirs, whose possession in certain cases had only reached the fiftieth part of the domain, and who had lived there on the heights in warlike promiscuity, destroying themselves by their antics under the rule of a viscount, a vice-comes Castri Polimartii, they had multiplied their hiding places, burrowing into the walls everywhere in order to hide from one another (and to hide their respective paltry treasures) in dark dungeons. I myself, later on, when all of Bomarzo was mine, discovered an underground passageway that connected the castle to the Sacred Garden in the valley. I made great use of it.

In the darkness revealed by the richly adorned panel as it slid open, I could only distinguish a dense blackness. My father took a candelabrum, lit its three candles, and pushed me inside. He put the light on the floor and in its glow I could perceive that I was in a low and empty room, without windows, smelling of must. I turned to beg for mercy, and then, for a second, my look and my father's crossed. I had the impression that he was hesitating. Who knows, perhaps at that fleeting instant he had perceived that rare thing that was surely emanating from me and which was enveloping me like a veiled announcement, but he recovered at once and the door closed in its frame. I was alone.

The room was completely empty except for a long shape at the opposite side. I went over, fearful, and I gave a cry. Just as in the attic with the chests, my voice echoed stridently against the walls, mingled with the laughter that I heard from the room where my father had remained, and it was not only his, for Girolamo was now there doubtlessly, enjoying with him what both of them considered to be a stupendous joke.

The elongated form was a skeleton or, rather, a mummy, someone who had been embalmed by some inept person a century before, perhaps, during the days of the first Vicino Orsini, and it was dressed in a gray and dirty garb of tattered tammy cloth, with faded ribbons that made a mockery of it and had changed it into an obscene parody. It had been set against the wall in a reclining position, with its jaw held in one hand, its elbow on the ground; and its head, the brow of which was bound with a crown of withered cloth roses, showed something undefined and horrible under the dirty flowers, something which resembled a skull and which also looked like a human face.

My heart was pounding so much that I thought I was going to lose my breath. My cry had added to my fright in that imprisoned loneliness, so that I remained mute, perspiring, keeping my eyes on that hair-raising shape. Its shadow moved along the wall, projected by the candles, and I thought that the body was moving too in the wavering of the flames, showing its teeth and gums. Never in my life have I seen anything as terrifying as my companion and his motionless grimace, except, possibly, the time I thought I had seen the Devil in a mirror in that same castle. But when I saw the Devil I was already a grown man, almost an old man, and I had had deep diabolical experiences, while at that moment I was nothing but a child, tender, defenseless, abandoned, face to face with a sinister being and one impossible to place in either this world or the next, a specter and a corpse, a caricature, with his indecent ribbons, his sackcloth, and his crown of withered roses, of Death, the Great Death that surrounded all of us in Bomarzo as it came forth from the ancient necropolis and the swampy shores of the nearby Lake Vadimone, where the Romans had defeated the Etruscans, the Death that was always mentioned in stories and conversations, because my father's history, my grandfather's history, and the history of my family was nothing but a gloomy tapestry woven out of famous or miserable deaths.

It is likely that my father sheltered the hope that the presence of the crowned monk would turn my mind once and for all and my madness would help him get rid of me forever. If that was so, I defrauded him. I do not know how long I stood up against the torture in that improvised chamber, barely daring to breathe, keeping watch on my cellmate, who was watching me in turn with his empty sockets, disdainful, smiling slightly at my hump and my fright. It could have been a few minutes; it could have been an hour. The candles were sputtering and the face of the unburied dead man—a hermit, an enemy warrior, a walled-up lover, or an artificial fabrication, an invented man, reconstructed sacrilegiously, transformed into a baroque mechanism, how could anyone tell—was leaning on the support of his dry, shining, purple arm looking me over from the distance of his implacable, destructive ennui. Perhaps it was my cowardice, my panic, perhaps the half-light, perhaps the excessively painful penetration with which I was observing the silent guest lying in wait, as the shadows came and went on him, bringing him to life, but at a certain point I noticed that the convulsive grin on his mouth was slowly becoming accentuated and that he was beginning to stand up. Then my resistance gave way and I lost my senses, as if a cord that was too tight had been broken.

I opened my unconscious eyes in my bed with my grandmother on one side and the Etruscan armor on the other. We never commented, Diana Orsini and I, about the scene whose worst details she did not know. My grandmother was aware of how much the memory of it made me anxious and from her son's perversity she could guess what he was capable of. From that day on I noted that her love for me had become more intense.

What is singular is that during that night, in one of those charitable and compensatory mysteries of nature, instead of struggling through the martyrdom of a nightmare, I do not know what I dreamed as I leafed through my recent experiences; a dream where there were flowery skeletons, duchesses, suits of armor, and naked gladiators—a combination that would have gladdened the heart of Sigmund Freud—a dream which corrected and completed my accumulation of unhealthy sensations and from which I awoke suddenly, bathed in sweat, halfway between being anxious and being amazed at having discovered that even a body as base as mine could be an unusual source of strange gratifications. Woe is me, I was born to lonely sensuality at the age of eleven, and because of it I have suffered as much as the hunchbacks of Mantua, my sad brothers, and like the miraculous Toulouse, another *ténébreux,* another *veuf inconsolé,* another *prince d'Aquitaine à la tour abolie,* slaves like me to desperate passion!

When I referred to the abnormalities of my physique for the first time—which, actually, I did in a rather forthright way, and ever since that moment, as if the exposure of it were deeply relieving for me, I keep returning constantly to the spiny theme with the maniacal obstinacy of one who has been through psychoanalysis and will describe and illustrate his complex—I counterpoised in the balance, seeking to level it, the merits of my appearance, the chiseled and intense harmony of my face, the delicate form of my hands, the chic of my patrician air, and the restless mystery that emanated from me like some fascinating omen. Toulouse-Lautrec was grotesquely ridiculous because of the imbalance that resulted from his adult torso and his infantile limbs, which made for a pitiful incongruence. Not so I. My height was slightly below normal, but I was not out of proportion, and if when I walked I did limp slightly, like Byron, and swayed my hilly torso, when sitting or placed in favorable shadows, I gave the impression of a normal individual, one endowed with an innate distinction and with traits that had been molded by multiple generations of aristocratic perfectioning. Just as I have contrasted these two realities, I wish, now that I have evoked the most bitter and cruel memory that my father left me, to set it off against the most beautiful memory that I owe to him. Naturally, if they are put together, one will notice that the black, offensive shades are, without comparison, much sharper than this esthetic fringe, but in any case I shall speak of the episode because of the influence that it exercised—as it worked unconsciously with its paradox on the receptive field of my spirit, adding other significant elements to it—on the future creation of the Sacred Wood of the Monsters. It has to do with a poetic impression that, as will be seen, had an effect on the regions deepest in me.

It happened some time after the event of the maddening skeleton that I have just related. My father and Girolamo had been away for a few months. They returned to Bomarzo in a good mood. I imagine that the war had been profitable. I think that it was that time that they brought back to the castle as part of their varied booty the picture by Titian that had been inspired by a passage from Catullus, which, as Girolamo asserted with an expert air, had been painted more with the fingers than with brushes, for Titian had modeled his mythological figures the way that God had done when He shaped the human body by molding the slime with his divine hands. That painting, like others in Bomarzo, no longer exists. I do not know what became of it. Wars, fires, sales, thefts... Sometimes I think when I visit museums and collections that half of the Renaissance has evaporated without having been noticed. And I miss it.

One night—it was winter—we were gathered around the fireplace in the main room. My grandmother had already retired. My father, Girolamo, and Maerbale were warming themselves in front of the logs. I, in the background, had mingled with the shadows in the darkest part of the room, and I was waiting for the opportunity to slip away without being noticed. I had crept off silently toward a door and when I was ready to go out and escape to my grandmother's rooms, my father raised his voice and began to speak of something that had to do with Michelangelo. I stopped and pricked up my ears. It was the story of the time when the statue of David had been moved through the streets of Florence.

Gian Corrado Orsini had been present, years before my birth, when Pietro Soderini was gonfalonier, at that complicated operation. For four days that gigantic piece of marble went along the route between the master's studio and the Piazza della Signoria. Forty men were pulling it through the narrow streets, and the scene is joined plastically to other very ancient ones like that of the Trojan horse. They rolled the standing statue along greased logs, using a system of pulleys and counterweights that held up the colossus like some fine war machine with a scaffolding of wooden girders and protected it from blows. It advanced slowly, gravely, through the Florentine crowd that had put aside their daily chores to discuss the qualities of the new arrival. All had their opinions, for in Florence art was a topic of popular debate, just like market prices and the policies of the commune. David kept advancing and at times his forehead was at roof level. At night they built bonfires at his feet, and envious enemies of the artist threw stones at it from ambush. (The envy and imbecility of a certain type of man is eternal and has turned up across the centuries with its virulence intact: in 1504 they stoned Michelangelo's David; in 1910 the Municipality of Florence deemed it proper to dress it in a fig leaf, which caused a great stir. The efforts of the *brachettoni* have defied the centuries.) And at dawn the statue would begin its solemn march again. David was not a small shepherd boy; he was a giant. After he had bested Goliath he had grown and had become transformed into him, to the stupor of the Philistines. That had been the prize of his audacity. A king is a giant. And while the forty men shouted in rhythm, pulling on the ropes as if they were raising a great sail, and the logs rolled along with a sorrowful groan, and during the pauses of enchanted silence halberdiers beat their arms, dogs barked, vendors hawked their wares, horses drew back madly, old women shrieked themselves hoarse, and here and there a lute, a lyre, a clavichord, a viola da gamba, a sharp, wounding trumpet could be heard over the strident crowing of the cocks, and people milled about as at a fair around the walking David, and the young lords, handsome, luxurious, and sleek as leopards, like imperial leopards sparkling with jewels, would come to the windows with their gilded prostitutes and visually caress the gleaming white marble victor as he passed along amid the creaking of the wood, his immutable broad eyes coming along at the level of the balconies and cornices—and silence came about again with symphonic majesty—it was as if august Beauty, stronger than the baseness that divided men into mean bands, avaricious and ambitious, had finally come into the city on the Arno, its hands quiet and the muscles of the rhythmic box of the body quivering, there to establish its permanent monarchy.

The story had warmed my father up along with the fire that had been lit when among the Tuscan courtesans and noblemen he contemplated David's glorious progress. He did not comprehend—I saw that later on—the allegory of the procession, the implications of that marble war machine of such serene action, the essential enemy of war, the destruction of Goliath and everything the condottiere stood for, everything behind his pride and reason for existence. But as a man of his time and caste, he put high value on the beauty created by an artist and he was pleased, showing in that way that he could be as refined as a Visconti, a Sforza, a Gonzaga, a Medici, an Este, or a Montefeltro by the resplendent reminiscence. As was his custom, he had begun to walk as he spoke, all about the room, and I—it was the only time—felt no fear at his proximity. Probably my father had perceived that ephemeral, spiritual nearness in the atmosphere, for he stopped in front of me and, as if distracted, as if he did not notice what he was doing, for between us there was the memory of Michelangelo's David, he stroked my face with a finger. Then he went back to his military strides. His monologue went on to Buonarroti's colossal projects. I cannot tell whether it was he who revealed them to me at that time—I do not wish to mix up my chronology—or whether it was later that I learned of some of the monumental ideas that attracted me so much, but the truth is that inseparable for me are that night in Bomarzo and the victorious form of David passing through the streets of Florence in his triumphal cortege. Michelangelo's fabulous plans—the one, for example, that made him restless as he worked to choose the blocks of stone destined for the magnificent tomb of Julius II, a plan which was the conversion of the whole mountain at Carrara into a cyclopean statue; or the one of raising alongside the church of San Lorenzo in Florence a bell tower that would also be an imposing piece of sculpture, with the bells hanging inside the head and a dovecote in the hollow of its torso, so that when the bronze bells swung, the metallic sounds would come from the open mouth of the figure along with the flapping of the doves' wings; dreams, deliriums which make one think of the Macedonian Dinocrates, who so as to flatter Alexander had wished to transform Mount Athos into a huge statue that would easily support a city in its left palm, and in its right would hold an exorbitant goblet from which the waters of the rivers that flow on that mountain would pour; and they also make one think of Giovanni da Bologna's "Appennino," the colossus of Pratolino; and also... also of my Wood of the Monsters in Bomarzo, the Sacred Wood that I invented—those utopias bewitched me then and afterwards, but their dazzling hallucination did not go to work all at once, and the night my father was speaking in the light of the flames of the fireplace, that inspired marvel was relegated to a secondary level, like some store of titanic constructions that would enslave and transfigure nature, a store in the confusion of which the profile of my father stood out as he paused, ran a finger across my cheek, and went away like a Saint George, a lancer of dragons, toward that region where gathered together were the infinite strong creatures who sank their stone faces into the clouds, leaving me with, more important than those wild ideas, a frenzy of genius, the fleeting sensation of an index finger which in a moment of carelessness, with an easy and affectionate spontaneity, had alighted on the face of the duke's hunchbacked son.

That was the only authentically happy moment that I owed to my father; the only one during which we vibrated together. David drew us together beneath his shadow for an instant. The rest has been hidden weeping, boredom, aggravation, disdain, and hatred; alternating among treating me as if I did not exist, ignoring me, and as if I were some irrational creature who made him lose his patience, punishing me, and, most of all, a mute, reiterated, inexorable method of making me feel that I was in the way, that I did not belong and would never be able to belong to that harmonious group made up of him and his other two sons. His attitude certainly contributed, almost as much as my deformity, to building up my unhappiness. If my father's position had not been such and if I had been able to rely on his alliance and understanding, as I could on my grandmother's, I think that the whole panorama of my life would have presented quite different facets. I would never have been effectively happy, because happiness is something that had been denied me from the cradle, but I would have enjoyed a certain ease that resembled happiness. And how much, how much I needed that wellbeing, that kind of hygiene that accompanies happiness! Each time that something rose up in my path, even though deceptive, looking like happiness, I would try to grasp it desperately, for I knew that it would not last. And the only happiness that I had in my childhood, the small treasure that I had accumulated in spite of the difficulties opposing my urges—apart from my grandmother's providential tenderness and the strange episode that I have described and which sparkled in that gloom like an exceptional gem in a poor collection that had been arduously gathered—was the memory of my rides through old Rome and my trips to Bomarzo, for both helped me to explore and discover the best in myself: a capacity to extract something from beauty and to find it where for others it was covered, as if it were absent, in a column, in an arch, in the bend of a river, in a cloud, in the languid swaying of a green and gray branch as its brushes of shadow sketched out Oriental calligraphies.

It occurred to Messer Pandolfo, whose classes were given scant attention by my brothers and whose switch had been broken by Girolamo, that perhaps he could capture our interest if he gave us our lessons as we moved about. It was a curious equestrian peripatetic system. We would leave on horseback with him in the morning and ride through the city of Rome, and at famous spots there, having us sit down on the edge of some ruin, he would discourse on the glories of the Empire and the Republic as they had developed on those same rundown sites. Girolamo and Maerbale barely listened to him. The future duke was attracted only by what pertained to our family, for, like Maerbale, he sensed the relationship between that evidence and the events of his splendid future, but any incident, some neighborhood women washing in the Tiber, a fight beside the arch of Janus, a fluttering of butterflies in the baths of Caracalla would draw them away and distract them. Girolamo would sit up on his steed, with gestures worthy of Verrocchio and Donatello, as our singular troop—composed of a garrulous old man, prone to sties, with a perpetually purple nose that had been tinted by distant and recent wines and which was protected by his absurd parasol or covered by his cape as if it were a toga he was wearing; a boy whose grace and bearing made women smile and common people tip their hats; a child giving off his toneless and mute laughter; and a hunchback with a delicate face who sat up as best he could upon his saddle—paraded through the places where the Orsinis had left deep traces of their importance.

In the Arenula, Parione, and Ponte sections, in the neighborhoods of the Calderari and the Catenari, the Campo di Fiori and San Lorenzo in Damaso up to the Circo Agonale, especially in the Campo de' Fiori, which had been our redoubt when it had been surrounded, as if by bastions, by the houses of the Capizuchis, Delfinis, Brancas, Della Valles, Capodiferros, Mellinis, and Alberteschis; and in the Marcello theater, joined to the Orsini palace, which had been ours, like the ancient theaters of Balbus and Pompey, and across from Sant' Angelo, where we had fortified Monte Giordano, and similarly at the posts where our forces had kept watch over the Tiber and the Porta Portese and everywhere between Hadrian's tomb and the Saint Sebastian gate,

Girolamo would make his horse rear, for he felt a sudden lash of pride in his ancient blood. And I too, woe is me!, I too, as Messer Pandolfo told us that Brancaleone degli Andalò, a professional podesta whom the Romans had brought from Bologna, had ordered the demolition of the towers of the barons, those of the Orsinis, the Colonnas, the Annibaldis, the Crescenzis, the Anguillaras, the Savellis, the Contis, the ones who people my family tree, would have liked to have used my admirable hands to kill that foreign podesta from the thirteenth century. Once, in the Colosseum, with my eyes half open, I dreamed about those lost towers, the ones that stood in the circus itself, at the foot of the Capitoline, and, following the river, at the foot of the Quirinal, and I dreamed that all of Rome was ours and that the castles which replaced the ruined battlements when the princes walled in the hills as their own property—we, on Monte Giordano; the Colonnas on Monte Citorio and the tomb of Augustus; the Crescenzis on Monte Cenci; the Savellis and later the Pierleonis on Monte Savello, from which we expelled them—were ours, only ours, and that belonging to us were those small and guarded dynastic cities whose hearts, within the secret of their barricades, contained glowing gardens.

But unlike Girolamo, in whose heart all that echoed was what had to do with the Orsinis and their might, I made an effort on those long didactic rides—which my older brother soon abandoned, called to his new life beside my father—to possess Rome, the essence of Rome as it floated about the monuments and the palaces in the heat and in the breezes, and it made me feel warm and it raised me up like a distant conqueror, perhaps General Caius Flavius Orsus, to whom we owe our name, or Paolo Orsini, the one who reconquered Rome for Pope Alexander VI, and the exciting influence that so many glorious presences exercised over me worked in such a way that I forgot about my sad condition, my taciturn pallor, my hump, and I would straighten up in the saddle or stand up on a crag among fallen capitals with the hauteur of a military chief looking over his memorable field.

I was wandering about in the springtime in the midst of that solemn debris. The birds were chirping and there was a quivering of lizards in the grass. I had only to push back the foliage to lay bare amid the shoots of ivy some mutilated pieces of sculpture or incrustations of marble that are now in museums. I found the head of a goddess, I took it back with me to the palace, and I began to clean it delicately in my room as they say the Grand Duke Cosimo de' Medici used to do, with small chisels and hammers. The Lombard peasants who came to work in the vineyards and plow the ground and who exhumed with their hoes, among the wild flowers, busts, medallions, cameos, and even emeralds and rubies, which astute antiquarians bought from them for a handful of coins, would approach me, knowing about the interest of the hunchbacked child, to offer me their muddy finds. Thus, thanks to the money my grandmother gave me, there was born, amid the irritated mockery and jealousy of my brothers, the collection that later, when I was able to dedicate myself to it, was one of the passions of my life, the alleviation of my loneliness. Thus was born also a certain fragile and stimulating feeling of security, for the peasants would come to me and not to Messer Pandolfo or to Girolamo or to Maerbale, and they would speak reverently to me, as if speaking to a prince and as if my hump did not exist.

Not everything that I acquired at that time was good. On more than one occasion they would sell me a cat for a hare, because counterfeiters abounded at that time, people who would sell me through those same ingenuous villagers stone fragments with freshly cut inscriptions and which revealed under the disguise of the skillful patina handsome (too handsome) Latin writings that made one surmise that they were part of the epitaphs to Lucretia and Caesar or from Nero's tomb. Only years later did I discover the trick when my eyes became sharper; yes, in my collections of the sixteenth century, as in any great present-day collection that deserves respect, there were several spurious pieces. They were the ones that Messer Pandolfo admired most because of the elegance of their texts. But there were also in the collection I had gathered together many items of quality. Classical Rome, which had suffered so much during the Middle Ages and the Renaissance from the constant depredations; which under Paul II had lost the stone wall of the Colosseum to be used in the palace of San Marco, and under Sixtus IV the temple of Hercules and a bridge over the Tiber were made into cannon balls; the Rome whose temple of the Sun had supplied materials for Santa Maria Maggiore and the pontifical palace of the Quirinal; the Rome which Michelangelo did not hesitate to despoil of one of the columns of the temple of Castor and Pollux to serve as the pedestal for the statue of Marcus Aurelius, and which Raphael Sanzio deprived of another column in order to carve an image of Jonah; the Rome where Hadrian's tomb provided the stones for the Sistine Chapel and which, when Saint Peter's was built, was left without the triumphal arches of Fabius Maximus and Augustus and without the frontispiece of the temple of Antoninus and Faustina; the Rome where, in the days of Clement VII, my dear Lorenzino de' Medici—the "Lorenzaccio" of Alfred de Musset—decapitated several effigies of the Emperor Hadrian; and which was robbed of infinite marbles, bas-reliefs, sarcophagi, and cornices as lords and cardinals built the residences that give them glory today. It held incomparable treasures in the abandoned, unpopulated forums, the Campo Vacchino, a harsh field upon whose weeds animals grazed to the sound of the herd boy's flutes as they scampered over the fallen podia and architraves as if they were walking upon crags and not on sculptured marvels. As I faced that Rome and drew in its splendor, I experienced something similar to the dazzling glow that had blinded Buonarroti when as an adolescent he entered the garden of the Florentine cloisters of San Marco for the first time and saw there, standing or thrown down, intact or in fragments, the pagan sculptures that the Magnificent was collecting. And as I faced it, like some plant of that ancient land, cultivated by civilizations, humiliated and exalted by the centuries, that land that was perpetually plowed and perpetually generous, tearing open its breast like the legendary pelican, bleeding, rendering over the centuries its sublime secrets, my gift of poetry came out.

I made the mistake of not collecting my poems in one volume. Now I have lost them forever. Of those that I wrote for Adriana dalla Roza at the time I knew her and many years after her death there is not even a memory left. Betussi, who dedicated some lines to the memory of that unfortunate woman in the dialogues in which he deals with love, and who, in order to please me, emphasized the feelings that drew me to the girl buried in Santa Maria in Traspontina, does not mention the stanzas that I had dedicated to her. Epigraphers argue today about the philosophical rhymes that I had engraved in various parts of the palace in Bomarzo, doubting whether they can be attributed to me. I should write them down and clarify the question, filling in what is missing in those inscriptions erased by time, but I have forgotten it. Besides, the same thing would occur as happened to my portrait in the Venetian Academy and to the Etruscan armor. I do not know why I did not publish my poems myself. Francesco Sansovino noted somewhere that I had a felicity with writing, a depth of quite rich ingenuity, and that I expressed noble and high concepts in an enchanting way. It is true. But my works do not exist. And it is my own fault. Perhaps I thought that a great lord like me ought not to publish his verses, although there were aristocrats who printed the fruits of their hatred and their more or less legitimate sharpness. I may have told myself, succumbing to prejudices as deeply rooted as our line, that that was fine for a Medici, but that I, an Orsini, from a military caste and one that had produced senators and governors of the Roman Church, had not come into the world to undertake the keen-sighted game of verse—despite Cardinal Latino and his *Dies irae* and Antonio Orsini, the epicure, poet, and heraldist—but, rather, to be like Cardinal Giordano Orsini, who published the recently discovered works of Plautus, or Valerio Orsini, who supported Aretino, for that was what befitted us, the role of an intellectual Maecenas. I was mistaken and I regret it. I would have occupied a place, small but mine, in the history of Italian literature like Betussi, like Molza, like Annibale Caro. I had other grave and terrible things to busy myself with. My children, my grandchildren could take care of the edition. Alas! if we expect our descendants to fulfill what we have postponed, all that awaits us—in case we can witness their indifference—is despair and disillusionment. My daughter Faustina, married to Fulvio Mattei, Baron of Paganica, only worried about placing the arms of her husband in Bomarzo, where they flourished alongside the unique dignity of the roses and the serpents of the Orsinis and the lilies of the Farneses. And she left my manuscripts to the moths in the same chests where the clothing of my mother and

Lucrezia dell'Anguillara was kept, the ones used for my torture and shame when Girolamo had dressed me as a woman and marked the lobe of my left ear with a scar that has never disappeared.

Messer Pandolfo, as was natural, encouraged me along those lines, but soon I stopped showing him my attempts. They did not really interest him, because they were not done in Latin. As with Cardinal Bembo, it was his understanding that all possibility of literary invention in the world had been exhausted, and the only path for writers to follow was that of Ciceronian imitation, in the case of Latin, and in our language, the imitation of Petrarch. And he, of course, preferred the imperial language. He was one of those pedants so abundant at that time, slaves to the revived paganism, whom Erasmus mocked because the only words they considered truly Latin were those that Cicero included in his lexicon. Sometimes he would halt to chat with me, exaggerating his twang, as we wandered through the forums of Rome, and his deference had a courtly tone, because in his scale of values after Cicero, and perhaps Bembo, came the Orsinis. And that adulation pleased me too. But neither the artifice of his rhetorical praise, nor the homage of the common people who would lie in wait for me with coins and cameos, nor the Roman majesty that passed something of its Orsinian splendor on to me every day made me prefer those excursions through the eternal city which took us to the villas of the emperors, beyond the vital center circumscribed by the great bend in the Tiber and the appendices of Trastevere and Suburra, to my trips to Bomarzo. There my simple pleasure was much greater than in Rome, because, for the moment, I would not have to return to the palace next to Santa Maria in Traspontina, the glacial melancholy of which weighed upon me like another enormous hump, stifling me, compressing my heart. And there I could go out by myself to ride across the broad domains without having to endure the presence of my brothers, who in Rome, offended and mortified by my figure, would pretend that I did not belong to their group, and they would gallop away whenever they could find a pretext, despite Messer Pandolfo's protests, and if we came upon some young noblemen going hunting with their dogs, the first thing they would do would be to ridicule me in front of their friends, showing how much they were annoyed by a presence they considered unjust and depressing. In addition, it must be kept in mind that Bomarzo and its duchy belonged to us thanks to my grandmother, the daughter of Orso Orsini, who was Duke of Bomarzo, the granddaughter of Matteo, and the great-granddaughter of Pier Francesco, and so on back to Anselmo Orsini, the lord of Bomarzo in 1340, and that circumstance gave the place an incomparable attraction for me, because there, on that soil, surrounded by that countryside, I felt as if I were on my grandmother's lap, and as if the others—even the duke and the future duke—were intruders, just as much intruders as the Baron of Paganica, my son-in-law, the one who dared to place his arms alongside ours.

The trips from Rome to Bomarzo, which we would make in order to avoid the heat and the malignant fevers, and which came to an end in 1528, when we settled down permanently in the castle, were awaited with emotion by the writer of these pages. Each stage brought us closer to the nearest thing to happiness that I have known. There were many of us in the procession, in the center of which my grandmother's coach swayed and creaked—Diana Orsini was the owner of one of those vehicles that were scarce in Italy—surrounded by the mounts of her descendants, her household, including chaplains, nuns, and two jesters, her servants, and the armed men coming to strengthen the forces that protected the estate. Chests and barrels were carried on muleback, along with tapestries and suits of armor. The ladies swayed on their palfreys and sedan chairs. The falconers carried their hooded birds on their wrists, and when the falcons grew impatient and flapped their wings, their silver bells would tinkle. The mastiffs trotted about with their tongues out. We would go through the Prima Porta, which the ancients had called Saxa Rubra, and follow along the Via Flaminia, passing close to the arch erected by Constantine to commemorate the site where he had camped before the battle against Maxentius; we passed around the rock of Cesare Borgia, and the countryside guarded by the peak of Mount Soratte, and we would arrive in that way in Civita Castellana, where we would rest and pray in the Duomo, which was bright with mosaics. Then we would continue on to the left, to medieval Orte, and from there through Bassano with its Romanesque church, and soon, in the neighborhood of Lake Vadimone, we would see the stern shape of the castle rising on a height.

It was a storybook trip, fatiguing and admirable. The farmers would stand up in the fields, wipe the sweat from their brows, and bow clumsily to us. Sometimes Maerbale and I would ride inside my grandmother's coach, and she, cooling herself with a stiff Venetian fan that was like a small banderole, would suppress her fatigue and tell us stories about the places we were passing through, stories of battles and martyrs. We would look out from time to time and see the wavering figures of the men of the escort, their plumed hats, their upright pikes, and their saddle swords; we would see the luxurious palace group with my father, who was chatting with comrades, old warriors like him; the graceful figure of Girolamo, coming and going, whistling at the whippets, bored with our ceremonious slowness; and in the distance, as in a dream, we could see bonfires, cypresses, and dark bell towers. The country received us with its undulant lowing, the fresh smell of the afternoon, and its uncountable stars as evening came on. As we got closer to Bomarzo, the feeling that we were entering arcane places, places with secret prestige, became accentuated. It seemed to me that other shapes, strange ones, were mingling with the family caravan amid the creaking of the harnesses, the sound of the women reciting their rosaries aloud, and the croaking of the night birds. Perhaps they were satyrs and nymphs, harpies or gorgons, who had come from neighboring streams or from those tombs in the underbrush and ravines with their hidden magic paintings. Messer Pandolfo came to the coach door, his face white with dust, looking like a clown, to repeat to us that the Etruscans, according to Virgil, had settled in Italy many, many centuries ago, and that according to Herodotus they came from the East. And I made an effort to distinguish in the darkness barely lighted by the paleness of the stars, dilating my sleepy eyes, what were slight and vague shadows that encircled the horses and the equipment. I seemed to be hearing supernatural voices, brief laughter, the echo of a guttural song, rapid hisses over the growling of the dog pack, the neighing, and the tinkling of the falcons, and giving a shudder, I crossed myself. But the armed outline of Bomarzo soon drew me out of that inexplicable anxiety, and then I took a deep breath and fell asleep on my grandmother's shoulder.

The next day and those following I would dedicate myself to reconquering the place and its atmosphere, which had been lost to me in the Roman agony. In the dryness of summer—the rains fell in October and November—the locusts and the crickets crackled. The citadel rose up above the roofs of the town and was quite different from what the tourist sees today. Neither my father nor I had yet undertaken the work that was to convert the castle into a villa according to the taste of the time, nor had the Lante della Roveres, who came after us in the seventeenth century, when my grandson sold the property, raised their massive bastions yet. At more than eight hundred feet above sea level, huddled together, were the buildings we had inherited. The vertical yellowish-greenish structures, with that color typical of the Viterbo region, were indistinguishable from the village and the church. Bomarzo and its rusticness seemed to be a stony outcropping of the height on which the fortress conceitedly stood between two streams: on one side, near the top, above the Morello, while on the other the slope descended steeply toward La Concia, the stream which bordered my Sacred Wood like a moat. At my feet, as I walked about the terraces, there stretched out the winding expanse of uncultivated valleys, where rocks emerged, broken and scattered by age-old convulsions, like half-buried antediluvian skeletons. The water sang in my ears, and between the crags and the small clumps of elms, live oaks, and willows, I could feel the flowing of the streams as they rushed noisily toward the Tiber, which was nearby, watched over by the castle of Mugnano, which had belonged to the Orsinis since the fourteenth century and in whose environs Carlo Orsini, Duke of Mugnano, had fought against the troops of Alessandro Borgia. Flocks of sheep and goats moved about, and it was like inhaling the peace of an eclogue, somewhat sad, with bells, the buzzing of the bees, and the bleating, a nostalgia for distant pomp, and it would change into an unfathomable anguish, so deep that it brought on tears and shuddering, but also hallucinations of shadowy beauty as the night broke forth like a breath from the secret watercourses, amid the flapping of the bats, and ascended over the tops of the trees, over the stones, over the acropolis, and over the smoke from the hearths of Bomarzo, forming up above a jet-black lake, the projection of the lakes of the region, Trasimeno, Bolsena, Vico, and Bracciano, and of the swamps of Vadimone, where the power of the Etruscans had been extinguished, a lake on which the moon's bark sailed, pulled by its silent oarsmen, and on the waves there floated, chasing each other with avid bird cries, the furtive divinities.

My time was divided among swimming in the Tiber and in the smaller streams, where my grandmother would take me, hidden from the others, for she knew that I would never undress in front of another person; horseback rides with a page when my father was not at the castle, for out of fear of meeting him on the road on his way back from an amorous adventure, I preferred closing myself up and reading; Messer Pandolfo's lessons, which I took with Maerbale, and in the course of which my interest in antiquity grew stronger; the incipient archeological enthusiasm which, accompanied by my teacher's sneezing as his purple nose revealed the dampness of the tombs, led me to places that almost no one knew and which the villagers considered cursed and to the discovery of pantheons which apathy and nature later caused to disappear and which the specialists discovered officially much later; fleeing from my brothers, my father, and the cardinal, who occasionally would visit us with his pontifical illusions and defeats, and who, not having obtained a cardinal's hat for Maerbale under Leo X, his cousin, doubted that he could get one from Clement VII, the bastard Medici, which embittered his character, which was sour and irksome by nature; and the waiting, difficult to describe, for something, something that must happen, while my sensuality became drowsy and the whole world changed into new, carnal visions, which dislocated the countryside, beings and objects, bringing them together, re-creating them, and which endowed them with a tremendous and disturbing reality that I would not share with anyone. Just as in the paintings of Mantegna, the clouds before me took on human shape. I could see promiscuous crowds in the sky, and when storms broke, I could hear their passionate collisions. I would see long bodies as they twined together. Trembling with the same voluptuous curiosity and terror with which I went down into the tombs where ocher gladiators, blue horses, musicians, and dancers awaited me, I would stroke myself as if I were an irreplaceable musical instrument whose complex register I was mastering so that I could draw from it my deepest and most subtle plaints and whose vibration was opening up, in opposition to my superfluity, scenes of vertigo.

Along with this restlessness, since my father had involuntarily revealed it to me, went the preoccupation derived from Sandro Benedetto's horoscope and his unusual announcement, and I would think about it for hours, leaning on my window sill. What will my life be like? I pondered. What is my fate? Will I live so long that my life will latently be joined to the haze of future times, as the stars studied by Niccolò Orsini's astrologer seemed to indicate, violating the allotted time of fatality? Or, on the contrary, which seemed ever so much more logical, given my weaknesses, will I be snuffed out any day now like some old candle? And if my existence does not follow either of those contradictory paths—neither the second, brief, nor the first, with no apparent end—and evolves within normal limits, how will its development take place? My father is old—I would say to myself—my grandmother extremely old. I will be left between Girolamo and Maerbale, my enemies. And then, will they not leave me some corner, a cell in Bomarzo, so that I can lock myself up in it like a monk with my deformity, and my activity will be reduced to reading, writing poetry, fondling cameos and coins, and looking out at the valleys through my windows? Or will they continue torturing me until they destroy me? Since I was still a child, even though grief had matured me early, I asked myself these questions in confusion, for my nature, with a simultaneous intensity, had given my permanence on earth the tone of a fantastic story with fearful and unique implications, and that of a vegetating, despised, and pathetic creature. But the astrologer's chart—to which my father had alluded once to tease me with its madness—rescued me during that period of doubt (even though I myself had to surrender, when I thought about it, to the evidence of its insanity); it rescued me even more than my grandmother, because I sensed from her advanced age that her help would not last long, while the pronouncement by Benedetto gave me an eccentric superiority over my brothers. And only later, during the years following in Florence, far from my family, when the turbulent variety of the court distracted me with its fevers and I felt less abandoned and more master of myself, did I relegate the memory of that insane horoscope to the most intimate part of my spirit, where, nonetheless, the outlined promise continued beating, for it was something so substantially mine that it never abandoned me.

Girolamo would invite friends and cousins, companions in arms, to Bomarzo. Under the direction of my father and my grandfather, they learned the remunerative art of war. I would spy on their training, their exercises, the hand-to-hand fighting, the clashing of their breastplates and swords. I would breathe with relief when they went out with the falconers. Although Maerbale was very small, they would include him in their outings, and his incessant laughter echoed amid the bells. When they returned they would drink like men and some would get drunk. My father and my grandfather watched their antics from the balconies and sometimes they would join in the improvised festivities in which girls from the place would participate, almost always willingly, for the members of the band, who varied between eighteen and nineteen years of age, were slim and agile, flattering all of a sudden and just as capable of unexpected displays of haughtiness, as people of the Orsini line who judged that by their alliance with saints and kings they were somehow kinsmen of God. Then, bored with teasing the jesters as they repeated their eternal imbecilities, and taking advantage of the fact that my grandmother was sleeping, the boys would go looking for me, because my appearance and my sadness made for the greatest fun, and if I had not taken the precaution of seeking refuge with the aged lady, it was useless to hole up in my room. It is easily understood, therefore, that I did not stray far from Diana Orsini, which increased my cousins' wrath and disdain. But despite all, and this will show how much I loved that place and how extreme has been my grasp of its essence and its hidden affinity with my own mysterious essence, even then I would not have exchanged my trips to Bomarzo for anything. There my vexed personality could stand up in solitude; there I understood that, deep down—and that was what vaguely must have upset the rest of the Orsinis more than anything else—I was, of all the descendants of Vicino, Grand Duke of Bomarzo, the one who had most secret roots sunken into the ancestral soil, the one most united tellurically, joined to that strange, unfathomable, metaphysical place, so much ours, so much mine... so much mine that now, when I discover in the Almanach de Gotha that since 1836 a Borghese—the first was a brother-in-law of Paulina Bonaparte—is Duke of Bomarzo by a papal decision, I feel myself overcome by a fury worthy of my father at such an arbitrary decision. After me there have been no more dukes except my son Marzio and my grandsons Orazio and Maerbale: the dukes of Bomarzo ended with them in 1640. For good.

In that domain, the Etruscan presences, gathered over the generations, would get into one's blood. And the Roman presences too. There was in the belfry of the church a bas-relief that survived from the time when the building had been an imperial fortress. In its marble there were profiled three sculptured figures dressed in togas, with paludamenta that leaders used in military campaigns. Messer Pandolfo had explained to me the rank denoted by that clothing. And I would go down from the castle to contemplate it. I liked to run my hand slowly across the relief, because it seemed to me that it was palpitating as if alive. The names of the families that established themselves in the region after the fall of the Etruscans—the Rutili, the Domizi, the Vibii, the Ruffini—written on stones of the time, echoed in my mind like that of General Caius Flavius Orsus, and I felt that through them and their progeny I was joined to the heroes of Etruria and to their ambiguous gods. I was aware, of course, what Bomarzo had meant since the beginning of the eighth century when with Ameria, Bieda, and Orte it constituted the formative nucleus of the Patrimony of Saint Peter, and I was aware of the importance of its apostles, its Christian martyrs, Saint Eustizio, Saint Anselm, the bishop who was appointed by a miracle, as a heavenly voice proclaimed it to the clergy, and all that was important to its spiritual progress, but my sensibility responded much more readily to the goad of past suggestion that alluded to the initial past, as old as the mother land in which was buried and from which emerged victorious, alarming, and confusing the metal of tripods, the paterae, the mirrors, the candelabra, the idols, the harnesses; the stones in the rings; the clay of the black, yellow, and red glazed pottery.

That rhythm of life, which went back as far as I could remember, was interrupted when I was going on twelve. At that time, Girolamo, Maerbale, Messer Pandolfo, and I accompanied our grandmother on a trip to visit relatives. Diana Orsini, an octogenarian, was not afraid of the roughness of the hard roads of Latium. She was faithful to the tradition of family courtesy that had been passed on to her when she was a child, and she did not hesitate to cover dangerous miles in her coach drawn by four horses, rigid, impeccable, untouchable, her face covered with a transparent veil, arriving at distant palaces where she would be welcomed with ceremonious respect, as if there were a hint of something liturgical, priestly, the age-old rites of the caste which only we Orsinis practiced and understood, for in the midst of so much uncertainty, treason, perfidy, and dissembling, so much quarrelsome violence that continually burst out in disputes, raucous shouting, and the flash of arms, she symbolized the sovereign dignity of our unconquerable women, so powerful that when, for example, one of them, Clarice, of the Monterotondo branch, the aunt of my grandfather the cardinal, married Lorenzo the Magnificent, no one thought of her bringing a dowry to Florence, for there was enough in the brilliance of her name to elevate the merchant artists with whom we had consented to ally ourselves.

That time we went to Bracciano, one of the largest castles in Europe, with six feudal towers, the property of the Orsinis of Gentile Virginio, the opulent lord whom I have mentioned already and who, in a procession, went ahead of the Aragonese princes, the same one who was poisoned afterward, having struck unwillingly, with his life of crime and glory, a typical medal of the Renaissance. And we went to Anguillara, where Carlo Orsini, Count of Anguillara, his illegitimate son, lived, the brother of that Antonio whose wit was exemplary and whom they called Epicurus, the one who was noted in Naples for his verses in Latin and who introduced the baroque style into heraldry.

One morning, followed by Messer Pandolfo, I rode from Anguillara to Cerveteri and from there to the nearby sea. Woody hills surrounded the castle of Palo, also the property of the Orsinis, a strong building, square and crenelated, against which the waves beat, and which Pope Leo X had converted into a hunting preserve. I knew the place, for I had been present there among the pages during one of the hunts of the pontiff, in whose court Cardinal Franciotto held the important position of master of the hunt and who was in charge of all that had to do with the expeditions. At that time more than three hundred people, headed by the young prelates, poets, musicians, and Swiss Guards, who would not leave the side of Pope Leo, had filled the place that now lay deserted and silent before my eyes. I remembered the roar of the trumpets and the explosions that frightened the wild animals out of their lairs, surrounded by snares and nets; and the merry, vibrant group of horsemen led by my grandfather and Cardinals Salviati, Cibo, Ridolfi, Cornaro, and Ercole Rangone, and a theologian, Egidio da Viterbo, who brandished his dagger and shield. They passed by in rapid pursuit of a black boar, with a flash of their arms, iron maces, scimitars, javelins, crossbows, and short lances, as the sun shone on their low engraved helmets, gold necklaces, and the baldrics they wore over their purple garments. The mastiffs were running about and I knew them all by their strange names, my grandfather adored them: Nebrofare, Icnobate, Lacone, Argo. And the pope, on a height in the distance, among his lute players, along with Fra Mariano, his jester, was slowly turning around like a sacred ox, with his bulbous and taciturn head disproportionately large on his thick, heavy body as he ruminated and snorted; and he brought his sparkling monocle up to his eye as if he were consecrating it between the index finger and thumb of his unusual, nervous, sculptured, and feminine hand, the beauty of which surprised ambassadors. Had some villager come by respectfully to kiss his foot, he would have been unable to do so from the thick boots and greaves which protected it. That day my grandfather's favorite falcon died, destroyed by an eagle. It was an unusual bird that had been sent to him from Crete, and Cardinal Orsini, for whom my misfortunes meant so little, wept with grief and rage as he saw it fall into the trees. My grandfather's sensibility was a very special one. He had it buried in a tower and on the stone that was engraved with the design of our arms he had placed the falcon's chain and hood and the heads of numerous birds that had been caught in the region. If he had been talented, he would have written the life of that Greek falcon as Louis XII of France did to honor the memory of his dog Relais. But he was not, and the cardinal's homage was limited to that stone covered with bloody feathers and bills; those hard eyes that kept on staring, round, like the pontiff's, amid the horror of the faces of the sliced-off heads, and which were part of my nightmares for a long time. They harassed my nights at Bomarzo.

I could see them again as I galloped alongside Messer Pandolfo, and for a moment—if it is true that scenes that have been lived leave their imprint on places—the loneliness of the place was capped by rapid running figures, their scarlet cloaks flaming, chasing an invisible wild boar, as a dying falcon fell through the air.

Soon the peace of the environment overcame me and my feverish imagination began to grow calm. On the beach side, which extends around the castle, my teacher, choked up with the heat and the effort, dismounted and made himself comfortable beneath the protection of a soft dune, opened his parasol, opened his Virgil too, and in a while he nodded, his eyeglasses slid off, and he fell back into a sleep of exemplary innocence. I had dismounted along with him, and I got back on my horse and after a short ride along the shore, I spied a man and a boy busy collecting pebbles and shells, selecting them with such attention that my curiosity was aroused, for they seemed to be searching for pearls and precious stones in a place where there were only common rocks. I kept my distance, even though I wanted to join in a conversation, for because of my deformity, I always kept my distance with strangers. They were commenting about their finds with disproportionate excitement and at one moment they both raised their heads and looked at me. Then I observed that the older one, who was strong and muscular and had a short beard, was probably a little over twenty years old, and that the other one, extraordinarily handsome, was probably fourteen. They called to me, waving their arms, and I went over.

"Why don't you get down?" the man asked.

I feared that he would become too familiar and that perhaps he would take advantage of my undefended weakness by making fun of my hump to his companion, so I decided to say who I was, hoping that my name, which echoed so nobly through all of Italy, would have more prestige in that place, which like the region around for many leagues belonged to the Orsinis, and which would remove the possibilities of any unpleasant notion.

But the man did not change his expression. "So you are Orsini," he answered haughtily. "I am Cellini, Benevenuto Cellini, goldsmith, and with these hands I can make such marvels in one hour that even if you were the emperor of Germany, you would treat me with deference and would commission me to make you a crown, certain that you had never worn anything like it. And, furthermore, I am a gentleman and on my coat of arms I have a fleur-de-lis held by a lion's paw, and I am descended from that Fiorinus, a captain of Julius Caesar, a native of the castle of Cellino, for whom Florence was named. You tell me if the Orsinis can boast of such fine blood."

He spoke with an equivocal tone, so that it was quite difficult to tell where irony began and where truth ended. If I had been older and had had more experience in worldly things, I would have perceived at once that what guided him as he expressed himself that way was the opposite of what it seemed to be, a deep respect for aristocratic values, and that they fascinated him as he took advantage of my extreme youth to treat me as an equal, which he would not have dared to do in front of my grandmother or my father, as he would not have dared strut out with his Captain Fiorinus. We were the lords, disciplined harmony ordained it, and if it happened that a metalworker was twitting us with his ancestors and comparing them to ours, *filii ursae* as everyone knows, we would be lost and the whole order of society would sink into chaos. Luckily for the tranquility of the balance which regulates human relations, such nonsensical sallies could only take place on an occasion such as the one I am telling about, with no consequences as it was anonymous, and which, fleetingly and absurdly, put the Orsinis and the Cellinis on the same footing.

The boy began to laugh. In order to maintain my status, for in spite

## THE HOROSCOPE · 69

of my young years I understood the ridiculousness of the assertion, I changed the subject and asked what they were looking for on the shore.

"We're looking for pebbles with a rare makeup," Benvenuto answered me, "because Nature is a subtle artist and she has more inspiration in her inventions than we, and she is always teaching us lessons of color and form. If you dismount, you can help us look."

I hesitated, still held back by doubt. Perhaps they had not noticed my hump, thanks to my position in the saddle. The boy took a step forward and held out his right hand with such an open smile that I jumped down onto the beach without giving it any more thought. For a few seconds we looked at each other. Both were handsome and had their jerkins half open, showing the nakedness of their sand-sprinkled torsos. The sun was burning. The sea was beating with the lacy fringe of its waves on the beach. As I faced them I must have looked like one of those pitiful and ungainly birds that sway clumsily as they walk. My hump weighed on me as if it were made of iron. I felt miserable, horrible. I would have liked to have slipped off and at the same time to have stayed with them, conversing, proud of their company.

Cellini did not change his expression, he did not even blink, and he turned toward the other one, who, disconcerted, had adopted an expression somewhere between surprise and gravity, and said, "This is Paolino, my apprentice." And he added, addressing the boy, "Did you notice what a delicate face the prince has, and what big dark eyes?"

I took a few steps forward and trying vainly to reduce my twistedness I began to turn over stones. The two of them gave me a confidence that I had never felt until then. It was as if all of a sudden I had discovered my real brothers. They joked, turning over pebbles, and their nearness brought on an unknown attraction. It fascinated me that Benvenuto was a goldsmith, for that connected him in time with the artistry that had conceived the works I had been collecting in the Roman countryside. Furthermore, my calmness was born not only from the fact that the land we were walking on was part of the inheritance of the Orsinis, but that the air about that I was breathing, and which projected the beloved image of Bomarzo in the salty atmosphere like a transparent mirage, for the same as my castle, the whole region from Lake Bracciano to the sea had been under Etruscan rule, had been a center of singular importance, and Cerveteri was built on the ruins of Caere, the capital of one of the twelve lucumonies of Etruria, so that I, so mysteriously endowed with the secret of my ability to absorb the sensibility of arcane messages that drew me to that vanished people whose subterranean presence I could discern like a dowser, had felt as I passed along the modest streets of Cerveteri my emotions becoming more acute, provoked by the sacred occult survivals of ancient Caere, surrounded by deep ravines, with promontories into the flatlands where, clustered together, invisible, lie the tombs of the fantastic necropolis, a feeling that had given me a kind of fleeting vigor that was being accentuated now by the cordial proximity of Benvenuto and Paolino.

Cellini handed me something shiny. "It's for you," he said. "Keep it as a souvenir of this meeting."

It was a ring of solid steel encrusted with gold.

"I made it," he added, "inspired by the ones that turn up in urns filled with ashes and which, according to what people say, are amulets that bring happiness."

I slipped it onto my left index finger as if I had received a gift from the pope. I have always worn it since then. As a man I wore it on my little finger. Among the many things that I have lost since then, including Sandro Benedetto's horoscope, the letters from the alchemist Dastyn to Cardinal Napoleone Orsini which played such an important role in my fate, the painting by Lotto, my ovens, bellows, alembics, and those devices with sonorous and illustrious names, the *atanor* and the *kerotakis*, the Etruscan armor in the Gregorian Museum, and the curious objects that enriched my collections, there are few I miss more than that ring of gold and steel which I would spin on my little finger, and the contact with which I think transmitted to me from its condition as a talisman and because it had been cast by the finest goldsmith of all time, a magical power that if it was not that of gaining the promised happiness, at least helped me confront, as it was constantly joined to me, binding me, the hostile sadness of the world.

Cellini liked to talk on. He told me that he had become ill in Rome because of the plague and a woman, and that he had taken refuge in Cerveteri in the house of his friend the painter Rosso to regain his health. He made the trip on a horse that was so fat and hairy that it looked like a bear, and Benvenuto told about it with a happy waving of his arms. It was obvious from the way he told his tales that he was volatile and that if something pushed him into a rage he would draw his dagger and seek blood, but unlike the men of that type whom I had seen and who terrified me (the same ones who were the delight of Girolamo during those boastful banquets presided over by my father), Benvenuto, perhaps because he was an artist and because the innermost traits of his complex personality included other facets, totally different ones that my precocious childhood tried to discern and which stood out over his personality of a touchy swordsman, kept me hanging on his words the same as on my grandmother's when she would tell me some legend of pride and righteousness in which the Orsinis were involved with their metallic clamor. Furthermore, as he spoke to me, he would punctuate his theatrical tale with winks in Paolino's direction during parts that were beyond my understanding, and from time to time he would halt his oration to show me in the sand, suddenly reverent and back to his original condition through some atavistic force, a stone that was quite original and polished, the way a merchant slyly lays out his jewels before a prince. And those spontaneous attitudes, coming from someone whom I already admired, bolstered my hesitant timidity in spite of the familiar tone, for I noticed that he was giving me, with an authentic and uncontainable facility—especially valuable as it came from one who calculated his arrogance by his virile independence—what I had always yearned for and which had been denied me by my father and my brothers and which was an absolute necessity for a child as gifted and as disinherited as I, the scion of a demoniacally haughty people: respect. I had noticed a minute detail lost in my new friend's outflow of words and it was that according to him the horse that brought him from Rome to Cerveteri, to the house of the Florentine painter whom the French later called Maître Roux, looked like a bear, and then it occurred to me, for my alert imagination was nourished by subtle coincidences like that, that the bear in my coat of arms, the Mother Bear whose steps I used to hear, "velvet footsteps," in the corridors of Bomarzo, had carried him on her heraldic back, disguised in some way as a grotesque horse so that he could meet me on the beach by the castle of Palo and so that I could add a fundamental item to my small store of affectionate experience. Thanks to Benvenuto Cellini, a singular craftsman, and thanks to the ancestral She-Bear, I had succeeded for the first time in what I had yearned for up until then without being aware of its real substance: the respect which elevates one and gives him vigor, and which—I translated it that way later on, giving it an allegorical quality, for I was fascinated with allegories—was produced by the alliance in one strange and single figure, seemingly laughable but really prodigiously pitiful, between the two essential elements fused in my individuality: a passion for art and a passion for caste, with the certainty that both, one fortified by the other, would aid me in the earthly journey that I was condemned to make and to make with that burden on my back.

Unaware of the effect that his revelations had caused in me, Benvenuto, without transition, declared to me what Paolino meant to him.

"This boy," he said, "this madman, is too handsome to live like others. Thanks to him I have understood many extravagances which the Greeks assign to the gods. But he suffers from melancholy. You probably know that my father, a builder of bridges, mills, and fulling mills, is famous for the marvelous way he works with ivory and builds clavichords, violas, harps, and lutes. He loves music and he planned for me to be a flautist, not a goldsmith. He drove me ever since I was small, he harassed me to put my chisels aside and devote myself to the instrument I hate. And yet, when Paolo grows gloomy, I will take my flute and play and play until Paolino smiles and his face lights up. You can't understand it. I will leave the arms of women, prostitutes, Pantasilea, Cassandra, or Livia, and when I return to my workshop I must find him waiting for me. I could do nothing without him."

Cellini was speaking in an unconnected way. He would jump from one topic to another, and I, wearing his steel ring on my index finger, felt as if he had grasped my hand as he spoke. It was obvious that he was trying to amuse me. He had put the selected stones together, building up a small pyramid, and he would add a pebble to it from time to time, taking great pains not to knock it down. He told me, without turning his head, that one day he had been invited to a party at the house of the sculptor Michelagniolo of Siena, where there would be several young artists present, Bacchiacca, Giulio Romano, Gian Francesco, a disciple of Raffaello da Urbino, and the poet Aurelio Ascolano. They had agreed that each one would bring a courtesan and that the one who did not comply would pay for the dinner of the rest. Benvenuto had counted on the company of a Pantasilea, but he had to cede her to Bacchiacca, who, among other things, was in love with the splendid woman. The hour of joining for dinner was approaching and Benvenuto had not found a partner, until, sharpening his wits, he conspired to dress a sixteen-year-old boy in feminine clothes, a student of Latin, the son of a Spaniard who made copper utensils and lived near him. No one was aware of the trick. On the contrary, the student passed as the most beautiful of the harlots. Only at the end was the trick revealed, to the applause of those present. Michelagniolo's enthusiasm was such that he lifted the goldsmith up by the arms and shouted himself hoarse with "Bravo, master! Bravo, master!" amid the howls of the painters, the verses of the poet, and the disappointed jealousy of the hussies.

As he evoked the scene, Benvenuto reproduced with the comic liveliness of his twenty-two years the voice of Michelagniolo of Siena, a big, strong man, larger than the rest of the noisy company. Mimicking the episode, he took Paolino by the elbows and lifted him into the air exclaiming, "Bravo, master! Bravo, master!" with such force that some fishermen who were mending their nets two hundred feet away turned their surprised heads toward us.

I reread the story not too long ago in Benvenuto Cellini's memoirs, where the author included more details of the adventure, but the text did not make much of an impression on me in comparison with the version that I heard from the lips of the protagonist. The fact is that what disturbed me on the beach was not the anecdote itself, which, after all, was nothing but an ordinary masquerade, but the circumstance, still disconcerting for me for what my father's wrath had meant and his exaggerated punishment of me in the cell with the skeleton (a woman's dress, which in my case, to make it worse, I had been forced to put on), to Benvenuto and his friend had brought, on the contrary, the applause and congratulations of a group of young men who, according to what I could deduce, stood out among the most notable artists of the period. Then I saw clearly something that I had already noticed in my Roman solitude, that what is bad for some is good for others and that factions will proceed with their rejection or approval with equal sincerity and vehemence, so that pure justice is outside of human decisions, which are governed by pre-established norms but are also guided by factors inherent to the sensibility of every individual and to the enigma that presides over the inexplicable and capricious makeup of every person's own soul. I perceived it, needless to say, in a disorderly way, like everything that took place during that period when my psychological conflicts were multiplying, but I will never tire of repeating, so that the reader may measure my situation in childhood, that I was an exceptionally precocious and alert child and that at the age of twelve my intelligence and my intuition were above normal, because of my peculiar temperament, because of my physique, which was also peculiar, and because of the aggressive milieu in which I developed and which compelled me to perfect my surmises and my defenses.

Paolino stood up excitedly from the stones he was scrutinizing. "Look what I've found!" he exclaimed. "I've never seen a stone like this!"

It was round and red with blue veins. Benvenuto took it and grew enthusiastic. "A marvel," he commented. "I should kiss you for finding it."

He went over and kissed him on the mouth. Then he turned to me and added, "I'm going to kiss you the way I did him, Signor Orsini; we have to celebrate this find."

He embraced me and on my face I could feel his breath, which smelled of wine. I could feel his hands tightening about my hump.

At that moment I heard Girolamo's voice from behind as he called me. We turned and we could see him beside Messer Pandolfo on the top of a dune which had kept us unaware of their nearness. They were both on horseback and my brother was strongly etched against the turquoise of the sky with his tight clothes outlining his trim figure.

"Let's go!" Girolamo ordered. "They're waiting for us!"

I left the arms of the goldsmith. Paolino held my stirrup and I mounted.

"Good-bye, Prince!" Benvenuto roared. "Don't forget Cellini!"

We galloped back to Anguillara without exchanging a word. Out of the corner of my eye from time to time I would peep at Messer Pandolfo's disturbed face as he clutched the reins, and Girolamo's haughty face, his tight lips, the expression of disgust and disdain that I knew so well. Three days later, according to plan, we returned to Bomarzo. But before we left, Paolino came to the castle and waited for me to pass by on one of the walks. I was with him for only a moment; the poor boy was afraid that he would be discovered, as if he were some kind of criminal.

"Benvenuto sends you this gift," he told me.

And in his open palm he offered me a gold medallion, one of those medallions with emblems and decorations which great lords would use to decorate their hats. The artist had engraved for me on the obverse the bear and the rose of my arms, and on the reverse, with an exquisite hand, under the design of my name, Pier Francesco Orsini, the paw of a lion holding a fleur-de-lis so small that one had to squint his eyes to appreciate the handsome outline. That medallion figures in my portrait by Lorenzo Lotto, although the majority of visitors to the Academy of Venice, where I look down in boredom at the tourists in Gallery VII, have probably not noticed it. If they look carefully, they will see it on my velvet hat which hangs toward the rear on the left, above the hunting horn.


In Bomarzo the family council called me. Participating in it were the cardinal, my father, Girolamo, and Messer Pandolfo, the last rather upset by the role assigned to him.

"We have resolved," Franciotto Orsini decreed, "to send you to Florence. May God have mercy on your soul. Here, where your grandmother spoils you and with your deplorable inclinations, you could only be ruined for good. You must steel yourself for life. It was in Florence that your father and I learned everything we know, far away from our homes, facing the world, and things have not gone so badly for us. Diana has approved our decision. There is always the risk, my son, that the family would have to look on you with shame."

They really were an impressive group, with the great red figure of the cardinal in the center and flanking him in perspective, as in one of those decoratively religious paintings that bring together aristocratic donors and doctors of the Church, assembled by the painter under a ceiling of gilded beams, the superposition of Messer Pandolfo's slashed sleeves and the metallic breastplates of Gian Corrado and Girolamo, with some hounds, and a casual page holding a halberd—and his presence made me blush more than that of any of them—for the lords were ready to leave also, but to war. I attempted an answer. I had sensed that something extraordinary concerning my existence was going to occur, and in spite of my shyness I was ready to defend myself. I tried to say, with childish fury, that even if Girolamo had dressed me up as a woman and because of that I had brought down my father's wrath, it was not really important, and that there were artists, famous artists, who had applauded a boy dressed up as a woman, but the words came out in spurts, mixed in with my hiccupping sobs, and my judges could not understand any part of my sporadic explanation and it did not interest them in the least. My father grew angry, overwrought. He stood up in front of me and slapped me across the cheek with his glove. The ear that Girolamo had pierced with the gold pin a few months before began to bleed.

"Out!" he roared, pushing me. "Out, you clown, you effeminate! You leave tomorrow with Pandolfo!"

I ran to my grandmother's rooms, dragging my leg along the galleries. I carried with me that last image of my father, whom I never saw again, an image that curiously, as I shall explain later, and perhaps because of some anguished trauma that psychologists and experts in psychoanalysis might be able to explain, was erased from my memory after a time as the somber features of Gian Corrado Orsini evaporated, and it has been difficult for me to bring them back. And I carried with me, as a background, the noble pictures of my grandfather and my brother, the old prelate and the young warrior, standing erect in the vanity of robe and armor. A feeling of rancorous happiness was added to the pain of the punishment. What? Had they found reasons for me to be straightened out, but instead of putting me under strict guard and observation they were exiling me far away from their surveillance? A strange way to resolve the problem that had been raised. I did not know what they had learned in Florence, but I was sure that life had not gone as well for them as Franciotto had proclaimed. He had not attained his tiara nor even a red hat for Maerbale, despite his vaunted influence, and my father had never ceased complaining how worried he was over always having to postpone paying his soldiers and about the poor returns he got from booty as the pope, the emperor, Venice, Milan, and Naples divided the best items up among themselves. What was certain was that they wanted to get rid of me, weary of a presence that was an insult to them, and that they had chosen a pretext which my innocence would not let me understand, because if I trusted in anything, bewildered by the dark allusions, it was in my simple innocence. I would leave, of course, I would leave. I would be better off anywhere else than among them; even among the unknown Medicis. I would leave. But, alas, I would have to abandon until who knew when, perhaps forever, Bomarzo and its restless charm which had given me such magical vigor; I would have to abandon my grandmother and her warmth and tenderness. I clenched Cellini's medallion in one fist and in the other a ring, as if I were hiding two relics, two talismans. I was weeping, and it seemed to me that the fountain of my tears would have no end. I wept until dawn on my grandmother's lap as she consoled me as best she could, stroking me lovingly on my straight black hair as it fell across my cheek and over my wounded ear, and in the middle of the endless tale I had begun, as I sobbed out my infinite misfortunes and the injustice of men, she begged me to calm down, to be patient, for my time would soon come and I should prepare myself for it among the Medicis, the most subtle people in all of Italy, proud of their kinship with the Orsinis. And after she had said it, after she had promised, she put such emphasis and guarantee in her words that I ended up by falling asleep, just as during the times when from her coach I would spot the castle walls of Bomarzo, the end of a long trip, and I would rest, lulled by the swaying of the coach and cooled by the perfume that came from her bosom as if her pearls were aromatic, a perfume which reminded me of Bomarzo and the roses of its gardens.

The next day I left for Florence with my tutor and two pages. These last two were both eighteen years old while I was going on thirteen. One of them, Beppo, thin, blond, his hair always mussed, was the son of a village woman of Bomarzo and according to rumor of my father.

When I heard of the relationship in the kitchens of the castle the news had upset me. In vain I sought something in his face, in his body, looking for something in common with Girolamo, with Maerbale, with me. He did not look like us. I thought, ingenuously, that the blood of the Orsinis, being so unique, pointed out its possessors and separated them from the rest of humanity. Beppo had a noisy and sensual spirit. He was always teasing the servant girls and that brought him close to my father and Girolamo, but yet he lacked their natural elegance, which, in essence, distinguished them as people born to command. The other page, Ignacio de Zúñiga, the orphan of an archpoor Spanish hidalgo who had settled in Naples and who had entrusted him to my father, was dark, thin, and smaller, with a great deal of reserve and religious restlessness and, as a Spaniard and a gentleman, was an enemy of the stigma of manual labor. Messer Pandolfo called them Day and Night, for the first was so fair and expansive and the second so dark and secretive. They did not get along well. They would argue over the slightest thing. Beppo, perhaps because of his hazy origins, acted as if the slightest allusion was an affront, in spite of his being naturally merry and always ready for a good time. He tried to get ahead of Ignacio from the first moment he met him, but the latter would serenely put him in his place. Coming into Arezzo, some hoodlums tried to rob us and we had to defend ourselves. The pages acted with such dispatch that the robbers fled. That common action established a kind of friendship between the boys, a truce. My grandmother had given them some clothes with our colors, silver and scarlet; with the rose and serpent from our shield sewn on the chest. The Spaniard did not like the motley; he would have preferred lordly black. In Spain, he told Messer Pandolfo, not even jesters would have dared to dress the way Roman and Florentine courtiers do. On the other hand, Beppo was delighted with that polychromatic outfit, and he was always flitting about, here and there, a silver leg, a red leg, like a tightrope walker.

We spent the night in Arezzo. We traveled very slowly, because Messer Pandolfo complained of the difficulty of the road. We slept at an inn or, rather, my tutor slept there. Ignacio stayed outside, walking up and down, scrutinizing the sky and praying until dawn. I retired to the quarters I shared with the teacher, but his snoring, the vermin, and the emotions aroused by the newness of my imminent future would not let me rest. After a while I went out too, and I did not dare disturb Zúñiga, because despite the lowness of his status I was impressed by his bearing and that faith which I, aggravated by the crush of my anguish and distracted by the exploration of the world, did not share. I walked for an hour under the stars, thinking. The memory of the family iniquity heated up the blood in my veins. On my way back to my quarters I could hear voices in a neighboring room. Through the opening of the partly closed door, I saw Beppo busying himself on a cot with the innkeeper's daughter. The two were naked and quite occupied. Up until then I had never witnessed that kind of exercise, of which I had, through fragments of conversation that I had picked up by chance and treasured in my memory, submitting them to analyses that were as mistaken as they were eager, a theoretical and superficial notion. The spectacle was of great interest to me, so much so that, hesitating, I leaned against the wavering plank of the door which groaned on its hinges. The lovers rose up out of the silent confusion of their struggle and saw me there in the doorway with a candle in my left hand and my eyes popping out of their sockets. The girl tried to scurry away but Beppo held her back. His audacity was so extreme that he called to me quietly and proposed that I share his agreeable task. He was facing me, inviting, ironical. I hesitated, pulled by fear, by the tightness of shame, by the desire to touch that soft flesh, by the astonishment caused in me by the page's slim back and its vertebrae—so harmoniously placed, alas, with no deviation—so sharp, as if they were ready to break through, down from the back of his neck which was half covered by yellow hairiness, but I gathered enough sense together to bring myself under control, understanding the importance of such an act for the future of my prestige in the city of the Medicis, and I went over to the rocking bed with the candle trembling in my hand and I slapped the page. Then, when he quickly changed expression, passing from one of lascivious complicity to one of pain, surprise, and anger, I noticed how much he looked like Girolamo as his face, different as it was, reminded me at once of my brother's the day when I had been driven to strike him in the attic of the castle as he made Maerbale go ahead with the farce of our wedding. I did not say anything; he bit his lips and gave me a black look of hatred in which I could perceive the disdain he felt for me and for my unfortunate appearance, and in which there also appeared the fateful evidence of kinship, for only my brothers had ever looked at me that way.

The woman, who evidently did not know who I was, brusquely pulled down the covers so that I could appreciate her body in its entirety, as if she were trying to humiliate me with her panting nakedness, and she said in a low voice, "Are you going to let a tricky, lowborn hunchback treat you like that? What kind of a man are you? Aren't you going to hit him back?"

I stood stupefied for a moment, facing the revelation of her flesh. I would have given anything to go back through the waterclock of time and return to the instant when Beppo had suggested that I accompany them in bed, because now, in spite of my timidity and my physique, I understood that nothing would have given me as much pleasure as an apprenticeship in those fiery mysteries. But it was too late.

Beppo jumped to the floor and I thought that he was going to take his revenge and I was ready to protect myself with the copper candleholder. He stood facing me, his wheat-colored hair flaming, his tight waist, his concave stomach, his narrow hips, showing the shadow and the pendulum of his sex. But he controlled himself. With a mocking pause he picked up the multicolored clothes that proclaimed by their heraldic design that he was my servant, and dragging them along as if he were dragging our escutcheon through the dust of the inn, he made a great, exaggerated bow, as if I were Cardinal Franciotto, and he declared, "Madam, this gentleman is the distinguished Pier Francesco Orsini, the second son of the lord Duke of Bomarzo, and I am his page."

And he left the room, going down the corridor, naked as he was, with secure solemnity. I went out after him and reached the room where Messer Pandolfo, a thousand leagues away from those sad doings, was dreaming in a low voice and with a grinding of teeth. Later on I heard the soft touch of Ignacio de Zúñiga's spurs as he went back to his room, and I could hear my pages talking until late, lowering their voices, so that, even though I made an effort and put my ear against the boards, I could not make out what it was about. I could guess, of course. They could not have been speaking of anything else. They were most likely discussing me, analyzing me, making fun of me, and what pained me was that Zúñiga took part in it, which was probably nothing but a common bond against that stupid, imbecilic, monstrous fright of a hunchback that had been elevated to the intimacy of the most secret delights.

I arose early after being awake all night, resolved at least to conquer the good will of the Spaniard since I had lost that of my half-brother. Ignacio came to meet me with sober amiability, and I told him that I was certain that if he conducted himself well in my service and made a good impression in Florence, his fortunes would prosper. I spoke to him as if I had not been thrown out of Bomarzo; as if in truth I were the prince that I pretended to be, a prince who was traveling to Florence on a whim to visit Ippolito and Alessandro de' Medici and Clarice Strozzi, when reality was quite another thing, and Zúñiga could expect little from my friendly disposition. He answered me with some courteous monosyllables in which I seemed to detect a very faint touch of scorn, but what was certain was that I spent my life suspecting and sensing wrong things, and it was unjust for me to consider the Catholic hidalgo as one more enemy of the many who surrounded me, even though it was also certain that his status of a hidalgo, a man of a caste similar (at great remove, of course) to mine, heightened my susceptibility in the case, because I was anxious to obtain his approval ahead of that of Messer Pandolfo and Beppo, the presumed bastard, and I was convinced that an alliance with someone like Ignacio would help me face life and bear up under my inborn tortures.

Messer Pandolfo and Beppo arrived and we mounted.

"Did you rest well?" the tutor asked pompously. "Did Day and Night rest well?"

He quoted Virgil: *"Nox ruit et fuscis tellurem amplectitur alis*—Night falls and embraces the Earth with its somber wings." And he began to hum triumphantly.

I spurred my horse and went on ahead. The soft, rolling countryside of Tuscany was all around me, lined with rows of cypresses. All that had to be done was to cover the blue depths of the sky with gold and our small company would have been transformed into one of those retinues that advance, minute, detailed, through crags, vineyards, towers, and triangular trees, under stiff angels, through the steep perspective of old paintings. But beauty, my great alleviation, was not working against the bitterness that had poisoned my heart. I turned back to look at my people at a bend and I observed that Messer Pandolfo was following me at fifty paces, declaiming with broad gestures, and that in the rear Ignacio and Beppo were chatting cordially; Zúñiga with grave measure, while the second was pointing out the features of the countryside to the Castilian, arching now his silver arm, now his red arm. They held the reins of the two mules carrying my baggage. I remembered the woman from the inn and it seemed to me that the golden hills were painted in the shape of her breasts as she lay there, and that the erect trees, golden too, which some primitive brush had made stand out in space, were a schematic reproduction of the figure of Beppo as he had stood before me naked during the events in the garret, and also the still adolescent figure of Benvenuto Cellini during that morning in Cerveteri, all of which had meant an advance, a fearful progress in the realm of sensuality and its hazy suggestions. And when I saw Florence, the tears rushed into my eyes and changed it into a place different from everything I knew, perhaps into one of those vague legendary towns that lie buried at the bottom of lakes and the sea, for the slow gray clouds were passing over it and over its cupolas and its belfries, over the glitter of its palaces and its porticos and where the Arno must have been, like enormous whales floating in the aquatic iridescence of my weeping over the lethal peace of the sunken city. Only when the bells began to ring, speaking to one another, and an extended flight of swallows took off from the tops of walls like a waving battle standard, did I convince myself that Florence was awakening, thick with people and passion, and that in it life awaited me with ready weapons. Then I pressed the spurs to reach as soon as possible the city to which I owed my single happy memory of my father, the city through whose streets the gigantic David had passed on its way to the Signoria, and where beauty reigned. I should not have been in such a hurry. What was I bringing to Florence, the capital of beauty, what was I bringing except my ugliness, my misfortune, my insult, my displacement in the world, my yearnings for love and friendship and the certainty that clear joy was forbidden to me, because where I appeared, there was my shadow of a clown, of a vain Punch, staining the soil with derision. And what could it give me, on the other hand, if my presence was all that was needed to break down the balance of its order that had been gained with the rhythmic rigor of courtly music, in which words and buildings, expressions and statuary, the very new and the very ancient, responded to one another like instruments in a musical composition.

Messer Pandolfo knew his Dante. He did not like him, but he knew him. His exaggerated love for the Latin language prevented him from appreciating anything that was written in another tongue. He also spurred his mount, and when he was beside me he enjoyed himself by casting into the morning air Alighieri's imprecations against the city that had exiled him.

"Nest of malice," he shouted, "evil wood, city of avarice and pride, ingrate, fickle, Devil's plant!"

And raising his voice even louder: "Filthy fox, madwoman, female drunk with wrath, scabrous sheep who infects the flock!"

I begged him to quiet down. I did not look upon Florence the same way as the poet who was blinded by his wrath. I saw it, as we drew closer, as the most exquisite thing that I had seen until then, even more beautiful than Rome. The truth was that Messer Pandolfo had not strung those insults together because he hated Florence, but to show off his erudition.

## 2. THE UNCERTAINTIES OF LOVE

*Ippolito de' Medici's hunt—Adriana dalla Roza and the slave Abul—The elephant Annone—The discovery of Ariosto—Adriana's illness—Nencia's snobbery and lust—Pantasilea the harlot—The missing ring—Surrender in Benozzo Gozzoli's chapel—The fall of the Medicis*

FROM THE time we entered the city until we reached the Medici palace on the Via Larga, where I lived for almost three years from 1524 to 1527, the streets of Florence offered me the miracle of its structures. On that occasion and subsequent days I could see how its orderly cadence was arranged around the four bridges that crossed the Arno and its eleven fortified gates; how the embers of the cupolas and belfries glowed in the sunlight; how the palaces were aligned, where the multitude chatted in the porticoes and on the stone benches. Except for Venice, I have never walked through a more garrulous city. The merchants haggled with one another in front of their shops; the women bubbled through the markets; the passion for gambling flourished everywhere, among the groups who urged on the chess players and those following the dry sound of the dice; and the passion for music enveloped everything, with the undulating sound of clavichords, organs, violas, lutes, harps, horns, trombones, and cellos mingling with the sound of the conversations. The people argue and laugh about anything, blowing on the cloth for sale, making jokes. Around a corner there emerged the banners of guilds on their way to an assembly, with the *Agnus Dei* on a field of blue of the furriers and the white ram on a field of red of the wool merchants waving, brushing against the cornices. Men pestered women with flirtatious remarks. A courtesan passed by, serious, aristocratic, like a great lady, on a bedecked mule, followed by a retinue that included young patricians and prelates, and the onlookers stood open-mouthed at the grace of the prostitute's bearing as her name passed from mouth to mouth. A page was carrying her parrot as if it were a falcon, and another a monkey perfumed with ambergris and orange blossoms. Although Florence had loosened many of the clerical bonds that had been tied by Savonarola, a whole world of nuns and monks circulated about its one hundred convents and monasteries, and the people would tip their hats to a cardinal or some great lord, while on the squares the loafers milled around the blind men, the beggars, and the tellers of tales who chanted verses of love and war that recounted the legends of Ginevra degli Amieri, or Saint Alban, Orlando Furioso, Lancelot, Constantine, Vespasian, Nero.

One could feel in Florence more than anywhere else the force of life. One could feel the city throbbing and vibrating and trembling from door to door. And one could also feel the art, the permanent and vital presence of art. Faces, expressions became transfigured in that atmosphere as if they required the familiar background of paintings or the sculptured marble or bronze to stand out with the desired intensity. Some children were going along the street singing, dancing, and they were a bas-relief by Mino da Fiesole or Luca della Robbia; some serious and handsome adolescents went by, and it was Donatello; there was a warrior, and it was Pollaiuolo; some peasants passed and it was Ghiberti; a gentleman, thin as a flower, in a suit of silver brocade, and it was Benvenuto Cellini; some ladies went by with richly assembled necklaces and earrings, and it was Pontormo; an athlete passed, and it was Michelangelo.

I remember how at that time, flanked by my three companions, I went along half startled, half fearful, covering the distance that separated me from my future residence. I was taken by the notion that those young men who were so handsome and so relaxed were returning, like Greek ephebi, from the stadium or on their way to the houses of humanists and courtesans, with their short hair and small beards, and that those statuesque women who, according to their station, walked with a missal in their hands or with a pitcher and a bundle on their shoulders—and, even more exotic, Circassian and Tartar slave girls with wide, sad eyes—were looking at me, at my hump, and were saying things that would draw attention to me in that noisy bustle. The ironical Florentines were doubtlessly saying something, but I kept on going, so erect on my mount that my back ached, pretending not to notice the ridicule and not to notice either the disrespectful gratification with which Beppo greeted the girls.

That was how we arrived at the palace. Fate had ordained that in the entrance to the square main court yard, the *cortile*, there were gathered together the outstanding characters who were to play roles in my next few years, for one of them, Ippolito, was getting ready to leave for the hunt, and he would not be back until the next day, and the others were watching the preparations. So I had them all together, suddenly, as soon as I dismounted: eight characters distributed about the stage which had witnessed the triumphs and penury of the Medicis, who had received popes, emperors, kings, princes, and the wisest and most sensitive men of their time, at the entrance to the palace where Cosimo, the father of his country, had founded the power of his dynasty, where Lorenzo had presided over his dazzling court, where Leo X had grown up, where Clement VII had planned the political future of his people; the *cortile* that had also been crossed during the tumultuous flight of the inhabitants into their successive exiles.


They were eight characters arranged deliberately, as in a fresco, for everything in the Florence of that time had a pictorial quality and tone. The three Roman tombs stood out among the columns, and one of them contained the remains of Guccio de' Medici, a gonfalonier from two hundred years back; the ancient sculptures, the Marsyas, Donatello's David, Verrocchio's David, the medallions in imitation of the cameos that belonged to the Magnificent. The covered loggia opened up above, the gallery called the *altana*, from which, topping the pictorial perspective, several short-sleeved women had tapestries and freshly washed clothes ready to hang, and they were looking into the courtyard at the impatient horses, hearing the shouts of the huntsmen, the sound of crossbows and blunderbusses. And although the gathering was numerous and quite eccentric, for Ippolito was in the habit of being surrounded by a fantastic company, a kind of luxurious circus, I only distinguished at first the eight characters located in the center of the *cortile*, which was being bathed in a soft clearness, and who, like Pirandello's famous ones, more than real human beings, seemed to be entelechies or allegories waiting for the artist who was to interpret them, and being so alive, they were quite different from the bustle that was going on around them with a flapping, barking, and neighing confusion of birds of prey, weapons, dogs, and servants, and they were gloriously isolated, unique and untouchable, from the theatrical machinery that was being set up around them so that they could continue declaiming their roles.

In the very middle, so that the entire composition rotated about his axis, which Luca Pacioli, "the monk intoxicated with beauty," would have used when he wrote his work on divine proportion, and which Leonardo da Vinci, his illustrator, would have drawn to explain their laws of harmony, stood Ippolito de' Medici. One could sense all around, governed by the inflexible mathematics of the Golden Section, the vigorous web of geometric figures that support Renaissance paintings, as each of the other characters developed in his own orbit, using him as a point of reference and adjusting to the cadence of his movements.

Ippolito looked fifteen years old. He was handsome, virile. His uncle, Clement VII, had sent him to Florence some time before as *capo* of the city, but they addressed him as "Your Serene Highness" and called him, like his grandfather, the "Magnificent." He liked prominence, forgetting the wise lesson of his ancestor, Giovanni di Bicci, who taught his sons that Medicis should be pointed at as little as possible. That was why it went so badly for him later. At the time in question, with the fate of leaders so insecure, the idea that his life would soon be over did not cross his mind. He was a boy with large eyes, dressed in black silk with scarlet sleeves, and he was playing with Rodone, his favorite dog. I learned later that he would alternate violent, almost mythological exercises such as breaking horses, the feats of an athlete capable of jumping with his feet together over the backs of ten men, and of perforating a cuirass with his arrow, with poetry and the translation of Virgil. He had translated the whole second book of the *Aeneid* into Italian. I was fascinated by him from the beginning. Messer Pandolfo too, but for more intellectual reasons.

Beside him, smaller, for he was only thirteen years old, was his cousin

Alessandro, who had come from Naples. He was dark-complexioned, with black hair and thick lips. It was said that his mother was a servant of my aunt, Alfonsina Orsini, the wife of Piero de' Medici, but others asserted that he was the son of a Moorish slave girl. As for his father, some claimed that he was a natural son of Lorenzo de' Medici, the Duke of Urbino, while the rest attributed his paternity to Clement VII himself, thereby justifying the strange preference of the pontiff. What was certain was that both he and Ippolito were bastards, which irritated the Florentines. The pope himself was one too, and that had many people in Italy upset.

Next to Alessandro was a laughing boy who belonged, on the other hand, to the legitimate branch of the Medicis, Lorenzino, the one who would assassinate him later, and who at that time was around nine years of age, fragile and malleable, and with a liking for foolishness. Without knowing it, he was already attempting to fulfill the idea of Baldassare Castiglione's courtier, who must not only be able to practice the buffoonery, but also the witticisms of a jester. If his interlocutors had drawn sufficiently close, perhaps they would have discovered a spark, a flame in the depths of his eyes.

He was the favorite of Clarice de' Medici, a lady much older than the others, for she was thirty years old and married to Filippo Strozzi, a great gentleman of whose ambiguous conduct I shall speak later. She really was a true Medici, with no spurious shadow, the daughter of Piero and the granddaughter of Lorenzo the Magnificent, the daughter and granddaughter at the same time of two Orsinis, Alfonsina and Clarice, my close relatives. Intelligence glowed on her face as quality glowed in her aristocratic manners.

On Ippolito's other side, splendidly dressed, moving with a wave of emerald and saffron brocade falling down in stiff pleats, leaning her thin fingers on the shoulders of the boys, was Catherine de' Medici, the one who was to be queen of France, and who joined together, like Lorenzino, the traits of the Florentines, who were given to jokes and irony, and a certain glacial reserve that sometimes would harden her face; and Adriana dalla Roza, the Roman girl whom I loved so much and who wore a topaz on her ring finger to protect her from the assaults of Eros.

And to complete the central theme of the composition, somewhat to the rear, was the purple tone of Cardinal Silvio Passerini, thin, cleanshaven, deceptive, named by Clement VII as tutor for Ippolito and Alessandro and charged with governing Florence with an iron hand in their name, along with his protégé Giorgio Vasari, Giorgino, the painter, who knew Virgil by heart.

In this way I have conserved intact in my memory the image of the eight palace characters. Over them there descended, as if a spotlight were shining on the center of the *cortile*, the golden reflection of the sun as it sparkled on cloth and metal, inflaming rubies and plumes, while among the columns there appeared and disappeared rumps and manes of stamping horses and the coming and going of Ippolito's squires, lackeys, and slaves, receiving from time to time as a pictorial touch on a breastplate, legs, the crook of an arm, a brief brushstroke of light that heightened the extravagant diversity of the hunter's following, which was made up of Moors from North Africa, Tartar bowmen, a bubbling of faces and torsos with tints ranging from lustrous ebony to the yellowish pallor of ivory, and rebellious hair held in by caps and multicolored turbans. Sometimes a very thin hand covered with rings that sparkled like beetle shells would emerge from the shadows grasping a scimitar, raising a quiver, with a shaking of shards and antennae; or the snort of a palfrey, white with foam, would break out of the vagueness of the tombs and statues as it was pulled along by one of the grooms. And that second zone framed the inner one with an agile rhythm that contrasted with the quiet, smiling, distant bearing of the lords, for most of the Africans and Asians had the furtive lightness of jugglers, acrobats, and slack-rope walkers, and their leaps and pirouettes, their shouts in barbarian dialects, and their comical contortions pointed up the slim elegance of Ippolito and his group, rounding out in that way the esthetic plan that was presented to my eyes and which was a kind of summary of all the grace of Florence, restless and ceremonious, stupendously cosmopolitan, the most different thing in the world from the milieu of my home in Bomarzo (where, however, they aspired to imitate it), for there everything was bound by the dictates of a proud military tradition. That archaic tradition, heroically hermetic and perhaps passé, was disdained by this people of opulent merchants and ingenious collectors, just as my people looked down on them, for the Medicis even considered us primitive to a certain degree—today we would say medieval—and the Orsinis considered them, their relatives, as noisy parvenus, more concerned with good taste, which is superficial and a feminine thing, than with the manipulation of arms, which is proper for men. But the truth is that the Orsinis envied the Medicis a bit, quite a bit, and they could not pardon them for having come out of the obscurity of their banking arrangements to be capable of giving them lessons in urbanity and refinement.

My great sensual delight has always been based—that is still the case today—on the pleasure of my eyes. Neither the most exquisite melodic arrangement, nor the rarest aroma, nor contact with the most golden and soft human skin, nor wine, nor a kiss, can bring me the pleasure that my eyes give me. Nor, as it is for certain superior minds, can the philosophical game with all that it implies of transcendent stimulus supply me with the reward my eyes can give me. Not even the game of poetry, which I love so much. For me my eyes are the sluice gates through which the noisy and shining river of the world penetrates into my interior. From the moment I arrived in Florence my eyes feasted, as if until then they had never reached the possibilities of their pleasure. I went savoring through the streets on my way to the *cortile*. It was as though the most intoxicating visual experiences that I had accumulated in Rome and Bomarzo were meaningless in their pettiness in the face of that swollen jubilation. And the reward that came from that concert of colors and textures dominated me as if it were being put together by a superb director, reaching its high point for my eyes in that stone courtyard surrounded by musical statues and in the picture of the figures flanking Ippolito de' Medici.

The singular thing—and it shows how rapidly Fate operates—is that while I did appreciate the marvel of the composition I am describing in its smallest details, my faithful and alert eyes became so extremely sensitive that they showed me something apart—in addition, of course, to the primordial image of Ippolito, the victorious sun of that planetary system—two figures that, despite the company's being so numerous and the group of the eight fundamental characters so imposing, stood out for an instant from the complex resonances of the composition as if suddenly during a very brief silence of the well-tuned instruments two high and single notes—one of a flute, perhaps, the other of cymbals—rang out, not in my ears but in my eyes, with their separate and powerful vibration. And those fleeting and persistent notes came from the girl that I have already named, Adriana dalla Roza, a maid of honor to the small Catherine de' Medici; and her long neck, violet eyes, and Venetian blond hair impressed me at once, the same as the grace of her movements and the modest elegance with which she wore her light blue silk dress with a round skirt and a large pouch hanging from her gold belt, as she was moving like a bird in the shadows of the *cortile*; and from a motionless man, one of Ippolito de' Medici's Oriental servants, who, in my evaluation of the picture, was essentially opposed for a second not only to Adriana but to the rest of the dynamic participants in the coming hunt for his firm calmness, statuesque, and who, as he leaned on a halberd, erect, his blue turban with red feathers above his face of an idol, dark and delicate, his black torso naked over the billowing of his bell-shaped pants of turquoise-colored damask, gave off a sensation of invulnerable equilibrium, so robust in spite of the bony thinness of his silhouette, and he did not seem to be a human being but another decoration that had been placed under the loggia, to one side of the vast vestibule, by the artists of the house. I fleetingly heard those two distinct notes amid the shouting, and the girl and the slave were erased at once in the tumult, for the horses were going forward now with a noise of harnesses and the shouts of command, and the composition broke up and dispersed before the surprise of my eyes.

Ippolito, up on his saddle, was the first to spot me and my three companions at the palace gates. He had been told of my coming by my grandfather in a laconic letter, so he dismounted immediately, and moving Moors and Turks aside he hastened to bid me welcome, his face illuminated by an expression so perfectly courteous that my fear, if it did not disappear completely, loosened the knots that were holding it tight. That was, in any case, the most trying moment for me, the one I most feared, the initial meeting with those with whom I was to share my life for the next few years. I do not know whether Franciotto Orsini in his letter had referred to my singularity or not. I suppose not. The Orsinis found it repugnant to mention it in front of strangers. Perhaps Ippolito knew all about it, for I presume that the "case" of the Duke of Bomarzo's son was most likely known in Italian courts and especially in Florence, the hotbed of gossip. Be that as it may, Ippolito refused to let me bow as I had planned to before His Serene Highness, nor would he permit me to call him by that title—as he waved his hand and swept the air with a quick, indifferent gesture—but he embraced me and patted me on the shoulders, taking care that his hands did not brush my humiliating back. He addressed me with the ancestral nickname that my grandmother had given me, Vicino, and when I heard the sound of it, so far from her loving presence for which I yearned, my heart tightened. Honored by Ippolito, who appeared to me to be the most open, cordial, and slim of men, I was perspiring with anguish. The others came up behind him, gathering their curiosity together. Clarice, Catherine, and Adriana kissed me on the mouth, in accordance with the custom of the time, which demanded that ladies kiss a gentleman's hand, but if he was noble they kissed his cheek, and if he was descended from an illustrious line they joined their lips to his. And when mine touched softly on those of Adriana dalla Roza and her curved forehead was so close, her eyebrows that opened out like black feathers and her violet eyes where there was a hint of microscopic golden veins like those in Benvenuto Cellini's pebbles, I trembled, oh, as if I were about to swoon. It was then that I noticed her topaz ring, a stone destined to protect her against the wiles of love, and I sensed in my confusion that I was going to suffer because of her. Even so, everything went along much better than I had expected. Only Alessandro de' Medici, the negroid, the Othello of the group, as he embraced me ran his cruel fingers over my back without making any comment, and he gave me such a mocking smile that I was disturbed lest the slaves should notice it. And, in fact, there was some movement of surprise and there were a few knavish expressions, and among the horse tenders a brief murmur arose, and a woman on the *altana*, where they were hanging clothes, broke out in laughter, but Ippolito spun around on his heels, and hitting his boots with his whip, imposed silence with a shout. I kissed Cardinal Passerini's ring, on which a sapphire glistened, just as on the papal right hand, to indicate that the princes of the Church shared in pontifical omnipotence, and Ippolito, from whose eyes, like mine, nothing escaped, begged me to show him the medallion on my hat. It was the one that Benvenuto had given me through little Paolino, and which showed the figures of our shield, and scarcely had I answered, stammering, telling who had designed it, than he praised me for it and spent time looking it over. Benvenuto Cellini's medal was my artistic passport. Even today, across the distance of the centuries, I am grateful to him for it. It interested Ippolito, Clarice Strozzi, Lorenzino, and Giorgio Vasari much more than the deviation of my spinal column.

I went through the lordly *cortile*, feeling dozens of eyes pecking at my back. Silvio Passerini, the Cardinal of Cortona, bony, mundane, hoarse from the cold, holding a handkerchief embroidered with his arms, was telling me about the friendship that joined him to my grandfather Franciotto, and he reminded me that both had received their capes at the same time, in 1517, when the prodigality of Leo X had created thirty-one cardinals, but I was scarcely listening to him. The blood was buzzing in my ears and the luxurious words were swimming singly on the surface of their sound. I turned away with him and the girls to the stairway that led to the upper rooms, and halfway up we turned to watch the departure of the hunters, who, their weapons aloft, and their horns vibrating, saluted us. The prelate sneezed, sketched the sign of the cross in the air, and behind his sketch, which held a square invisible grating in the air, I observed the grace with which the horsemen mounted and, in the midst of the tumult of whippets and pages, beside the Negroes who were leading them on silver leashes, several of those Asian ounces, yellowish, with long tails and agile legs, turning their cattish heads about, and reputed to be the swiftest animals on earth, superb hunters, I saw again, fleetingly, in a flash, the outline of the slave with pink plumes, who, as he passed under our battlement, lowered his head, which was as proud as that of one of the Magi. At that instant I felt another elbow softly brushing against mine. It was that of Adriana dalla Roza, and the contact could only have been coincidental, for she was occupied, like Catherine de' Medici, in waving a handkerchief. A mysterious, unforeseen happiness came over me, as if I had taken a sip of my father's Greek wine. I looked for the eyes of

Messer Pandolfo, of Ignacio de Zúñiga in order to communicate it to them with a blinking of my eyes, but I could not find them, and guided by the Cardinal of Cortona, I continued up the stairway, making an effort to infuse into my thirteen years and my ungainly architecture the arrogance worthy of an Orsini, of a member of that family that was so old, so noble, and so famous that its descendants, even those made clumsy by afflicting humps, received as their due, as is just, the respect of well-educated merchants.

During my first night in Florence I had a strange dream. I dreamed that I was walking through the garden of Bomarzo with my grandmother and Cardinal Passerini. Michelangelo's David appeared in the garden, taller than the cypresses. I let go of the hands of the lady and the cardinal and went over to the foot of the statue, which rose and rose until its head was lost in the clouds, as was said to have happened with the Tower of Babel. I found myself between the open legs of the colossus, as if under the curve of a triumphal arch, and I was waiting for something that was to happen without knowing what it was. Then, in order, like ballet dancers, Ippolito de' Medici, Adriana dalla Roza, and the Negro hunter arose between the legs of the statue. Ippolito placed himself in the center of the arch and the other two came forward toward me to the sound of hidden violas on the right and on the left, and they kissed my lips alternately, while His Most Serene Highness contemplated us gravely and his gloves, embroidered with precious stones, clutched the gold chain that hung from his neck. And on that chain glowed Benvenuto Cellini's medal, it glowed so much that it finally blinded me and left me alone and trembling in the darkness that was illuminated here and there, as by stars in a firmament, by the stones on the gloves and the figures on the medal, the bear and the flower.

Before retiring that same evening, I had my first impression of the divisions that separated the Medicis. I had heard something in Bomarzo about the discords that had embittered the Florentines among themselves. The Palleschi on one side, favoring the governing family, derived their name from the famous *palle*, the lozenges on the shield of the Medicis which not even with the fleurs-de-lis of France which they incorporated by the grace of Louis XI had succeeded in becoming really noble. On the other side the Piagnoni, the weepers, as they were nicknamed in mockery by their enemies, were the successors of the fanatics who appeared as followers of Savonarola and his monkish tyranny. But the latter made up the street bands, those involved in uprisings, attempted assassinations, those who came out shouting into the streets during the time of revolution. Far was I from knowing that within the palace on the Via Larga and in the bosom of the family, the opposing passions stirred up those who should have been allied in defense. The palace boiled with intrigues. The bastards were opposed by the legitimate offspring. And not even those factions presented clear outlines, for the bastards did not get along well. Ippolito understood that he was the chief of state, the *capo* of the city, anointed by Pope Clement, while Alessandro gnawed at the bit, waiting for his chance, aroused without doubt by that same Clement VII, his presumed father, and he would rear up every time his cousin was called "Highness." What was certain was that the one who really governed, crushing the Florentines with taxes, was Cardinal Passerini, and that the two precocious boys—one fifteen years old, the other thirteen—played at politics and authority with their horses and clothing. And of the legitimate ones, Clarice Strozzi symbolized the pure tradition of the Magnificent and the father of his country, and she took pains to indoctrinate Lorenzino, her distant relative, from infancy, so that the power would return to the genuine branch, the one without stain of adulteration, while little Catherine, the *duchessina*, hated the vulgar. Alessandro, but, on the other hand, she adored Ippolito, the charmer. Some time passed before I could capture those shades in detail, but on the afternoon of my arrival, as I have already said, I needed only a short conversation with Clarice to get an idea of the strength of her temper and to understand what unexpected energies were enclosed in her will.

She called me aside when she found me wandering through the rooms, and as if she were trying to amuse me, she began to talk about the palace, what it was and what it had been. My sensitivity was extremely thankful for any evidence of concern for my person. Nothing could have given me more pleasure than that, for them to speak to me like that, cordially, simply, as if the barrier of my physique did not exist, as if I were one of the so many boy princes of the House of Orsini whom it was proper to amuse and divert. And the pleasure increased with that opportunity because it came from a beautiful and serious woman, thirty years old, the head, in a certain way, of the family with whom I was living.

I wandered marveling from one object to another, and Clarice explained to me that the things I saw lacked importance compared to the treasures that her grandfather Lorenzo had collected there and which had disappeared in the sack of 1494.

"My father would tell me when I was very small," she added, "and I liked that story better than all the others. The quarters of the Magnificent glittered. They contained the Flemish tapestries and the six paintings by Uccello showing the battle, and the cameos and infinite crystals of his collection, the sardonyxes, the chalcedonies, the amethysts, the reliquary of rubies and pearls, the books with miniatures. All of that glittered. My father used to say that when he would describe the lost objects to me, my eyes would glitter."

"They still glitter," I said, and, in fact, her dark eyes were shining under the arc of her brows as if reflected in them were the agates, the onyxes, and the crystals that today are scattered among the showcases of so many museums in the world, in Italy, France, England, or as if inside them the great battle by Uccello, all banners and lances and armor, were taking place.

"My grandmother," she went on, "your aunt, Clarice Orsini, was severe. She did not understand pagan things. She detested the Platonic teachers. She could not bear to look at the statue showing Hercules triumphant over Antaeus. She would close her eyes. In that she was a true Orsini. I'm not. I have more Orsini blood than Medici, but I feel like a Medici. I like rigor, order, a certain severity—and that's from the Orsini side—but above all I like life, the splendor of life—and that's from the Medici side. You don't seem to be completely an Orsini either, in spite of the repetition of the blood in your veins. It's better that way. But the Orsini blood is our luxury."

I puffed up my chest as much as I could, flattered, seduced. It filled me with arrogance to hear my line spoken of in that way, even though to the Orsinis of Bomarzo—excepting, of course, my grandmother

Diana—I owed only bad memories. Clarice had evidently planned to capture me and she was having success. She spoke of the two Orsini women, her mother and her grandmother, to bring us even closer together. She took one of my hands, the one with Benvenuto's ring, and she went on: "My grandmother was stupendous. She must have been very much like yours, that admirable woman."

When she said those words, she gained complete power over me and her dominion increased as she went on: "You remind me of Diana Orsini, Vicino."

And immediately she launched into the tale of what she knew of the marriage of her grandmother to Lorenzo the Magnificent.

"When she was married, she wore the Medici diamond, which is beyond compare, on her forehead. And she died when she was thirty-eight. I shall die young too."

"How do you know?"

"I know." She lowered the tone of her voice. "They don't love me here. Only Catherine and Lorenzino love me. But you will love me."

"I will love you. Don't die, Clarice... I... I will never die..."

I regretted having said it. She laughed and her laughter lit up the room. "I hope you won't die, Vicino. I think that we're all going to die. But first I have a lot of things to do. The Holy Father"—her voice was a thread—"doesn't love me either."

She sank her nails into my sleeve, and as she brought her face close to mine, I could see, like a removable mask and one which modified her features, the pomades with which she anointed herself, the white of her cheeks, the red of her mouth, and I could smell the camphor that was mixed with the oil of sweet almonds to soften her skin.

The mask was over: "The bastards are against us, against Catherine, against Lorenzino, against me; never forget that. But we're the real Medicis. This palace belongs to us."

She went off toward the door. She was wearing so many pearls on her dress and they trembled in such a way when she walked, that I thought that a rain of pearls was going to stay behind in the room in the wake of her passage.

Then I found out that she was not happy with Filippo Strozzi, her husband, who was always visiting houses of prostitution. In Rome the gentleman was an assiduous visitor of Tulia of Aragon and Camilla of Pisa, the intellectual courtesans who wrote poetry and offered their beds. He would send them rhetorical letters. And in the meantime, Clarice, who had married him when she was fifteen years old, kept thrust deep in her breast the obsession with the power held by the bastards and with her own weakness, and slowly, lovingly, without anyone's foreseeing it, she was preparing Lorenzino's spirit for the crime. But that, the crime, took place thirteen years after the moment I am speaking of, and when it did, Clarice had been dead for a long time. At the time of my arrival in Florence, Lorenzino de' Medici was still a child. He was not yet Lorenzaccio.

As I was accustomed to do when my father returned from the wars or the hunt, I arose very early to spy on Ippolito's return. The fantastic dream that I have described had made me restless, and I was the first one who, hidden in the gallery, witnessed the return. It occurs to me now that Beppo, my page, was spying on me—perhaps on orders from my father or my older brother, perhaps on his own—because a short time before Ippolito's party burst into the *cortile*, he emerged out of the shadows with his permanent smile to greet me and disappear immediately thereafter.

The hunters had got several splendid specimens. Two wild boars were dangling from two pikes on the shoulders of the gamekeepers. And the dead birds of prey, mixed up, their wings and talons as sharp as knives, overflowed the game bags and large baskets. The procession entered the courtyard with a great bustle. Ippolito dismounted in the light of the torches that brought to life the figures in the corners, in the secrecy of the tombs. He lifted his head and spied me in the *altana*. Immediately, with three elastic bounds, he was beside me, affectionate, vehement, boasting of the success of his hunt and recalling the skill of my grandfather, master of the hunt for Leo X. In the smoke of the torches he pointed out to me the boars, the deer, the wolves, the foxes that passed by hanging head down. Then I spied the slave who had concerned me and I realized that I had not left my bed and gone out at dawn to admire the return of Ippolito, but to see again that unknown person with a black face, short beard, and wide-set eyes who had walked through the intimacy of my dream. As on the previous day, he was leaning on his halberd; as on the previous day, he was wearing a blue turban with pink plumes. This time, bathed in the sudden orange clarity with which the torches had bedaubed the *cortile*, I appreciated better the edge of his cheekbones, the firmness of his hands, the thickness of his lips, the baroque pearls that trembled on his ears, the bracelets that tightened about his arms near his elbows, the vigor that emanated from his agile figure. I wanted to know at once who he was, but first, in order to hide my interest—not because I considered it blameworthy, but because I, for obvious reasons, ought not to run the risk of showing interest in absolutely anyone, because my curiosity might unleash a storm of mockery—I asked Ippolito about other members of his band, and the young *capo* of Florence, noticing my intrigue, wrapped his whip on the loggia and gave several rapid commands. Quickly the *cortile* was transformed into a circus ring. Those exotic men, worn out by hours of tension and physical demands, forgot their fatigue. The joy of the game worked a metamorphosis in them. Human pyramids of complicated construction grew like squids, like gigantic spiders in the center of the *cortile*. Others jumped around like monkeys or danced athletic dances to the sound of the tambourines, giving free rein to an animal jubilation, triumphant over their exhaustion. The pyramids swirled with the glow of black, bronzed, and ocher skins over the muscles, with phosphorescent eyes and teeth, with panaches of manes, of knots of hair, of feathers; and Ippolito, who from time to time would lash the air with his whip, was telling me where his servants came from and explaining their virtues. When it came to the turn of the one who interested me especially and who was fearlessly crowning a monstrous pyramid, the arms and legs of which, locked together, seemed to belong to a single being, perhaps to one of the strange gods that those very slaves worshiped in their distant countries, Ippolito told me that he had been in Italy for over ten years, that he had come to Rome in the magnificent embassy that King Manuel of Portugal had sent to honor Leo X, and that in that unforgettable ceremony he had ridden and guided the famous elephant Annone, whom the monarch had sent as an offering to the pontiff.

Later on, gathering facts from here and there, I was able to reconstruct the short biography of Abul (for that was his name, like a character from the *Arabian Nights*). He had been born in North Africa, he could not remember where. A pirate had kidnaped him as a child after his village had been burned, and had sold him to Portuguese slave traders. He had learned the difficult and ancient art of training elephants and he had always lived among them. When Annone, the most superb and majestic elephant of his day, was shipped out with the court at Lisbon as his destination, Abul sailed with him. He constantly whispered words to him, consoled him, calmed him down; he did not speak to any other. But in Lisbon Abul fell in love with the daughter of a shoemaker and she succumbed to the fascination of the black boy who passed by sitting on the elephant's head, wrapped in a red cape like an emperor. And if Abul did not forget Annone, he did divide the affection he had given him. Until they ordered him to join the embassy that was to leave for Rome, where Annone was to be given to the Holy Father. Abul spoke softly to the elephant one night. He was anxious to stay in Lisbon, making love to the slipper maker's daughter, showing himself on the streets in his red cape, and he told his companion that they were preparing to take him to a land where he would be treated very badly. Annone—who did not bear an old Carthaginian name in vain—obstinately refused to leave. Then the King of Portugal himself, Dom Manuel de Aviz, the Fortunate—such is the story, with a king, an elephant and a handsome Negro who knew the language of the proboscideans—when he discovered that it was all a stratagem of Abul's brought on by his love for the shoemaker's girl, called the slave and told him that he would kill him if the elephant did not leave for Rome with him on its back. So that Abul, who appreciated his life more than the Portuguese girl, could only reason again with the enormous Annone and clarify the situation, confessing to him that he had been erroneously informed, and that the country that awaited them overseas was a veritable paradise. Persuaded, Annone went on board the ship

## THE UNCERTAINTIES OF LOVE · 101

with the melancholy Abul. The shoemaker's daughter followed them weeping to the port, and the great lords who had come to bid farewell to the embassy, whose flagship was commanded by the heroic Tristão da Cunha, all golden necklaces, gauntlets, and shining armor, pushed her back, irritated, not understanding what such vulgar and strident grief had to do with the voyage of an elephant who was going to kneel before the pope.

Abul obtained his full reward when he presented himself before Leo X, sitting on his heels, half naked, on top of Annone's large swaying head in the middle of the procession that unwound its splendor along the bridge by the Castel Sant' Angelo and which His Holiness contemplated ecstatically through his monocle from the top of the castle, for it was the most fabulous spectacle that had ever been offered his eyes of a connoisseur of beauty. The prodigious beast went along, the first of its kind to appear in the city since the fall of the Roman emperors, moving slowly amid the noise of the trumpets and the fifes, preceded by several ladies and hidalgos dressed in scarlet velvet, behind a Moor riding a resplendent white horse, and led by a Saracen; but the one who was really guiding him, speaking a secret word to him from time to time, was Abul, the triumphant Abul who glistened up there like a jewel, made of obsidian, jet, and rubies, and with one hand he stroked and calmed a leopard who was crouching on the swaying back. That back supported on its crimson trappings a silver castle with several turrets, one of which was used for the exposition of the Holy Sacrament while another carried a chalice, and on the others there were several coffers with sacred ornaments. Behind came mules with trappings, the felines, the exorbitant hoarse parrots, and behind them the ambassadors, in the midst of whom advanced the famous Tristão da Cunha, the conqueror of distant isles, whose stony face was chiseled out amid the sharp geometry of the halberds and the feathers of the brilliant birds, as if everything being shown there was one of his dreams, a dream of the conqueror of barbarian tribes in the name of Dom Manuel the Fortunate; and it was as if that tapestry of the Indies that unfolded its many colors along the bridge of the Castel Sant' Angelo and which, as the participants appeared on the parapets, poured forth its bejeweled luxury into the restless Tiber, which was such an expert in extravagant processions, had been woven with the threads of the discoverer's dreams. But Abul was riding much higher than he. Abul, with the leopard, was riding above the astonished multitude as if he were sailing in the prow of a rocking galleon of the King of Portugal, cutting through a sea of startled heads and feeling against the sides of the imposing ship, not the blows of albatrosses and sea gulls, but the wing beats of jungle birds from the tropics, parrots and macaws of different types who prolonged their electricity around them, their excited sparkle, their discharges of blue enamel or butterfly blue and sulphur yellow. When the delegation bearing messages and gifts had departed, Annone remained in the Eternal City under the care of Abul in the Belvedere of the Vatican, where people came to see him dance to the sound of fifes. But afterward they tried to humiliate him. Messer Giambattista Branconi dell' Aquila, the pontifical chamberlain in charge of his maintenance, would put aside for himself a good chunk of the outlay assigned to the feeding of the elephant. The pope decided to use him as a part of the mockery of the coronation on Capitol Hill of a jester poet who was to put on the laurel of Petrarch; and Annone, dignified, very serious, as they crossed the bridge of Sant' Angelo, which had witnessed his martial victory and which was now shaking with laughter and sarcasm, threw the clown to the ground. He must have obeyed a brief command from Abul, who would not tolerate such decadence either. A short time later Annone died; of illness, some said; of sadness, of shame, others suspected. They buried him by the entrance to the Vatican; Raffaelo d'Urbino painted his likeness; a poet wrote his epitaph in hexameters. Abul, empty, lost, orphaned, wandered through Rome until Ippolito de' Medici, always on the lookout for curiosities, took him into his service and brought him to Florence.

I have told the story of Annone in such detail because many years later, in Bomarzo, during the period when I was constructing the wood of monsters, I wanted the memory of Abul's elephant eternalized in it, and I ordered one of the rocks sculpted in his shape. Last year, when I was in Bomarzo, I observed that there are almost no traces of the figure of Abul himself, which rises up on the head in front of the small castle fastened to his back, eroded by time. On the other hand, the one who can still be made out rather clearly, in the dress of a Roman soldier, is Beppo, my page. The elephant has his trunk wound around the body of the soldier, Beppo, and is crushing him. The meaning of that allegory will be understood later on.

During the moments when beside Ippolito de' Medici I witnessed the *féerie* in the *cortile* and the play of the shadows that the torches made large upon the walls, I was far from imagining that the sharply outlined, gleaming person who crowned one of the spinning pyramids would, with the passage of time, be transformed into a symbol. Abul was farther from thinking it than I, for even if I had noticed him, he did not seem to be aware of my presence. But no—on that occasion I had the impression for the first time that he was looking at me. It was during one of the rotations of the human pyramid that was holding him aloft. Our eyes met and touched for the fraction of a second. Then, as before, I felt the rub of an arm against mine. It was Adriana's. She had arrived with Catherine de' Medici, running, flying through the galleries with fur cloaks on, their unbraided hair floating behind, with a page who was running too, carrying a candelabrum. The uproar of the acrobats had awakened them and they arrived shivering, naked under their furs, drawn by Ippolito's return. Intoxicated by the spectacle of the acrobats and strongmen, by the friendship of Ippolito the Magnificent, by that enchanted palace, by the Negro mahout who was outlined before me with the subtle design of a piece of Renaissance jewelry, one of those fantastic brooches that hang over the low necks of beautiful women, and by the nearness of Adriana dalla Roza, whom I could hear breathing heavily against the balustrade, I did something that I do not know how I dared to do—because one must not forget that I was only thirteen years old, that there was an outcropping on my back, and that I was only the second son of the Duke of Bomarzo, exiled from the parental estate. Slowly (without looking at her, naturally, without looking at her even once), I slipped my hand, my icy, mad, unmanageable left hand, which wore Benvenuto Cellini's mixture of gold and steel, and which moved as if it did not belong to me, as if it were an animal with five tentacles and a single eye of steel and gold, perched in the shadows on the balustrade, independent of me, an undomesticated small animal, very beautiful and quite unknown, or at least unrecognizable for me in the opportunity in which it escaped from my control, and free, but infinitely cautious, which was crawling away along the balustrade; I slipped that hand along, or rather, my hand slipped along by itself, endowed with will and intelligence, until it touched the hand of Adriana, who, unaware of it all, was resting there on the railing of the loggia, and it took hold of her. And in the instant in which that happened, my hand became completely mine once more, abandoning its autonomous individuality, so that I found that I was fully responsible for that extravagance. I did not know what to do, whether to draw it back or leave it there, whether to hold it still or prolong the caress it had begun and for which I was not to blame, and during that doubt I noticed that Adriana, whom I had thought, rather absurdly, insensitive to my feelings, distracted by the improvised festivities and by the gleam of so many naked bodies combined in rhythm, perhaps not noticing my audacity, assumed in her turn the initiative in the secret game, in the pantomime hidden in the shadows of the balustrade, and she took my hand openly, slightly sinking her long nails into my palm. Something became knotted in my throat; my eyes clouded over, and King Baldassare disappeared from the peak of the pyramid the same as his companions disappeared along with the whole gymnastic architecture that filled the *cortile* with quivering structures. Without looking at her, because for nothing in the world would I have dared turn to her, I saw Adriana, only Adriana dalla Roza, as if suddenly I had been covered with eyes, as if I were an Argus or a peacock or a mythological tiger flecked with open eyes instead of a hunchback livid with terror; I saw Adriana next to me, her hand in mine, her violet and golden look, her neck that was like an exquisite stalk, her breasts that were struggling, that perhaps were peeking out from under the nocturnal furs. That was how we were, that dawn, for a few seconds. I had thought that I would be happy in Florence. I was at that moment. I was so happy, I was enjoying and suffering so much, that I thought I would be ill and, although I would not have exchanged the mute privilege that was being awarded me for anything in the world, I undid my hand from that of the girl, and babbling excuses, desperate to leave, regretful, furious, and fascinated, I returned to my room, leaving behind Ippolito de' Medici's acrobats and their fireworks, which continued on among the columns of the courtyard as if they were part of some tightly geared mechanism, a colossal clock that was impossible to stop and which repeated and repeated the figures of Abul, the Tartars, the Berbers, ascending, descending, arms outstretched, eyes like carbuncles, woolly hair in disarray, torsos glistening with sweat, before the eyes of Adriana.

In Florence my teacher was the famous Piero Valeriano, Giampietro Valeriano Bolzani, who liked to hear himself called Pierus Valerianus. He was the tutor named for Ippolito and Alessandro de' Medici by Clement VII, and he did his duties under the vigilance of Cardinal Passerini. Giorgio Vasari and I shared their classes, and Messer Pandolfo also attended in the shadows. The latter was dazzled by the personality of the famous man of all letters, and he soon began to imitate him. But Messer Pandolfo, a humble provincial tutor, was far removed from his model, and what he got from him was a certain varnish of literary bitterness, a certain mixture of highbrow resentment and mordacity which did not become him well at all, for he lacked the inspiration to put it to use and it did not blend with the simple goodness of his soul. The truth is that although Pierus Valerianus was partially correct when he gave free rein to these acerb criticisms that were motivated by the difficulties of men of letters, into which he would break suddenly in the midst of a commentary on Plato or Pliny, his own life, according to what I could put together, had not been so disagreeable. He had been born in Belluno forty-seven years before in the bosom of a very poor family, and his initiation into existence—which he remembered with haughty rancor—had led him bouncing along from one low domestic chore to another. He possessed a flame, however, a light, and at the age of fifteen he began to study on his own. Since then his existence had changed. Startled by his exceptional powers of assimilation, scholars like Valla and Lascaris taught him Greek. The fame of his memory was widespread, the fantastic swiftness with which he devoured the texts that were given him, filling the margins with polyglot notes. Always mentioned was the archeological success with which he had classified the antiquities of Belluno. He wrote torrentially, loosing a cataract of papers in verse and in prose, and he wrote only in Latin, as was natural. Attracted by that wealth, there was a rush in his direction, until the currents formed an opportune confluence and delta, the favor of princes brought on by the classical knowledge that so impassioned them. Bembo, Julius II, Leo X, and Clement VII were his patrons. And when Clement VII entrusted to him the education of his two nephews who were destined to govern the most cultured city in Italy, he gave him with it a firm proof of the highest favor, one that all intellectuals in the peninsula were striving for. Nevertheless, such success did not uproot the malignant plant that grew in the teacher's heart, planted there during his miserable childhood, or which perhaps he had brought into the world with him. Any occasion was fine for him to bring its hard and spiny branches out into the sun of Florence. He did not use a wounding tone, but a melancholy one, and a person who heard him could perceive beneath the mournful phrases, reminiscent of the Piagnoni, the Savonarolan weepers, a bristling of thorns, a permanent, cactus-like armor. Pierus Valerianus would lift his eyes from a Platonic dialogue and, with the slightest pretext, begin to lament about the misfortunes of those who had chosen the harsh road of teaching or study and seen their lives under the threefold siege of envy, disdain, and hunger. Some years later, when the sack of Rome took place, that atrocious spectacle suggested a book to him, the *Contarenus sive de litteratorum infelicitate*, in which he devotes himself exclusively to his afflicted colleagues. When I read it, many of the people to whom Piero Valeriano referred during the classes in Florence reappear out of its pages. There is almost no writer of the time who was not placed by him on some level in his scale of misfortunes. Men eternally subject to the whims of the great pass through the pages; men who in times of revolt lost first their pay and then their jobs; men whose manuscripts were burned in the fires of the cities and in the destruction that followed plagues; men who received insults and calumnies from their own colleagues; men in the decorative jails, which the palaces were, who yearned for the missing freedom that was enjoyed by the lowest mendicant friar. Perhaps that was the cause of Valeriano's grief, that last one: the notion that he was a prisoner in the palace on the Via Larga. Nevertheless, Piero would not have been able to live anywhere else. He needed the atmosphere of the palace, its tone, its libraries, its ancient collections; he needed to feel that his shadow was the prolongation of so many memorable shadows, that of Marsilio Ficino, that of Poliziano, that of Pico della Mirandola... As I have said, the protest, the bitterness over wrongs, was held stagnant inside of him and nothing was good against it. After all, writers and teachers, the crowning point of humanism, in spite of the rhetoric in that regard, have always lived to one side of those who possessed lordly power, who considered them something of jesters and something of servants, as members of a special caste, in any case, a caste apart, who should not be taken too seriously, for then they could become dangerous (for the lords suspected that they desired to seize power, basing their action on presumed grounds of intelligence), and they did not fare badly in the Florentine mansions of the sixteenth century.

When Piero Valeriano applied himself and discoursed on some theme of his specialty, the art of poetry, for example, which inspired in him one of the most notable treatises since Aristotle, his disciples—with the exception of Alessandro, for whom those matters had no importance—the rest of us, experienced moments of rare delight. Especially Ippolito and Giorgio Vasari. I have pointed out the interest that Ippolito de' Medici had in classical studies, which led him to translate a book of the *Aeneid* into Italian. As for Vasari, he was able to recite a good part of the *Aeneid* by heart and it was that to which he owed his inclusion in the aristocratic circle of the Medicis. At the age of twelve he had been discovered by Cardinal Passerini in Arezzo, his native city, where the cardinal was astonished by the fact that Giorgino could not only paint or sketch anything he felt like, but that he could also reel off the Virgilian cantos like litanies, and he brought him back to Florence with him. There he lived in the house of Niccolò Vespucci, a Knight of Rhodes, and perfected his apprenticeship with masters such as Michelangelo, Andrea del Sarto, and Baccio Bandinelli, but he came to the palace every day, friendly, smiling, inquisitive, jotting down all that was told him—it was with good reason that later on he wrote the biographies of so many painters, sculptors, and architects—with only one tiresome piece of vanity: that of the kinship that united him to the admirable Luca Signorelli (I later learned that it was rather remote), who when Vasari, whom he called *parentino*, was eight years old, had predicted a marvelous artistic future for him, which the young painter would remind us about every so often.

In contrast to Giorgino, Piero Valeriano, and Messer Pandolfo, we—Ippolito, Alessandro, and I—were beings of a different mold, modeled out of a more beautiful material. Or at least we imagined ourselves as such. The evidence of that basic inequality, present even in the case of Alessandro, the mulatto bastard, exacerbated the hidden acrimony of Valerianus. It was marked in me more than in the Medicis. I may have been a hunchback, but I was without a doubt a prince. It was obvious. I always had that certainty, nourished by my grandmother, who had helped me to walk through life between my heraldic bears. But my status as an Orsini and a legitimate one—which both Medicis must certainly have envied in the secrecy of their hearts—could not rid me of my hump, and therefore I had to humble myself and renounce that part of my princely education which would have been impossible. What could I have done to take part in the sports that Ippolito, Alessandro, and even Lorenzino, in spite of his fragility, engaged in: racing, wrestling, swimming, jumping, riding, dancing? Can anyone imagine me dancing? Imagine me executing the steps, the crossovers, leaps, twists, turns, and bows which the Medicis handled so well and which they practiced with the girls sometimes, with Catherine, with Adriana, under the eyes of Clarice Strozzi? No. That was not for me. How Alessandro would have looked at me! And if Beppo took it into his head to look into the room ... For me there was, on the other hand, the poetry that I wrote by the ream in secret in honor of Adriana, under the influence of Messer Piero, in pompous Latin, poor imitations of Tibullus, Propertius, or Catullus, or in my own language, so majestic that it sounded like a translation from the Latin, and which I did not dare show to her.

After the dawn scene in the gallery, I kept watch unsuccessfully for the appearance of another moment, of another spark of intimacy between Adriana and me. It was as if it had not happened. I even came to doubt the episode, as if it had been something out of my fantasy, as if it had been part of the fever of the dream that had bewildered me during my first night in Florence. Adriana did not abandon her air of distant friendliness which I, so timid, so bound up with my physical disadvantages, did not dare to break. Sometimes, according to the Tuscan custom, we would spend the day on the outskirts of the city. We would leave in the morning and join the groups scattered about in the shade of the trees, lunching and chatting near the cart outfitted with cushions which had served to carry the ladies. We would spend the whole day there, telling stories, singing songs, I, somewhat withdrawn from the company, watching the sketches that Giorgino was piling up. The slaves in Ippolito's entourage, summoned by their master, would burst into our refuge at dusk, gleaming with sweat from their running and galloping, and they would amuse us with their games.

Once, toward sunset, we were gathered together like that. No one was missing, for it was hot and those who had not taken refuge in the coolness of the courtyards had fled Florence. We could see the city down below against the sea-green and gray background of the hills, the gigantic dome of Santa Maria del Fiore, the Baptistery, with green and white stripes. The cypresses disappeared into vapor and mist. Beppo and Ignacio de Zúñiga followed on foot behind me, as was appropriate to my pages. The Africans improvised a confused pantomime, interrupted with acrobatics: they mimicked arrow shots, the blows of clubs, war in heathen lands. Ippolito stretched out on the grass next to me and yawned. Suddenly he called for a lute. He could also play the viola, the flute, and the horn. What could he not do! He tuned the instrument and played a mysterious dance, slow, while the decorated savages of his following drew back into the depth of the shadows. The whiteness of their teeth glowed on the edge of the darkness as if it were peopled by strange luminous insects that turned off and on. Adriana dalla Roza sighed opposite me, sitting up on her pillow, and it was as if her long sigh had capped the afternoon and floated over Florence, winged, light, sad. Ippolito continued strumming and suddenly a man emerged from the darkness. It was Abul. He was not wearing a turban; his shaved skull was neatly outlined like a shell over the precision of his profile, his beard, the black lacquer chest which was crossed by a broad necklace of blue stones. In each hand he brandished a scimitar, and with them he performed a solemn dance, shaking them in short flourishes or raising them, rigid, ritually, like tapers. He was dancing without looking at us, as if we were not present, as if he were spinning, brandishing the two curved steel blades, around his triumphal elephant.

"Do you remember him?" Ippolito asked me. "He's the one who brought Annone the elephant from Portugal for Leo the Tenth—the one who used to talk to the elephant."

"Yes," I answered, "I remember him."

Ippolito ran his hand over the strings once more. "Raphael painted the elephant," he went on.

The music stopped. Abul fell on his knees and the Cardinal of Cortona began a brief applause, tapping three fingers against his palm. Catherine de' Medici applauded, Lorenzino shouted. Giorgio Vasari threw a flower to the African, who stayed on his knees, his eyes closed, the curved scimitars like two silver wings.

Piero Valeriano quoted Lucretius. Messer Pandolfo quoted Horace. Adriana, unexpectedly coquettish, turned to me and smiled.

"His name is Abul," Ippolito added. "If you want, I'll give him to you."


The possession of Abul filled me with terror and joy. I must have been in Florence a year when Ippolito gave him to me. Now, from far away, infinitely far away, I am trying to order my mind, search in my memory, and understand how that year passed and slipped away, what happened to the time, and I can see that the novelty of that life, the overturning of my former habits, and my being suddenly hurled into the heart of a different world to which I had to adapt had twisted my pre-established notions and enveloped me in a kind of whirlwind, where the vertigo put wings onto the days and hours. The months kept on passing by. Events came rapidly. Astrologers predicted another flood and the end of the world for the following month of February; we waited for it with prayers and with jokes, and when February arrived we burned the astrologers' books. The Chevalier Bayard died without *peur* and without *reproche*, Francis I was captured at Pavia. The Franciscans were reformed and the Capuchins founded. The famous Giulia Farnese, the "Beautiful," also died. She was the sister of the future Pope Paul III and a relative of mine through her marriage to the Orsini master of Bassanello, the one they called "Monocolo," for he had only one eye. When the news of her death reached Florence, Alessandro de' Medici was lavish with his cutting remarks to me, for everyone knew about the unattractive role her husband had played during the period when she was the mistress of the Borgia pope. I let him talk. So that he could release his anger at being a bastard. After all, the kinship was rather distant.

My grandmother wrote me often. On the other hand, I never received a line from either my father or my brothers or from Cardinal Franciotto. Every ten days the messenger from Bomarzo would dismount in the *cortile*. In her letters my grandmother would tell me about the architectural changes that my father had begun at the castle. The princes, influenced by their readings of Greek and Roman poets, were discovering the charms of nature, and the outskirts of cities began to be covered with villas as large as palaces, with statues, fountains, stone steps, and shady gardens. The idea of the *villeggiatura* and what it had of an aristocratic imitation of the ancient way of life and of disdain for the turmoil of the capitals was growing and spreading. Gian Corrado Orsini did not want to do less than the rest, and he devoted himself to the pleasures of construction. I continued the work afterward and brought it up to its maximum splendor, but during that period, when Beppo would bring me my grandmother's letters, which I kissed before breaking the seals, it upset me to think about what was possibly happening to my beloved Bomarzo, and I felt that they were artfully despoiling me of what was most mine, for many times I was unable to grasp exactly what my grandmother was saying in her prose that was sprinkled with elegant irony, and I drew the mistaken impression that the medieval castle of the Orsinis had been torn down stone by stone and that later on, who knew when, if I had the good fortune to return to the family refuge, I would not recognize my home. Reality was quite something else again, and my father had limited himself, as I ascertained in time, to disguising the castle, giving it some false palatial airs, but without losing anything of its vigorous, almost brutal essence.

Diana Orsini hardly mentioned my brothers. Perhaps she calculated that the thought of them might upset me. And I was dying to find out about their lives. I surmised, between the lines written by my grandmother's firm wrist, that they were interposing between themselves and me a kind of courtly curtain, the development of Girolamo, even more despotic, cruel, and of Maerbale, more cowardly, more frivolous. Behind the careful writing, interlarded with news of the neighbors and allusions to life within Bomarzo itself—the mare that had been bitten by a snake and had to be killed; the discovery of some Etruscan vases; the blooming of the roses in the garden; the reading aloud of Ariosto's long poem, the second edition of which had recently appeared—I could see the outlines of my brothers' hostile figures, and although I was happy in Florence, a sudden nostalgia pressed at my chest. I did not suffer from the absence of Girolamo or Maerbale or my father; I suffered because any thought of them was invariably joined to the memory of my grandmother, and I did miss her, I felt her absence among strangers. At first I thought that she might visit me, such a traveler as she was, and I begged her to do so in my vehement letters, but I soon stopped demanding it, understanding that the cardinal and my father has forbidden it, and that it was part of my cruel exile, of my extirpation from the circle of the handsome Orsinis, and I resigned myself to never seeing her again, which intensified the bitterness that was fermenting in my heart. I dreamed then, I dreamed very much, and my grandmother invaded my dreams, so that I would wait for night to fall, for it would give me back the kind image of the one I loved so much, and even if my companions in Florence were incomparably more cordial than the ones who harassed me in Bomarzo with their cruelty, to the friendship of Clarice, Ippolito, and Giorgino Vasari I preferred the untouchable image of my grandmother that my dreams brought back to me.

Time had stopped by magic in the palace on the Via Larga, and it was impossible to measure its passage. The studies with Piero Valeriano had immobilized me and isolated me from the passing of the days. I only saw the *duchessina* and Adriana dalla Roza in the presence of others. They too were preparing, sharpening their weapons to enter a world where women, abandoning their past seclusion, played a powerful role alongside men. They were learning Latin and Greek, even conversing in those languages; they knew the classical and contemporary writers; they sang the poetry of Virgil to the sound of the lute;

they discussed Cicero; they danced with exquisite grace; they cultivated the complex art of being fascinating. And they did fascinate, poetically, as if they were something incomparably prodigious, almost monstrous, a cross between hopping birds dressed in stupendous feathers and worldly sages capable of discoursing on Vitruvius, Pliny, Columella, Petrarch, and the divine Raphael. It is not surprising, therefore, that the few minutes were not enough for the little hunchback with sensitive hands who contemplated them from afar, blushing, hiding in the group of youths behind so many perfect backs, so many harmonious shoulders, so many legs that were as straight as swords.

My sensual loneliness was growing and at the same time my concentration on myself, on the poor deformed body that was the only instrument of my passion and which, with a sad fidelity that would have made one think it was the object of some small parcel of love rather than the hatred it inspired in me, continued to tremble, moan, and in solitary shame savor the fleeting joy that phantoms would bring to it, something I could manage whenever I wished. One night, as in Arezzo, Beppo, who had drunk more than he should have, tried to draw me out of that dangerous, autarchical lack of communication and initiate me, by means of one of the women who warmed his bed, into the voluptuous exchange that my adolescence so desperately yearned for. It was an *idée fixe*; I do not know what personal benefit he hoped to obtain from the postponed spectacle. Just as in Arezzo, I rejected him with cold fury. I ended up by doing without him completely, as if he were not my page, the same as I avoided Alessandro de' Medici, in whose ardent precocity I could sense a mocking censure, perhaps a suspicion of my clumsy, anguished maneuvering. And also, for reasons diametrically opposed, I did without Ignacio de Zúñiga, whose piety and severe equilibrium quietly brought me face to face with my sinful lack of any spiritual fervor with high aims. So that if I insist that I was happy at first in Florence, it must be interpreted by comparing the life I led there with the one that was imposed on me in Bomarzo. In Florence, furthermore, there was Ippolito de' Medici, the paradigm of generosity, but Ippolito would often disappear, called away by his hunting, by public ceremonies of Tuscany, by his frequentation of famous females. There was Clarice Strozzi, but she pestered me with her obsession with the bastards and with the plans that she openly exposed to me in the secret of her rooms—Lorenzino would lie at her feet like an obedient whippet—feeding the fire whose flames would ignite the Tuscany of the future and give it back to the legitimate Medicis. And there was, finally, Abul, slender, as trim as one of Veronese's black kings, born to decorate a mythological painting on a palace ceiling beside the dying Cleopatra, among palm trees, colonnades, and draperies; but Abul, like Ippolito, would disappear for a month or more, off to distant battles with bears and boars. So that when his master gave him to me on a whim, without previous notice, I hesitated at accepting him—knowing that I would accept him, not caring a whit for what Beppo and Ignacio de Zúñiga might think—for I did not consider myself worthy of that incalculably valuable piece of property. Nevertheless, the possession of him, instead of making me immensely happy, bothered me. He inhibited me with his dignity, with the mysterious rhythm that emerged from the depths of his being and which was reflected as much in the cadence of his movements as in the calmness of his mien. And ever since Abul became mine, as if I was seeking distraction, relief, and stimulation in them to help me keep on facing up to the risky existence that destiny had laid out for me and whose labyrinthine implications I had not managed to perceive, I wrote more and more clandestine verses in which I praised, torturing metaphors and metrics, the beauty of Adriana dalla Roza, the miracle of her violet eyes, the color of the Aegean, the alabaster of her hands, on which there gleamed the topaz that excluded the tumultuous possibility of love.

My grandmother had infected me during that period with her intense enthusiasm for Ariosto's great poem, which she had received in turn from her friend Elisabetta Gonzaga, the Duchess of Urbino, the one whose predilection for dwarfs had afflicted me so much. I read, therefore, the forty-six cantos of the *Orlando furioso* (I finished the reading later, when the third and definitive edition appeared), and fascinated by the discovery of such a world of wonders, I also read two previous poems which spin like decorated baroque wheels about the paladins: the twenty-eight cantos of the *Morgante* of Luigi Pulci, and the sixty-nine cantos of the *Orlando innamorato* of Matteo Maria Boiardo. Those readings, fabulous poetical *feuilletons*, would have tried my patience today, but at that time they aroused my passions with their endless episodes, situations, characters, and interwoven family links of love and perfidy, similar to Renaissance *romans-fleuves*. Beyond the interest of their fantasy, I was taken by their epic humor. My sensibility has always reacted the same way, and if I am attracted today by the most diverse authors, from Dante and Shakespeare and Góngora to Proust and Joyce and Virginia Woolf (and also the refined and admirable author of *Lolita*) it is—in addition, of course, to their essentially deep quality—because of the salty taste of terrible irony that in the midst of an apparently serious paragraph will suddenly render them capable of smiling and laughing, and which relates them to Flemish paintings, where in the opulence of the composition there are small and unexpected openings into zones of everyday and picturesque wit which suddenly bring us close to their creators, erasing the majestic separation of time and circumstance.

How I enjoyed the *Orlandos* and the *Morgante*! What an influence, what an enormous influence they exerted on me! How they helped me to live at that time, peopling my life with golden reflections! What I could not do, what I would never be able to do, others were doing for me, leaping out of the folios in full armor. I can understand the fervor that they caused. I can understand how the Marchioness of Mantua and Galeazzo Visconti got into a dispute over the pre-eminence of Roland or Renaldo, as if they were discussing the merits of Pompey and Caesar. A person who entered that world of wild enchantment felt his heroes throbbing about him, more alive than the cruel strutters that surrounded us. The disguised brutality of the condottieri and of the poison-giving princes which terrified me so much; that of my father, throwing me into a cell which held a skeleton crowned with roses; that of my brother Girolamo, chasing me at night at Bomarzo with his drunken friends, became in the pages of Ariosto a mad, divine struggle between giants and champions who galloped or flew, impelled by some kind of holy hygienic joy. Everything grew large in those pages; everything was immense. Forgetting about myself, I would enter the tales as a warrior, as another giant, as if I had straightened up and as if one of the fairies that circulated through them had, thanks to a brief touch, taken away from me the pack that fate had placed upon my shoulder. Oh, miraculous! Oh, miracle of miracles!

Messer Pandolfo did not approve of my ecstasy. He thought that Ariosto was too popular and somewhat cheap. That part about *fra l'una e l'altra gamba di Fiammetta*... in Canto XXVIII would drive him wild. His country-teacher myopia would not let him see beyond classical archetypes, and his scholiastic pen moved among them, sure of not making a mistake. He was for Achilles and Aeneas, who held Homeric and Virgilian passports, officially legalized from remote antiquity with many erudite stamps. Roland and Astolfo seemed to be suspicious creations to him, of anonymous origins, who had slipped furtively in among the busts in the sacred temples and dared to be compared with them. For him they were nothing but adventurers fostered by acrobats and blind market-place reciters who did not have the august nobility that is the undisputed patrimony of the *Iliad* and the *Aeneid*, and which cultured poets sang as they succumbed to a kind of reverse snobbery with the unpardonable vice of replacing the ritual Latin of the bards with the subaltern language of everyday use. Of course, he did not express his repudiation very loudly, and he limited himself to reticent monosyllables, for he did not wish to compromise himself in front of the frivolous lords for whose favor he yearned. On the other hand, Piero Valeriano—who, incidentally, is mentioned in the *Furioso*—grudgingly gave his approval to the poem, with the ductile sagacity that he had attained through long experience in court, and which taught him that noblemen, for some mysterious and irritating reason, are never wrong when they give an opinion on something that even most tenuously involves refinement, and that the great enlightened ladies, the makers of opinion, who originate fashion (and who, invariably over the passage of the centuries, found or give rise to institutions of art), are the possessors of a special sense of smell which permits them intuitively to discern the new spiritual values connected to certain particular aspects of civilization.

The truth is that the elegant courts of the time, in imitation of those of Ferrara, Mantua, and Urbino, were delirious over the tales of chivalry, where they recognized something like an exaltation of their mythological forebears, of what was most theirs, of what most justified their prerogatives. And although the barons pretended indulgently to make fun of the simple and credulous people in the squares who could only appreciate the outside wrappings of the complex stories and would listen in astonishment to the wandering storytellers who would relate the tale of Brandimarte and of how he was stolen from his paternal house and sold as a slave until it was discovered that this Saracen was the son of the King of the Distant Isle, and how he married his beloved Fiordalisa, another slave belonging to the same master, learning in turn that she was the daughter of King Dolistone... The barons only pretended to mock as they leaned their elbows on the palace window sills, for afterward, laughing and rubbing their hands, they would have the rhapsodes who wove the tales come up the palace steps and regale them with their fables of magical deeds. Messer Pandolfo did not understand them. For that, one had to be more aristocratic, like us, like the Gonzagas and the Montefeltros, or more plebeian, like the audiences in the public squares. In a word, it was necessary to be more authentic, less artificial. They moved me as they moved Diana Orsini. I looked upon those heroes as kinsmen. If they had told me that Bradamante, Renaldo's sister, who went along the highways dressed in shining armor and fighting on equal footing with men, was a part of my genealogy, it would not have startled me in the least, because in my family tree there figured the Princess of Taranto, Maria d'Enghien, the wife of Raimondello Orsini, a conqueror of the Holy Sepulcher, and that princess, heiress to magnificent possessions, as a widow defended Taranto like a valiant captain, with a sword and a cuirass, against the King of Naples, Sicily, Hungary, and Jerusalem, whom she married in the end, all of which could easily have made for another canto of the *Orlando furioso*, and if Bradamante was a mythical successor to Hippolyta, Queen of the Amazons, and Camilla, the one who used her arms in support of Turnus against Aeneas, then Maria d'Enghien was in Italy her genuine flesh and blood successor.

The memory of those allegories weighed powerfully upon me. Years later, when I succeeded in finishing the Sacred Wood of the Monsters, the seeds of which had been maturing in the depths of my being, and which was the artistic corollary of many and distinct contributions, the memory of the *Orlandos* suggested some of the strange sculptures to me, huge men, dragons, harpies, so that if the *surrealism* of my creation—which nowadays provokes the astonishment of such masters of that school as the imaginative Salvador Dalí—can be found in telluric sources such as those provided by the local Etruscan tradition, or in sentimental homages like the one that is the basis of Abul's elephant, one must also search for them in the spell cast by Boiardo and Ariosto, a fusion of the fantasy of genius. From a certain point of view, the Sacred Wood of Bomarzo has been in stone what *Orlando furioso* was in exotic words. Both of them initiate a period, an artistic revolution. I can boast of my part in that revolution, and that the critics have not recognized me until now. It has been written that the *Furioso* represents, along with Boiardo and Pulci, the last form of poetical interest in knighthood. Yes, but it also represents the first form of another more modern interest. The same is true of my statues. A new esthetic world, one more free, was waiting behind my Wonders, a monument raised to Orlando, Ruggiero, Renaldo, Angelica, Astolfo, Brandimarte, Bradamante, Grifone, Aquilante, Fiordiligi, Atlante, the wizard Merlin.

What greatly accentuated my interest in those readings is that I had identified their characters with my companions in Florence and Bomarzo. Ippolito was Orlando; Clarice Strozzi, Bradamante; Piero Valeriano, Merlin; Beppo was Brunello, the robber slave, the one who stole Angelica's enchanted ring (alas, later on I was to prove the exactness of that literary substitution!); Benvenuto Cellini was Astolfo; my father and Girolamo were Agramante and Rodomonte, the kings who were the enemies of the paladins; Catherine de' Medici was Marfisa; Adriana was not one but many women, for she was all of the women in love who appear in the cantos; and Abul ... I looked for Abul in the poem until I found Aquilante the Black, the twin brother of Grifone the White, and then I wanted to be Grifone, because that meant that we would go forth together in search of adventure and that under the protection of our two fairies, the Brown Fairy and the White Fairy—whose roles were democratically entrusted to the Portuguese shoemaker's daughter and Adriana dalla Roza—we would fight side by side and we would slay the bloodthirsty crocodile who watched over the evildoer of Egypt, the son of a fairy and an elf. We were friends of

Astolfo (Cellini-Astolfo) the jokester, the one who told the truth, and since Astolfo was on an island that in reality was a whale, like those described by the soldiers who went to America and the East Indies, I later had a whale carved in Bomarzo, transforming a colossal rock into a monster with open jaws.

In the garden of the palace on the Via Larga, in the shady *viridarium* that the Riccardis stupidly destroyed a century later when they bought it from the Medicis, among the shrubs that were cut in the shape of deer, dogs, elephants, and galleons under full sail, I would conceal myself after lessons to read. Sometimes Abul would come and lie at my feet and I could tell from his eyes that he wanted me to tell him one of those hallucinating stories. Then I would recount to him the episode in which Aquilante the Black and Grifone the White fought side by side for the arms of Hector the Trojan, or the episode in which they defended Angelica; and if the breeze brushed the foliage, I deduced that the White Fairy and the Brown Fairy were spying on us from behind the boxwood hedge. Or if fate saw fit that Adriana and Catherine should appear in the garden, I would venture to chat with them, and I was so imbued with the music of Ariosto's hendecasyllables and language that I made an effort to reproduce it in what I said and I felt that I was speaking in verse. They would break out laughing and I, not knowing whether they were laughing at my absurd metaphors or at my even more absurd appearance, fell from the clouds, changed by evil magicians into a rhetorical hunchback, and I was ashamed, I despaired, searching in their eyes for the exact reason for their laughter, until at the next opportunity, bewitched again by the magic of the *Furioso*, I would repeat my poor inflamed remarks once more and sink into anguish again.

That was how I lived, as in a dream. That was how the months escaped me. Everything was a dream in Florence: Ippolito, Ariosto, Adriana, Abul, Orlando, Bradamante. The teacher Piero Valeriano had decided that we would study Pliny's *Natural History*, which teaches that there is nothing more unfortunate and proud than man, and which also teaches that no creature possesses a life as fragile or a passion as ardent. And his annotated text embellished my imagination with more and more chimerical figures: the basilisk, whose look burns the grass and destroys rock; the phoenix, who lives for the period of time required by the sun, the moon, and the five planets to resume their initial position; the hippocentaur; the dragon; the unicorn; the griffin, with long ears and a curved beak; the red-skinned sphinx; the catoblepas, whose head is so heavy that it drags and whose eyes give death; the mares made fertile by the wind... Everything—people, literature, study—was like a multicolored dream, with domes, porticoes, through which flashing swift Amazons and strange animals passed. Everything was a dream that fed my imagination and my anxieties of a fragile and ardent boy, reinforced by Pliny's disdainful affirmation. A dream...

Until Adriana fell ill.

Hers was a mysterious illness, the diagnosis of which was beyond the physicians of Florence. During the first days, as a way of asking for heaven's favor for the girl, Clarice Strozzi had made a wax figure on the Via dei Servi, where the image makers worked: a doll which, with its blond hair, was an attempt at reproducing Adriana's features, and she sent it to the church of the Annunziata, where it was hung between altar lights, dedicating the patient to the Virgin. But Adriana did not get better. Of no help were the ignorant doctors whom Cornelius Heinrich Agrippa compares to the vultures hovering over carrion and who, according to him, trot melancholically from one apothecary shop to the next asking if there were some urine samples to be examined. The illness was probably related to the plague that had assailed Florence two years before, which was called the worst punishment that the city had suffered since the fourteenth century and which reappeared some time later, tremendous, devastating, along with a band of charlatans who prescribed useless potions and who soon fled in terror. Adriana dalla Roza was languishing in her palace bed. Adriana, more beautiful than ever, in the somber room that smelled of drugs, her strange violet eyes aglow, had become so bloodless and pale that her face reminded one of certain imperial cameos, with dark blue veins on her temples. Her hands lay on the covers as if dead. She had become so thin that the topaz was slipping off her ring finger, ready to fall. That was how I saw her many times for four weeks.

At night, when no one was aware of it, I would tiptoe into her room, going through the solitary corridors with a flickering candle. A woman from Clarice's house named Nencia was taking care of her, a mature, strong-hipped woman in her forties, whose acrid smell was mixed with that of the potions, and who, as soon as I arrived, would receive me with the smile of an accomplice, would make a polite curtsy, giving me the chair where she had been nodding beside the bed, and she would withdraw into the shadows in the corner of the room. I would settle down there; I would stretch out my feet on a stool; and my whole task consisted of watching over my beloved, whose delirium, sprinkled with confused words, would increase with the dawn. Sometimes I would bring one of my books along to fight off drowsiness, and then the room would become filled with spells. As Ariosto in his poem repeated the names of places in Italy reaching from the Alps to Sicily, the episodes took on an alarming reality for me. I would half close my eyes and invoke Merlin, so that he would come and save Adriana with a philter, with a gesture. At other times Nencia would come forth and speak quietly to me, as if, with her energetic face and an unexpectedly springy walk for her volume, she had come out of the hazy tapestries that contributed to the magic of the place, for captive ladies had woven on those drapes centuries before the figures of other ladies, reserved and sad like them, who were withering eternally among whippets and trees. Nencia was unmarried, and even at that time, I must confess, her nearness made me a little nervous, for suddenly her look would grow inflamed above her authoritarian nose, and although she overdid the formulas of respect, her hovering presence added to the perturbation born out of the environment. She told me about her childhood in a village on the outskirts of Rome. Her devotion to the Orsinis bordered on extravagance. Her mouth grew full when she would mention one of our people. She felt, I noticed at once, a blind admiration for old families, titles, the glory of lineage. From time to time she would venture to ask a question and I, flattered by her curiosity, would hasten to answer, unraveling a skein of kinship and lives, as if I were lifting before her avid eyes a piece of the veil that covered the Orsini sanctum sanctorum. We would also share tales of elves and magic to keep sleep away. I told her that I had read in Pliny about the monster they had exhibited in

Rome in the Campo di Fiore near the Orsini palace, and that it had the body of a girl, the head and tail of a cat. As she listened, she glanced at the corners, afraid of ghosts.

That intimacy stimulated her audacity, and one night—I remember that Nencia had been sitting at the foot of the bed and that I was in my usual place, my feet on the stool with the open book on my knees— in the middle of a conversation in which I, in a low voice, was explaining to her the position my grandfather Franciotto occupied in the court of Clement VII, exaggerating perhaps his standing in the pontiff's intimate circle, the woman brought her round busts forward, extended a hand, and touched me on the leg, as if obeying the interest which the story had awakened in her. That unexpected contact, wrapped in a whiff of her strong odor, produced in me disgust and a certain annoyance difficult to classify, sensual no doubt, which was not disagreeable, so that, blushing, I went back to my reading of the *Orlando furioso*. It flattered me, of course, to observe the importance that the spinster gave to everything connected with my people (she had told me at one time, "The Orsinis are made of different stuff from the Medicis, Signor Pier Francesco"), but I was even more flattered when I comprehended that, although just a boy and hunchbacked, I had been capable of provoking—I myself, I alone, I, by my own and miserable merits—a special interest in that full-grown woman with a touch of fuzz on her lip and firm flesh on which the gold of the candles was playing around her low-cut neck. But immediately after, as if ashamed of her boldness, Nencia withdrew to the corner of the room, toward the gray-green refuge of the tapestries, as if she had disappeared into the woods, and I slowly recovered my calm as I contemplated the one who had inspired my verses while she faded away, wraithlike under the disorder of her blankets, behind the crystalline geometrical irreality that the reflection of the bottles cast about with its iridescence. Then, as on past occasions, I finally fell asleep, and I do not know whether I dreamed that Nencia caressed me or whether she really did, slipping her trembling hands over my unequal legs as if she were stroking a relic, for that was what we Orsinis were to her, worldly and warlike relics, the reliquaries of divine blood that was venerated in the most noble palaces of Europe, since we had allies and kinsmen in every great palace and the quarters of our coat of arms were interwoven with those of the principal houses in Italy and beyond its frontiers; and then even I, since I shared in the blood of the She-Bear, even I, who, when I stumbled upon my own likeness in the mirror turned my head, deserved to be secretly idolized and touched and caressed with superstitious fear and delight, as if a sacred fluid flowed from me, ancient and triumphant like our obeyed race. But that time, in my half-sleep—and, I repeat, dreaming perhaps— I thought I could discern another element in the reverential pressure given me, voluptuous, lustful, something that was given me as an individual and which was separating and moving away from that atmosphere of general admiration and toward my own self, something that no one else could share. I insist that it may have been a matter of a hallucination brought on by my intimate and painful lust that lay in permanent wait, always ready to invent favorable images, although when I went back to my room like a specter, I carried with me the feeling, somewhere between repugnant and proud, of a conquest that brought on a new restlessness in me.

In the meantime, Adriana seemed to be improving slowly, as if her adolescence were conquering the illness. Very weak, still subject to intermittent relapses that were more and more infrequent, she could recognize me and she thanked me for my solicitude. The woman was erased then, as if she did not exist, becoming a part of the hazy folds of the tapestries as during the first days, but I—such was Adriana's weakness—did not dare prolong my chat with the little one, so that a dark silence usually hung over us. I occupied myself with meditating on my unjust past and my future prospectives. No one forbade me to imagine, and in my fantasies Adriana's face and mine were joined together, for I miraculously was no longer hunchbacked, and we returned to Bomarzo together to rule alongside my grandmother. Other fantasies—that of a heroic future, worthy of the deeds of the Orsinis; that of high literary triumphs; that of my fortunate friendship with the Negro Abul, shared with Adriana; that of the privileged immortality which Sandro Benedetto's horoscope had promised me—floated about, fluttering and echoing like the world of the *Orlandos*; and the truth was that if I did return night after night to crouch beside my poor beloved, I did it not only to watch over her restless sleep, but also to enjoy a fictitious and glorious life that was continuously re-created in her silent bedroom. I also did it because added to the relief that I experienced there, bound to the utopian illusions that reached the consistency of a happy reality, there was the disturbing emotion caused in me by the presence of the other woman, the woman who could have been my mother but who upset me with mixed feelings, and whom I could perceive beyond the candelabra as something thick and scrutinizing.

One day at dawn our solitude was broken. The door of the room opened and Beppo came in, his ever-present smile fixed upon his face. He told me that he had been in my room, thinking that I had called him, and upon not finding me there at such late hours, worried, he had gone out looking for me in the rooms of the palace. The obvious pretext irritated me. It irritated me that he should have found me there, and I certainly would have lost control and punished him, as in Arezzo when he proposed that I share his bed and his harlot, had it not been for the presence of Nencia and Adriana. I limited myself, therefore, to commanding him to withdraw, scarcely dominating my rage, and while I was speaking rapidly to him I observed the quickness with which his eyes covered the room, mastering everything within it, from my figure, where the hump loomed even larger on my back, to the figure lying in the bed, whom he in turn wrapped up in the affectionate clarity of his look, and to the third figure, who, as she appeared in the half-light of her corner, greeted him with a short nod and answered his eternal smile with another cordial one.

The brief interruption broke the spell. From then on I had the feeling that the atmosphere had changed, as if some indefinable grief had been introduced into it. The following night Nencia abandoned her isolation to ask me if Beppo had been in my service for a long time and to inquire with annoying indiscretion about his family. I sensed that she had heard of the legend about his origins which made him my bastard brother, and which Beppo himself must have spread about the pages' quarters to enhance his status. I answered her brusquely, clearing the matter up with a disdainful grimace, not realizing that in that way I was confirming the rumors, but I did understand that I had not managed to convince her and as the week wore on, a cruel suspicion—that Beppo, perhaps in the morning while I was attending Messer

Valeriano's classes with the Medicis, was quite capable of visiting the bedroom of Adriana dalla Roza—grew in my mind, without there being anything certain that contributed to its growth; it grew like an intuition, like a subtle danger signal. I interrogated Ignacio and Abul by means of subterfuges in that respect, for it seemed unseemly to me to reveal to them such an offensive doubt, but they were unable to clarify anything. I also interrogated Nencia, who did not understand me or pretended not to, and since I had presented my sibylline demand with such twists and excuses it was quite possible that she did not understand me. It was useless to speak to Clarice and Catherine. For fear of the contagion of the unknown fever they never penetrated into the part of the palace where Adriana was suffering, surrounded by the emphatic impotence of her physicians. What was unquestionable was that the spell had been broken, and that although I kept on going to my place of discomfort—and on two occasions I arrived before noon, using an excuse to leave class—I could not ascertain anything, and had I not been so jealous and mistrusting, perhaps I would have forgotten the incident and the consequences that my apprehension suspected.

During that period my alarm was intensified by the loss of my friend's topaz. I noticed that it was not on her ring finger one night, no sooner than I had sat down, and with a worried voice I pointed it out to her companion. It was impossible to ask Adriana, prostrate in a semi-stupor, so the woman and I began searching about on the floor and among the covers, raising the candelabrum, whose light molested Adriana so much that she begged me to take it away. Nencia promised me that next morning she would look more carefully when she took care of the patient, and she was sure she would find it. But the ring, the magic ring that for Adriana was a defense like a magic suit of armor, did not appear within the four walls.

In order for the intensity of the agitation that the disappearance of the ring caused in me to be measured, I must insist upon the superstitious traits of my spirit that I also shared with the most educated men of the century. Pope Paul III Farnese, who put on the tiara some years later, lived surrounded by occultists and astrologers, and in that way he shared the fortune-telling convictions of Boccaccio, who two centuries before had steadfastly believed in the omens of dreams and that

Aeneas had really visited Hell. The cultured ladies who conversed in Latin, the notable lords who governed their states considered the existence of elves and the possibility of looking into the past and the future to be true. They acted like our contemporary dictators—Hitler is a famous example—who, like the distant monarchs of Egypt, Chaldea, Greece, and Rome who sought answers in the flight of birds, the entrails of sacrificial victims, and the tongues of priestesses inspired by arcane vapors, do not take a step without consulting signs in the stars, in cards, or in the palm of a hand. The inclination toward the occult exercises a strange and justified power over men. Thomas De Quincey calculated that for every superstition of the kind that revealed things to the pagans, we have twenty. He made that calculation in the nineteenth century; we probably have more now. One must remember in respect to this matter the curiosity that in my case was unleashed by the horoscope cast by Benedetto, the augur of as serious a captain as Niccolò Orsini, whose daughter, furthermore, had married a brother of the Farnese pontiff whom I have mentioned above, which joined the links of superstition between the two lines. The matters relating to such an arduous problem would require a great deal of space to write about. Whole books have been written and are still being written. I make up, in any case, living proof that the apparently logical foundations that govern the world for the tranquility of its inhabitants are susceptible to sudden modification as laws of the most solid reputation are violated. And one must not forget that I have seen the Devil, *vu, de mes yeux vu*. I have believed and I still believe that some of the beings we call dead are capable of appearing to us under determined conditions, I believe that they are around us constantly. I believe that they are spying on us from the balconies of heaven that Baudelaire speaks about, and if they judge it opportune, they come down from them on ladders of mist. And I have believed and I still believe that certain objects, certain trees, certain buildings are not what they seem to be with their feigned obedient immobility. In those days, in great numbers, moving in a more favorable climate, amid flying witches and learned men who affirmed, like Paracelsus, the actuality of sylphs and nymphs, or swore that they possessed, like Cardano and somewhat later Torquato Tasso, a familiar demon, my Etruscan faith in the secret forces and in their meddling in our entranced milieu, continuously grew stronger. At a short distance from Florence, toward Fiesole, in Fontelucente, sorceresses with artificial eyes and teeth extracted the magic liquid. Farther south, in Norcia, near Spoleto, there rose up, menacingly, the great necromantic center of the Apennines, where the esoteric books were consecrated and where, in a well, the sister of the Sibyl of Norcia and the aunt of the sorceress Morgana resided. Aretino notes it, perhaps in mockery, also perhaps with disguised terror. It can be deduced, on the basis of so many antecedents, that I felt a great deal of anguish when I found that Adriana's ring had been lost.

The girl could not clear up what had happened. Her weakness mingled the images of her delirium with real ones. She had the impression that Beppo had been beside her, but she could not put her recollections in order. I found out later on that she was not telling me the whole truth and I understood why Nencia had been silent. The topaz of the virgins had volatilized and become invisible, like the ring which, in the *Orlando innamorato*, Angelica's father had given her, and which had the virtue of making whoever put it in his mouth disappear and of conjuring away any spell when it was worn on the finger. The slave Brunello, sent by King Agramante, stole Angelica's ring and gained the kingdom of Tingitana. Someone had stolen my beauty's ring and had gained a different kingdom perhaps. I tortured Beppo with questions, like an inquisitor. I undermined him with my most intimate tone; I promised him money; I gave it to him. All I got were negatives. His face, which time was molding and making more handsome in its resemblance to my brother Girolamo's, remained impassive. Then, since Adriana had been despoiled of the chaste stone that had defended her from erotic traps, I presumed—I was still only fourteen years old and my ingenuousness ran parallel to my complex passion, which had been fashioned to point out several different beings simultaneously—that the helpless young girl would reward me with her love and I redoubled the ineffectual fervor of my poetical batteries, languid looks, and sighs, placing myself in the half-darkness of her room so that only my thin face, with its accentuated pathos, and my noble, eloquent hands would operate as emissaries of my tender feelings. But she opposed my attacks with the wall of her swooning indifference and on some days it even seemed to me that she was pretending to be dozing when I went into her room. An hour later I was, as always, asleep (for the poor, nervous, thin, worn-out hunchback was really sleeping), and I dreamed again that Nencia was caressing my arms and thighs with expert persuasion.

In the meantime, without previous notice, Cardinal Franciotto Orsini arrived in Florence.


My grandfather traveled, as befitting his position, with a retinue of thirty people. In his palace at Monterotondo and in the one where he lived in Rome, not far from the church of San Giacomo degl'Incurabili, his household came to a hundred servants. Although I was not happy to see him, it did please me to think that he was bringing direct news from Bomarzo, and his pomp when he dismounted in the *cortile* fed my vanity. I hurried to greet him there along with Cardinal Passerini, Ippolito, and Alessandro. It was sufficient to look at my grandfather to judge his nobility. The military life, ecclesiastical majesty, his upbringing at the court of Lorenzo the Magnificent, and the invulnerability ordained by his ancient blood and the assurance of finding relatives in high positions everywhere, all combined to enhance his prestige. That accumulation of circumstances had helped him triumph over the vexation of finances that were in perpetual disorder, the result of the prodigality forced upon him by his emulation of the other cardinals. In spite of the fact that his income was great, it did not cover the expenses of Monterotondo, and he was always living on the brink of ruin. In order to help him, his cousin Leo X had the inheritance of Bishop Silvio Panonio transferred to him, but it turned out later that the inheritance was not too substantial, because some years before the bishop had pawned a part of his possessions to the Cardinal of Aragon, who had enormous savings. Franciotto Orsini had to become involved in lawsuits with the cardinal's heirs in order to face his own creditors and there was no other way out except to turn over some of his holdings to the widow of the banker Chigi. Therefore, when my parents were married, my grandfather was only able to bring together one-fifth of the established dowry. My father reached an understanding with him— they were, as I have already said, very much alike—but as soon as any reason for an argument arose, he would throw in his face his failure to comply with the promise. I heard them many times in Bomarzo and in Rome as they became involved in harsh disputes. Those twelve hundred ducats still owed to the dowry—even though my mother was already dead—were the despair of Cardinal Franciotto. His prodigality knew no limits. The livery of his servants, dressed in the Orsini colors, had cost a fortune, the same as the maintenance of his arms, his packs of hounds, his horses, the falcons sent him from Cyprus, Crete, and North Africa, and the festivities with which he tried to imitate the Medici splendor. People spoke of his silken miters, his camlet-lined furs of ermine and sable, his golden spurs. Cardinal Orsini was proud of his pomp. Only with me was he miserly. It surprised me, therefore, that as soon as he touched the ground he held out his hand for me to kiss and gave me a thick chain adorned with sapphires. He was doing it to show off in front of the Medicis, who were receiving him as an illustrious relative; Passerini kissed him on the cheek.

His urge to shine in the circle of the Magnificent's descendants—whom he mocked, however, in conversations with other Orsinis, for he considered them parvenus and bastards—was obvious. It was difficult to recognize in that courtly gentleman, so attentive to the ladies, carrying his niceties to the point of mannerisms, the wrathful old man of Bomarzo. Like many great lords he reserved his bad manners and constant ill humor for those at home, so that even Ippolito, when I tried to make him understand that this attitude was nothing but a superficial disguise and that at home he had the reputation of a violent person, reprimanded me, telling me that I was exaggerating and that I should not become embittered, because the sapphire necklace that hung over my chest was evidence of the generous feelings of my mother's father.

Preening himself during the first conversation, the cardinal referred to the time that he had helped save the life of Leo X. I had heard the story a hundred times, and the company gathered in the main room knew it too, but we followed the story with all of its details (I was thinking about Adriana, Nencia, what they were probably doing), as my grandfather declaimed like an actor repeating his lines over and over again, and he described the hunt in which a wolf had attacked the pope and in which Francesco Orsini and Cardinals Salviati, Cibo, and Cornaro had protected him in the midst of a dust cloud that the dogs were raising until Captain Annibale Rengoni finished off the creature with his dagger. His Holiness—whose heaven was peopled with many gods—declared that his head could not have been better protected had he had Mars as his defender. That was the same occasion when the funeral of one of my grandfather's falcons had been celebrated in the castle at Palo (I think that I have already spoken about that; I am probably repeating myself like him) and that anecdote pleased the people more than the other. Clarice Orsini declared that there are no better falcons than those from Crete, real princes, and she looked out of the corner of her eye at the illegitimate ones, Alessandro and Ippolito.

Franciotto Orsini also brought news of the situation in the Church. He had found out that some time previously, during the plague of Rome, a Greek had deceived the people with his words. The Greek claimed to have tamed a bull by whispering secret words into his ear, and he sacrificed him in the Colosseum with pagan rites before a group of imbeciles in order to placate the infernal powers, according to what he told them. The Romans thought that their troubles were over and they wanted to make a god out of the bull. When the papal police tried to jail the trickster there was a tumult, and it was necessary to organize expiatory processions with people beating their breasts. I remembered Abul speaking to the elephant Annone. Then I thought that someday I would have a monument built to the elephant and that Annone, because of his relationship to Abul, would be like a god to me. But his tale of the sacrilegious Greek did not exhaust that chapter of the cardinal's complaints. Some suspicious hermits had emerged on the streets of the Eternal City and they were shouting and calling the Holy Father the Antichrist. And the people had discovered the prediction of an astrologer from Urbino who had confided to Agnesina Colonna more than twenty years earlier that Rome would be sacked by enemies from the north because an examination of the constellations of Cancer and Capricorn had announced it. My grandfather was scandalized. He rolled his eyes and hypocritically put his fingers together in an attitude of prayer. What was the world coming to! Deep down he was thrilled at being able to startle Clement VII's relatives as he proclaimed his filial respect for the pontiff. He had been unable to gain anything at all for Maerbale, who was already thirteen years old, not even a promise. Raffaele Riario, Giuliano della Rovere, the one who became Julius II, and Ippolito d'Este had received their capes at the age of seventeen. Ippolito was a bishop at nine; and ten years later Niccolò Caetani di Sermoneta was raised to the purple at twelve. Contrariwise, for Maerbale Orsini there did not seem to be any prospects, and his grandfather made allusions to the Vicar's indifference. The cardinal was silent, of course, about those intimate misfortunes and he went on listing public calamities. His colleague Silvio Passerini shook his mistrustful head of a big greedy bird and invoked the Virgin Mary.

The only time that my grandfather received me alone, when there was not a flock of gentlemen and servants around—he had not really come to see me; Florence was a stage on a trip to his more distant estates—he gave me very scant news about my people. My father and Girolamo were off to the wars again. The breaking of the Treaty of Madrid by Francis of France once he was free had rekindled the embers of hate. My grandmother was beginning to fail. She would go out with Maerbale—by naming him alongside of Diana Orsini, he took the opportunity to give me a prick of jealousy—and walk slowly through the garden at Bomarzo. I could imagine them painfully: she erect, leaning on her cane; he jumping about comically, smelling the flowers; a page and some greyhounds behind. The work on the villa was not progressing very rapidly. The cardinal did not approve of his son-in-law's spending, which was useless in his opinion, so he changed the subject. My studies did not interest him. Pliny... Horace... Catullus... He yawned; he looked at me through the monocle he affected in imitation of Leo X, and his eye, which the thick lens enlarged like that of a batrachian, took in my back, my legs. He dismissed me with a brief wave of his glove and opened his Book of Hours. I do not know if the cardinal ever prayed, but from time to time he would thumb through a very beautiful prayer book with miniatures by Cosimo Roselli.

A few days before his departure, my grandfather showed his claws and had a pitiless idea. Perhaps he did it to make fun of me; perhaps to test me; perhaps in good faith, for his plan fit his concept of virility; perhaps to bring back to Bomarzo on his return the spicy details of an anecdote that would make my father and Girolamo weep with laughter, giving them an accursed and murky joy; perhaps, lastly, to ingratiate himself slyly with the Medicis, for he did not know what they thought of his grandson the hunchback, and he would not have asked Ippolito or Clarice about such a spiny subject for anything in the world, much less have wanted to let them imagine that he was stupidly blinded by blood relationship in my case.

It occurred to him that I, who had still not yet reached the age of fifteen, had come to the time to know in the most intimate way possible one of the famous courtesans of those cultivated by gentlemen and prelates, and whose retinues were outstanding for a pomp and gravity that rivaled that of great ladies and had dazzled me since my arrival, with their passage announced by the golden tinkling of mules along the streets of Florence. Had his character been different and had his feelings toward my misfortune been different, perhaps I could have deduced at that time that by proceeding in that way my grandfather was seeking to destroy the complexes that doubtlessly embarrassed and crushed his deformed grandson, but I put aside that possibility and I hold to my first conjecture that his was a gratuitously incompassionate idea with certain streaks of sadism. He confided his plan to Ippolito, who found it proper—he, yes, I am sure, in acting that way did it thinking that it was for my good—and between the two of them they worked out the conspiracy which was soon joined, without his telling me a word about it either, by Beppo, always ready for expeditions of that stripe. Giorgino Vasari would go with me too to face up to an equal experience. But it was not easy to put into practice a project such as the one they were hatching, and it required the influence of the capo Ippolito and the cardinal so that it could be done quickly.

The courtesans—who had previously been called, with more accuracy, sinners, *peccatrici*—were at that time divided into three large groups. There were the harlots *honestae*, those with the greatest prestige; the ones of the candle, *de lume* as they were called, according to some because for a lack of servants they themselves would light the way for their guests along the treacherous stairs, and at night they frequented the stone benches along the façades of the palaces; and there were lastly the ones who combined other professions with prostitution (shirtmaking, washing) and they usually gathered in the more remote neighborhoods, in houses that pretended to be dedicated to the business of placing servant girls, and they were attended by public employees and impecunious writers, the unfortunate people described by my teacher Piero Valeriano, people who ate there, conversed, and went through the more or less important exercises that motivated their presence in such places. Among one category and another, there circulated through the porticoes of Florence determined old women who were the unsavory arrangers of assignations and the purveyors of herbs, unguents, and love potions. A boy of my status, the son of the Duke of Bomarzo and the grandson of a cardinal of the Holy Catholic Church, could only test his weapons of that nature within the first group, that of the *honestae*, which complicated things because the *honestae* were extremely difficult and took on great airs. I have already mentioned the disquieting amazement with which I watched their long processions pass by when they were on their way to mass or to the public baths or to visit one another, moving about with a train of people that could have been the envy of ladies of lineage and fortune. The young patricians learned the art of good manners in their houses. In that sense they were as useful allies of civilization as the *cocottes of* the France of Napoleon III and at the beginning of this century. In order to obtain an appointment in one of their sumptuous residences, the center of intellectual snobbery, it was necessary to put in motion the machinery of important pledges and credits, and even then it was sometimes necessary to wait for a long time in order to attain such a high favor. All that, as was quite natural, had made them very vain. There was one in Rome who was the daughter (that was the rumor, at least, which she did not deny) of that same powerful Cardinal of Aragon who, before my grandfather could take advantage of it, had squandered the inheritance of Bishop Panonio. They discussed Petrarch in her house and Ippolito de' Medici praised her hair in verses which are still extant. There was another one, just as haughty, who would not allow any man to approach her except on his knees, for which reason her house was spread with pillows. The one that fate had reserved for me was, of course, one of the *honestae* in question, but one of the less famous. She answered to the name of Pantasilea, according to the custom that demanded of prostitutes *comme il faut* to seek their pseudonyms in ancient history or from mythological sources.

Perhaps the reader still remembers that when I spoke briefly with Benvenuto Cellini on the beach by the castle at Palo he told me about the time he attended an artists' dinner with a Spanish boy disguised as a woman, since he had ceded the courtesan who was to accompany him to one of his friends. That courtesan was Pantasilea. Since then, taking advantage of time, Pantasilea had progressed. From the circle of artists she had risen slowly to that of the lords and prelates who gave them their work; and from Rome, for reasons which will be explained later, she had gone to Florence, where she was soon notorious. Ippolito de' Medici had set his eyes on her when Cardinal Orsini told him of his plan. My grandfather and the prince started the wheels of the intrigue in motion, and—the expense must have been substantial—they succeeded with coming and going by Beppo to arrange the desired meeting for a few days later. I presume that Beppo took advantage of his position as messenger and temporary banker, along with his handsome face, to attain the favors of Pantasilea without any personal expense. I presume that, because knowing him it seems obvious to me that it must have been that way. Who can tell but that he used the argument that since she had to arouse a hunchback, it was logical that the woman should have her reward beforehand with such a well-built young man. Or perhaps he collected his commission in that way. In any case, the fact is of no importance.

While all the maneuvering that involved me was going on so close by, I was a thousand miles away from imagining it. I continued to visit Adriana secretly and at night; I continued going in the afternoon with Abul or with Ignacio de Zúñiga to places where the cream of the gallant Florentine aristocracy gathered together to comment on the latest happenings in the city and where my friendship and relationship to the Medicis contributed to the fact that my appearance was tolerated without any apparent mockery. Among the statues on the Piazza Santa Liberata, where it was so delightfully cool, on the Spini bench or in the Tornaquinci gallery, one of the fifteen loggias that have been mentioned where the trivial and grave people of the city gathered, I would listen to comments on politics, adultery, painting, writing... Until finally, when everything was ready, my grandfather announced to me that on the following evening I would enjoy the prerogative of a visit ("an amorous visit," he told me) to Pantasilea's house.

The news dumfounded me. Even though antlike lust was nibbling at me, I could not conceive of anything like that ever succeeding. And least of all, least of all the way it had been arranged. Sometimes I would think that at some unforeseen moment my basic encounter with a woman—with *the* woman—would come about, and I speculated on the idea that it would come as the result of circumstances, of fate, of destiny, almost logically and inevitably, the way a sickness passes into convalescence, but never by using organized treachery to provoke the feared and yearned for contact. And if there had to be previous organization, what had never crossed my mind was that it would be under the direction of my grandfather, whose patent indifference in my case alternated with his difficultly concealed repugnance, so that my first deduction when I received the unexpected blow was that there was a trap concealed in Franciotto Orsini's plan. The fear of a trick, of a mocking, was then added to that other fear, the basic fear that I felt opposite the mystery of a woman, a consequence of my singular physique and the way in which it had shaped my twisted psychology. I trembled. I must have looked ridiculous at that instant and I can understand the slight smile that appeared on the cardinal's lips, which increased my anguish. My grandfather, my father, Girolamo, the long line of our splendid ancestors, must have considered those terrible things when they rose up in their paths as the most simple and natural on earth. They were created to face up to them, dominate them, and enjoy them. I, handcuffed by my timidity and by the obsession with the hobbles of my body which, instead of facilitating the discovery of that unknown world, the goal of a difficult journey, made it difficult and even impossible—because of the aversion that they would no doubt arouse in my unknown traveling companion—had endlessly postponed the probability of such an encounter and, if on some occasion I would imagine it in my dreams, I would invest it with an unreal air, as if it belonged to the realm of fantasy. If it happened, let it happen; then we would see... In the meantime, I took refuge in that secret and unspoken fruition that I myself had unleashed and which did not contain the risk of any rejection, because while my poor sensuality was on fire, I was like a veteran puppeteer who manipulated at his will the actors taking part in his scenes, and I also took refuge in the seclusion of a sentimental labyrinth that imprisoned my spirit and peopled my solitude with various emotions, to which Adriana, Nencia, and Abul contributed with the diversity of their personalities, and I thought that I did not require anything else to provide for my adolescent needs. Let them leave me in peace; that was what I wanted. Let them forget me; let them leave me alone...

It was useless to try to oppose it. I knew too well what my grandfather's character was like. Any attempt to the contrary would only aggravate matters.

"Ippolito de' Medici," the cardinal told me, "has had the goodness to consent to go with you. You may consider yourself well served, with a prince as your squire. I won't go myself out of respect for this purple. Before, when I was under arms, it was different. I would have gone with you. But Beppo your page will go along and he's a sharp-witted one. And that boy Vasari, the painter. I think that he too"—my grandfather smiled and showed his toothless mouth—"will be paying his first visit to Venus. You lucky people. I envy you."

The only concession I managed, since the battle had been lost beforehand, was that Abul should have a part in our undertaking. With him by my side I would feel more secure. Franciotto Orsini graciously agreed. He was glowing with good humor. He handed me a vial. "Put on some perfume, Pier Francesco. The young prince must wear some perfume when he goes there. And put on the sapphire necklace. It will be the same as if I were there."

I spent an atrocious night waiting. I did not dare go to Adriana's room, such was the state of my nerves. I could barely sleep and my frightened dream was capped with the confused images of intermingled bodies that made up a kind of carnal and monstrous Laocoön. I awoke at dawn, bathed in sweat. The memory of Beppo and the innkeeper's daughter when I had glimpsed them in Arezzo pursued me. The only thing that filled me with a certain confidence was the name of the harlot, Pantasilea. Perhaps she was the same one that Benvenuto Cellini had spoken of and if I mentioned the artist to her and the friendship that he had shown me—building it up until I proved that we were intimate friends—perhaps the courtesan would treat me indulgently and help me, with my hump, with my shame, with my irresolution, with my pride, with my fright, with the inborn burdens I could not rid myself of, help me through the unjust crisis that Cardinal Franciotto was imposing on my next fifteen unhappy years.

Up to that time, the two episodes in my existence that had made the greatest impression on me were the confrontation with the rose-crowned skeleton in Bomarzo and the adventure with Pantasilea in her house in Florence. Both left a bitter taste in my mouth and accelerated the stormy pounding of my heart. I am gliding back now across the enormous space of time toward the latter episode and in spite of the wall of centuries in between, I am reliving the anguish of it with an intensity that makes me catch my breath. In my memory, in spite of their diametrically different natures, I cannot separate them, perhaps because in both cases my sensibility underwent similar anxieties, born of the terror of the unknown as I faced the aggressively mysterious, which on both occasions was related to the perplexed anxiety that the human body passed on to me, and which in the one case was provoked by the mysterious terror of death and in the other by the alarm as I came face to face with the secret of life. Life and Death, like two allegorical figures, the Naked Woman and the Skeleton, preside in that way by the door that opens into my deepest emotions. Later I will tell how I made use of those symbols in the Wood of Bomarzo.

I resigned myself therefore to my condemnation, which for others would have been an incomparable celebration, and on the following day at the established hour, I left with my companions for the Pantasilea affair. It irritated me that Giorgino Vasari, who would be going through a similar initiation and who was barely a year older than I, apparently did not share my restlessness. His frank and simple character made him take everything quite naturally. But he was a man like any other and I was not. I was a mistake, a disorder of nature. Who could become happy by making me happy? Who could receive any pleasure from caressing me? Nencia? Was it really certain that Nencia had caressed me and that I had not invented her caresses? And Pantasilea? The harlot, for professional reasons, had seen many bodies pass by her public bed, but she could never have seen one like mine. My body was not of the kind that is bared but of the kind that is hidden. It could not be used like the others as an instrument of joy. If it was for me, that was due to the fact that nature is wise even in her mistakes, and her pity is not completely withheld from her children.

I took extreme care with my cherry-colored outfit; I bathed myself in perfume; I put on the sapphire necklace; I hung a pearl in my pierced ear, even though it pained me a little, for the same original ideas that brought on repudiation in Bomarzo were applauded in Florence and would start new fashions, and I met my companions in the *cortile*. Ippolito, in blue and hazel with diamonds on his cap and holding a Florentine lily which he was taking to Pantasilea, was the most handsome and was more communicative than ever. He patted me on the back, he took me by the arm, and we went out into the street. Giorgino was on the other side, somewhat preoccupied, of course, wearing the borrowed gray suit that did not fit him too well, and behind us came Beppo and Abul, the first proud of his red and silver suit, colors which he may have considered his own and which lost their character of livery thereby. My grandmother had given him those clothes, which his growth had made it necessary to alter. As for Abul, he was wrapped like a dancer in his netting in a gold and white outfit that had belonged to Filippo Strozzi and which Clarice had given him when he entered my service, because she was amused at the contrast between that silky snow and the gleaming jet of his face and hands. He was the only one who was bareheaded. The rest of us were crowned with dancing feathers. As we went along like that through the streets of the most beautiful city in Italy, we formed a garrulous, polychromatic group in the center of which a timid hunchback was hiding and in which not even the dark note of the slender African or the lordly note of the page in heraldic clothes was lacking, showing the people who stepped aside as we passed and greeted Ippolito, the exceptional condition of people who, with such bright pomp, sparkling from head to toe like proud birds, were obviously on their way to some affair of love.

I said that Pantasilea had progressed. Her house showed it. It was a house that smelled of ambergris and roses. Alabaster and porphyry on top of the carved credenzas showed the generosity of her lovers. The tapestries evoked the rape of the Sabines, with a twisting of women being attacked and excited horses, but I, so ready for the enjoyment of esthetic luxuries like that, could not appreciate them, attent only on the nausea that was making me tremble. A long table with wines and food was in the center of the main room where we entered, which, beside the loggia on the second floor, was bathed in soft clearness. In that loggia one could glimpse some peacocks, whose semicircular opened tails seemed to indicate along with the rest of the place and its blue and green enamel the entrance to the Garden of Eden. Confused, I could not consider them as such, because according to one of my grandmother's private superstitions, shared by her grandsons, peacocks bring bad luck, and Diana Orsini believed it so completely that in our palace in Rome she had burned a tapestry in the foliage of which there glowed one of the birds of Juno. Its closeness confirmed for me from the first moment that my visit to Pantasilea would produce nothing good. And the ominous cry of the peacocks which accompanied my presence from the first terrace is inseparable even today from the memory of my anguished initiation, because all the time, even when I cannot see them, I can feel them around me, dragging their fearsome feathers or unfolding them in ominous fans. I can hear them now in this study where I am writing these pages.

There were several women in the house, friends and protégées of Pantasilea—one of whom was destined for Giorgino—who greeted us with ceremonious dignity, for the courtesans had learned not to exaggerate their show, imitating in that too the aristocratic ladies who served them as models. They were all wearing brocade, with slashed cloth and prodigious necklines that laid bare their firm breasts, and their jewels, which the mirrors and glasses all about reproduced as moving sparks over the walls and furniture. The flash of the clothing and the jewels also twinkled on a curious crystal polyhedron that was hanging from the ceiling like a lamp, and which intrigued me for its look of a wizard's instrument. Two old hooded women were whispering in the shadows. But Pantasilea was not there. They told us that she would soon come; that she had just returned from the baths. Ippolito drank a glass of wine and, true to his custom, asked for a lute and began to sing. Then Beppo played something that was either a rosina or a pavan, which Ippolito and Giorgino danced with the women. Until that moment things were not going badly. It was like one of the parties in the palace presided over by Clarice de' Medici. It was true, however, that the girls, laughing, were going after Abul, whose color and elegance fascinated them, and who, because of his status as my slave and probably so as not to upset me more, for he knew how much that expedition had frightened me, rejected their bold demands; but they left me alone. It was obvious that they were aware of the special case that was being presented to them and I thanked them from the bottom of my heart for not showing any surprise at my appearance. The two old women came over and fussed about me while the dance was going on, calling me "my Lord Duke," as if I were, and they offered me something to drink, chatting avidly, asking me what my exact relation to the Medicis was, and I, recovering my composure somewhat at the mention of topics that were so important to my vanity, deigned to answer them and to down two, three, four glasses of Trebbia wine as I sought a fictitious courage.

Then Pantasilea appeared. Her red hair, tinted with those subtle highlights dear to the Venetians, in which some fresh laurel leaves were interwoven with strings of pearl, as on the brow of a poetess; the whiteness of her skin, which was kept smooth by almond oil; the ever so pure outline of her features; her green eyes; her fruitlike mouth; her harmonious fragility; the cadence of her movements; the grace of her breasts, lightly tinted to bring out their shape; the rubies scattered about her transparent tunic which melted away in the vagueness of the tones of Chinese wistaria; her voice, slightly husky, which sounded as if she always spoke in low tones, confidentially... I have forgotten nothing. Time has passed, much time, and I have not lost one detail of that delicate gold filigree that was Pantasilea. She was hugging a small dog against her breast, a Maltese lap dog, white, curly-haired, with very dark eyes, similar to the one that looks at Saint Jerome in the oil by Carpaccio, of the Scuola degli Schiavoni.

My heart beat more rapidly from terror and wonder. The music stopped. The couples paused, and Ippolito, Giorgino, and I went over to greet her. Ippolito did it familiarly, embracing her and kissing her on the lips, and he gave her the lily he was carrying with such nobility in the bearing of his seventeen years that it seemed he had given her a scepter. Pantasilea—who did not blink when she looked at me—kissed me on the mouth too, but she barely touched my lips, like Clarice, Catherine, and Adriana when they welcomed me to the palace of the Medicis, for the courtesan followed aristocratic ways in everything. The proof of it was that with Vasari, who was noble, she only touched his right hand with her pursed lips. Her entrance changed the tone of the meeting. We sat down, we made ourselves comfortable on furniture covered with pillows, and the harlot turned the conversation toward the latest things in literature. She liked to put an intellectual coating onto those banal and sensual interviews. Writers came to visit her and give her their books. I took a breath, relieved. Perhaps the adventure would not go any farther. The latest writers were mentioned (Ippolito replied to something with a tone of somewhat eccentric sophisticated superiority, with a certain sarcastic dandyism) and, since they had also spoken of Ariosto, of the second edition of his poem, I was able to murmur a word, a phrase about my idol, to which Pantasilea listened attentively, frowning and running her index finger along her cheek, as if I had been Piero Valeriano or Cardinal Bembo. Standing behind, Abul and Beppo listened. The servant girls offered us glasses as large as chalices and the rubies on the harlot's tunic rivaled the ruby of the wine. Vasari asked her about the meaning of the crystal polyhedron that was hanging from the ceiling, and she condescended to explain to him that it was an exact reproduction of a design by Leonardo da Vinci, one of the ones that figure in the treatise on *Divina proportione* by Luca Pacioli and which can also be seen in the portrait of the mathematician painted by a disciple of Piero della Francesca. Ippolito showed himself to be aware of those scientific mysteries of which I was completely ignorant, and the conversation, in which I could no longer take part, turned toward the virtues of the golden section that occurs in the construction of a regular pentagon, for it is the division of a segment into the middle and the limit of reason, whose properties—and Ippolito quoted Fra Luca Pacioli himself—correspond in likeness to God himself. The *capo* went on like that for half an hour and the harlot was listening to him with a courteous frown as he spoke, pointing to the magical object swaying up above which in the glow of its facets seemed to be the sum of all the wisdom of the world, until one of the old women went over to Pantasilea and whispered in her ear. She smiled briefly and looked at me. I could feel the color rising into my face.

"Let the dance go on," Pantasilea said. "Prince Orsini and I have to consult about some very serious matters."

The women's excitement grew. A tambourine came forth, bounced and shook its jingles. The lute sounded. The courtesan gave me her hand like a queen, put the Maltese dog carefully down onto the floor. He shook himself and ran ahead of us, and we withdrew together. Through the loggia, along with the late sun the sounds of Florence were entering, mingling with the ill-fated cries of the peacocks. In a mirror I glimpsed the black and white figure of Abul bowing in a salute.


The room where Pantasilea led me was covered with mirrors, in the vogue that later was to grow and prosper and which when Catherine de' Medici was Queen of France was responsible for one of the rooms in the palace in Paris being decorated with one hundred and nineteen mirrors. I saw myself reflected in them with horror. On the walls between the pieces of tapestry multiple cherry-colored hunchbacks with pearls hanging down the side of their faces and sapphire necklaces around their throats were looking at me, ruddy with a blush of modesty that was enlivened by the closeness of the harlot and the shame that was emanating from my body. Worth nothing to those monsters repeated there in the glass was the seduction of their noble faces and their sad eyes. Of no use to them was their adolescence, their haughtiness. The mirrors copied my look of a buffoon from all angles, and if those in front of me returned my image from the best perspective, for they offered the most favorable angles of my face and the most opportune configuration of my hands, they also held for me—as they caught together the figure offered them by the other mirrors located behind me—the accursed picture of my twisted spine and the certainty that those enemy satellites that treacherously encircled me were conspiring to wither me with their terrifying retinue of Punches. I remembered for a second the day when Girolamo and Maerbale had dressed me up as a jester in Bomarzo. Just as at that time, an earring was hanging from my pierced ear. I was frightened at myself, frightened, frightened, and I closed my eyes. The Maltese dog, rolling on the skins and knocking over a pile of books on the floor in the corner of the room, began to bark ridiculously, as if he too, with his sharp voice, was a little courtesan and was making fun of Prince Punch, of the one who read immortal poetry and dreamed of being a miraculous giant like Briareus, like Antaeus, like Caligorante, even more so like that huge king Morgante, who had used a bell clapper as a weapon and who reposes among the tombs of the giants in Babylonia. But I was nothing but a dwarf. I was aware of that now. In spite of the fact that I was almost of normal height, I was nothing but a poor dwarf, from the stupid fact that I carried a hump on my back.

The worst thing that Pantasilea could have done to calm me down was to speak to me so naturally about hunchbacks. I am surprised that she did. She had evidently sensed my anguish—one did not have to be an astute psychologist to deduce its origin—and in her innocence she calculated that by proceeding in that way she would establish a comradeship between us, a complicity that would make our relationship easier. But one cannot deal naturally with what is nature off its course. And while she was getting undressed and going back at random in her reading to the glorious memory of Aesop, of the much less glorious Thersites, whom Ulysses calls "eloquent orator" and whom the same Ulysses beat with his scepter, and finally to the lingering memory of Alessandro and Gian Lucido Gonzaga, the mystic and the poet of the court of Mantua, I could feel growing in my heart the rage that was forming there inside, a hard, black stone, and that rage blinded me and prevented me from enjoying as any mortal would have enjoyed the sensual splendor that was being offered to my eyes as the tunic and veils slipped off and Pantasilea, with a fearful lack of awareness kept on talking and talking, naked, to a desperate audience whose humps went from one mirror to another and created in that bedroom a small and strange mountain range of cherry-colored humps which vaguely moved.

The courtesan stretched out on a divan, offering herself, and she reached out her arms to me. I went over timidly and sat down beside her among the pillows. She pressed her hip against my thigh and then there happened what I had feared so much and which in reality was absolutely necessary for the fulfillment of what was proposed in the contract: her deft hands began to take off my clothes, with a knowledge of the fasteners of masculine dress which, had I not known, would have told me what her profession was from the technical skill that she showed, and which Pantasilea exercised without losing her intellectual air, as if absorbed, in contrast to the voluptuous look on her face. But I did not let her reach her objective completely, and half undressed, my hump sunken into the pillows, I stayed there beside that costly and celebrated nakedness, so white that it glowed in the shadows. She drew me closer, she kissed me, she hugged me. Should I go on describing a painful and predictable scene, the useless insistence of her skill, the fruitlessness of my cooperation? My great complex was choking me, turning me to ice. My hump weighed down upon me; everything that crawled about and hid in the depths of my personality was weighing on me. I was shivering before the fire. And even if I took my eyes away from the walls where I knew that tens of hunchbacks were mimicking my unconducive gestures, decupling their regimented pantomime to mock Pier Francesco Orsini, the imbecile, the ninny, and perhaps—since the most unusual things are possible within the bewitchment of a mirror—they adopted other sensual postures and laughed softly, the presence of those hostile brothers contributed to my certain failure. How could I have imagined for a moment that things would have gone differently as was obviously happening in the room set aside for Giorgio Vasari? Even though I had not counted on those heartless witnesses, it was fated that the ignoble episode should have come off that way, for there was one witness whom I would never have been able to be rid of, and that analytical onlooker was I, myself, the sweating dromedary who was biting Pantasilea's lips and who, simultaneously, was hunched over and observing the scene and judging it with lucid censure. I called upon my most ignominious resources to get out of the difficulty, but I could not. I replaced the living body being offered, rich in blood and softness and hardness, with phantoms whose aid I entreated, thinking that they could help me. Alas, the disturbing Nencia, the beautiful, moving Adriana, and Abul, Abul too, superimposing themselves on one another until they formed one single monstrous being, indiscernible, sharing their opposite traits, more terrible than the monsters that Pliny lists, impetuously substituted in vain on the bed for Pantasilea! I accuse myself of the felony of that sterile artifice. I asked for help from literature, from Ariosto's Fiammetta, who had aroused me when I read the description of her amatory gymnastics with the Greek in the lodgings at Játiva, and I could not bring back the excitement I had had at that time. I was lost... lost... And what bothered me most was not that the occasion for which I had ardently yearned in my lonely moments was being frustrated, confirming to me that forbidden to me beside an admirable woman was the healthy happiness that exalts the flesh until one's misery is forgotten, but the inexorable consequences that were augured when it became known, the redoubling of the jeers, the new material that my failure would add to the store of disdain that, even when disguised, I could feel throbbing among those who made up my world. Then I tried to avoid at least the publicity of what my exaggerated hypersensitivity considered a final discredit, and I applied myself to earn Pantasilea's good will and silence, making use of, like an alliance, like a supreme means to an end, the mention of my friendship with Benvenuto Cellini, whom I imagined to be close to the harlot, for I calculated that in that way I would distract her toward other interests and in any case obtain her indulgent solidarity.

I never should have done it, my God! I must say—since my gaffe would have been unpardonable otherwise—that I had not been able as yet to read what Benvenuto tells in his memoirs about his relationship with Pantasilea for the simple reason that thirty years still remained before he would begin to write them and two centuries before they would be printed for the first time by a physician philosopher. The only thing that I knew, for he had told me about it, was the story of how the goldsmith had gone to a dinner at the house of the sculptor Michelagniolo of Siena with a boy disguised as a woman, having turned his Pantasilea over to Bacchiacca. But I did not know what had happened afterward. I did not know that a young man named Pulci, who sang so prodigiously that even Buonarroti would stop his work to listen to him, and whom Cellini had received with enthusiasm, had aroused the passion of the harlot, and that Benvenuto, jealous of both of them, had wounded Pulci, in spite of the fact that the latter, frightened of the violent craftsman, never took off his coat of mail, and that he had also wounded Pantasilea herself on the nose and mouth. She told me about it hesitantly. Her eyes were aflame at that moment. I can see her as if the scene had happened yesterday, huddled on the bed, her fingers clutching the pillows, showing me the scar that came down to her lips. Pulci had died in the courtesan's house, and in spite of the fact that his end was due to a fall from a horse, the woman attributed it to Benvenuto's spells. She hated the artist. I could not have sought a worse ally, and she must have hated me too for having mentioned him. What terrible luck, the luck of a dog, Pier Francesco's! Motionless in my corner, I heard her poisonous recriminations. The peacocks were screaming outside and the little dog, as if he were breathing in the atmosphere of rage, began to bark about the bed.

The only thing that I was able to mutter to relieve the mischance was that if one looked at the bright side, those things had made her move to Florence and gain the extraordinary prestige that she then enjoyed, but she refused to pay attention to me. According to her, she would have achieved the same success in Rome, for she had more than enough reasons. I answered her, yes, she was the most splendid woman on earth, and she gave a short laugh that sounded like a whistle.

"No one would say so, Signor Orsini," she answered quite correctly, "if he took into account the weak impression I've made on you."

She drew me to her again with a strength that no one would have guessed in such a fragile person; she brought my hand to her breast and she added, "That ring is one of Benvenuto's. I thought I recognized it, but I wasn't sure. Give it to me, Prince. We'll destroy it. It's the work of a sorcerer."

She took it off with a pull, but I would have let them strip me naked first rather than lose the ring that I valued as my talisman. We began to fight with slaps and she, amused at her fury, began to laugh again.

Then I thought of the necklace. I would give her my grandfather's sapphires, I would give her anything as long as she gave me back my steel and gold ring.

From the floor I picked up the chain on which the blue stones were strung, and I proposed to her, "Look, Pantasilea, I'll give you my sapphire necklace. You give me the ring and I'll give you the necklace."

I made it shine in the half-light. The mirrors were filled with stars. It was a rare, noble piece of jewelry, which the cardinal had probably got from my grandmother or her father. In Monterotondo, according to Beppo, there were coffers filled with jewels. It felt so magnificent to me, snaking through my fingers, that I decided to increase the benefit of the exchange.

"Give me back the ring, don't say anything about what happened here, and the necklace is yours."

Pantasilea thought it over, tempted. Greed made her so beautiful, tinting her with pink, that I thought that at that instant, provoked by her body as it rose up, glossy, at full length out of the scattered pillows, I could have been capable of possessing her, but I did not dare to try.

"All right," she resolved, "here it is."

"And you won't say anything?"

The sapphires slid over her breasts, her shoulders.

"Not a word."

She laughed and her laugh mingled with the cries of the peacocks.

"Before you go, I have to show you my secret cupboard."

She stood up and I followed her, with the recovered ring, adjusting my clothing, imagining that she was going to show me her harvest of jewels, her harlot's treasure. She went ahead and walked with such grace, naked, that one would have thought she was dragging a queen's train. A closed cabinet stood in a corner of the room.

"Open it," she commanded me, "and you'll see what Pantasilea's secrets are."

I pulled open the door and at first I did not understand what it was all about, for instead of something shining, what was there was dark and gave off the dim glow of ivory. Then I drew back, stifling a gasp. On the shelves there was a macabre exhibit: skulls, bones, bits of human skin, dirty rags stolen from tombs perhaps, bottles filled with doubtful liquids. The skeleton of a toad, hanging by a thread, was softly swaying. I remembered that I had heard Nencia tell that some courtesans got those terrible spoils from sorceresses and used them to make up their love potions. The anguish that had crushed me in Bomarzo when my father had locked me up with the bones was reborn, intact, atrocious, as if by way of some dark magic I had gone back to that horrible imprisonment. It is possible that someone had told Pantasilea about my cruel experience, for no one who knew me was ignorant of it, and in order to mock me, to avenge herself perhaps, to drive me mad, she was frightening me with that repugnant spectacle. I turned toward her, trembling with panic and with rage, but Pantasilea was already fleeing, light, luminous, her red hair glowing, with no other adornment on her milky nudity except the sparkle of the sapphires, as rhythmic as one of Botticelli's nymphs, escorted by the leaps of the little Maltese dog, toward the room where my companions were waiting. I tried to chase her, but I had to hold back. The encircled child that I was at that time fell onto the bed exhausted. I sought refuge in the memory of my grandmother, of Adriana, of Benvenuto, of Abul, and they could not give me shelter in my despair. The harlot's odor floated in the air, and, nauseated, I perceived that mixed with it was that of the demoniacal carrion in the cupboard. Then I stood up slowly and went out through the hallway toward the room where the fateful crystal polyhedron was hanging, like a person going to his torture.

Ippolito and Giorgino had already left. Abul and Beppo were waiting for me, surrounded by the women. They were feeding the peacocks in the loggia, and Pantasilea, dressed now in a transparent scarlet tunic, was going among them. I did not chance joining the group, so as to avoid the proximity of the birds of ill omen, and I waited in the salon for them to see me, pretending to be interested in the tapestries that pictured the rape of the Sabines. But as they drew farther and farther away along the open terrace and my situation grew more ridiculous, I decided to leave. Although no one smiled or said a word, there was perhaps the shadow of a smile on Beppo's lips, and I could see at once that Pantasilea had lied to me and that they knew of my misfortune. I could spot it in their eyes, in something slight that was painful for Abul and grotesque for the others, and which joined those different beings together with invisible bonds. I raised my glance, avoiding the peacocks, and summoned all of my energy to command (and my voice sounded strangely like that of Cardinal Orsini to my ears): "It's getting late. Let's go."

The good-byes were brief. Pantasilea gave me her Judas kiss and then she and her companions bowed in a low curtsy to the hunchback, but I could tell that it was part of the mockery. The harlot took off the laurel that was around her forehead and offered it to me as the crown of a conqueror; that was carrying the irony too far and I flung it to the floor.

"Come back to see me, Prince," Pantasilea said. "We'll talk about Ariosto."

Beppo handed me my gloves, Abul gave me my hat, and we left. I walked stiffly ahead of them.

Florence was spinning around like a golden wheel, but I had no eyes for it. I felt like slashing my wrists; I felt like jumping into the Arno. I was insane with humiliation. Only a magical instrument—Astolfo's enchanted horn; Orlando's sword Durindana; Balisarda, the sword of the fairy Falerina—could have saved me, but no wizard took note of my misery. That was how we reached the Piazza di Santa Croce; Poliziano had sung of the tourneys there. The palaces were flickering in the sunset. I crossed the width of the esplanade and, because my chest hurt and my eyes were clouded, I stopped with the pretext of listening to the fable behind a group of artisans who were listening to a storyteller. I noticed Beppo and Abul very close by and I raised my hand to my open neck like a figure in a portrait. Everything had been so unreal that I could have been a painted figure. Some people recognized Signor Orsini, who lived in the palace on the Via Larga, and they stepped aside and let me go to the front with my servants. The narrator was blind and old and he accompanied himself on the violin. He was telling the story of Ginevra of Ravenna, and I, who was only too familiar with it, thought of withdrawing, but it was too late. It was too late for me to avoid the hated couplets. I clenched my fists and gave in to bad luck, to the inexorable wrath of the peacocks.

Ginevra's father had destined her for marriage to a hunchback from

Ravenna (here my neighbors looked at me out of the corner of their eyes, and the blind man with the violin, who could not have realized his cruelty, hunched his shoulders and twisted himself, imitating a hump in front of the hunchbacked prince who was standing in the first row), but Ginevra was in love with an adolescent, Diomede, who was as handsome as Antinous and who would go riding on a white horse dressed in green silk. Ginevra was married, and Diomede, disguised as a woman, entered her service. One day the hunchback, who in spite of his efforts had been unable to make his wife his own, tried to make advances to the young servant girl and he discovered that although she did not have a hair on her face, the servant possessed elements that indicated undeniably that she belonged to the male sex. The lovers pushed the hunchback down a staircase, like a scene in a puppet show, and the husband cracked his skull. The sweet Ginevra finished him off and the lovers inherited his estate. When the story was over, nobody dared applaud. Only the blind man was laughing, and his violin too, with a cascading laugh. I opened my purse and threw him three gold florins. Their metallic sound rang out in the silence. They were picked up by the boy who was his guide and who fixed his innocent eyes on me, and the old man, taking off his cap, thanked me for such a splendid fortune. But no one gave him any other coins and the group broke up at once; that night the young men were probably talking about the episode along the Tornaquinci porticoes.

"What's the matter?" the blind man asked, and the guide did not know what to tell him.

We left and I walked along like a sleepwalker, having to lean on Abul's arm. Why was I so constantly assaulted? Why was there no rest for me? The story of Ginevra, of Diomede, and the hunchback which had been thrown into my face, slapping me publicly, as the crowning point of an afternoon of opprobrium, was revealed as an allegory of my existence. There floated above it the memory of Girolamo, making me dress up as a woman, but Diomede had done it to attain a wily victory, and all that I had gained from it was my father's disgust and wrath. And that hunchback who had not been able to enjoy Ginevra of Ravenna and who, without knowing it, had made advances to a man in female dress... and then had fallen down a staircase and died...

Some laggards who had remained in a corner of the square were chatting when I passed them about the new world that had been discovered across the sea, where previously one had been assured that the World came to an end. Hernán Cortes had already conquered Mexico, and the news was bright with blood and gold. There, far, far away, I would have liked to have gone, for America was the real land of the *Orlando furioso* and I could have passed unnoticed among its monsters.

In the palace, while I was going up to my rooms, dressed in the shadows of the stairway, my nerves gave way and I began to weep like a child, sobbing, doubled over, repeating to myself that everything was over for me and that really the best thing that I could do to free myself would be to let myself die. Then Abul came forward, took me in his arms and kissed me. I felt his wet lips on the folds of my mouth along with the taste of my tears. Beppo said something, I do not know what he said, but it must have been something disagreeable and stupid, and I punched at him again and again, but the punches fell into space as the boy began to run upstairs. We chased him, shouting insults, but we could not catch him; Abul much more light-footed; I, limping behind. When I burst into the pages' quarters, my two servants were separated by the bed where Beppo slept, and they could be seen, one ready to jump and the other to move his body aside and escape. Between them both, on the wall, was nailed a crude copy of the Orsini shield, which Beppo considered his own: the rose, the serpent, the bears. The symbol of so many glories that had gleamed on banners and for which I, a reprobate Orsini, meant an affront, with its admonitory presence increased the pain that was tearing me apart. If I had been the illegitimate one, what else would I have been except another jester in my father's house? If Beppo had been the legitimate one, if Gian Corrado Orsini had recognized him, he would now have been in Bomarzo with Girolamo, with Maerbale, with their cousins, with their friends, polishing his armor for tourneys and for war. I realized that the intensity of my hatred was only comparable to his, for each of us had more than enough reasons to hate the other, and envy tormented the servant and the master to an equal degree. Abul jumped over the bed, spindly, magnificent, like Aquilante the Black. His skin and his suit of snow were sparkling. As he upset the bed with his leaps, an object fell at my feet which I picked up. It was Adriana's ring. Then my two pages disappeared, one chasing the other, running, running, dodging among the overturned beds and scattered clothes toward the back door of the room which was clouded in a haze of harnesses and pieces of armor.

The topaz was burning my fingers. Its yellow stone enclosed the only thing my venom lacked, the one last drop of gall. With it in my hand, as if I were carrying a live coal, I sought the path to the bedroom where my beloved was dying. I had to know at once and receive the final thrust; I can almost say that I yearned to receive it and drop forever. But halfway there I ran into Piero Valeriano and Messer Pandolfo, carrying books, quills, and inkwells, who stopped me without noticing my upset appearance which was hidden by the shadows.

"A topaz," Piero Valeriano declared slowly, "a healthful stone, the stone of virgins, of chastity... Nature's crystals are very interesting. A topaz... I must consult my lapidaries to see what they have to say about it."

"I have a copy of the poem by Mardobus," Messer Pandolfo put in proudly, "which mentions seventy precious stones in almost eight hundred hexameters."

"And I have the *De mineralibus* by Albertus Magnus."

"That's so. I was looking through it here in the master's library. And there is an Arabian-Persian treatise..."

"We'll look at them."

"A topaz... Signor Pier Francesco, why in such a hurry? If I'm not mistaken, the topaz is one of the twelve stones that adorned the square emblem that the high priest of Israel wore on his chest... Why such haste, Signor Orsini?"

Where are my gigantic bears hiding—I thought in my impatient madness—my age-old bears, my guard? Why don't they come? Why don't they help me? Can't they see that I need them more than ever now? Have I stopped being Prince Orsini perhaps and no longer merit their escort? What can I do alone? What can I do, hunchbacked and crippled, with my twisted fourteen years, with Death hungrily circling about me, what can I do against Life? What about my immortality? What about my horoscope?

And the teachers in the meantime were passing Adriana's topaz back and forth and going on in Latin.

---

The fleeting light that had been Adriana was barely aglow when I entered her room. She would soon die, and that bedroom with its hazy tapestries would remain in darkness. I reached her bed and I could see that Death was already beginning to assume control over her violet eyes, which had become opaque and had lost the flash of their golden streaks. In her detached rigidity, in the white folds of the embroidered linens that outlined her, she looked sculptured, marble, and it was the sketch of a statue for her tomb. The candles were burning in front of the religious images and offerings, and the whispering of the praying nuns could be heard in the shadows. I learned from Nencia that the doctors had said that there was no more hope but to resign oneself, for the end was close at hand. I also found out that Catherine and Clarice had been to see her and that the latter had given her a useless broth, prepared by an old herbalist woman, as a last attempt to save her. Large reliquaries surrounded her, brought from the church of San Lorenzo, and the flickering of the candles on their glass and goldwork suggested dried blood and sacred bones. I fell to my knees, forgetting the important circumstance that had brought me there, and I began to pray, something that I had not done for a long time. I wanted to contribute something that could save her and I remembered the venerated remains of Saint Anselm that were kept in Bomarzo, but they were too far away, so that for lack of any other aid, I superstitiously turned to my talisman, to Benvenuto Cellini's ring, and I raised it to her lips. Adriana looked without recognizing me, and in the quiet of the room her lips half opened under the metal hoop and she whispered, "Beppo..." Beppo, as if she were answering the apprehensions that bothered me, with a low and distinct voice which had nothing of its former rich vibration. Then I felt my jealousy rise up again and my rage, I drew the ring back, I took another ring out of my purse, the one which I had found in the pages' quarters, and I gave it to Nencia, who was looking at us without concealing her guilty hesitancy. I took the woman by the wrist with a violent gesture which I would not have been capable of under normal circumstances, and I drew her away into the corridor so that the nuns could not hear what we were saying.

In five minutes' time I learned everything. Nencia could no longer hide it from me. Also, Nencia must have been using some undercover method to attach the love I felt for Adriana and she certainly thought that the revelation would serve her ends. She informed me, avoiding my eyes, that the girl was dying madly in love with the page. Beppo had visited her several times and both of them, Adriana dalla Roza and he, had gained the silence of her caretaker who, thinking that the flame of that love would bring back the health of the little one (that was how she explained it to me at least) had become their accomplice. She swore to me that nothing had happened between them, absolutely nothing, for nothing could have happened, given the young girl's extreme weakness, and that the latter had not even given the ring to Beppo voluntarily, but one morning he had removed it from her lifeless finger. But the lucidity of jealousy made me sense the truth that lay beneath that urgent chatter. What Beppo had wished to do, above all, was to rise up as the rival to his master, to defeat him; then, because when he started his visits the outcome was still not in sight, which could have been different with Adriana's recovery, he had calculated that if she recovered her health, perhaps they could flee together and he could link his destiny to that of the noble maiden, rehabilitating his bastardy and his lowness of birth; and lastly, no matter how much Nencia protested her attitude of disinterested neutrality and how she had admonished Beppo, I guessed that her blind devotion to the Orsinis had impelled her to aid one who, even though illegitimate and concealed, was perhaps a part of the lineage that had inspired such servile devotion in her; and I sensed that she had calculated perhaps that in that way she would see herself free of a powerful opponent and consequently she would be in excellent conditions to give to me her dynastic fervor and her equivocal sensuality without hindrance, winning a victory whose material fruits I do not dare to think of, but which were allied no doubt, to the caresses that she had given me. If Nencia took only a few minutes to bring me up to date on the adventure, I took much less time in reaching those conclusions. I threw the topaz in her face and left to find

Abul. My mind was made up: I would have to do away with Beppo, the spoiler, the bold one; put an end to his tricks, his daring, his traps. I spoke to the African about it in vague words that implied a command. On the following day Ippolito de' Medici would go hunting. I would ask him to take my pages along and leave the procedures to Abul's initiative. I was a coward even in that: I placed on his shoulders the responsibility for the crime, detaching myself from it with insinuations, with euphemisms.

The slave bowed and touched his forehead to my extended hand as a sign of obedience. I did not see him again that night nor the following morning at dawn when the hunting party left the palace in the direction of Cafaggiolo. I never saw him again. The cruel idea that such a thing would happen had not even crossed my mind, for had I suspected it, I never would have suggested to him a position that would have torn him out of my existence; but life is mysterious and it plays with invisible dice; it does not let us foresee the broad consequences that are hidden in the seeds of our fleeting acts. When I left Bomarzo, I did not imagine that my timid eyes would never again look upon the imposing figure of my father; and when, trembling with rage, I drove Abul to put an end to the Beppo nightmare, I did not suspect that in so doing I was losing him too, losing Aquilante the Black, and even though Abul may not have died, it was as if I had sent them to their deaths together.

The two following days I practically did not leave Adriana's side, without caring that Clarice Strozzi called me and chided me for such an exaggerated display of feelings. She thought that Adriana and I were just children, and that a vehemence like mine lacked seriousness. Her opinion interested me very little. I only lived through the painful hours to watch the decline of my beloved, to await news from the hunters, to discern on the faces of the inhabitants of the palace what they knew about the miserable role that Pier Francesco Orsini had played in Pantasilea's house and which certainly had been spread about through Beppo's insidious behavior.

Adriana was declining rapidly in the midst of the suffocating candles and the litanies. With a rosary in my hand I answered the nuns' mumbled prayers. There was no news of Ippolito and his servants and I did not dare send Ignacio de Zúñiga to the valley of Mugello seeking some word concerning his party for fear of arousing suspicions. On the other hand, every time that I left Adriana's room to walk about the palace like a specter and I passed the many servants of the Medicis in the galleries and in the *cortile,* my susceptibility led me to feel that they were all looking at me differently, as if they were scrutinizing me with mockery, even those who unquestionably could not have had any news of my clumsiness during the business with the courtesan. Until on one occasion I reprimanded a young squire of the Strozzis with extreme anger because he was amusing himself like an idiot imitating the barking of a dog in order to make the other pages laugh and I thought that he was imitating Pantasilea's Maltese dog, the one worthy of Carpaccio's brush.

Clarice and Catherine took part in the prayers in Adriana's room with Nencia and other palace women, but the slim relief that I obtained for my upset did not come from them but from a child of twelve or thirteen who, with disconcerting closeness, did not leave my side during those two days, as if he sensed the various conflicts that were warring in my spirit. It was Lorenzino, Lorenzaccio de' Medici, the curious person whom I had seen among his relatives when I arrived at the palace on the Via Larga, and whom I had met after that on only a few occasions.

I have read several books lately which have as a theme his slippery personality and in none of them have I found a reference to the visits he made at that time to Ippolito and of which no trace remains in documents. The orphan of an absurd spendthrift, Lorenzino lived with his mother and his younger brothers and sisters near Florence in the ancestral villa of Cafaggiolo, disguising their economic scarcity with lordly appearances. He was dark, frail, and aristocratic, more graceful than handsome. He moved with a natural gallantry, so thin and rhythmic that it moved one to watch him. He was the victim of an elegant sadness (the English would call it "becoming"), which probably derived from his patrician isolation that was dedicated to reading the classics; from his poverty; from being aware that he, the first legitimate male of the two branches of the line, was condemned to an obscure existence;

from the subtle insinuations which Clarice and Filippo Strozzi used to point out to him the injustice of his position and artfully prepare his spirit, as his father had already prepared it, for revenge. He had only one friend, a son of Riccardo de' Medici, and there was even whispering about that impassioned intimacy, as there were comments too at one time about the excessive affection that Clement VII showed for his mysterious nephew, but I can assert, for I knew the milieu rather well, that they were calumnies. Lorenzino had not yet given any evidence of the possibility of a change in character such as came about later and which transformed the grave child into a shameless parasite, an organizer of pleasures for that same Alessandro de' Medici whom he murdered. He would appear from time to time on the Via Larga with his tutor Zeffi, an old priest with rudimentary culture, and his main pleasure was listening to Messer Piero Valeriano conversing with Ippolito and Giorgino Vasari about Plutarch and Virgil. He learned more there than in Padua and Bologna. He would shut himself up with Filippo Strozzi to listen to him comment on themes of Florentine history, and there is no doubt that the dilettante skeptic, sometimes ardent, sometimes ironic, was poisoning him with his disdain for divine and human things and with disdain and envy for the usurpers. Filippo was an ambiguous man, formed in the school of Machiavelli. When it suited him, he presented himself as one of the leaders of the oligarchical opposition to the bastards; and when it was to his interest he passed over to the other side. Many great lords of that time shared his comfortable attitude. It was he who lent Alessandro de' Medici, the Duke of Florence, his former enemy, the money to build the fortress destined to put an end to the rebellious dreams of the Tuscans. He died in that fortress which he had paid for, imprisoned, writing sonnets and invoking liberty like a hero of ancient Rome. He possessed a personal charm that worked on Lorenzino, the authentic, disinherited successor to the Medici rule. He modeled him as if he were made of wax. But Lorenzino soon left us. His mother, as soon as the risk of an invasion by imperial troops became imminent, sent him to Venice with his tutor, and even there the boy must have undergone new humiliations, for in spite of his being the senior, the doge as well as the ambassadors of France and England lionized his cousin Cosimo, the future grand duke, who had arrived in Venice at the same time and who, instructed by his ambitious mother, had pushed him into the background. All of that worked, as can be understood, to embitter him, to alienate him, and to whet his homicidal steel.

Nothing of his future evolution was foreseeable during the time in which he showed me such discreet evidence of kindness. Perhaps his suppressed grievances felt kinship with mine. What is certain is that during those difficult times I felt his friendly presence by my side, and that the soft young figure there, kneeling in the room that smelled of candles and potions, has always been deep in my memory. Sometimes, without saying a word, Lorenzino would take one of my hands and smile gently, the tired smile of an aged child, and his graceful elegance when he crossed the room as in a dance or in a dream distracted me from my woes.

Adriana dalla Roza died at midnight on the second day. Our relationship had been so singular that even today I cannot define concretely the kind of feeling that it inspired in me and which is so much like love (an urge, a dissatisfaction provoked by my loneliness and my physique, by the urgency that someone beautiful, desirable should assure me that it was not illogical and that I was loved, that my love was needed, at least), nor do I know with certainty up to what point the bonds that united her to Beppo had reached. The image—the last one—that she left me and which I converted into a stone statue, made me think at the time (for everything that happened to me grew larger than life under the influence of my Latin studies) of what Ovid tells in his *Metamorphoses* about the young girl who, hopelessly in love with a young man from Cyprus, committed suicide at his door, and while her body was being borne off it was changed into a stone statue by Venus. It is true that I was not the one who died, but something of mine, very much mine, a certain candor, a certain nobility, died forever beside Adriana's bed. Destiny ordained that she be buried in Rome in the very church of Santa Maria in Traspontina where I had been baptized. The sphinx that I built later in Bomarzo was dedicated to her memory. No one has said so until this moment. Adriana was like a sphinx to me, tender at moments and even bold, as when her hand caressed mine in the Medici palace or when I felt the softness of her breast beside me at the balustrade of the *cortile*; pitiless and treasonous too at times, as when she took up with my page, flouting my careful efforts, and affronting my pride. She inspired lost verses in me. Years later, at a time when her sweet memory had been replaced by others that were deeper, I continued singing them as a sort of sterile literary exercise. What had been an emotion had been turned into a theme. During the course of that distant Florentine night, I wept for her, embracing Lorenzino and Clarice, believing, in my innocence and disillusionment, that I would never be consoled. I was weeping too over my shame in the Pantasilea affair, for Beppo, for Abul. I was weeping for her and for myself, perhaps more for myself.

And the following morning, my tears still warm, I was perfidiously disloyal to the memory of Adriana dalla Roza.


I was leaving the room of death early in the morning when Nencia came over to speak to me.

"You have suffered, Prince," she said to me, "I know. And you have not suffered over Adriana's death alone."

The allusion to my failure with Pantasilea was too clear for me not to have understood. She was beside me, her mature body offering itself underneath her generous clothing. She took me by the hand. "Don't be nervous," she added. "An Orsini cannot be the object of scorn."

Then she stepped back a little and bowed to me. "I would like to help you."

I looked at her more carefully than at other times, and even then I had known her well: opulent, her broad hips firm, a shadow on her upper lip, her dark eyes with an expression that was half commanding, half beseeching. She lifted me up, wrapped me in her arms, kissed me long on the mouth, and I could feel my body awakening from its torpor and I answered her back.

"We have to consider this matter in more detail," she whispered into my ear, and I remembered Pantasilea's words that were almost the same, "I'll meet you here in an hour."

She returned to Adriana's room and I went to mine. I was trembling and I thought that my teeth were going to chatter. That forty-year-old woman, so strong and so submissive, so obsequious and so bold, for whom the members of my house had a legendary prestige; that woman who had inherited from her forebears a fervor that had been enriched by the centuries of service dedicated to the glory of the Orsinis, who had become in the end for her and her people distant and all-powerful idols, fashioned out of a metal so divine that their humps became halos and their limps became majesty; that fanatical woman, effervescent, transported in her modest frivolity by the rites of worldly respect, covetous of lords, avid for illustrious familiarities; that woman had waited patiently for Adriana's death in order to invade my intimacy, as if with Adriana gone the only barrier between us had been broken, and she could no longer contain herself in her zeal to obtain the extreme relationship. Her attitude filled me with pride and with fear. Somebody, for whatever reason she might have had, desired me physically, desired me. By the calculations of somebody, the little exile with the deformed back represented passion, with all of its violence and complications.

Free from the respect which was imposed on her by my acute feelings which burned like a lamp as I watched by the bedside of the dying young girl, free of that young girl and her fascination, the plebeian dared approach her gods and live with them. I sensed in her attitude, more than the probability of pleasure, the hypothetical chance to redeem me. If Nencia, who aroused me so strongly, could not manage it, no one would be able to attain my rehabilitation. It was absolutely necessary that I try it, but I hesitated. So many doubts had agitated me in the course of the last few hours, one following upon the other, with my having had no rest, acting like a robot in the hands of Fate. I would go...I would not go...If it all ended up as in Pantasilea's house, I would be lost forever. I did not think about Adriana, about her tight skin, still warm, about her soul which was floating about us. I only thought about myself.

The door to Messer Pandolfo's room was ajar and I could see his worn copy of Virgil on top of the table. The tutor was sleeping. I went in noiselessly. I would entrust my fate to the decision of other gods, more powerful than the Orsinis, by means of the *Sortes Virgilianae*. In Bomarzo we used to play that popular guessing game, which left to the fortunes of the oracle of the book the solution to problems great or small. Did not the blood of magicians flow in Virgil's veins? Did we not, under Dante's spell, consider him a necromancer, a seer? I would submit myself to whatever the Aeneid decreed.

I opened the pages, closing my eyes, I ran my finger along one of the folios and I read:

> *At Venus aetherios inter dea candida nimbos*
> *dona ferens aederat, natumque in ualle reducta*
> *ut procul egelido secretum flumine uidit*
> *talibus adfata est dictis seque obtulit ultro...*

I translated mentally: "In the meantime, Venus, who, glowing, had crossed through the ethereal clouds, was there with her gifts. She saw her son isolated in the depths of the valley, separated from his companions, on the cool bank, and she said these words to him, showing herself..."

But I did not have to know what the words of Venus to Aeneas were. That message was all that I needed. It was enough for me for the goddess to show herself to her son, "isolated," "separated from his companions" like Pier Francesco Orsini. It was enough for me for Love herself to rise up before the solitary one. And if I did not read what followed, it was because I was anxious for the Virgilian prognostication to coincide with my hidden aspirations, which the text had infused with a sacred vigor, and because, as on other occasions, it managed to divest me of the responsibility for a decisive act. The gods had resolved it and they were much wiser than I and in a position to know whether what I was hastening to do would offend Adriana's memory or not. Adriana's shade would not rebel against celestial determinations. At the appointed time I went to find Nencia, who was punctual.

She guided me up the stairs and we went into the palace chapel.

"We will say a prayer," she explained, "so that the dead girl will forgive us".

She prayed in a low voice and I, standing beside her, was caught up by the strangeness of the situation and could not concentrate. The dancing of a few candles lighted, as if it were painting them, the frescoes by Benozzo Gozzoli that completely covered the walls of the small chapel. I have never seen a cavalcade of such beautiful fantasy. The youthful Lorenzo, the Emperor of Byzantium, and the Patriarch of Constantinople represented the Magi in the triumphal procession. Clarice Strozzi had explained to me who portrayed the other characters: Pandolfo Malatesta, the lord of Rimini; Galeazzo Maria Sforza, the son of the Duke of Milan; the Medicis; Vittorino da Feltre, Niccolò da Uzzano, Gozzoli himself. They paraded by, metallic, multicolored, adorned with luxurious caprice, on horses with splendid trappings, through a countryside of cypresses and towers—Careggi, San Gimignano—of crags, woods, and gardens, as if they were on their shining way to a festival at the Florentine court. Camels and wild animals contributed to the extravagance. Mysterious birds were flying about. And the one who impressed me most was a boy there who was carrying a leopard on the rump of his steed. But no—the one who impressed me this time was the Negro bowman who rose up beside Sforza's horse, for he reminded me of Abul, and then the poetical scene, almost Oriental for being so curious and bejeweled, was transformed, making me shake with terror, into Ippolito de' Medici's hunting party. Ippolito was the adolescent Lorenzo, wearing a strange crown; Beppo was the boy with the leopard, dressed in blue, who was turning to look at me, the cat being held by a chain. The others were looking at me disdainfully from up on their mounts, from the magic of a world that was silently condemning me. And the cavalcade continued turning with slow ceremony. That one was Lorenzaccio; that one was my father; that one Cardinal Orsini; that one, the one dressed as a page, was Adriana; and they were imprisoned with me in a huge birdcage that was sparkling in the sun. They were looking at me silently, like aristocratic judges, so illustrious that my guilt grew larger and I prostrated myself before them. I tried to flee and Nencia held me back. She squeezed me against her breast. She covered my mouth with one hand. There were voices on the stairs. The woman closed the door.

Ippolito's companions were returning and the noise of their arms could be heard as they hit the worn stones. They were talking excitedly. They were saying that Beppo had been killed by Abul's crossbow and that my Negro slave had disappeared. No matter how much they had looked for him, beating the brush, exploring, they could not find him.

The naked Berbers were carrying Beppo's body up the stairs on their shoulders on a stretcher, his head was tilted. His blue eyes were probably still open, the eyes like those of Girolamo, like my grandmother's, for he had even stolen those from me: Diana Orsini's blue eyes. My tense body showed Nencia the horror that was wracking me and she clung to me. Then, almost suffocating me, while the funeral procession went off down the halls, she dragged me to the floor.

Oh Lord, oh Lord, Adriana dalla Roza had died; Beppo had died by my order; Abul had gone away, perhaps forever; and I was there, struggling with a female who could have been my mother and who was drawing a quick confused, desperate delight out of my insides! I was becoming a man and attaining that terrible victory in the arms of Death, who, in order to possess me, had taken on the mask of a woman maddened by lust! And it was happening in a holy place, in the chapel of the Magi, profaned by me! Day had died; Night had died too—the ones that Messer Pandolfo should have named Day and Night, because Night was Abul and not Ignacio de Zúñiga—and now, like the two figures by Michelangelo on the tomb of the Duke of Nemours, Abul and Beppo were guarding the invisible sepulcher of Adriana in an incandescent region that I would never know, and toward which, without a sound, without a single fold of the fabulous vestments moving, the cavalcade of Benozzo Gozzoli was departing. And I would be perpetually alone, alone with my sin. My tears, usually so easy, would not flow. My heart was becoming hard, as if a gigantic topaz had been set in its place, Adriana's topaz. Nencia, aware of her savage madness, had finally run off, leaving me lying on the rare slabs of serpentine or porphyry. I did not dare rise. The golden knights were still around me, with lances and plumes, lying in wait for me. It terrified me to stumble onto the painted eyes of the boy with the leopard. Or to discover on Filippo Lippi's altar who knows what kind of wrathful prodigy.

I do not know how long I stayed in that position with my head in my hands waiting for the august vengeance. Who was I, what was I at the age of fourteen, a monster? Had the deformity that tortured my body gotten into my soul, twisting it? What good had my proud skepticism been to me? Who was I and for what purpose had I been put on earth, and why did not some purifying bolt strike me? If I had only felt like praying... But that would have been adding to the profanation.

Then I heard them shouting my name in the galleries. Ignacio de Zúñiga was looking for me. I dragged myself to the door, I pushed it open, and I answered with a wisp of a voice. I do not know whether he understood what had happened when he found me, my clothes in disarray, lying down like a dog. He told me briefly what I already knew and he tried to lift me, but I would not let him.

"I have sinned," I murmured, "I have sinned against God and against man."

He fell to his knees beside me and began to pray. I had been unjust with him too. Like Ariosto in the court of Ippolito d'Este, Ignacio was suffering in that of the other Ippolito. Like Ariosto, he would have preferred a simple existence instead of the pomp that I had imposed upon him among the vain Medicis. I lifted my eyes to his face and I saw that it was illuminated like that of a saint and that his lips were barely moving. On the ceiling, among the multicolored coffers, the monogram of Christ was carved. I kissed my servant's cold hand, just like a dog. He passed a finger over my impure mouth as if he were cleaning it. Then I fell into sleep.

I dreamed that I was in a rocky garden with enormous statues. It was the garden at Bomarzo. I was still unable to understand it, but it was the future garden of Bomarzo, my strange creation. And in the midst of the monsters, the dragons, the titans who were emerging from the bushes, I felt a wonderful relief. I lost myself among them as in an enchanted forest, and although I feared their ghostly armies, I loved them, I loved my stone monsters, because only surrounded by their guard, by their claws, by their fangs, by their colossal wrinkled skeletons would I be capable of continuing living, living, living eternally.


The remorse and grief made me ill. I was ashamed of myself. When I recovered a week later, I was in a complete spiritual crisis. It lasted as long as the rest of my stay among the Florentines, a whole year. If it had not been for my physical inconveniences, I would have begun studies to receive Holy Orders, for, stimulated by Zúñiga, I thought that I had been touched by grace, which was awakening a religious vocation in my reprobate soul. My grandfather, a few days later, continued his trip to the north of the peninsula. I said good-bye to him and I asked him for his blessing. For the first time I saw the man of God in Franciotto Orsini. But if I thought that he had changed, the cardinal was still the same. He traced the sign of the cross on my forehead with a brusque gesture, more the warrior than the churchman.

"I have learned," he said to me, polishing the mockery, "that the necklace I gave you has remained in the hands of Pantasilea. I don't reproach you. It is well for a gentleman of your caste to be generous, but only if such an act is justified by gallantry. Because, as I understand, you received nothing in exchange for the sapphires, my son, and you left her house in the same state as when you went in."

He slapped his riding boots with his whip, as my father used to do, and he looked at me with a smile. I could have answered him that if the matter bothered him, there was evidence that would calm him down, but the candor of his grandson was a thing of the past, even when it was a question of material proof, so I tightened my lips and offered up my vanity in silent sacrifice.

The letters that I sent to my grandmother during that time were sprinkled with quotations from the Scriptures. She answered me with surprise, not daring either to share my enthusiasm or to make an epigram. She was not pious and she was probably wracking her brains to find the motives for my change, which she must have attributed to some twist in my growing up, and which intrigued her in a milieu as pagan as that of the Medicis. I found out that Ignacio de Zúñiga, in answer to the only letter that Diana Orsini had sent him, insinuated to her that I had undergone a fundamental change because of Adriana's death, but in my turn I avoided clarifying the affectionate doubts that her correspondence brought me, or telling her, besides about Adriana, about Nencia, Beppo, and Abul, and about how much my heart pained and how I stayed awake at night beside my breviary. As for Nencia, she did not pursue me any more. She had got what she yearned for. Perhaps she dreamed of having a child from the Orsini line. Happily, it did not come about. The change in my behavior and the scant enjoyment she had derived from my troubled sensuality had calmed my rapist's enthusiasm. And the rest, Ippolito, Alessandro, Clarice, Giorgio Vasari did not bother with me either. There were other problems worrying them. Cardinal Passerini himself, when I consulted him on certain theological scruples, told me that he was too busy with affairs of state to attempt to resolve my perplexities, and he pointed out to me that it is dangerous to set about delving deeply into some texts, for the temptation of heresy is the accustomed punishment of neophyte curiosity. He insisted that I return to Ovid and Catullus. He proposed that I take up falconry.

What is certain is that parallel to my spiritual upset—which made me repeat my confessions to a patient Dominican from the monastery of San Marco whom I almost drove mad—the historical events that changed the life of Florence and brought about my return home were developing.

The emperor had stirred up the Colonnas against Clement VII and had obliged him to shut himself up in Sant' Angelo, his citadel. The Borgo section of Rome, where our palace was, was sacked. They stole the wardrobe of Clement de' Medici, one of his three tiaras, the chalices, the crosses, the vestments of Saint Peter; they threw what they could not carry out of the windows of the Vatican. Once free, the pope avenged himself by destroying fourteen castles and villages belonging to the princes headed by Cardinal Pompeo Colonna. Filippo Strozzi had been one of the papal hostages, and Clarice traveled to Rome in her litter and managed to save him. They had no time, therefore, or peace of mind, to worry about my speculations. Then there came the order of Charles V to the Constable of Bourbon and Lannoy to march on the papal states, and Lorenzino left for Venice. The barbarian Frundsberg advanced with his Teutonic hordes, brandishing a noose which he swore to use to hang the Vicar of Christ. He was later stricken with an attack of apoplexy. The troops camped at the gates of Rome and the pope again repaired to Sant' Angelo with thirteen cardinals— among whom was my grandfather—and three thousand people of all kinds who hindered military operations. Benvenuto Cellini (the news made me happy in the midst of so much sadness) contributed to the defense of the bastion as an artilleryman. It was at that time that he wounded the Prince of Orange with a piece of shrapnel and my grandfather, furious, wanted to order his execution, for he felt that the prospects for peace had been hindered. It occurs to me that Cardinal Orsini's anger with the goldsmith had, among other roots, that of his unpardonable attitude toward me. The cardinal had not forgotten the family conference that had taken place at Bomarzo after my brief encounter with Benvenuto on the beach near Ceveteri and which motivated my absurd exile to Florence. Cellini had dismantled the tiara and jewels of the Holy Father; he sewed them into his ritual vestments and into the clothing of Cavalierino, a boy who had been Filippo Strozzi's groom, and Clement VII would not let any harm come to the craftsman. The episodes grew more frequent, rapid. Rome was conquered in an hour and sacked without mercy. The imperial soldiers who had crossed Italy in rags were now walking through the streets dressed in gold and silver. Their hats flashed with jewels and on their hairy chests there swung strings of pearls that had belonged to great ladies and to prostitutes. My grandmother lost her famous necklace. Women dressed in extravagant richness and processions of servants followed wherever the ruffians went, carrying paintings, statues, valuable vases, and the long swords of their masters, stiff like priapic symbols, intertwined with bracelets and ribbons. The blade of the Holy Lance was tied to the pike of a Lutheran lansquenet, and in the taverns, among the chalices for the Holy Sacrament, brimming with wine, the Veil of the Veronica passed from hand to hand. In the meantime, in Sant' Angelo, there was no surcease of litanies and the noise of explosions. The smell of incense engulfed the castle, which rose up, perfumed, amid the horror like a sacred hill, the last refuge of faith and order.

The news that the refugees spread in Florence roused up the masses. Toward the end of April 1527, when the hosts of the constable came down into Tuscany, the mob rioted in the Piazza della Signoria, taking advantage of the brief absence of Cardinals Passerini, Cibo and Ridolfi and of Ippolito de' Medici. It was said that they had fled the city, but that was not true. We knew quite well, those of us who remained in the palace, that they had gone out into the countryside to seek the aid of the Duke of Urbino and the Marquis of Saluzzo. That April 26th was a fearsome day. Friday, a baleful day. Contradictory rumors were spread from room to room by the pages and harquebusiers, and we waited around Clarice, as around a fortress, touching her voluminous skirts from time to time, as if we were touching the vestments of a saint or a king, while the people deliberated in front of the Signoria about the expulsion of the Medicis. The old shouts of liberty were reborn, and they echoed angrily among the tapestries. The inhabitants of the Via Larga, isolated, without news of the cardinals, who were dealing with the troops in Montefeltro, ignorant of what was happening in their own home, wandered then from one room to another, impelled by the pages, and we looked at the rare objects that might disappear a second time. When they shouted to us that from the windows of the Signoria they had thrown stones down on the mob and that they had broken one of the arms of Michelangelo's David, the David of my childhood, the only beautiful memory my father had left me, I hid myself and wept. Ippolito and the pensive cardinals finally returned, as if they were coming back from a worldly party, speaking quickly of how well the duke and the marquis had received them, and a fiction of peace was re-established. The Republic had only lasted one afternoon, but the Medicis were already doomed. On May 12th we learned, six days after the pillaging of Rome, about the bestial license that had been unleashed on the Eternal City. Cardinal Passerini told us that it was rumored that the emperor, when he heard about the excesses of his uncontainable troops, had been overcome with remorse. Months later we learned that the Spanish court had dressed in mourning for the sacrileges, which was rather paradoxical. And on the 17th of that month Clarice de' Medici put on her great theatrical scene, which she had probably been rehearsing for years, and which had probably fanned the dramatic flames of her solitary ambitions, although she never imagined that it would be produced under such atrocious circumstances. She went into the Signoria palace, where Passerini was waiting like a lackey for the resolutions of the Council, which repeated the word revolution. Ippolito, Alessandro, and Catherine were gathered around the fearful cardinal, and the granddaughter of the Magnificent rebuked the bastards with ironical bitterness, calling them incapable of protecting the heritage of the legitimate Medicis, forgetting that her father had left Florence under circumstances even more painful for the descendants of the *Pater Patriae*.

The pitiful inhabitants of the Via Larga disbanded, the arrogance of the period of their rule having ended. Only little Catherine stayed behind as a hostage of the Republic. Ippolito, Alessandro, and the cardinal fled, followed by the horde of African and Asian slaves who tried to save the chests filled with works of art and books, piled in helter-skelter, without selection, and who ran after their masters amid nervous greyhounds and frightened whinnying as the people destroyed the shields and broke up the bezants and the fleurs-de-lis. What a different procession from that by Benozzo Gozzoli, from its lithe music, its elegance of a palace masked ball! This was no procession; this was disaster, consternation, angry shouts, anarchy. Filippo Strozzi, always unsure, accompanied Ippolito to Pisa. I escaped too, with Messer Pandolfo, who clutched his Virgil, and with Ignacio de Zúñiga, who was reciting his rosary, indifferent, as we plunged into the shouting river of the rabble. Pantasilea, from her terrace, half hidden in the coming and going of her women, who were unintentionally reproducing the expressions of esthetic fright on the tapestry of the rape of the Sabines, recognized me in the tumult by my hump and threw me a rose. Perhaps she understood at last, in her lucid sorrow, that with the hunchbacked boy, the tragic Orsini from the Via Larga, *le veuf, l'inconsolé*, one of the last true lords was leaving and that she had made him suffer like none other of her sad lovers. A peacock jumped up on the parapet and his harlot's tail hung over the center of the façade like a malevolent embroidered coat of arms. Rodone, Ippolito's favorite dog, who followed us for a while, sniffed the trampled rose and then his mournful howls were extinguished on one of the streets crammed with frantic people. The bells were tolling as thieves invaded the palace of the Medicis and pillaged it a second time. Two days later we were in Bomarzo. Since the death of Adriana and Beppo, my life had been, like that of Italy, a grim nightmare, crossed here and there by flashes of an impetuous fervor.

The serene sight of the structure of Bomarzo in its lofty isolation moved me so much that I got off my horse, my eyes burning with tears, and kissed the beloved soil. There was my house, rusty, golden, in the thin transparency of the spring air that was making the fields quiver. The fascinating mystery of the place, its centuries-old Etruscan strength, peopled with invisible presences older even than my race, took hold of me as when I was a child, smothering me, dissolving in my chest the sharp stone that had been pressing on it. The familiar voice of the water sang in my ears. Some shepherds waved to me. And I thought, fancifully, incorrigibly, as when I had arrived in Florence almost three years before, that perhaps I would be able to be happy among my people, in spite of everything, with the help of God.

# 3. THE APPEARANCE OF MAGIC

*My grandmother's indulgence—My older brother in the Tiber—The writer Palingenio and the demons—Silvio da Narni, a petty wizard—The seduction of the Martelli twins—The death of my father—Pier Francesco Orsini, Duke of Bomarzo—The secret passage—My dreams*

MY INTENT and my spirit soon changed. Everything there conspired to draw me away from my new life. I was beginning to find again the life I had before my trip to Florence, and at the same time, weakened by the interest which I used to evaluate what I held deepest in my blood—my old, basic Bomarzo—the images of Adriana, Beppo, and Abul, which a year before had capped my despair, began to grow pale. I did not forget them, of course, but at that age anxiety can be replaced by a quick self-interest. In the mansion of the Medicis, during the months between the death of Adriana and my return to Bomarzo, I had lived almost exclusively under the severe influence of Ignacio de Zúñiga. His presence and his attitude were the ones most indicated during that time to pacify me and to reconcile me to myself. It was a period of transition, during which emotional elements worked with a strong impact, nullifying me, and during which, under the stimulus of the Spaniard, I thought I could find in religion a harbor safe from the storm unleashed in my soul. In Florence I was alone and no one had any time to give me, occupied as they were with the military and political events which encircled the people of the palace so closely. Everything around me—the palace itself, the streets of Florence, the proximity of Nencia—was full of tragic allusions, and even though time was working its subtle activity of erosion, the marks of the recent past were too close for the sudden disappearance of episodes and figures that would rise up to make an impression when I went into a room. If my fervor had been authentically religious and not—as it had been—the consequence of painful remorse and Ignacio's tenacious preachments, if my Christian faith had had deeper and stronger roots, I would have changed permanently, thanks to the accompanying action of anguish, repentance, and exhortation, but I lacked the necessary base on which I could build a luminous edifice of piety. My religion, for I really did have one, had been created out of a certain ancestral paganism that placed my family on shining altars and which decreed that I, the most miserable member of the line, should also earn my place in the Orsini Olympus, a place that, even if it was mine by the will of Destiny, still required an effort of conquest, for, unlike my brothers, my relatives, and my ancestors, I had brought into the world the paradox of being and not being at the same time a privileged person. My grandmother had shaped me within those inherited ideas—erroneous, blameful, vain, call them what you will—and if the reader censures her for that he should be careful and weigh the pros and cons on delicate scales, because everything that concerns me is intricate and multiple. Diana Orsini, for her part, had grown up in the climate of that cult, from which she derived her strength, and she calculated that in order to strengthen her grandson, who more than anyone needed support and help, she had to pass on to him the essence of a vigor that was affirmed not in the divine but in the human, and which conferred upon the human the qualities of the divine, replacing the absent divine force, whose only vague survival was that of a complex superstition, with the drive of a dynastic veneration, rich in illustrious examples. The replacement of something so high by something so small—I can see it that way now, but at that time I did not have the perspective to appreciate it in its exact proportions—explains many aspects of my tragic actions, but even if I focus on things with an a posteriori lucidity, I think that my grandmother should be considered with indulgence and even absolved, for her mistaken attitude grew out of an urge to benefit me, giving me as support the only thing that she possessed. Such was the drive that came from that proud position, shared by my people in a natural way, that no sooner had I returned to Bomarzo and, as if under a huge glass bell, had begun to breathe once more the rarefied air that had fed my childhood, than I again became the being that I had been before the violent crisis in Florence. It did not happen all at once, of course, but it was fated to happen if one keeps in mind the fragility of my fifteen years; the lack of an intimate handle for my personality to grasp in Zúñiga's preachings; the mysterious dominion that Bomarzo exercised over me as its pagan ghosts joined mine over the centuries; and the logical veneration that I felt for my grandmother, whom, since she was my great ally of always, I also looked upon as the supreme font of wisdom.

The first words that sprang from her lips when I fell into her arms after my long absence were to tell me that I had grown handsome in Tuscany. She looked me over and repeated it to me. She led me to one of her mirrors and in it showed me my delicate face, molded on the cheekbones that had a smooth, flat tint, reflecting the traits of my definitive portrait. Since she was beside me, hiding my hump, and as the transparent beauty of her beloved image suppressed my defects, I discovered that she was correct and that the boy with the large mournful eyes who was looking back at me from the poetical region of the mirror could be considered attractive with his restless physical appearance. She praised me for my lucco, the typical sleeveless mantle of the Florentines, which I had adopted even though it was almost never worn any longer in the city of the Medicis, for its roominess and hood hid my back, and from then on, all through life, I always wore one, of cloth or of damask, black, purple, or red, lined with taffeta, tabby, velvet, silk, or fur, depending on the season.

My father and Girolamo were off to the wars that were shaking Italy. Maerbale, who had shot up a great deal and already had the aristocratic touch that gave him such prestige, and which was accentuated by his rather long and nobly formed nose and the smile of distant contempt that never left him under the shadow of his ruffled hair, greeted me with a coolness that was not aggressive. When Girolamo was not at Bomarzo our relationship grew better. So between the love of my grandmother and the aloof lordliness of my younger brother, the atmosphere of the castle filled me with an unknown peace, accentuating the feeling of happiness that I had felt as soon as I spied my home from the road.

As far as Bomarzo was concerned, scaffolding covered the main façade. Carved materials were piled up on the terraces and very early in the day the hammering of the workmen as they broke and carved the stones informed us that the work of transformation was progressing. But Bomarzo was as stern as the armor of a giant, and even though they added adornments to its cuirass, they could not succeed in modifying its wildness, as harsh as the rock on which its medieval bulk sat.

I continued my strolls with Ignacio and to read the books that he gave me, although the interest that came out of them—and Zúñiga soon noticed it and chided me in vain—was decreasing, and the walks became less and less frequent until I gave them up. On the other hand, I delighted in going out with my grandmother, using one of her walking sticks as I walked about the estate beside her litter. We would wear furs because the cold was strong. From time to time we would make a stop to criticize from a distance the nature of the changes that had been added to the castle or to talk about the *Orlando furioso* or, just as when I was small, about the Orsinis and their glory and about the unknown glories that life held in store for me. During the walks I was slowly opening up my heart to her, for I noticed how much good her comments did for me, and I told her all about the sorrows I had felt over Adriana, over Beppo, and over Abul. She listened to me with grave intensity, trying to discern the truth in the labyrinth of my explanations, and then she would apply her intelligence to undo the guilt complex that the remembrance revealed. She could not see my sins; she saw the need to rescue me. One will most likely think that her compassionate inclination contributed to the fact that I was what I was, covering me with a precocious hardness, and that if later on my spirit developed as I shall show, it was due in a large degree to the blind passion of Diana, who wanted above everything else to avoid the breakdown of her deformed grandson; but I demand tolerance on the part of those who judge and I ask them to remember the details of the case—mine and hers, putting them under the common mark of the Orsinis—when they pass sentence on my grandmother. My grandmother committed reproachable acts—and the worst one of all, the one that marked the direction my existence would take, had not happened yet—and still I cannot condemn her, for I know that her mistakes and her crime were the unfortunate product of love. In any case, I cannot condemn her, because it would be like condemning the air one breathes, for that was what my grandmother was to me: the air that I breathed and the one who supported me until, after she had gone, I had to make my own way, without a guide, without anyone, in a world that was alien and adverse.

Two months and a half after my return to Bomarzo, Cardinal Orsini arrived with fresh news from Rome. The pope had managed to flee from the Castel Sant' Angelo to Orvieto, disguised as a peddler, with a single companion, thanks to the help of the very Cardinal Pompeo Colonna who had given him so much trouble, and who was now gathering the proofs of his selfless devotion. In that way, wearing the dress of a porter with a cushion on his head, Cola di Rienzi had escaped two hundred years earlier, but they had recognized him by his gold bracelet. Less sumptuous and wiser, the pope also had better luck. In the Eternal City, as soon as the bold flight had become known, the people went into a delirious joy, thinking that their miseries were over, and a multitude of monks and priests poured into Saint Peter's to sing a *Te Deum*. The powerful fury of the invaders knew no limits. My grandfather had gone through moments of concern during the struggle against the Colonnas, for he was part of the group of hostages who had served as a guarantee when Clement VII abandoned Sant' Angelo for the first time, but Cardinal Pompeo (the same one who had prevented him from becoming pope at the last conclave) took him with him to Subiaco and heaped honors upon him. Then, during the long siege by the imperial troops, he locked himself up again in the Castel with the pontiff and would not leave his side. He detailed his anger with Benvenuto Cellini to us, giving me stern looks. And he told us about the plague. The plague had broken out in Rome like a divine scourge. The worst of it was that without distinguishing the justice of the causes it decimated besiegers and besieged in equal measure. Corpses were piling up in the streets.

My grandfather stayed with us, forgetting about his estate in Monterotondo. He no longer went out, as before, to ride around the castle and stop at the huts of our peasants where he would taste the wine that they brought up to him from the cellars with ceremonious solicitude. He stayed in his room with an ermine wrap over his legs, looking like a storybook king. The old condottiere sang interminable masses. He had seen too much infamy and atrocity for it not to have moved his tired heart.

During the most bitter days of February the Spanish left Rome for Naples. The Germans also left, loaded down like altars, and when they disappeared out the San Giovanni gate, the people crowded along the road gave free rein to their jubilation, momentarily distracted from the horror of the plague that was so cruel that a year later packs of wolves attacking people still marauded through the streets. In June the Holy Father moved from Orvieto to Viterbo, and Cardinal Orsini hastened there to kiss his cheek. When he was able to return to Rome in October, Clement VII wept in horror at the city in ruins, burned out, having lost half of its population.

In the meantime, in Bomarzo, my life went on placidly. With Messer Pandolfo I began to translate Lucretius. The initial invocation to Venus reminded me of my adventure with Nencia, but I put aside that sinful image and in order to punish myself I composed an ode in praise of Adriana, which I destroyed with more than enough reason. One morning, beside the arch where later on I was to have engraved the contradictory statements on Life and Death, I observed that some of the artisans, during a rest, were carving stone—the soft, local volcanic *peperino*—giving it rough, fantastic shapes that brought to mind the Etruscan tradition of that soil. Those figures made me remember the dream of the colossal statues that had filled me with wonder in the chapel of the Magi, and when I went along the steep terraces that rose up the side of the valley beyond my grandmother's Italian garden, for the first time I had the vague, diffuse idea of how beautiful it would be to transform the rocks that emerged there in all their roughness into immense statues, and that wild vision made me so emotional that without imagining that I would carry it out one day and that it would be the summation of my singular existence, I carried some pieces of workable stone to my bedroom and placed them like offerings at the feet of the armor that Diana Orsini had given me after the episode of the rose-crowned skeleton, for I thought that I could discover an essential kinship between that armor green with rust and that material that was so familiar to the touch of my hand, one which would link them also to me and to the workers who had been born in Bomarzo and were climbing about the scaffolding on the castle. Obscure and age-old energies began to crawl and move about inside me, stirring, awakened by an incentive apparently as trivial as the recreation of some peasants who amused themselves by carving small stones. I felt as if the land there was demanding of me an allegorical expression of its secret, and I felt that the secret was so tightly involved with my own life that both were part of an inseparable whole, to such an extent that if at some time the rare monument would be raised to the magic of Bomarzo that was gestating in my spirit and which was beginning to take shape, hazy, as if it had been stolen from the ancient clouds, it would at the same time place in my Etruscan heritage, as on the stage of a theater, the statuary characters who with their appearance symbolized the periods of my exceptional existence, but in order for me to be in a condition to make that double and unique metaphor plastic and concrete, and to understand what was expected of me, it was still necessary for me to go far along that spiny road, tearing myself apart, gathering emblems and bloody thorns. I could not see it then, of course, with the clarity with which I can now explain the process, but something like an intuition of pain and glory overcame me as I spoke leisurely with the craftsmen and relived my troublesome warning dream, looking from time to time, above the beams of the scaffolding, at the clouds—also sculptures—that formed and broke up their fleeting patterns across the clear sky; and when I returned to my room I was carrying with me an esoteric ballast, as if the Bomarzo air had splendidly enriched the ridiculous hunchback and had planted the seed of a hermetic mission in his insides.

During those days my grandmother received some lines from my father, who informed her that the Venetians had entrusted to him the rule of Monopoli under the command of his friend Lautrec. The Frenchman was to march against Charles V's possessions in northern Italy, while another army, backed by the Genoese fleet, would attack the Kingdom of Naples. In August Lautrec reconquered the Milanese for Francis I, but he died of the plague, and what was left of his forces, nearly wiped out by Antonio de Leiva, surrendered in Aversa after Andrea Doria went over to the emperor. Gian Corrado Orsini did not return to Bomarzo as we had supposed he would. Perhaps his grief over the loss of his illustrious comrade, for whom the Duke of Sessa, the grandson of Gonzalo de Córdoba, had a sumptuous tomb built, caused him to keep on marching with his decimated troops through the devastated peninsula. On the other hand, the one who did return was Girolamo, and with that my whole life found itself facing one of its great turning points and it took a new direction.

Girolamo did not come alone. As on other occasions, he was accompanied by relatives and friends his own age, made haughty by the early maturity which their deeds had conferred on them. They were the same as always, bronzed, garrulous, boisterous, ignorant, quarrelsome, endowed with a spontaneous elegance and an innate sense of the beautiful which was reflected in the certain art with which they chose their cameos and jewels and with which they passed opinions on architecture, music, and theater. They had been defeated, but they had fought well. And they did not stop talking and trampling upon us with their swaggering. They installed themselves in the main rooms of Bomarzo, which became transformed in that way into a kind of military encampment. Arms were piled up on the tables and the chests and were lined up along the walls. Among the pitchers of wine gauntlets and unsheathed swords appeared. In the courtyards the servants polished pieces of steel armor. Arguments arose over trifles, and the boys, like gamecocks, would leap up and show their spurs. They would brandish daggers and beat on their shields, cut each other, and make up. Cardinal Orsini, locked in his rooms, could not prevail at all against the young gentlemen of his blood who considered themselves the masters of the world. On the contrary, sometimes his red ghost would appear behind a door and he would smile nostalgically as he watched them fight with gymnasts' leaps, or dance together, or gather around Maerbale as he invented crazy mimicry. My grandmother and her ladies avoided them. The warriors were growing rusty from inaction, bored with hunting, quarreling, chasing the village women. Then, as before, they would dedicate themselves to persecuting me. I suffered more than I had on past occasions, for I was no longer a child and I understood that the importance of my experiences over the past years had given me a personality that was worthy of respect. They, who were astute, and Girolamo more than any of them, had smelled out that budding sprout of vanity, and they applied themselves with greater efforts to tease me. They would suffer attacks of childish cruelty as they organized their humiliations. Things were reaching the point where I feared for my life, for no sadistic game seemed to satisfy their boredom. They would lie in wait for me behind the columns, their daggers unsheathed; they would mimic my walk; they would make me follow them in their dances; they destroyed and stole my books; they would force open the door to my room at night, breaking down the barricade of furniture that I had piled up in my embarrassment to protect myself; and they would come in there too, naked, obscene, to plague me with their pantomimes. Messer Pandolfo told my grandmother about the situation, because, ashamed, I did not dare tell her about my martyrdom, and she sighed and spoke to Girolamo, so that the tormenting of me ceased, but it would start up again a few days later as tedium aroused my torturers again. I thought of fleeing, of seeking refuge with Ippolito de' Medici, who had joined the pope in Rome, where—attaining what Maerbale would never get—he would soon be obliged, against his will, by his uncle to accept a cardinal's hat. Shame held me back again from exposing my degradation and weakness, from showing the whole world how mistreated in his own land of Bomarzo was the duke's second son. Diana Orsini intervened again and for the first time Girolamo dared stand up to the authority of the old lady, whose reproaches he had come to mock, telling her that a man built like me, a whiner by nature, could only serve to amuse genuine princes. My grandmother bit her lips and went to the cardinal, but Franciotto Orsini, having grown bland, washed his hands, alleging that she must be exaggerating, and it was quite probable that deep in his heart—in spite of his remorseful look—he was on the side of Girolamo and his accomplices, in whom, near his end now, he recognized the turbulence of his condottiere youth, for which all that counted was the boldness of the bullies and into the harsh depths of which the Florentine refinement that he boasted about so much had not penetrated. I had to bear the worst of troubles, and it came to the point where my grandmother—and I was already sixteen years old—had me sleep in her room, where I would lie awake at night and listen to the uproar of my cousins downstairs as they improvised songs about the effeminate hunchback, or listen later to the only thing that brought me a certain relief, Diana Orsini's measured breathing, a clock that ticked off my hours of loneliness. Sometimes there the curtain that separated us from the room where her ladies slept, among whom there were some quite young, would open halfway and my distress would be complicated with other problems, with the spectacle which was another sign of contempt as they did not even consider me a man as their carelessness offered my watchful eroticism, thick with the visions it had gathered in the city of the Medicis and in my chance coming and going through the castle, a sight for which there was no other recourse for relief than my own sad, unsatisfying love. At dawn, when the carousing of the drinkers ended, I would fall asleep, exhausted, and nightmares would prolong my torture. There was not even left to me the expedient of yearning for my father's return or of writing to him, for I was much too well aware of his feelings toward me.

My anguish ended suddenly one morning when, taking advantage of the fact that my enemies had gone to Bracciano to hunt, and since the heat was oppressive, I went for a swim in the swollen Tiber. My grandmother accompanied me, also desirous of some peace and quiet. Both of us were unaware that Girolamo had stayed behind at the castle.

Although I never would have ventured to get undressed in front of anyone, I would do so in front of my grandmother, a custom that went back to my childhood, and because she was until that moment the only person who filled me with confidence with her love and accepted naturally what was a cause for revulsion or mockery in others. She stayed in her sedan chair, reading there protected from the sun, and she told her servants to withdraw out of sight. Set in her little niche like a religious image with diamonds sparkling on her clothing, she kept watch over me from there and sometimes she would shout something affectionate to me, taking off her glasses and raising her eyes from the book. Splashing, happy, I went into the water. I swam badly, barely able to, as might be imagined, and I did not go far from the bank, but I enjoyed the pleasure of the cold water intensely, feeling it running over my chest, my poor back, my limbs, with a long, cordial caress. At that instant Girolamo came out of the thickets. Perhaps he had planned to go swimming; or perhaps he had guessed that I was going to when he saw us leave the big house, and he had followed us in hiding.

He stood up on his horse on the bank between some rocks and he began to throw stones and insults at me with a diabolical insistence, something incomprehensible in a person who was already twenty-one years old and had distinguished himself in war and at court. I had no way to hide my thin and twisted body from the wrath of his comments and projectiles. I decided against going into the current or coming back to the shore either, where he would easily trap me, so I protected myself as best I could from the stones by sinking into the river up to the dorsal fin I had that was changed into a small aquatic vestige. How I hated him at that moment! How I hated his imbecility, his wrath, his disproportionate advantage! How I also hated his beauty, the grace of his bearing, though even as I hated it I could not help but see its worth in the reflection that was lighting up the bushes! He had opened his shirt and his dark chest stood forth, strong, in the disorder of his clothing. His long legs in yellow stockings hung down toward the ground that he was to inherit, each one painted with a single skillful brushstroke, and his whole body was like a slender bush that had grown out of that land. A sweaty lock of hair hung over his forehead. His white teeth and his blue eyes were shining.

Our grandmother got out of her chair with slow fatigue, calling him, and she went over, leaning on her gold cane. Her beautiful features were transfigured by rage. Girolamo turned toward her and having lost now his reserve of respect and courtesy, he shouted at her that if I was the way I was—he said a nauseating vermin—it was because of her and the degeneration of her people, because the other hunchback of the House of Orsini, Carlotto Fausto, had come from her side. They faced each other at a distance, and I could understand from my brother's expression and from what he was muttering the depth of the rancor that Diana Orsini inspired in him. Now, in a frightful way, Girolamo was throwing in her face the misfortune of her relative, Giulia Farnese's husband, who had dishonored our people with his ridiculous marital disgrace during the time his wife was the mistress of Pope Alexander Borgia. That business, dragged in by the hair, bore no relationship either to Carlotto Fausto or to me, or even to her, not responsible for those misfortunes, but Girolamo could not be stopped now, as if he had broken the dam of his poisonous resentment, and he kept on shrieking. My grandmother, startled, mute, took another step, brandishing her gold stick, and then something happened that neither of us could ever explain. Girolamo's black horse looked at me as if he were trying to speak, as if, like the Xanthus of Achilles, he had the gift of speech and was able to warn me against the possibilities of my death that was close at hand. But it was not a question of my death. Death had stalked that place ever since it had been frequented by men. The barbarian hosts of Totila and Narses had battled there; so had Albinus and the Exarch of Ravenna. There, near Mugnano, Saint Hilary and Saint Valentine had been thrown into the Tiber on orders of the proconsul of Ferento; Saint Secundus had met his end there. The horse looked at me and something frightened him, perhaps the ghosts that were floating in the restless waters. He whinnied, reared, and Girolamo swayed in the saddle. Then my brother pitched forward and his head hit a rock. He rolled into the river, half unconscious, and the current dragged him along to another rock which held him back.

I could have saved him. The whole drama is summed up in that sentence which I write centuries later with a trembling hand. Girolamo's salvation could have depended on me. And on my grandmother too, if she had alerted her servants. I could have reached the half-submerged stone that was turning red with blood and beside which his hair was floating loose, fretted, like dark crimson algae. He was imploring us with eyes made large by terror and pain. I lifted mine to my grandmother's, where she stood up on high, dressed in white and shining with a diamond-like glow, like a goddess of those parts who had emerged from the tombs where other warriors embraced, and I saw her reach out a hand to hold me back and put the other one to her lips to impose silence. We scarcely looked at each other, the space of a spark, but that was enough. The horse was stamping and galloping in the distance. A bird, a blackbird, stopped on a branch and began to sing. It was the same song that I had heard years before at the attic window in Bomarzo when Girolamo and Maerbale had dressed me as a woman, and which had evoked at that time in the midst of my despair the beloved landscape that my soul had seen flourish. While the blackbird made his jet black feathers sparkle and continued trilling the clear notes, unconscious of the horror like a bewitched poet, that distant scene came back to me with all of its desperation, brought on by the thrills that were not telling me now about the static peacefulness of the place but about my brutal brother's lack of compassion. I closed my eyes for a second, trembling in the water, and when I reopened them I could see Girolamo struggling to grasp the rock with his curled fingers and then, overcome, he abandoned himself to the current, thrashed his arms in a useless effort, and sank into the course of the water. Only then did I raise my hoarse voice as loud as I could, and my grandmother's echoed it on the bank. We attracted the servants when it was too late already. The blackbird, fearful, hesitated. It turned its yellow eye toward Diana Orsini, its yellow claws, yellow like Girolamo's thin legs, which would soon be floating like two long dead fish in the iridescence of his liquid shroud, and tracing a black stripe through the air, the bird took off in flight. The horse was also fleeing madly toward the heights of Bomarzo.

Everything took on a required pomp and a kind of symphonic majesty. The chamber where Girolamo's body had been placed, covered with armor, was hung with black cloth. My grandmother dressed in white, because for her, as for the ancient queens of France, white was the color of mourning. Maerbale and I changed our clothes for others, black ones which were brought down from the chests in the attic. Gloves, silks, and jewels disappeared. The cardinal had the monks from the neighboring monasteries called and the prayers went on night and day. We sent a messenger to my father with the news that would plunge him into a terrible grief, and I felt sorry for him, old, alone, bereft of what he most loved. But it was not for me to soften, to let pity weaken me. I had to call upon all the energy I had at hand. We learned from the emissary that the condottiere had received the letter, but he did not reply nor did he return to Bomarzo. We waited four days for him, renewing the candles and the prayers. By my order, they put Girolamo's helmet on, as if they were enclosing him within an iron jewel box, and I insisted that they close the visor so that his disfigured face would no longer be seen. With his having been converted in that way into a piece of sculpture, I was able to bear the nearness of his corpse. The people of the castle respected my orders, came to me, the heir now, and in the absence of Gian Corrado Orsini, the head of the family, my grandmother, horrified no doubt at what she had done, closeted herself in her rooms, where no one entered. Late at night, wearing a veil, she would join the monks as they repeated their prayers. Her withdrawn reaction, which the rest attributed to her sorrow over the loss of her eldest grandson, of which she had been witness, matched by the reaction of the cardinal, who wept and wept without saying a word, with senile babbling, confirmed my authority. Maerbale embraced me. Girolamo's companions silently stepped aside for me in the rooms that resounded with the *Dies irae, dies illa*, composed centuries before by Cardinal Latino, whose mother had been an Orsini. *"Libera me, Domine, de morte aeterna in die illa tremenda,"* the monks chanted, and I had no time for remorse. I was waiting for my father. I was waiting for the meeting with my father. For the first time I felt strong, essential. I was heading toward my destiny surrounded by corpses. Beppo, Girolamo... and I was only sixteen years old. I saw myself by chance in a mirror and I was surprised at the hardness of my face. But I could not worry about myself. I was waiting for my father. And my father, although we knew that he was somewhere in the region, did not arrive. On the fourth day I decided that Girolamo should be buried in the church in Bomarzo. His comrades, in black, carried him down along the steep road from the castle on their shoulders. His armor gleamed in the sunlight and on the sides of the litter the funereal cloth dragged along, brushing the earth that the handsome boy would no longer ever rule. The workers on the scaffolds, farmers, subjects, serfs followed him; and his whippets, held by pages, howled as the cortege passed, smelling death. At the doors of the houses there were women with children in their arms; some one of them must have been Girolamo's child. They joined the procession behind Cardinal Franciotto, who was walking slowly, sunken in the chasuble of the officiant, between men who had tied strips of mourning cloth to the embroidered coats of arms. The monks were singing solemnly, their faces deep in the shadows of their cowls. Bishops had come from Rome to honor the cardinal's grandson. They moved along in the procession with their white gothic miters. One by one they kissed me after the ceremony. My grandfather also kissed me, wetting my cheek with his tears. The warriors gathered up their arms and left Bomarzo. The party was over. They no longer had anything to do there, because now the lord, the duke, would be the very hunchback whom they had persecuted so much and from whom they took leave clutching his hands in their gauntlets as if they were his friends. They would have been quite willing to have exchanged me for the dead one and flung me into his grave. They turned to look at me, leaning on the rumps of their horses as they went off with their pages, their lances, their pennants that repeated the shield of the rose and the serpent. The sun fell down on the blind mass of Bomarzo, transforming it into a glowing golden coal. Perhaps they were cursing me. If they suspected, they swallowed their useless suspicions. And during those four days my grandmother and I did not look at each other once.


Girolamo's death did not upset me as much as Beppo's, in spite of the fact that if I was the one responsible in both cases, this time I had seen the victim die, I had seen his twisted, imploring face during the last moments in which he clung to life, and that must have intensified the atrocious and clear images in the nightmare of my remorse. Pier Francesco Orsini was maturing in crime. My experience was hardening me. Furthermore, this time the anguish of guilt was compensated for by great advantages. The disappearance of the page had only removed a brazen and importunate person from my path; that of my brother had done away with a real enemy, aggressive, dangerous, who perhaps would have ended up destroying me, which affirmed for me the idea that I had acted in self-defense, and, if that were not enough, his elimination would make me duke and would give my weakness, with the title and all that it implied—I was aware of that immediately after Girolamo's death—a support with a solid base, sunk into the ancestral rock of Bomarzo. And that was not all. In that second contact with homicide I had not been alone; I had an accomplice, for Abul, who had been only a material agent on the past occasion, should not have been considered such. My grandmother had been my accomplice... or, who knows, perhaps I had merely been an aide to my grandmother and it was to her powerful initiative that Girolamo's murder was due, or leaving him to die, which was the same thing. The blame was shared and that made it easier to bear. My grandmother bore the greater part. And since she was a model of perfection for me and nothing that she did could be wrong, Girolamo's death had the appearance of a just act. As the days passed I was unconsciously ridding myself of my share of responsibility and convincing myself more and more that the only one compromised was my grandmother. In the eyes of my cowardice, she assumed the inexorable role of an agent of Destiny. My life and my death had been in the balance for a moment on the plates of a scale beside the Tiber, and Diana Orsini had helped save me with a quick gesture that had the force of a command. Blinded by selfishness and hate, blinded also by the jubilation of feeling myself free, I did not consider that it was a matter of Girolamo's life or death. I had subtly replaced him on the balance, as if my health or my destruction depended on that gesture and not those of my brother. And then, instead of being horrified at myself and my grandmother, I felt that I should thank Diana Orsini for her rescuing intervention.

In order to understand my reactions, one must put himself in the period and remember that I belonged to a line in which, as in every illustrious clan of the time, crime had a certain familiarity from its repetition throughout time. Gian Antonio Orsini had done away with a spy of his stepfather, the King of Naples, and had cut his body into twenty pieces, sending a piece as an example to each of the cities under his jurisdiction; Matteo Orsini had poisoned Ugolino Monaldeschi; his son Niccolò had brought a Ranieri, his father's murderer, to Rome, paraded him naked in a cart on Holy Monday, and ordered that he be torn to bits with hot irons and his remains thrown into the Tiber; Rinaldo Orsini had helped murder Thomas à Becket in Canterbury cathedral and afterward made a pilgrimage to Jerusalem; Penelope

Orsini, her cousin's concubine, had the throat of her lover's legitimate son cut so that the bastard would be his heir; both of them—Penelope and the spurious successor—were exterminated in turn by Niccolò Orsini, the great warrior, the Homeric one, the one whose expert in planets had cast my horoscope, and by acting in that fashion the condottiere had earned the enthusiastic admiration of my father, my cousin Orso had stabbed his wife on the Pitigliano bridge and was then beheaded by her vassals; Francesco Orsini, the Abbot of Farfa, was famous for his murders; when Paul III excommunicated him and prepared to arrest and execute him, he holed up in a castle with his bastard sons and no one could get him out of his bastion. Still missing from the list is the famous crime of Paolo Giordano Orsini, the Duke of Bracciano, a hero of Lepanto, the son-in-law of Cosimo de' Medici, the Grand Duke of Tuscany, who hanged his consort as he pretended he was embracing her because of her infidelity with the page Troilo Orsini. That last death could not have impressed the fiery grand duke very much as he reflected on his existence, if one keeps in mind the brothers and sisters of his daughter Isabella de' Medici, the uxoricide's wife: Maria was poisoned; Lucrezia was sacrificed by her mate, Alfonso d'Este; and Pietro erased his wife from this sad world. It was also said—but it has not been proven and I think the previous list is sufficient—that of the other two brothers, the cardinal had been killed by his own father, Cosimo I, who in that way avenged his son Garzia de' Medici, assassinated by Cardinal Giovanni. The drownings, neck-breakings, strangulations, fatal intoxications, stabbings, and other bits of butchery alternated in the genealogical recollections that my grandmother had given me since childhood with splendid military feats, with triumphs of artistic patronage, and with the glories of saintliness. I grew up in an atmosphere in which crime was something as natural as a warlike deed or a profitable marriage. That contributed, as is logical, to molding my psychology, to toughening my hide. And I cannot even accuse my grandmother of having perverted me, because as I have already written, and I repeat it so that it will be understood well, such episodes, constantly repeated in the bosom of other princely houses of Italy, were something foreboding, unavoidable, and even obvious. The crimes of my family are known and described in books, the same as their heroic acts, because of their outstanding position. It is part of the price one pays for fame and one which makes the laurel fade. I am sure that if the evolution of common lineages could be traced over four or five centuries, similar happenings would be found. If we Orsinis did more killing, it was because we were more powerful and consequently we had more enemies and suffered more envy and revenge, but crime and saintliness are the two supreme paths in man's fate, and both, known or not, are present in all kinds of human links. So that if when Beppo was killed on my orders by an arrow in the lush valley of Mugello I suffered from a lack of experience, when Girolamo disappeared into the current of the Tiber, I barely felt a fleeting remorse, for as the years passed and I became tempered and calloused with so many ancient and contemporary examples from my old and mistreated line, I was losing the notion of responsibility and putting less and less value on the life of my fellow men. Neither in the case of Beppo nor that of Girolamo were my hands stained with blood. They were never stained. Numerous ancestors of mine had reddened theirs until it could be said that they walked through the world unable to take off their terrible and wet scarlet gloves. Not I. My cowardice would not have permitted it.

The months in Florence following Beppo's demise, during which I thought that I had changed and that I might even put on sackcloth, had not had any effect on my real core. At the first opportunity I was betrayed by my ambitious weakness and my lack of the strength to pardon offenses. Ignacio de Zúñiga, who doubtless perceived certain grave implications in the circumstances that surrounded the death of Girolamo, asked permission to return to Spain. The heavy air of the castle was suffocating him. I gave it to him sadly, because I loved him and because his austere energy fascinated my laziness, but what was certain was that he upset me as an embodiment of my discarded conscience, which I refused to listen to. He left, and later on, when Loyola founded the Society of Jesus, I learned that he had joined the new militia of Christ. Many years passed, until the glorious battle of Lepanto, to be precise, October 7, 1571, until we saw each other again.

My father, in the meantime, had not returned, and that, which should have pacified me, plunged me into a fearful worry, for I could not help thinking that rather than resign himself to the fact that the hunchback would be the replacement for his beloved first-born and heir to the dukedom, he must have been plotting something against me, as the long list of violent removals that I have just noted made me foresee. Most likely, with the loss of Girolamo, he would want Maerbale to succeed him. So that during that period I ate only what my grandmother had cooked by women of her trust. The powder of a ground-up diamond, disguised in the food, could have dispatched me to the other world; or that white powder with such a pleasant taste that works slowly and gradually without any trace of it remaining, and with which the Borgia pope in Sant' Angelo had poisoned Cardinal Giambattista Orsini, who was blind.

My uneasiness over my existence left no place, then, for remorse. On the other hand, my grandmother, who should have been invulnerable from all that she had seen and borne in the course of her long life, grew feeble and her resistance weakened. She was old now, very old. The shade of my brother, her eldest grandson, haunted her nights. Sometimes she would clutch me to her breast, convulsively, looking around.

"It was for you," she told me once, and I noticed that in a few weeks she had grown incredibly worse and showed signs of decrepitude that I never thought she would reach, "for you, Vicino. I have condemned myself for you."

Although she lacked faith, the old woman had a superstitious devotion for the chapel of Saint Sylvester built on Monte Soratte, quite ancient, and an uncle of the Emperor Charlemagne had retired to the contemporary monastery there. My grandmother had taken me as a child to that peak, just as her mother had taken her. That trip had been something like a wordless initiation for us. It occurred to me, in order to distract her from her terrors, to suggest a pilgrimage to the little chapel, where we could spend a few days at the monastery. We went there in two sedan chairs tied onto horses, for climbing on horseback tired me. Messer Pandolfo and several servants went along. Sylvester was the name of an eleventh-century pope who, according to legend, had sold his soul to the Devil in order to obtain Saint Peter's throne; and the hill where the chapel of Saint Sylvester, patron saint of the wizard pope, rose had previously been dedicated to Apollo, the titular deity of the divinatory art. Those two mysterious influences, coincidental in a countryside of deep ravines that imperial poets had sung of, moved about in my spirit like disturbing premonitions and they inflamed my inborn passion for the secret and the fantastic. My grandmother hoped to find on the mountain the peace that her tormented sleepless nights required. I was looking upon it, instinctively, still unaware, sensing it perhaps with restless confusion, as something more singular, what the ancients trembling at Eleusis had sought: the invisible path that would guide my steps to the dark and dangerous zone toward which I leaned, thirsting, what was most hidden and most mine within my complex soul as it began to discern the existence of the tempting path that zigzags toward the magical clouds which God has forbidden man to penetrate. And of the two of us, I at least found on Apollo's mountain a hint of what I was seeking and which was to have so much influence on my strange life.

At dawn on the second day I left the mountain on horseback, bored with the monastic seclusion and obsessed with my grandmother, who continued to think about Girolamo's death and seek extenuations for the inertia with which she had allowed it. If my grandmother—as was evident—had done it to save her favorite grandson, reduced by the inferiority of his condition, and to help him face an existence that would have been impossible otherwise, and also perhaps—which was even more reproachable, given her advanced age, and could be held against Diana Orsini—to assure the noble dignity of her last years which was being threatened by Girolamo's pride, it was over and done with and it was useless to attempt any justification, much less to correct it. Now it was necessary to go forward and face up to the new life that had arisen from the crime. Our positions were different, of course, for life was spread out before me, while hers was already over. In any case, her understandable attitude, her complaints, her perplexity, her fear which had changed her physically and spiritually in a short time, did not jibe with the cruel jubilation that came over me when, after the first moments of disorder and fright about what had been done had passed, I surveyed the vast perspectives that were opening before my eyes as a consequence of our act and, still revering my grandmother and thanking her silently for what I owed to her decision, which could be considered monstrous by even the most indulgent morality, her presence bothered me and I felt the need to enjoy myself alone, without anyone befogging the brilliance of my bright situation and its unusual promises. I left, therefore; I rode off on horseback for a few hours to drink in the wind.

The full moon was still floating in the sky. I took the road to Rome, the Via Flaminia, and when I passed Duke Valentino's rock, I spied a shadow moving among the cypresses on the side of the road. It was a grazing mule. Farther on, sitting on a stone, there was a man. He stood up before I got to him and standing in the middle of the road, he waved his arms, indicating for me to stop. I was afraid that he was a highwayman, but when I could make out his appearance I felt better and reined in the animal.

"Stop," he shouted to me, "even though I don't know whether you're man or devil, and help this poor wretch."

Such astonishing words pricked my curiosity and I thought that he was probably some beggar, but his looks were not those of an alms seeker. He was around thirty years of age and his clothing showed that he was an intellectual, a tutor perhaps. I pulled in my horse and went over to him holding the reins. There was no one else there and all that could be heard was the croaking of the frogs as they dived into their dark pools, but I felt no alarm.

"Tell me your name," he asked, "and spare me a few minutes."

"Pier Francesco Orsini, the son of the Duke of Bomarzo," I declared, and I noticed that he stepped back a little to get a better look at me. His eyes, shining in the moonlight, were looking for the outline of my hump.

"I have heard of you," he went on, "through my friend Piero Valeriano, the tutor of the Medici princes, who thinks well of you. I am Angelo Manzolli, called Palingenio. From your *lucco* I thought you were a Florentine."

I had also heard my teacher Valeriano mention the humanist who worked for the House of Ferrara, and that designation of "Palingenio" had bothered me from the beginning, for I linked it with the mystery of my horoscope, since palingenesis, practiced by bold physicians, assured the possibility of the rebirth of life, of a repeated return to life from the depths of death. I remembered that Angelo Manzolli was preparing a book, a philosophical poem, and I remembered its pleasant title, *Zodiacus vitae*. I told him that and I could see that, flattered by his fame, he had relaxed the tension that had kept his muscles hard, and his eyes brightened. I got off the horse and sat down beside him on the broad stone. I told him, in order to give him time to calm down, for his distress was obvious, that I was coming from the monastery of Saint Sylvester and that I had ridden out to enjoy the beauty of the night.

"Like you, I come from there," he interrupted me, "from the hermitage of a holy man."

There was a pause, filled with batrachian sounds and the whispers of the Roman countryside, and he added, "You must be a close relative of Cardinal Franciotto Orsini."

"My grandfather."

"Then you more than anyone else must hear what has just happened to me."

And he told me a fabulous story that he later put into his *Zodiac* and which had a great effect on my entire existence, because through it I came to know Silvio da Narni.

Palingenio had left Monte Soratte two hours before me. In the sacred solitude of the crags dedicated to Apollo he had spent the afternoon in meditation beside the hermit, analyzing the vanity of human things and affirming himself in his belief in how precarious and insignificant our lives are. At nightfall he decided to return to Rome, and on the highway, at the same spot where we were talking, the strangest adventure that he could have dreamed of happened to him. Three men approached him, calling him by name, and they asked him where he was coming from.

He answered them with good grace and one of them chided him when he mentioned the holy man on the mountain: "Oh, you fool, perchance do you imagine that there is anyone wise on the Earth? The only wise ones are beings from on high, and even though we have taken on the mean shape of men, we belong to that superior order. I am Saracil, and these are Sathiel and Jana. Our empire is near the Moon, where the multitude of intermediate beings who exercise their dominion over the Earth and the Sea reside."

The philosopher, startled, ventured to inquire what they were going to Rome for, and the same devil answered him that one of his brothers, Amon, had been imprisoned by the magic arts of a boy from the village of Narni, a page of Cardinal Orsini, because men, owing to their immortal essence, were capable of reducing spirits to captivity, and Saracil himself had once been shut up in a thick glass bottle by a German until a monk gave him back his freedom.

"Now we propose to rescue our comrade Amon and we are waiting for the news that will be brought to us by the emissary that we have sent to Rome."

A light breeze blew at that moment and another devil, the fourth, showed himself and was greeted warmly by his brothers. They learned through him that the pope was renewing his alliance with the Spaniards and was making ready to tear out the Lutheran heresy by the roots, and that capped their diabolical joy, for then blood would flow in thick rivers and out of its red current the lunar spirits would gain thousands upon thousands of souls to be cast down into Hell. When that was said, the four apparitions vanished and Palingenio remained alone on the silvery road, half in a faint from terror, until after the longest time he heard the sound of my horse's hoofs.

Everything that I had learned from infancy among the heirs of the Etruscans and the bookish courtiers of the Medicis concerning the offspring of Lucifer who ceaselessly surround and persecute us came to my mind. Demons harassed great and small. Luther, the Antichrist, had asserted that they hid inside monkeys and parrots. Scholars had managed to penetrate the secret of their names: Asmodeus, Behemoth, Leviathan, Onocentaurus, Cacodemon... And a few years later the illustrious Johann Wier, physician to the Duke of Cleves, taught that their kingdom was composed of 72 princes and 1,111 legions. People signed pacts with the Devil, attended his sabbath; writers lived with familiar demons, like Cardano's red cock, Bragadini's black dogs, that of the economist Bodin. Therefore a great number of exorcisms were practiced, and possessed women would place on their heads relics of Saint Zanobi and the cloak of Saint John Gualbert. The air was pregnant with demons. For delicate noses, in every scent from a pleasant aroma to the smell of filthy carrion, there was mixed a trace of sulphur. And at that place where Palingenio was speaking to me, on the highway to Rome, beside which amid the mourning sway of the cypresses the ruins of tombs arose, and where, profiled, dominating the countryside, Apollo's peak stood out, one could feel more than anywhere else their menacing and disquieting presence as it came out of the croaking of the frogs, the splashing of the toads, the flapping of the bats, sabbath beasts, the quivering of the funereal trees, the livid lunar lantern that transformed and bewitched things, and the story of Palingenio, who had witnessed atrocious miracles. As a finishing touch, I was now learning that someone closely connected with us, with our daily life, one of my grandfather's pages, had dared invade that forbidden world. And I, instead of rejecting with horror such ghosts and crossing myself and escaping back to the refuge of the monastery of Saint Sylvester, suddenly felt that my existence was being illuminated with a new light and that these miracles were related to my horoscope in some way and that consequently inseparable from the basis of my life.

"You must find that page from Narni, Signor Orsini," the poet told me, "and unmask him to the cardinal."

I promised to do so, although I did not intend doing it, but rather to take advantage of the strange revelation. Back at the monastery I kept silent about what I had learned. I did not tell anybody about it, not even my grandmother, when we returned to Bomarzo.

I could not remember which one of the cardinal's numerous servants the boy from Narni could be, but it was easy to ascertain. I soon found out that his name was Silvio, that he was in my grandfather's palace in Rome near the church of San Giacomo degli Incurabili, and that he was to come to Bomarzo the following week to rejoin Franciotto Orsini's party. My position as heir to the dukedom and the cardinal's bland senility had filled me with an unwonted audacity, so that I did not hesitate to ask him directly to allow me to add Silvio da Narni to my retinue, since with the loss of Beppo, Abul, and Ignacio de Zúñiga I had been left without pages for my personal attention. My grandfather, who could not remember the lad very well, confused by the hundred people who surrounded him, consisting of food tasters, chaplains, servants, huntsmen, swordsmen, and many parasites, turned him over to me at once.

Narni is a village close to Bomarzo. I went there the following morning on the pretext of visiting the Duomo to look at the statues of Saint Giovenale and Saint Anthony Abbot by Vecchietta, and taking advantage of the tricks of espionage, I found out that Silvio, who was only two or three years older than I, was known among the young men who gathered to chat at the fountain for the strangeness of his character, and that certain mysterious and inexplicable powers were attributed to him, for which reason the good people had sighed with relief when Cardinal Orsini had added him to his household and taken him to Rome. Restless, I spent my time waiting for him to return to Bomarzo. As if my life depended on it, several times during the working day I would go out onto the terraces where the men were and look toward the road, waiting for my new servant. He appeared at last, riding a lazy mule, and the cardinal's steward, instructed by me, informed him of his change in destiny, which he accepted without comment.

Silvio da Narni was at that time a lanky young man, so thin that the bones stood out under his tight skin. His ugliness was due to the smallness of his eyes, a mouth that was too large and from which several teeth were missing, and his dry, strawlike hair, which fell down on both sides of his face like a stringy wig; but, perhaps from having learned through Palingenio of his strange background, I discovered a singular attraction in him when he presented himself to me. Sometimes he would remain as if absorbed, lying in one of the doorways or among the flowerpots in the vast garden, and I, who secretly never lost sight of him, thought I could catch a catlike glow in the flashing of his eyes. Very soon we were inseparable, to the jealous surprise of my grandmother, who could not understand my liking for such a mediocre individual. I explained to her that I enjoyed Silvio, for, having been born in the region and descending from the peasants who had lived there for centuries under the rule of the Orsinis, he knew any number of curious tales and he had been to places that belonged to us and which we, the owners, barely knew existed. I was not lying when I said that. Guided by him, Messer Pandolfo and I visited some Etruscan cemeteries that were later forgotten and which the curiosity of archeologists did not unearth until centuries later. Preceded by my page, who was carrying a torch and pointing out to us the dangerous parts of the slippery descent, we went down into damp caves to uncover fearsome paintings that had been buried by rains, underbrush, and landslides, dating from the period when the city of Mars arose there in a region which, along with the Tuscan Maremma, is the one that has best preserved Etruscan traces. My collection was enriched with important pieces that we cleaned and classified together, because everything connected to that world interested him immensely.

Silvio's reserve never left him. When we were alone on different occasions I would turn the conversation toward the theme of demonology, linking it to those diabolical frescoes and to the atmosphere of Bomarzo, impregnated, according to what I told him, with dark suggestions, but the boy pretended not to understand me and I did not dare insist, fearful of arousing his suspicions. In order to gain his confidence, I made the appearance of adapting myself to his taste in everything and to have great appreciation for his judgment, which cost me absolutely nothing, for I really did enjoy his company, now taciturn, now talkative, and he would regale me at the most unlikely moments with fantastic reflections. A singular friendship—which would have been authentic had my possession of his overwhelming secret not stood in the way—grew up between the hunchback and his page, and not a month had passed before I deduced certain aspects of his character that I began to flatter in order to get deeper into his confidence. The most salient was a violent sensuality which, held in check by Silvio's cautious hermeticism, was waiting for an occasion to give free rein to its anxieties. As soon as I discovered that, I set about winning his intimacy along those lines. I thought that I was dominating him, that step by step I was transforming him into my plaything, but what really was happening was that Silvio was building up his domination over me. When I noticed it, after a time, it was already too late to draw back. And in the meantime, with those feints and subtleties that occupied the greater part of my time, I was drawing away from my grandmother and I rid myself of the last aftertaste of upset that had remained with me as a result of Girolamo's death. But it is also necessary to point out that if I had not been impelled in that tangled and voluptuous direction by my own drives, I would not have followed him down the slope where, with stupid innocence, I thought that I was going ahead of him.

We began to go out, like my father, like my older brother, to pester the village girls. Maerbale would go along with us and soon it was known in Bomarzo that the nocturnal chases of the lords had begun again and that the *homagio mulierum* continued in all its vigor. Sure of my position as heir, I lost my timidity. The skills of Silvio da Narni made my adventures easier and in my pride I had almost forgotten about my hump and the motives that had drawn me close to the page, until suddenly our outings began to change their course, growing complex, and Maerbale ceased going out with us. With a quick tug, Silvio grabbed the reins and we took off. The truth was that I was a typical Renaissance man and as such did not have the barriers that in other periods of history worked as basic bonds. Flung into pleasure, I wanted it at its fullest. And I ran, thirsting, insatiable, dazzled, after the boy who had held a demon captive and who, even before facing the opportunity to give way most fully to passionate delirium still maintained his alarming and well-guided lucidity.

My grandmother sensed something in the air, in my attitude, but Diana Orsini was going downhill rapidly, past ninety years of age, in the final phase of her life, and she no longer had any control over me. Until that time she had fought against Time and she had conquered it; now, tired of fighting, she was giving in. There was something that suddenly, with her age, her immense age, was making her like Bomarzo, stony, dark, and motionless. Her blue eyes would light up from time to time like the clear valleys of Bomarzo between the eroded rocks. Perhaps she sensed then that her beloved grandson was strangely happy in his morbid intoxication and that underneath it all the only thing that mattered to her was that I was happy at any price.

In charge of administering my father's estates at that time was an excellent man, widowed, obese, and God-fearing, called Manuzio Martelli. He lived with his sixteen-year-old twin children, Porzia and Giambattista, in a big house that still stands on the lane going from the base of the castle to the church of the Virgin of the Valley and which has our shield over the doorway. The presence of the Orsini arms in that place indicated to me, with its heraldic allegory, that not only the house belonged to us, as everywhere, but that those who lived in it belonged to us too. That was what my father, my grandfather, and the previous Orsinis had thought; that was what I thought. The shield represented the imprint of a stamp put onto stone and—although invisible—put onto the flesh of the inhabitants in the way that ancient slaves were branded. The idea may seem repugnant, inhuman today, and it is, but in those days it was accepted in the most natural way by people who had been brought up like us.

Porzia and Giambattista were quite good-looking, blond, slender, so identical that they would confuse people when they swapped clothing as a joke. It would not have surprised me that in their veins, because of the imprudence of some female forebear, Orsini blood flowed. They did not mingle with the village people, because as the children of our administrator, who was continuing a dynasty of tax collectors and harvest assessors, they enjoyed a position somewhere between the mass of field hands and servants and the lords of the castle. Messer Pandolfo had explained to them the rudiments of Latin, mathematics, and music, which their intelligences had learned easily, and both possessed a fortunate gift for inventing dances and pantomimes. My grandmother would summon them to her room from time to time so that, directed by Maerbale, they could amuse her with their comical imitations. They were usually seen by themselves on the paths of Bomarzo, setting traps for birds, fishing, or looking for pretty stones. An old man, Manuzio Martelli's uncle, took care of them, for their father often had to leave them and he would disappear for a week or more when his business at markets and villages in the surrounding country demanded it. Silvio da Narni admired them for the first time one day when they were dancing to the sound of a viola in my grandmother's room. And since Silvio, bored with the one-stringed pursuit of girls who were more or less docile, began to develop ennui at Bomarzo and to yearn for his complex diversions in Rome, it occurred to him to relieve the tedium by overturning and corrupting them. The two of them were quite young, very innocent, and that enlivened my page's libertine inclinations. He told me about it and I, who did only what he suggested to me in order to tighten our bonds, willingly accepted the plan. I must add that before he suggested it to me, Porzia and Giambattista were already bothering me in a hazy way, ambivalent in such a way that their similarity and their deceptive sex game reminded me of certain of Ariosto's disguised characters.

Laughing, we organized the attack the way a hunter prepares for an important expedition, a safari. It was necessary not to miss a single detail if we wanted to be successful in the undertaking. And we dedicated ourselves to it with the enjoyment proper to perverse occasions. We began by flattering them with distinctions, with little gifts, giving them to understand that for us they were something different from the rest of the people in the village, whom they surpassed—something true, in any case—because of their quality and their instinctive elegance. Our attitude flattered them, particularly Giambattista who, as a man, desired more than his sister to assert his position of a pretender to the manner of the lords. They would go out walking through the area with us on various occasions in the absence of their father and when their great-uncle was sleeping his deep siesta. Silvio taught them how to train a falcon, and I, as if they belonged to my line, would tell them tales about the Orsinis, especially those which showed that princes were not bound by ethical principles, which were bonds fashioned for ignorant peasants. I prettied up the stories, adorning them, adapting them with my imagination to the ends we were seeking, and I went ahead like that with extreme caution toward the winning of their confidence, backed by Silvio, who, with the same false and direct simplicity, told of episodes of that nature that had taken place in the cardinal's palace in Rome or in other illustrious houses. In that way, while we played at seeing who was the bolder, we were mixing up their poor minds. Soon, instead of the four of us going out together, we began to separate into couples, changing partners on each occasion, which activated their unrest, and we managed to establish a disturbing atmosphere that, even if we had not yet gone beyond the dialectical phase, did create between both groups a familiarity of its own kind that the twins, accustomed until then to a peaceful and repetitious life, accepted, aroused by moments when there was an awakening and a delving into their sensuality. I do not know what confidences they might have made to each other during that time, but I have no doubt that Silvio and I were the center of their conversations and that our figures kept them awake until late at night in their respective beds. The fact that the future duke was taking part in that exciting recreation was a principal contribution, I am sure, to befogging their consciences, for their father had raised them since childhood with respect for the Orsinis, which he shared, of course, and which, as in the case of Nencia, took on the characteristics of adoration among the Martellis. The hunchbacked Orsini, the one with the noble face and perfect hands, the one who would be master of everything spread out below the terraces of the castle, had deigned to be their friend, which was so extraordinary that it gave a stamp of honor to those so favored. Manuzio himself thanked me for it, superficially aware of that incredible friendship, without suspecting what it hid, and I replied that both Giambattista and Porzia seemed exceptional creatures to me and that since there was no one my own age in the area to talk to—for my cousins and Girolamo's comrades had not returned to Bomarzo—his children made up for those absences. He repeated his thanks to me, flushed with happiness, his hands folded over his magnificent belly, calculating perhaps that on those bonds formed in adolescence the future of his offspring might depend. And if, for my part, my past and my probable future influence worked to smooth the path of seduction, in Silvio's case what facilitated it, in spite of his toothless ugliness, was the mystery that emanated from one who had made a pact with the Devil and which endowed his slightest gesture with an ambiguous secret fascination.

Finally, when we thought that the time was ripe, we decided to crown our campaign. Porzia and Giambattista had been lost in a maze. They could no longer distinguish good from evil, nor the natural from what is not. We had raised a wall of sophistry against their first reactions, painted with different hues, closing them in with it, showing them in that confused reclusion how ridiculous conventions were and letting them glimpse the fact that if they persisted in them, they would never be different from the peasants who turned the earth from sunup to sundown and lived like animals. We used their instincts as delicate instruments, polishing and tuning them, plucking one and another string here and there so that they would produce the precise rare sounds. We harassed them, we plunged them into perplexity, into a revealing delight; we proved to them that beyond the reduced and monotonous territory in which the vulgarity of humans moved, there existed an immense world inhabited by dangerous marvels which only the initiate can reach. The part that fell to Silvio da Narni in such a subtle and demoralizing task was most important. All I did was to follow him, like a disciple of the tempter, carrying along, of course, the suggestions that had grown out of my shadowy imagination, instigated by the game, for that was how in my tortured irresponsibility I looked upon what we were plotting, a game, the pastime of a bored prince. I did not stop to reflect that what I was really doing, besides providing for the requirements of my epicurean demands, was measuring my forces, showing myself that the deformed one, the hunchback, was capable, if it was proposed, of dominating and conquering pure spirits, which, because of their condition, might have figured as the most precious conquests on the list of a professional trained in the art of winning loves. And I must finally confess that possibly I was urged to corrupt them so that, despoiled of their candor, besmirched, the distance that separated them from me would be less, for I was jealous of them, of their beauty, of their lightness, and I wanted their souls to become as hunchbacked as my condemned body so that I would be less isolated in my misshapen singularity. What was I like at the age of seventeen? I knew too well what I was like physically, but within, in my recondite, essentially arcane inside, where the most intimate forges do their work, I still had not been able to define myself. Girolamo's death had accentuated the congenital imbalance of the unstable Vicino Orsini who, because of it, had perceived the rewards of impunity and the ones that came from his new position as the dauphin of Bomarzo, to whom everything was due and from whom everything was tolerated. I went ahead blindly, destroying, hiding from myself among the ruins, as if purity were a mirror which had to be broken so that I would not see my accursed obsessions reflected in its serenity.

I enhanced the profanation, tutored by Silvio. With a pretext, using my authority, I sent Manuzio to Rieti for the day, and no sooner had he left at siesta time than I invited the twins to visit the Etruscan tombs near Piamiano with us. The sun was biting and we went there, taking advantage of the fact that the people in the palace and in the village were sleeping and that we would not run into any interlopers. We embraced furtively on the way, laughing, taking off our shoes to dip our feet into the water, eating fruit from the basket we were carrying. We lit a torch to illuminate the cold darkness of the tomb. We could feel the twins huddled against us, trembling with fear, with insecurity, with expectation. All around the fragmentary paintings of the naked heroes looked at us with their worm-eaten eyes that the leprous dampness was making more unreal. Just as in Benozzo Gozzoli's chapel, plastic figures surrounded me underground with their quiet morbidity, and now the two scenes are superimposed and complement each other in my memory because of those distinct and analogous decorations, as if to tell me that in the Renaissance even abominable happenings, if not justified in themselves, at least are changed and take on an esthetic beauty like a part of the crest of a great triumphal wave which covers all acts and melds the blameful with the glorious in its lustful promiscuity. But in the Florentine palace the procession of the Magi, witnesses to my inexperienced anguish with Nencia, had framed the episode with refined and courtly gold, while in the region of the Dukes of Orsini, the primitive frescoes of Etruria intensified with their ritual and brutal crudeness the frenzy of the violation. What emphasizes the rapidity of my progress in those struggles is the fact that while among the worldly gods of Florence I had been the one possessed, among the impetuous gods of Bomarzo I was the possessor.

Spiders and silent little beasts fled along the walls. A toad puffed up in a corner. Since these are the sincere memoirs of a gentleman made captive by the Devil and not a pornographic novel—although I do not know how the unpredictable censorship of today will classify it—I shall not go into great detail. I will only say that from the frightened expression of the twins, I realized when we fell to the damp earth that I had been mistaken in thinking that they were now finally seasoned for the adventure. Their equal pupils grew large in a like way in the shadowy redoubt where Death reigned. And I have to say that their thin hips, the color of sand, of thin chains, were so much alike that it was difficult to distinguish them in the dim light. When the bonds were loosened they both fled like two small animals, and Silvio and I remained there lying on the ground. The torch went out and the spiders, one by one, returned to the peace of the corners to weave their veils of mist once more over the immutable faces of the Etruscans.

We had not counted on the unforeseen, which usually works in such cases in the same way that it did that time. We did not count on the fact that Messer Manuzio Martelli, drowsy with the vapors of the siesta he had renounced with a thousand sighs, would forget certain papers necessary for his business in Rieti, and that he would have to turn his horse even before he had reached Narni. While he was searching for the documents in his drawers, Porzia and Giambattista arrived furtively at the house with the shield and they ran into him. Their looks, their disarray, their tears, their blushes were more eloquent than their contradictory babbling. In a few minutes Messer Manuzio had made them confess. The good man was overcome with horror. It had never occurred to him that a thing like that could happen through the fault of his masters. In his limited simplicity he had not even imagined that such things ever happened. If on certain occasions he had heard deeds like that mentioned, he had doubtless thought that they were remote things, on the verge of fantasy, the sad privilege of dissolute courts, but that they were impossible in Bomarzo, a healthy and simple place inhabited by people who lived only to work and to honor God. His bureaucratic villager's simplicity could not grasp the strange sensual atmosphere that imprisoned Bomarzo and which was like one of the webs in the nearby tombs, viscous and ancient, spun over a long period of time with Etruscan, Roman, and barbarian threads and the more recent woof of the golden strands of the Orsinis, a weaving of dark filaments that would suddenly sparkle, swaying between the castle and the tombs, between the Tiber and the crags, and which muffled the place in its eternal scheme.

The first thing that he probably decided was to go to the palace and seek justice from Diana Orsini and the cardinal, but he soon abandoned the idea, because my grandparents were much too old to have the problem laid before them and to dictate the punishment. He knew of my grandmother's weakness in everything concerning me, and Franciotto was no longer good for anything. Besides, the lord for him was still Gian Corrado, and the condottiere was at that time fighting across from the fortifications of Florence among the forces sent by Clement VII to recover the city for his family. He must have hesitated, unable to make up his mind, overcome with grief and perplexity, until he decided to leave with his children for Florence. He only opened his heart to Maerbale, and the latter took sides and resolved to accompany them, calculating perhaps that he could draw some advantage out of it all, for anything that contributed to blackening my figure in my father's eyes—quite ready to judge against the offspring that he hated— would redound to the benefit of the youngest of the Orsinis and would contribute, there was no way of telling how, to strengthen the hidden pretensions to the dukedom that he was certainly nourishing ever since he had given up hopes for a cardinal's cape.

At night, therefore, like highwaymen, they left Bomarzo. The twins were probably silently weeping. They tied rags to the horses' hoofs so that they would not be heard, and only in the morning, when Silvio went to Porzia's window to find out her impressions of the adventure and to plan a way of prolonging it that afternoon on a grander scale, did we learn about the Martellis' departure and that Maerbale had gone with them. We immediately deduced what had happened and that they were galloping off to the condottiere. That, as can be imagined, upset me terribly. Gian Corrado now had another reason to return to his castle, armed with his just lighting, and strike down his despised successor. The idea of flight passed through our heads for an instant, but we rejected it in the certainty that the paternal wrath would reach us wherever we hid. We also weighed the pros and cons of telling my grandmother about the situation, presenting it to her in the most favorable light for us to gain her support, and in the end we inclined toward remaining silent, because the matter was too rough for us to expose to a woman of ninety—or to any woman. After all, it is not easy for one to tell his grandmother that he has been involved in the things we had done to the twins, no matter how the details are doctored and no matter how indulgent and *modern* the person who is told might be. We would wait. We would face the storm. We would deny the accusations. We would state that they were things invented by Maerbale with the complicity of two children in order to displace his brother. And as for those children, it was difficult to predict how they would react. At the first moment, startled, they had betrayed us, but now, calmer, it could have been that our influence was at work and we were recovering the domination that had made them ours. We had to wait. What could happen, what was the worst that could happen? Gian Corrado would not dare kill me. He was no saint. His biography was strewn with worse episodes than the one that he would throw in my face. Or perhaps he would kill me. Perhaps he would lock me up with the skeleton and leave me there to die of hunger and anguish. To flee... to beg for the help of Ippolito de' Medici? My father's arm would reach out, holding steel, into the cardinal's palace. The Medicis could not refuse their friend anything. To hide in Narni? That would be stupid. My hump would always give me away.

We waited until night. It was already late when we made ready to sleep—or not to sleep, to despair; we were sleeping together in the same bed in accordance with the promiscuous custom of the times—and I decided to risk the great step. There was nothing for me to lose. No human means would be able to help me. There remained the other means, those which do not depend on humans. In the darkness, my face half covered with the sheets, in an unsure voice, I revealed to Silvio what Palingenio had told me on the road to Rome, his meeting with the devils, and I asked him if he knew how to do it, to invoke their aid. Then the cry of a strange bird was heard in the depths of the garden. We went to the window, but nothing could be seen in the thick darkness. My grandmother's window suddenly lighted up and the old lady appeared in its illuminated frame wearing a white nightgown. She was waving her arms like a puppet.

"A peacock!" she exclaimed. "There's a peacock in the garden, I heard its cry! Look for it! Bad luck for those at Bomarzo!"

They lighted some large torches which began to leap up madly. In the mourning velvet of the countryside which barely showed the shape of the terrain under its tetric cover the fireflies were shining like scattered diamonds, and it was as if the night had drawn its cloak across the ground.

"We can't see anything," the servants said. "There's nothing here."

"It must have been an illusion," a woman's voice said.

"There's no peacock," Messer Pandolfo asserted. "It's the night that's moaning. The night moans like Dido: *Quid moror*, why go on living?"

But we had heard, the same as Diana Orsini. We drew back slowly into the center of the room and Silvio lit the candles in the candelabrum. We covered ourselves, because we were naked.

"Bad luck for those at Bomarzo," I murmured, repeating my grandmother's fateful words.

"I'll do what I can," Silvio whispered. "Today is Wednesday, the day of Mercury, the day that Eve engendered Cain, an adverse day. I have what I need: a branch of wild hazel that I cut with a new knife two days ago at the time the sun was appearing on the horizon. We have to get two candles that were blessed."

Then I understood the reason why he would suddenly get out of bed at dawn. Like a herbalist wizard, he was going to look for conjure plants. I put on my Florentine coat and went down to the church. On the way I took the heavy key to the church from the nail on which it hung next to the door of my father's room. Then I went out of the castle, crossing the small square, and went into the church, lighting my way with a lantern. On both sides of the main altar flickering lights glowed in the half-darkness. On one side, to the left, there was a painting of the Virgin distributing rosaries to the lords of our line, the one I hated so much because my father had had Girolamo and Maerbale painted by his feet and had left me out. On the other side the oil painting of Saint Sebastian could be seen; his livid nakedness, pierced with arrows, stood out against a blue background. There were always candles on that altar. I passed by the relics of Saint Anselm without looking at them where they were venerated in a stone tomb, and I took two candles. The shadow of my hump fell upon the paving stones of the nave like a black bundle.

Silvio explained to me that he would use the formulas of the *Sanctum regum*, but that he did not guarantee that they would work.

"It would be better," he added, "to go down to the tombs, but we're in a hurry. We'll do it on the terrace."

The boy suddenly seemed very old to me. The deep lines that marked his face alongside his mouth were even more sunken. He took a bottle from a cupboard and studied it in the light. It contained an oily liquid.

"Don't forget the candles, Signor Orsini."

I was the servant now. We went out onto the terrace again. The thickness of the shadows had begun to lighten, softly outlining the terrain. Owls were hooting on the parapets. Silvio undressed completely, and his bony, squalid body, graceless, shone like an elongated statue. He sketched a triangle on the ground with the oil and on both sides he placed the two pieces of holy wax. Two brief cones of fire trembled over the wicks. Under the figure he wrote the sacred monogram IHS, flanked by several crosses. Then he stepped into the triangle, holding the branch of wild hazel. The rhythm of his voice undulated with a monotonous cadence. During the pauses in the invocation one could hear the calls of the owls, the flapping of the bats, and from time to time the clean trill of a bird as it rose up from the valleys to greet the night's death agony. The black and beautiful night reminded me of Abul. It was as if Abul were with us.

"Emperor Lucifer, lord of the rebellious spirits, I beg you to be favorable as I call upon your minister, the great Luciphagus Rocophallis. Oh, Astaroth, great count, be favorable to me too, and have the great Luciphagus appear in human form and grant me what I wish through the covenant that I have made with him! Oh, great Luciphagus, I beg you to leave your dwelling place, wherever it may be, and come to speak to me! If you refuse to come, I will oblige you with the power of the living God, the Son and the Holy Spirit. Come quickly, or I will torment you eternally with the power of my grave words and with the Key of Solomon, which the king used to oblige the rebellious spirits to accept his pact. I demand it. Appear at once or I will harass you with the all-powerful formula of the Key: Aglon Tetragram Vaycheon Stimulamathom Erohares Oera Erasyn Moys Meffias Soter Emmanuel Sabaoth Adonai, I conjure you, amen."

His voice grew loud in the vagueness of the dawn and I was afraid that he would alert the sleeping palace. The sounds stopped. The night was listening like an immense monster. The Etruscan ghosts must have risen among the rocks. On the terrace now the skeleton of the scaffolding could be distinguished.

"He's here," he told me, shuddering. "You can't see him, but he's here."

I stood up and scrutinized the gloomy masses that surrounded us as they moved in the flickering of the candles. Sweat was running down my face. Mechanically I grasped Benvenuto Cellini's ring, my talisman.

"Obey me," Silvio da Narni commanded, "obey me, demon, by virtue of the pact. Help me. The duke must never know what took place in the tomb at Piamiano."

A hoarse voice that made my hair stand on end and which could have been Silvio's disguised answered, "I will obey you."

The page left the refuge of the enchanted triangle. He burned the branch of wild hazel with the candles from the chapel and the hesitant smoke rose up in a thin column.

"Don't be afraid. It's all over. The duke will never know nor will he attempt anything against you."

A thunderous noise shook my room behind us. We looked in, trembling; Silvio clutched his clothes against his nakedness. The Etruscan armor that is in the Gregorian Museum had fallen over and its pieces scattered on the floor multiplied the black and green reflections as if covered with mossy blood. One of my grandmother's maidservants knocked on the door to see what was going on. My grandmother had not shut her eyes all night. Since she thought she had heard the fateful cry of the peacock in the garden, all she had done was to repeat that disaster would befall Bomarzo. The page and I picked up the pieces of metal, and their confusion brought to mind the chieftains who had been quartered in the battles described by Ariosto. We went to bed clinging to each other; I was praying without moving my lips. Morning came timidly into the room.

Three days later the sentries posted on the heights announced that a group was approaching the castle from the direction of Orte. The cloud of dust that wrapped the horses was glowing like a distant bonfire with the flashing of the arms.

"It's my father returning to Bomarzo," I whispered to Silvio. "We're lost."

He looked at me and shook his head. The procession moved slowly along. My grandmother, standing by my side on the same terrace where the page had made his invocation, put her hand on my shoulder.

"My son Gian Corrado is returning. Now I can die in peace, Vicino."

I avoided her eyes and I could image where the traces of the triangle and the monogram painted in oil had been on the stones of the terrace.

The duke was returning to Bomarzo with his men. Maerbale was coming with them, carrying his withered banner. Gian Corrado was returning, on his back, destroyed, dead, so disfigured that it was impossible to recognize his face. He was being carried by two mules that were covered with the trappings of mourning. Pier Luigi Farnese, the son of the future Pope Paul III and related to us through his marriage to Girolama Orsini, the daughter of the Count of Pitigliano, embraced me when he turned the remains over to me and told me that my father had ended his life as a hero in the siege of Florence. He told me that until the very last moment the troops had been amazed at the old man's vigor as he climbed through the trenches with the agility of an adolescent and roared with anger. He was carrying a mace, like Hercules, and his commands re-echoed amid the standards with the bears and the ancestral rose. That Pier Luigi, closely linked later to the destiny of my conduct, was the first to call me Duke of Bomarzo, and when he did so a convulsion shook my accursed flesh. The scene clouded over and I fell onto the body of my father, which had been disjointed like the armor that my grandmother had given me, cut into pieces, I do not know—I never did—whether by demons or by men, as arrows and cannonballs flew around him lighting up the war at Florence. I never found out either whether Manuzio Martelli had managed to betray us.

My father had covered himself with glory, but his cause had not been the just one. That does not matter, for glory has nothing to do with the justness of causes; it depends, really, on the points of view and, by and large, on a determined dynamism. Gian Corrado, at the time of his death, had boasted of his seventy-two years. Perhaps he was younger and had added years out of vanity. The arrival of his mutilated body plunged me into a stupor. During that entire day—we buried him on the following—I did not leave his side. I had already acquired the habit of unexpected wakes that were linked to future responsibilities of mine, but none impressed me as much as that one. Several years had passed since I had seen my father, and that distance, added to the psychological upsets that were the product of hate, disillusionment, and remorse, had worked on me in the strangest way. When I leaned over his destroyed face in the chapel, I noted with desperation that it had been erased from my memory. I could remember this or that isolated trait, the color of his eyes, his skin, certain tics, certain expressions, but I could not put them together to reconstruct the lost face. Sometimes it would appear to me in a flash, and when I thought that I had captured it again, it would disappear once more, as if a sponge had been passed over the brief sketch. I thought I was going mad. The other people stood out with sculptured clarity in a sort of contrast: my grandmother, all sky-blue eyes and wrinkles, a yellowish blotch on her left cheekbone, shaking her head from time to time like a bird and talking to herself; Maerbale, resembling me so much and so thin, casting furtive looks at me, for he did not know how far the new duke had penetrated into the reasons for his departure from Bomarzo, and he was anxious to ingratiate himself with me, which made him extremely solicitous and, for lack of any other pretext, he treated me as if grief had overwhelmed me, which was quite ironic; Cardinal Orsini, sunk in his chair, his chin resting on his chest and his thin beard spread out over his purple; Pier Luigi, insolent, seductive, his aristocratic and aquiline nose triumphant, as if we did not know that the Marquis del Vasto had ignominiously removed him from his command of imperial troops for some obscure act, and looking over the pages without hiding his avid sensuality, which corroborated what was said about him; Messer Pandolfo, his sties enlarged behind his glasses, doubled over in servile reverence; Silvio da Narni, measuring with his crisp smiles the advantages that he would obtain from my situation, until I had nothing else to do but suggest that he withdraw, an attitude that proved the brand-new strength I owed to the dukedom; the winding, shadowy background of my grandmother's ladies; the monks; the warriors, whose chorus monotonously exalted their captain.

No, my father's cause had not been the just one in the siege of Florence, which lasted for ten months and which saw so many heroic acts and so much black treachery since that time in September 1529 when the army of the Prince of Orange had appeared in the Arno valley and had begun the bombardment of the city that Clement VII, backed by the emperor, had hoped to recover for the Medicis. The just cause had as its champions Francesco Ferrucci, the great defender; Michelangelo Buonarroti, who had fortified Florence; Stefano Colonna, who came out at the head of the young patriots who wore white shirts over their armor. The unjust cause had a scoundrel, a Judas, the perfidious Malatesta Baglioni. My father was on the side of the pope and the Medicis for very old family reasons and probably for others that were related to the economic position of the condottieri and to his disdain for the notion of justice and injustice, but he could not have been ignorant of which side was fighting for equity and for the generous feeling of independence; nor could he have ignored the fact that every one of his blows contributed to guarantee in the future a bloody crown for Alessandro de' Medici, the negroid, the pontiff's bastard, the only Medici I detested in the city of the lily as a base, inferior, and crafty person. Neither the sacrifice nor the gallantry of the illustrious city could halt the invaders. It did not matter to them that around the walls the Florentines themselves had razed everything that might hinder the defense or provide hiding places for the enemy, demolishing villages, churches, lovely villas; destroying treasures; cutting down fruit trees and vines. In spite of the siege commerce continued, as if the merchants wanted everyone to see their challenge. At carnival they cavorted on the Piazza della Santa Croce—the one where I had listened to the story of Ginevra of Ravenna and her hunchbacked husband, even though it pained me—playing ball, and the musicians climbed up into the bell tower so that the Bourbon ruffians would know that there was a festival in the city. And none of that, so devil-may-care, so beautiful, appeased the fury of those who were striving to impose their will at all cost and to reinstate the overthrown dynasty. One of them was my father, the one who now lay in the chapel at Bomarzo surrounded by those who were commenting on the splendor of his deeds and assuring us that his name would be inscribed on the list of Orsini household gods alongside those of the most valiant captains.

I was unable to get his face back. I evoked the important occasions on which I had seen it: the time of my imprisonment with the skeleton, when his face had glowed, transfigured by rage; the time he told us about the progress of Michelangelo's David toward the Piazza della Signoria, when my admiration had embellished him. I sought his image beside the logs of the monumental fireplace, extinguished now, reconstructing on both sides the garrulous picture of Gian Corrado, the cardinal, Girolamo, the cousins who were testing their crossbows. I sought it in the memory of his warlike departures, with metallic sounds as pages served him a jug of wine on his shield; in his returns from amorous outings, flushed, his beard flying in the wind. And I could not find it. It eluded me; it was mixed in with other family effigies that came from the portraits we had in Bomarzo and in the palace in Rome which shared certain of his traits as they stood like models in the frames of their oil paintings, their hands on their waists or theatrically extended, the gleaming cuirasses, almost aquatic in their luminous reflection, surrounded by the trophies that underscored the majesty of their bearing. That strong, thin face escaped me. For several days I went through the rooms and terraces of Bomarzo, through the garden, through the countryside about it, distracted. People attributed it to the worries brought on by my new status. Silvio da Narni was unable to bring me out of it. He must have sensed that I wanted to be away from him as from an annoying accomplice when I no longer needed him. That was not true; I needed him more than ever. I preferred not having him beside me because perhaps I sensed that the disappearance of my father from the field of my memory was connected in some way to the magical practices of the night when he had conjured up the devil, and therefore his mere presence was enough to increase my uneasiness. He finally understood himself and wisely withdrew. As for what part I had played in my father's death, I must confess that it upset me very little. I rejected it as absurd and attributed to chance the links between the scene on the terrace and the funeral in the chapel. The only thing that disturbed my euphoria, in moments which went beyond the initial period in the course of my life, was that mysterious erasure of my father. I felt deserted, almost robbed.

The ceremony in which the subjects came to render their homage coincided with the arrival of a messenger bearing a letter from Pope Clement. In it he expressed to me his sorrow over the exemplary death of his ally and he commanded me to attend the papal coronation of Charles V the following February in Bologna. The emperor had been in that city since November. It was his first visit to Italy, to the poor Italy that owed so much spilling of blood and destruction to him. The sacker of Rome, the besieger of Florence, was to be anointed by the Vicar of Christ. If the decisions of Providence are unpredictable, so are those of politics. Guelph and Ghibelline were joining together to honor their master. I clenched my teeth and replied that I would go. In the meantime, I took advantage of the letter and had it read to the functionaries, peasants, and men at arms who were acclaiming me in the main room of Bomarzo. They knelt; the cardinal blessed them, not really knowing what he was doing; and Messer Pandolfo undertook the elegant reading. Standing on a dais, the hunchbacked duke listened. Maerbale raised the symbolic paternal sword with both hands. The ancient banners hung about in tatters. The ceremony took on a military air, paradoxical, given the figure of the main actor. I wondered where Porzia and Giambattista were wandering, Ignacio de Zúñiga and Abul. I would have liked for Beppo and Girolamo to have seen me. I threw my lucco over my shoulder, exposing its marten lining. It was raining softly and it was cold. In a corner of the vast room I observed a figure who was still standing in the midst of the kneeling vassals. He was tall and wrapped in a monkish cape. No one seemed to have noticed his unique position. Irritated, I thought of interrupting the reading to tell him to kneel, and when I made ready to do so, he raised his head and I recognized my father. He had no face, but I could recognize him. In the place of his features there was a shapeless blotch that extended down underneath his gray hair. I clutched the arm of Messer Pandolfo, who interrupted his reading and turned his eyes in surprise. He followed my wide-eyed look to the corner where the specter was vaguely glowing, and the gathering turned also, seeking the cause of the duke's upset, but the ghost had already vanished. I shuddered, passed my right hand over my sweaty forehead.

"Go on, Messer Pandolfo."

And the tutor continued translating the elegant Latin phrases, making a special effort to choose the most mellifluous words. Maerbale laid the sword on a pillow and supported me. The rain was growing stronger. The village people filed by, those from Foglia, Castelvecchio, Montenero, Collepiccolo, Castel Penna, Chia, Collestato, Torre, from the possessions that I would later divide with Maerbale, to kiss my cold hands. Allegorical offerings piled up at my feet, fruit, wheat, turtledoves, loaves of bread, bottles of wine, hothouse roses which evoked the triumphal rose of the Orsinis.

Just as when I was a child, I entered my grandmother's room with an upset face. Some women around her were spinning and when they noticed my expression they withdrew. Flanking the bed were the looms, the bobbins, the multicolored balls of yarn. The rain was beating on the windowpanes. I opened one and the water wet my cheeks and mouth. Chilly, my grandmother pulled the blankets over her body and asked me to close it. Her fragile voice was mingled with the mewing of two large white cats who elastically jumped to the floor from the bedcovers. I hesitated a few more moments before deciding to tell her about the fearsome apparition that had shown itself to me that morning and confide to her the anguish that had been tormenting me ever since my father's remains had reached Bomarzo, because she looked so small, so faded, so distant, as if she did not belong to this world either, but my desolation won out over any reserve and, without thinking about her state or the harm that my revelations might do her, I poured out to her weakness the anguish that I had not dared share with anyone—not even with Silvio—because it was a matter that was previous to my relationship with Silvio da Narni, something whose roots went deep into my childhood and which only Diana Orsini was capable of understanding and explaining. She listened to me, nodding her head.

"Gian Corrado is wandering about the castle," she finally answered, "and he is not the only one who has come to agitate us. Girolamo is still walking about here. The house is haunted. I wish I could die today, right now."

The cats jumped back up on her bed. They were so meticulous that they did not add another wrinkle to the covers. Erect, their splendid tails quivering, their eyes phosphorescent, they looked at me. The old woman sensed my weakness and sighed; she took her hand out of its warm nest, drew me to her, and caressed me softly.

"My poor grandson, my poor duke, how many cares await you! I am going to leave you soon, Vicino."

Then she seemed to be meditating. The rain was drumming on the fields. Her blue eyes lit up.

"After the coronation, go to Recanati. In the monastery of Saint Dominic there is a painting with many figures. One of them...wait"—and my grandmother searched hesitantly in the vast storehouse of her memory—"...wait...Saint Sigmund is the portrait of your father. Go and see it."

The same as at other times, her words worked like a balm on me. Of course I would go. I was already burning with the desire to leave in search of the remedy, as if my peace depended on finding an image.

I placed my lips on the parchment of that abandoned hand. She noticed that I was getting ready to leave and she held me back. She was aglow with lucidity.

"You should get married, Vicino. Think about it. You are duke now, and Bomarzo needs a woman. Marry a Farnese. The hour of the Farneses is at hand."

Between her cats she looked like a sorceress. I was amazed to observe how her practical intelligence worked at a time in life when the logical thing would have been for her to be out of touch with everything around her, especially after the unbalancing of her whole being which the death of Girolamo had meant for her. I was amazed that in her decrepit isolation and in her apparent renunciation of contact with reality, she could be so well informed, so alert, because it was true that the star of the Farneses was rising—her visionary powers sensed it as if, detaching her suddenly from the present, her old age that was so near the tomb had projected her into the future—and it was true that their victory would coincide with the twilight of the Medicis.

Later on I meditated about what she had told me. I remembered that at some time I had heard my father mention the polyptych of Recanati. He had told us of his inclusion in it by the painter Lorenzo Lotto. Saint Sigmund! What connection did my father have with Saint

Sigmund and why had he personified him? Could it have been a mere whim of the painter or was it for a more intimate and secret reason? Who was Saint Sigmund? I asked Messer Pandolfo, who knew his hagiographies, and he told me that the saint had been a king of Burgundy converted to Catholicism, who, in spite of having ordered one of his sons killed, had been raised by the Church to the glory of the altars because he had died as a martyr. The information left me thoughtful. If the Duke of Bomarzo had not succeeded in eliminating me as the King of Burgundy had his offspring, I did not doubt that the idea had passed through his head more than once, and although the polyptych was previous to my arrival in the world, I could see allegorical correspondences between the saint represented by the condottiere, a prince like him, and my own threatened existence.

As for the Farneses, their ties to the Orsinis went back into antiquity, even though their standing and ours could not be compared. The distance that separated us from them was not as great as that which kept us apart from the Medicis, merchants of Tuscany, but anyone with any knowledge in those matters was aware of it. In more recent times distance had loosened the bonds: Ulisse Orsini, my great-great-uncle, had married Bernardina Farnese; Angelo Farnese, the brother of the next pope, had married an Orsini; his sister Giulia—Giulia the Beautiful, the one who gave us so much trouble—had married Orsino Orsini; and Pier Luigi Farnese, the son of the Holy Father, was married to Girolama Orsini. The Holy Father Paul III himself had our blood: his maternal grandmother Caetani di Sermoneta was an Orsini. The Farneses and the Orsinis had intermingled their distinct branches, and that spoke eloquently of the progress of the new, worldly vedettes, who in their search for aristocratic backgrounds had made life difficult for hired scholars who were put to work inventing their genealogy, which, starting with petty noblemen from the Viterbo region, had risen, step by step, thanks to much historical mending and patching, to the category of descendants of the noble Roman family of Farnacia. I was not ignorant of the fact—Messer Pandolfo had taught me—that five centuries before, some members of that line had joined with our family, the Estes, the Monaldeschis, and the Counts of Anguillara in the struggle against the Ghibelline Colonnas. I was also aware that three centuries later a mob led by the Orsinis and Bindo di Soana had destroyed the Farnese castle on Ischia, killing three Farnese brothers and hurling the other two down a well. Those antecedents glorified their shields, but they were still miles away from us. Every time that we did away with one of them, it was as if we had ennobled him by the simple fact that we had given him attention, but they were still quite far from attaining the prestige of the *editus ursae*. There are things that are not acquired just like that. Only around 1400 did they begin to move strongly, with their Ranuccio III, a Senator of Rome, who, thanks to Popes Martin V and Eugenius IV, put together a considerable estate in the volcanic region that extends to the southwest of Lake Bolsena. Then came Ranuccio IV, the one who perished gloriously in the battle of Fornovo; there was the matrimonial alliance with the illustrious Caetanis of Rome, to whose line Pope Boniface VIII belonged; there were the alliances with my relatives. The Farneses were finally breathing with a feeling of security. From the beginning of their climb in Viterbo, they had followed a difficult path, and even though there were stubborn and iron-willed people among scholars who kept on insisting that they were of modest German or Lombard origins, and who proved that the grafting of Roman patricians onto their family tree was an invention that could not be swallowed, the Farneses acted as our equals. The number of their castles increased and in their salons, as they did later on in the sumptuous Farnese palace, they had theatrical scenes with popes and warriors painted, but the Farneses and we Orsinis, without proclaiming it, were aware of the essential gap that separated us. When I was born and the Pax Romana was signed, the fleeting idea of taking part in that pact did not cross the minds of the Farneses. The other nobles would have laughed out loud. It was a matter for Orsinis and Colonnas, the only hereditary guardians of Saint Peter's throne. The Farneses withdrew with the rest in a boisterous crowd behind the balustrades of the basilica. Now, Cardinal Alessandro Farnese, quivering with ambition, was working more than anyone for the advancement of his house. La Vanozza, Rodrigo Borgia's mistress, and his own sister Giulia, the shame of the Orsinis, who lived within the circle of the Spanish pope, helped him. Alessandro Farnese enjoyed the prerogatives of a cardinal since 1493 and he had had celebrated teachers in Pisa and in Florence. His children, legitimized by Julius II and Leo X, grew as the paternal power of the prelate grew, for no sooner had he sung his first mass than he stood out among the most severe members of the sacred college. His influence governed conclaves. Clement VII, whom he had loyally accompanied in Sant' Angelo, the same as my grandfather, during the sack of Rome, declared that if it were possible he would have designated him as his successor. And Alessandro did succeed him to the throne, four years after the time I am speaking of here, thanks to the maneuvers of my friend Ippolito de' Medici, who in his innocence did not know with whom he was getting involved. Yes, my grandmother was right as always. A Farnese was right for me, right for Bomarzo. As I thought about those things, blinded by my recent investiture, I did not think about my hump but about Bomarzo. Bomarzo came ahead of everybody and everything. And, furthermore, had not the most beautiful woman of the time, praised by Ariosto, Giulia Gonzaga, married an old, one-armed, maimed Colonna? An Orsini is the equal of a Colonna. He is worth more. And if I was hunchbacked, I was also young.

Those ideas distracted me from other disquieting matters. I ceased worrying about the phenomenon of the absence of my father's face, which had disappeared into a vagueness of water and mist. I would get it back at Recanati. I avoided going about the castle alone in case some supernatural encounter might take place now that dark forces were wandering on the loose, but I sensed that there would be no repetition. That apparition had surely been the product of my nerves during the ceremony of homage. What my grandmother had been able to see for her part—and about which she preferred not going into details—was probably the consequence of her advanced age and insomnia. One had to forget those terrible fantasies...try to forget them...And I dedicated myself to the minute preparations for my trip to Bologna. I wanted to present myself to Clement VII and Charles V—a bastard and a Fleming—as corresponded to my position. I would take Cardinal Franciotto with me, manageable, obedient, and decorative, a red symbol of our military and ecclesiastical fame. I hoped that his purple would hide my hump, would make it disappear with a sleight-of-hand trick into the elegance of its folds, into the banners, the trappings, the bold shining of the metal, the tutored rearing of the horses, the harmonious grace of the pages.

Something else agitated me especially ever since I succeeded my father to the dukedom and it was to find the secret chamber where the condottiere had locked me up with the skeleton who wore a crown of withered roses. That macabre vision had worked like a poison on my adolescence. I discreetly inquired from my grandmother and the old servants without obtaining any worthwhile piece of information that would lead me to the hiding place. Everyone knew that Bomarzo concealed clandestine passageways and cells, constructed as it was for the most part during the time when, after the destruction of the Polimartium by the Hungarians and the establishment of the first fief in the fortress, it had as joint owners the one hundred descendants of certain Frankish and Lombard barons who, in order to hide their respective treasures and defend themselves from one another, had opened chambers and corridors in the walls and in the rocks, but they had disguised them so successfully that their traces had been lost. Although we had the impression that we were moving about in the midst of an unfathomable labyrinth punctured with subterranean passageways—which, when one stopped to think about it, conferred on those walls of such apparent ferocity a dangerous weakness—there were only occasionally brought to the surface, by the chance blow of a workman's pick, testimonies that confirmed a reality judged by many as legend. But the only things discovered were mere fragments of the network that extended within through the bowels of the castle, and the bones did not appear either during the period when the masons, continuing the work that my father had begun, were knocking down walls and perforating parapets in order to lighten the decoration of the bulk of Bomarzo. The skeleton, if my father had not had it removed (an almost inadmissible hypothesis), must have still been lying in its dark jail and governing the palace from there. That was what worried me: the idea that as long as the skeleton was still there, poisoning the marrow of Bomarzo like a cancer, Bomarzo would never be completely mine. Without my realizing it, the invisible skeleton had come to be changed into something like that conscience I had rid myself of. Hidden and fearsome, capable of humiliating me with only its memory, it was keeping watch.

With an effort I brought back to mind the famous scene in which Gian Corrado Orsini had thrown me into the hollow place presided over by the lugubrious figure. It had taken place in the room where my father used to receive his vassals to deal with affairs of the estate. My progenitor had stood up, turning the chair from which he rebuked me, beside the fireplace; he had pushed me against the wall; then he had pressed something on the wall, and with that—following the great tradition of episodes of architectural and medieval mystery—a panel had opened up. I tested that part of the wall, inch by inch, but it did not give way. My raps revealed nothing to me. I made the investigation many times, locking myself in the room with the pretext of studying the figures of the encumbrances. I was accompanied only by Silvio da Narni, who knew the story of my tomblike prison, and after a time, bored with listening at walls, he lay down on the floor—unintentionally reproducing with his sharp thinness the lying image of the mocking skeleton—and he began to sketch and read. In the meantime, abandoning the wall that did not respond to my feel, my taps, or the tenacity of my fists, I covered the rest of the room, repeating the same useless investigation on the other panels. Until one afternoon my patience was rewarded, if not with what I was seeking, with an important find.

In the place exactly opposite from where my father had made the spring work, as I slipped my fingers along a cornice they passed over a flower carved into the facing. My attuned finger tips, trained in those explorations, felt at once that there was something different in the texture of the decoration. I leaned, I pressed, and a door opened in the wall. I gave a shout and Silvio, who was still lying on the floor and could not see me on the other side of a long table, stood up and was beside me with a leap. A gust of cold and nauseating air came in through tire opening. We lighted a candle, drew our daggers, and went into the blackness. There, a few steps away, perhaps we would find the abominable skeleton. There was a chamber or a cell, similar to the one which in my memory held the tragic remains, but it was not the same one. It was empty. The only thing there was a chest pushed up against what must have been the outside wall. I lifted the lid and the flickering of the light showed me some parchments at the bottom. I recognized the bold, authoritarian, and angry-looking hand of my father.

Silvio called me. "A passageway goes through here."

I took the papers and followed him. A narrow and low corridor—so low that even I had to hunch over in order to go into the foul-smelling tunnel—went down along some rough-hewn steps into the darkness. We descended, pushing aside the cobwebs that were as thick as lichens, surrounding us as the rheum stuck to our eyes, becoming entangled in our hair and on our mouths. The candle would ignite that skein with brief sputtering that the dampness quickly extinguished. We went down and down, turning, spitting, using our hands, crawling, falling, losing our breath. It was difficult to breathe. We went a long way, holding each other by the waist, the arms, the legs, fearing at every moment that the light would go out, which, held almost at ground level, revealed to us the roughness of the rocks and the trembling of the ashen nets. Sometimes the tunnel was so steep that we slid, one after the other. Silvio went first, with the candle. I, limping, clinging to the stones, breaking my nails, could feel my hands bleeding on the tattered parchments. Finally we emerged, still in thick darkness, into a place where the tunnel went along horizontally, and we calculated that we had covered the distance between the upper part of the castle and the terraces of my grandmother's garden, and that we were now probably underneath that garden. We could stand up there, and after following a straight line for a good distance more, we stopped in what seemed to be the end of the amazing secret passage: a round cave into which a faint light was filtering, indicating to us that, like the rest of the excavation, it had been cut out of solid rock, and that there was no trace evident to allow one to tell the period in which those who had preceded me in the rule of Bomarzo had done such an arduous piece of work. We approached the place where the light was seeping in and we found that if I got up on Silvio's shoulders I could reach it. We did that and I found myself looking at the thick brush that closed off the entrance. Its brambles scratched me and I had to cut my way through. Silvio took my right hand and climbed up too. A few seconds later we got through the thickets and flung ourselves down panting on the grass. We were in the middle of the woods. The cobwebs woven in our hair and the scratches that crossed our faces had changed us into two gray-haired old men.

The sunset was turning the underbrush to fire and giving the crags a golden splendor. The place was quivering, as if under the force of a spell. The tawny and purple spots that the sunset spread over the rocks were making them feline and gigantic, as if the foresight of nature were rehearsing what that place would be one day as the result of my work. The birds were singing, sending crystalline messages, and the breeze was bringing up sumptuous odors from the vineyards and orchards. We cleaned ourselves as best we could, washing in the brook, and we went slowly back to the big house.

"It must be a very old construction," I explained to Silvio, "maybe from the time of the Lombard barons."

"It's good that we found it," he answered. "We may have to use it someday."

From his tone I could understand that he was figuring that our destinies were inseparable, and that fact, which should have brought a certain comfort to my perspectives of melancholy loneliness, irritated me.

Back in my father's room, in order to emphasize that neither that discovery, nor the magical ceremony on the terrace with its hermetic triangle, nor anything that he knew about me gave him a greater claim to intimacy (which was not true, for the fact is that even though I might not have wished it, we were linked by strong bonds), I ordered him to leave me alone. He obeyed grudgingly. He was no doubt burning, as I was, with a desire to examine the parchments that I continued clutching and which were reddened by my blood.

I locked myself in then and began unfolding the manuscripts on the table. In one of them, Gian Corrado had drawn up—most likely in a boastful moment—the list of his possible adulterous offspring. There were twelve of them, and the name of the mother, a peasant from Bomarzo or a servant girl from a nearby castle, was next to each one. Beppo was among them. In the next paper the condottiere had put down in detail what his father-in-law still owed him of the dowry:

twelve hundred ducats. Then there were two identical letters, one addressed to the pope and the other to Cardinal Orsini. My father declared in them his wish that if Girolamo should die before succeeding him, his prerogatives and possessions should pass to Maerbale. "My son Pier Francesco," he said, "lacks the moral and physical conditions that the succession requires. I hope that Maerbale will use the firmness that I impose on him to keep him locked up in Bomarzo. May God forgive me and may people forget that Pier Francesco ever existed." The last parchment was the horoscope by Sandro Benedetto that forecast eternal life for me. It was not difficult, given his character, for my father to have kept it with his precious writings as a joke. The detailed design was very beautiful. The allegorical images of Mars, Venus, and Saturn were interwoven with lines that corresponded to the influences of the stars over Hebrew letters. On one side my father had written, "Monsters never die."

I stayed over the papers for a long time, hours perhaps. The previous duke had proposed to disinherit me as unworthy, seeking as his recourse the authority of the Supreme Pontiff, whom our Guelph tradition respected as infallible in material the same as in spiritual matters. Why, then, had he not returned to Bomarzo after Girolamo's death? Could he have repented? Could he have postponed week after week the return that would bring my destruction with it? Instead of sinking me into despair, that final proof of his hatred, which confirmed so many previous indications, made me happy. Neither the ghost of Girolamo, drowned in the Tiber, nor that of my father, wandering facelessly through the rooms of the castle, could upset me any more. On the contrary, those two letters filled me with the desire to do something so unique that it would obliterate their memories and show the startled people what Pier Francesco Orsini was capable of. I lighted a fire in the fireplace and burned the documents. What did I care about the dozen rustics that Gian Corrado had given me as adulterous brothers? What did I care about the debt that the cardinal would never pay? What did I want with the letters by means of which he had planned to despoil me of what was mine, of that Bomarzo which was more mine than anybody else's? The fire grew, devouring miseries. I carefully cut away the inscription that my father had added to the horoscope and threw it into the fire. I folded Benedetto's sketch and kept it in the drawer where I kept our patents of nobility and the details of Orsini prowess. I would have the prophetic painting copied in a fresco that would cover one of the walls of the castle, in the showiest room: the nudity of Venus, the helmet of Mars, the muscles of Saturn the farmer, the arc of the Moon, the golden smile of the Sun. That armor belonged to me alone and it was more beautiful than the others.

I went to my grandmother's room to ask her to heal my wounds. The place looked like some ancient tailor's workshop. The women had left, leaving in disorder the work they had begun, to be continued on the following day, and everywhere could be seen pieces of the clothing that Maerbale and I would wear to the coronation of Charles of Hapsburg. Rough designs spread out on workbenches served as patterns. My red archaic long cape of a Magus king and the hat with the ducal half crown were being worn by an improvised dummy. One could note the artistic (and polite) skill with which the women had tried to disguise my hump, adding more and more furs to one side of the back. I went over to my grandmother through the scattered adornments, stepping on velvets, and I told her that I had fallen from my horse into a bramble bush. I needed to be cared for, to be petted. The white cats rubbed against me, increasing their soft purring, and she, in spite of her great age and fatigue, busied herself with wet cloths, murmuring words of consolation. "Vicino," she sighed, "poor Vicino..."

I fell asleep in her arms. I dreamed—I always dreamed—that Mars and Venus were leading me through a shadowy corridor. The smell of carrion was nauseating. I was wearing my gold crown on my head. The hand of Venus was strong, like that of a man, and that of Mars delicate, like a woman's. At the end of the path the skeleton was waiting for me, and without any fear at all I lay down next to him, until little by little I was disappearing, as if the skeleton were absorbing me, so that the two of us became one tetric mass. My diadem was replaced with his withered flowers. Through his empty sockets I looked at the gods, the warrior and the lover, who were smiling at me, bowing before the crowned lord, who, as if he had appeared on a theater balcony that had a grating of bones, was contemplating them from beyond death.

# 4. GIULIA FARNESE

*The trip to Bologna—Charles V and Clement VII—The twins in the house of prostitution—The luxury of the Farneses—The magical dolls—The imperial coronation of Charles V—My vengeance on Pantasilea—The emperor knights me—My love for Giulia*

THE ANTS were coming and going in every direction in the anthills of Italy. They were moving in wavy lines. When their caravans crossed they would stop and greet one another and parley, and then they would continue on their way with their multicolored burdens. To God—and also to me now as I watch that bustle again from a distance that eliminates pride—the banners looked like threads, and the armed noblemen were like insects shining in the winter sun. They went up and down hills; they went through passes; they crossed woods; they forded rivers, on their antlike way. Was that a small green leaf or a canopy? And that other thing, was it a city with many towers or a stone that had fallen into the grass? They were coming and going, carrying shining objects, but it could be seen that they were doing it without any joy, in obedience to orders, customs, vanities. One of those anthills was called Bologna and there was a special ant in it called the emperor. His infinite subjects were coming to render him homage, and their processions were crossing constantly with their threads and their pennants. They came from the far reaches of Europe, oozing with rancor, distrust, and greed. The shining ant-men who sparkled on the highways of Italy could not forgive the foreign leader whom they were coming to crown for the sack that they had suffered in Rome or the destruction that was still taking place in Florence, and if they were numbered among those enriched by the pillage, they felt that their services were worth much more than the advantages they had gained and which were evident in the stolen jewels as they gleamed. They would pause to drink in the taverns in cities along the way, and the tavern keepers would open their eyes wide at the necklaces and crosses of precious stones that sparkled on their plumed hats. The pope, on the other hand, the one who was to place the crown on His Holy Caesarian Majesty, must have lowered his eyes so as not to see those spoils from the Church of Christ that were ceaselessly flowing into Bologna in an insolent exhibition. And the Vatican's most bitter enemies, also vassals of that same emperor who considered so much wealth as a problem, were not satisfied either, for their prince stood before them as one who was destroying the strange religious ideas that were feeding and beginning to gnaw at a new world. Everything was so insecure, so fragile, that neither the pope nor the emperor had dared to hold the ceremonies in old Rome, covered with recent scars, many of which were still bleeding and Clement VII de' Medici, on the way to Bologna, had made a detour to avoid his native Florence, where his name, associated with those of the invaders, was being cursed.

I also avoided it with my party. The latter was rather large. The cardinal rode in my grandmother's coach, which was one of our greatest luxuries in spite of the fact that it had no springs, because in Florence, for example, only in 1534—or four years later—did the first carriages appear, introduced by ladies of the House of Cibo. Part of the baggage was placed on its creaking roof. The rest was carried in a wagon and on muleback. We—Maerbale, Messer Pandolfo, my young relatives Matteo, Sigismondo, and Orso Orsini (the flower of Girolamo's friends, who, difficult as it was for them, had to accompany me), the pages, headed by Silvio, and the men at arms, making a total of more than thirty people—went on horseback. In Bomarzo, in the place of Manuzio Martelli, of whose fate nothing was known, I had left a new administrator, Messer Bernardino Niccoloni, probably anxious to thrive by juggling figures.

Perhaps most worthy of note during the trip were the efforts of my cousins to gain my good will. At eighteen I was the head of the family, and their fate as poor relations depended on my decisions. I enjoyed myself observing the prodigious diplomacy with which the three of them tried to drive away the hatred for them that I had accumulated

GIULIA FARNESE · 227

during the period when they had surrounded and fawned over Girolamo and had won his sympathy at my expense, for they knew that the easiest path toward pleasing my brother was to tease me. That change in tactics and shifting of batteries, brought on by the change in positions and by my unexpected and rapid rise to the rule, was rather difficult to bring about if not impossible, and not even their marvelous Italian wiles, rich in inherited hypocritical subtleties—the only inheritance they had—were able to dominate immediately the delicacy of the situation, because events were too close together and had been too intense for us to disguise them. After the death of Girolamo, whom they had served like lackeys since childhood, obeying the advice of their parents and their own slippery inclinations, which coincided with the character and tastes of the presumed successor—whose corpse they had carried to the tomb as if with it they were burying the gold their hopes had promised—they had approached me timidly. The gamecocks of yesterday were the gentle doves of today. I can imagine their conversations, their intrigues in their run-down houses in the valley, ornate with reproductions of the Orsini shield which ruled the somber crest of Bomarzo. I can imagine their calculations, their anguish. What could they hope for? How should they proceed in order to seduce me, to make the duke forget, while they replaced insults with abjection? Matteo, Sigismondo, Orso... the three of them somewhat older than I; the three of them first cousins among themselves and my second cousins; the three of them dark, thin, languid, nervous, inseparable, making up with the elegance of their gestures for the modesty of their clothing, which had been ennobled with some gift—a brooch, a baldric, a plume—from Girolamo; the three of them were starving for rapine and prestige, valiant when war demanded it and cowards when the torture of the hunchback called for it. They rode beside me, and even without looking at them I could feel their wolfish eyes burning in the darkness like lighted coals whose fire was joined to that of the smoking torches. When we stopped, they would slide off their steeds and fight for the honor of holding my stirrup. They were speculators, they would tolerate a great deal in the name of ambition, but they were also to be feared: secretive, intriguing, and dangerous, like the secret passageway at Bomarzo. They conversed little, not knowing what was proper to say, and they watched for the single words, the casual words that I would throw to them like bones. If they thought that all doors were closed to them, they would conspire with Maerbale and would leave me on my back with dagger thrusts. At the same time, since they were playing their base game, I had to play mine, giving them to understand that they had offended me and that the wrath of the master held unforeseen risks, but to insinuate to them also that my great magnanimity implied the enigma of future advantages that had to be earned. Farther back in line, Maerbale spied on me like Beppo. Boys matured very quickly in those days. One lived rapidly, because at any moment, with a lightning flash of steel, one could stop living. All of that distracted me from other thoughts, like the uneasiness brought about by my approaching presentation to Charles V, and it made me savor in short sips the wine of a poor victory. As long as we went along in a group, flanked by my escort, nothing could happen to me. In the midst of the three hovering wolves I must have looked like a bear cub, with my *lucco*, my lined Florentine tabard to which I had had added a thick fur collar on the back to hide my hump. Since I had been among bears so much, ones of stone, wood, velvet, and gold, it transformed me mimetically into a cub. The sacred animals of the *editus ursae* were in that way protecting the Duke of Bomarzo, giving him the fiction of strength. I only took off that article of clothing when, fatigued from riding and with aching joints, I shared the coach with my grandfather. Then I would put a blanket over my knees and read Baldassare Castiglione's *Cortegiano*, the Renaissance manual of good manners. I wanted to be irreproachable, as if when I bowed before the pope and the emperor, all of the Orsinis, from the hypothetical general Caius Flavius Orsus on down, were watching me.

We spent the night at an inn in Forli. I had them unload the baggage and I gave each of my cousins a new outfit of red, silver, gold, and green—our colors. They accepted them with shouts of enthusiasm, for it redeemed them from the low state of appearing in court like unsheltered waifs, and it suggested the possibility of pardon to them. We ate together, with the cardinal, Messer Pandolfo, and Maerbale, in the bustle of the hostel filled with people going to the festivities at Bologna. From a table of young prelates the harlots were smiling at us. Silvio

## GIULIA FARNESE · 229

served the meal. My cousins spoke cautiously about the emperor; about the benefits of the Ladies' Peace, signed between his aunt, Margaret of Burgundy, and Louise of Savoy, the mother of Francis I; they spoke about the return of Milan to the Sforzas as imperial governors; they spoke about events in Florence; the Caesar's projects concerning Hungary; about the Lutherans; the pirate Barbarossa. They were exploring the terrain and they would glance at me from time to time from behind linked hands as they broke their bread, passed the jugs, stood up to fill my cup with a mixture of homage and familiarity. Since they had not penetrated the flow of my political ideas, while on the other hand they knew very well what Girolamo's had been, prepared for any advantageous concession, they did not dare pass any opinions as they untangled the skein that the pope and the emperor had put together. They would laugh and suddenly stop laughing. I would say a few words, often without any meaning, and would look deeply into their eyes. I could guess that they were racking their brains to understand me, to grasp the oracle of the guiding voice of the castle, that of the hunchbacked bear. Even though I detested them, it was impossible not to admire the beauty of the three, accentuated by the tension that made them lean their faces toward me, that made their dark eyes burn, that made them sink their nails into the table.

After dinner I fell ill. I was seized with a terrible vomiting. My grandfather wanted to confess me, perhaps to get rid of several things that he had been curious about for a long time, because in his moments of lucidity, as if he were desirous of making up for the time lost in dotage, he would become exaggeratedly acute. I thought that I had been poisoned, but we had all tasted of the same golden kid roasted with saffron, the same dumplings. Because of my illness, which left me wan and shaken with nausea, we had to stay in Forli for a week. I slept with Silvio da Narni, naked swords within reach and with two faithful men lying in front of the door. I attributed the illness to the emotions that had been building up over the past year. Silvio cured me with a brew of herbs that smelled like mint. I do not know whether or not he had put something diabolical in the potion. Because of the accident we missed the first part of the ceremonies, the one in which Charles V received the iron crown of King of the Lombards which a group of magistrates had brought from Monza. We reached Bologna on February 21, 1530, along with the Duke of Savoy, a vicar of the empire, the new Duke of Milan, the Duke of Bavaria, and the Bishop of Trent, the ambassador of the King of Hungary. Inside the swaying coach my head felt as heavy as if the iron crown were pressing down on my forehead. My grandfather had me inhale some scents.

In Bologna there was no room for another soul. Except for the Duke of Ferrara, who did not come because of differences with Clement VII, and the Duke of Mantua, who did not present himself because of quarrels with the Duke of Monferrato, gathered together about the palace that had lodged the Supreme Pontiff and His Majesty for months were all of the great Italian noblemen. No one came to receive me, for everyone else was waiting for Charles of Savoy, the husband of the empress's sister, and because no one except the Medicis knew me as yet. Nevertheless, I calculated that my grandmother's coach would draw attention. The German lansquenets, dressed in white and turquoise, their pikes on their shoulders, opening a path for us, pointed at it. I thought of Abul, of his feeling of triumph as he went through the crowds on Annone's back, and several times I went over to the door to chat with the cardinal about anything at all (I had mounted my horse when we entered the city), showing in that way that the carriage belonged to us. No matter what had happened, I still had many childish traits and certain aspects of my vanity were still quite infantile.

Since I had been prudent enough to have reserved lodgings through relatives of my grandfather, my brother, my cousins, and I put up in the house of a physician with tolerable comfort. Franciotto Orsini joined the Sacred College. On those occasions his efficiency was startling. The soldiers slept in the squares around their bivouacs. They would get into fights and it was necessary to keep them under control so that they would not tear their costly uniforms. One of them was killed, the son of a village woman from Bomarzo, Beppo's mother, but he was legitimate. I was cold and I had a headache.

In the morning, accompanied by Maerbale, Matteo, Sigismondo, and Orso I went to greet the Medicis. Society had developed, adjusting as always to what was convenient, to the ups and downs of values which depended on the changeable influence of the powerful, and something as disproportionate and so contrary to status as the fact that the Medicis did not go to visit the Orsinis, but it was the Orsinis who visited the Medicis was therefore possible, and, to make it worse, bastard Medicis.

There were so many people milling through the streets that it was difficult to advance. In the same way that because of the imperial rites and pomp we had the fiction of Saint Petronius's church serving as the basilica of Saint Peter's, with its altars rebaptized with dedications to those venerated in the greatest church of Christendom in order for the acts of the papal coronation to proceed just as they would have in Rome, so Bologna, the ancient university city, had been converted temporarily into the capital of the world. Its twisting alleys seemed ready to burst out onto the plains with the large number of people that filled them, speaking their strange languages and dialects. Especially bubbling were the Spaniards, coming from Barcelona on the fifteen galleys, ships, hookers, and carracks of Andrea Doria, and the Germans, recently enriched from the sacking. The luxury of their livery distinguished the servants and pages of the Spanish hidalgos.

Ahead of our horses, Silvio da Narni was shouting proudly, "Make way for the Duke of Bomarzo! Make way for the Princes Orsini!"

But the crowd was already used to personages and illustrious names in that immense and glorious stew in which were mixed the aristocratic spices that would later feed the *Gotha* with centuries of blood for us Orsinis to impress the masses. And, furthermore, we were not the only Orsinis who had come to Bologna. Scaffolds obstructed the squares, adorned with garlands and emblems. Over the doors and windows ingenious devices had been hung, paintings and representations of the emperor's victories, of his kingdoms and of the lands discovered across the seas under his command. Along with the familiar coats of arms, the eagles, the castles, the lions, and the fleurs-de-lis that surrounded the collar of the Fleece, new figures had been added, feathered savages gleaming with precious stones. Beyond the old world that had been carefully classified with metal labels and colors strictly ordained by heraldic usage, another world was waiting, mysterious and fierce, bursting out of the jungles of America cut by enormous rivers on the banks of which temples dedicated to cruel gods arose, and that world of sumptuous barbarism had been obliged, artificially, monstrously, to participate in the courtly festivities that were bringing together fragile European patricians with whom it had no connection and whom it was perhaps capable of destroying with its golden claws. Between the palace where Clement VII and Charles V were lodged and the church of Saint Petronius, where the coronation would take place, a high open walkway had been erected over which the dignitaries would pass in public view, like actors on a stage, up to the main altar. And there also were numerous branches of laurel and ivy around the papal and imperial shields.

"Make way for the Duke of Bomarzo! Make way for the Princes Orsini!" Silvio da Narni was shrieking as my men drove the ninnies back with their pikes, and if some did withdraw voluntarily, it was not so much to escape the blows as from their astonishment at seeing a duke with a hump on a pure white charger. I returned those looks that changed from surprise to mockery with my most impassive expression, as if I were floating on a cloud, but if anyone had put his hand over my heart at that moment, he would have noticed that it was beating with a frightened madness. Suddenly I reined in my horse. I thought I had seen Abul beside a portico. I could have sworn that I had seen his thin face which had been swallowed up by the crowd. I peered into the sea of heads and we went forward. I would have quite gladly let go of the reins, over which Benvenuto Cellini's ring was trembling like an insect, and I would have dived into that dark current to find my Negro page, but it could not be; I had to fulfill the role I was playing in the midst of my handsome relatives. I consoled myself by thinking that it was a vision, the product of my weakness.

We dismounted in front of the palace where Alessandro de' Medici was staying. The presumed son of the pope had displaced Ippolito in the hierarchical order and it was proper to visit him first. He was Duke of Pina at that time and soon, after Baglioni's treason and the defeat of Ferrucci, when the bleeding Signoria would order a cessation of hostilities, he would be the protector and hereditary Duke of Florence and he would marry Margaret of Austria, the natural daughter of Charles V. In that family, as with Morny in the nineteenth century, everything happened naturally. In the meantime, his cousin, Cardinal

Ippolito, was chewing his nails, writing verse, hunting pheasants, and thinking about revenge that had no substance.

I do not know how we were brought in, for at that very instant an absurd scene was taking place, one whose intimacy did not admit outside witnesses. In a vast room, surrounded by the indifferent busts of ancient philosophers and poets, Alessandro and Ippolito were arguing. A few steps away, lying on the floor, Lorenzino de' Medici was amusing himself with a stiletto, sticking it into the floor from time to time as if he were unwittingly rehearsing the great theatrical act of his life. Rodone, Ippolito's favorite dog, recovered after he had run away in Florence, was romping about the noblemen. Farther off some Africans of the cardinal's retinue were looking out the windows and commenting on what the people in the streets, invisible to us, were doing, with monkey-like expressions and loud laughter.

Alessandro turned to the slaves and exclaimed furiously, "Be quiet, you imbeciles!"

The three years that had passed during which we had not seen one another had done much to shape the young men from the Via Larga. Alessandro the Moor, dressed in green, had acquired corpulence on reaching manhood. He looked at me, and the essential dislike that had separated us as boys was re-established intact, as if not a single day had passed. The nineteen-year-old cardinal stood up in a wave of purple and opened his arms to me, happy to find a pretext to put an end to the quarrel that was sputtering in the air.

Maerbale and the three Orsinis, restrained, remained at the threshold. I advanced, and although I should have greeted Alessandro first, I took advantage of the fact that they were together and of the ecclesiastical rank of his cousin to go toward the latter, and carrying the scheme to such extremes in order to have my revenge for the duke's obvious disdain, I called Ippolito—pretending that my confusion had made me make the mistake—"Most Serene Highness," his title from the time when he had been master of Florence.

The cardinal raised me up and brushed away my words with an ironical gesture: "The Serene Highness has died, Vicino. I am now a father of the Church."

No one would have taken him for such. He looked like a soldier, a hunter disguised in clerical garb. He embraced me and I could feel the strength of his muscles that had been hardened by gymnastic exercises. His eyes, the dark rings, betrayed his upset, but unlike those of Alessandro, they were aglow with generosity. I brought my relatives over, still without having greeted the duke, and introduced them. Then I repeated the ceremony with Alessandro. He answered me coldly. Lorenzino, illuminated with joy, came over to embrace me, and the Africans, turning and seeing the hunchbacked prince whom their master loved, fell to their knees and touched their foreheads to the floor. Even Rodone came over, barking, panting, putting his paws on my shoulders and licking my hands. In spite of the attitude of the Moor, who did not count, the reception filled me with jubilation, especially since it showed the people from Bomarzo the intense familiarity of the links that joined me to the pontiff's nephews. At that moment, curiously, I felt completely that I was Duke of Bomarzo; I felt it more than when my vassals had rendered me homage in the castle after my father's death, because it was as if Ippolito had anointed me and as if my snobbery had received the definitive consecration from people who, in spite of being illegitimate, were so important and so sought after and flattered. The reader ought not to grumble and should try to understand me. That was what I was like, frivolous, superficial—being deep and complex, on the other hand—I had an urge for recognitions that would affirm me in the position in the world that was befitting to me, although I also counted on a congenital immunity that was guaranteed by my blood and by rights which I presume to be divine. I was very secure and very insecure at the same time. That was where my imbalance came from, as I have been showing in these memoirs. And it enchanted me that Maerbale, who no doubt considered himself possessing more title than I to the historical paternal succession, and Matteo, Sigismondo, and Orso—the Orsinis who were angry at having been defrauded, who had tormented me with such fury during the period of Girolamo's splendor when they considered me a low, ridiculous vermin—had the full proof that I had something that neither of my apparently superior brothers had attained: position, authority, and worth among the all-powerful who aroused even more envy and before whom, in spite of their being bastards and of our having illustrious ancestors as immemorial as the stones of Rome,

GIULIA FARNESE · 235

and the pride of our grandmother Diana and our grandfather Cardinal Franciotto, we were nothing but small and greedy provincial chieftains. Although it hurt us to admit it deep inside, we were discredited in elegant circles, but nothing in the world would have made us recognize the word, for we would have let our tongues be torn out before resigning ourselves and accepting the obvious.

I sensed that our entrance had interrupted a dispute. Alessandro, vibrant, his eyes like embers, all of him comparable to an ugly green bird with a black head, was swaying furiously, trying to hold back Ippolito as he began certain explanations that emphasized the grotesqueness of his pretension. But it was too late.

"The duke is irritated because in the ceremony of the twenty-fourth, that of the imperial coronation, he won't play the same role as he did two days ago when His Majesty received the crown of the Lombards."

"It's the one that befits me," Alessandro thundered.

"In that ceremony," Ippolito went on, "the Marquis of Astorga carried the scepter, the Marquis of Villena the dagger, Alessandro the globe of the world, and the Marquis of Monferrato the crown of Lombardy. They walked in front of His Majesty like four torchbearers. On the other hand, for the ceremony the day after tomorrow it's been arranged for Monferrato to carry the scepter, the Duke of Urbino the sword, the Duke of Bavaria the globe, and the Duke of Savoy the imperial crown. Alessandro's been left out."

"They'll pay for it!" the duke roared. "I'm going to talk to His Holiness today. The pope never denies me anything! Those insolent people will see!"

"The pope can't change anything," his cousin argued dauntlessly, "because the emperor has decided on those distinctions. The Duke of Bavaria represents the German electors."

"The swine, a bunch of heretics!"

"Not the Duke of Bavaria."

Lorenzino's little voice was heard as he lay on the floor shaking the huge head of the big dog: "What difference does it make? My aunt Clarice said I was head of the Medicis and they always put me in with the crowd of poor princes."

He laughed. It was difficult to tell whether as a playful child or as an angry man. The bastards were silent for a few seconds and looked at him curiously. That child was not like his cousin Cosimo, the astute one. They could never predict his reactions. His barb touched me too: I would have to march with the "poor princes," and even there my place would not be one of the best.

Alessandro, pretending that there had been no interruption, faced Ippolito again. "Of course, Your Eminence doesn't care, because you have a place assigned among the cardinals and you'll probably help hold the imperial cape in Saint Petronius's."

"Some advantage should be given to a person who has abandoned the glories of the world for other higher ones. Although I would really rather go hunting in Mugello if I could."

Ippolito smiled and the Orsinis were listening open-mouthed.

"I'll take the world away from the Duke of Bavaria."

"The world," the cardinal sighed, crossing himself, "does not belong to Your Excellency nor to the Bavarian. Nor does it belong to Charles the Fifth. It belongs to God."

He stood up even straighter, with the grace of his nineteen athletic years, and holding back his cousin's reply, which would have been aggravating, perhaps a blasphemy, he drew a cross in the air.

"I bless you in *nomine Patris, et Filii, et Spiritus Sancti*. Restrain yourself, Alessandro de' Medici."

He put a hand on my shoulder and ended it by saying, "Let's go, Pier Francesco."

We bowed and left, preceded by the gabbling of the Africans. One of them was leading Rodone on a silver leash.

"Why did you say that, Lorenzino?" the prelate asked.

"As a joke, just in fun."

"Perhaps you were unaware," Ippolito said, addressing me, "that Clarice Strozzi died."

The news saddened me. The granddaughter of the Magnificent had given up her soul two years before and no one had told me. I remembered her broad forehead, the grace of her oval face, her firmness, her arrogance, the way we obeyed her without discussion.

"All we do here is get heated up over nonsense. If you only knew, Vicino! This coronation has been a hell—God forgive me."

GIULIA FARNESE · 237

Suddenly the busts of the philosophers that surrounded Alessandro looked like clay to me; the duke looked like an angry mulatto; the pieces of cloth on which the trophies that decorated the streets had been painted looked miserable; the high passageway and the canopies like the tents at a fair; the soldiers spread about the square looked like occupation troops who were there to stifle the protests of the people. In general, those people and those acts are much more impressive in the fervent descriptions by the chroniclers charged with gilding the curtains than seen as I saw them. On the twenty-fourth, Saint Matthias's day, the birthday of the august emperor and the fifth anniversary of the day on which Charles's captains had captured the King of France in Pavia, the Duke of Bavaria carried the globe of the world and Alessandro gnawed at his bit.

When we left Ippolito, pressed in by the crowd that was tight around his sedan chair, I commented languidly to my companions, "They used to fight about everything in Florence. But they're both very discreet. Their ability to bluff comes from their Medici blood. If they spoke in front of you people about such intimate things, it was because I was there. I'm like one of the family."

And in that way, in order to shine in front of my brother and the rustic Orsinis, I did not hesitate to relate myself to the bastards.


We turned our horses over to the pages and returned on foot, for it was more comfortable that way. In the turmoil of people I thought that I had seen Giambattista Martelli, just as I had thought I had seen Abul before. I pointed him out to Maerbale, but he had disappeared. Giambattista was blond and delicate, a type that appeared many times among boys of his age who served in powerful houses, so that, as in the previous case, I attributed the discovery to a coincidence of likenesses. The crowds of Bologna were hiding the specters of my past. In another crush, as we tried to help our progress with our elbows, we ran into Pier Luigi Farnese, the son of the future pope, the one who had brought my father's remains from Florence to Bomarzo.

"The people are all excited, gentlemen!" he shouted to us. "Push hard and forward!"

His energetic profile stood out over the fearful faces. A few dried pustules stood out on his cheeks, the traces of the terrible disease that inspired Fracastoro to write the poem *Syphilis*, published in Venice that same year and which claims that the appearance of the disease was due to the conjunction of the three superior planets, Saturn, Jupiter, and Mars, which is very rare. What was not rare at all, on the other hand, was the illness in question, which the Italians blamed on the French and the French on the Italians, and which many claimed had been brought from America by the Spaniards, so the peoples of Europe all blamed one another for the responsibility. It did such damage that its destruction threatened to go beyond that of the epidemic sicknesses known for centuries: plague, tuberculosis, scabies, erysipelas, anthrax, leprosy, trachoma.

Pier Luigi lovingly took the arm of Sigismondo Orsini, who was startled at such a privilege. "Let's keep together, friends. We can protect ourselves better that way."

That was how we went, pushing the celebrants aside, and I noticed that Farnese was whispering into the ear of the youngest of the Orsinis. I could imagine what he was saying, because no one was ignorant of his inclinations.

In the afternoon, in accordance with what had been arranged by our grandfather, I went with Maerbale to pay my respects to the pope and the emperor. On the way my brother pointed out a group of ladies gathered at a window from which they were throwing flowers to the passers-by.

"Look at that one!" he exclaimed without holding back. "She's so beautiful!"

I followed his glance and I spied in the center of the girls one whose beauty eclipsed the others. She was dressed in an ocher dress with very broad enveloping sleeves. A thick hairnet, also ocher, which came down over her neck, held her wavy chestnut hair. Under her coral necklace, her breasts were small and firm. Her big blue eyes alighted on us for a second and then went away. We were not important to her.

"I've never seen anyone like that," Maerbale said. "I'd like to meet her."

I would have, too. I felt jabbed with the pin of jealousy for an instant.

It occurred to me that by simply looking at her and wanting her Maerbale was taking away from me something that belonged to me, because from the simple fact of my being the Duke of Bomarzo, no one of my household should have had ambitions for anything without consulting me. Jealousy has always been one of my prime movers. But at the same time I was pleased that at a moment when we were on our way to face something that was making our emotions burst like fireworks, Maerbale could be distracted from his rich preoccupation with some sensual detail, for it proved that in spite of everything, we Orsinis were still what we had always been, temperamental people, quick to fall in love, and that intimate trait had precedence over the demands that circumstance had placed on us, as solemn and as desired as they might have been. Others would have gone to see the pope and the emperor as if they were going to receive the Sacrament. Not us; we did it familiarly, without granting that episode any more importance than a bureaucratic procedure that derived from our position, while nothing—not even the alarming idea that a short time later we would find ourselves before the complete masters of soul and possessions, elected by God for that incomparable task—could make us stray from what essentially and for several centuries had been our great and pleasurable restlessness. And then my jealousy became twice as strong because, since it was Maerbale who was giving to me the aristocratic example of his courtly indifference and of his faithfulness to an attitude that we displayed every day, he was showing me that he was more of an Orsini than I, more worthy of being one, and that, with exasperated emulation, aroused my curiosity about the girl who was bringing out such reactions of independence.

I asked the people around but they did not know who the blue-eyed girl was. I sent Silvio to find out and he returned with no news.

At the palace they brought us into a salon full of noble people who were waiting to greet the heads of Christendom. Cardinal Orsini, aided by a page, came to rescue us from that gilded mass, anonymous in spite of the luxury of the names and the clothing. The crosses of the Spanish orders—Santiago, Calatrava, Alcántara, Montesa—were repeated on the capes all about. They took us to another room, where we had to wait for a long time.

"You kiss the pope's foot," the cardinal instructed us again, "and the emperor's hand."

The recommendation was useless: we had rehearsed the liturgy of the genuflections for a week, and I had learned what was proper for the Duke of Bomarzo to transmit to the holy people in a brief discourse. This last part was of no use to me. I became tongue-tied or suddenly felt a great weariness as I evaluated the superfluity of my preparations and of all that was happening, for it struck me that those scenes did not belong to reality and that, like those that Leon Battista Alberti had invented a century before with chambers in which the sun, the moon, and mysterious countrysides appeared, were vain optical illusions.

Both interviews were quite rapid. We stood in a line which went through a maze of many empty rooms and past His Holiness and His Caesarian Majesty. The pope showed that he was a better politician than the Hapsburg or that he needed more support. He had me rise and he spoke of my father.

"We remember Gian Corrado Orsini in our prayers. He was a Catholic gentleman of singular worth, the same as your grandfather, the cardinal."

While I eluded his shining eyes, I fleetingly remembered my father's excesses, girls raped in Bomarzo, the vexation of the magistrates, taxes, and the gallows.

"Cardinal Ippolito has spoken to me of you with praise, Duke."

I muttered a phrase of thanks, furious with myself, with my timidity.

The emperor did not say a word. The paleness of his thirty years surprised me, the silvery color that Paolo Giovio mentions, the coldness of his blue eyes, the hereditary chin, which like the nose of the Bourbons and the hemophilia of the House of Hesse is a certificate of royal authenticity for monarchs. In my case, my hump was unique; I shared it only with Carlotto Fausto. If all the Orsinis had had one, it would have upset me not to have possessed it. Because of a headache, when he left Barcelona the emperor had cut his hair, which had been worn long in Spain until then, and it was as if the Middle Ages ended with that decision. Spanish noblemen imitated him, for it was not without reason that Shakespeare noted that great men do not follow fashions but initiate them. It was said at that time that some of them had wept as they cut off their long locks, but it is difficult for me to believe. They must have been the vassals from Flanders and Germany, countries so faithful to that custom, from then on a habit of blind obedience, that even today they lead the way with their military haircuts. We kissed the imperial right hand, and then it rose up to the Golden Fleece, taking leave of us with a frugal gesture. Other princes were treading on our heels to repeat the ritual.

"He's conceited," I confided to Maerbale as we left, "or timid."

Perhaps the master of the world had both weaknesses. I was close to him again the following day, when he knighted me.

That night—we were acting ahead of our time in Bologna, like tourists who try to take advantage of every minute of their time and who, after covering the gallery of historical portraits, do not wish to miss either the famous cabaret or the red-light district—Maerbale went to a whorehouse with Silvio. They proposed that I accompany them but I did not give in. It irritated me that they had arranged the adventure without telling me; I was also irritated by the friendship, the complicity that was implied in that decision. If my brother had won the affections of Silvio da Narni, he was despoiling me of the only thing that I possessed authentically, on my own merits, because everything else—the castle, the vast estates—was the product of chronological chance... although no, it was always the product of an episode that happened in the Tiber, of the thrashing arms of a drowning boy, of my grandmother's silence; nothing of mine, if one looks closely, was the fruit of chance; I had conquered everything with difficulty. But Silvio meant something special in my life. For myself, for myself alone, I wanted that thin, toothless, and fearful person. I thought of forbidding them to go, but I realized that it would diminish my authority instead of affirming it, and it would probably strengthen their alliance. The wet-blanket type is the worst kind of enemy; and if the wet blanket is a hunchback who bosses people around, he is intolerable. I bit my lips and, trying to console myself without managing it, I said to myself that by staying in our residence I was marking the distance that separated the prince from the second son and the page, for it was not proper for the Duke of Bomarzo to go among prostitutes: that was for those of less responsibility and importance. I lay down on the bed, I opened Fracastoro's poem, and even if I did not admit it to myself, I waited for their return. Jealousy, the worst kind of jealousy, the kind that is not based on love but on other feelings, sadder and darker, was gnawing at me. I was unable to become involved in the reading of the Latin poem that was so unexpectedly dedicated to the person who was to be Cardinal Bembo. The long and complicated story of the shepherd Syphilus, attacked by the venereal disease because he had raped Diana, and of the carrying of the disease from America to Europe by the profaning sailors left me unmoved. For me syphilis did not consist of the discourses of nymphs or the prophecies of a wounded bird or the refined stupidities of a shepherd, but the horrendous lesions that I had seen on the faces of Spanish and Italian soldiers and which the women of our people transmitted with such mortal determination.

Silvio returned very late, when my nerves could no longer stand any more and I was getting ready to go out looking for them, repeating to myself, so as not to face directly the reasons for my upset, that something bad might have happened to them. I received him harshly, but my violent reaction left me when I saw that he was bandaged and that a bloodstain was on the cloth that covered his cheek. He told me about their singular adventure.

In the house of the women, he had run into Porzia, the daughter of Messer Manuzio Martelli, my former administrator. She and her brother Giambattista—our victims in the tomb at Piamiano—had fled from their father's custody a short time before reaching Florence, where Messer Manuzio had proposed to reveal the crime to Gian Corrado Orsini and demand vengeance. The twins wandered from town to town, hiding in barns, living off the charity of the peasants. Finally there was no other way out but to use Porzia's body in order to keep themselves alive, and in that way they became expert in the carnal business at an age when they should have been studying grammar. They reached Bologna that way, made greedy by the news of the great crowd of people that would be there for the occasion of the coronation festivities, which would help their poor business. The girl's beauty and youth attracted the attention of an evil old scheming woman who went about the market places arranging rhythmical interviews between restless people of opposite sexes, and for that reason the child ended up in the house of harlots, soon becoming its main attraction. Maerbale, who, as will be remembered, had not participated in the rape in the underground tomb, had been fascinated by Porzia and her innocent charm, which she had not lost in spite of her following a profession in which innocence usually becomes discolored and soon disappears. They were, therefore, engaging in some agreeable hand exercises when Giambattista, presumably short of funds, appeared in the brothel. The difficulties of life had hardened him in a short time. No one would have recognized in him the youth whose delicate features were confused with those of his twin sister and whom we had used and abused with such wild success. Now he was every inch a man and perhaps a man to be wary of. He was carrying a clanging long sword and had two older companions with him who had scars on their faces and blasphemies on the tips of their tongues, and no sooner did he see Maerbale and Silvio, forgetting that the first had been his father's ally after the outrage, than he unsheathed his naked steel, something that his lieutenants also did, and attacked the guests, who also could not have been more naked. In the flashing of the waving blades, Giambattista was leaping like a gazelle and shining like a god. My brother and my page defended themselves weakly with some stools, aided by another boy who, to his misfortune, had been sharing in their erotic games. Porzia and the other harlots shrieked as if they were being murdered; the guard appeared; Maerbale identified himself, the same as his chance partner, who turned out to be a Farnese; and the three ruffians—as well as the innocent "sweethearts"—were on their way to jail for having attacked gentlemen of such substance. Then Farnese, Fabio Farnese, well aware of the bonds that joined Orsinis and Farneses, proposed to Maerbale that they go to the palace where he was staying to get rid of that bitter taste by replacing it with the taste of a good wine. At the palace they lighted the lights, the servants were aroused, and the boy's sisters appeared, all excited: Giulia, Jolanda, and Battistina, under the command of their father, the magnificent Galeazzo Farnese. What was Maerbale's surprise when he saw that Giulia was the very same angelical girl whose beauty had bewitched him from the balcony of the flowers when we were on our way to the royal visit! They told them something about a confused scuffle with some of Antonio de Leiva's drunken lansquenets— fights like that happened over any pretext—and they were immediately washed, bandaged, and served, Silvio da Narni the same as the others. There was wine and music; it all ended with a party. Galeazzo Farnese liked to laugh, and he certainly must have guessed the true cause of the disorder, but that only intensified his enthusiasm of a man now retired from sensual contests who lived off anecdotes and reflections. With good-hearted vanity he explained to Maerbale that he was a first cousin to Pier Luigi Farnese as the son of Bartolommeo, the lord of Montalto, and the brother of Giulia the Beautiful, the wife of Orso Orsini, the one of the memorable matrimonial misadventure. The last item was not mentioned, of course. While the gentlemen were conversing, the girls circulated about with pitchers of warm wine and sweets. The surprise made their eyes large (I thought about the eyes of Adriana dalla Roza). Giulia played the lute; Battistina sang; Jolanda danced. Later they spoke about artists; they showed a cameo that Benvenuto Cellini had carved for them; they mentioned the visits of Titian, the painter whom Charles V had assigned to paint his portrait. And Maerbale said that he would come back.

That news, as it came gushing out of the page, made me especially angry. Added to the betrayal implied in Maerbale's going out with Silvio was this other one of having beaten me in meeting the young girl on the balcony. Not for one instant did I stop to measure the enormous harm that I had done to Porzia and the pit into which I had cast her. Other matters were bothering me: Maerbale's independence, his influence over Silvio, his new friendship with the Farneses. The Farneses, after all! The Farneses! The family in whose bosom, through my grandmother's recommendation and through my own intuition, it was best for me to seek the one who would be Duchess of Bomarzo. I threw off the covers and I stood in front of Silvio, and just when I thought that I was going to give him a splendid dressing down, showing him, in spite of his position as a controller of devils, who was master and point out to him the risks in opposing the whims of my authority, I found that I could not control myself after the long, angry wait, and the emotions brought on by the tale had exhausted my reserves of energy, and so, instead of the scene of lordly spite that I had planned, I offered him a different one, quite the opposite, of babbling hysteria, more proper in a woman blinded by insane jealousy than in an offended prince. The tears and sobs prevented me from speaking. Silvio was looking at me, somewhere between stupefied and smiling. Then his muscles relaxed, he took a step toward me, bent his sharp backbone and kissed my right hand. He had understood exactly what was going on with me.

"Your Lordship is right," he said to me. "You're right," he added in a more familiar way. "Please forgive me. Come to sleep now. Tomorrow we'll clear all of these matters up."

I obeyed him like a child. He undressed me and stroked my forehead.

"I heard you when you spoke about Giulia Farnese with Maerbale. If you want her, she'll be yours."

"I have to get married, Silvio, and that frightens me. Everything frightens me. I have to get married for the sake of Bomarzo."

"You'll get married, Duke."

He blew out the candle and we went to sleep. On the following day, very early, I awoke overcome with a feverish urge and with the restlessness to pick up again, with the help of Silvio, the lost reins. It was necessary to do something quickly. I sent my page—whom from that time precisely I began to call "secretary," to the indignation of Messer Pandolfo, who had dreamed of that position—to Pier Luigi Farnese's house to ask him to take me that afternoon to pay my respects to his cousin Galeazzo. Pier Luigi could doubtless smell what I was after, calculating that it would further his own interests, and he agreed so long as Sigismondo Orsini went with us. I arranged it that way and Sigismondo came at my summons. I do not know who was more startled by that preference, he or I, because for me the three indigent Orsinis from the Bomarzo region, Girolamo's turbulent favorites, were so much alike among themselves that I often mixed them up, which, if at times I made a mistake with their names to humiliate them, at other times I also did without meaning to. Perhaps Sigismondo, the youngest of the trio, was also the most handsome, with his falcon's face, his piercing dark eyes, his svelte slimness and that anxiety that constantly emerged from him like a trembling or a tension that was almost invisible.

It was only necessary to pass through the sumptuous salons of the palace that this branch of the family was using during their short stay in Bologna to arrive in the one where the inhabitants had gathered to entertain their visitors in order to appreciate the favor that the Farneses enjoyed at the papal court, thanks to the influence that the dean of the Sacred College, Cardinal Alessandro Farnese, had with Clement VII. At a time when most of the guests in crowded Bologna were uncomfortably packed into the masses of unhospitable and crowded houses, these Farneses, who did not even belong to the main line, were living there with the same ease as if they were on their estate in Canino. Through those rooms, where squires alternated with lackeys, and where over the yawning whippets, lying dreaming with their legs shamelessly widespread, specially brought tapestries covered the damp walls with allegorical scenes of nudity dominated by the family's blue lilies on gold, I went along, swaying my hump, between Pier Luigi and Sigismondo. I had put on an orange waistcoat and the tabard with an enormous ermine collar fell over my hump. I was repeating to myself that there was no reason to be nervous and yet I was. Taking off my gloves and putting them on again; stopping to praise this or that canvas with scenes from the Trojan War; stopping to stroke the back of some dog who, so bored and indolent, did not even growl at me, contenting himself with fastening his glassy eyes of a stuffed animal on me; and pretending not to see—although I saw it quite well, and although it should not have bothered me because it was so obvious, it did—that Pier Luigi had boldly put his arm around the waist of my Orsini cousin, I arrived at the room where Galeazzo was entertaining several people, more than I had hoped to find there.

In the center of the immense room, heavy, communicative, triumphant, waving the great head that was framed by a pair of Buddha ears, Galeazzo was conversing with two cardinals: his uncle Alessandro and my friend Ippolito de' Medici, one a sexagenarian, the other a youth of nineteen. Galeazzo was exuding joviality. He was one of those tremendously vital individuals who with their simple presence invite the world to enjoy itself. He had the look of a Fleming. His extreme euphoria made people seek him out, even for reasons of health, for in that age before vitamins he worked as a stimulant. His great fortune also worked. He was speaking with opulent verbosity, and the prelates were following what he was saying. Alessandro, concealing a half-smile, folded over himself like a cat, would reply from time to time with a monosyllable; Ippolito, moving restlessly, was tapping his fingers on the arms of his chair. Both wore the same purple, but anyone would have taken them for a prince of the Church and his young acolyte.

Pier Luigi brought us over to them and made the introductions. I kissed the two outstretched hands, the one wrinkled, the other smooth, well cared for. Ippolito drew me to him and embraced me, as was his custom. I noticed the wise look which the future pope gave his oldest son from under the hood of his eyelids. Alessandro knew all about his offspring. He immediately saw what Sigismondo's being next to him meant, and he raised the lax and disdainful brow of a man who had been a tenacious woman chaser, whose withdrawal from sensual skirmishes out of respect for his investiture did not deprive him of feeling retrospective agreement and revulsion. Married to Girolama Orsini for more than ten years, Pier Luigi was the father of five offshoots, the last of which had been born in that same year of 1530, because his deviations in other directions did not prevent him from fulfilling a marital duty that was imposed mainly by his great respect for the Orsinis. A long line of kings would sprout from his impure blood. His bastardy—his mother was an aristocrat who finally married a Roman baron—had been legitimized by Julius II. It was my fate to go through life surrounded by illegitimate people. It was really unfair that some of my famous contemporaries—like Leonardo and Paracelsus—should have suffered because of their state as natural children when there were so many (and these memoirs abound in examples of them) whom their status as the products of an uncontracted love seemed to serve as a goad on the path to honors. It was simply that even to be a bastard one had to have good luck, and it was one thing to be one of the pope's and another that of a notary from Vinci.

Galeazzo Farnese received me magnificently. Imprisoned in his arms, as between those of my splendid protective bears, as my host mumbled remembrances of his heroic friendship with the Orsini condottieri and especially with my father, I spotted in the background the group made up of Maerbale and the three Farnese girls. Maerbale had not lost any time. I was more irritated than ever then, for Giulia's beauty was such that she glowed. On the right arm of Galeazzo as he guided me through a strange dance step executed by a giant and a little hunchback, I went over to greet them.

"My Lord Duke of Bomarzo," the titan announced, and ancestral walls grew up in the room, pushing back the ornate ones there with their solemn statues, and their stony tutelage gave me courage.

But what help could I expect from Bomarzo against Maerbale's grace, since he also shared that help? My brother was very much like me; he had my same dark eyes, my cheekbones, my mouth, my tapering fingers; what he did not have was the bulk that loomed on my back and one leg shorter than the other. I pretended not to see him—something impossible—and I did not even return his nod, while the girls, one by one, obediently, brushed their fresh lips against mine. Sigismondo soon joined us, fleeing from Pier Luigi. I think that only then had my cousin grasped the captain's intentions, for it had never occurred to him that he could arouse such feelings in a bearded and scarred person who was famous for his rigorous inflexibility at the head of military formations.

Our entrance had interrupted the conversation that soon started up again. They had been chatting, as all over Bologna, about the ceremonies of the following day. The question of precedence was heating up ambitions, and if Duke Alessandro de' Medici had tried to make his father use his influence to have him assigned the same arbitrary category that had been given him during the iron coronation, Pier Luigi was insisting to his—whose duty it was to anoint the emperor's right shoulder with holy oil—for him to modify the ceremony and get him a more outstanding position.

"What's the advantage, then," he asked as his sire flashed his eyes at him, "of being a cardinal's son?"

"There are many advantages," the prelate replied, "among them that of being able to stand here speaking nonsense."

I thought that the argument would go on, but Alessandro linked his fingers and buried himself in his habit as if it were the shell of some red mollusk. I discovered later on that he was afraid of Pier Luigi, who was capable of atrocious acts. It occurred to me that since those two spurious sons of high ecclesiastical figures were asserting themselves in such circumstances in order to obtain decorative eminence, the symbol of their position in the world, I could also use my status as the grandson of a cardinal to obtain it, but I suddenly felt a great fatigue and indifference and I forgot about the matter. In any case, the protocol had been examined and debated for months and it was useless to attempt to change it.

Getting away from his challenger—who perhaps was doing it to make an impression in front of Sigismondo—Cardinal Farnese told how the day before Charles V had recognized a daughter he had had in Flanders by a lady from Perugia and who was being cared for by nuns at the convent of San Lorenzo di Collazone near that city. Her name was Taddea and she was about eight years old. He went into great detail, as if the fact that the emperor had a contraband child would be enough to justify his own and that of the pope himself. The theme was sticky and after having opened it with such rhetorical vehemence, the cardinal let it drop.

"It seems that something that has many people worried," he went on to say, "is the scaffolding over which the pope, the emperor, and their processions will go to Saint Petronius's. It's been tested twenty times, but some people still have doubts about its strength. It must be quite heavy and the emperor, when he heard what people were saying, sent his engineers to examine it, and he said that we're in the hands of God. I hope," he concluded, crossing himself, "that if the beams weaken, God will keep this old servant of his in mind."

While he was speaking I did not take my eyes off Giulia, but she avoided mine, involved in a conversation with Maerbale. The conversation changed its course again and Alessandro and Ippolito, both collectors, were interested in my incipient collections. They had heard about the Etruscan armor at Bomarzo and they wanted to know more details about it. Then Ippolito asked me for Benvenuto's ring so that he could show it to Galeazzo, and they brought out Cellini's cameo. We were examining it—and I was burning with the desire to leave the central group and go to where the young people were, in the midst of whom the brutal laughter of Pier Luigi was exploding—when a man entered who was more than fifty years of age, with a noble profile and a white beard, hiding his baldness under a black silk skullcap. He made a low bow and when he greeted me he called me, exaggerating the title, "Your Most Illustrious Lordship." He was Messer Tiziano Vecelli, from Pieve di Cadore.

The cardinals asked him about His Majesty's portrait, which he was painting at the suggestion of Ippolito, who had recommended him to the Caesar. They wanted to find out how he was picturing him, something that he had kept secret until then, and the artist, with a touch of a Venetian accent, smiled, not daring to deny such eminent questioners, and he described the noble figure, the blond marten tabard, the yellow satin, the diamond brooch on his hat, the amber-colored gloves, the curious detail of the fly swatter, the hand that was petting Sampere, his mastiff. He was as specific as if he were actually painting, lingering over the play of colors, the chiaroscuros, molding the air with his fingers, and it was common knowledge that he painted not only with his brushes but also by rubbing with his exquisite finger tips, alternating the relief of the heavy touches with a light, transparent delicacy that his hand created like that of a wizard.

"I would have liked to have painted him on horseback, wearing his armor, with a river and trees and clouds in the background. Someday I will."

The group broke up, distracted, and I remained to chat with the master. We recalled Ariosto, my idol, whom Titian had known at the court of Alfonso d'Este, the Duke of Ferrara, after the death of Lucrezia Borgia and the duke's marriage to the commoner Laura Dianti. The poet had confided to the painter the fate reserved for many of his characters while he was writing the *Orlando*, and later on, when I admired the works of the man from Cadore, I deduced that although he had not confessed it, jealous as he was of everything that had to do with the originality of his painting, Titian had been inspired more than once by Ariosto's heroes as he organized his spiritual and voluptuous world. But at that moment and as I listened with a reverence that did not exclude the lordly accent that my grandmother had taught me to use in my relationships with people of palette and pen, my nervousness would not let me enjoy with esthetic fullness what he was telling me, because my eyes, betraying me, were fleeing toward the window where Maerbale and Giulia had withdrawn. It was with another Giulia Farnese, with an incredible lack of tact, that Cardinal Alessandro detained me then as he referred to our relationship through his sister, Giulia the Beautiful, married to Orsino Orsini, the magnificent cuckold of our family. I was burning as I heard him praise her beauty and her innocence. I knew too well what the cardinal owed that sister of his in his greedy rise toward the keys of Saint Peter, but among us, those of Bomarzo, placed in that contradictory position and having a susceptibility that had been sharpened by mocking allusions, she was never mentioned. I thought that he was mocking me and I stared at him, finding in reply the bland look of an old prelate who was evoking the glory of his line, which did not fool me.

I finally managed to get away, and taking advantage of the fact that Giulia was between Pier Luigi and Sigismondo, I went over, blushing and timid, a courting so clumsy and absurd—moved more by my brother's rivalry than by direct interest—that I saw at once the shadows of irony, surprise, and displeasure come over her face that had no makeup on. Maerbale returned with a drink for the young lady, and my animosity surged out as I observed his grace. Out of pure evil, without stopping to reflect, I did something insane: I pushed his arm and the liquid spilled over the girl's pale blue dress. Before they could react, because it was obviously my fault alone, I spun toward Maerbale and dressed him down for his carelessness. My cheeks were burning, and Giulia stepped back, startled.

"A person who doesn't know how to behave among ladies and only knows the company of whores," I shouted, "should not appear among ladies!"

I immediately regretted my imbecility and rudeness, but it was too late to retreat. Galeazzo Farnese came over, courteous, conciliatory, the colossal swelling of his belly rocking, reaching out his claws that were covered with huge sapphires and rubies.

"It's nothing! It's nothing, Duke!" he repeated.

Giulia sketched a curtsy and withdrew. Maerbale took refuge in the shadows of the tapestries, merging with them. He did not leave there until we took our leave, and I, miserable wretch that I was, wandering, having lost my footing, only managed to increase the impression of rustic uncouthness that my outburst had caused by beginning to list for Galeazzo the properties that made up my patrimony, without rhyme or reason, with childish pretexts, madly hoping to win his good will with it, as if Galeazzo, Alessandro, and Ippolito had been some Oriental merchants and not three pontifical noblemen, so that—and I realized it very well, because as I was doing it I was suffering and hating myself—more than a member of a family of empresses and conquerors, popes and heroes, I looked like a vulgar parvenu who was laying out his fortune for princes to see, surprised at what he possessed, hoping to dazzle those who were smiling inside, for they—it did not matter to them—did not have to dazzle me in turn, something that they could have done had they wished, since their positions and fortunes were much greater than mine, in spite of the Orsinis and their immemorial magnificence. Four centuries have passed and I have not forgotten a single detail of that first meeting with the Galeazzo Farneses. Even today, when I recall it, a burning wave comes over my face. The memory of our ridiculous acts, of our grotesque blunders is stronger than that of our successes.

Maerbale and I did not exchange a word on the way back to our lodgings. What was heard most was the voice of Sigismondo. He had still not recovered from his surprise over the quick interest that he had aroused in such an important individual as Pier Luigi. So as not to disappoint him, I kept quiet about what I knew about those sudden interests of the military man, often directed to people of the lowest quality. Sigismondo had sized up the situation by telling himself—and repeating it to us—that if he had aroused such reactions it must have been the fact that Pier Luigi had recognized the Orsini in him, the great lord in spite of his lowered condition, but that argument was not worth anything except as a safeguard for his masculinity, for we were all Orsinis. Besides, for all of that and since the authentic reasons were so clear that they could not be disguised, our cousin grew heated over the pretensions of Farnese, who was obviously following more concrete ends which were related to the sixth commandment of the Law of God. I observed that Orso and Matteo, who had come out to wait for us at the palace gate, instead of teasing him about the situation that had arisen, so much the opposite of his masculine beginnings as a follower of Girolamo in numerous orgies with village women, treated the matter naturally, and Matteo even went so far as to argue with him not to be stupid and not dismiss out of prejudice an intimacy that could facilitate his progress in the world. That was what they were like, unscrupulous. So was I. And since we are speaking about it, so was the Renaissance. And I observed that the complicity that had been confessed concerning something that was muddied but productive contributed to breaking the ice that separated them from me (for they knew through Maerbale of my participation in the Giambattista and Porzia affair), and about my reproachable attitude in Galeazzo Farnese's house when I attacked my brother, and instead of weakening my position because of its stupidity, it softened that of Maerbale, who had been arbitrarily insulted by me in public. They had been accustomed since childhood to enlist in the ranks of the strongest, and they understood, by the lights of their narrow criterion, that with my capricious violence I had shown that if I wanted to, I could act, even in front of important people, with the unmotivated despotism worthy of the dukes of Bomarzo. Maerbale sensed those subtle changes and I suspect that he, in a like manner, had the feeling for the first time that I was capable of imposing my whim, and that plunged him into a cautious uneasiness. Separated from his allies by circumstance, he limited himself to remaining silent and showing his wrath with looks that did not dare be too disdainful, because they took in all four of the rest of us.

We reached the house where we were staying; I went to my room and there I found Silvio da Narni, whom I brought up to date on what had happened. The former page and current secretary was involved in a curious task. He had made two dolls out of burlap, crudely dressed with remnants.

"This one," he told me, "is Giulia Farnese; and this one is Porzia. Giulia will belong to you and Porzia will be mine, not only because I like her, but also because her twin brother offended me."

I was afraid that his actions would bring some kind of harm to Galeazzo's daughter and I told him so, but he reassured me immediately.

"Nothing bad will happen; good things will happen. You'll see, my Lord Duke."

"I want to marry her."

"Have no doubts. Amon, Saracil, Sathiel, and Jana, the demons whose realm is near the Moon and who wander along the highway to Rome are my friends."

He went on putting the effigies together, and then he moistened one of them with his saliva; he pricked his arm and let a few drops of blood fall onto the face of the doll that represented Porzia. Then he ran his hand over my mouth and his acid skin made me feel revulsion. He wet the figurine that represented Giulia with my saliva and with my blood, which he obtained by pricking my finger with a needle.

"Here is the blood of a toad," he said, lifting a dark vial. "Toad's blood is infallible. The formula comes from a French wizard from Carcassonne."

He opened the vial and poured its contents over the dolls. A repulsive stench spread through the shadowy room.

"Now we must sacrifice a butterfly, just a butterfly. The idea seems strange, but it produces fine results. And it's so poetical."

He opened a small box and took out a black and white butterfly which was flapping it wings desperately.

"It was hard to find. In Forli, when you were sick, I struck up a relationship with a boy who collects them. He'd found this one in the middle of winter and I bought it from him, thinking it might come in handy. I gave him a good price for it."

"Here's a ducat."

He pierced it with the same needle and took it to the candle, holding it with the minute dagger. It caught fire at once: its body sputtered; the wings were brief flames.

"Amon," Silvio da Narni invoked, "I trust in thee. I released thee from my bottle; now release us. That's all," he ended, addressing me, "except for placing each doll at the door of the corresponding house."

He wrapped the rags in his cape and left. I waited for his return. Images of my life floated for an hour in the atmosphere which, even

## GIULIA FARNESE · 255

though I opened the shutters and let the cold February air come in the window, was not cleansed of its insinuating miasmas. The women who had upset me were sketched upon the walls in a disparate circle: my grandmother Diana, an ageless goddess, a Fate who was weaving the cloth of my existence, for whom nothing was impossible when it had to do with me; Clarice Strozzi, the scourge of usurpers, like a Roman woman of the magnificent centuries, dead before she could realize her haughty dream; Adriana dalla Roza, a frenetic lyric, the generous awakening of childhood, whom I loved with a complete passion perhaps, and which was, in any case, the closest thing to love for a woman that I had known; Pantasilea, the gilded allegory of my humiliation in the courtship of the sin that can be bought; Nencia and her liturgical passion for the Orsinis, who robbed me in a chapel (I mean just that: robbed me) of a quality that I no longer had; the vague village women of Bomarzo on whose docile bodies I tried to imitate the dictatorial acrobatics of my father and Girolamo, proclaiming in that way my rights to a dominion that was based on customs that were proudly lewd and which required the testimony of those bodies which were punished to guarantee the imperious permanence of a very old tradition; Porzia Martelli, the bifurcation of the passionate torrent, or the accepted exaltation of other disturbances, those of a more upsetting shudder, because Giambattista was so inseparable from her, so rooted in her twin flesh that both of them formed one single and two-headed seduction; and lastly, Giulia Farnese, the desire for legitimacy, order, the protection of intact beauty, and also a devouring fervor of jealousy that demanded property that was not shared. The female circle of my eighteen years spun about in the room where a white-black butterfly had burned, a paradoxical homage to the He-Goat, and I, in the midst of those untouchable beauties, was waiting for the toothless page who governed with magical gestures the possibility of extending those spinning objects into a garland of breasts and hips that would be enclosed, vibrating, in the lightless caverns of Time. I felt insignificant and exhausted, while hermetic forces worked about me, as if I were not in the everyday room of a bourgeois house, but in a workshop where inexplicable and silent machinery was working for me—or against me—with obstinate pressure.

When he returned, Silvio informed me that he had not run into any difficulties.

"In front of the palace of King Enzo of Sardinia, Amon appeared to me in a pillar of fire and confided to me that Maerbale had best be careful tomorrow."

"You tell Maerbale to be careful."

"I'll tell him."

I imagined that he would not tell him anything and that, furthermore, he was exaggerating his relationship with the devils in order to increase his prestige with me. That familiarity of the evil agents with a petty page from Narni did not make sense. I still thought that devils, being princes, should deal directly with princes, so deep in my spirit was my concept of hierarchies.

I could no longer sleep, because at dawn, in the main square, crack formations of Spanish and German infantry were falling in with a great deal of noise. They were beginning the preparations for the imperial coronation. I sent for Sigismondo Orsini and dispatched him to Galeazzo Farnese with my ring from Benvenuto Cellini. It was the thing I treasured most, and since Giulia's father had praised it, I had decided to give it to him. I had meditated a long time before resigning myself to giving up my talisman, of that ring of steel and gold which for me was something as important as that topaz had been for Adriana dalla Roza in Florence. My mistake of the previous day was one that called for an important reparation. He returned after a while with the ring and Galeazzo's most affectionate words. No argument—his message said—could justify his accepting my gift, for he understood how much I valued the jewel. On the other hand, he suggested to me that after the ceremonies in Saint Petronius's, perhaps on the following day, I should not fail to visit them. Giulia had asked about me. She had been up very early getting ready for the festivities.

"What did you say, Sigismondo?"

"I'm repeating what he told me: Giulia Farnese asked about you."

For a second the crude shape of Silvio's doll appeared in my memory. I blended Giulia and the burlap doll in a single image. The girl became a puppet with painted violet eyes and a sky-blue skirt on which the stain of the drink that Maerbale had offered her was spread out. Suddenly the figurine was burning, as if to illustrate the Spanish proverb: "Man is fire, woman the tinder; the Devil blows and she turns to cinder." Perhaps that fire had come from the butterfly that had been burned or the flaming pillar of Amon, if that pillar and Amon really existed. Those dangerous reflections were interrupted by the arrival of a page from Pier Luigi Farnese, who was bringing for Sigismondo in the name of his master, a graceful hat of hazel-colored velvet, with a transparent blue plume fastened with a brooch of baroque pearls. Sigismondo tried it on in front of a mirror, delighted in spite of my ironical remarks.

"Do you think I should accept it?"

"I think so. Gifts are flowing this morning, and if Galeazzo should not have kept mine, you, on the other hand, should keep the one from Pier Luigi."

He ran out dancing to show it to his cousins. He no longer had the look of a haughty little falcon that he had had when we reached Bologna, all suppressed violence, but rather a luxurious bird in a courtly cage, a pale blue egret. Even the boy's manners, brusque and aggressive, began to soften and be changed into others, feltlike, cultivated, the product of the subtle metamorphosis that was working in him as a consequence of the constant vigilance that he kept over himself now that he had a new and unexpected awareness of his worth, and which impelled him to exhibit himself under an aspect that he considered more attractive for being so refined, but which in reality was much less than the personality that we had known until then, almost gruff from being so manly. In that way I ascertained how weak had been the psychological armor that he had worn during the time of his friendship with Girolamo and even a few hours before, and how possible it is for very young men, by reason of an influence that opens up unknown perspectives, to be so quickly changed, adapting themselves to situations that they had formerly ignored or despised, and the seeds of which were present, ready to germinate, even though they themselves did not know it in the most secret depths of their beings.

I slipped the ring onto my little finger and went to dress for the ceremony. Silvio, gravely, without commenting on Giulia's reaction, about which I had told him, adjusted the furs on my back and helped me put on the red cape and the ducal hat with the half crown. I would have liked for my father to have seen me like that, majestic, like an ancient monarch, but, of course, that was nothing but a fantasy, for in such a case the one who would have been wearing the cape would have been he. And as at other times, Gian Corrado Orsini's face appeared to me for the fraction of a second, hazy, and then it vanished without my being able to bring it back out of its mysterious oblivion.

That February 24, 1530, may have been one of the greatest days in the history of Bologna, and although it was from the point of view of the official chronicles, it was not completely so for those of us who lived through it and especially for those of us who were not taken in by all the pomp. There was lacking, as I have said, an ingredient that is irreplaceable: the warmth of the people. And also, perhaps because of difficulties that would have been surmounted in Rome, one noted beneath the bloat of pomp a certain municipal tawdriness in the materials, a certain precarious look of a stage set that would be taken down the night after the spectacle with a tearing of paper and a crumpling of cardboard. But they made use of everything they could so that the coronation of His Caesarian Majesty could rely on, for the sake of his infinite distant subjects in a satisfactory and even dazzling way, many high-sounding names, a large amount of fine clothing, and rich ceremonies whose ritual archaism would proclaim over the face of the earth the hereditary continuity of the divine right that governed the succession.

When I left with my companions, I went to the papal and imperial palace in accordance with what had been arranged. Converging there at the same time was a multitude of prelates, princes, and gentlemen from all nations, richly dressed. The fantastic costumes suggested a certain madness, even if it showed signs of channeling the anarchic furor of the previous century. Stockings and breeches, imposing pantaloons, slit and cushioned sleeves, tippets, lace, hatbands, hooded cloaks, sable wraps, belts, boastful codpieces, extravagant cuirasses, fabulous hats, and a forest of mixed feathers transformed men into mythical animals, gorgons and griffins, and into those monsters that

GIULIA FARNESE · 259

cartographers created to decorate the deserts of Asia and Africa. If it had been difficult to move through the crowds during the past few days, the difficulty had reached the impossible on the morning of that Saint Matthias's day when the emperor reached the age of thirty. The color was delirious in the broad expanse of the square, with soldiers of Bologna in blue, yellow, and white velvet; the cardinals' servants in purple and black; brocade overcapes and coattails with embroidered shields; satins, damasks, gold and silver, plumes, trappings, the waving standards with Charles's eagle and the red cross of the League; crossbows, lances garlanded with flowers, fifes, drums with straps; the emblems hanging from the windows clogged with spectators. The noise was deafening. The trumpets and the drums were never silent in that Last Judgment that would have delighted Hieronymus Bosch as it boiled with halberdiers, harquebusiers, pikemen, archers, crossbowmen, chamberlains, stablemen, students, monks, and ordinary people too, crushed together wherever there was room, and when they could not find room they would rain blows on others who replied with foul words. Luckily it was not hot. At one corner of the square they were roasting a whole ox stuffed with kids, pigs, rabbits, and birds; and medieval gluttony and an even more ancient glutton dating from the time of the insatiable Caesars added to the merriment with its bestial prestige, incarnate in the huge bovine that was turning over the glow of the coals, and near whose stuffed hulk there was a steady flow of two streams of white wine from the open mouths of two lions on a wall, while another stream of red wine came from the breast of a stone eagle, and from the palace roof they threw cakes, fruit, bread, pastries, and nuts to the avid crowd, and pieces of the plates also fell in the haste. Yes, everything possible was being done so that the clamor would be extreme, with no thought of expense. As we advanced with the risk that I would lose my crown on the morning that Charles V would put his on, we could see the real hero of the festival in the same square, the gigantic Antonio de Leiva, who had come from waging war on the Venetians and lived only for more war, in spite of the gout that made him limp and kept his hands and feet wrapped in bandages of pain. His soldiers had brought him on their shoulders, and up there, aloft, twisted with suffering, the great captain was contemplating, above a background of flags, the crush of the multicolored processions that were struggling to reach the palace walls. We were one of those thousand different groups. With mine I finally reached the goal, my half crown askew and my furs almost dragging, perspiring in spite of the temperature. We separated at the door, for my brother and cousins were to go ahead of me to the places that had been assigned to us in Saint Petronius's.

There were as many people inside the palace as out, except that those inside were of higher quality. Nobles and churchmen were going up and down stairs, rushing across the *cortile* without greeting one another, barely readjusting their clothing, wishing for needles, combs, a bath, inquiring right and left what they had to do, where they were to go, stepping aside because they thought that the one coming down the stairs was the emperor himself, when actually it was the Marquis of Aguilar or the Commander of Calatrava or the Duke of Nassau, all aglow; or Galeazzo Farnese, whose triumphal belly was bouncing, with his son Fabio; or Pier Luigi, who winked at me; or the Duke of Bavaria, who was bellowing in German or in a very doubtful Latin. Finally the pope emerged, dressed in his pontifical vestments, followed by fifty-three bishops and archbishops and cardinals and magistrates of Rome and Bologna, with a glitter of croziers and miters. The march to the church began along the famous high boardwalk. Clement VII went in his gestatorial chair, rocking as if it were a ship on a sea of heads, plumes, and ivy leaves woven about the shields on the scaffolding. My grandfather leaned on the railing, overwhelmed by his cape. Cardinal de' Medici was supporting him. They were blessing right and left, as if their red gloves were cutting the air that gleamed with precious stones. The scaffolding creaked, and the Sacred College continued its procession in the midst of an unexpected chorus. My grandfather blew his nose; the linen shone in his hands. Underneath, the anthill was applauding weakly and some, whom the soldiery could not locate, were making rude noises or shouting comical remarks.

As soon as the pope stopped at the main altar, the cardinals of Ancona and Sancti-Quatro returned to fetch the monarch, and the emperor appeared, preceded by the bearers of the insignia. The Duke of Bavaria was carrying the globe of the world. Behind came Alessandro

GIULIA FARNESE · 261

de' Medici, feigning a displeased calm, but dark as he was, his redness could be seen. Charles of Hapsburg passed, the iron crown on his head, dressed in the clothes that Titian was painting. The Marquis of Cenete, with the tips of two fingers, was holding the edge of his cloak. They went onto the bridge—creak, creak, creak—and the anthill applauded without enthusiasm. The paleness of the emperor was such that one felt that Europe was growing pale, and as if over distant America, its mountain ranges, its forests, its plains, and its rivers, a broad pallor was spreading out, an ashen rain that the golden gods watched in astonishment. Some noblemen—among them Galeazzo Farnese, who was snorting like a wild boar—began to run across the square in an undignified way to take their places in the church. Flanked by four guards of my retinue, I was among those rapid princes, holding up the skirts of my cloak like a woman or a monk and using my other hand to secure the crown on my hat. We opened a path with shoves. We were shouting, "I am Galeazzo Farnese! I am the Duke of Bomarzo! I am Pier Francesco Orsini!" and the last identification had some effect.

In that way I emerged right at the place that had been saved for me by Maerbale and the others and from which one saw very little of what was happening on the main altar, because there was a column in the way. Charles had already sworn to Cardinal Salviati to defend the Catholic Church. Now they were taking off his imperial clothing to dress him in the cape and rochet of a canon of Saint Mary of the Three Towers in Rome, as had been the custom among past emperors. That took place in a special chapel on the right. Then the sovereign went into the church, where he was received by my grandfather and another very old cardinal. His cape must have been as heavy as if it were lined with lead, like those of the hypocrites described by Dante, and it was supposed to be that my grandfather and his companion, both trembling in their dotage, were there to help carry the tremendous burden, although I do not know who was helping whom as the three walked along the bridge, overwhelmed, for it was most likely that the young man, even though emperor, at that moment added to the fatigue of his tiring garments by dragging along two old men who were clutching the enormous piece of sparkling brocade. They paraded along very slowly above our heads—creak, creak, creak—like three colossal snails.

In the remote setting of candles and incense I was able to make out the pope kneeling in prayer. From time to time he would remove and replace his glasses to read the texts, and then, to the glow of the altar and those who were officiating, there was added a brief flash of lightning, something like the flight of a luminous insect about the pontiff. There was a clap of thunder and the platform gave way, a part of it dropping on us.

I was saved by the column that had annoyed me so much... and the promise of my horoscope. Among cries, several guards plunged into the space, pulling back pieces of beams. Matteo, Orso, and Sigismondo, through a miracle, emerged unharmed. A Flemish gentleman had been killed and there were people who had been bruised and injured. Maerbale had been hit by the fragments of a cornice that knocked him down all bathed in blood. The demon Amon had recommended that he look out for himself with good reason. While my cousins helped him and Sigismondo used his sleeve to clean the wrinkled hat that was a gift from Pier Luigi, I saw above in a cloud of dust, as if they were already floating in the celestial atmosphere, the emperor and the two cardinals. Charles V, impassive, turned his grave head to examine the damage. His long jaw was moving as if in prayer. He touched my grandfather's shoulder, reassuring him, and adjusted his dalmatic, and the procession continued. Matteo told me that Maerbale had broken his leg, and I ordered him and Messer Pandolfo to take him to the house of the doctor where we were staying. It would be difficult to find the physician in the tumult, but that seemed the best thing to do. They left grumbling, especially Pandolfo, who had planned to describe the ceremony in Latin hexameters.

They carried off the victims and cleared and swept away the debris, which allowed me to move a few feet into the nave, and it was calm again. Someone predicted that the disaster, which could have been much more serious, meant that no other emperor would be crowned, for the Hapsburg, after passing through, had cut off the path for those who were behind. The rites continued unfolding: the placing of a new maniple and the vestments of a deacon, the anointing of his shoulder by Cardinal Farnese, the kisses of Clement and Charles, the presentation of the insignia. The ambassador of Venice brought the wash jug and the priests sang the epistle in Latin and Greek.

Several people had moved forward, cutting me off completely from a view of the spectacle, for since I was short, no matter how much I stretched, I could only make out a black curtain of heads. That threw fuel onto the irritated fire that I had been feeding ever since I became aware of the modest position that had been given me in the procession. With whom did those whoresons think they were dealing? Was my hump reason enough—because, as always, underneath it all I attributed the insult to it—for them to forget the services rendered by my family over the centuries to the cause of the Church? Was it because of my Guelph tradition? Could the distribution of places have been in charge of the emperor's Ghibelline secretaries? Yet I had noticed lords who belonged to the most inner papal circle, friends of my father, in the front rows. What, then, of the Orsini popes: Stephen, Celestine, Paul, Nicholas, and the saints, and the martyrs, and the empresses, and the Queen of Naples, and the thirty Orsini cardinals, ending with my own grandfather, who had been awarded such a principal role in the ceremonies that his grandson could not even see him? Was I not the Duke of Bomarzo, was I not, with or without my hump, the Duke of Bomarzo?

I declared in a voice sufficiently loud for people around me to hear (for the sting of the offense had not erased my sense of prudence and it would not have been good for me to cross swords openly with the monarch who was to knight me a few hours later and on whom my fate depended in part) that I was worried about my brother's fracture, and I left the church of Saint Petronius, which, since it bore the name of a Roman writer who was a dandy—in addition to that of a venerable bishop of Bologna—was singularly close to my feeling of an aristocratic poet steeped in rhetorical snobbery. I left by the principal nave, erect, slowly, as if I had just been crowned, escorted by Orso and Sigismondo. There was still a good deal of time left in the ceremonies. One does not become emperor in a simple way. At that moment the pope was handing the unsheathed dagger to Charles V, chanting in Latin, "Receive the knife, the holy gift of God, with which thou shalt conquer and smite the enemies of the God of Israel." The God of Israel! The

Jews were always involved in those rites. I clutched Benvenuto Cellini's ring and held my other thin hand on the gold chain that crossed my chest. I was a Roman, like Petronius.

The crowd was waiting in the square for the emperor's return. It was known that, according to custom, he would toss them some newly minted coins, and the poor people were heating up in the sun that was decorating the palaces and which, like an incomparable miniaturist, was detailing the exquisite gradation of colors that extended from the somber tonalities of the walls, foreshortened in broad planes, to the tiny details lost in the polychromatic labyrinth of arms and clothing. Some hungry people were stalking about the ox that was turning impressively, perforated by a spit as huge as the lance of Briareus, and others had begun to eat what was being thrown to them from the windows, or were buying food from the ambulant vendors who were circulating and hawking their wares of pastries, cheeses, and hams. In an arcade a jester with a tin crown was mimicking the rites that were taking place in Saint Petronius's. Students were laughing at him until some soldiers broke up the group. They brought me my horse and I began to cross the square slowly. Orso was leading him by the bridle. Some vagabonds, when they saw my half crown, ran over to beg, showing me the pustules from the poem by Girolamo Fracastoro. I had resolved to post myself in a good corner to watch the procession in comfort without the participants' noticing me, when, amid the insistent shouting I distinguished a brief bark which I seemed to recognize, although I could not locate it—a sharp, short bark, willful, from some small animal accustomed to having its way. I searched with my eyes from the trappings of my high position looking among legs and feet, and Orso caught and picked up with both hands, showing him to me, the one who had been making those impertinent sounds, I immediately recognized what that white, curly, and angry bundle was: it was Pantasilea's little Maltese dog. A rose fell at my feet, as when I had been fleeing from Florence, and the thought came to me that by some miracle the machinery of Time had gone backward and was projecting past images over again, because thanks to the magic virtue of that flower and that dog, escaped from a picture of the past, the tumultuous crowd that was milling on the right and on the left all across the square, instead of waiting for Charles V to emerge from Saint Petronius's, was waiting for the Medicis to come out, driven from their palace in Florence.

I raised my eyes and, just as four years before, I saw on a covered terrace, with two peacocks walking on the parapet, Pantasilea. She was calling to me with graceful expressions; she was asking me to bring back her favorite Maltese. I took the little yapper in my arms and told my cousins to take my horse and not to worry about me, that we would meet at the house where we were staying, and I went into the harlot's house. Added to the new wrath that had grown in me by having been passed over in the hierarchical order of the coronation was another, older one that stung in my memory at that instant, and which emphasized for me, not the happy aspects of our fleeting contact—the beauty of the courtesan's naked flesh and her unsuccessful play and industry to make the child respond to her professional instigations—but the unfortunate reminiscences of that meeting, which stood out vividly in my offended and vengeful soul: her laughter, her mockery, the macabre joke of the cupboard filled with human debris, the skeletons of toads, horrendous liquids, the amatory tools that sorceresses had obtained for her. She had no doubt forgotten it and it did not bother her. Four years had passed since then and the innumerable men who had taken their turns on her body during that period had certainly managed to erase that futile memory along with many others. Besides, when that had happened I had been a young boy without experience, while in 1530 I was the Duke of Bomarzo, a different person, a different entity, responsible, illustrious, powerful (in spite of the secretaries of Charles V), worthy of any adulation. I soon proved the disparity of the two situations.

She came toward me in the large empty room and put out her arms, which led me to understand that she knew about the deaths of my father and my brother and my accession to the title. She looked even more beautiful, for week after week she had continued learning new tricks in cosmetics. Her red hair, revealing her forehead, fell on both sides of her face in small ringlets held with clear turquoises that framed her oval whiteness, and her green eyes, mirror-like, as in certain insects. She was moving—maneuvering—her harmonious body more gravely, more slowly than before, or at least that was my impression, as if in her walking over the past four years she had discovered the advantages of a languid rhythm to bring out her physical merits. Perhaps that was the cadence that she used with opulent lords and she had already been using it during her Florentine period, but at our first meeting she did not judge me worthy of such a notable display, while now—now that I was eighteen years old and a duke—she was giving me the best of her pantomimic repertory. She kissed me, and the soft pressure of her thick lips brought back painful feelings in my memory. She took the little dog and kissed him with equal enthusiasm; then she clapped her hands and a woman brought wine and some sweets at her command. She suggested that I take off my crown and my cape, and I did so, almost begging her pardon, for, thinking only about the renewed prick of my wrath, I was not giving any thought to the grotesqueness of my figure, to my look of a hunchback disguised as a playing-card king, which contrasted, because of my puppet-like rigidity, with the sinuous relaxation of the harlot, so marvelously vital in her wiles. We sat down on a wide Oriental couch with cushions of the kind that she liked so much, and she poured me some wine from a pitcher.

"We have time," she said to me, "Your Excellency can watch the spectacle from my window. How is it that you're not in Saint Petronius's?"

I lied to her that I had left the church because of the excessive crowd. I would not have confessed the truth to her even if I had been put to torture: that I had left out of irritation over the unjust modesty of my place. I asked her how long she had been in Bologna and she answered a month. She had come directly from Florence. The light in her eyes grew dim as she told me of her difficulties on leaving the besieged city.

"It was impossible to escape. I tried every means that occurred to me until, with great risk and using one of my girls who knew him, I was able to get to talk to a captain of the Prince of Orange. Oh, my Lord Duke! Your Excellency cannot imagine the terrible moments I went through! Those doubts when I tricked the sentries, the quick words, the maneuvers in the shadow of the walls! I finally arranged with him that in exchange for the superb necklace that Your Excellency had given me, no less, and which I discovered later had been a gift from your grandfather the cardinal, the captain would arrange my escape. What made my flight difficult was that for nothing in the world could I get myself to leave my peacocks behind; even if it were only a pair, I wanted to take them with me. The captain laughed, thinking that it was the whim of a crazy woman, and he finally agreed. So very late one night I covered my cheeks with soot; I put on peasant's clothes; I made a bundle of my jewels, which I slipped under my skirt; I put the peacocks into two large wicker baskets that I had had made, tying up their bills so that they wouldn't make any noise; I also put the crystal figure made by Messer Leonardo da Vinci there, and settling on a donkey as best I could, with a basket on either side, I set out, frightened to death, on the worst adventure of my life."

As she went on, I could see hanging from the ceiling the famous polyhedron that was spinning slowly, catching the tremor of the lights on its smooth facets. It was the polyhedron of Divine Proportion of Fra Luca Pacioli, which in the exactness of its relationship summed up the divine musicality, like a symbol of the regulated equilibrium of the Renaissance; and that presence, which should have calmed me down with its rhythmical message, accentuated the bitter animosity that was eating at me, for it helped arouse in my mind remote and hated images of failure and disdain, the anguish of which was with me every time I thought of them.

"The captain," Pantasilea went on without sensing my reactions, "wanted something more than Your Excellency's sapphire necklace to let me escape. He was a brute. I not only had to give myself to him, but also to three of his soldiers before he would let me through the enemy camp. I agreed to everything, as Your Excellency will understand. Hours later, battered, nauseated, having saved my jewels, I don't know how, considering where I had them, I was out of danger. From then on my only ambition was to get to Bologna, where they were going to crown the emperor."

I thought about Porzia Martelli as I listened to her. She too had dreamed of reaching the city that was inviting the women of pleasure of Italy to gather around the richest lords in the world, the women I had seen at the festive windows.

"When they stopped me on the snow-covered roads," the harlot went on to say, "and tried to steal my peacocks, no one wanted to make use of me because my hands, face, and hair had become so coarse. I held the tramps off by warning them that the birds had been bought for the Marchioness of Mantua and that if they stole them she would leave no stone unturned to find the thieves, because a peacock is not an easy thing to hide. They did not imagine that under my skirts I was hiding jewels that were much more valuable—and Your Lordship must not think that I mean my personal charms. That was how I saved my peacocks and my belongings and one afternoon I reached Bologna. I rented this palace; I hired a maid, for circumstances would not permit me more for the moment; I set myself up; I advised Cardinal de' Medici and other friends; and then"—she began to laugh with her admirable singing laugh—"then the news ran through the city and they remembered me, people of importance poured in just as they had in Florence. I'm a practical woman. The only thing I deplore is the loss of my Lord Duke's necklace. My Lord Duke has grown up so well! And what an intense and perfect face he has!"

My lips cut off her last phrase. I threw her down there on top of the pillows; I tore off her dress, which, in spite of the harsh weather, was nevertheless diaphanous and showed the soft and studied grace of her body; I scratched her painted breasts; I possessed her gloriously, covering her mouth so that she would not cry out, wrapping my legs around hers to stop her from using her knees, redeeming myself, cleansing myself of my old timidity and frustration. My hump was riding on top of me, redeeming itself too. The little dog was barking around us, the same as on the past occasion. Being so close to her, I could see the scar that she owed to Benvenuto Cellini, reddened by her struggles, and the delicate web of wrinkles that emerged on both sides of her mouth and led up to her temples, which pointed up the smoothness of her white forehead as with a very light brush-stroke.

"You're getting old, Pantasilea," I murmured.

We remained embraced, blended, panting.

"Why did you do that, Orsini?" she stammered. "I would have given myself willingly."

"You're getting old, Pantasilea; you're full of wrinkles."

She got one hand free and slapped me. "Swine, hunchback, pig!"

The air thundered as if the city had exploded. Cannons and blunderbusses were being fired; trumpets sounded, mad instruments; the bells began to toll in honor of the son of the Fair One and the Mad One, the heir to the world. The pope and the emperor were walking toward the entrance of Saint Petronius's.

"They're coming!" and Pantasilea's eyes were shining with enthusiasm. "Let's go to the window!"

"Empire! Empire! Spain, Spain!" Antonio de Leiva's legionnaires were roaring.

I still held her back with my weight.

"Do you remember when you stood me in front of your cupboard full of filth in Florence?"

"That's not true! I never had any such cupboard, that's not true!"

I covered her mouth again and dragged her through the hallways. She was biting my fingers. In her struggles she was sobbing, "Hunchback! Toad!"

Her eyes were flashing, green, green, green, and I thought that they were two malignant insects and would come flying into the gloomy hallways. I was still not sated, I still wanted my vengeance, with an idea that was so puerile, so worthy of an adolescent, that if I put it down in these pages with shame it is because I have promised myself to be faithful to my memoirs, even in the most stupid things. I finally found what I was looking for, an inside room without windows. She had been anxious to see the imperial procession: perhaps to exhibit herself to her friends between her peacocks at her window; perhaps to call to some of the important people, showing herself between her birds as befitted a harlot of such renown. Well, then, she was not going to do it; they were not going to see Pantasilea and Pantasilea was not going to see anything. There was no trace of her maid; she had probably run away or she might have been at the door. I gave the courtesan a push and I locked her in and went back to the reception room. Pantasilea's pounding and shouting were lost in the noise. I climbed up on a bench, pulled out the magic crystal, and smashed it against the floor. The marble tiles of the floor glittered as if I had thrown a rain of diamonds down on them. Then, half hidden by the curtains, I peeped out the window. The Maltese dog was whimpering beside me, staring at me with his little black eyes, showing his teeth.

The splendor of the triumph was reaching its heights on the esplanade. The pope on a Turkish horse, and the emperor on a white one, richly adorned, the one with his tiara, the other with his crown, were advancing under a canopy that was being held by the flower of nobility. At the head of the march were relatives of the cardinals and the princes, also on horseback; those of the Medicis and those of Charles V, with golden fabrics that showed their colors and shields; the forty councilmen of Bologna and the doctors of the colleges; the gonfalonier of Justice; the standards of the pope, of the emperor, of Rome; the trumpeters, the drummers, the four white palfreys of His Holiness; the College of Consistorial Advocates of Rome; the clerics, the acolytes, the chamberlains; then the Holy Sacrament on a caparisoned mare from whose neck a small bell hung and which was preceded by a subdeacon on a mule with a crystal lantern; twelve knights with wax torches surrounded the body of Our Lord; my peers followed, the princes, dukes, counts, marquises, barons, captains of the immeasurable empire, among pages and lackeys of trim beauty, and they—the princes— handsome too, even the ugly ones, even the old and senile ones, with so many gold chains, so many gold stirrups, so many pearl bridles, so many eagle eyes, so much curly hair, so much martial elegance from Italy, Spain, Germany, France, Flanders, Hungary; and the mace bearers and earl marshals of Charles V, Francis I, Henry VIII, Charles III of Savoy, who kept one because of his pretension to the Kingdom of Jerusalem; and those who were flinging flashing handfuls of ringing coins which stirred up the mob; and the cardinals, two by two, with many grooms; my grandfather, erect as in his days of war, making me happy, making me weep with pride; and the four main bearers of the supreme insignia; and the canopy floating over the pope and the emperor, the latter still very pale, as if his crown were of thorns; and the ambassadors, the prelates who were not cardinals; and lastly, four companies of men at arms. The ephemeral and splendid glory of the world was passing through Bologna, as if a river of glowing metal that was bouncing in the sunlight had overflowed in the city. I spotted Titian sketching in a notebook, rapidly turning the pages; Galeazzo, who was imposing for the majesty of his immense and hardened mound of flesh alone; my cousins, who suddenly looked handsome to me, like bronze idols; Sigismondo's blue plume floating in the breeze, but he was farther ahead, next to Pier Luigi Farnese. They began to slice up the ox, and mouths, anxious, pushing, were wetting themselves at the fountains of wine. One of the peacocks opened his tail and hid part of the square from me. If I had dared, I would have thrown him down into the crowd. In any case, I dismissed the superstition, and letting myself go, I shouted, "Empire! Empire!"

I blushed at my foolishness. I should have shouted for the pope, Guelph that I was. I smiled, put on my hat, looking at myself for a while in the mirror, and went downstairs.

Taking refuge in Pantasilea's *cortile* with some other people was a Hungarian who was leading a bear on a chain. I went too close and the beast growled. Glowing with euphoria from the esthetic spectacle that I had just witnessed and from the cowardly vengeance that I had just obtained, I reached out my hand, touching the rough fur, even though the man warned me to be careful, and I held it there for a few moments, stroking the warm back. The bear stood up on his hind legs, greeting me, and those who were watching applauded. Perhaps the animal had been thoroughly domesticated; perhaps he was nothing but a poor bear who was tame as a lamb; or perhaps he had recognized his brother, the *editus ursae*, the Orsini cub before whom bears in palaces and parks hold up the rose of the family shield.


My grandmother's counsel, Maerbale's fracture, the show of cordiality on the part of Galeazzo Farnese, and the amends that I thought I had made for Pantasilea's disdain, which vindicated other humiliations, incited me to take a step that I would not have dared to under different circumstances, and I was also impelled toward it by the healthy excitement that I was feeling as a result of the theatrical procession—for nothing moved me as much as sumptuous beauty—but which did not succeed in clouding over the arbitrary treatment given by those who organized the protocol to a conspicuous member of one of the two lines—Orsini and Colonna—to which the protectors of the pontifical throne belonged. No sooner had my grandfather returned from Saint Dominic's, where the emperor had knighted several people, than I went to congratulate him for his part in the ceremony, and to suggest to him that he solicit from Galeazzo Farnese the hand of his daughter Giulia for the Duke of Bomarzo.

The cardinal, rejuvenated by the goad of pomp, listened to me in silence, scratched his head, stared at me, and answered, "I will do that if you wish. You are now, by your status, free to choose. But first I want to consult with His Holiness and Cardinal Farnese. For my part, I approve of your plans. I hope that they materialize, now that you show signs of reflection and maturity. The girl is gracious and wealthy and from a stable family that is on the rise. Her great-uncle may be the next pope—or maybe I will, because that question is part of the highest and most secret designs of Divine Providence. In any case, the alliance is a good one, and for you to have your grandfather or your wife's uncle as pope will bring greater glory to Bomarzo. I will go see the Holy Father right now."

That afternoon a page brought me news from him: Franciotto Orsini had worked with a swiftness that proved that under the effects of enthusiasm he was conquering his mental rheumatism. Both the pope and the dean of the cardinals had given their approval, and Galeazzo, if he did not answer definitively, had implied hopes that were almost promises.

The jubilation left me half in a stupor. I felt very much a man, making serious decisions. I wrote to my grandmother, telling her of the dealings that were following the wisdom of her advice, and I decided to send her the letter in her coach along with Maerbale, Messer Pandolfo, Orso, Matteo, and an escort made up of half of my men at arms. I kept Sigismondo with me, for I suspected that he could be useful to me because of his influence with Pier Luigi, the cousin of my lady's father. Maerbale and the Orsinis gave me protests, but they shattered against my inflexibility. I had learned to give out irrevocable orders, and I myself was surprised at it. Besides, my brother's leg in a Splint needed rest and attention at home. That argument, coming to me at just the right time, allowed no discussion, powerful as it was. In that way I got rid of some companions that I did not need and a possibly

## GIULIA FARNESE · 273

dangerous rival. They packed their bags and left, swallowing their rebellion. Messer Pandolfo told me that since, as Virgil tells, imitating Homer and Hesiod in his descriptions of the heroic forge, Vulcan the Ignipotent, at the request of Venus, fashioned for Aeneas a shield on which he engraved the entire history of Italy and the triumphs of Rome, it would be interesting if I suggested to the emperor—whose good will toward me he exaggerated in a flattering way—that he should have forged a shield on which the whole coronation procession would be pictured, for it was impossible to imagine anything more splendid. I listened to him, thinking about other things. He was still talking out of the carriage window when I told the coachman to whip up the horses. They started off in a cloud of dust and aftertastes of the *Aeneid*.

From Silvio da Narni I discovered that the dolls prepared according to the experiments of the Carcassonne sorcerer were beginning to work favorably. I realized that with so much coming and going I had forgotten about the figurines anointed with our saliva and blood. Porzia had set up a meeting with Silvio for that evening, assuring him that she had managed to calm her brother down. If a skinny, toothless, strawhaired individual could win his easy victory so quickly, why could not the Duke of Bomarzo obtain his too? Perhaps my doll was resting on Giulia's heart and transmitting a beneficial restfulness to her.

Few times have I felt as happy as then. I gave one of Girolamo's jewels to Sigismondo, and Silvio a pouch with four gold coins. Then, aided by my cousin and my secretary, I made ready for the ceremony in which Charles V would knight me and which would take place after dinner. I did not really follow the ritual. I should have spent the night before praying in a church, confessing, and receiving communion. I did none of that. I considered myself confessed and absolved, considering as such the brief conversation I had had in Forli with Cardinal Orsini when they thought I had been poisoned, and my mother's father had made the sign of the cross over my forehead and murmured the words of divine pardon; and the Extreme Unction that I had received at that moment, scarcely noticing it, I had felt so ill, I judged sufficient to comply with the demands of the rule. The Sacramental declaration of sins accumulated since then could wait for another occasion. I imagined that I had more than enough reasons for going through the ceremony of knighthood. I *was* a knight, and in things of that nature I dealt directly with God. One who carries four popes and eighteen saints and venerable figures in his blood cannot be treated as just anyone. If I submitted myself to the ceremonial game it was to follow through with custom, as all of my ancestors had, because my lack of prejudices did not lead me to fight against certain essential practices of my world, and because of the fact that the consecration coming from Charles V—a rather exceptional and prestigious happening—would be to my greater credit, not so much among my peers as among the people of Bomarzo and among those whose snobbery was complacently based on details like that. Furthermore, my own snobbery came into it. I was pleased to have Charles V knight the Duke of Bomarzo; it seemed to me that it fitted in perfectly with what was equitable and it would help erase the bad impression of my being passed over in the order of the imperial procession. Fighting against that pleasure was a displeasure: the one imposed on me by another exhibition—and an important one—of my hump before the monarch and his court, and one which brought on the idea that Charles V would touch my deformity as if pointing it out with his sword, for it was ordained by a centuries-old formula. My grandfather would play the role of my sponsor in the ceremony. According to the requisites of the ritual, he should have been keeping the vigil with me all through the night in the church of Saint Dominic—the night I had spent in anxiety, reading the *Syphilis* and listening for Maerbale and Silvio to return from the house of prostitution where they had found Porzia—but I persuaded him that because of his advanced age and weak health he should not do it, as it was better for him to preserve his weak energies for the arduous task he had been assigned in Saint Petronius's and I assured him that my cousins would supplant him. The cardinal had hesitated but he ended up agreeing. He did not put a great deal of importance on the etiquette of knighthood either. As the soldier he had been, he felt that knights were made by war and not by genuflections, and he doubted very much that I would ever wrap a warrior's laurel about the virgin sword that was to be girded on me.

At the end of the afternoon, then, with Sigismondo and six torchbearers, I went to the palace. Silvio had asked my permission not to attend the rite which came at the hour he was to see Porzia, and although I would have preferred to have had him see me in action before the emperor, I did not make him change his plans so that he would not think that I was putting too much stress on the value of the ceremony.

There were, as always, many people at the emperor's residence. Other noblemen like me were to be knighted by the hand of the monarch, and I waited with them in a room adjoining the one in which Charles V was finishing his meal and from which we could see the Caesar, who, sitting alone at the table, was displaying his impressive gluttony as the grandees about him hastened to serve him. Some dignitaries were chatting on one side, among whom were my grandfather, the Bishop of Malta, the Chancellor of Germany, the Cardinal of Ancona, and Alessandro de' Medici, who invariably slipped in wherever the sovereign was. My presence aroused a certain curiosity. Several of my neighbors had had dealings with my father or Girolamo and had heard of me, and they came over pleasantly to chat. I answered them as best I could and I thought that my future life had the possibility of unfolding normally among Giulia and my peers, which was a categorical denial of my sire and his plan to disinherit me in favor of Maerbale because of my lack of "the moral and physical conditions that the succession requires"—his words had been engraved in my memory—but soon I thought I could discern a reserve in the patrician youths, a veiled jeer, a sarcastic complicity that probably was not there, for they were too restless about the gravity of the role they were soon going to play, and the state of grace which their presumptive communion had imposed on them should have prevented any such signs of a proud lack of mercy; and I folded up in myself, sighing.

The emperor washed his fingers and stood up, moving to a chair that had been specially prepared for him. Then a majordomo came to alert us and our trial began. There were nine of us. We went into an adjoining room, where we put on shirts that were more or less alike and small coats of mail. Mine had been specially woven and, although I had tried it on before, I noticed that it pulled on my back, twisting to one side. Over that they placed the ducal cloak that I had worn in Saint Petronius's. Dressed in that fashion—and red with shame, even though I feigned a calm that was far from what I felt—we were led into the emperor's room, which reeked of roast meat. The coat of mail weighed down on me and made my movements clumsy. I pulled at it hysterically and a man with a sad look hastened to help me and fastened it with a cord from his cape. I asked him his name.

"Don Pedro de Mendoza, of the House of Infantado."

Some years later I learned that he had founded a city, Buenos Aires, in the southern extremes of America, and that he had died at sea. On his face and his fingers he had the same pustules that marred the looks of Pier Luigi Farnese, and he had participated in the sack of Rome, but his good manners showed his quality.

My grandfather came over and took my right arm, fulfilling his role as sponsor, and we went forward together. I would be the first and that warmed me with vanity. Cardinal Orsini had seen to it. I made a bow; I knelt before the emperor and waited. My heart was beating, pounding, pounding, and my head was buzzing. I was so near to the master of the world that, mixed in with the remains of the smell of his dinner and of the closed room where the braziers were burning, I could perceive also beyond the aroma of incense that still perfumed him, his smell of a young man, the smell of perspiration that came from his body that was fatigued by the long liturgy and suffocated by the heavy clothing. I was suddenly attacked by a mad desire for him to embrace me (I often felt absurd desires like that), but I stayed on my knees, my eyes lowered, my hands clasped.

The Duke of Urbino presented the sword and when His Majesty raised it, the pommel of the hilt came loose, falling to the floor, losing several pearls. We Orsinis certainly had bad luck. The consequences of the lack of organization of the coronation ceremonies were reflected on us. When the boardwalk collapsed in Saint Petronius's, one of the victims was Maerbale, and in my case—so soon for me, anxious for the act to be over quickly and motionless on the floor, stricken with a desperate timidity—in my case it was ordained that the imperial weapon should break. Some people inferred—prognostications were always deduced from abnormal happenings, especially in Italy—that it meant that the emperor, obliged to be absent so much, would be unable to control his army well for lack of a supreme commander; and others drew the conclusion that the emperor would risk his sword in the

GIULIA FARNESE · 277

Levant, where pearls came from, and that his soldiers would enjoy the riches of the Turks.

They repaired the hilt and I stayed on my knees until I dared lift my eyelids and I saw, perplexed, undecided above me the myopic eyes of Charles V. He too was suffering at that instant because of the ridiculousness of the situation; he too was timid, a weakness that I could sense under the armor of his authority; and that coincidence, which made him pathetically human for a few seconds, caused between us, even though the distance that separated us was so great, a fleeting and profound communication which lasted the time of our nervous looks. My grandfather and other knights and prelates stood by with my gloves, with the golden spurs. In order to gain time the cardinal blessed those symbols. Finally the emperor again grasped the sword and with a great deal of care touched me on the shoulder. The fleeting contact with the steel made me shiver as if my detested hump were being burned, and as if the cauterizing applied by the royal hand might free me surgically from my congenital horror. I was moved by a physical and strange pain, so singular that I was unable to tell when he pronounced the definitive words in the name of God whether the Hapsburg did it in a Teutonic Castilian or a reprobable Latin. The rest happened as if we had all been hypnotized. Alessandro de' Medici, perhaps on orders of the pope and with undeniable annoyance, put on my spurs; my grandfather put on my sword; I kissed the tips of the Caesarian fingers; I touched his knee with my lips and I heard Cardinal Orsini telling me in a low voice, "Don't trip over the sword, Vicino. Here's Sigismondo. Go home with him. Go to bed and get some rest."

Knighthood ... tourneys ... Durindana, Orlando's sword, which had belonged to Hector the Trojan and about which Death had said that in the paladin's hand it could do more damage than a hundred of his scythes the clash of armor before the walls of cities ... the adversary framed behind the bars of his helmet ... the banners floating in the war-like din ... the Crusades, the Holy Sepulcher ... how far all of that was from the hunchbacked duke, who believed nevertheless that he was a proper knight, for he had learned since he was a child—and from before, from the origins of his line—that we must disdain earning with our sweat, as Tacitus proclaims, what can be acquired by means of blood! How far all of that was not only from me but also from the world I lived in, where the King of France had himself knighted by Bayard and then made a pact with the infidels!

I went out hypnotized. At the door a mass of flesh threw itself upon me and hugged me against its thick volume, cutting off my weak respiration.

"Giulia agrees to your request, sir," Galeazzo Farnese declared to me, with just as much happiness as I. "I asked her because I'm a modern man. The only thing I ask of you is for you to give her one more year before you take her away. She's only fifteen; I'm a widower. Don't take her away from me so soon, Duke. And don't visit her now; you'll be seeing her for the rest of your life. If you see her, maybe you'll change your mind and not agree to my conditions, she's so beautiful. She sends you this ring and asks for yours in exchange."

Hypnotized, still hypnotized, I took off Benvenuto Cellini's ring and in its place I slipped on the one that Farnese had just given me.

His son Fabio came forward. His clothing fit him in such a way, in accordance with the style of the times, that he seemed naked, and his elegant adolescent body was so straight that it seemed as if his sleeves, swollen, round, aerostatic, the only loose and opulent part of his multicolored suit, were capable of suspending him in the air.

"She sends you this gift too," the young man added. "It's a child's gift; take it as such and forgive her. She's sure that it will bring you good luck."

He placed in my outstretched hand Silvio da Narni's doll, to which Giulia had added a rose. The rose of the Orsinis was opening up fresh in front of me on an instrument of witchcraft. I took what he was offering me, still absorbed; I embraced them both and I went out into the night in which the stars were imitating the coronation ritual about the moon with millions of candles and sparkling swords. The towers of Bologna were straight as erect swords. There were swords everywhere that night. And there were drunken people stumbling about or sleeping open-mouthed in doorways. Some were singing the fierce verses of Aretino against the pope, the emperor, the King of France, the three Medici bastards, and the guards would haul them off, quieting their shouts with blows on the mouth from their crossbows. Many teeth were broken on that 24th of February.

At our lodgings I found Pier Luigi and Silvio. The first asked me to allow Sigismondo to stay in his service for a time, and on gathering from the boy's expression that it was his wish, I granted the permission with a nod. My secretary begged me to allow him to bring Porzia with us, and not only her, but also her brother Giambattista. I consented—that day I would have signed any contract at all—and there was a great uproar. The twins, who had predicted my decision hidden in a neighboring room, came to kiss my hands. Wine flowed and just as when they entertained my grandmother with their pantomimes, the Martellis danced to the rhythm of a viola. No one could have told himself that the young man there who resembled his sister so much was the same one who had attacked my page in revenge for our outrages. While they were dancing I went to take off the coat of mail, the cloak, and the spurs. I was helped by Silvio, to whom I showed the doll that Fabio Farnese had handed me.

"It is proper that this ally receive the price of its work and celebrate the success with us, Excellency; it has accomplished its mission!" the secretary exclaimed, and he reddened the burlap face with some wine.

"It looks like blood."

"It's wine, Excellency."

I began to laugh. Along with the iron coat of mail I had gotten rid of the bewilderment that had been weighing down on me.

"I want to dictate a letter to you which they will take to Galeazzo Farnese's house at once."

And I dictated a flaming love letter to Giulia; the letter of a poet nobleman who had read *Il Cortegiano*.

The party was still going on in the main room. When we rejoined the dancers, Silvio made a toast: "To His Excellency's immortality."

I remembered my father's bitter phrase, "Monsters never die," and I shuddered. I drank a mug of wine without pausing. Giambattista came over to me, rolling his eyes and smoothing his hair. Without doubt he was trying to allude to our adventure in the tomb at Piamiano. It upset me that the supposed swordsman had changed like that from aggressive dash to effeminate condescension because it suited him. Did his ambition calculate that in order to earn all that favoritism implied he would have to employ that method? Where had he left his virility, his slashing, his fight, which had frightened the harlots into wild, cackling hens? I pushed him aside brusquely. Only a short time before, Charles V had knighted me, Alessandro de' Medici had knelt at my feet, and they had told me of Giulia's acceptance; I was in no mood for equivocal diversions worthy of sensual boys.

"Get me some more wine."

In the morning, even before the fog of drunkenness had been dissipated, I left for Recanati with Silvio, Porzia, Giambattista, and an escort of four pages and six soldiers. My grandfather would return to Rome in one of the pope's sedan chairs. They packed the doll in a chest beside my half crown and Baldassare Castiglione's *Cortegiano*. Giulia's gift, a ruby ring, bothered my finger. I missed the other one, Benvenuto's, my talisman. If I had had my wits about me when Farnese asked me for it, I would not have given it away.

The roads, the same as when we had come, were jammed with people. The empire, having paused for a few hours, was in motion again. I was going after the face of Gian Corrado Orsini. How much I hated him; I envied him, admired him, loved him, underneath it all, so much!

## 5. THE DUKE OF THE CATS

*My father's disturbing portrait in Recanati—The vile Pier Luigi Farnese—My brother Maerbale leaves us—A cattish lawsuit—Silvio da Narni and Porzia Martelli—A trip to Venice—Student discussions about Paracelsus*

DURING the trip from Bologna to Recanati, long and complicated and over bad roads, nothing of note happened except an assassination attempt near the inn where we spent the night in Rimini. I was attacked with knives in an alley, but I was protected by the silk-covered buffalo-hide chest protector that I was wearing. I attributed it to one of the rancorous Pantasilea's plots. The hired ruffians escaped into the darkness pursued by Giambattista and Silvio da Narni, and after that I redoubled our precautions. In the expeditious Renaissance, things like that happened every day; I was not going to lose any sleep over something so minor.

After our arrival in Recanati, I decided not to go to the church of Saint Dominic, the goal of my pilgrimage, right away, as if I were afraid of the confrontation with my father, more difficult than that with the modest swordsmen of Rimini. I wandered with my squires for two days through the town that was laid out on the rolling hills as if on terraces delimited by heavy walls. I climbed the dominating tower and from it I took in the breadth of the prodigious countryside, miles and miles of it, resting my eyes on the reflection of the Adriatic or following, as on a map, the chromatic diversity of the Apennines. If I passed Saint Dominic's, I would stop at the door and study the sculptures by Giuliano da Maiano, but I would not go in. I finally overcame my hesitation and the polyptych stood before me with its great central compartment and the five surrounding it, standing above the three small divisions distributed along the base, but the darkness was such that I told Silvio, my only companion, to light a torch. The flame burst out and it was as if Lorenzo Lotto had returned to paint, because as Silvio moved along before the altar of the Virgin, new areas of form and color rose up, and the polyptych took on shape and lost it with a plastic rhythm. A monk who was praying across the church and, along with some old women mumbling their rosaries, was the only witness to the episode, came over to see what was going on, and when he discovered that the Duke of Bomarzo was looking for the effigy of his father in the vastness of the oil painting, he asked for some alms and left us alone.

In the meantime my eyes were going from one shutter to the next of the extension of the painting, from the middle panel, with the Virgin on her throne giving the scapular to the founder of the order of preachers, those bashful angel musicians, and the architectural tiaras of Saint Urban and Saint Gregory, to the various scenes that took place as if in several small theaters: the *Pietà* over the naked body of Christ, his mother's wide sleeves, and the eye of the Magdalen, watching, like that of a Peruvian *tapada*, in the blue shadow of her cloak; Saint Thomas Aquinas and Saint Flavian, the latter magnificently luxurious, standing in the painting on the left; Saint Peter Martyr, whose beatitude was not upset by the knife sunken in his skull, and Saint Vitus, the patron of Recanati, thick, feminine, and bland in spite of his armor and lance, appearing in the one on the right; Saint Catherine of Alexandria and Saint Vincent Ferrer up above to one side; and on the other Saint Catherine of Siena and Saint Sigmund, as if their half-bodies were appearing on balconies. That one, Saint Sigmund, was my father. Of course it was! My father, painted in 1506, painted six years before my arrival on earth had caused him such an angry disappointment. But even though I recognized him at once, how far away, how opposite was this image from the one, hidden until then in my memory, that came back to me immediately when I compared Lorenzo Lotto's portrait with the one that burst forth at last, intact, clear, out of the fog of my recollection!

The Venetian had placed there up high a gentleman dressed in dull velvet with thin strips of marten fur on his cuffs and shoulders, an arrogant gold belt and a double chain, also of gold, the links of which crossed the blackness of his chest. One hand was resting on the hilt of a sword, like that of a dandy on a cane, and the other hand was hanging down, open, emphasizing the patrician beauty of its structure. His head, marked by his blond hair and beard, had a mysterious beauty which was brought out by the thinness of his eyebrows and the design of his sad eyes, and the model gave an impression of elegant indifference, almost disdain, alongside the female saint who, with her heart between her fingers, as if she were holding an exquisite fruit, was turning in the opposite direction. All of him exuded aristocracy, displeasure, a certain fragile mannerism that was incomprehensible in someone who had been so robustly vital, a famous condottiere, and it was concretized in that useless right hand, hanging like a tassel, which no one could ever have imagined grasping a sword or clutching at rocky walls during an assault on a fortress.

How long did I stay there, astounded, doubting, trying to understand? The torch moved and with it the circle of effigies, drawing out the austere black and white that went from panel to panel with the monkish habits and which accompanied the polyphony of the courtly clothing with a sober musical ritornello; but I could only see Gian Corrado Orsini, and although the artist had placed him to one side in the composition, the graceful image of my father, displaced by the coming and going of the lighted torch and by the anguished attention with which I was observing it, now constituted the center of the polyptych, and the other people were rotating around it, as if in an armillary sphere along whose circles celestial and earthly figures paraded very slowly, rendering him rhythmical homage.

What did that portrait mean? What was it showing me? Standing there before the altar, I was making an effort to interpret its symbolism. Was it trying to say that when we face the truth, what we think we possess as the only truth shows that there are others; that before the image that we form of one being (or of ourselves) other images are elaborated, multiplied, provoked by the reflection of each one on the others, and that every person—like the painter Lorenzo Lotto, for example—when he interprets and judges us, re-creates us, for he puts something of his own individuality into as, in such a way that when we complain that someone does not understand us, what we reject, not recognizing it as ours, is the store of his most subtle essence, what he involuntarily adds to us in order to place us in harmony with his vision of what we represent in life for him? Is it possible that we do not exist as single, independent entities? Can each one of us be the contradictory result of what the rest have been making of us, of what the rest have forged out of that necessity for a harmonizing transposition that each one feels as a means of communication—that necessity of seeing oneself as one sees someone else? Can each one of us be *all* of us since we are composed of the effects that other people carry with themselves? Can it be possible that we go through life amid mirrors that face and deform us while we ourselves are those mirrors? But no... Because when I think of myself, without the addition that each one adds to me on his own, I think of myself just as I am, in my naked and authentic limitation. And do not those incorporations leave traces, do they not disfigure, do they not minimize, do they not make us often act in different ways before different people, giving them, without our noticing it, what they expect of us, multiplying ourselves, diluting ourselves? My father had been a violent man for me—and nothing else but violent—because my inner violence, born of the rejection which made me sure of provoking him to violence, had only made the aggressive indices stand out within his complexity. And yet, once, only once, when I had gone with him into the magical aura of Michelangelo's David, penetrating the crust of resentment that doubtless covered him, but which I too, like a scaly contagion, transmitted to him, I had glimpsed a broad and different perspective in his soul, one of love for the beautiful, the gigantic, the balanced, on whose familiar surface sown with grave statues and crossed by the wind of noble majestic phrases, we would have perhaps been able to understand each other and live together. But at that time I had not entered upon that path that was thorny with difficulties and which brought on harsh modesties, and which perhaps hid peace at its end, but I followed the opposite trail, which, even though it made me suffer so much, was still the easier one, for the only thing that I limited myself to doing was to continue projecting the weak light of my rancor on the condottiere and seeing exclusively what its lugubrious reflections showed me: pride, wrath, and violence, which

THE DUKE OF THE CATS · 285

he did have among many other things, but which were mostly my violence, my wrath, and my desperate pride. On the other hand, for Lorenzo Lotto, because of what Magister Laurentius sensed of the ambiguous, melancholic, and poetical, Gian Corrado Orsini had become concrete in a fundamentally equivocal being, in response to the link of Magister Laurentius's anxious uncertainty with which he on his part hid, hazy and vague, in the most secret chambers of his intimacy. Every painter paints himself, because every painter gathers and emphasizes in the model what is like him, and it becomes active and flows to the surface, evoked by his passion. Every one of us sees himself in others. We are echoes, mirages, changing reflections.

And what if I were mistaken? If all those reflections as I faced Saint Sigmund were but a rhetorical game? If Lorenzo Lotto, more lucid than I, more mature in experience, without the hindrances that I had brought into the world, had dug into the genuine psychology of my sire and had drawn out his deep mystery, the one that I could not sense because I was blinded with jealousy? If my father had been much, much closer to me than I had thought, closer to my shadows, my painful indecisions over the perplexities of life?

"He looks like you," Silvio da Narni whispered.

He looked like me? My father and I alike? What nonsense! No one had said so until that moment. And in spite of it all, there was something in that expression, in that posture, in the turning of the head, the longness of the face, the straight nose, the design of the eyebrows, in the air—that was it, in the impalpable and obsessive *air*—which indicated to me that Silvio had not been motivated by flattery alone. Alike! The one who had looked like my father was Girolamo. They kept repeating it, even if he had my grandmother's eyes. Maerbale and I came physically from the other branch, that of Cardinal Orsini of Monterotondo. But now I had to give in before the obvious: at the age of eighteen, with my hair parted like his, although mine was chestnut and I wore it over my ears, the similarity was evident, undeniable. My hands, in which I placed so much pride, as Galeazzo Maria Sforza did in his famous ones, could have been mistaken for those of the portrait. I lifted them up in the light of the torch and I analyzed for a while the shape of the finger bones, which thickened only at the joints. Giulia

Farnese's blood-red rubies were shining. I examined the transparent paleness of my fingers as if they did not belong to me, the vein canals that crossed the smooth back, the magical lines of the palms where probably was written the history of a future that I did not dare imagine and which penetrated into the black infinite labyrinth of Time. How strange! I could have sworn that my father's hands were shorter, broader, harder, stronger. The hands that had pushed me toward the horror of the skeleton in Bomarzo, and which had traced the triumphal silhouette of David in the air.

I fell to my knees and said a prayer. For the first time I dedicated a completely sincere prayer to Gian Corrado Orsini, to Saint Sigmund, who had killed his son and who, nonetheless, had entered the immaculate glory of sainthood. Do we know anything, anything at all, about anybody? Do we know, by chance, anyone's last sealed truth? What did I know about my father? The questions that had not ceased tormenting me since I went into Saint Dominic's were tearing at me with the outline of their wounding claws. I was turning about in the webbed prison under their harpoons. Most likely—or most hatefully—when he had planned to disinherit me, what my father had intended was to prevent me from prolonging his own sins and deficiencies in Bomarzo, the most acute, those that were distilled in complex alembics. He had not condemned me; he had condemned himself.

I felt a wave of tenderness soften me and I raised my eyes with hot tears in them. I prayed for him, but I prayed for myself too. My prayers were not directed to any abstract and invisible power, or to the God of Battles, or the God of Mercy, but to those knights and ladies who were slowly turning about the weak prince dressed in lordly black velvet; to Saint Catherine, who was turning her back on him; to the bejeweled Saint Flavian; to the winged and startled children, who, when we left, would softly play the violin and lute again in the silence and mist of the church. I asked them to help me to carry my burden through life as my father had his.

Silvio touched my elbow. "Don't cry, Duke; don't be afraid. The future belongs to you."

I wanted to reject him, to flee from what he represented; but suddenly I saw myself so alone and lost, so confused in the midst of that forest of columns and altars from which the images were peering at me with cold reproach, that I stood up and embraced him, sobbing.

"Let's go now; you've seen him."

It was then that I decided that Lorenzo Lotto would paint my portrait. I was burning with the desire to discover myself in turn through the eyes of the painter.

Before we returned to Bomarzo, a messenger from my grandmother reached us. He was bringing me a long and useful letter in reply to the one I had sent her. Its many pages, covered with a hand that quivered and trembled here and there with the logical vacillation of her many years, to affirm itself again and flow on in the recuperated solidity of her cursive writing, proved to me once more what I knew so well: that my grandmother, ninety long years having passed, my grandmother, who could have been the mother of my other grandparent, the cardinal, and who had suffered from the cloud brought on by Girolamo's singular death, had recovered her spirit, one of the most alert that I had known in the world. Isolated by age and by the demands of her position in the solitude of Bomarzo, she had not renounced any contact with life, which she was now proving with extreme lucidity, and by means of a vast correspondence whose bearers covered Italy from court to court, alerting her relatives and giving and receiving sealed missives, Diana Orsini was informed of everything that happened on the peninsula, better informed in certain cases than the very participants in the events she commented on, for her testimony came from all manner of sources, crossing back and forth in the coming and going of swift messengers. Her permanent curiosity was her great invigorating tonic, the rejuvenating recipe that kept her erect and communicative. As if she had been at the head of a hard-working chancellery, she wrote, asked, and answered. Nothing eluded her investigation, neither the causes of distant alliances, nor the hidden intrigues at home, nor the probabilities in the game of power. A very old sorceress, she wove on her great loom in the remoteness of her palace on the Etruscan hill, and the trembling threads, gathered up in complex balls by her equestrian pages, who appeared like Mercury and angels dusty from the enchanted clouds, involved the lengthy Italian territory that extended between the blue seas. Other duchesses were astonished at her mental dynamism, which did not ignore the smallest detail of the most stupidly frivolous matter, because my grandmother, making judgments like an acute woman with accustomed experience, like a powerful engine of the world, stored up in the ample archives of her memory a wealth of first-hand information that was as varied as it was fertile.

In her writing, which at times tortured her correspondents and which I deciphered without any trouble, I perceived her joy over the swiftness with which her grandson had converted her hopes into reality. She immediately went into great details concerning the Farneses of Giulia's branch, which I had not known until then and had considered them all *en bloc*, without discrimination, out of my indolence which only took into consideration the general situation of that prosperous lineage. She told me that she had known the two wives of Galeazzo Farnese, Ersilia, the natural daughter of Pompeo Colonna, and Girolama dell' Anguillara, the daughter of a sister of the one who was to be Paul III and the mother of Giulia; she had also had dealings with Galeazzo's mother, Battistina dell' Anguillara, and with his grandmother, a Monaldeschi. Whom had Diana Orsini not known during her ninety-odd wandering years! All of those ladies were of irreproachable prestige. Their relationships unfolded like nets that intermeshed the papal courts with those of the great lords. And crime was not absent, of course, in the careful enumeration: Giulia's grandmother had been murdered by her stepson, so that unavoidable detail was not missing from the family portrait, one worthy of any respected family. As for my presumptive father-in-law, Diana Orsini had seen him quite often three years before, when I had still not returned from Florence, during the period when, as conservator of the commune of Orvieto, the pontiff had sent him at the head of fifteen hundred people to rescue the castle of Castellottieri, which belonged to his sister Beatrice Farnese, the widow of Antonio Baglioni. An uncle of that Baglioni, Pirro Fortebraccio, had taken the castle away from Beatrice, and Galeazzo, with militias from Rome, Narni, Orte, Orvieto, Spoleto, and also Bomarzo—under the command of my father—had besieged Fortebraccio for fifty days until, beaten, he capitulated and was sent to Civita Castellana to eat his bitter bread in the shadows while Beatrice Farnese, with her brother Galeazzo on one side and my father on the other, entered her reconquered castle again. Galeazzo had, therefore, been at Bomarzo several times. My grandmother was enchanted with the agile drive with which from a colossal horse that arched and snorted under his remarkable weight, he directed the operations of war, but she was also enchanted by his fat joviality and what he had of a balanced nobility which was reflected in the exquisite courtesy of a patrician accustomed to be in the salons. Probably, when I had been in his house in Bologna and Galeazzo had smothered me in his cordial arms, the gentleman had spoken of such things in the cataract of words with which he dampened me and in which the name Orsini jumped up and echoed, but feeling the intensity of the affectionate linkage, I did not pay great attention to what his heavy-tongued eloquence was saying, and distracted by Giulia's closeness, I let pass, lost in the torrent, the allusions which my grandmother was now clarifying for me.

"You will get along very well with Galeazzo," she told me. "Always say that he is right, that is the only thing he demands, and then do what you think is best. Giulia, if she has his personality and has inherited, as they describe her to me, the beauty of her mother, will be an ideal duchess for Bomarzo. The Lord be praised! I am anxious to hand over to her soon the reins of the estate which are already falling from my weak hands. If you could only see them, Vicino! No one would recognize my poor hands any more."

I raised my eyes from the paragraph and smiled. My grandmother's hands were still strong, and in order for Giulia, with her fresh fifteen years, to assume the responsibility of succeeding her in the government of our house, she would have to learn a great deal, but she could count on an incomparable teacher. And, furthermore, if one thought about the scandals of Gian Corrado Orsini, those of Girolamo, and mine, which were no exception in Italian castles but were an adjustment to the characteristic way of life of the times, he would observe that the government in question did not imply a very rigorous domestic policy.

My grandmother went on then about the financial considerations of the lords of Montalto. There was more than enough money there, the fruit of opulent contributions.

"There is no reason to disdain it," she added, "for the glory of the Orsinis is rather expensive, and your brand-new administrator, Messer Bernardino Niccoloni, seems to be more of a spender than Martelli. I am happy that you have found Porzia and Giambattista; perhaps this will help bring Messer Manuzio back to Bomarzo, which he left in such an inexplicable way."

The disappearance of the twins' father was apparently still an undeciphered enigma for Diana Orsini. It was one of the few secrets that I believe I had kept against her inquiring astuteness, and if she had penetrated the real causes of the desertion of our economy by Manuzio, she hid it with admirable effectiveness, preferring to pass as an innocent rather than officially accept the evidence of indecorous disorder on the part of her beloved grandson.

Up to that page, my grandmother's letter had been written like a jubilant hymn, interrupted, according to the ups and downs of her mood, with the inevitable light touches of irony as soon as she gave her thought free rein—as when she spoke about Galeazzo's "generous waist," or "the indecisive, vagabond left eye" of his grandmother Jolanda Monaldeschi—but her tone changed in the part dedicated to Pier Luigi. Through Maerbale she had learned that I had authorized Sigismondo to place himself under his orders, for that would further his career in the world, and Diana Orsini did not share my attitude. Who knows how Maerbale, Matteo, and Orso had presented the matter? Perhaps, in spite of their boastful maleness, they were offended by the predilection that was opening up for Sigismondo perspectives that were difficult to calculate. In her isolation in Bomarzo, the weaving sorceress was more up to date than I about the misconduct of Pier Luigi, although what I had heard and guessed in that respect was voluminous, for wherever he went the whispering of rumors arose and Alessandro Farnese's son went through life as if he were surrounded by a cloud of buzzing bees. But I was only aware of the flow of gossip about his character and stories about him, while my grandmother gave me concrete facts.

According to them, Pier Luigi, educated by Tranquillo Molosso— of such contradictory name—in accordance with what his father had decided, had been legitimized at the age of two, and at sixteen had married Girolama Orsini, the daughter of the Count of Pitigliano. His brutalities and his shame at once made him an enemy of that illustrious branch of our line. He broke with the Orsinis and allied himself with the Colonnas, taking part, along with Sciarra and Emilio, in the sack of Rome. He stole everything he could, but he ordered Molosso's house respected, which was perhaps his only agreeable act. In 1528, during the war of Naples, he was dispatched with two thousand men to Manfredonia, which was fiercely defended by Carlo Orsini, whom he defeated. No, we Orsinis had no reason to love him. When Naples was conquered, he was sent to Tuscany, and there he passed some unpleasant moments. He was supported by the Marquis del Vasto, while Ferrante Gonzaga declared himself his mortal enemy. For some ignominious act, the roots of which are unknown—and the nature of which I could guess as obvious and which my grandmother certainly knew—he was thrown out of the army. His father did not lift a finger in his favor. Then he appeared at Bomarzo accompanying my father's body.

"If I had been aware at that time of the details I am relating now," my angry correspondent wrote, "I would not have received him as I did. Perhaps he calculated that with that action he could win the good will of the Orsinis; perhaps he calculates that he will win it now through the intermediary of Sigismondo, although he should have chosen a more brilliant intermediary, and I suspect that what moves him is not only his public interest. I insist that he is a rival of ours, hostile and one worthy of watching."

A little less than degraded in his military position, Pier Luigi lived by his wiles after that. The year before, he had wandered about Perugia with a handful of mercenaries, more of a bandit than a condottiere, until in 1530, without paternal authorization, he suddenly appeared at the imperial festivities in Bologna.

"Such is his background," the letter went on to say, "and there are other things over which I prefer not to linger, given their dubious nature, but which excite a great deal of gossip and because of which Pier Luigi played no role in the celebration of the coronation. There must have been hundreds and hundreds of the sackers of Rome there (and among them the one who was crowned himself), but the pope could not avenge himself on them; on the other hand, Pier Luigi, abandoned by the imperialists and by his father, whom it did not pay to play too high a card in his defense, Pier Luigi, with his spectacular behavior after the pillage, received all of the pope's wrath. The Farneses push each other, opening up paths toward positions of the highest level, something that does not seem reprovable to me and, if you come right down to it, it will help you in life when you marry Giulia; and you must understand that if Pier Luigi's father, who is held in particular esteem by His Holiness, did not exhibit his offspring on the stage at Bologna, such an opportune moment to show him off to the world, it was because disagreeable circumstances made it impossible. If it had not been like that, you can be certain that the cardinal would have pushed him with all the strength of his influence. Alessandro is a man of family feeling. His children, even though illegitimate, come ahead of everything for him, but he may be afraid of the dangerous Pier Luigi, capable of blind barbarities. In any case, if Alessandro succeeds Clement de' Medici on the throne of Saint Peter, which is quite presumable, since your poor grandfather does not seem to me to have enough votes and the proof of it is the fact that he has not even been able to make Maerbale a cardinal, I conjecture that this boy will give him a great deal of trouble with his vicious fury and that he will be master of Rome. Do not doubt but that he will come to a bad end."

Some acid reflections linked to the low position I occupied during those same ceremonies—which Maerbale, naturally pleased at being able to wound me, had stressed for her—were finally sweetened with her reiterated praise of Giulia's beauty, celebrated by my cousins, and with the manifestation of her desire to have me in her arms soon.

Later on when Pier Luigi's wild development showed me how prophetic her words had been, I was able to measure the depth of her wisdom. For the moment, at the same time that I was flattered by everything she said to me concerning my future relatives and Giulia's looks, I was annoyed that she judged in that way—even with more than enough reasons—my resolution to leave Sigismondo with Pier Luigi, which I had thought slyly political, for it was one of the few decisions that I had made without consulting her, and she was still scolding me as if I were a child. The truth was that if on the one hand

I needed for her to treat me as such during the moments of weakness and fear when I sought her refuge, my vanity would have preferred for her to modify her tone, at least when she brought up my mistakes to my face, and to give me the impression that even when I was wrong I was the man, the master, the duke.

My grandmother's preoccupation with the way in which I had been passed over in Bologna, even if it was quite justified in our small world that was so jealous of the positions it had won, surprised me. It was the first subject she brought up when we returned to Bomarzo.

When I told her about my strange feelings before the figure of Saint Sigmund and insinuated to her that my father and I might have resembled each other, she sat up in her bed for an instant, took my hand, and said, "What happened to you in Bologna would not have happened to your father. With all his defects, your father was a proper Orsini and he knew what it meant to be one."

I looked at her as if I were seeing a different person, as if in her matriarchal old age Diana Orsini were revealing to me another facet of her inexhaustible spirit. It was certain that since I was an infant she had dedicated herself—and she had succeeded—to inculcating in me the pride of my race, passing on to me through her stories the glorious splendor of a line that even in crime had a grandeur that was almost mythological, but until that time she had worked beside me as a friend, and now for the first time I perceived a certain rancor in her manner. Could the relationship between Diana Orsini and the Duke of Bomarzo have been different from the one she had maintained with her grandson Vicino, the hunchbacked child? By attaining the dukedom could I have lost what mattered most to me, her indulgent love?

"The Duke of Bomarzo," she added, confirming part of my suppositions, "is responsible to the Orsinis. He has received a legacy and his task is to preserve it and enrich it. You may perform some reproachable act, and you have done so and you will probably keep on doing so, Vicino, because your nature is weak; you can do so even if you ought not to; but what you cannot do and must not do, under any circumstances, is to let yourself retreat one inch from the position that we have won, all of us, and with great difficulty, over the centuries. For you more than anyone else of this house the Orsinis and the interests of the Orsinis must come before anything or anybody. It is as if you were carrying a flag. Make it wave, Vicino. You wanted to be duke and I too wanted you to be; don't show me now that I am at death's door that I have been wrong."

I mumbled that she was exaggerating, that it had not gone so badly for me in Bologna, for Charles V had knighted me and I had returned from there with Giulia's promise. But I knew that she was right. The bastards themselves, Alessandro de' Medici and Pier Luigi Farnese had given me the example with their anger because they had not been granted the places in the coronation ceremonies that they felt entitled to. I had been passed over and I did not raise a complaint, I had not known enough to impose myself. What was it, had I resigned myself to wander through life with my title and my name on my back like a hunchback unworthy of those privileges? Was my assumption of the ownership of an estate that many people envied limited to a mere posturing to dazzle my villagers and a few provincial functionaries? Did I think that it had been enough for me to have taken advantage of the *homagio mulierum*, responding to libidinous anxieties and the urge to prove my manhood, in order to affirm that I was really the duke as my father and grandfather had been? Would I be happy being a half-Orsini like my other grandfather, the senile one, who played a decorative role in the court of Clement VII and had not been able to become intimate and bring about his great aim, placing Maerbale in the Sacred College—although Cardinal Franciotto, by his brave past as a condottiere, had shown a prowess that assured him a place among the authentic Orsinis?

I was aggravated when I left her room. My blood was boiling.

In order to drive away those unpleasant thoughts which proclaimed my initial and stupid failure—a failure whose magnitude I had not perceived at the moment because of a lack of courtly experience, but which my vigilant grandmother had made me understand without disguise—I took refuge in Giulia's love. When I felt alone and measured my weakness I always had to take refuge in a man or in a woman, and since I could not count on my grandmother, to whom had fallen the role—her of all people!—to show me the symbolic damage that I had caused my people, I sought shelter in the remembrance of a girl of fifteen. The feeling that she aroused in me became alive and grew, as if someone had blown on a tenuous flame, because Giulia represented for me, as I faced the idea of defeat and incapacity that had arisen from my bland acceptance of the offensive passing over in Bologna, an idea of triumph now that her promise of marriage, so flattering, so exactly in tune with the plans of my grandmother, attested to the fact that I was capable, if I wanted to be, of fulfilling my aspirations and declaring to the whole world that I deserved being Duke of Bomarzo. My love for Giulia burst forth, therefore, out of cowardice and thankfulness. What might have been owed to Silvio's black magic in her conquest did not enter into my calculations. I only thought about the victory that came from Giulia and which compensated for other misfortunes, not just that circumstantial one that came from the disdain I had suffered in Bologna, but also the frustration that my hump implied. Giulia had accepted me just as I was and that was enough for me to feel redeemed and for me to dedicate myself to loving her with all of my strength.

I never loved her as I did then in the solitude of Bomarzo. My relations with my grandmother were re-established, affectionate, but there had been opened in our bonds the fissure that criticism, even when rational, would open in my sick sensibility. And I embraced the phantom of the girl with blue eyes who gave a strange vigor to my isolation. I loved her romantically, as in a novel, on the deserted roads that surrounded the palace and along the edges of which wild orchids grew, the primroses were yellow, the ferns curled, and the brambles mingled with the osiers. I carried my love with me, secretly. In her way, just as those plants and flowers mingled on the banks of the brooks and in the hollows of the ravines, old feelings were mingled and exalted in my love. The memory of Adriana dalla Roza, dead in Florence, that of Abul, lost perhaps forever, were joined to my new passion and they nourished it with their images. Everything that had to do with the feeling that makes me tremble and feel transported contributed to shape the figure of my new love, which required those contributions in order to ripen, because I had really received so little from Giulia, barely glimpsed, so little I knew about her, that its fire needed to be fed from the heat of coals that lay under the ashes of a vague oblivion.

I wrote to her; I wrote her many letters in which I explained what those feelings suggested to me and what our future existence in Bomarzo would be like. The architectural work undertaken by my father had been finished now, and I was waiting for the occasion to undertake the changes that would make my name endure, inseparable from that of the castle. For the moment, I wanted to have a series of frescoes painted on ceilings and walls with scenes that would proclaim, along with the warlike victories that had given such glory to my people, the artistic victories that I considered to be mine with a fatuousness that had no other basis than my inclinations toward dilettantism. And in the most important room I would have painted a large-scale copy of my horoscope. She answered me from time to time with brief, circumspect letters, inspected by Galeazzo Farnese, which I devoured like delicacies in spite of their schoolgirl simplicity. When one arrived, I would go down into the garden where my grandmother's white cats were taking their ease and I would read it slowly, trying to read between the lines and extract from its text a vital juice which it did not really have, but which I would savor because of the simple fact that it had been written by Giulia. Then I would run to the mirror in my bedroom, raise the cloth that covered it, and for the hundredth, the thousandth time observe my face, its angles, the thick depth of my eyes, my long alabaster fingers, my blue veins, my oval nails. I would move the candelabra, placing them in strategic positions, not only to bring out the best of my features but also in such a way that if I located myself skillfully, my hump would disappear in the shadows and I would see myself as worthy of being loved.

One night I took the letters I had received so far—they were four— and I went down to the garden with them. I was going to read them in the light of the moon that was outlining the Cimini mountains and was reflected on the water that was noisy with frogs. I was unfolding them and was being carried away with their laconic, infantile content, which as it passed through the sieve of my imagination became transformed and caught fire, when a strong blow on the shoulder knocked me down. Someone with a drawn sword was facing me, wanting to kill me. His cape and hat covered his face. He was short, agile. I got up, drew my dagger, and defended myself. The steel blades made sparks. I shouted, shouted, calling my people. The attacker disappeared into the underbrush. They had tried to assassinate me, just as in Rimini, and the proof was my bloody shoulder, but this could not have been a plot of Pantasilea's as I had suspected in Rimini, nor had the attack in Rimini been either, most probably. I staggered back to the castle, where torches were waving on the terraces and pages were shouting my name, awakened, and with my dagger still in my hand, I went to the room where Silvio was studying the hermetic science of horoscopes late into the night.

Pier Luigi Farnese believed in seers and horoscopists the same as his father the cardinal. Francis of France and the Emperor Charles also believed in them and consulted them frequently. And Sulla, Julius Caesar, Tiberius, Nero ... And my kinsman the great condottiere Niccolò Orsini, to whom I owe my own horoscope. As for me, how could I have ceased believing in those who see the outline of human life in the stars and think, like Aristotle, that this world is by necessity joined to the movements of the upper world. I submit to the proofs. Neither the opinions of technical astronomers nor the acute reflections of Saint Augustine, nor the infinite errors and contradictions that have taken place in the field—like the announcement of a new universal Deluge six years before the time I am speaking of, which convulsed Europe and was translated in reverse into a frightful drought—have succeeded in convincing me of the opposite. Here I am, alive, in my house, writing in my library, testimony that at least in one case, sensational for its uniqueness, those who scrutinize the sky and coordinate its position with the destiny of men are capable of surprising deductions.

Therefore, when Silvio told me in Bologna that Pier Luigi, having found out about his inclination toward magic, had advised him to study the wisdom of the stargazers, I in turn stimulated him along that path, giving him the means to acquire all that was necessary. Ever since we returned to Bomarzo, the boy from Narni had shut himself up in a garret of the castle with books, manuscripts, and planetary cards, and I saw very little of him. Porzia would stay with him in his learned solitude, which would show a light behind the shutters until dawn, as if a spark had fallen from the stars that he was ceaselessly analyzing and continued to burn in the heart of our fortress.

I went there looking for him, the naked dagger trembling in my right hand, and I found him.

Silvio had grown quite old in recent months. No one would have said that he was only a few years over twenty. The flame of the candle on the table over the confusion of numbers, designs, and open volumes spread out there was engraving on his frowning brow and around his mouth and eyes wrinkles and cracks that grew deeper toward the shadowy cavities of his eyes. His extreme thinness stood out among the musty folds of black quilting. Behind, on the wall, the outlines of the Agathodaemon stood out on a rough painting, the Egyptian serpent with the head of a lion and a crown of twelve rays which represented the signs of the Zodiac. Silvio was reading and taking notes from Ptolemy's Tetrabiblos or Quadripartitem, translated into Latin from the Arabic version, which teaches that the stars are divided into masculine and feminine, and which contains essential information concerning the characteristic qualities of the different planets which are the origins of their various influences.

He was matching that reading with that of another, smaller book, and when I entered, without noticing my upset appearance, for he was intoxicated with his investigation, he stood up and exclaimed in fascination, "You're just in time, Duke. Listen to what Plotinus states: 'Stars possess a strength analogous to that of the winds that drive ships; they can move the body on which the soul travels, but the latter is free.' In that way he reconciles the existence of free will with that of an occult action of the heavenly bodies, and one can understand how Cardinal Farnese, a prince of the Catholic Church, can consult horoscopes without religious condemnation."

I tried to interrupt him, but he was too involved in the matter.

"During these past few days I have been analyzing three horoscopes of Our Lord Jesus Christ: that of Cecco d'Ascoli, which got its author burned at the stake; that of Tiberius Russilianus Sextus of Calabria; and that of Girolamo Cardano, who dreams his books, like an illuminate, before he writes them; and I can assure you that it's something to marvel at. Everything is up there"—he pointed through the window at the lighted dome—"the stars are the eyes with which God observes us, and he fulfills natural processes by using those animated stars that are endowed with science and knowledge. Listen now to what Guido Bonatti, the astrologer of the Montefeltros, says in his *Liber astronomicus*..."

I dropped the dagger on the table and the dry sound awoke Porzia, who was sleeping on a straw mattress. Her startled beauty, emphasized by the snow of her uncovered round breasts, which she quickly put something over, stood out like a lamp in the shadowy room.

"Leave us alone, Porzia," I ordered, "we have to talk."

The girl went downstairs and I lay down on the cot which still smelled of her, warming up my virility.

"They tried to assassinate me tonight, Silvio. Someone wants me dead. I've got to find the guilty one."

The secretary was silent, then he was about to speak.

I said, "Do you suspect anyone, Silvio? Pantasilea... Messer Manuzio ... my... my brother?"

He was silent. The wavering of the candle gave strange life to the serpent of the Agathodaemon, as if its coils were twisting on the wall under the crown of the Zodiac.

"I would have to examine your horoscope."

"And your demons, couldn't they help us? Do you suspect anyone?"

"We'll soon find out. Everything is in the stars, instruments, according to Albertus Magnus, by which the Prime Cause governs the world. The edicts of Augustus, Domitian, and Adrian got nowhere against astrology."

"Tell me who the assassin is."

"We'll soon find out. Now lend me your horoscope."

We went down together, without exchanging a word, to the room where I had hidden Sandro Benedetto's writing.

"In the meantime, Your Lordship should never take off the buffalo chest-piece. Sleep with it on."

"Will you speak to your demons?"

"We'll soon find out. Look, Mars and Venus, the rulers of the House of Death, installed in that of Life—a triumph of the unexpected..."

Before us, in the decorated sketch by the physician of Niccolò Orsini of Pitigliano, the triangles, the letters, and the figures came together.

Sharpening one's ear, it was possible to hear a sound that came perhaps from the far-off brooks like spheres softly rotating above the heaviness of the silence.

"No one, not Astolfo, or Orlando, or Alcina, or Marfisa, or Merlin could kill you, Duke of Bomarzo. No one."

Maerbale's fracture was healing slowly. His leg was in a splint and he spent the spring afternoons in the sun reading or chatting with Orso and Matteo. Then, as the healing progressed, he began to walk, leaning on a cane and on the shoulder of one of his cousins. He was limping, and that should have brought us together, for we were fleetingly sharing at least one, the most benign, of my irregularities, but it did not happen that way. Ever since Bologna I noticed that a new wall was rising between us, and that barrier could be attributed to two things, perhaps both at the same time: to his jealous inclination for Giulia Farnese, exaggerated perhaps by my jealous suspicions, and the official evidence of his inferior position alongside that of the duke, for if Charles V had not knighted him, it was not because of the accident (as Maerbale himself spread about Bomarzo), because the possibility was never mentioned before the collapse of the scaffolding in Saint Petronius's had made it impossible in a practical way, but the fact that my brother's inferior position did not make him worthy of an honor reserved for the great. I imagine that such proofs moved about in his pernicious character. What I did find out, in a concrete way, is that he had written to our grandfather in Rome, demanding a definitive explanation from him concerning the matter of the cardinalate, because, with the abandonment (as it was suitable for him to do without any consultation) of that forbidden splendid road, he was burning to forge a name for himself as our most prestigious ancestors had done, by means of arms. The cardinal did not answer him. I do not doubt that my brother's letter, throwing up to him his lack of influence, with tricks of apparent courtesy, must have annoyed Franciotto Orsini deeply. As for me, as soon as I heard that Maerbale, when he regained the use of his leg, proposed to undertake the memorable and remunerative life of a condottiere, I was seized with dark doubts.

Since my return to Bomarzo I thought I had sensed a kind of buzzing around that was impossible to localize, the restlessness of the vassals with reference to the duke's future. They were aware of the way I had been received and knighted by the emperor—not of my slight in the protocol, jealously hidden by my grandmother, my brother, and my cousins, for it was to the interest of all to hide it, since it had bearing on the prestige of the house—and now they were calculating that I would follow in the footsteps of my father and my warrior ancestors, strapping on the consecrated sword and taking part in military expeditions alongside other heroic princes. They did not stop to think of the physical circumstances that prevented me from doing so. My glory would be the glory of Bomarzo, and because of it, as because of that of the people who had gone before me, they would strut before the inhabitants of neighboring villages that were not under my jurisdiction. They had been accustomed over the centuries to see the young men of Bomarzo leave behind the banners of the bear under the command of the heir, and they considered as something obvious and natural that the tradition, inseparable from my place in the world, would continue to be fulfilled. For them I was no longer the hunchbacked boy but the duke, and as such I had unavoidable obligations. The idea that the ducal character eliminated my hump, converting me into a symbol of protection, should have made me glad and given me strength, but on the contrary it added another anguish to those already gnawing at me. I did not feel strong enough to hold a lance, a position that would have ridiculously stressed the intricacy of my structure, and which revolted my spirit, moved since childhood by other worries. The reader should observe that the buzzing, that expectant atmosphere, did not really exist perhaps and had been imagined by my alert mistrust, and that what was most probable was that those who depended on me sensed that a hunchback was not destined for warlike matters, but I always reacted in that way, goaded by suspicion, and I saw disturbing phantoms everywhere. Now Maerbale's stated decision aggravated my concern. He would do what I should have been doing, and that eventuality plunged me into despair. Without telling anybody about it, I too wrote our grandfather, insisting that it was important for the reputation of the Orsinis of Bomarzo that Maerbale be elevated to the cardinalate, and I received no reply either. The transfer of Maerbale to Rome, to the Sacred College, would have meant the end of a nightmare for me for various reasons. In any case, I tried to get something out of my position, telling my brother that I had intervened with Franciotto Orsini about the matter of the cape. In that way he owed me his thanks, and if Maerbale had perceived the real motives that had impelled me to proceed in that way, they were so transparent, it did not matter to me: the important thing was that it be known that I, the duke, looked after the welfare of my people.

Two unexpected events took me out of the tribulations I suffered as a presumed combatant: a child was born in Bomarzo who was baptized with the name Fulvio, and a misdirected letter appeared in my correspondence.

Fulvio's mother, a village girl of twenty, swore that Maerbale—who was seventeen at the time—was the child's precocious father. Maerbale refused to recognize it, but the insistence of the poor girl and a wealth of details assured us that it was his child. Informed of the case, I ordered that the peasant girl and the child be sent to our palace in Rome, with false magnanimity, for I hated bastards and what I wanted was for the little creature to disappear. That was the famous Fulvio Orsini, writer, archeologist, and antiquarian, who became canon of Saint John Lateran and published the admirable *Imagines et elogia virorum illustrium et eruditorum ex antiquis lapidibus et numismatibus expressa cum annotationibus*, and who later aided me in the classification of my collections. At the time, his birth enraged me deeply. Maerbale was even ahead of me in the task of prolonging the line, while I did not know, with my accursed complications, whether I was capable of doing so. I imagined with rage, in the foggy weakness of my sensuality, the risk that Bomarzo might someday pass into the hands of Maerbale's heirs—without bearing in mind that my fabulous status as an immortal seemed to award me the dukedom in perpetuity—and I sighed, because my wedding to Giulia should take place as soon as possible, for I was suddenly eager for offspring. I too had lain with peasant girls like Maerbale, I had also fallen in the haymows with them, but of natural children—which at that moment I desired and rejected simultaneously—I did not have the slightest knowledge.

And the letter, the letter they delivered to me through an error on the part of the drunken emissary in charge of bringing me those that Giulia Farnese wrote me, was not addressed to me but to Maerbale. Maerbale, always Maerbale, my obsession, my hidden enemy! Nothing indicated to me in the very brief text that I ran through with stupefied anguish that there could exist a guilty understanding between my brother and my betrothed. Giulia limited herself to giving him some dull news about her life in Rome and to emphasize her desire to become established soon in Bomarzo. She ended respectfully. It could have been a simple sisterly letter, the result of the ingenuous friendship that had grown up between them in Bologna, but it was also possible to suppose that its dull tone came from the fear that it might fall into my hands. What was indisputable was that they had established a secret correspondence behind my back.

The wrath, the deception stupefied me. Could Maerbale be planning to despoil me of what I had won, and as a consequence could it have been he who had used hired swordsmen in an attempt against my tenacious permanence on earth? The secret letter from Giulia indicated to me that the spell of the doll that had been bewitched by Silvio da Narni had not worked. The other spell, that of the opportune demise of my father as a result of the conjuration on the terrace at Bomarzo could well have been a coincidence. And the story of Palingenio—the first one to reveal to me the magical powers of the page on the highway to Rome when he told me about the demons—was perhaps the result of the hallucinated philosopher's wildness. If the page really lacked that diabolical power, if he had deceived me by taking advantage of coincidences to prosper at the expense of my innocence, I was lost, because I knew full well that alone, deprived of supernatural help, I would not dare to face life with my weak weapons.

I thought of making Silvio show me the game, to resort to what I could hold on to, but I was afraid that if I was mistaken I would be without his valuable alliance. The most intelligent thing—and the one most fitting to my irresolute character—would be to let time pass. We would soon see. "We'll soon find out," my secretary had said. I let the letter reach Maerbale so as not to arouse his suspicions, and after having conjectured that if he embraced the profession of a condottiere it would contribute to my discredit, I strove, so changeable was my spirit when shaken by adverse currents, to see that he did follow the path of our forebears. I was consumed with the urgency for him to leave Bomarzo as soon as possible; for him to cover himself with glory but to leave me in peace with Giulia, with my castle, with my collections, with my sweet shame, with my onerous immortality. The prospect of eliminating him crossed my mind. Beppo had died; Girolamo had died. Kill Maerbale; wipe him out... My cowardice did not dare. Let him go away.

In the meantime, without taking off the buffalo garment even to sleep, as Silvio had advised me, never leaving the fortress alone, never eating anything that someone else had not tasted, shut up most of the time with my grandmother and her women or with my dogs and my genealogical tables, I applied myself to writing Giulia some burning letters into which I let astute traps slip. She never fell into any of them. She eluded the ambushes with smooth elegance. I redoubled the watch on the mail; nothing for Maerbale came to Bomarzo. If they were in communication they were probably working through accomplices in the neighboring villages.

Until one day Silvio da Narni told me that according to Saracil, Sathiel, and Jana my only brother was the one who desired my death. He suggested that we get rid of him at once. It would be easy, with money, to get the collaboration of Matteo and Orso. That very afternoon Maerbale announced to me that on the following morning, if I had nothing against it, he would leave for Venice to join the forces of Valerio Orsini of Monterotondo, my father's comrade and cousin, who was fighting under the orders of the Most Serene Republic. I authorized it hesitantly. At night, in order to give strength to my spite, I pondered over the painful memories of the time when he persecuted me along with Girolamo. I saw him twisted over me when the first-born martyrized me and pierced my ear. I got dressed, unsheathed my dagger, went toward Silvio's room, but before I got there my strength abandoned me. I could not do it. I could not kill Maerbale.

And Maerbale left with Matteo, with Orso, and with two hundred men whom he had gathered together for the enterprise and who were uprooting themselves from Bomarzo, radiant with joy over the prospect of looting. The party rode off from the cliff as in the days of my father, as in those of my grandfather, as always ever since we Orsinis had been masters of the estate. The people gathered to watch them. The chaplain blessed them. The women shouted good-bye, and the family of Fulvio, the bastard, wept as if they were losing a relative. A broad flight of doves floated over the standards. Everything, the castle, the gardens, the woods, the church, the village tight about the bastions with which its rusty crust was mingled, glowed with a distinct light, a golden light, because our people were going to war. To war? Was not Maerbale most likely going off to kidnap Giulia, to steal her from me? And I? What could I do, what could I work out to defend her? I—leaning on a balustrade along with Messer Pandolfo, Silvio, Porzia, Giambattista Martelli, and Bernardino Niccoloni, the administrator—was looking at the vast blue, the marble-like clouds, the hills, the green and gray patches, the column of ants as it went off. My grandmother appeared at her window and waved a scarf.

A blotch of embarrassment reddened my face. I clenched my teeth until they ground together. I had a feeling that I was letting a crucial moment of my life slip by. I drew Silvio apart.

"My friend," I whispered in the astrologer's ear, "I've changed my mind. The traitor has to be done away with."

"I've anticipated it," the sorcerer answered me, and it humiliated me to find that others had boldly adopted on their own account the resolutions, that were incumbent upon me and which my weak hesitation postponed.

The tiny horses were galloping off. The dust hovered over them like an iridescent canopy. Maerbale waved to us like a delicate silver insect, shaking his shards, his multicolored antennae. Over the back of a mule they were leading his armor like a dead hero.

The administrator asked me, thinking to flatter me, precisely what he should not have asked: "When is Your Lordship leaving for the campaign? It's been whispered around here that you are going to take part in the siege of Florence on the side of the Medicis?"

The coldness of my eyes froze his words. That man, that imbecile, was of no use to me. I would have to discharge him at the first opportunity.

Giambattista Martelli was by my side, rubbing against me with his abandoned body. Perspiration made a lock of blond hair stick to his forehead. I heard him panting as if he were suffocating and the urge to relax so soon after my trouble was pressing me, not to explode, not to run to my grandmother's room dragging the burden of my hump with my eternal lamentations, with the shameless exhibition of my fainthearted incapacity. I took him by the arm. "Come on," I said to him.

And I pushed him toward my room, while in the turns of the valley the banners appeared and disappeared, snaking along as if they were playing, as if they were mocking.

Maerbale's departure loosened the tension that was gripping Bomarzo. I continued my correspondence with Giulia as if nothing had happened, and I even thought that through the fiction of self-deception I had managed to relegate her letter to Maerbale to the status of a vague nightmare. I was ardent in my desires to deceive myself, because I painfully needed people to love me—much more than my loving them—and therefore I was putting the letter out of my memory, disfiguring it, reducing even more within its brief structure until I managed, if I did not make it evaporate, that at least it had changed into something shapeless, imprecise, the harmlessness of which came from the fact that by avoiding thinking about it I was acting as if it had never existed. But it had existed and it was lying in wait for me, and all of a sudden, when I dropped my defense, thinking that I had destroyed it, the letter would leap up before my eyes, flaming, and the sight of it would agitate me again.

Seeking distraction from those worries, I turned to the supervision of the administration of my lands. I went over the accounts of Messer Bernardino Niccoloni, a chore that was repugnant to my prejudice that princes should avoid tasks fitting for merchants, and I could see that the administrator was robbing me. The opportunity to discharge him had arisen then, but my fluctuating hesitation worked as at other times whenever there was a question of adopting radical measures and I limited myself to scolding him and showing him with imperious contempt that the eyes of the master were on him. Messer Bernardino was astute and he knew how to manipulate arguments and figures; from then on he proceeded with greater care, limiting his ambitions.

His wife unexpectedly obliged me to make a decision worthy of Solomon. She was a dry woman, a grumbler, rather dirty, whose aridness was warmed by only one passion: that for stray cats. At night, when dogs howled in the prison of courtyards and gardens and in the distant countryside, the feline flock would invade the solitude of Bomarzo with its felt and emeralds. On late walks I had often seen them wandering through the alleys, stretching in doorways, decorating the walls with their sacred basalt sculptures as if the place had been changed into an Oriental village where no one dared touch the sacred animals. They mewed from hunger and love, and their cries split the air. Some people who were still awake would open their doors noisily to chase them away. Then—I witnessed it on several occasions—two mumbling demons would appear at opposite ends of the steep street which was tightly confined by the town and over which the colossal shadow of the castle fell. Messer Bernardino's wife and the wife of one of my grandmother's jesters were going through their ritual as protectors of the cats. Signora Niccoloni, tall and severe, the wife of the jester, fat and fussy, vied in their drive to feed the army of stray cats. Each with a basket, one would go down and the other would climb up the narrow street, and the cats, leaping like possessed people or arching their backs and tails would run to meet them as if floating on a lunar stream. Finally, at the end of their respective advance, both samaritans, escorted by their corresponding famished creatures, the opulent containers empty now, would come together in the center of the street, and the concert of meows would be replaced or extended by a contest of obscene words in which the adversaries gave free rein to the jealousy of their patronage. I knew that Signora Niccoloni was driving her husband mad in an attempt to have him get my grandmother to send the jester to Rome so as to be rid of her nocturnal rival. I would have liked it too, except for different reasons, because I was bothered by the presence in Bomarzo of that bespectacled dwarf with orange-colored hair, who, if he did not have my hump, which would have been quite useful to him, acted as if he had one. There were jesters in every great Italian house—not two, as in ours, but many—and that fact, which gave tone and was an indication of position, held back my impulse to get rid of them. I also feared that if I sent them away, the matter would be commented upon at the papal court and they would say, making an easy joke, that I was the only jester they needed in Bomarzo. The complaints of the inhabitants, silent at first because of the fact that the administrator's wife was involved, grew and reached my ears with the demand that since the administrator would not take care of it, being mixed up in the matter, the duke himself should put an end to the uproar. There was nothing left for me to do but intervene and listen to the litigants. It was a grotesque affair, worthy of Aristophanes. I had a map of the disputed street drawn and at its center I traced with a firm hand and in green ink the exact line that separated the two nutritional jurisdictions. Peace reigned after that. If the cats crossed that line, the enemies were not to call them under pain of losing their monopolies. They did call them, of course, in low voices, with cautious gestures which in their suppleness matched those of the tigerish rebels. One night I watched them from a window, leaning on my elbows between my grandmother's cats, white princes, the Orsinis of catdom, and I saw them slip out with their baskets followed by their adepts. The village declared that the duke had made a perfectly equitable decision. It was the wisest thing that I had managed to do until then and when it was compared with the simultaneous deeds that my imagination attributed to Maerbale, one could measure the extent of my rage. The duke of the cats, that was what I was, the hunchbacked duke of the cats, with two ministers, the administrator's wife and the wife of the jester.

I made such mediocrity bearable by putting my budding collections in order. Aided by Messer Pandolfo, who found the influence of Virgil everywhere, not hesitating when faced by anachronistic evidence, and by Silvio da Narni, who interrupted his horoscopic calculations to become involved in the field of an improvised archeology, I studied the armor that my grandmother had given me—the vases, the urns, the mirror, the combs, the terracotta figurines found in the tombs of Bomarzo, the medals and cameos that I had acquired in Rome and which excavating antiquarians were still sending me. I was happy among those objects that took me away from reality. While I picked them up and turned them in my hands, Porzia would be with us. Perhaps, with my being certain in the presumption that Silvio lacked magical powers, the girl had fallen in love with my secretary without any secret intervention in spite of his ugliness, and the spectacle of that love accentuated my melancholy, because it showed me that even he, without grace, without teeth, was capable of arousing the affection of a beautiful woman, while I, who owned everything about me, operated within the perplexities of insecurity.

With such humble diversions I spent my time as if nothing else interested me. I hid my anguish behind the mask of economic and artistic cares, analyzing taxes and polishing medals, when in truth I was only waiting for two things: letters from Giulia and news of Maerbale. The first continued arriving, spaced, colorless; of the second I knew that he was fighting with Valerio Orsini at the walls of Florence. In August, Baglioni was master of the Medici city and the Signoria declared a truce; in December, Baglioni the Judas died and his dream of becoming duke of the same Florence he had betrayed was over. On the other hand, as had been foreseen, Alessandro de' Medici, who returned the following year to the palace on the Via Larga, did, and there were no more doubts about the paternity of Clement VII. But Maerbale was still alive, probably plotting against me, and the promises that Silvio repeated to me week after week left me indifferent. My brother returned to Venice with Valerio Orsini. They said that he had become rich and that his clothing sparkled with precious stones.

Against that image and to show an austere trait that did not exist, I adopted the custom of dressing as a peasant, like Petrarcha in Vaucluse, and cultivating a garden. A single dog and two servants would accompany me as in the case of the poet. Just as he boasted of the copy of Homer that had been sent to him from Greece, I intended to limit my pride to the objects of greenish iron that I was digging up in Etruscan tombs and which spoke to me of a beautiful and strange past. With Messer Pandolfo I again picked up the translation of Lucretius's poem on nature, little known at that time. I was planning to leave for Rome, tiring of arguing with mad women and uprooting nettles, when we heard through a messenger from Orso that Maerbale had been seriously wounded in the Most Serene Republic as he was crossing a bridge. Some days later Orso himself and Matteo appeared in Bomarzo with three more cousins: Arrigo, the condottiere; Leone, destined soon to be the wealthiest member of our house; and Guido della Corbara, the son of a sister of my father's. They were probably coming to collect the price of their perfidy, for the attempt could be attributed to nothing else. Something along those lines was insinuated to me by Silvio da Narni, and I shouted at him to settle up with them whatever it was, but that he should tell them that if they dared speak of it in front of me I would have them thrown out of the castle. In any case, Maerbale was not dead. He was lying in pain in the comfort of a palace in Venice. Valerio was caring for him and Aretino would come to visit him.

My relatives renewed the practices of the time of Girolamo, making our halls resound with their noise. I let them blow off steam. They asked me to let them have some lady friends come and I allowed it. I wanted to get drunk and forget, forget myself. When the women arrived, Porzia, Silvio, and Giambattista joined in the festivities that would last from dusk to dawn. One day the Count of Corbara announced to me that he had a surprise for me and that afternoon Pantasilea arrived in the courtyard of the castle, laughing, surrounded by slaves and baggage. The rooms resounded with the barking of her Maltese dog, and the white cats ran off to hide. She had brought her peacocks in large baskets. I ordered them killed immediately and I gave her a pearl necklace in exchange. The hanged peacocks were strung from a tree in the garden like a pair of those iridescent cloaks that Venetian merchants would buy from caravans in the Far East. Pantasilea wept, kissed the moonlike pearls, embraced me, and begged me to banish from my memory the episodes that had darkened our friendship. Nothing mattered to me any more, so there was no reason not to promise everything she asked for. I sadly gave myself over to the debauchery. In Recanati I had discovered that my father looked like me, and now I was discovering that I, in certain aspects, was like my father. It was as if in some mysterious way we were changing into each other. Just as Cardinal Orsini used to do, my grandmother would appear at times leaning on her canes to watch our orgies. Behind her were the curious heads of her ladies in waiting. She would sigh.

"What do you intend doing, Vicino?" she asked me one morning when I met her in the garden.

"I don't know."
"Do you intend to stay here forever? What about Giulia?"

A short time later I said good-bye to my cousins and Pantasilea. I decided that Silvio and Giambattista would accompany me to Venice, where Lorenzo Lotto would paint my portrait. It would have been easy for me to get the artist who was constantly moving about and who suffered from a lack of money to come down to Bomarzo, but I preferred taking the trip in order to get away from a place which, even though I loved it so much, was now working upon me as if it were enervating me, as if it were gnawing at me from within with very fine teeth. Furthermore, in Venice I would find out how to proceed once and for all in the matter of Maerbale. Then I would have to busy myself with my wedding. The image of Giulia Farnese came back to glow like a swinging censer. Peace and to be loved: that was what I asked. It was much to ask. It was asking everything. What would I give in exchange? I could exchange a string of pearls for some dead peacocks, whose bodies I ordered taken miles away from Bomarzo and burned, where their sinister influence would not reach us, but for Giulia's love and the calm that my spirit yearned for, I had nothing to give. I raised my beautiful hands in the solitude of my room, and I saw them as empty and transparent, weak, useless.

We traveled to Ancona on horseback; from there we would sail to Venice. Autumn was making the road golden, rusty. We galloped along in a cloud of dust and scattered crackling leaves as if the wind were sweeping us toward the Adriatic along with the withered leaves. On the way, at inns, improvisers who composed verses on any subject would receive some coins from me for singing of the glories of the Orsinis when they found out that they were in the presence of the Duke of Bomarzo. Since they did not have an exact knowledge of those deeds, they mingled historical characters with those of fantasy, laying hands on Greek heroes and the paladins of old ballads to supplant their ignorance. The family bears appeared constantly in their cadences, fighting, charging, snorting, destroying enemies, as inseparable from my ancestors as the gods of Olympus were from the Homeric chieftains.

Those comforting presences did not calm the upset that had accompanied me since our departure and which was growing as we went ahead. In Ancona I felt some fever and my body began to break out in suspicious blotches. I thought that my turn had come to suffer the illness that had inspired Fracastoro's *Syphilis* and which was gnawing at Pier Luigi Farnese and so many unbridled passionate people, and I trembled as I remembered his livid face covered with tumors and splotches. Perhaps I owed it to Pantasilea or one of my cousins' lady friends. Numerous apprentices of Aesculapius then offered me their services, which I prudently rejected. I would have myself treated in Venice. The cures might be more rigorous than the disease.

Students invaded the taverns, their knapsacks bulging with manuscripts, bottles, and unguents covering the tables. Along with them went healers, who hawked their miracles in the market places, the purveyors of elixirs, toothpullers, and beggars. Some were escorting teachers of mysterious knowledge on their wanderings. They earned their way singing, casting horoscopes, examining sores on people and animals, offering love potions, conjuring up Satan, stealing. They would undress the serving girls and mock the gravity of merchants and burghers. They put on pantomimes, pretending to be princesses or blind men or the god Apollo. Their laughter and their guitars made the cheap eating places merry. I heard the mention of Paracelsus for the first time in Ancona.

Silvio and Giambattista had wrapped me up in a chair beside the fireplace of the hostel, for I preferred the bustle of the dining room to the suffocation of a bedroom where one did battle with fleas. Ten or twelve ragged young men were arguing over some pitchers of wine. The day before there had been a fight on the docks and a man had had an ear cut off which a barber had refastened with mortar. As might be imagined, the ear fell off again, and the students were arguing about the treatment with violent gestures, mangled Latin, and dirty words. From time to time they would come over to me, carrying their greasy hats in their hands and fire in their eyes to solicit my opinion, as if from the fact that I was who I was and had had Valeriano as a teacher, I could resolve their conflicts, but I listened to them, half dozing, in silence. In addition, I did not know a whit about those matters.

On one side the Avicennists were all aroused, those who claimed that all science came from the Arabs; on the other the Neo-Galenists and the Neo-Hippocratics were ranting. There were also those who thought that outside of Aristotle there was no knowledge whatever, and those who opposed them with Platonic concepts. Since their grasp of the themes was very superficial, at every instant they would become entangled in contradictions. The Aristotelians had briefly attended the University of Padua and the Platonists that of Ferrara. The last must have been mostly Germans (it was an effort to understand them), because the links of the House of Este with the emperor facilitated the residence of Teutons in the territory. The Arabists were out of fashion, while the general current inclined to look with disdain upon any advances after Galen. Only a few voices in the uproar were raised against the one whom his admirers had nicknamed "Paradoxopeo," the miracle maker. The unusual words and the invective became confused in my mind. Withdrawn, grumbling, I was sipping a potion that Silvio had prepared for me. Suddenly the name of Paracelsus came out in the tumult and the debate heated up.

"An ass who doesn't teach in Latin but in a kind of barbarous German that doesn't even deserve the name," one declared.

"The asses are the ones who are against him," another shot back. "He himself has called physicians proven asses, drunkards, cheats, and cuckolds."

"I've dealt with a lot of cuckold doctors."

"I've helped make them that way."

"But he calls himself a doctor. 'Theophrastus, Doctor in Both Medicines and in Sacred Scripture,' and he's not even a physician."

"He is too a physician."

"No he isn't."

"He calls himself the 'Monarch of Medicine' and he puts everyone who practices it beneath his majesty. He says that all other doctors in the whole wide world will be forgotten someday in hidden corners where dogs go to piss."

"Paracelsus isn't a doctor and neither is his father, who in the inn at Einsiedeln washes the sores on the feet of pilgrims on their way to the sanctuary of Our Black Lady."

"He's just a surgeon. A physician doesn't put on bandages or perform operations. That's for barbers. And he, as a barber, sinks his knife into the flesh."

"I'm a barber and I'm proud of it."

"He calls himself a chemical doctor, whatever that means. He goes around dirty, covered with soot, as if he worked in a smithy. And he gets drunk with coachmen, with midwives, and with whores."

"Like me and I'm proud of it."

"Like us."

"But he doesn't like women. I don't think he's ever had one."

"He's a beardless eunuch. And rachitic too."

"I feel sorry for Paracelsus. He's missing the best, the salt of this poor damned earth."

"The damned fool looks down his nose at the influence of the stars, but in Vienna he learned to determine fate by the constellations. He says that physicians limit themselves to studying the horoscopes of patients and to determining the best time for intervention, and that the scientific work falls to the barber."

"He's an imbecile."

"He asserts that the orbit of Saturn won't lengthen or shorten the life of a man, but he doesn't give a physic or a bleeding when the Moon isn't in the right position."

"Where does all that get us?"

"Aristotle," Silvio da Narni shouted, "declares that this world is joined of necessity to the movements of the upper world. All power in our world is governed by those movements."

The Aristotelians broke into applause.

"Paracelsus doesn't believe in books."

"In books?"

"In Basel he burned the texts of Avicenna and Galen four years ago."

"Heretic!"

"He maintains that the books from which one gets knowledge are the bodies of patients and that it is necessary to center the study at the bed of the afflicted person. And he's against dissection. He states that doctors have never dealt with real anatomy, which is that of a living body and not a dead one. 'If you want to find the anatomy of health and sickness, you need a living body.' That's what he says."

"Butcher! Torturer!"

"But he cured the King of Denmark's mother."

"That's a lie!"

"And eighteen princes... and the abbess of Zinzilla..."

"Lies! Lies! He showed his impotence before the Margrave of Baden."

"No university is good enough for him. They've thrown him out of all of them."

"I met him in Montpellier."

"I did at Nuremberg."

"I did at the Sorbonne."

"And he swears that a person doesn't learn as much in German schools as in the market place of Frankfurt."

"He's right."

"Shut up, you idiot! He doesn't know anything about anything. I was in Nuremberg when he refused to debate with the professors."

"I was in Basel when he didn't dare have a public confrontation with Vandelinus Hock, who had already beaten him in Strasbourg."

"On the other hand, I was in Nuremberg when he cured nine patients of the French disease in the lepers' hospital. A miracle. He prescribed mercury with juices and herbs."

"Interesting."

"Impossible."

"He's a genius."

"He's an ignoramus. An herb gatherer who goes through the Alps with his father talking to shepherds and looking for fennel, thyme, opium poppies, mint, and Saint John's plant."

"Are you talking about his cures? The fat of a viper, the horn of a unicorn, the dust of a mummy, children's hairs boiled by a redhead, toads, a handful of manure, moss growing on a skull..."

"What does he use the children's hair for?"

"Chilblains."

"I'll have to try it."

"Imbecile!"

"I've used mummy's dust prepared with birds stuffed with spices and then pulverized. There's nothing like it."

"It's better to cut down a corpse from the gallows and use his mummy."

"You're as crazy as he is when he explains that the human body, the *limus terrae*, is made up of salt, sulphur, and mercury."

"What about the *archeus*?"

"What do you mean, *archeus*?"

"The *archeus* of Paracelsus is the life principle that takes root in the depths of every living thing. The quintessence. A crouching elf who governs bodily reactions."

"You make me laugh. I'm laughing: ha! ha! ha! The *archeus*..."

"Besides, who can understand it? He doesn't believe in the power of demons, but he discovered one, Afernoch, the one who causes melancholy."

"Not believing in demons is heretical."

"But before looking at a patient he finds out if he has been bewitched, and if he takes hairs, nails, needles, bristles, or pieces of glass out of his body, he declares that they have been put in him by a wizard."

"In those cases one must place one of the objects expelled or taken out in an oak tree, on the side facing the east, so that it will work as a lodestone and draw out the malignant influence."

"That's Paracelsus's method."

"That's my method."

"You share it."

"And he has a demon imprisoned in the hilt of his sword."

"I've seen it, I've seen it! A huge sword, the gift of a German executioner. It drags when he walks."

"No. He got it in Greece. In that hilt he keeps hidden the recipe for laudanum that a magician from Constantinople gave him. It's protected by the demon Azoth."

"Lies!"

"Why can't he believe in demons, beginning with Afernoch and Azoth, if he boasts of his friendship with the Abbot Trithemius, the one who evoked the ghost of the dead empress at the request of the Emperor Maximilian and when the specter advised him to marry Bianca Sforza?"

"Still, Paracelsus doesn't believe in ghosts. For him they're neither body nor soul, but a certain reflection that he calls *evestrum*. And since they're ineffectual shadows, they can't do anything."

"That's enough to have him burned on the square. The Holy Bible overflows with ghosts. Not even the Devil can save him."

"According to him, the Devil is incapable of effecting transmutations if nature does not permit it."

"He's right."

"You'll burn alongside of him."

"He's right. The Devil works miracles with the power of natural arts."

"Heresy! Paracelsus is a Lutheran heretic. So are you."

"He's a Catholic!"

"I was in Salzburg when they threw him out because he was preaching anti-Christian ideas in the taverns."

"You're a fool. Paracelsus is just as Catholic as the pope."

"Even more."

"The strange thing is that he believes in incubuses and succubuses."

"Who doesn't believe in them?"

"In his opinion they're born from the ill-spent seeds of Onan."

"And the Devil."

"Someone who really sees the Devil, Machiavelli says, doesn't see him with so many horns and so black."

"That's from the *Song of the Hermits*."

Suddenly the disputants became very young, almost adolescent, as their fury abated and they begin to sing in unison and off key: "We are monks and hermits and we live on the peaks of the Apennines..."

The overflowing mugs came together. In the meantime I was looking at my hands, darkened against the light of the flames. Soon the signs of the pustules would begin to form.

"Where is Paracelsus?" I asked.

"We don't know, Duke. He's everywhere, like God."

"Like the Devil."

"He's in Venice."

I thought about Paracelsus's theory of the creation of the demons of lust who are born of those who commit the unnatural sin and from the lost semen, carried by the spirits who wander in the night. How many times, heated up by lustful urges, had I succumbed to the temptation of the imaginative *actus* which engenders demons? I shuddered in the warmth of the blankets.

"Buy them some drinks," I ordered Giambattista, and the wine flowed at the tables amid the gabble.

"To the health of the Duke of Bomarzo!" they exclaimed, raising their noisy glasses.

"To the health of Philippus Aureolus Theophrastus Bombastus von Hohenheim, Paracelsus!"

"No, no! Theophrastus is Cacophrastus! To the health of Aulus Celsus, the Cicero of Medicine, the Latin Hippocrates! Celsus is better than Paracelsus!"

"Nonsense!"

"Fools, imbeciles, blind asses, cuckolds! Long live Paracelsus, the King of Medicine!"

Drunkenness got the better of them and they took out their daggers. "Let's get out of here. This is no place for Your Lordship," Silvio proposed to me, and between him and Martelli, slowly, they carried me upstairs.

In the dining room the moans, the curses, the noise of benches thrown as projectiles resounded, the blows of knives and fists. We were sailing at dawn. My head, mouth, waist, legs, and arms all ached. I was no longer interested in Maerbale, or Lorenzo Lotto, not even in Giulia Farnese, but in Paracelsus. Perhaps he would be able to cure me, cleanse me of the impurity that was devouring me hour after hour.

During the boat trip Silvio confided in me that for some months he had been in correspondence with Pier Luigi, who had contracted him to cast his horoscope.

As always when something concerning a person of my intimacy took place behind my back, without my being consulted, I felt that I was being cheated, robbed, but I did not have the strength to get angry and I limited myself to sighing and shaking my head.

"Farnese was born under the sign of Scorpio, November 19, 1503," Silvio said.

"In November, when the delirium of autumn is aggravated—under the scorpion who flees from light, who seeks refuge in caves, who comes out at night with the poison of his dart. Yes, Pier Luigi was born when he should have been."

"Don't you like him, Duke?"

"I'm speaking of the scorpion, the *formidolosus*, the symbol of hypocritical perfidy. Artemis was right to choose one of those creatures to wound Orion on the day he tried to rape her."

"Now Orion walks through the sky. And the scorpion too. Everything is appeased and reconciled up there."

We looked at the stars that were shining above the sails.

"According to the conjunction of Saturn and Jupiter, Pier Luigi Farnese will die at the age of seventy and his end will be peaceful," the astrologer added.

"Tell him that, because he'll be pleased with the news. I don't believe it."

Silvio bit his lips. "I'll do that, my Lord."

"In the Most Serene Republic you'll look for Messer Paracelsus."

"Do you have faith in him after what you've heard?"

"You look for him."

"I'll do that, my Lord."

I lay down to doze on some bundles. I was shaking with fever. The breeze brushed my face and it was cold, like the breath of the Fates. Which one could be Scorpio among so many hanging lamps? Could he be slipping along with his pincers in the terrible astral darkness, black and shiny, his aggressive tail arched, his cruel eyes staring, extinguishing the stars with his huge shadow, still pursuing the athletic boy guilty of desiring Diana? Not even there in the infinite Pythagorean symphony, where exact music answers itself, could one not have rest even there from the sad, earthly passion?

"You'll find Paracelsus."

I clasped my hot hands. I was frightened by the idea that my supernatural horoscope would not be fulfilled and that everything might end in mediocrity, in nothingness, without Pier Francesco Orsini, the Duke of Bomarzo's having done anything worthy of note in the books of his clan except that he let his older brother die, he broke a crystal polyhedron, and he meted out justice in the suit between two madwomen who were litigants in the midst of mewing. Or I was frightened that the illness would devour my face as it had Cesare Borgia's, and that like him I would have to wear a mask, because if I lost my face, the best thing I had, chewed away by ulcers, and if nothing remained but my eyes burning in the openings of a mask, the hump, invading me, would end up taking complete control of me.

"Do you think that Paracelsus will cure you?"

"I think he will save me."

I sank the bundle of my hump into the puffed-out bundles there. Up above the sails the stars were twinkling, chasing one another.

# 6. THE PORTRAIT BY LORENZO LOTTO

*Dazzling Venice—My illness—The generous Valerio Orsini—Pietro Aretino—Paracelsus and immortality—The letters from the alchemist Dastyn to Cardinal Napoleone Orsini—The visit to Doge Andrea Gritti and to the tomb of the condottiere Niccolò—The lizard—Pier Luigi's scandalous boat—Lorenzo Lotto paints my portrait*

THE READER will have to forgive me for the lack of taste, the anachronistic petulance, the typical insolence of travelers toward those who have not come from their district—and in this case their time—but I can assure you that a person who had not seen Venice in the sixteenth century cannot boast that he has seen it at all. Compared with the Venice of that time, with that vast, careful, and impetuous composition by Tintoretto or Titian, the present-day city is like a picture postcard, or calendar art, or those watercolors that daubers sell to innocent foreigners on Saint Mark's Square. I suppose that something else might be said—annoying to me in that case—by one who had seen it in the fifteenth century, the eighteenth, and even the nineteenth. I can only speak of what I had the good fortune to know. The Venice which the reader has visited perhaps during these postwar years, a series of glass bazaars, with noisy launches, innumerable hotels, photographers, invading tourists, hysterical women, honeymooners, paid serenaders, rascals of sensuality, leftovers from Ruskin's time, and ambitious bikini wearers, has no link at all except for certain traces of eternal decoration with the admirable one that I visited in the fall of 1532. It is customary to repeat that certain cities—Bruges, Toledo, Venice—do not change; that Time respects them and tiptoes past. That is not true: they do change and they change a great deal. Venice has changed so much that when I arrived there recently it was hard to adjust the picture of it with the image of a marvelous city that my spirit had kept intact.

I scarcely glimpsed it the morning of our arrival. I was riding along quite ill in a boat that we rented when we gave in before the evidence that I would not be capable of continuing on horseback, but the first contact was dazzling. After Bomarzo, made of harsh stones, ashes, and rust, tight and gloomy, Venice was outlined before me, liquid, aerial, transparent, as if it were not a reality but a strange and beautiful thought; as if reality were Bomarzo, fastened to the earth and its secret entrails, while that incredible sight was a projection that had crystallized over the lagoons, something like a suspended and tremulous illusion that could dissolve at any moment and silently disappear like the mirage of a dream. It is not that I considered Bomarzo less poetical—God forbid—but in Bomarzo the poetry was something that came from within, one that was born in the heart of the rock and was nourished by the work of hidden essences across the centuries, while in Venice the poetical aspect was the external luminous result of the love between air and water, and consequently it had a ghostly quality that tricked the senses and, in order to be captured, demanded a communication in which esthetic ecstasy and magical vibration were combined. That was my first impression of the fascinating place. Then I understood that, on me at least, the mysterious force of Bomarzo, less evident on the surface, more secretly vital, worked with a much deeper strength than that courtly seduction that was made up of exquisite games and exciting tones; but like so many, like everybody, I succumbed when I came upon the enchantment of the incomparable city and in my memory I betrayed my authentic truth—everyone has his own Bomarzo—and I thought that there was no place, that there could not be any place in the world as beautiful as Venice, or as rich, or as exciting, or so obviously created for the search of that difficult happiness that we anxiously seek, using up people and places, those of us who are desperately dependent on our senses.

It stood before me for a moment that morning, and for a month I no longer saw it, but its image did not leave me in my sickroom, and I am certain that my restlessness to win it over, walk through it, learn about it, treasure it, helped in good measure to speed up the recuperation of my health, the breakdown of which was based not only on physical causes but also on psychological ones. For the rest I shall say that my emotion was not an exceptional feeling in the sixteenth century. After Rome (and for many ahead of Rome), Venice was the most attractive city. It was filled with outsiders, although not like today when old-time Venetians take refuge in their homes so as not to run into the intruding guided caravans; and in that throng of travelers princes and great lords stood out who had come from the far corners of curious Europe and the Near East, attracted by the noise of its festivals and the prestige of its matchless sights. Venice was imperceptibly decomposing, gnawed at by the rot which like a fatal emanation from the muddy water was wearing its palaces and its people away, and which, years later, it tried to get rid of with the effort of Lepanto.

It was losing its Eastern domains to the Turks; other colonizing states were taking over its markets in India; corsairs in the dangerous Mediterranean were ruining its maritime commerce. But its luxury, its splendor had never been more evident. Wise spirits captured the feeling of the alliance of life and death that it represented, and that, that emotional contradiction, added to its charm. It was as if everywhere on its canals and in its *cortili*, under the flag-bedecked noise of its celebrations, whispered in repetition were the terrible words that were spoken to the dogess during the high triumph of her accession to her position: "Just as Your Ladyship has come alive to this place to take possession of the palace, so you must understand that when dead, your brain, your eyes, and your entrails will be removed and they will be displayed on this very spot for three days before being lowered into your tomb." It was romantic, with a predominance of romantic officials, no longer simply mercantile as during the period of its eager growth, but aristocratic and suffering from the illness of decadence which was sinking its teeth into it underneath the pretendedly intact pomp of its ceremonious domain: that was how I saw it during that autumn of my twentieth year. And perhaps because I was ill I felt it deeply. I felt that this sick Venice and I resembled each other in that twilight moment, urgent and still proud; that we both symbolized something similar, something destined to be looked down upon and lost: the attitude of a caste (of an idea?) facing life; and that, for all of our arbitrary weaknesses, our vanities, and our corruptions, Venice and the men of my line—who had initiated their progress in the world toward their aristocratic goal with a similar heroic uprightness and who were falling apart together in the withered melancholy of refinement—had contributed to give to that world, to that world which as it thought that it was becoming better would be becoming more and more uniform and mediocre, a tone, a proud greatness, the lack of which would deprive it of an irreplaceable form of intensity and passion.

We went along the Rialto bridge, which was still wood, although plans were already made to build one out of stone, and famous architects and sculptors were sketching its future design. As always, the noisy circle of commerce had its center there, around the column of the mappemonde which boastfully showed the routes of Venetian speculation. I went slowly up to the place, leaning on the arms of Giambattista and Silvio, and the fresh smell of the fruits, mixed with that of spices from the Levant and that of the rich fabrics assaulted me in the midst of the gabble of exotic languages. I sent my pages off in search of lodgings, for I had not reserved any, and, lost in that miniature Babel, I sat down to look at the Grand Canal, along which boats loaded with straw and wood were coming and others that were dragging long nets through the water like cloaks. I had not counted on the espionage, an essential element of the Most Serene Republic, which covered the entire city with invisible threads, so that nothing of what was going on, no matter how small it might be, could keep its secret, so that, for example, if a nobleman made the mistake of grumbling against the government, even in whispers and imagining himself safe from betrayal, he would be warned two times and on the third he would be drowned without further ado. The informers immediately communicated my presence, which I had planned to hide, so that two men came back with my pages: a messenger from the Doge Andrea Gritti, who sent me greetings and invited me to come see him, and another from my kinsman Valerio Orsini, who told me that he would never forgive me if on my stay in Venice I would not be his guest in the Emo palace, located in the Madonna dell'Orto section. I thanked the prince for his attention, promising to go when my health grew better, and after hesitating, knowing that Maerbale was living in that same palace, I ended up accepting the hospitable offer of my uncle, because the truth was that I was in low spirits because of my obscure illness and I was frightened by the prospect of facing it almost alone. In a short while a gondola arrived bearing the Orsini gonfalon, and I settled myself in it with Silvio, Giambattista, and my luggage, feeling suddenly better because of the simple circumstance that on that small pennant the figures of the rose, the serpent, and the bears were waving. We rowed to Madonna dell'Orto along the part that faces the iridescence of a liquid plain of lilacs and crimsons out toward San Michele and Murano, and we got out at the place where the Zenos had built their palace, those travelers who had wandered so far that there is evidence of their having been in America a century before Christopher Columbus. I made the trip along the Grand Canal and the Cannaregio with my eyes half-closed. My body ached, the fever was burning me as if there were hot coals hidden under my skin and the light hurt my burning eyes, but, as if I were dreaming about them—and that was probably where the initial impression of a dream that Venice gave me came from—it seemed that the palaces lined up on both banks, several of them covered with scaffolding on which artists and workers were moving, quivered in their sparkling tunics of water and, bejeweled like harlots, they were escorting me in a double column of gold, purple, and coral between the coming and going of the boats that gathered the fleeting trace of musical instruments, of lutes and theorbos, or of multicolored insects that were flapping their wings and vibrating delicately on the lagoon.

Valerio was one of the most perfect, most complete Orsinis that I have ever met. Naturally, as a good condottiere, he shifted from one side to the other, according to his convenience, but from the Renaissance point of view, he was behaving as was fitting and he had earned an envious position. He had been—and he was—an intimate friend of the Medicis; of that Lorenzo who had been given the Duchy of Urbino, less permanent than his statue by Michelangelo, and of Clement VII, whom he had defended against the infernal Colonnas and had protected during the siege until his cavalry was crushed by the enemy's numerical superiority. Then he entered the service of Venice and backed up the undertakings of Lautrec along with my father.

Francis I awarded him the Duchy of Ascoli and the County of Nola, traditional holdings of the Orsinis, but that privilege did not last long, because the French army was defeated by fever and my uncle was left without allies. Then Valerio, with a sharp sense of realism, broke with the French and went over to the side of Charles V and the siege of Florence. My brother followed him there. Until his death, twenty years after the time I am speaking of here, he was yet to abandon the Spaniards, command troops for the Grand Duke Cosimo de' Medici, return to the service of Venice, be governor of Dalmatia, and expire in that same Venice, in that same palace where he had received me, opening his paternal arms and hugging me against his old and robust chest. Two renowned loves accompanied the accidents of his tumultuous life: that of his wife, the granddaughter of Oliverotto da Fermo, whom Cesare Borgia got the better of in Senigallia with *divine* trickery, and that of a boy of great beauty, Leonardo Emo, the son of the friend to whom the palace where he lived and where he put me up belonged. I must add that the noble Emo, an outstanding magistrate of Venice, knew about the relationship and encouraged it, for he understood, like the ancient Greeks—like the Cretans, who judged a young man dishonored if he did not enjoy a liaison of that type, like the Spartans, who established it by law and fined the rare aristocrats who did not maintain such a love—that it bore great benefits for Leonardo, whom the glorious condottiere nourished with experience. That whole situation, as can be seen, was as much a part of the period as the calculated political and military changes of the great Valerio. His wife worshiped him; Leonardo worshiped him; the patrician Emo respected him; Maerbale admired him; Aretino jealously guarded his illustrious friendship; money and jewels increased his private treasury after every sack and campaign; and Valerio considered himself the most fortunate man in the world, organizing concerts, masquerades, and balls in time of peace, with the noisy attendance of greedy adolescents and stupendous prostitutes, and organizing in time of war disciplined companies and strategic attacks. He knew how to enjoy himself and he knew how to work.

As I have said, I spent a month in the Emo palace without going onto the street. I never saw Maerbale during the thirty profitable days in which I learned the most diverse and unexpected things thanks to Aretino and to Paracelsus. I was interested in his health and they told me that my brother was recovering from his wounds. Two or three times I thought that I had heard his cries in the silence of the evening. They were washing his wounds with boiling wine to avoid gangrene, and that was ample justification for attributing the unrecognized roars to him, which caused me no remorse since it was a question of an eye for an eye. It was singular that the only two lords of Bomarzo should be in Venice at the same time, so far from their castle, on their respective beds in the same palace with wounds and suffering, and that there should not be the slightest communication between them. Valerio Orsini and Leonardo Emo, the old man and the boy, went from one room to the other, bearing invented messages. They assured me that my brother was worried for me and they assured him that I was worried about him, although that was not the case. We really were worried, but we did not say so.

Pietro Aretino, fat, bearded, his satyr's head muffled in fine furs, would come to visit me and amuse me with the enumeration of the princely gifts that were ceaselessly sent to him from remote courts in Italy, France, and Germany in order to silence his devastating irony, and of the tales of tributes paid to him by the Barbary pirates and the Pasha of Algiers as if he were some fearful sovereign. Pleasant when he wanted to be, fierce too when he wanted to be, an incomparable blackmailer, a journalist without scruples and without fatigue, his letters and printed matter multiplied and gold poured in for him which would immediately slip through his prodigal hands. When he persecuted someone the venom of his darts would finish him. My grandfather Franciotto knew it well enough when he refused to pay his tribute and suffered the sting of his lampoons. Aretino, basing everything on the function of master of the hunt for Leo X which the cardinal fulfilled and that of purchaser of exorbitant falcons and whippets for the pontifical party, attacked him with his satires. That detail did not annoy me in the slightest. I had taken the precaution of sending Silvio out to acquire a gold chain for the poet and, like Cerberus with the honey cakes, Aretino—who, furthermore, had great respect for my uncle Valerio—stopped grumbling and kissed my right hand. By proceeding in that fashion I was doing nothing but imitating Francis I and Charles V, who had given him necklaces of precious stones, or the Duke of Mantua, who made peace with him by means of velvet jerkins and brocade shirts, or the sultan, who had given him a slave girl of rare beauty and effective sensual techniques. He had been living for three years in the Bolani palace, opposite the Rialto, and there he received in great disorder the homage of Turks, Jews, Italians, Spaniards, Germans, and Frenchmen, who considered him an oracle, whether they were lords, students, or monks. He owned a harem made up of five or six women who were nicknamed the "Aretinas." It was also whispered (and he was even accused of it publicly) that his amorous army did not stop at the limits of the female sex, and mention was made of his links with as proper a gentleman as Captain Giovanni delle Bande Nere, a hero of Italy and the model of a condottiere. Perhaps that double activity—if it did exist—might have helped tighten the bonds that linked him to Valerio Orsini. He was the man who was in fashion and he took advantage of it, reeking with satisfaction. Everything was called "Aretino" in Venice then, from a breed of horses to a kind of glass, from the canal near his house to a literary style and even those women whom he enjoyed with a success comparable to that of Titian, his great friend and associate in matters of art. And the picture of Pietro, the son of a loose woman and a shoe repairman, born in a hospital in Arezzo, a lackey of the banker Chigi and a jester to Pope Leo de' Medici, was painted on ceramic plates, stamped on the handles of mirrors and on comb boxes, struck on medals of gold, silver, and copper, and sculptured on the façades of palaces. More than once he made me forget my pains with a Pantagruelian recounting of the mountains of almonds, cherries, strawberries, limes, figs, apricots, melons, and plums that were unloaded at the Bolani palace, destined to his table of invincible gluttony; or that of his quarrels with the Duke of Mantua over the poem *Marfisa*, never finished, which was to proclaim the glory of the Gonzagas, and the manuscript of which he would pawn every so often to get a little money; or that of his relations with the Doge Gritti, to whom he had offered his soul because he had redeemed Venice; or that of the public confession he had made in a church, where there was so little light that he could barely read the text that was smeared with his theatrical tears.

Yes, Aretino was an intelligent rascal, capable of amusing like no one else if he put his unleashed genius to work, and I owe him prodigious moments, especially when, in the midst of an anecdote, he would begin to laugh thunderously, shaking his thick body, holding his stomach with both hands and making the links and jewels that crossed his strong chest ring—they say he died of an attack of laughter like that because he lost his balance, fell to the floor, and broke his neck—but as much as I owe to the rich diversion that came from his imaginative turbulence, it cannot be compared to the memory I have of Paracelsus. Paracelsus was one of the men who had the greatest influence on the development of my strange life.

Against the opinion of Aretino—who detested him because perhaps he discerned a rival in him, and also against that of Valerio Orsini, who would have had me examined by one of those German physicians who rode along preceded by a page and who wore leather caps and red tunics, who were accepted as the peers of grain and wool merchants and bankers, and who would not have performed the vile work fitting for despicable surgeons for anything in the world—Paracelsus visited me shortly after my arrival. My intuition had given me a firm belief in his powers. Silvio looked for him, found him, and brought him to me. My health had declined so much that immediate treatment was begun.

I remember very well the first impression that his presence made on me. He was a man of some forty years at that time, thin, fragile, bald, with bulging eyes, without a hair on his chin. He spoke to me in an Italian with a strong German accent, but he sprinkled the monologue with words from different languages. I suspect that some words—those he pretended to have acquired during his travels in Transylvania, Tartary, Alexandria, and Greece, where according to him he had even been on the island of Kos, the homeland of Hippocrates—were invented. He wore a shabby coat and on top he had a hat that was sticky with grime, which that time, at least, and with the pretext that he had to protect his naked head, he did not take off all during the visit. At his side hung the famous huge sword in the hilt of which it was said that he held the demon Azoth imprisoned. If his look was bizarre, with the contrast between his smooth face and his ruffian's hat plumed with a crust of grime, his talk was even more so. He spoke arrogantly, bombastically, as if he were looking down on the person spoken to from the height of his wisdom—we must not forget that his name was Philippus Aureolus Theophrastus Bombastus von Hohenheim—with a great waving of the hands, rolling of the eyes, and clanging of his sword, and the first thing he did was to inform me that he was from a noble family, the grandson of a commander of the Teutonic Knights, as if with that he was attempting to establish the basis of our relationship and put things in their proper place. But in spite of my youth, I was too well aware of that attitude of intellectuals toward princes—did not Benvenuto Cellini act that way when we met on the beach?—and I saw the human weakness behind it too well to let it annoy me. Otherwise, contrary to what usually happened, I was taken from the first with that small, almost rachitic man, lively and talkative, who lectured without taking his eyes off me.

He examined me minutely, he asked me if I had been bewitched, and he inquired about the past history of the people with whom I had "taken my ease"—that was his expression and he stressed it with a touch of mockery—lately. I answered him by mixing up the images of Giambattista and Pantasilea, but I could not deceive him. While he was feeling my body he told me that God had not permitted any sickness to exist without providing its cure, and he promised me that by the end of a month, if I followed his advice, I would be healthy. My case was different from that of Erasmus, who had stated in a letter that his studies kept him so busy that he neither had time to be cured nor to die. I had time. He prescribed his prestigious *tinctura physicorum*, which it was said he had used to conquer cancer, hydrophobia, syphilis, epilepsy, and other incurable diseases, because he was the only one who treated hopeless cases, and he cited the example of the abbess of Zinzilla in Rottweill, who had been given up for dead. In Nuremberg he had just published two treatises on Fracastoro's disease which were banned, out of envious blindness, by the Faculty of Medicine in Leipzig.

"No physician," he pronounced ironically, "should tell a prince the truth. Nor should any magician, astrologer, or necromancer if they possess it. They should use occult and indirect routes, allegories, metaphors, or marvelous expressions. But I swear to Your Lordship that Your Lordship is very ill and that in a month you will have forgotten what has been torturing you."

He visited me almost daily, to the great rage of Pietro Aretino, who, nonetheless, had still not come out openly against him, because with his way of life he might have needed him at any moment. He would arrive, do me the honor of taking off his hat, look over my sores, put me into a sulphur bath, administer his potion, and then begin to lecture. His smell of wine, sweat, and dirtiness filled the room along with that of his nauseating concoctions. Valerio, Silvio, and Giambattista would escape in disgust. In the midst of the yellowish vapors, his livid face would appear like that of a wizard. I guessed then that under his avalanche of words, something, a restlessness, was hidden, but I took a long time in discovering it. I expected much from him and he expected much from me. In the meantime he was explaining to me that the Soul-Spirit of the World impregnated everything that existed and that whoever could succeed in dominating it would be master of the power of God; he referred to the cure of the Queen of Denmark, or he revealed to me that the phoenix is reborn from the skeleton of a horse, and that a pregnant woman, if she wishes, is capable of printing a sketch on the body of her child. It was difficult to distinguish when he was speaking seriously and when he was joking, because he maintained the same majestic tone. He was probably applying to me the principle that one must disguise the truth with a lord, but what was certain was that in ten days I began to recover. He taught me that salt, sulphur, and mercury were the ingredients that entered into the composition of all metals and also of all beings, and that they were contained in the *mysterium magnum* of which everybody contained within himself an *archeus* or life principle. The union of the organic elements, according to him, was the origin of life, and the predominant element was the one which constituted the quintessence. Through those disquisitions he made me feel, vaguely, that I was the center of the world, because he made me feel my communication with everything that existed. And that helped fortify me, infuse me with new vigor. The world revolved around me, strangely, and at the same time I was a minute part of its limitless mechanism. I was not alone, I was not lost, and by reducing myself in the infinitesimal dust of the microcosm I grew to gigantic proportions, because everything, from an insect to a cloud, rendered me homage and worked for me.

One day when no one was with us in my room, I told him the story of my horoscope and of its announcement of immortality. His eyes sparkled.

"The stars tell nothing," he declared. "They do not lean toward anything, they do not impose anything. We are as free of them as they are of us. The stars and the whole firmament are incapable of affecting our bodies, our color, our gestures, our vices, our virtues. The course of Saturn cannot lengthen or shorten life."

"But they've told me that you won't bleed patients or give them purges if you find that the Moon is in the wrong position."

"That has nothing to do with it. And that matter of immortality is something else. Immortality really is passion-consuming. Reaching it should be the aim of all of us who singe our lashes studying."

I looked at his unsheltered eyelids, rimmed with red. The "medical chemist" picked up the theme again:

"Since 1513 at least, based on a pronouncement by Leo X at the Lateran Council, the immortality and individuality of the soul has been established against those who assert that there is but one soul for all men. I already knew it before. I did not need His Holiness, and Your Lordship should not consider me a heretic, I am not. But the interesting part is not the immortality of the soul, but the immortality of the soul within the body: remaining, remaining here in this world, on this side of the mirror. Continuing to be alive. The lapse that Fate normally awards is very short for all there is for us to do."

He remained silent for an instant.

"It is possible," he added, "to create an artificial man. With the help of the Hebrew Cabala, Elias of Chelm created one, a Golem, who came to life when the Jewish sage wrote one of the names of God on the clay of his creation. It is possible—I have done it—to create a homunculus by enclosing sperm in a hermetic glass, magnetizing it, and sinking it for forty days in horse manure. It is possible for devils to form a body from air, by condensing it or condensing water vapor, and thus make a specter that will serve them as a temporary abode. Simon Magus succeeded skillfully in producing movement in wooden statues. Saint Thomas Aquinas destroyed the dangerous automaton that could speak which Albertus Magnus had built. And the famous Cornelius Agrippa brought off the following miracle: A student suddenly died in his studio and the master, afraid that they would accuse him of a crime, obliged the Devil to get inside of the inanimate body and take two turns around the square with it so that it would then drop dead in front of other people. But those are fictions; they're fearsome games. It's not a question of engendering an appearance of life, but of maintaining without end the one which God engendered. I have a means to keep a person alive for centuries. And when I die... I will not die. They will bury me for a whole year, because one has to go down into the darkness of the tomb before ascending to the light of eternity; they will bury me, cut into pieces, in horse manure, the source of constant heat, as any alchemist knows, and they will make me the object of the whole gamut of combinations of the Great Art; then I will revive, transformed into a handsome youth. Someday I will have eternal youth, not like that Venetian imbecile Luigi Cornaro who eats the yolk of an egg every twenty-four hours and aspires to reach the age of one hundred, as if it were worth the trouble in order to remain on earth transformed into a hungry old man only to die in the end. I will live and I will live young. Your Lordship can also do it, not because it is promised in the fantasy of the horoscope by Sandro Benedetto, but because in your case you have a method that you must find."

From the bottom of the bathtub located beside my bed, wrapped in the evil-smelling vapor, hiding my hump in the murky water, I was listening to him, bewitched. Nine years later, when Paracelsus died in Salzburg—according to many prematurely because he had increased the dosage of the elixir of life that he kept hidden in the hilt of his sword and which was guarded by the demon Azoth—I heard that they had respected his orders, that his servant had cut him into pieces and buried him in accordance with what he had prescribed, and that when twelve months were up, the servant impatiently opened the tomb two days before the complete time was over. Then (at least that was what his disciples testified) it could be seen that Aureolus Theophrastus was reposing in the coffin changed into a handsome adolescent, like Faust.

Except that his skull had not finished sealing and a breath of air slipped through the fissure into the brain and killed the magician once and for all, making it impossible to revive him. Then his legend began to fly about and there were people who swore that he had been recognized simultaneously in several places in the world. But that took place nine years after the time I am speaking of. While Paracelsus was speaking, leaning over the bathtub, so close to me that I thought with horror that he was going to embrace my naked body, what bothered me as I followed the bubbling of his strange discourse, because it was so fabulous, was what he had been telling me, what he had just declared: that I, the same as he, was the master of immortality if I could find its formula. And there, in that phrase spoken with an intensity that made it stand out from the rest of his discourse, I could discern the cause that had impelled him to visit me every day.

"Help me discover the secret," I murmured.

"The secret belongs to Your Lordship's family."

"To my family? To my father, my grandfather?"

"To the Orsini family."

The news left me stupefied. The Orsinis were proud of being and having been warriors, prelates, rulers... It was hard for me to imagine them mixed up in matters of such secret subtlety.

"We all dream of immortality," Paracelsus pointed out, moving his pale face, his bulging batrachian eyes back. "Princes more than anyone else. Even the lady Marchioness of Mantua, the unconquerable Isabella d'Este, wore a black jewel on her breast on which she had this inscription engraved: 'So that I may live after death.' It's an age-old dream, the urge to be like gods."

"And us, us, the Orsinis, which one of us...?"

"We have to go back in time, Duke, two centuries back. The most famous alchemist of that period was Jean Dastyn. Pope John XXII was ruling in Avignon and he was intimately linked with the nephew of another pope, Nicholas III. I mean Cardinal Napoleone Orsini, dean of the Sacred College. The alchemist Dastyn could make gold and he wrote several letters, which are still preserved, to the pope and the cardinal. One of those letters explained in a labyrinthine way the truth about the noble material that can transmute any metallic body into gold and silver and which can change an old man into a young one and can remove illnesses from the flesh. I have studied his ideas in the letters in Latin to Cardinal Orsini, and I share many of them; when he asserts, for example, that mercury is the sperm and material of metals and of the Stone. John XXII, frightened by the enormous influx of coins into France, signed a decree against those practices, but he took advantage in private of what he had condemned in public. When he died, the Holy Father—who had started out in the world as the son of a petit bourgeois from Cahors—left an immense fortune. It was estimated at eighteen million gold florins, plus another seven million in church vessels, tiaras, crosses, ornaments, and jewels. Some estimated even more. What was certain was that Jean Dastyn had found the formula for transmutation. He had the Stone, the Elixir, and the Tincture that previously had been known by Noah, Moses, and Solomon, and which had been foreseen in Alexandria by Bolos Democritus. For Dastyn everything was tied to that mysterious element, so that when he analyzed the "Song of Songs" by the Great King of the Temple, or detailed and dissected the myth of the Golden Fleece, he was pursuing his tireless investigation, which was crowned with success. There is something, however, that is not known. Around 1340 Jean Dastyn sent Cardinal Napoleone Orsini some letters in which he told of his investigations in search of immortality and the results of the same. It seems that the privileged monk who ate roots and did not drink water had not only hit upon the solution to easy wealth but also that of indestructible eternity. Those letters must be somewhere."

"Have you looked for them?"

"I've looked for them, I've asked questions, but I haven't found them."

"What you're telling me happened two centuries ago. They must have been lost."

"I'm sure they exist, my Lord. The cardinal himself probably hid them because they were dangerous."

"The cardinal would have used the formula, and if what you say is true, he'd still be alive."

"Not everybody would dare to be immortal, even though we all dream of it sometimes. It's something too serious, more terrible perhaps than death itself."

"And do you think my family has the letters?"

"They must be somewhere, in some library, some archives, in the attic of some Orsini castle."

"There are many castles. There are many palaces. And there have been wars, sackings, fires..."

"It's worth looking into. After all"—and Paracelsus smiled with a prophetically Voltairean look which wrinkled the corners of his mouth—"it's been promised to Your Lordship in the horoscope by Niccolò Orsini's astrologer. Let's look at those sores now. Yes, they're beginning to heal over. The Duke of Bomarzo will soon be in shape to go up the Grand Canal and join in the Venetian festivities. But let's change the subject. Let's talk about Neo-Platonic philosophers, whose seed Your Lordship gathered during your stay in Florence. I especially admire Marsilio Ficino. Most likely in Florence your teacher Piero Valeriano exposed his ideas to you. I admire Valeriano too, especially when he exposes the sad situation of intellectuals. Believe me, my Lord Duke, we intellectuals are treated without any regard today."

And as intellectuals were accustomed to do before princes, he embarked upon the bitter argument about the lack of consideration that afflicted those who lived for the glory of the spirit. I was not listening to him. I was thinking about the cardinal and the alchemist.

I asked Valerio Orsini about those letters, since he was the Orsini closest at hand, and he professed complete ignorance of them. He had never heard them mentioned and he knew many members, important and obscure, of our vast family spread from one end of Italy to the other.

"Immortality can't be gained with formulas," he said to me, "it's won with a good weapon. There are plenty of immortals among the Orsinis and they didn't have recourse to potions. That gallant Orsini of Monterotondo who is painted on horseback in the palace of the Signoria in Siena, Captains Napoleone and Roberto, Gentile Virginio, Niccolò, and Paolo, the natural son of Cardinal Latino, the great condottieri of our house, are all immortal. If you want to be immortal you have to forge your perpetuity for yourself. I never believed in

Benedetto's horoscope, which I heard of. I met the astrologer at the castle of Niccolò Orsini, the Count of Pitigliano. That one, Pitigliano, is immortal, and he didn't need any formulas. As soon as you get better I'll take you to see his magnificent tomb in San Giovanni e Paolo."

Valerio made me think of my grandfather Franciotto, who, when Charles V knighted me, gave the opinion that knights were made in wars and not by genuflections. I bit my lip and did not insist. His opinion upset me, irritated me. I, hunchbacked and sickly, imagined myself anointed by the gods, unique—and I clutched with all the claws of my imagination at that fantastic offer—and now an old soldier was tossing out a pair of biting phrases and wiping away my hopes. I did not whisper a word of it to Silvio da Narni. His inclinations and his knowledge of magical matters might alert him more than was convenient. In that matter it was necessary to act delicately, diplomatically. On the other hand, I did write to my grandmother. Diana, upon hearing about my illness, had thought of joining me in Venice, but I forbade it, keeping in mind her many years and using to do so the authority given me by my position as head of the Bomarzo branch. Messer Pandolfo brought me the answer with the evidence of my father's mother's worries over the condition of her grandson. Nor did Diana know anything about the location of that correspondence, although she had heard it mentioned at some time.

"My great-grandfather Pier Francesco, the first Vicino Orsini," she said in her letter, "spoke skeptically of the procedure proposed to one of his ancestors by an alchemist to assure him immortality. He used to add that luckily his forebear had not used it, for then all of those who succeeded him would have been excluded from the dukedom because of that permanent duke. Don't dig around in ancient mud, Vicino. Let it lie. And think about Giulia Farnese."

Naturally, I was thinking about her. I wrote to her every week.

Along with the papers from Diana and several others dealing with the complicated administration of my lands, Messer Pandolfo brought me an important document. In order to avoid disputes, Cardinal Franciotto had suggested (and Maerbale and I accepted) that his colleague Cardinal Alessandro Farnese be given the function of arbitrator in the division of the lands inherited from our father. In accordance with his decision, there fell to me, besides Bomarzo, Montenero, Collepiccolo, Castelvecchio, half of Foglia, and the Roman palaces, while Maerbale received Castel Penna, Chia, the other half of Foglia, Collestato, and Torre. It was an equitable distribution. The second son would not receive the same as the first-born. I sensed that Maerbale would reject it, to cause me an upset more than for any other reason. I asked Valerio to tell him about the division made by the arbitrator, but my uncle did not offer to arrange a meeting with him, even though Maerbale had already been cured of his wounds.

Instead of my brother he brought other visitors to my room: Aretino, of course, and also Claudio Tolomei, one of the champions, along with Bembo and Speroni, of the Tuscan language against the imperialism of Latin. The movement had been stressed in Bologna during the festivities for the coronation of Charles V as a national reaction to the overwhelming power of the foreigners. And he introduced me to the famous Jacopo Sansovino, who at that time had begun to beautify the square of Saint Mark's, moving out the butcher shops that dirtied it and opening up new streets; and his son Francesco, a child at the time, who later gathered the histories of the House of Orsini and who, when I established a kind of literary court at Bomarzo, was, along with Claudio Tolomei, one of the most assiduous in attendance. I discovered through them that Venice was being crammed with more visitors every day. Cardinal Ippolito de' Medici had arrived in the city on his way back from Hungary, where Clement VII had sent him—to get him out of the way and avoid his upsetting the actions of Alessandro de' Medici, the Duke of Florence—with the position of papal legate to the army that Charles V was sending against the voivode of Transylvania. In Venice he was living in the palace of the courtesan Zafetta, whose ardent gallant he was, which did not stop him from being desperately in love with Giulia Gonzaga, the most beautiful woman in Italy, for whom he translated with exemplary beauty—alternating that work with the diversion of the very detailed embracing of Zafetta—the second book of the poem by the divine Virgil, the one that sings of the fall of Troy. And the tireless Pier Luigi Farnese had arrived in the city of the doge with my cousin Sigismondo, from whom he was never separated. Sigismondo came to see me, dressed like the son of a king and painted and perfumed like a public woman, so that it was difficult for me to recognize in him the person who had been a short time before, like Matteo and Orso Orsini, a strutting warrior. He only talked about clothing, plumes, and parties. It offended me that Ippolito did not visit me, although it was impossible for me to become angry, because I loved him too much. Zafetta and Giulia Gonzaga were dividing up his time. I would have liked to have received him, even if it were only to shine in front of Valerio and Leonardo.

I began to get up and spend the afternoons in a tall chair by the large window. Paracelsus and Silvio would amuse me there with their mysterious tales; Aretino would repeat his worldly anecdotes, malignant bits of gossip, bursting into violent laughter; and Giambattista and Leonardo, like two slender ropewalkers, worked together to amuse me with all sorts of games of skill and astuteness. Wrapped in the warmth of my furs, I felt life flowing in my restless body again. Sometimes I would lift my eyes from the page on which I was copying some baroque conceits for Giulia Farnese, in which love was disguised in allegories; and old images—and yet so close: that of Adriana dalla Roza, that of Abul—would appear in my nostalgic memory. I stood up, leaning on Silvio's arm, and looked outside. The gondolas were going toward Burano, toward Torcella. The gondoliers spoke to each other, insulted each other, the same as today, as always, with long rhythmical laughter. The sound of finely tuned instruments came up to my window. The bucentaur, the doge's ship, was passing by slowly, like a golden dragon, like a monster out of Pliny, toward the port of San Niccolò di Lido, bright with beacons and standards, and on the poop deck, under a canopy, the small, chilly figure of the doge Andrea Gritti was outlined, like a holy image. I thought I was happy—did I think that I was happy at that time?—in my way. I felt coddled and protected, and that had an essential value for me. Everything around was so beautiful, everything so harmoniously in accord as it assuaged my esthetic needs, from the slim elegance of Leonardo and Giambattista in their clothing that was tight as a glove, to the graceful shape of the boats that were moving along loaded with golden fruits and even the promise that the beautiful Giulia Farnese would soon be my duchess, my wife, and that in the secret of one of our great palaces the flower of immortality was waiting hidden so that

I could cut it without effort, as if it were a game, and aspire eternally as the majestic round of time spun about with its fleeting perfume!

As soon as I was in a condition to go into the street, I went to pay my respects to the doge. Valerio went with me. Andrea Gritti received us splendidly in the palace of the masters of Venice. The old lord who had ruled the destinies of the Most Serene Republic for nine years had molded his own face, with the passage of the years, until he had attained the exact, perfect mask—and the testimony of it remains in the portrait by Titian—which reflected his awesome office. The sculptor of himself, he utilized, in order to chisel that severe face which was surrounded by the *corno* of gold brocatel and his frothy beard, the elements that showed his energetic life as a soldier and diplomat, the trickster of the Turks and the leader of armies, the wise director of finances and the guardian of a prudent equilibrium that equally balanced his relations with France and the Empire. All of that was constructed in his dauntless face and it was affirmed by his powerful hands. The Venetian domains were breaking up around him, but the doge continued symbolizing the unchanging patrician Republic. He spoke serenely, with a proud good will. He had collaborated with Niccolò Orsini when the latter had fought under the command of Venice and that made him favor us. In his palace covered with paintings, the sanctuary of magnificence, he was a god, a Jupiter dressed in ermine and velvet. When one saw it he understood the familiarity of the doges with the divine court, the Christian, and the mythological courts, evidenced in the insistent satisfaction with which those princes had themselves represented among saints and archangels, between Mars and Venus, with whom they lived sumptuously in the pomp of the enormous oil paintings. The common people who entered there must have thought they were entering a heaven where the blessed, the nymphs, and their leaders shared an equal glory. And when the bucentaur sailed toward the island, they must have thought that tritons and nereids were holding it up on the brink of a wave, and that cherubim were flying in the folds of its banner.

Nevertheless, from what Gritti told us at that time, if the relations of Venice with Olympus had not varied, its bonds with Heaven were not especially fortunate. Acute controversies divided the religious patriarch and the secular power. The tension with the papacy had deepened with the imposition of extraordinary tithes on the clergy, which the doge had established without pontifical authorization. Then there was the question of heretical books, because of which even craftsmen were arguing about the sacraments and the faith, and the scandal of certain convents, whose professed nuns and novices seemed to be living in a perpetual carnival, and, coming from noble families, they wrote shameless letters that fell into the hands of spies. But if that were not sufficient, the Dominicans were acting with an unbearable haughtiness, as if they thought they were masters of the city. The calm face of the prince darkened, as if suddenly the shadow of a cloud had passed over a statue of marble and porphyry. We listened to him in silence, surrounded by angels, martyrs, apostles, naked goddesses. Sometimes the light would spread out in the corners or a courtier would move in the shadows, and we did not know whether Heaven was going to join in the stormy grief of the sovereign and if the opulent Virgin was going to descend from her painted throne to lay her right hand on the shoulder of the doge. The one who did, however, was his sister, as old as he, who came out of the wavering darkness with a rustle of brocades and a vague glimmer of pearls. She was famous for her piety.

"Happily," the old woman said, "not all the cardinals are against us in Rome. We can count on Grimani, Pisani, and Gonzaga. And, of course, on Alessandro Farnese."

"Especially on Alessandro Farnese"—the august, musical voice of the doge was raised—"who backs the Venetian cause. There's been a terrible mistake made concerning the matter of tithes. The Signoria can impose them."

"Pier Luigi, the son of that holy prelate, came to see me," the lady added, kissing her ruby rosary. "He's such a fine gentleman."

"We have been told," Andrea Gritti interrupted, turning to me, "of the close friendship that links him to Your Lordship. That speaks well for the young Duke of Bomarzo."

Valerio and I exchanged glances. The Venetian authorities could not be ignorant of the details of Pier Luigi's licentious existence, which everybody knew about, or about the headaches that it had caused his father. I wanted to protest, to point out that the friendship was not that close, but Valerio held me back. In any case, the prince was already making a sign indicating that the audience had ended.

While we were passing through the rooms decorated with paintings of naval battles and were going down the stairs, Valerio whispered to me, "Here, Vicino, it is necessary to work with the greatest caution. If the doge declares that you are a friend of Pier Luigi, of that scoundrel, I recommend that you act as if you were, even though you may not want to."

Some days later Valerio took me to see the tomb of the condottiere Niccolò in the church of San Giovanni e Paolo. It was an obligatory pilgrimage for the Orsinis. Leonardo Emo went with us. A notable place to be buried in, there...when one was in the category of those who would be buried. Walking over funeral inscriptions, we reached the structure of the condottiere's tomb. Warriors and commanders looked down at us from the other monuments, standing on their sepulchers. I stood as tall as I could on the red and white tiles and looked up at the equestrian statue. Niccolò Orsini had died at the age of sixty-nine, but the soldier in the plumed helmet, the gilded figure who was rising up in the right transept under the lion of Saint Mark, flanked by the shields of our family, the bears and the roses, was quite young. He was triumphant on the glory of his horse and in his armor as if he should not have and could not have died, and to me he looked like a hero out of Ariosto, an immortal Orlando.

"This," Valerio commented, "is an immortal Orsini."

I had the thought that the immortal was dead, quite dead; that worms had been lodging in his flesh for more than twenty years under the stone that hid his remains; and that if they removed the weight of that slab and laid those horrible remains of an old man devoured by maggots next to the image of the victorious youth who was still mounted and in command, one would appreciate the caricaturesque lack of proportion of the theatrical reproduction. And I thought back to the promise formulated for me by the astrologer of that very same captain, which was like a message from him, from the great Niccolò Orsini, like a message from beyond the grave. It was necessary to fight against death. Death was the only authentic enemy.

Leonardo, pointing at the statue, asked, "Did he die so young?"

"He died old, as old as I am," Valerio Orsini answered with a strange grimace, "but immortals are young forever."

"Will you be young forever?"

"I don't know. That will be known afterward."

"I want to be young now," the adolescent murmured, opening his arms in the solitude of the church, and it occurred to me that from their tombs the celebrated dead accumulated there were shuddering amid the waste matter that stained their arms and their jewels. I also wanted to be young. Forever. I wanted it the way Paracelsus did, and like him I would find the path to reach it. I also felt young, in spite of the hump that oppressed me as if its carnal burden were dragging me toward the blackness of the grave. Behind Valerio, without my uncle's noticing it, I reached out a hand and stroked that of the boy. We smiled at each other.

Paracelsus was getting ready to leave and take up his incessant wandering again with my cure added to his list of accomplishments. He proposed to me, as a farewell, that I go with him as far as the square of Saint Mark's. Autumn was disguising itself as summer that morning, and a warm wind was blowing that accentuated the perfume of the spices. It might have been said that the cinnamon and the saffron were rising up along our path, coming to life again in the storehouses like mysterious restless animals, made that way by the air that came from across the sea.

There were many people in the square. From time to time a great wave of pigeons, like another Oriental wind, would rise up, and when we looked, attracted by the noisy flap of wings, we could see above in the wooden *altanas* that crowned the palaces, or on the open balconies, the beautiful patrician women and the prostitutes who were taking advantage of the rays of the sun to lighten their hair, extending it out over broad crownless straw hats, and wetting it continuously with wet sponges. They were using all manner of recipes to tint it blond, the famous Venetian blond, in accord with Firenzuola, who maintained that the true and proper color for hair demands that it be blond. On the terraces the loose locks gave a shine of metals, to whose glow was added that of the mirrors that went from one hand to the other, sparkling, as if the beautiful women were making enigmatic signals. Later on the ladies would go down to the square and the gondolas, walking prodigiously in their high buskins, their golden *zoccoli*, and covered with sparkling stones, and showing, as they slid their veils skillfully over the white tabby clothing, the perfect roundness of their painted breasts. Waving opposite the basilica were the flags of the Republic on the three staffs near which slaves were being sold and, if we turned our eyes toward the Piazzetta, without lowering them from the cloudy height that the sun was burning, we would see, standing out on their columns, the figures of Saint Mark and the Lion, at the feet of which Andrea Gritti had ordered the gallows built as a warning to the cosmopolitan population. But no matter how marvelous what was going on at the upper level was, tremulous with iridescent vibrations, what moved me more was the spectacle of the square itself, where, mingled in their splendor, were the dry goods coming from the shops of San Salvatore and San Lio, the red and blue brocades, or gold and silver, some of which were so splendid that Ottoman agents soon made them disappear from the factories, to the indignation of the Venetians, for the adornment of the favorites in the seraglio of the Grand Turk. Ah, it was not without reason that Venice was hated so much for its prodigious luxury! It was not without reason that the useless decrees aiming to contain it multiplied! Living together there were the fashions of a world that had still not given itself over to the repetitious and imbecilic vulgarity of uniformity, with no lack of Flemish coats, Spanish doublets, or enormous turbans. I was devouring it all, never sated with the colors. Suddenly I remembered Bomarzo and a pinprick pierced my joy. I remembered the time when Girolamo had dressed me as a woman and had humiliated me. That day, like this one, in the attic of the castle, filled with chests that were stuffed with old clothes, the luxurious garments spoke to my sensuality with their passionate language. I shook my head. I did not want to think about anything that would disturb my pleasure. In addition, Girolamo was dead; I was alive and I was the duke, and of the insult of the depressing episode no proof remained except my pierced ear, from which there now hung a pearl enclosed in sapphires. I leaned on the arm of Paracelsus and continued walking. I almost did not feel my hump, which I always *felt*, as if it were something separate from me, something that did not belong to me, that was not part of my body, an added burden.

The extravagance of the garments could not overshadow those worn by Paracelsus. With his colossal hat, gloriously filthy, and his sonorous great sword that bounced on the cobblestones, he drew the attention of travelers, who made way for him. He stopped to point out to me with emphatic gestures the church of San Gimignano, which Sansovino was beginning to raise and which later would be destroyed by Napoleonic madness. Then he pointed out to me on the mosaics of the church of the Evangelist figures that he interpreted esoterically, as if they were scenes of magic. In that way we came to the Piazzetta, on the side of Saint Mark's, next to the Porta della Carta of the doge's palace. The sun was biting and we sat down to rest beside the secret statues of the emperors done in porphyry, embracing, two by two, on a corner of the wall.

"Those four emperors were brought from Saint John of Acre," he told me. "I don't know whether they're embracing or conspiring."

"They're embracing," I answered, "and whispering to each other. But they keep their hands on their swords."

"They love each other and they hate each other too."

I slid my hand over the shoulder of one of them.

"They love each other. You can feel the warmth of their bodies."

"Hatred can also cause burning."

At that moment Paracelsus took off his huge hat and with a rapid, furtive movement dropped it.

"I caught it!" he shouted, "I caught it! It was half asleep, drowsy, it's obvious that it hadn't had so much sun for a long time. I wanted to leave a gift with Your Lordship, something so that you won't forget me, even if it was a short acquaintance. And here it is."

He put one hand under the crown like a sleight-of-hand expert and quickly drew it out. Between his firm fingers a shape was twisting. It was a lizard. Paracelsus was holding its jaws closed to avoid its sharp bite.

"It's a salamander," he declared proudly to me, "the immortal beast, the conqueror of fire."

"Isn't it a lizard?"

"Your Lordship may call it a lizard if you prefer. And don't forget that in the Greek lexicon of love, lizard is one of the words used to designate the male organ. But I consider it a salamander: a salamander, the symbol of the immortality of the Duke of Bomarzo, the symbol of my immortality."

The small reptile was wriggling, showing its greenish and gray back and its white belly, mixing in with agile swipes of its tail the colors that reproduced in my imagination those of the mossy, oxidized stones of Bomarzo. Bomarzo was obsessing my convalescent memory. Everywhere, the feelings, the emblems that burst forth from that so different Venice suggested my distant and beloved homeland to me.

Paracelsus wrapped the little beast up in a filthy handkerchief, the tonalities and materials of which would have delighted the nonobjective painters of today. Then, near Madonna dell' Orto, where the statue of the Moorish merchant is, we bought a cage for it.

In addition to that outing, the others that I took during the first week that I was allowed to leave my room in the Emo palace took me in search of the antiquities whose possession aroused such an avaricious pleasure in me. Giambattista and Silvio would accompany me, and it was rare for us to return to the place without some remarkable find. It was then that I acquired, from the collection of the patriarchs in Aquileia, the busts of the Roman emperors—fifteen, from Augustus to Marcus Aurelius, more decorative than notable—that I sent to be placed in the gallery in my castle.

I paid Titian a high price for an Ariadne that had fascinated me in his studio on the Ca' Grande. The Orsinis of my branch have not been particularly fortunate with Titian if we were counting on his collaboration so that future generations would admire our sense of art. In that respect our expenses were useless. His canvas inspired by a passage from Catullus that my father and Girolamo brought home to Bomarzo as part of the booty from one of their campaigns has disappeared. And this other Titian, the Ariadne, has also disappeared. Where can they be now? Where could they have come to rest? To whom can they have been attributed? What fire, what war, what rats, what dampness of a granary, what ignorance, what incomprehension can have fed on them? Ariadne, naked, abandoned, moaning on the rocks of Naxos, was lifting her eyes to heaven like a Christian martyr, and on one side a slave is offering her a tray of fruit which she is proudly rejecting.

To Giulia Farnese I sent a marble Bacchus that had been found in some diggings, which was a miracle of art. I realized after the case had already left Venice how improper, how out of proportion my gift was for a young girl, and at the next opportunity I sent her a set of emeralds. When we were married, Giulia brought the emeralds back, but the Bacchus stayed in possession of her father. In spite of my polite hints— to which he would reply with jokes about his love for wine and the cordial links that joined him to the god—the wise Galeazzo Farnese preferred to keep it in his garden in Rome. He said that it reminded him of his son Fabio, and it was true.

The exceptionally good weather continued and it allowed me to accept an invitation from Pier Luigi to go for a gondola ride at night. He sent it to me through Silvio da Narni, who was still in touch with him after having cast his horoscope, which still bothered me. I carefully chose the clothes that I would wear from my wardrobe, and I decided on a yellow jerkin with silver embroidery over which I put on the Florentine *lucco* of black fur. I spent a long time looking at myself in the mirror. Yes, there was no doubt that I was handsome. The illness had made me thin and refined my face; it had polished it even more, sculpting its aristocratic cheekbones, and giving my ivory-like paleness a vague sky-blue background, making for a look of almost unreal asceticism (*le ténébreux, le veuf...*), like a poetic visitor from the other world, like a sad angel who would have enchanted Victor Hugo and, naturally, Gérard de Nerval, but alas, it would still be a long time before Hugo and Nerval would appear on the restless earthly scene. I resolved not to look at my hump. It was hanging behind, the rucksack of my misfortune. When I found the letters from Dastyn to Cardinal Orsini (if I found them), I would be reborn without it. Because it was a question of that: to live eternally without that monstrous addition; otherwise immortality would be the prolongation of a torment. Paracelsus had told me that he would return to life, forever, transformed into a handsome youth. And that was what I dreamed of. Now I think that more than the risk of immortality what attracted me was the possibility of being a man like others, that what I sought in the prospects of abnormality was a normal build. That takes greatness, imagination, and luster away from my hope, but each one is as he is, and I do not aspire to present myself as a demigod.

I asked Giambattista to help me dress, to look in the chest for the black gloves, the ones with the topazes, which would blend with the colors of the jerkin and the *lucco*, and while he was digging out the contents, the doll that Silvio da Narni had made in the likeness of Giulia Farnese fell to the floor.

I had forgotten about it for the second time. My illness and my new preoccupations had made me forget it completely. Now I had it in my hands, and its shape reminded me of another doll, the one which Clarice Strozzi had ordered made in the likeness of the dying Adriana dalla Roza on the Via Larga in Florence in order to put her under the care of the Virgin of the Annunciation. Giambattista also saw the figurine that Silvio had wet with my saliva and my blood and, not knowing what it was all about, began to tell me the story that he had heard from Leonardo Emo about the doll that Isabella d'Este had sent to Francis of France at the request of the king who did not know her, and which reproduced exactly the features of her face and the details of her clothing. Figurines, dolls played an important role in that period, for good or for evil. They could both win love or cause death, by means of black arts, and they could also invoke divine or royal favor.

It was with fear that I held in my hands the one that reminded me of the guilty procedure with which I had perhaps conquered the will of my future duchess. Who knows what evil powers it enclosed. I ordered the puzzled page to bring me some drops of holy water from the palace chapel, and with it I touched the mouth and the blue eyes of the puppet. As soon as I went out I would throw it into the water. I did not want to see it any more. That was what I did when I got into the gondola, without the others noticing. The olive-green canal carried it off with its filth.

The boat had a gilded prow and a cabin lined in red velvet and covered with pyramids of flowers. At the stern, at the feet of the gondolier, who was moving rhythmically, voluptuously, there were two musicians and a singer. In the darkness I could make out several masked people, among whom I recognized Pier Luigi and Sigismondo, and some women. We—Silvio, Giambattista, and I—were also in disguise, using the false faces they gave us, the picturesque *bautte*, with long noses, which covered half of the face like a mask and had begun to be made popular by the comic mime theater. I joyously gave myself over to the enchantment of disguise, which was so Italian, destined to spread far and wide with the passage of time, and which was already so popular that when the court of Ferrara wished to please Cesare Borgia it sent him a gift of a hundred different masks...which, of course, could have been interpreted as an ironical allusion.

Pier Luigi dragged me to the back of the cabin, laughing. They had all had a lot to drink and they were still drinking. It took me a while to notice that the women who were with us were boys dressed up in female clothes, and the son of Alessandro Farnese laughed with such noise at the trick he had played on the Duke of Bomarzo that his laughter and gagging for some time covered up the steady plucking of the stringed instruments and the languid inflections of the singer. Silvio and Giambattista Martelli, laying aside etiquette, demanded glasses and bottles of wine so as not to be left behind and in a short time they had joined the noisy group. Although I was also drinking and quite a lot, I stayed somewhat apart from the general uproar that rocked the gondola and threatened to break out into a frank orgy. I escaped from the arms of Pier Luigi and went to the prow.

There were other boats like ours on the Grand Canal, noisy, flower-bedecked, which were taking advantage of the warmth of the night. On the palaces the beacons were blinking that decorated the *pòrteghi* of high naval officers of the Republic and which also proclaimed the family fame of those who over the centuries had fulfilled the most coveted functions. The shields of the old families placed proudly at the entrance ways strutted in their light, and one could imagine under the porticoes between the decoration of braided marble that climbed toward the multicolored Gothic balconies, the rooms destined for commerce, because Venice was an inseparable mixture of lordly vanity and mercantile prudence. Venice, crisscrossed with scaffolding that announced the incessant growth of sumptuous buildings, appeared to the traveler at that time with only the attributes that came from its own glory, its own efforts, its own corruption, still without the romantic-touristic suggestion, without the propaganda of foreign and literary origin spawned by Goethe, Byron, George Sand, Musset, Wagner, Browning, or Ruskin. The false palace of Desdemona was still the palace of the Contarinis. And the city attracted only with the seduction of its strange presence.

Giambattista, little accustomed to wine, soon felt its effects. He seemed possessed. Obeying a hint by Pier Luigi and before I could stop him, because the boys dressed as women were blocking my path with their opulent skirts in the shaky boat, he took off his clothes until he was stark naked. To the applause of the passengers in our gondola and the nearby ones, he stood up like a bronze by Giovanni da Bologna or Benvenuto, like one of those delicate bronzes of Benvenuto's that stand out at the base of the Perseus, and he began to pretend with clumsy gestures that he was a statue. His slender body, drawn in at his narrow waist, extended along his long legs, was reflecting the light of the moon and the lanterns. In the uproar made everywhere by musicians and singers, I heard my name being called from a nearby vessel, from which they had recognized us in spite of the masks, and I spotted Ippolito de' Medici, Maerbale, and two women, one of them of such extraordinary beauty that she could not have been anyone but Zafetta the courtesan. Maerbale had grown very thin and that accentuated the resemblance that showed our kinship. Ippolito, who was the one who had called me, was wearing the strange garment of furs with a feathered headdress that he had brought back from Hungary. His proximity disturbed me, made me desperate. I was upset that they should have surprised me like that in the midst of those people, but fate decreed that every time I participated in an ambiguous scene—as when Benvenuto Cellini kissed me on the beach by the castle at Palo—one of my brothers should be a witness. I felt myself blushing down to the roots of my hair, and freeing myself from the fictitious women, I stood up, the topazes on my gloves shining, and with a shove I pushed Giambattista into the water. With that the rejoicing of the bystanders grew ripe while the boy, mouthing curses, swam lazily toward the docks.

At that instant, above our shouting there came other shouts, more powerful, more serious, filled with danger and terror, and in the distance we saw the flames of the fire. A palace, that of the Cornaros, who boasted of their kinship with the Queen of Cyprus and with the memorable Lusignans, was burning in the breeze that had begun to come up and which was threatening to turn into a wind, as if autumn were finally claiming its postponed dominion. The music grew silent and the alarm chilled one's soul with a prelude to death as the boats, pushed by the agile gondoliers, headed swiftly for the palace where the fire was outlining the Byzantine windows and tinting the canal purple, throwing the design of the palace down as a bloody reflection. We were the first to arrive, along with Ippolito's boat.

The inhabitants of the palace had been surprised in their sleep. In confusion, masters, servants, and slaves, with the impossibility of reaching the street in back through doors that the combustion had turned into hot coals, were jumping into the canal. The women, the men, the frightened children were all shouting. The gondolas were picking them up. Into ours we took an old man who was so thin that it was ludicrous. The skin over his ribs was so pointed that it made him look as if he had been carved out of dark wood. Pier Luigi identified him. He was the famous Luigi Cornaro, the one who aspired to living for a century and more and was on his way to doing so by eating the yolk of an egg every day, and who later would publish his *Discourses on the Sober Life*. That night his experiment almost failed. I wrapped him in the furs of my *lucco* and I heard him sob as, shivering, he listed the treasures that were being lost forever with the palace. That was what living was: losing, leaving behind along the way, getting rid of... And being immortal would be the equivalent of being more naked, outside and inside, than the graceful Giambattista Martelli had been when he displayed his drunken boastfulness in the middle of the deck of our boat.

The incident broke the ice that had separated us from Ippolito and Maerbale's group. In a little while our gondolas went along side by side. Neither the cardinal nor Pier Luigi would allow the fun to come to an end. We gave the old man something to drink as he sputtered hysterically and pulled out his last surviving hairs. We went into a side canal and stopped in Front of San Giovanni e Paolo because Pier Luigi Farnese, completely intoxicated, wanted to admire the monument to Bartolommeo Colleoni in the moonlight. Everybody got out, staggering, and I was with them. Luigi Cornaro leaned on me as I offered him my fragile support, and we went over to Verrocchio's work.

"He was," Farnese exclaimed, hiccupping, "a great warrior and a son of a bitch."

And suddenly, without saying a word, he began to urinate on the base of the statue. That irritated Maerbale extremely. Had not Colleoni been a supreme colleague of his? Did not both of them represent the same thing, heroic passion, a disdain for life, the sale or rental of one's valiant life to the highest bidder? Had not Colleoni attained for posterity the finest equestrian statue in the world? He reacted immediately, with barracks solidarity—most likely if it had been a case of the statue of a poet he would not have reacted like that, but his professional prestige was in question—and without any of us being able to separate them, so sudden had his attack been, he began punching Farnese. They went on across the empty square, through the Campo delle Meraviglie, toward the portico of the church, toward the arcades where were located the funerary urns of the earliest doges, those Tiepolos who had a Phrygian cap for a shield. Luigi Cornaro got loose of me and began to curse them, weeping. Then, without thanking me, without taking leave, he began to run, like a ghost, toward his flaming palace. The folds of my *lucco* were floating behind, whipping the air, as if he were carrying on his back, as it held on with fierce claws, a black, hairy cat, which he could not get rid of and which was venting its wrath on him and on his fierce will not to die. Lying on the square, abandoned, were our long-nosed masks, useless, as if a battle among puppets had taken place there.

That experience prompted me to hasten my departure. It was not proper for me, so soon before my marriage, to exhibit myself in equivocal games like that, even though I was sharing them with the son of the one who would certainly be the next pope and in spite of the fact that the times did not lay the slightest importance to such episodes. And that last matter is still to be seen. The tremendous Aretino experienced it fully in his own flesh years later—and it did not serve him as a passport to have Ariosto proclaim him, in the second edition of the *Furioso*, as "divine" and the "scourge of princes"—because a suspicious Venetian, whose wife the writer had admired and courted platonically, accused him of blasphemy and sodomy, nor was it of help in the case for him to have lodged a harem of "Aretinas" in the Bolani palace with a natural daughter to boot, because the "scourge" saw himself obliged to hide on the edge of the lagoon until spirits calmed down, powerful friends intervened, and his safe return was arranged, and it was triumphant. I was already sufficiently recovered, furthermore, to face what had brought me to Venice (and to which I owed my meeting with Paracelsus and its unforeseeable consequences): my portrait by Lorenzo Lotto. And if my thinness and paleness were extreme, that would help accentuate the interest and the elegance of the likeness.

I arranged, therefore, for an interview with Magister Laurentius in the Emo palace, and the master came there to visit me. It seemed appropriate to me that before undertaking the work the painter should know me well, because I knew that each one of his portraits had been nourished by a rich psychological store that guided the artist as he created. The procedure was much to Lotto's pleasure, and we went out walking through Venice several times. He was about fifty-two at the time, twenty-four years older than when he had painted my father for the polyptych. He was a taciturn man who said little, with no notable physical characteristics except his large dark eyes, but he had an attraction difficult to define, neither on the side of the Angel nor the side of the Devil, which emanated perhaps from his sickly and concentrated timidity, from his susceptibility that would be wounded by anything that brushed it, and from the silence which made one think that he was tense with emotion. In moments in which the opulent and pleasing wave of Venetian painting was progressing theatrically toward the supreme surge of Veronese, and was preparing to burst forth at the foot of marble terraces where frivolous banquets took place, Lorenzo Lotto continued being, from aspects related to his somber introversion, an index of subterranean fires, a hermit of art, turned in his perplexed doubt toward the interior mists of his models. Therefore, he attracted me and we understood each other in spite of the euphoric superficiality that made what there was of the baroque in me stand out. We were crossing a shadowy region—that of the anxious, that of the unsatisfied, that of those incapable of a full confession—and we lived in it together. Much has been written about him (particularly since his present-day "rediscovery"), about the pathetic feeling of fleeting time that runs through his portraits—a critic has compared him to Tasso and even to Pascal in his sensibility—and about his frigidity, which takes away the warmth from female nudes, who evidently did not move him, while his disturbing male figures are like the reflection of a painful secret that he kept hidden through a tortured life which took place among mocking disciples. All of those "themes" came together in Lorenzo Lotto and I could sense them at that time, in a confused way, because the painter avoided conversation and would be silent, or he would change the topic as soon as the other person opened one of the doors that led into the twilight regions of his intimacy. I felt comfortable with him in spite of his disturbance, his reticence, his mumbling, the difficulties of a dialogue in which we went along as if its greatest merit lay in hiding thorns. I tried in vain to get him to talk about my father.

"He was a splendid gentleman," he said to me one morning, repeating the coined formula, when we had stopped at the street of San Giovanni Crisostomo, which the workers had widened, "and perhaps in the bosom of his family he was not fully appreciated, they had not penetrated the depths of the singularity of his character."

I asked him to clarify his thoughts, but the only thing I got was his murmuring that inside the family is where the individuality of those who make it up is least glimpsed, because prejudices, and small personal interests (when not blind love) cloud the deeper vision.

"But... what about my father?"

And Lotto became distracted, pointing out the advantages that would come to Venetian traffic from that widened street.

During the twenty sessions that took place in the Emo palace, the portrait destined to be so famous was taking shape on the canvas. The artist composed an important part of the work—everything concerning the elements that surround the figure—without my presence. Those elements attain a fundamental position in the painting and are characteristic of Lotto's taste for symbols. The lizard is on the table there, on the blue shawl—the sexual lizard from Paracelsus which the painter discovered in my bedroom in the palace—the bunch of keys, the literary pens, the rose petals scattered next to the book I am thumbing through, and behind, on the same plane, where my cap with Cellini's medal can be seen, those unexpected allegories: the hunting horn and the dead bird fraternize in Lotto's work with the mysterious objects—the golden hook, the lamp, the minute skull, the withered flowers, the bouquet of jasmines, and the jewels—which appear in other likenesses by him. Lorenzo worked that way, through allusions, through clues, through unknown things. Around each image an enigmatic, suggested world arose. And that can be seen, more than in any other portrait, in the one he painted of me. The restlessness of a hunter that agitated in me in search of the secret of death; the passion for art and poetry; the idea of the vanity of the perishable; the idea of possession and secret that the keys imply; that of magic and sensuality that comes from the lizard, which Paracelsus had called a salamander, are interwoven like a magic circle about that thin, pale youth dressed in a deep violet-like color, whose rare and beautiful features emerging from the whiteness of his shirt, and whose tremulous hands emerging from the snow of his cuffs were mine. Nothing can be seen of the hump. The way the compassionate—or polite?—Mantegna had done when he painted the hunchbacked Gonzagas in the Mantuan fresco of the matrimonial bedchamber. In my case it blends into the shadow. I was those dark eyes, that chestnut hair, straight, parted, drawn behind the ears, those thin eyebrows, those protruding cheekbones, those red lips, tight but hungry, that sharp chin, those intelligent, delicate, bare hands, that intensity, that reserve, that pride, that hidden and latent power, that cold flame, that equivocal, imprecise violence that can be felt in the ice of aristocratic loneliness, and that tenderness too, desperate. In the gallery of Lotto's desperate people, no one surpasses me. I was to be a melancholy and ambiguous person like him, captured that way, imprisoned like that by his brushes as he doubtlessly had imprisoned my father. Certainly there is in both images, in that of my father and in mine, much of Lorenzo Lotto, of what he was, covered and fought against, and which can only be seen in his painting, but we two Orsinis salute him over a quarter of a century of distance, with our obscure essences related to the complexity of his own essence, the coveted chance to express himself and confess himself by expressing us and confessing us. Therefore it hurts me that it is not known that the person in the "Portrait of an Unknown Person," the "Young Man in His Study," is Pier Francesco Orsini, Duke of Bomarzo, and that some commentator should suggest as a model for it a certain Signor Ludovico Avolante. I do not know who Ludovico Avolante was except that he was the brother of Bartolommeo, the humanist physician. I do not know (and it does not matter to me, although in that respect I might weave a web of suspicions and exploit it for stories that would amuse the reader) what relationship there was between Signor Ludovico and the Count Alvise di Rovero, who commissioned a portrait of the aforesaid Avolante from Lotto for which he paid twelve pounds. But what I do know and proclaim and would maintain before the wise Berenson if he were to rise up from his grave, is that I was the model in the Emo palace in Venice in the year 1532 when Magister Laurentius painted that portrait of the gentleman that has been discussed so much. Until 1572 at least, the oil was in the castle at Bomarzo. I do not know what happened to it later; it and the Titians. My descendants have sacked me; they have scattered about what was most mine. They did not count upon the fact that some time later I would be given the supernatural privilege of writing these pages.

When the work was finished, I looked at myself in its pale and purple glossiness as in a mirror. On the left Lotto had placed a window that opens onto the luminous distance of the sea, and which promised, in the disordered enclosure of the studio, so full of furtive keys, a hope of calm light. And I completely recognized myself in the moving figure, in the mask of glowing alabaster. That was what I was like: sad, strange, indecisive, dreaming, confused, and yearning. An intellectual prince, a man of that time, a little less than an archetype, situated between the mystical Middle Ages and the Today that is surfeited with the material; simultaneously preoccupied with things of the lascivious world and with those of a problematical beyond; bland and strong, ambitious and vacillating, master of the elegance that cannot be learned and of that which is taught in books; the one who plucked the petals from musty roses; the friend of the lustful lizard and of the immortal salamander. The hump, the painful bestial burden, is not present in the canvas but it weighs upon it—and we have an example there of one of the marvels of Lotto's art—it weighs on it, invisible, on its spiritual grace, on its metaphysical atmosphere.

As soon as I had the portrait in my possession, I decided upon our return. Through the intermediary of Valerio Orsini, Maerbale let me know that he approved of the division of our properties made by Alessandro Farnese. Even if I did not believe it, the news pleased me. The rebel second son was evidently bowing to the duke.

The day of our departure Silvio da Narni brought me a manuscript from the visionary nun of Murano, an epileptic woman who was consulted because she prophesied with certainty. She had announced that Pope Clement would be replaced very soon by another, of French origin, and certain scholars maintained that the Farneses had come from France and confirmed it by the fleurs-de-lis on their shield. The nun wrote me only one phrase: "Within a time that humans cannot measure, the duke will look at himself." It was a sibylline phrase, whose meaning I did not understand until much, much later. Of all that it prophesied for me in the inextricable web of auguries of which my hallucinated life was made up, it was the most precise, the most exact.

So I left Venice. I already had my portrait, the image of my truth and my absolution. In moments of uncertainty I would look for and find myself again in it. Now I was ready to undertake two serious tasks: my wedding and the search for the alchemist's letter. When I left, Valerio Orsini showered me with gifts and best wishes; and the small Leonardo Emo, with whom I had barely spoken, I saw weeping, hiding behind a column.

# 7. A WEDDING IN BOMARZO

*The preparations in Bomarzo for my wedding—Illustrious guests—The Orsinis and the Farneses—The allegorical cart—The ceramic demon and frustration—The sensuality of Bomarzo—Maerbale's jealousy—The hunchback's anguish—The death of my grandfather, Cardinal Franciotto—The search for the letters—Redbeard the pirate attacks Giulia Gonzaga—Maerbale's marriage—Paul III Farnese, pope—Ippolito de' Medici poisoned*

BEFORE anything else it was necessary to get Bomarzo ready for the nuptial ceremonies and to receive the duchess. I ardently wanted to avoid the most minute error in my preparations. My mistrustful way demanded perfection in that case more than anything else, for I knew the Farnese family quite well—I do not mean simply Giulia's branch, but the Farneses of the various subdivisions who made up an ambitious and robust tree—and I knew how they analyzed and judged everything dealing with the external pomp linked to their prestige, and how among themselves they criticized mistakes and fumbles with haughty mordacity. It was easy for them to become annoyed. Since in spite of their evident antiquity it was a question of people whose position had only been assured in recent times, only recently assimilated with the exaggeration of intruders among the first houses of Italy, its members exhibited—while no longer being such—the punctilious foresight of parvenus whenever the worldly interests of the line were involved. They noticed things which Colonnas and we would have passed over because it had been centuries since they annoyed us. They still did not feel themselves the masters of a position which they had gained by means of audacity, rapacity, and opportune prodigality, and an involuntary mistake could offend them. The danger of gaffes surrounded them like a ring of barbed wire. I know too well that if it had been possible for them to read these lines, they would have shouted to high heaven—because nothing, absolutely nothing would have aroused them as much as having shown their suspicious attitude toward life, so different from ours, for they felt they had the certainty of acting automatically, obviously, like any of us, for reasons that were almost reflexes engendered in the aristocratic community of the blood—and they would have proclaimed to the four winds that I was raving, that I did not understand the insouciant magnificence of their behavior, for no attitude of an Orsini, a Colonna, an Este, a Gonzaga, or a Montefeltro—on the level of the ceremonial relationships between lineages—would have dared disturb them, because they were aware of everything, of the frivolity, the pomp, precedents, and the minute ritual details, and only an inexperienced hunchback, a petty provincial nobleman, blinded by his inner complexes and mistrust (probably, if attacked like that, they would even have dared to speak of a *mésalliance*), could have thought of such extravagant distinctions. But if I was on the right track in anything, I was in this matter, and if I had forgotten it or had not given it the fundamental importance that it had, my grandmother was there to remind me, and she was an exceptional expert in minor details and caste. Furthermore, it is certain that to that uneasiness over subtle trivialities, so deep, so alert, and so disguised that my new relatives had, were added those that came from my personality. I—who as a member of a clan that could not be attacked, was so sure of my position when it was a question of the broad general and conventional frame of the family—would hesitate if I had to work on my own initiative and if my individuality had to stand apart from the conglomerate solidarity of the Orsinis, because in that case I was I—and no longer a leaf on the immense illustrious tree—I, a fragile hunchback on exhibition. It was necessary, therefore, to go forward with feet of lead, leaning on the very old and protective hand of my grandmother (and without giving the impression that she was supporting me, because my sense of ducal responsibility would not have tolerated it, and public proof of that dependence would have made me suffer terribly) and feeling my way skillfully among the traps that were being set for my plans, on one side by the watchful malice of the climbing Farneses who had more eyes than Argus, and on the other by the apprehensions that flourished from my congenital anguish, worsened by the prospect of exposing myself before intruding and censuring spectators, all of which, with its supply of the miseries of snobbery and tortured psychology, was covered majestically, as if by one of those heraldic ermine cloaks that wrap shields under the corresponding secular crowns, by the undisputed glory of the Orsinis, which protected me and which I, in turn, had to care for more than anyone, because nothing which happened within that supreme space could be either ridiculous or wrong. So that in reality I, because of my anxious smallness, when I undertook a task so simple and yet so arduous, was obliged to watch out not only for the inconveniences that might grow out of the perpetual alarm of the Farneses, disguised as elegant nobility, but also—although I would not confess it, and my inherited impertinence made me only consider the possible reactions of a group to which I gave less importance than to mine—the difficulties that came from the position of the demigod Orsinis and those that had their origins in my unfortunate physique and my hesitant way of being. But as I have already said, there was my grandmother, the aged fairy godmother of the castle, to aid me. That time, as others, as whenever my anxiety required it, she came out of her enclosure to guide me and to calm my upset.

The months of decorative euphoria, so near to my love of objects, went by. Letters came and went across Italy, across Europe, to ambassadors, friends, relatives, asking, ordering this and that. And Bomarzo was splendidly decorated. I wanted Bomarzo to be the most beautiful house in Italy, and if I did not succeed—for it was impossible to rival the princes and opulent cardinals who benefited from the pontifical treasury in spite of the miserly parsimony of Clement VII—I did succeed in giving the castle an air of festivity and luxury, hiding its feudal aggressive walls, and converting what had been a heroic fortress into a mansion of pleasure. Since I could not make myself better, for my case was one of those in which neither tailor nor beautician was of any use, I fondled the hope that Bomarzo, my faithful ally, would present itself in the most sumptuous way possible, the most attractive that my means could afford, so that it would be the allegory of its duke, and so that, protected by the dignity of its bearing, as my ancestors had been

## A WEDDING IN BOMARZO · 361

protected by the strength of its walls, the feeble Vicino could play his embarrassing role opposite the beautiful woman and the suspicions of her tribe with light and thankful ease. I turned the house upside down in order to adorn the one who would supplant me; I established new taxes; I spent my paternal savings and I contracted debts.

From Flanders came the tapestries to which the design of our shield was added at the connection of the unfinished edges. I had them placed in the long main gallery and among them I placed the fifteen Roman busts from the collection of the patriarchs of Aquileia, also placing on the level of the fantastic niches torch holders of bronze which illuminated the rooms as if day had taken refuge in their precincts. From the lonely palace in Rome where I had been born, I had brought the portraits of my ancestors, more noteworthy for their historical meaning than for their artistic quality, for in general they were very badly painted, and their solemn expressions topped the walls and the stairways with an assembly of mute emphasis. Pope Nicholas III, the condottieri, the prelates, and the Orsini lords gathered in Bomarzo in that way to welcome the small Giulia Farnese and receive her as one of ours from the triumphal and clotty distance of the oils. I ordered them to hang my recent acquisitions, my portrait by Lorenzo Lotto, the Ariadne by Titian and also the master's painting inspired by a passage from Catullus, and I had purchased from dealers and from the artists' studios canvases by Raphael Sanzio, Sebastiano del Piombo, Dosso Dossi, Pontormo, Jacopo Bassano, Bronzino, and Giorgino Vasari, my young friend from Florence. I must recognize that next to those works the ancestral paintings stressed the mediocrity of their manufacture, but I covered it up by strategically distributing the lights in such a way that in the case of a certain warrior only the armor and his right hand holding his sword would be seen and in that of a certain archbishop only the folds of his purple, so that on the whole, with all of them and thanks to my skillful staging, they made up one single prestigious ancestor who had the hands of this one, the beard of that one, the forehead of that other one, of that one the jeweled helmet, and of the other one the ecclesiastical sleeves, with a composite result that was rather honorable and which, furthermore, corresponded to a documentary truth, for their coming together, like a curious puzzle, summed up the military, clerical, and civic tradition of the Orsinis, exalted by the marvelous proximity of their masterful neighbors, which, from Raphael and Lotto to Bassano and Dossi certified with the splendors of their obvious centers of attraction, the merits of the semi-invisible ancestral gallery and raised it to the indisputable regions of great art. The canopies were cleaned and they sparkled in the rooms under the banners that told of past victories, and among them I placed by itself the armor discovered in the Cave of the Paintings in Bomarzo, which stood out like evidence of the epic old age of the place. What was to be the nuptial bed I had adorned completely with pilasters and intertwined ceramic roses, combining the heraldic figures of the Farneses with ours, and in the salons and on the terraces the joining of the initials of Giulia and Vicino Orsini was repeated. From Venice came lace, mirrors, cameos, and glasswork; from Milan and from France credenzas, chairs, and stools of rare design. Marble statues and urns spread their figures through my grandmother's geometrical garden. In the other part of the park, the more remote one to the rear, the one which was invaded by the unkempt little wood, I had not yet dared undertake my revolutionary renovation. I sensed vaguely that there among those trees and rocks something was hidden that was impossible to pin down and which was announcing to me the misty indecision of ancient dreams and that it was closely bound to my reason for existence and being in the world as well as to the search for immortality. I am not exaggerating when I say that on every occasion when I went down alone toward that brambly place which spoke to me with the hypnotic voice of the water and the locusts, I felt as if I were penetrating a secret zone in which the magical empire of Bomarzo was emphasized, and I guessed that what I must do there would occur in its own time and that it was a task that should not be begun without my being ripe for it, for as the years passed, by enriching myself subjectively, the probabilities of bringing it to an end without making any mistakes would also grow.

In the meantime, what was of the greatest urgency was to organize the house, and nothing would distract me from what I had proposed. The sentries incessantly announced the fatigued approach of carts along the road toward the village and the castle. They came loaded to the top with crates, bundles, with an armed escort, and my great pleasure, which my grandmother shared, more than for what those things represented in themselves, because of the joy that they aroused in me, would be present in the courtyards or in one of the rooms for the opening of the chests and observing as there appeared among the shattered boards and packing straw the arched arm of a piece of sculpture, promising to be a goddess who would join the ghostly Olympus of Bomarzo; or a greenish bronze that still preserved, clinging to the grace of the flanks, patches of earth turned up by the diggers; or the portrait of Giulia, which like that of the other Giulia, the ineffable Giulia Gonzaga, commissioned by Ippolito de' Medici, I had entrusted to Sebastiano del Piombo.

All of it was being located, with the passage of the months, in the vastness of the rooms that resounded with hammer blows and the shouts of workmen, and I was obliged to take a trip more than once, especially to Rome. The people of the family whom I ran into on my travels asked me about the decoration of the castle, because news had already begun to spread of my urge and it was a matter that was of equal interest to great and small in a period which was characterized everywhere by a search for the elements that concerned formal beauty. That curiosity added a wild vanity to the many that distinguished me, and my chest puffed up with pride and startled satisfaction. If Paracelsus in Venice, with his explanations of the macrocosm and the microcosm had made me feel that I was the center of the earth, that constant prying convinced me that at that time I was, albeit fleetingly, the center of my complicated lineage, whose innumerable and surprised eyes were fastened on the work of the humpbacked esthete, because I was bringing to the bosom of the Orsinis, involved until then by other more practical worries which were related to material power and political influence, the envied tone of refinement, which gave such luster to the first houses of the peninsula, a tone that I had incorporated, like another very coveted piece, in the legendary shield of the She-Bear, which the centuries were squaring off in new and intricate quarters.

As is logical, with so much running about, I had little time to dedicate to the manuscripts of the alchemist Dastyn, but they remained present in the depths of my memory, inseparable now from what most intensely concerned me, and in that last redoubt, which was the base on which my personality rested, their sediment was imperceptibly building up a kind of strength that was replacing my lack of religious stimulation. My religion, in those years, was being nourished, as in my childhood, by the spiritual vigor of Bomarzo, so rich in centuries-old impregnating essences that connected my line to the mystical dawn of Italy, and also fed, confusedly, by the sustenance offered it by the notion that perhaps it would be given to me to communicate with the arcane powers that rule our destiny and that my will would perhaps succeed in twisting and subjecting, obtaining from them, with the supreme banquet of life, the necessary energy to confront who knows what mysterious visions, what strange answers to the questions that I sensed and could not even formulate with exactness.

That organizing and expectant period was distinguished in what concerned my intimate life by an exceptional purity. Worried by the task that was weighing upon me, I did not give my sensuality a chance to become aroused. Besides, the doubt of whether or not I was capable to face up to the confrontation between Bomarzo and the Farneses worked like an antidote to temptation. The lewd provocation was just as alert and latent as ever in the environment of the castle and the small village surrounding it, but I isolated myself from it, I do not know whether moved by the idea of reaching the arms of Giulia cured of my murky eroticism, or by the fact that nothing would distract me from my drive as the defender of my beloved Bomarzo. My cousins Orso and Matteo, who had established themselves in the big house, could not get over their surprise, accustomed as they were to accompanying me on sensual expeditions, and it was necessary to use the weight of my authority to convince them that it was not a question of a fleeting whim. My incorruptible rigidity did not sit well with them. They had counted on the fact that when I was back on my lands, fun would be reborn and they would be able to shake off the provincial tedium. They did not need me to re-establish their wanderings and that was what they did behind my back, as if they feared the scolding of the austere duke who was implanting his unexpected asepsis in an atmosphere that since the time of the Etruscans, the Romans, and the first truculent Orsinis had affirmed its voluptuous contamination. Giambattista, after hovering about me for a time, disconcerted, decided to withdraw from me and join my cousins' renegade group. Silvio and Porzia, when I would suddenly appear in their room, would assume grotesque, bashful positions. And, while Silvio would show me his astrological sketches and calculations and explain to me the signs that showed the summer to be the most opportune time for my marriage, I was enjoying within the confusion I was causing and discovering in it one more pleasure, a new way to exercise my rule, which rather amused me. It was good for those who depended on me never to feel too secure, never to presuppose my reactions. Now, pale as a monk, dragging my leg, I would go through the corridors and the chambers as if Bomarzo were a monastery, and I would feel a sharp pleasure at the flourishing of an unaccustomed aspect of my personality, fictitious, to be sure. An atmosphere of distinct respect—the fruit particularly of disorientation, of not knowing how to act so as not to upset the young duke—surrounded Bomarzo. I bathed in it as in a magical spring, happy, for nothing could bring me better results than imposing my personality and making others adjust their structures to mine, and in that way the unknown continence replaced for me one absent pleasure with another, more subtle, stranger, engendered by a singular form of despotism and by the certainty that my sacrifice—although there was no sacrifice in it, but rather an unexpected manifestation of the alternatives of my character—responded to high motives of example, authority, and perfect love.

Sometimes after dark I would have torches lit in the vastness of the rooms and I would judge my work, walking at length among the paintings, the statues, and the tapestries. The busts of the Roman emperors that I had bought in Venice—the majesty of Augustus, the hardness of Tiberius, the madness of Nero, the cruel mouths, the astute noses, the severe foreheads, the heroism, the sagacity, the obscenity, the avarice, the stupidity, and the pride—and the ostentatious effigies of my forebears—the outstretched arms, as if that warrior were a singer; the dancer's feet put forward, the expressions of hard-headed and ingenuous command—escorted my thoughts with immobile reverence, and I did not separate them any more, as if all of them, Galba the same as Pope Nicholas III, Trajan the same as Cardinal Giambattista Orsini, who had bathed me in the baptismal font of Santa Maria in Traspontina, made up my family tree and were the basis of my personality.

Naturally, what most disturbed me was the nearness of the moment in which my destiny would be joined to that of Giulia. I yearned for it and I feared it, and no sooner did that thought upset me than I wiped it from my troubled mind, replacing it with the agitation that the work on the castle was causing me. At any hour, in order to deceive myself, I would have the foremen and the workers called. I would interrogate them, criticize them, invent jobs, and replace my permanent worry with other, superficial ones to which I gave too great a value. But my love for Giulia was a curious reality. Since I had seen her so little and scarcely knew her through her circumspect letters, I had made of her an image whose traits were the product of my fantasy. I would stop in front of her portrait by Sebastiano del Piombo, who had admirably reproduced the charm of her beauty, and I would say to it everything that I had not dared say to her: the hopes of my passion, the necessity that she understand me, that she alleviate me, that she help me, that she understand us, me and Bomarzo, and reign over both with gentle domination, because then, if she transmitted to me the security that comes from loving, understanding, perhaps I would be capable of realizing what I had not yet realized and of being what I most strove to be: an Orsini, a Duke Orsini, worthy of my people and perhaps superior to them.

One day in Rome I could not resist the impulse to see her. I sent Silvio to tell her father diplomatically of my desire, and Galeazzo Farnese agreed. In his palace, from the height of a loggia, half hidden between Galeazzo and his two sons, the handsome Fabio and Ferdinando, who had just received the bishopric of Soana, I looked into the salon where, along with her sisters Jolanda and Battistina, my betrothed was having her lute lesson. It was a fascinating scene, almost mute, for it was broken only by the brief laughter of the girls, something which made one think of the theater and painting and which was removed from the conventions of daily life. Galeazzo pushed against me, crushing me with the colossal mass of his body, and when I was about to retire, Giulia, no doubt advised of my visit, raised her head and smiled at me. With a graceful expression she showed me on her finger Benvenuto Cellini's ring. Her small breasts were pushing against her bodice, and the lute, resting on her skirt, made the outline of her legs visible. I did not dare ask her father to allow me to break the pact and go down and speak to the girl. I was frightened of the probability. Suddenly, now that I had her so close, I measured everything that separated us. I went back to Bomarzo—it was a month before the wedding—disturbed, gloomy.

My grandmother brought me out of that mood—which later kept me up whole nights—going back to her plan to have me make peace with Maerbale. My brother had accepted the conditions of the division made by Cardinal Farnese; was not that evidence of the proof of his good will? Custom imposed that he, my closest relative, should be the one to fetch my betrothed and escort her with her family retinue to Bomarzo. Diana Orsini had already made inquiries in that sense and Maerbale seemed inclined to accede. Besides, what concrete grievances did I have against my brother? A letter, an innocent letter; his supposed attempts against my life. Had they really existed when I had not been able to confirm their origins? And for my part, had I not tried to avenge myself on him in Venice with the help of my cousins? Were we not in the same position? And did it not befit the magnanimity of the duke, as when Maerbale had made common cause with Martelli the administrator, to pardon the offenses, if they had been offenses, and if all had not been a plot woven by those who hoped to divide us? Would I not in that way affirm the nobility of my position? Was it to my benefit to separate him from me forever now that his prestige was beginning to grow, and should I not, on the contrary, attract him, absorb him, so that his glory as a condottiere would blend with the glory of Bomarzo and constitute an inseparable whole with the strength of the duke, so that when he gained a triumph it would be as if I had earned it, because it was a triumph of the branch of the clan which I governed? And—but this was my deepest thought and the one least revealed—would it not bring me the incomparable satisfaction and the complete revenge of the hunchback who had been the object of his mockery, facing the second son whom he resembled so much and the owner of everything the other one lacked and display his possession of Giulia Farnese? I told my grandmother that I agreed, that I would proceed according to her wishes, and the old woman kissed me on the cheek. Maerbale would go with Matteo and Orso to fetch Giulia. Sigismondo would also go. I wrote him a letter in Rome which could be interpreted as an order and as an expression of desires, for I wanted to remind Pier Luigi Farnese in that way that Sigismondo still depended on me, although it was not opportune that because of it I should make enemies with a dangerous member of the family with which I was going to ally myself, nor should I run the risk either of receiving a negative reply, which would lower my standing as head of the Orsinis. Happily, Sigismondo answered at once, proclaiming his fidelity to the house and thanking me for the honor that the embassy implied.

My grandmother and I wrote many letters during those months, inviting relatives and friends to attend the wedding. I was anxious to have present the most significant representatives of the line, the heads of other great families of Italy, and a few famous artists and intellectuals, to point out in that way that the Duke of Bomarzo was a defender of the traditions that he had received with his inheritance and which the other lords shared, but at the same time a modern man, *à la page*, and as such he disdained feudal prejudices and the spiritual backwardness that in a world in full evolution, with patron and humanist princes, the arrogant and archaic descendants of the She-Bear continued to characterize. I would have liked to have had Ariosto as my guest and I sent a letter to Ferrara to tell him so, but the poet declined and he died that same year. Nor could I count on Paracelsus, who was practicing his profession in Saint-Gall, nor on Lorenzo Lotto, whose timidity broke into excuses. On the other hand, Aretino, Benvenuto Cellini, Sansovino, Tolomei, and Sebastiano del Piombo did not miss the chance offered them to shine alongside the Duke and Duchess of Urbino and Cardinal de' Medici. It would be necessary to lodge all those lords and their retinues for several days, taking care not to cause any stir because of precedence, and that brought on complicated chores. Furthermore, I wanted Giulia to arrive at Bomarzo the way other princesses entered their new domains, in a carriage whose sumptuous decorations would impress the village; and to build it according to my plans, craftsmen from the Estes arrived at the castle, disciples of that school of Ercole de' Roberti, which had been responsible for the triumphal carriage in which the bride of Francesco Gonzaga entered the palace in Mantua. The gilded vehicle would await my betrothed and her party on the outskirts of Orte, where some tents had been set up with ancient tapestries so that the Farnese retinue could rest and change into their ceremonial clothing.

Yes, one had to think of a thousand things: the proper location of the five cardinals; the special food for the Duke of Mantua's falcons, for he would go nowhere without them; not placing the Orsini squires near those of the Colonnas; keeping Leonardo Emo within reach of Valerio Orsini without that implying any offense to the people of the family of Oliverotto da Fermo, to which his wife belonged; not aggravating the touchy Benvenuto, even less the biting Aretino; finding the way in which Ippolito de' Medici could meet privately with Giulia Gonzaga, his illustrious platonic love, in a castle teeming with spying eyes; seeing that the fountains functioned and that the fireworks did not fail; that Pier Luigi Farnese did not drink too much or get out of hand with the young pages; that the Orsinis who were older and richer than I (principally those of the devastating Bracciano branch) felt comfortable in my domains, as if they had not left home, but without forgetting that I was the master there; wisely distributing the hidden musicians; that my grandmother and Cardinal Franciotto always be above everyone, no matter how great they might be; that my father-in-law cause no trouble over the dowry, for I was not ignorant of how things had gone with my father and my grandfather in a similar situation; that the newly remodeled kitchens respond to the enormous effort that would be required of them; the sarcasm of the Marchioness Isabella of Mantua, the most courted woman in Europe; the vanity of her son Ercole; her daughter-in-law, the Duchess Margherita, who was descended from the blood of the Paleologhi, which meant a lot, but which should not have impressed me because I was descended from Caius Flavius Orsus; me—good Lord, me, Vicino Orsini!—the folds of the cape that would hang from my poor back ... A thousand complex, contradictory matters that were linked to the service of God, for at least thirty clerics, princes of the Church, and chaplains would have to say their daily masses in Bomarzo, and with the frivolity of the world, since each one of the guests considered himself an exceptional being and required exceptional care, it would have to be taken into account in organizing that labyrinth of courtly etiquette, all wrapped up in formulas, and an effort would have to be made so that the mistrustful tribes would not fall into the eternal brutal arguments provoked by the turbulent Orsinis.

That last month stands out in my memory with the tones of a nightmare. Along with the administrator of my estates, Bernardino Niccoloni, and my favorites, Silvio da Narni and Giambattista Martelli, I went a thousand times from the stables, where they were making ready to feed several dozen horses, to the place where, like a miniature military encampment, they were setting up the tents crowned with gay standards; and from the place where they were building the symbolic cart which displayed on high our fierce totem holding up the heraldic lily of the Farneses, to the rooms where there was no end of coffers, beds, and drapes; and to the workrooms where they were sewing my clothes and the red and silver liveries of my people, lined up on fearsome dummies; and to the courtyards that resounded with the singing of the servant girls as they polished the tableware and prepared the wax for so much unusual illumination. The heat of early June was oppressive; perspiration wet my whole body and, sliding down my forehead in thick drops, it blinded my tired eyes. I would have gladly taken off my shirt as I went back and forth with pages and scribes, dictating orders, but the horror of showing the hated promontory with no protection whatever deprived me of that relief. And every time I looked up toward my grandmother's rooms, no matter how much the air burned and I had repeated to the point of annoyance that she should stay in the coolness of her bedroom under the protection of her ladies, who waved small square fans with multicolored speckles, I would see my adored Diana Orsini on the terrace under a parasol, waving a handkerchief and showing me in that way that she was still watching over me, white, remote, and vigilant, as if she were guiding me from the distance of the clouds in which petty human destinies are woven and unwoven.

A week before the wedding the guests began to arrive from the far reaches of Italy. The various Orsinis made their appearance with military clatter: the terrible Niccolò, who lived like a biblical king among his Hebrew concubines; the tremendous abbot of Farfa; the luxurious lords of Bracciano, who moved with a sparkle of precious stones; the Duke of Mugnano, my neighbor; Giulio Orsini, the friend of intellectuals; Violante, married to a Savelli; Leone, whose wealth was frightening; Francesco and Arrigo, condottieri of great renown; Valerio, who traveled from Venice with his wife and Leonardo Emo and brought me as a gift two golden goblets which, according to scholars, had belonged to the Emperors of Byzantium; Carlotto Fausto, the other hunchback, the warrior, whose presence I wanted as proof to the Farneses that the Duke of Bomarzo was not the only crookback in the line, that a hump among us could be something as natural and as unimportant as among the Gonzagas, and as a proof also that it was no hindrance for the one who bore it in gaining glory with arms in the example of our great forebears. The successive columns wound up the roads in the direction of the big house. My grandmother, my grandfather, and I received the relatives with lavish familiarity. At interminable banquets we spoke to one another of the magnificence of our line and that put us in a great good humor. The quarrels that several of the Orsinis maintained among themselves, almost always over legacies and divisions, were postponed, as if diluted by the vapors of the wine.

The Farneses also appeared, more affected, more courtly. Cardinal Alessandro closeted himself with my grandfather in secret sessions that doubtless had to do with pontifical diplomacy, which—although these matters probably were not very serious, for I do not believe that Giulia's astute uncle would bring my grandfather into the torturous confidence of his hidden plans—crowned Cardinal Franciotto with joy to have the occasion to shine mysteriously before his kinsmen and let be hinted among them the startling deduction that he could still emerge with a surprise at the next papal election. Pier Luigi arrived with his wife, Girolama Orsini; Angelo Farnese with his, Angela Orsini, the daughter of the Count of Pitigliano, showing how our lineages were intertwined; and also arriving were the Count and Countess Santa Fiora and the della Roveres of Laura Farnese, and Federico Farnese, the husband of Ippolita Sforza. The beautiful names of Italy were sung out in the rooms under the haughtiness of the portraits. My guests would bow and I would spy on them, unnoticed, when they went hunting or hurried to religious services, or went down the stairs in twos between the stone bears and the hanging banners toward the banquet hall. Neither before nor after had Bomarzo ever lived such moments of pomp. Soon the lords of the House of Gonzaga got out of their carriages, my grandmother's famous friends: Isabella d'Este, whose wedding my mother had attended at the memorable festivities that had seen her dance with Gilbert de Montpensier and Guidobaldo da Montefeltro; her daughter Eleonora, very beautiful, timid, the wife of the nephew of that Guidobaldo, Francesco Maria della Rovere, the current Duke of Urbino; and Duke Federico of Mantua, and Maria Paleologa, his duchess. It was a group that took up a lot of space, made a lot of noise, because in Italy it was the center of artistic and worldly snobbery, and although Isabella had lost a great deal of the power that had attracted the eyes of all Europe, because her jealous son had slipped through her fingers and was imposing his harsh will on Mantua, the great lady continued to dazzle like a matchless star with the glow of her intelligence. Federico Gonzaga and Francesco Maria della Rovere were mediocre beside her in spite of their dash. And although they were extreme in courtesies, puns, and witty remarks, the reader must not think that both princes were mere ceremonial palace dwellers. Gonzaga, a captain general of the Church, had murdered his tutor, and della Rovere had stabbed his sister's lover and Cardinal Alidosi to death. They looked apathetic, frozen in their distinction and urbanity, or they seemed preoccupied with whippets, falcons, swords, and clothing, but at any moment an angry spark could light up in their indolent eyes. They were traitors, libertines, dandies, blusterers. They initiated fashions. Pier Luigi Farnese, when he slipped in among them lost stature, in spite of his wildness. Giulia Gonzaga, the widow since the age of eighteen of the deformed Vespasiano Colonna, eclipsed the rest with her beauty, which had been praised by Ariosto. Cardinal Ippolito de' Medici did not leave her side. They would speak quietly of enigmatic things that bordered on heresy. From time to time the lady would lift her eyes to the one who adored her and her face would light up with a transparent clarity. The Orsinis, who did not like her, and less than any the abbot of Farfa, commented among themselves, hinting with frowns that she had married old Colonna, lame and one-armed, at the urging of Isabella d'Este for his money. I was fascinated by the motto that she displayed embroidered on her sleeves under an amaranth studded with jasper: "*Non moritura.*" I asked her to explain it to me and she smiled and said that just like that flower, which always becomes green again on contact with water, there would always remain with her, moistened by her tears, the image of the dead Colonna. Ippolito smiled too, skeptically, and he kissed her hand. *Non moritura.* It should have been my motto.

Pier Luigi and Benvenuto Cellini almost provoked a disaster. I was happy to see Benvenuto again. He had matured since our first meeting without having lost any of the dynamic youth that made him quiver like an undefinable vibration. He belonged at that time to a "humanist" circle with Giovanni Gaddi, a student of Greek literature, the wise Ludovico di Fano, the poet Annibale Caro, and the painter Bastiano da Venezia, who had decorated the palace of the banker Chigi. His inclination toward dangerous miracles had led him to invoke the Devil in the Colosseum one night with the help of a priest and a Pistoian who dabbled in necromancy in order to get back a Sicilian girl whom he was in love with and whose mother had taken her away from Rome. He told me about it in great detail. This time he did not kiss me and he bowed before me majestically, but I opened my arms to him because his memory had cast on my adolescence one of the few lights that had shone there. He clashed at once with Pier Luigi because the son of Cardinal Farnese tried to treat him with the disdain that he reserved for inferiors and he was completely mistaken. And then came the episode with Giambattista Martelli. My page came to confide his fears to me one morning: the nobleman and the goldsmith were pursuing him. That night they had got into his room at the same time, and if they had not cut each other, having drawn their daggers, it was because the boy had escaped, naked, with his sword in his right hand, and had managed to get away from them in the park. Five years later, when Cellini was arrested and imprisoned in the Castel Sant' Angelo under the custody of a mad warden who thought he was a bat, it was due— Benvenuto himself says so in his memoirs—to intrigues of Pier Luigi. The craftsman tells in his book that Farnese accused him of having stolen Vatican jewels valued at eighty thousand ducats during the sack of Rome in that same castle where he later suffered a long imprisonment. It was really an absurd pretext. The real reason—and I do not know why Benvenuto did not point it out in his long book—came from the hatred that grew up between the two of them at Bomarzo because of Giambattista Martelli. I had to talk to both of them separately, to calm them down, pointing out to them the inconvenience of their attitude, and from then on, as if by common accord, they limited themselves to an exchange of fearsome looks and grasping the hilts of their daggers when they passed in the galleries. But Pier Luigi had sworn to have his revenge, and of all the promises he made, that was the kind that he kept. He did it five years later, during the time when his father had been elevated to the throne of Saint Peter and the ambitious rascal took advantage of such an extraordinary and powerful position. Nor did it go very well for Cellini with my grandfather Franciotto. The cardinal had not forgiven him for having wounded the Prince of Orange during the siege of Sant' Angelo, when the goldsmith had disobeyed his orders not to fire on the enemy leaders at a time when there were chances for an armistice. Those were the only disagreeable episodes during the period preceding the arrival of Giulia Farnese. Afterward, of course, there were others.

Aretino conducted himself with irreproachable good sense. He had just published his *Dialogues of Nanna and Antonia* in Venice, which had been composed, according to what he said, for his monkey Capriccio, and he amused us by reading them with such wit that he drew the applause of Isabella d'Este. He even made peace with the Duke of Mantua, from whom he had been estranged by ancient differences over matters—there is no need to underline it—of money. His stupendous laughter would burst forth in the rooms amid the talking of the Gonzagas, the Farneses, and the Orsinis. In a corner Sansovino and Tolomei were observing the activities in a bashful way, like artists who did not dare mingle with the great noblemen of Italy. My grandmother seated in her high-backed chair to which she had been carried from her bedroom in a hand chair, was the hub of such varied activities. Her white cats rubbed against her stiff legs, mewing, or climbed insolently into her lap, that of Isabella, that of Eleonora d'Urbino, those of the

## A WEDDING IN BOMARZO · 375

ladies of my lineage who formed a circle of agitated fans about her. Isabella's main obsession was to eclipse her daughter, whose beauty was capable of pushing her into the background, in spite of the fact that the daughter had never dared attempt to rival the slyness and charm of a mother who used them almost professionally, and that poor Eleonora, infected by the lewdness of her husband and his unmentionable illnesses, would have preferred to be left in a restful and sad shadow. And I, going everywhere, would leave the rooms where the dancers were performing and where the Duke of Urbino was playing chess with the Duke of Mantua under the critical eyes of Cardinal Ercole Gonzaga, and go up to my room and try on once more the mantle that I would wear in the ceremony, a miracle of sculpture and architecture with its padding and stuffing. Fascinated and frightened, I counted the days and distracted myself watching the grandeur and misery of my guests, who were not essentially either better or worse than the members of other dazzling societies, but who as representatives of the Renaissance accentuated with touches of their own superlative personalities the characteristics of its merits and its vices. During that time everything was done on a grand scale. There were no half-tones, concessions, or pretenses. If one pretended in a Machiavellian fashion, the attitude had a passing, preparatory character, like a crouch before the leap. All believed that from the mere fact of existing and enjoying a hereditary or acquired position they could do as they pleased according to their overwhelming convenience, showing themselves just as they were, for they had more than enough drive and impunity to assert it, and that fact, which rejected the present-day equalitarian calmness of conventions that have arisen from individual rights, and which conferred on that period an originality of violent colors, contributes to the alarming attraction of its leading figures, who were usually a cross between a wolf and a whippet, and while it could well have been rather uncomfortable and even dangerous—for the probability of a sudden death hung over all of us constantly—it was also passionate and it kept us tense and alert, living, devouring life with desperate enjoyment. That was how I looked at them, lucidly, and that was how I was seen among them. The Orsini Duke of Mugnano was very capable of murdering me or Cardinal de' Medici if in some petty argument we had involuntarily cast a faint shadow on the aggressive brilliance of his personality. In the meantime, surrounded by the mythological paintings, with the crackling of the flames of the torches, my guests danced the galliard and the allemande, and the ladies, to the sound of the music, turned slowly, gravely, with a small handkerchief or glove in their right hands. The Orsinis of Bracciano danced marvelously in the midst of the flashing of their precious stones, and a blind man, from a balcony where the instruments untwined the tremulous tapestry of the cadences as if it had been woven with the bows of the violas, was singing us stories of love that recalled the magical world of Ariosto.

Until the day came when I had to put on the golden spurs that Alessandro de' Medici, the Duke of Florence, had tied on me when I had been knighted by Charles V. I put on the silver cuirass—which was really only a breastplate, with the inlaid figure of a She-Bear vanquishing dragons and griffins, for the rear part was of leather and adjusted to my hump, disappearing under the broad green cape—and I mounted a spirited sorrel whose trappings were a reproduction of those used by my ancestor Francesco Orsini of Monterotondo in the medieval fresco in Siena. In order to do me honor, the great Valerio Orsini followed me, bearing on a scarlet cushion my helmet, which was decorated heraldically with roses and serpents of gold. It was demanded by the military tradition of our people and the prestige of Bomarzo, so different from my own inclinations. Leonardo Emo and Giambattista Martelli, as delicate as if sketched by Botticelli, led our horses by the bridles and more than one person must have smiled on observing how those young men were involved in a ceremony that should have put an end to their voluptuous reign. In that way I went to wait for Giulia in the tents raised near Orte. From the procession there rose up a small forest of halberds, crowned by iron tips of fantastic geometry. As we moved along it might have been said that the breeze was playing with that metallic foliage, shaking branches and fruit. My grandparents, the cardinals, the dukes, the ladies, and the rest of the guests would wait in the castle. Peasants and shepherds greeted us everywhere, along the road, at bends, on knolls waving garlands.

So much time has passed since that morning, and yet now just as then I can smell the perfume of the roses in the garden that we passed through, I can hear the monologues of the fountains, and if I were a painter I would be able to recapture the exact coloration of the rocks that rose up alongside like quiet monsters and which were to preoccupy me extremely later on. It was a June with starry warm nights and afternoons in which the heat drugged the birds and only the butterflies seemed to be alive in the vibration of the sun at motionless siesta time. The butterflies escorted us to the encampment, succeeding one another, relieving one another, yellow, red, white, blue ones, flying among the lances, alighting on the helmets, hovering for a second over the horses' erect ears. Giambattista caught one on the fly, turned and showed it to me. Messer Pandolfo, who worshiped ritual solemnities and who, old, ailing, would not have left his place beside his ducal pupil for anything, flashed his sty-filled eyes at him. The boy opened up his hand, where some golden powder remained, and let it go up into the winged cloud that was surrounding us like a trembling rainbow.


When her ladies raised the flaps of the tent in which my betrothed had rested for several hours and Giulia, already dressed for the ceremonies in Bomarzo, appeared at the opening of the lifted tapestries as if she were in a niche, I thought that I would faint from emotion, for her grace was as great as I had dared hope for. She was small and yet her bearing made her seem tall; very thin, very delicate, like the work of a goldsmith, so delicate that the ampleness of the fashion could not disguise the feeling of lightness that came from her and which, with her wide violet eyes, of a shade almost the same as those of Adriana dalla Roza, made up the salient characteristic of her charm. Her chestnut hair had been braided about her small and perfect head and over her long, flexible neck à la Ghirlandaio, with the pearls of the Farnese-Monaldeschis intertwined in it, which also came down over her extremely white chest, outlining with the sketch of the strings and the swinging edges of the oval twist the exquisiteness of those small breasts that had peopled my dreams—sometimes all by themselves like those that martyred saints would carry on a tray like fruit—the pearls that then were strewn along her sleeves and her skirt, giving those red folds a pale twinkle in such a way that it could have been said that they were not splendid additions but something that was part of her, giving off a cold and mysterious light. Beside her, her father, her brothers, her sisters, her aunt, Beatrice Baglioni, were also radiant with satisfaction, with pride. I kissed the tips of her fingers, helped her into the carriage, and the procession started out for Bomarzo.

I think now that the golden coach drawn by six white horses, showing on its rear the She-Bear holding up the waving Farnese lily, as if it were trying to escape from her claws—for which I had been inspired by the medal that shows the Orsini bear embracing the column of the Colonnas—and the cortege of carriages and riders which followed it had something of the circus about it, but at that time such a disrespectful simile could not yet have occurred to me. Valerio still carried my helmet and Maerbale, without blinking an eye, just the same as when I had succeeded my father to the dukedom, was carrying my erect sword, the phallic symbol. I, among the other Orsinis—Orso, Matteo, Sigismondo, who went to extremes with his audacious open shirt and Pier Luigi's diamonds sparkling on his bronzed skin; the abbot of Farfa, the hunchbacked Carlotto, the opulent Leone, the condottieri, the Duke of Mugnano, those from Bracciano, who for the occasion had augmented their luxury and looked like pheasants or some glistening crustaceans—and among the Farneses—the huge Galeazzo, a spectacular Falstaff; the purple bishop of Soana; Fabio and his supple elegance; Pier Luigi, taciturn, using his plumes to hide the sores on his aquiline face; his son Orazio, a lively adolescent; and the ladies whose heads were nodding in a coach where the chattering of Jolanda and Battistina could be heard and in which there also rode a sister of Giulia's whom I had not met until that moment, Lucrezia, who was pretty and half-witted, with the stigma of the old, corrupt blood—and among the rest, pages, grooms, halberdiers, standard-bearers, wagons with luggage and gifts, I sat up as straight as I could, making the folds of the emerald cape wave. From time to time I would go over to Giulia to point out to her some detail of what would be her domain and she would turn her clear, fearless eyes toward me. The news that the Gonzagas were waiting in the castle with Ippolito de' Medici had capped the vanity of my new relatives. They did not cease to ask questions.

A WEDDING IN BOMARZO · 379

They wanted to know, for example, how many people the Duke of Mantua had brought with him, and what the Holy Father had given me (two pieces of enamelwork surrounded by pearls showing Saint Peter and Saint Francis, my patrons). Thus, with much talking, a creaking of harnesses, a clanging of arms, neighing, and the rumbling of wagons, and, above all, with a great deal of barracks humor directed at the bridegroom, at his timidity and the obligatory task that awaited him, jokes that would explode obscenely—for if in those times the spirit of Ariosto was triumphant, so was that of Aretino—without regard for Giulia's modesty and which made me grit my teeth and smile falsely, the nuptial apotheosis advanced through the dusk, through fields lighted with torches. The picture was so artistically composed in its histrionic perfection that it seemed as if we were pulling the clouds along like floating veils, for nothing that made it up could be separated from its careful balance. Seen from the battlements of Bomarzo, the procession was like a meandering animal, like a dragon or an ophidian with multicolored scales, like the serpent on the shield of the Orsinis which was sliding along, creeping, shining, toward the phosphorescent mass of the fortress. The trumpets announced our progress, accentuating the impression of a traveling troupe calling out the villagers, and from Bomarzo bells and bugles replied. Everything was happening just as I had planned it, except, of course, for the imbecilic obscene jokes, necessary nonetheless, and putting aside the anguish that contracted my chest, I might have been considered happy now that the very air was quivering with jubilation. Some peasants, led by the administrator of my lands, stopped us at the entrance to the park and gave Giulia a garland of amaranths, the flower of *non moritura*. Messer Pandolfo took advantage of the occasion to declaim a harangue whose Latin words I cut short. I was anxious to arrive. How I would have enjoyed it for me to have been seen by the dead people who had exercised so much influence on my tormented life: my father, my brother Girolamo, Adriana dalla Roza, Beppo, Clarice Strozzi, and those other absent ones, Abul, Ignacio de Zúñiga, Nencia, Pantasilea, Piero Valeriano, Alessandro and Lorenzino de' Medici, who had also crowned my existence with their affection and their hatred, because that cortege, that showy pantomime taking place on the soil of Bomarzo, proceeding toward the castle as if it were boring into the secret of the Etruscan tombs and as if it were being held up by a base of an age-old civilization and of subterranean rites and conjuring, was in a certain way the justification of Pier Francesco Orsini and the proof of his first victory!

At the entrance to the castle a crowd was waiting, crushed together all along the street opposite the small houses of the village. There were people at the windows and crowded onto the terraces. My grandmother was standing in the center of the main entrance, dressed in white silk. She was leaning, as if on two crutches, on the shoulders of her two dwarf jesters: the redhead and the stammerer. The latter, with such a bad character, would stare boldly with his lashless little eyes, which was the main part of his humor. As far as I was concerned, neither the redhead nor he was funny at all. Cardinals Orsini, Farnese, Medici, Gonzaga, and the newly arrived Colonna—that enemy, Pompeo Colonna, who attacked us with his hidden perfidy, for he was the one who stopped my grandfather from attaining the papacy and who fortunately died that year—drew blessings over the caravan amid the rolling waves of their purple. The rest made efforts to be noticed and mingled in repeated, tight, and probably hypocritical embraces with the Farneses as soon as we dismounted and majestically went up the staircase.

That night a monumental banquet was served. The customs are well known: the people at the table tore the birds apart as if they were fighting with them, sucked their fingers, greasy with venison, and threw the bones under the table; but every utensil, every golden goblet, every crystal and amethyst vessel could have been included by Paolo Veronese in his great spectacular oils. I danced afterward with Giulia, making an effort to do it gracefully, but every time my mistrustful looks lighted on one of the other dancers of my age, Maerbale, Sigismondo, Fabio, the lord of Bracciano, my cousin Count della Corbara, the splendid Duke of Urbino, who held a hand open like a tulip over his heavy Venetian chain, an atrocious fatigue would bring me back to reality and nothing, not even Giulia's sweet expression, nor the proximity of the humpbacked Carlotto Fausto, nor the certainty that the father, the grandfather, and the great-grandfather of those Olympian Gonzagas had been more hunchbacked than I, nor the memory that the husband of the divine Giulia Colonna had been a sick old man, lame and one-armed, was able to calm me.

My bride was most gracious. She praised the arrangements in the castle, she admired the portrait by Lorenzo Lotto, she kissed my grandfather's ring and Diana's lips, she gave a shout of surprise when I gave her my mother's jewels. But when we retired I could not sleep for a moment. I strolled with Silvio until late through the shadowy woods in which the strange rocks stood out like family monsters and where the invisible and defending bears undoubtedly lived. Silvio tried to penetrate my silence, but I did not answer him. I limited myself to deep sighs. Now that I was finally faced with the crowning of a long effort and I could not distract myself with the placing of statues and the ordering of decorations, for everything had its place within the chessboard of busts and mythical figures, the fear that was crouching inside of me took over, smothering me, and impelling me to keep walking like an automaton along the moonlit paths. I was afraid of Giulia. My virility, which had been affirmed so many times, was of little use on that occasion. I felt despoiled of her, as if the fright that was growing in my breast and which dominated even the smallest parts of my being left no room for the drive of my manhood when I needed it most. And Giulia was gentle, nonetheless, and a transparent goodness seemed to emanate from her. No aggressive shadow darkened her clear domain. Perhaps a demanding observer might have been able to accuse her of a certain indifference, a certain obsequious distance, but it too could be attributed to her justified modesty.

"I'll keep watch over Your Lordship," Silvio said to me; "with Messer Benvenuto Cellini I'll make the proper invocation."

My conceit rebelled. "No. I forbid it. This is my affair, mine alone. Go away and leave me alone."

The wedding took place in the morning. My grandfather officiated, aided by Cardinals Farnese and Medici. The other two princes, Gonzaga and Colonna, and the bishop of Soana, along with the acolytes, also went up and down the steps of the altar burning incense for the relics of Saint Anselm, distributing blessings. The Saint Sebastian and the painting that my father had had painted with Girolamo and Maerbale, excluding me (I explained when asked about it that it was

Maerbale and I, and my brother did not put the lie to me), flanked the rite with their nudity and their clothing like sensual allegories. I slipped a sapphire on Giulia's left ring finger and she gave me back Benvenuto's ring, passing on to me as I squeezed it in my hand an intense happiness, for it was as if its contact brought me new life, but that happiness did not last for long. The ducal cloak was suffocating me in the summer heat and I thought with horror that I was going to faint, that the multicolored miters and chasubles would be erased in the heavy air and that the Latin sung by the aged and the young cardinals along with mutual bows would be transformed into a vague murmur so that the only thing remaining intact in the mist into which those attending the ceremony would disappear too, as if they were specters, would be the impassive grace of Giulia Farnese, illuminated, crystalline, quivering, glacial.

My subjects rendered their homage to the duchess in the afternoon, and she gave them silver coins and played her role with her usual ease, as if she had been mistress of Bomarzo for many years. Aretino read her two sonnets, stroking his beard, and Benvenuto Cellini gave her a buckle with the intertwined images of Venus and Adonis. At nightfall the fireworks burst forth. A gigantic She-Bear climbed over the fountains and released to the heavens fireworks in the shape of fleurs-de-lis. We danced until very late. The Marchioness Isabella of Mantua, who was the granddaughter of Ferrante of Aragon, the King of Naples, and carried in her blood the wealth of numerous generations of courtly affability and the repetition of formulas that eased contact in society, told me in a pause in the music that I danced very well, that I had a spontaneous grace. And although I knew only too well that it was not true, for the lie was obvious, I would have liked for that ball never to have ended, that we should have danced and danced into the night, into the small hours, into the morning, without stopping, like animated dolls or as if we were bewitched princes and princesses, bowing and rising to the gallant rhythms, putting one foot forward, holding out right hands, making rhythmic bows like the cardinals in the chapel, so that everything since the Farneses had arrived at Bomarzo would be an irreproachable ballet, while the days lighted up and went out again on the balconies and the stars that assured my infinite presence, moved by the same rhythm of violins, would continue tracing their eternal, solemn dance on high.

I would have preferred not going into great detail about the intimacies of my wedding night, for it is improper for a gentleman, or even for a person of taste, but it is a matter of importance for an understanding of aspects of my psychology and of the confusions that afflicted me, and, keeping in mind the sincerity of these memoirs, in which I am describing exactly what I have been and in which I have been searching for explanations of my life and character, it would be inconsistent to avoid a theme of such importance.

For the moment I must speak of the disquieting matter of the Devil. It was Giulia who discovered him.

I had destined a rather small room on the second floor for our bridal chamber and I ordered it decorated with green and yellow ceramic work. In order to do that work, special workmen came from Rome, bringing with them the mosaics that I had ordered in the city. When the work was completed, I examined it and approved. It was something distinct within the castle and I wanted it that way, something that would stand out from the pomp and austerity that my father's and my refurbishing and the medieval heaviness imposed on the rest of the fortress. I wanted the room I was to share with Giulia to have the air of a graceful retreat and I succeeded in it. The Farnese lilies and my own initials, VIC. ORS., were distributed in the adornment of pilasters and vases, intertwined with white roses, and they proclaimed discreetly that this was our most personal refuge, the one in which the heraldic flowers of both families lost their warlike symbolism, reaffirmed so many times on their battle shields, and regained their simple and natural beauty. At that time I did not notice anything anomalous in the composition, and, really, the place was of such reduced proportions, with its window and two doors, that it would have been difficult for anything wrong in the sketch, no matter how small, to have escaped my watchful eyes. The craftsmen left, the bed with green hangings and the few pieces of furniture were placed in the room, and I only entered from time to time, moved by the superstition that my presence in the chamber would prejudice my future happiness. For the same reason I did not show it to Giulia, keeping it as a surprise for the wedding night.

So we climbed the narrow stairs, escorted by ladies and pages whose candlesticks projected dancing shadows along the way. In a neighboring room I changed my clothing for a thin garment modeled on the ample lines of the Florentine *lucco*. Then I sent away my aides. Silvio and Giambattista were the last to go and I kissed them both. Maerbale, who was present at the ceremony with a light in his hand embraced me too. I remember that in that supreme instant I still sought some sign of his feelings on his face, but I encountered the same courtly mask, the same impenetrable respect which never left him. I heard him tiptoe away, and I went out onto the terrace that adjoined the room where Giulia was being undressed by her ladies.

It was a singularly clear night which conferred a rare paleness on the countryside, as if it were all strewn with colossal bones. I leaned over the parapet and on the right I could make out the gray ripples of the tile roofs of Bomarzo, which surrounded us like a muddy wave that had been immobilized upon touching the castle walls. The whole mountainous panorama gave the same impression of a stormy, static sea, a sea that had taken on the appearance of cyclopean skeletons when it froze over. In front, in the distance, the rock of Mugnano arose, and beyond, like a broken sword blade, the Tiber was sparkling. The door opened and I sensed Giulia behind me. I turned toward her and saw her standing against the nest of shadows. With her hair down and her long white gown she was a lunar apparition. Shining like aquamarines under her dark lashes were her light eyes. I took her hand and led her to the guard rail that formed a severe balcony. My heart was beating terribly and I was trembling so much that Giulia, when she noticed it, smiled and slid her arm under mine. In order to hide my upset—I was stammering and fumbling like an imbecile, when she should have been the frightened one—I pointed out to her the outline of Mugnano, where some lights were twinkling and I told her that the duke, my cousin, must have been entertaining the relatives he had taken with him when he left. I also showed her in the shadows of the bulwarks the abandoned nuptial carriage in which she had triumphantly entered my domains and in which the She-Bear was still holding up, like a male attribute, the erect and allegorical lily. Then, in order to gain time, I frivolously began to comment on the incidents of the festivities, exaggerating the buffoonery until I realized that I was talking to myself and I fell silent. I drew her to me and kissed her cheeks, her forehead, her broad eyes, her mouth. A soft perfume was coming from her skin. By acting in that way I was not giving in to a spontaneous, anxious excitement; I was proceeding as if I were fulfilling a ritual, and the proof of it gave me even more anguish. In that same spot the invocation of the Devil by Silvio da Narni before the death of my father had taken place, and that event, which I could not erase from my memory, contributed to my upset. The whole countryside seemed to be lying in wait all around. Not a sound could be heard, not the chirp of a cricket, nor the tingle of a cowbell, nor the hoot of an owl, nor the whispering of the foliage, and the rest of the big house, in which so many guests were still lodged, was silent nonetheless. It might be said that the house was breathing quietly, like a huge animal. The image of Silvio and his conjuring came back to assault me clearly, as if the necromancer were sketching on the ground the geometric figure and the sacred monogram, and I was sorry that I had rejected the aid of his arcane wisdom at that opportunity at hand.

It was impossible to prolong the waiting. We went back into the bedroom and with clumsy fingers I removed my wife's light garments. In the middle of the room, which was lighted by the wax of the lamps, she stood before me naked and I thought that I would faint, for her adolescent thinness was even more beautiful than all I had imagined. In the silky corners where the light was spreading her whiteness was turning almost pale blue.

"I never thought," she said to me, "that Your Lordship would have invited the Devil to this meeting."

I was kneeling and I raised my eyes to hers, not understanding. Giulia was smiling and pointing at something on the wall. Beside the door, among the marquetry of mosaics, there was an outline that I had not noted before—and that was the impossible part, the fantastic part, because, as I have said, the room was small and I had examined it when the artisans had finished their work—a ceramic the same size as the others which represented a two-horned demonic head with an open mouth. I jumped up and touched the figure with trembling fingers. It was not a question of a vision. I could feel the outline of the faunlike face under the tips of my fingers, the sharp nose, the eyes, the hanging blobber lip, the tips of the twisted horns. Giulia began to laugh and covered herself again.

"Are you a friend of the Devil's?" she asked me.

I was surprised as much by her attitude as by that strange presence.

"I don't know how it got there," I murmured. "It's witchcraft."

"Do you believe in it?"

I did not answer her. I searched on the tables for something, a sharp instrument to destroy the effigy with. My sword and my dagger had been left behind in the neighboring room.

"I'll break it to pieces. No. I'd better call Silvio to conjure it away. And tomorrow I'll find out who put it there."

She laughed again. "Leave it there. Don't call him. Let it stay."

"But I can't understand how it got there or who put it there on that wall."

Giulia threw her robe over the back of a chair and its folds hid the perverse ceramic. Now she was naked again, prim between the drapes.

"Forget about it, Pier Francesco. Here are your holy protectors."

And then she showed me on both sides of the bed the enamels of Saint Peter and Saint Francis, surrounded by pearls, that the Holy Father had given me. I approached with apprehensive cowardice.

"Forget about it. Promise me that you won't take it off. It's a toy, a decoration. Forget about it."

I promised her. Perhaps I was making a basic mistake in promising her. On the following morning I would have it sprinkled with holy water, but I would not remove it from the decorations. It is still there in its place next to the door after four and a half centuries. Whoever visits Bomarzo can see it.

The alarming discovery increased my nervousness. It was also accentuated by my beloved's composure. Where had she left her bashfulness, her timidity? But had that bashfulness and timidity really existed? Had they been nothing but a disguise? Did I really know her? Alas, if she had only acted differently, if she had only shown some sign of hesitation like the one that was shaking me instead of that unexpected composure, I think that the episode of the initiation of our relations would have had a different face, just the opposite, because then circumstances would have been equal for both of us and we would have gone forward simultaneously toward the fires of passion. But her boldness deepened my loneliness and abandonment. I felt alone, helpless, facing her as she, on the contrary, was sustained by an unknown strength, the product of experience perhaps. But was my experience as a man not present with me? What was happening to me? Why was the unavoidable ridiculousness of my physique now being joined by that other ridiculous thing which I had not counted upon and which placed me in such a false and insecure position, grotesquely reversing the role without any real justification? I began taking off my *lucco* as if the whole scene were a nightmare, intensified by the culminating horror of having to exhibit myself naked in front of Giulia. That—and I stress it as I have stressed every weakness of mine in these public confessions—was the most horrible part of the case: the fact that what for the moment gave me the deepest anguish was what concerned my esthetic vanity, the terror of exposing my defect, and not the doubt that had arisen from Giulia's attitude and which implied a possible betrayal. First came my immediate and obvious problem; that of Giulia, unknown, could be postponed. The wound in the heart of my vanity caused by my physical poverty could do more than the wound caused by infidelity, which, if it were true, should have made me incomparably more desperate. But I refused to think about it and I could not. The hump was growing on my back, on my shoulders, over my forehead, blinding me. I had to exhibit myself finally, and while she reclined on the pillows with the indifference of a harlot (or with the serenity of a sensible woman who faced the essence of matrimony not as a dangerous sacrifice but as a peaceful step toward a communion of existence, for there is also room for that interpretation), my teeth were chattering.

How unfortunate, how helpless I felt at that time! How had I dared suppose that things would have turned out differently? Were my adventures with whores and village girls, my activities with Giambattista, where the reactions had been quick and effective, enough to give me any guarantee? What was happening to me, what was happening to me, good Lord? The months of monkish continence, waiting for that instant, preparing myself for it, those months during the course of which I thought I had cleansed my body and soul of impurities had been of no use to me. Just as when I had failed in my initial attempt with Pantasilea, I sought recourse in imaginative substitutions, I evoked Nencia, Abul, Giambattista, and Pantasilea herself, and even the memory of my page Beppo's rhythmical back and the open surrender of the innkeeper's daughter in Arezzo on the day when the lascivious act was revealed to me, in order for them to help me in the crisis and give me the vigor that I lacked. The room became peopled with invisible burning figures but they twisted about like flames in vain. I caressed that thin and desirable body, I kissed it ceaselessly, moaning, weeping, but Giulia Farnese left my arms that night as she had entered them.

"Forgive me," I babbled, and by speaking that way, without wishing to, I was doing the most contraproductive thing I could, for I was authenticating my impotence, "forgive me, Giulia, forgive the hunchback, the one unworthy of you..."

She stroked me too, keeping her hands away from my back, perhaps with disgust, perhaps with a certain indulgence, with a certain indifference, because, the same as I, she came from an old caste, and in lineages that had been eroded by time, exhausted by decadent artifices, what was not habitual, what could result in an immediate break among other people, was a matter thought of as something between accomplices, heirs to the same disorders, for in that atmosphere everything was more complex and unusual. It was the milieu in which Giulia Gonzaga had accompanied her husband Vespasiano Colonna with her virginity until his death; the milieu in which Guidobaldo da Montefeltro and his wife had shared their chaste marriage, without being saints. But perhaps I was thinking that way because I faced the horror of a scandal that might bring to light yet another defect in the Duke of Bomarzo. What did I know of what was going on in Giulia's head in moments during which I was uselessly striving, gritting my teeth, shaking her, torturing her, torturing myself, trying to do with my mouth what I could not attain in another way? What did I know, helpless, lying on that beautiful and cold body? I spoke to her vulgarly about my victories in that field. I supplied names that meant nothing to her in order to show my powers. I acted like a peasant after having acted like a frail weakling. And only then did it occur to me to throw up to her what I called her brazenness. Only then—and not because I was basically disturbed by her daring attitude, but because I used it as a pretext to take the blame away from me—did I hit upon accusing her of previous practices and knowledge in the matters that were bringing us together on the tumultuous bed. Anger from the insult inflamed her. The gentle girl, the provocative woman turned into a wronged goddess. She had equal control over her majestic register as well as her sensual one, and when she felt like showing it, one could see to what point she was Cardinal Alessandro Farnese's niece. I must say that she defended herself very well, that she put such apparent logic into her words, referring to her innocence and her sole desire of making me happy, offering me whatever she had, that she made me beg her forgiveness, curling up, prostrating myself at her feet, for I was suddenly afraid that I had made my situation worse with a terribly grievous mistake and that I had lost everything with another fumble. That capped my humiliation. In order to reconquer her friendship and obtain a deferment of her confidence at least, I turned to servile adulation, as if I were not the duke and great lord I aimed to be and the one who had received her in his castle with such noble pomp amid the great of Italy, but a vulgar villager, a serf, until her tension abated and we took up our frustrated caresses again. Finally, exhausted, bathed in sweat, I fell into a lethargy.

I dreamed that I was going with Giulia down to the woods where the rocks were, the future Sacred Wood. We were going along together, pushing back the branches, among elms, live oaks, tamarinds, and willows, where, in the midst of the thickness, the ghostly crags with all their priapic insolence were revealed. A large company of naked men and women, similar to the infernal beings who inhabit the Etruscan tombs, was there. We joined in their dances, their erotic maneuvers, their violent embraces in the dizzy witches' Sabbath, and we fell down, one joined to the other in the center of those piled-up bodies in strong colors, painted with the ochers of iron oxide, the blacks of charcoal, the blues of lapis lazuli which were spinning about a ceramic demon. I stretched out my hands, moving my arms like a swimmer about to sink, and I ran against a hard female breast, against a leg, against a male organ. It was as if I were swimming in a river thick with multicolored bodies, mingled, interlocked, in which it was impossible to separate members and heads, because among them all they made up one single huge monster which was stretching out like a slow, hot river, moving along in the shadow of the lewd trees and the lascivious rocks. Giulia was mine at last.

So sharp was the spasm that I woke up shouting. She was still asleep, abandoned. I saw the remains of our sterile struggle in the disorder of the bed. I saw with bitterness that if I had not been able to possess the living woman, on the other hand I had possessed her image.

Just as after my misfortune in Florence, when my grandfather Franciotto had thrown me into the arms of the public woman in order to rouse me, the worry that weighed on me over all others, over my own setback, outside when I left the room where Giulia was still sleeping, was to avoid any knowledge of my shameful mishap. I sensed that Giulia would not say anything for now, that she would in any case postpone the disagreeable revelation. And I was not mistaken. Hours later, when she came down into the garden, having just bathed and been dressed by her ladies, my wife did not betray anything of what had taken place. Together we attended the mass said by the bishop of Soana; together we watched, as in answer to my request and without the others' knowing about it, Cardinal de' Medici sprinkled the diabolical head in our bedroom with holy water, and we heard him as, smiling ironically and shaking the hyssop, he pronounced the purifying Latin words.

Many of the guests had already left for Mugnano, Bracciano, Anguillara, Bagnaia, to the neighboring estates, but the castle was still full of people whom it was necessary to take care of and entertain. There was a mock tourney in the afternoon and later on my grandmother's dwarfs put on a pantomime based on some poetry by Aretino. Of all those present my grandmother was the only one who sensed from my behavior that the nocturnal experience had not been favorable to me. She caught it in spite of the fact that I made great efforts so that no sign should allow for any conjectures, exaggerating the proofs of amorous enthusiasm alongside my wife. Furthermore, Giulia contributed to the deception, replying to those raptures with the official testimony of her modest affection. Did I love her? Everything concerning love is so complex, so difficult to understand... Had I loved Adriana dalla Roza? Had I loved Abul? Did I love Giulia? What was certain was that as on other occasions I wanted her to love me, and now, after the failure, even more; I wanted to conquer her, I wanted to take possession of her feelings, now that I had not been able to dominate her body, and that was extremely difficult after the sad adventure I have just described, and keeping in mind the revulsion that must have come from my physique and the dullness that she felt for me spiritually, even in the midst of the play of aristocratic courtesy. The important thing, for the moment, was to gain time and for the guests not to notice the basic weakness of our relations. And that I managed. I managed to deceive them. But I did not deceive my grandmother. Out of her old age and her idolatry, as if from an unconquerable watchtower, my grandmother was looking at me and she saw me very clearly. It was impossible to hide anything. I was sitting between her and Giulia in the semi-darkness of the room where the dwarfs, the redhead and the stammerer, were leaping about and declaiming the merry nonsense of Pietro Aretino, when I felt Diana Orsini pat my knee twice, affectionately, as is done when one wants to calm a person, and then, hidden from the others, she took one of my hands and lifted it to her lips. Yes, she knew; she knew everything, and that gave me anguish and calmed me down at the same time, and made the tears well up in my tired eyes. But the others had not noticed anything. On the contrary. As soon as I went off with the gentlemen there was a surfeit of off-color remarks about my great luck, remarks that Galeazzo Farnese, with his vehemence, was the first to stimulate. And the curious thing that I must note here was that on that day, the same as the week that followed, and during which a good part of the guests of both families remained in Bomarzo, a passionate sensual atmosphere spread through the castle as a consequence of our presumed happiness, and the erotic ardor that emanated from the bedroom with the ceramics went up the stairways and into the rooms. The sensuality passed through the rooms like a growing fire, fed and activated by the paradox of flames that did not exist, but its presence spread everywhere.

The initial symptoms of that outbreak could be noted after the performance by the jesters and it had the coloration of a farce by Boccaccio. We found out through the gossip of the pages that the redheaded dwarf's wife—the same one from the fight over the cats—when she saw him acting on the improvised stage dressed as the god Mercury, felt being reborn in her veins a lewd greed which, given the age of both of them and their long congress, we would have supposed to have been permanently reduced to ashes. In their intimate moments she demanded his courting, which the old man naturally refused, and then the woman's fury was unleashed. Quite a few years before, Messer Pandolfo had been her lover at times when he was teaching her to write, and the woman ran to him to find what her husband could not give her, finding, for the same reasons, a similar rejection. Her disappointment and anger bubbled up in such a form that, half crazy as she already was, she ended up by losing her reason. Silvio da Narni had once shown her the horoscopes that he composed, and the woman could think of nothing better, taking advantage of the scrawl that she owed to the patience of Pandolfo, than to start inventing some tremendous horoscopes, thick with dire predictions, dedicated to various guests, and which she distributed secretly in their rooms, as if she proposed avenging herself on the world. According to those papers, the Duke of Mantua would die eaten by ants and Isabella d'Este would give birth at the age of eighty-two to a three-headed child. Those who were damned laughed a great deal during the following days over the absurd episode, which was commented on all over Italy, but the one who laughed least was I, the duke, not because it annoyed me that those things were happening in my castle and because the insults and impudence of the senile witch might upset any of my guests, but because the constant reference to the voluptuous ineptitude of the dwarf and the tutor was wounding, without the others' noticing, to the terribly susceptible nerves of my alert sensitivity.

The days passed sumptuously, with parties, hunts, balls. I uselessly tried to renew my base intents with Giulia Farnese. I even began to think about a curse, a possession. The head of the devil had been exorcised, and yet...When I thought again of destroying it, Giulia intimidated me, arguing that it might bring me bad luck. My luck had not been very good, one might say, but I left the mosaic alone. It seemed to me that if I showed an excessive fright in contrast to the calm disdain of Giulia for those alarms, I would be running the risk of showing

A WEDDING IN BOMARZO · 393

myself to be even more cowardly. Added now to the other subtle barriers that stood in the way of my fulfilling obvious functions, was a mute rage, which blinded me, overwhelmed me. Giulia had not changed her attitude. It was almost as if she had foreseen that things were going to happen that way and the suspicion that she sheltered that debasing thought aggravated my upset. In the nocturnal solitude of our bedroom my wife continued to be the same beautiful statue, without veils, the same obsequious, smiling coldness. Dark rings made the sunken face of which I was so proud bluish, and the guests attributed them, with obscene insistence, to my repeated amorous triumphs. I was growing desperate. I passed from anger to languidness, while I had to play the role of robust happiness for my guests. And such was my excitation, such the sexual frenzy that aroused my wolf prowl about the unattainable possession, that I went back eagerly, in search of an alleviation saturated with remorse, which redoubled my anguish in the end, to the vice of my adolescence. But I soon understood that that ruse, that *ersatz* thing, that fleeting coming together with phantoms was not enough to relieve me, and when everybody had retired I began to go out, accompanied by Giambattista, in search of a peasant girl who could serve me as quick consolation. The page did not ask any questions. Even today I do not know how deeply he had penetrated the truth of the situation. Nor did he suggest to me that consolation could come from him as before, for only another woman, taking Giulia's place, was capable of getting me my revenge, securing my patents of manhood. And the village women to whom I had recourse must have arrived at the conclusion that in addition to Giulia Farnese my lust demanded other loves, other firm and docile bodies ready to care for its urgency. Then the legend of my fabulous vigor began to take shape, one which has lasted until the present time and which, mixing my figure with that of my father and awarding to one alone the deeds of both, surrounds my name with a strong prestige. Giulia would pretend to be asleep, I am sure, when I left her bed. Perhaps my departure meant a rest for her. And if next to her I was a mere puppet, next to my other companions I showed insistently, daily—all aroused, which was most strange because of my being a marital cipher and because of the burning that was caused in me by the forbidden splendor of my wife's body—that in what concerned amatory gymnastics at least I was an Orsini worthy of the century-old virile tradition of the breed.

In the meantime, at Bomarzo, as I have said, those efforts and the certainty of my victory had given rise to an atmosphere of concupiscence that prolonged in the castle the sensual climate that emanated like a hot vapor from the Etruscan earth and whose mysterious outpourings I had discerned from the first warnings of my childhood. Reborn behind my back was the pursuit of Giambattista by Pier Luigi Farnese and Benvenuto Cellini, making my handsome cousin Sigismondo indignant, and although I have no proof in that respect, I gather that my page ended up succumbing to the persistent goldsmith. Violante Orsini, married to the illustrious Savelli, gave herself, according to what was said later, to the Duke of Urbino and to a halberdier. Ippolito de' Medici did everything in his power to beat down the virginal defenses of his adored beauty. There is no need to speak of Aretino. Cardinal Ercole Gonzaga was surprised in the gallery of the busts, precisely between Caracalla and Claudius, in the act of fondling the breasts of Lucrezia Farnese, Giulia's retarded sister, as if he had another piece of sculpture in his hands, such was the poor girl's lack of modesty, and although the matter came to be known, the father and brothers of the girl preferred to cover it over, probably because it was not convenient to incur the hostility of the Mantua clan over an idiot. Nor do I know up to what point the episode was true: the irresponsible indecency of the son of Isabella d'Este, of which a strong trace has remained in his letters, was probably a confirmation of it. His mother had obtained a red hat for him in moments when Clement VII, besieged in the Castel by the troops of Charles V, put up five cardinalships for sale to the highest bidder. Cardinal Ercole had at least two natural children, but when it fell to him to preside over the Council of Trent, in his fifties then, those close to him described the insistence with which the repentant sinner punished his flesh. There was still a good deal of time before the Council for a sincere and supreme approach to God by the penitent Don Juan...

It seemed to me that Maerbale was watching Giulia too much. I spied on him without results. In any case, quite soon he would travel to Venice with Valerio Orsini, Leonardo Emo, and the majestic granddaughter of Oliverotto da Fermo, a lady of as many edges as a crystal, whose light mustache was inseparable from a well-known biting tongue. My handsome brother-in-law Fabio became good friends with Sigismondo. As soon as the latter corroborated the coolness of Pier Luigi, to whom he had to return the diamond necklace which had made exotic reflections on his bronzed skin, my cousin sweetened his abandonment with the help of the youngest of the Farneses and some well-built soldiers of the fortress. The wife of the red-headed jester, the madwoman, continued stirring things up until there was no recourse but to lock her up. At dawn her savage cries shook me like those of a bird of ill omen in the bed I shared with Giulia. Then the duchess would get up, brush her finger across the papal enamels, touch my forehead, and sink into the depths of her dreams. I practically never slept. I ended up sending the possessed woman to my Roman palace.

Even Silvio da Narni, so spiritualized, so obsessed with his astrological experiments, succumbed to the fire that was sweeping the house and one morning he came down from his tower to ask my permission for him to marry Porzia. I gave it to him despite the protests of Giambattista who, forgetting or ignoring the profession that his sister had followed in Bologna for the glory of many nervous men, and moved by the vanity of his doubtful position, which gave him his links to the Duke of Bomarzo and Pier Luigi Farnese, said that the union with the sorcerer was a *mésalliance*. Giambattista aspired, with certain reason, if the physical attributes of his twin were taken into consideration, to a better marriage or to a lover from the main nobility. While Silvio, a scrutinizer of the sky, was showing urges that were more and more contradictorily bourgeois and the desire for a stable home, Giambattista began to show the claws of an unexpected ambition.

And my grandmother's cats, so decorous, so snobbish, so Orsinian, joined the concert, as if infected by the general wildness. At night one could hear them mewing on the roofs, mating stridently with the vagabond army of the village, and the white female received her masculine harem in Giulia's allegorical carriage.

Yes, those were very disturbed days for Bomarzo during the sticky summer heat that beat down through clouds of flies. Everyday life went on as if nothing extraordinary were happening, for we would gather together for garrulous picnics, enjoying the picturesque sights, or in the afternoon we would invent difficult games of wit in which the roguishness of Isabella d'Este and the impudence of Ariosto triumphed, or we danced, bowing with jerkins and long coats, as if we were some kind of hopping birds wavering and chirping on the edge of the gilded tapestries, but as soon as the shadows fell and the moon awoke ancient monsters, the contained frenzy would come over the castle again. Those disturbed princes and artists—Gonzaga, della Rovere, Farnese, Cellini—were capable of disposing of, with a flash of steel, the lives of their fellows. The bishop of Soana who knew it full well, prayed ceaselessly for their effervescence to calm down.

Not only we, the nobility, were aware of the erotic current that was dragging us along in its delirious whirlpool, but the people too, who watched us from afar, as they were watching a strange spectacle which they certainly must have envied. In the village everyone arranged things as best he could in order to participate in the contagious intoxication that was spread by the soldiery and the servants, and at the end of the period fixed by ordered evolution, it was my duty to stand as godfather in Bomarzo to numerous baptisms that complicated the modest economy of vassaldom and obliged me to multiply my donations. The fable of the orgies and scandals at Bomarzo began to spread and it reached Rome, blown on, inflamed, swollen until the last guests left. When Aretino took leave of me it was difficult for me to defend the Byzantine goblets that Valeriano had given me against his greed. Then a fictitious peace reigned again. There was peace for everyone except me. My nonagenarian grandmother, startled by the commentaries of her ladies whispered during the fluttering of the fans—and one must attribute her puritanical repudiation to her great old age, for she had lived among the Borgias—would come down to the garden again, abandoning her bedroom, her cell, as if after the storm she wished to pick up the lost reins again in her gnarled hands. She would pass me in her chair carried by two lackeys along the paths next to the roses and she would stare at me. Giulia was looking at the countryside up to where the party of her relatives had disappeared in a cloud of dust. And I half closed my eyes, robbed of my secret by the very wise Diana Orsini, and I pretended to be absorbed in grave thoughts, as befits a duke.

A doctor, a modern psychoanalyst, people with experience, with a knowledge of books and theories, could probably explain easily (or with difficulty) what was happening to me, what exact, delicate, minute, and tremendous little wheels had begun to turn and had put in motion the mechanism of my inhibitions toward Giulia. On the other hand, some not very subtle reader will probably be skeptical over the fact that at the same time that I repeatedly gave testimony of my virile efficiency with various vassal women of Bomarzo, I was an absolute failure in my amatory efforts with my legitimate spouse. I shall not delve too deeply into the analysis of the problem and I shall limit myself to repeating that things happened that way. I shall only stress for the skeptical reader the fact that my triumphs were won over people of a subordinate position, linked to me and my people by centuries of obedience, and who were like a human projection of that loyal Bomarzo earth, which had served us since the shadows of the Middle Ages, that land incapable of betraying me. Giulia Farnese, a great lady, the daughter of a famous house, placed opposite me under conditions of equality, brought a new element into the voluptuous exchange. For the first time I was facing, on a level where I had always felt the basic inferiority of my situation—as at every opportunity in which my body was placed in evidence—a responsibility of that type with someone who was not only my contractual associate in such tasks, but also my peer, my hierarchical equivalent, in spite of the pride of the Orsinis, and, consequently, a possible intimate and ironic judge. And the inhibition that resulted from that situation was stronger than my will, stronger than my urgency to affirm myself then more than ever.

All of this is sad, small, disagreeable, even repugnant. If Giulia acted as if she did not grant it any importance, as if she were on some soft and secret height where the panting sound of those useless attempts never reached, I, on the other hand, was unhinged, for I was the one to blame for such a miserable situation. As on other occasions, I tried to rid myself of the blame by unloading it on an innocent party, by convincing myself that if things had turned out that way it was due to the coldness and indifference of my companion, which, if it was true in part, was so in such a very minute part. I set out to vex her, then, as if I were getting my revenge for an offense that did not really exist, and since my deceptions with humble Bomarzo peasant girls, which Giulia must have known about, did not bother her, I turned to the more ostentatious and offensive recourse made possible for me by Giambattista and Sigismondo. I was always with them at the time of day when members of the family and servants could witness the strangeness of our constant contact in the castle and in the garden. The heat was still oppressive and I took advantage of it by having both boys go about half-naked, shirtless, emphasizing their bodies by the lewd tightness of their pants, and with them dressed in that fashion—or undressed— I would let myself be seen between their gleaming torsos leaning on the balustrades or laughing in the shade of the terracotta flowerpots which were decorated with roses or laurels. But not even that exhibitionism succeeded in moving her. If I passed her next to one of the low flower beds or on the terraces where old tapestries served as awnings in such scandalous company, Giulia Farnese would limit herself to smiling at me from the distance of her aristocratic indifference, which made my humiliated wrath burn all the more. My grandmother would watch me in the meantime, leaning on her window sill between her motionless cats, and I, convinced, desperate, would carry on the insolent pantomime to extremes, as if I were placing Diana Orsini among the group of imaginary enemies who encouraged my urge for revenge.

Time passed like that, basely, and during a period when I was urgently seeking a pretext that would allow me to leave Bomarzo and the torture that came from sharing my wife's silent bed—and to leave without arousing any dangerous suspicions—I received the news, brought by a monk, that my grandfather Franciotto was dying in his Roman palace. I left for there at once, exaggerating my show of alarm. I was accompanied by Giambattista Martelli and my three Orsini cousins— Orso, Matteo, and Sigismondo—who were doubtlessly hoping that the cardinal would remember them in his will. If that was so, the three of them were disappointed.

A mixture of alleviation and anxiety possessed me as I left the castle. My marital tribulations could wait until later. Perhaps everything would fall into balance on my return. The only thing that worried me then was the old man's end. Although my grandfather had shown me a thorough and permanent lack of love, I was seized by a new feeling toward him as I galloped along the road to Rome, something that resembled an anxiety for the cardinal to show that he loved me, because that was what my anguish needed, to know that I was loved, that I was being supported by the warmth of affection, and when I entered the twisting streets of my native city, I noticed with surprise, when my retinue was going past the Forum, which had witnessed my innocent searches of an infantile archeologist—the Forum where a few feeble buffaloes were grazing and where a herd of swine was rooting among the ruins—that my eyes were filling with tears; and I had been so hardened by selfishness, mistrust, anger, and adversity that the strange weeping did me an enormous amount of good, for it showed me that in some hidden corner of my soul the warm emotional spring still flowed.

My grandfather was going out like a luxurious church candle in his large red bed in the palace of San Giacomo degli Incurabili, where a hundred servants proclaimed with ceremonious slowness the splendor of his position and the disorder of his finances. A world of prelates, relatives, and nobles in the service of the Vatican surrounded me as soon as I went up the staircase and through the salons where the works of art that would fall to me in the inheritance were all together. They embraced me, kissed me, patted me on the back. They asked about my grandmother's health, about Giulia's happiness. A few of them perhaps felt a genuine grief at the death of the prince who, when he had organized the hunts of his cousin Leo X, had contributed to their diversion and who, in the period prior to his elevation to the purple, being a condottiere of the Church and of the Most Serene Republic, had had his share of danger in sieges and battles alongside the terrible Malatesta Baglioni, who later sold out Florence, but the majority were probably calculating the advantages which would follow the elimination of one who, because of his character of a tenacious candidate for the tiara, was standing in the way of many ambitions.

The end took time in coming. For a week I remained beside my grandfather. An urgent lucidity illuminated him during that period.

In order to distract him, I gave him details about the guests who had been at my wedding in Bomarzo. I explained to him that the problem of Giulia's dowry had been arranged profitably thanks to Galeazzo's munificence, and that drew a sigh from him, for he had never fulfilled that of my mother. I described to him the jealousy that Sebastiano del Piombo was still building up against Raphael so many years after his death. I told him what Duke Federico of Mantua had told me about his uncle, Ludovico Gonzaga, the collector of rare objects, the one who was always on the lookout for ancient comedies to be presented before his court in Gazzuolo, and I told him that I too, one day, wanted to convert Bomarzo into a small center of Italian genius. But he, with a distant, transformed voice, barely moving his transparent hands, mentioned the echoes of the orgies in the castle that had even reached Rome. It surprised me that he spoke that way, for he had been famous for his frivolity and his worldly indulgence, and because the presumed orgies had actually not been such, and if only to calm him down I declared to him that nothing extraordinary had happened on my estates—which, from the point of view of the general criterion of the times was true—I thought, on noting his melancholy, that the nearness of his passage and of the final rendering of accounts was making him punctilious at the very end. Avoiding the shoals that the theme might raise, I changed the subject and went back to the matter of the letters from the alchemist Dastyn to Cardinal Napoleone Orsini, under the illusion that the perspicacity that came from the consumption that had devoured his body and had left alive, tremulous and burning, only the flame of consciousness, might help him to remember what had escaped his vague memory before, but my grandfather repeated that he knew nothing about those documents.

"Immortality, Vicino, my poor Vicino," he whispered with a thread of a voice, "is succession in time. We are links in an immense chain. When you have a child, you will be immortal."

"Giulia is expecting a child," I answered him impetuously, and the pride that the lie caused in me made me see something that I had not noticed before: how much I desired to assure Bomarzo of an heir, for otherwise the promise that I would be its owner for infinity would be weakened by being monstrous, with all of its splendid temptation, in the midst of one insecurity that covered the penury of all of my insecurities. I said it without thinking about the consequences of my words, convincing myself that I had said them out of mercy, as soon as they were out, in order to seek a utopian peace for the dying old man who would never be able to discover the deceit; but I also said it to give myself some artificial relief from the suffocation with which uncertainty was smothering me.

Franciotto Orsini drew me to him, and I caught the smell of death from close by. He kissed me and I began to weep. He had never kissed me, not even when I was a child, when his three grandsons would run to receive him in the courtyard at Bomarzo, pulling on his purple folds.

"I give you my blessing, Duke," he said, "and I bless the one who will succeed you and the one who will succeed him. Orsinis never die. They will never die until the Lord so decides. I will die, you shall die in your turn, but the Orsinis shall not die. And that is what is important. Immortality is ... is ... the will of God."

I raised my eyes toward the tapestry whose multicolored threads sketched out our arms. Perhaps the cardinal was right and the secret was not hidden in the magic formula of a wise man but in the hermetic design of the rose, the serpent, and the bears. But I rejected the idea at once. The obsession that since adolescence had kept me as tense as a bow aimed at the eternal future and which fed me with its miracle rebelled against that logical family solution, common to the majority of men.

My cousins would come into the room while we were speaking and remain at a respectful distance. One could guess their presence more than see them in the shadows where the great reliquaries gleamed. They looked uselessly for a gesture from the cardinal, something that would indicate that he had remembered them. They were looking at us, handsome, bronzed, like birds of prey.

When Maerbale arrived from Venice, Franciotto Orsini was already deliriously drifting away toward the final night. In the shreds of his babbling he was still fanning the flames of his rancor against the Colonnas, which he had dominated on the surface during the clear-sighted hours when he had been reconciled to his Maker, but which his subconscious was freeing now and letting out like a hidden and tenacious poison. He, who had been married to a Colonna—that Colonna grandmother whom I think I mentioned at the beginning of these memoirs, but whom I have purposely cast aside as I have written them, as if in that way I could suppress her in the struggle in my blood—swore that all of his misfortunes had their origins in the fury of that enemy breed. Suddenly his wandering changed direction and, summoned by his exhausted voice, a dynamic vision filled the bedchamber. It was only necessary for him to murmur the names of the elastic dogs of the first Medici pope, the ones I knew so well—Lacone, Nebrofare, Icnobate, Argo—for the clatter of distant hunts to resound over the murmur of the rosaries that the monks were reciting ceaselessly, and for the chamber to tremble as if a feverish wind were shaking the scarlet curtains. My grandfather's eyes were enormous, burning from the depths of the pillows which were dampened by his sweat, and the pious scene, which had in its center an old man who had received Extreme Unction and who would soon face the supreme judge, took on strange pagan tones, a macabre gaiety, from the vital fire that was gleaming on the bed and was creating the fiction of a light that was illuminating among the hangings the dark silhouettes of the hunchbacked duke, Maerbale the condottiere, the other indistinct grandsons, Francesco, Arrigo, Leone, and the despairing relatives who were not resigned to their financial misfortune, Orso, Matteo, Sigismondo. I, in the meantime, was thinking about my destiny. I was thinking about Giulia, whom I yearned to see again and yet feared to, and who over the comfortable distance was becoming dim, until her image became blended with other vague images, that of Adriana, that of Abul...I imagined her watering the roses in the garden at Bomarzo, chatting with the peasants; I dreamed of her embracing me in our nuptial bedroom, giving herself finally, as if she were melting, receiving me in her exclusive intimacy. And my eyes sneaked a look at the static figure of Maerbale, as if I were fearful that my brother might guess what was going on inside of me.

One afternoon Pope Clement VII announced his visit. We waited for him on our knees at the palace gate. With him came Cardinal Alessandro Farnese, who, as we were going up to my grandfather's room, said something in jest about the heir that his niece would soon award the Orsinis. His Holiness, on hearing it, stopped, smiled, and stroked my forehead with his glove. I bit my lips and kissed that intensely perfumed glove. Then I went on with a candelabrum in my right hand behind the heavy cloaks whose trains went waving up the stairs, step by step, slowly, like boa constrictors.

Franciotto Orsini did not recognize his illustrious guest. He did not see the broad, sad eyes of the pope fixed on him. He died that night, and on giving up his soul, he sat up for a second, his visionary eyes widened, and he moved his arms in a quick wave.

"The falcon!" he shouted, "the falcon...!"

The cardinal's death supplied me with a more than sufficient pretext for not returning to Bomarzo for some time. The complications that came from an inheritance that was plagued with debts, which perhaps would contribute to lightening the pontiff's coffers, if it was possible to obtain through the intervention of Cardinal Farnese his absolutely necessary aid—a thing not easy to get when one thought of the parsimony of the Holy Father—required my presence in the neighborhood of the Vatican. In the distribution of goods I received the palace of San Giacomo degli Incurabili with everything of value within it, while the castle of Celleno, in the diocese of Montefiascone, and the ancestral estates of Monterotondo passed to the other branch. Actually, of all the heirs, I received the least, but I did not wish to start a suit, and since mortgages were devouring the building like borers hidden in its structure, I dedicated myself to saving the furniture, paintings, and objects that it contained from the creditors. That kept me very busy at the beginning. Maerbale had returned to Venice, where Valerio Orsini had called for him, and with the collaboration of Giambattista and Silvio da Narni, whom I had ordered to Rome, and my cousins, whose protests I silenced with various gifts, I directed the complex packing. The allegorical canvases, the holy paintings, the delicate metal pitchers, the tapestries, the marbles, the agate vases left for Bomarzo in successive caravans. I was in the castle on two occasions to await the arrival of the wagons and I saw Giulia fleetingly. I did not even share her bedroom, the one with the ceramic devil. As soon as I could, I returned to Rome.

Bomarzo no longer represented for me the marvelous refuge that had attracted me since my infancy and which conferred on me, within its limitations, the illusion of tranquility. Although I continued worrying about its adornment, and in that sense the contribution of my grandfather was splendid, I felt the necessity of fleeing from there because Bomarzo and Giulia were beginning to be inseparable.

The duchess, in the meantime, had gained the love and devotion of my people, who murmured with reason (Silvio told me) about the incomprehensible abandonment in which I had left my young wife. Giulia possessed an innate gift for capturing wills, for imposing herself with her mere presence, as if, as she matured—and she was doing so rapidly—there were sprouting in her the typical traits of the Farneses, who knew how to command without giving orders. Perhaps because in us, the Orsinis, the habit of command was much older, as old actually as the fabulous origins of our lineage, and it had a military and disciplinary base, we Orsinis commanded resolutely, briskly, sure of being obeyed as leaders, while the Farneses, who had reached full power much later, thanks to various political combinations, and who still had not reached the omnipotence that would be given them by the pontificate of Paul III, continued preserving in their links with the people a compromise, the product of their recent promotion to the dominant sphere, which, unconsciously, weighed on their activities and made them seem bland, compassionate, and even liberal. This, which applied to the Farnese tribe in general, did not prevent some of them—like the fierce Pier Luigi—from going to extremes of tyrannical rigor, but even when they acted in that way they did it in imitation of us, and everyone is aware that a caricature exaggerates the expressions of the model. Giulia worked with a subtle balance, like the daughter of her goodhearted father and her aristocratic mother, and it was logical that she should be adored so soon. I wonder what would have happened if someone had dared go against her wishes. She would have exploded, of course, and her anger would have been worse than that of my grandmother, for by the same circumstance of being *newer* and, as a consequence, more vacillating, the Farneses could not tolerate being disobeyed, for that, in spite of recent privileges, took things back to the not so distant past when it was not indispensable to obey them. But that did not happen. No one disobeyed her at Bomarzo. Quite the contrary. Behind her, her grace, her air of asking and never ordering, we Orsinis stood like an inflexible walled backdrop of gigantic suits of armor. She could give herself the luxury of being a Farnese and an Orsini simultaneously, of being imposing and fragile at the same time, and that gave her an ambiguous and original charm for my vassals. I might have hated her for no other reason than her rapid conquest of my people, of what was most mine, and yet I did not hate her. I felt before her the discomfort of guilt, and for once the old mechanism of weaklings which allowed me to unload the weight of my sins on others did not function. So that after explaining to them—her, my grandmother, and my administrator—the serious reasons that obliged me to stay in Rome—and which I hoped they would spread among my vassals, for in spite of the distance between them and me I was stung by the fear of losing the affection that I imagined I aroused in the villages on my estates, in spite of the despotism of the *homagio mulierum*—I escaped to the palace of San Giacomo degli Incurabili and cloistered myself in its empty rooms.

I let two weeks pass. My cousins and my pages came to my redoubt from time to time with news that populated my agitated solitude with phantoms.

In Florence the despicable Duke Alessandro was giving free rein to his libidinous frenzy. The sobriety of the first days had been supplanted by an ardor that fed his whims without distinction of classes. Ladies of noble families and nuns were familiar with his imperious courting, his blind violence. The city that had accumulated such high proofs of its honor during the siege was descending now to the level of its leader, the bastard. Night after night the parties went on, which the duke attended in a mask—sometimes dressed as a woman, as a nun—with those aristocratic boys I had known as children, the Strozzis, Francesco de' Pazzi, Giuliano Salviati, Pandolfo Pucci, and rape and sword fights went unpunished. Shortly after, they were joined by Lorenzino de' Medici, my dear Lorenzaccio, the one who had been so kind to me at the time of the death of Adriana dalla Roza and who turned out to be the worst of the lot. But before leaving Rome, Pope Clement's little favorite outraged public opinion by decapitating with insolent madness several statues on the arch of Constantine. Filippo Strozzi, the widower of my admired Clarice de' Medici, who belonged to a generation older than that of the carousers—among whom were several of his sons—instead of offering them the example of dignity which his high position in the Republic obliged him to do, rivaled them in extravagance.

As a reward for his excesses, Duke Alessandro received as a wife Margaret of Austria, the illegitimate daughter of Charles V, by which the prestige of the pontiff's house was increased. The glory of the Medici alliances grew even greater when Francis I arranged for the marriage of Catherine de' Medici to his second son, the Duke of Orleans. I was to have been part of the retinue which escorted the pope on ships of Andrea Doria to Marseilles, where the wedding was celebrated, but at the last minute I invented a pretext and I did not leave Rome, because I detested the idea that Giulia would accompany me, as protocol demanded, and that her astute relatives would suspect something of what was happening between us. On his return, Cardinal Ippolito, whom Francis I had given a lion cub which had belonged to the corsair Barbarossa—Redbeard—told me of the luxury of the ceremonies and the generosity of the Holy Father—who, when it was a question of the interests of his family, loosened the strings of his purse with calculated effects—and he told me also that on the trip they made in order to sail from Leghorn, they took a long detour, avoiding Florence, just as at the time of the coronation of Charles V in Bologna, for, ever since the time of the siege in which the city had suffered so much because of his cruel obstinacy, Clement VII had avoided the wrath and perhaps the vengeance of his fellow countrymen in Florence. While he was speaking to me that way, without adding commentaries, the cardinal was looking at me fixedly. I was well aware of his feelings, of the anger with which he had seen himself relegated in favor of Alessandro when Florence fell into the power of the Medicis again. What I could not discuss with him—because in spite of the anger that separated him from the pope and the duke, he was still an important member of that clan and as such his sensitivity was aroused when an intent was made to question the dizzying progress of the Medicis—was the irritation of all Europe over the disproportion of a marriage which linked the kings of France to the descendants of the bankers of the Arno. The marriage of Alessandro to Margaret of Austria was tolerated because, after all, both parties were illegitimate—the one possibly the son of the pontiff; the other certainly the daughter of the Caesar—and its action would be played out in a small Italian state, but the link that could bring a Medici woman (as did happen) to the throne of the most Christian kings was something that shook the proper calculations of probabilities by snobs; that infuriated rachitic and avaricious sovereigns yearning for a crown for princesses whose lineage obliged them to die of boredom in icy convents; and that upset the observers of the advance of a new house that was burning with ambition.

A recluse in the palace of San Giacomo, I gave myself feverishly over to reading. The Latin classics—and especially that Lucretius whom I loved so much and sweet Catullus—added the images of past splendor to those that rose up from the stories my visitors told. Messer Pandolfo, goose quill in hand, his little red eyes teary, helped with his limited lights to illuminate my path. How I would have liked to have had next to me Piero Valeriano or Messer Palingenio, his friend, the one who had conversed with demons on the Via Flaminia! But no matter how much effort I made to distract myself from them, the basic anxieties that gnawed at me—that of my deformed body; that of my abnormal relations with Giulia; that of my incapacity to demonstrate that I was worthy of an overwhelming genealogical inheritance; that of my consequent drive to affirm my personality with some triumphant deed that would raise me up before my peers; that of the mystery that glowed in my future with flashes of miracles—drew me away from the texts and sank me into anguished pondering. I would fling the *lucco* over my shoulder like a Golden Age toga and wander through the galleries talking to myself. That was how my pages and my cousins surprised me on several occasions.

In truth, during that lapse my reason vacillated and I do not know why I did not lose it completely. Possibly I was saved by the memory of Paracelsus and the necromantic manuscripts. I left my voluntary jail and set out to visit the palaces and estates of my relatives in search of Dastyn's furtive letters, untiringly asking about the lost documents. First I visited the houses in Rome, and then I wandered about the countryside, from Naples to Tuscany, and the Orsini lords who received me with startled courtesy and invited me to join in enormous banquets or interrogated me in turn about the quality, not always good, of the works of art that they had bought, thought they could discern in my maniacal unrest one more symptom of the singularity of my character, clouded over by the study of the Orsini lineage—a matter in which they all considered my grandmother to have the supreme knowledge— and by my urge for antiquities that had made me enthusiastic about them since childhood. The fame of that odd streak traveled from estate to estate and from duke to duke, carried by messengers who went from one court to another, the bearers of the voluminous and conspiratorial correspondence which was the only relief from an isolation which in many places continued being almost feudal. But of the letters from the alchemist, even though I examined infinite parchments faded with dampness, I found nothing but confused references from the lips of old people, some of which did not even coincide with the clear information of Paracelsus.

I soon had to abandon my vagabond chore of investigation. The pirate Khair ed-Din, Barbarossa II, the one whom the Turk had named commander-in-chief of his naval forces, had made a surprise landing at Sperlonga and from there he went along the Appian Way as far as Fondi, the castle of the Colonnas where, living in an involvement with theological studies, was the most beautiful Giulia Gonzaga, who had attended my wedding in Bomarzo, the widow of that deformed Vespasiano Colonna who had inspired in the beautiful woman the device of the amaranth and the inscription "*Non moritura.*" That strange happening had very important consequences for me.

This tale of piracy and love would have aroused the imagination of Ariosto and would have inspired numerous memorable stanzas from him, if it were not for the fundamental circumstance that when it happened Ariosto had been sleeping his eternal sleep for a year. But even though he was unable to narrate it and sing it, the whole episode had an Ariostan air to it with its mixture of reality and poetic fantasy. Perhaps as compensation for the insistence with which reality was taking the color out of fantasy at that time (for the world was becoming more and more *modern*), and perhaps because the materialism of the motives of many merchants disguised as princes and warriors was destroying the lyrical myths that we had inherited from our medieval ancestors, leaving us only their empty shells, an event like that suddenly arose, beautiful and unique, exalting our time and projecting it back toward the golden centuries of authentic knighthood, the nostalgia of which had illuminated Ariosto. And just as the *Orlando* is a nostalgic farewell to an age in which reality and fantasy were inseparable, forming a single essence, small and marvelous happenings, such as the one which motivates these reflections, as they suddenly developed and lighted up the everyday atmosphere of the prosaic market-place world with shimmering, magical clarity, also symbolize with their last sporadic outbursts the disconcerted farewell of a period in which the real and the fantastic were beginning to be filed away separately forever to a period in which generous illusion had caused poetic banners to wave.

Barbarossa was a Greek, the son of a potter from Mytilene. With his brother Horush he gathered together a fleet of twelve galleys, and from early youth dedicated himself to piracy. The King of Algiers, who admired the boldness of both and the technical refinement with which they carried out the most atrocious tortures, took them into his service. Horush was the first of those Redbeards. He left his brother Khair ed-Din in charge of the pirate ships and he dropped anchor in Algiers, with the long beard from which his nickname came waving in the breeze. He immediately betrayed his ally the monarch, whom he murdered. Then he was defeated and slain in his turn by the Spanish governor of Oran. Khair ed-Din remembered then that his beard was no less red and imposing than that of his brother, and with the title of King of Tunis he assumed the epithet that had made admirals tremble. Suleiman understood the advantages that he could obtain from his skills and, wilier than the Algerian ruler who had paid with his life for his innocence, he kept him at a distance and named him commander of his squadrons. The reasons for Khair ed-Din's landing at Sperlonga are still under discussion by historians. It has even been said that what he planned to do was kidnap the most beautiful woman in Italy so that the sultan could add that pearl of incomparable brilliance to his harem. It has also been said—Girolamo Borgia expressed it in poor Latin verses—that when Charles V reconquered Tunis the following year, he did it as an act of noble reprisal for Barbarossa's outrage against Giulia Gonzaga. That, of course, is an exaggeration of knighthood. What is indisputable is that, outwitting his enemies, the pirate king appeared on the peninsula with two thousand followers on the road to Rome. They sacked villages; they kidnaped young wives and girls. In that way they reached the fortress of Fondi—on the Appian Way, halfway between Naples and Rome—along difficult, overgrown short cuts. The horror of the news shook the courts of Italy. The lords and ladies of the Houses of Gonzaga and Colonna, whose glory was reflected in Giulia's virtue as in a shining mirror, learned that while the invaders were beating down the doors of the castle, the lady of the place had succeeded in fleeing half-naked on horseback into the mountains. Barbarossa pursued her, the fire of his hot irons and his cutlasses gleaming in the night, but Giulia eluded the hunt. The Muslim thought that the lady had taken refuge in a Benedictine convent near the towers of Fondi and he went there, galloping through the cloisters, raping and massacring nuns.

In the meantime, in the holy city, the fearful cardinals about the pope were repeating the horrendous news, one of them, Pirro Gonzaga, was Giulia's brother. Ippolito de' Medici did not hold back. At last he had a chance to prove to Giulia that his love was something more than a courtly play of melodic words. The one who had signed his translation of the *Aeneid* which he dedicated to his true love with the pseudonym the "Knight Errant," would hasten to her rescue like a knight of the great centuries. He was twenty-three years old and the blood was burning in his veins. He was roaring like the lion cub that had belonged to that very same Redbeard and which the King of France had given him. Once before already, when he suspected that his cousin Alessandro would be chosen Duke of Florence, he had suddenly dismounted in the city, leaving the notables stupefied, and he tried to impose his candidacy with no more strength than his youthful boldness against the pontiff's will. And later on, in Hungary, at moments when the mercenary troops mutinied over lack of pay and because they were obliged to eat black bread and they resolved to return to Italy, the cardinal, offended because he had not been given the rank of general as he thought he deserved, took off his robes, put on a cuirass, and placed himself at the head of all of them as if he were the leader. That made the emperor suspicious that once back in the peninsula, if the pope supplied him with the necessary money, Ippolito would be quite capable of leading the mutinous troops and causing some disorder, so he ordered him arrested, in spite of his ecclesiastical position, and he was in jail for five days until Charles V relented, and free once again, the cardinal withdrew to Venice, where he stayed with the harlot Zafetta and where I saw him on the Grand Canal on the night of the fire at the Cornaro palace. Now once again he was being offered an opportunity to show his mettle. He had been forged for war and love, not for religious meditation. When he was my guest at Bomarzo he never left Giulia's side. They would stroll through the garden among the laurels, speaking of the heart and the soul. They passed their time in flirting, in rhetorical games, distilling the obscure alchemy of conceits, he shaken with passion, she frozen with literature, but at last a barbarian's madness as he advanced violently over battered doors and shattered windows woke the young prince from his musical dream. His idol had been molested by the terrible Barbarossa. The virgin widow of Vespasiano Colonna had fled from the claws of the hungry tiger like a gazelle. How could he not leave at once, wearing out his horses, as his blood boiled, as he heard, in the silence of his Roman palace, the cries of the beauty fleeing through the gloomy forest like a nymph of Sebastiano del Piombo fleeing satyrs who hid their horns under turbans and sharp crescents? How could he not fly, like one of Ariosto's paladins, like one of Ariosto's knights errant, with his friends, his followers, and his squires, with that fabulous band of African slaves who followed him everywhere, to save the Lady of the Amaranth? He left in a tempest of swords and armor, of black heads and leopard skins; and in his multicolored retinue, with capes flapping and fighting at the winds like sails, went Maerbale, who had been passing through Rome on his way south, where Valerio Orsini was sending him and he had been surprised there by the news of the attack on Fondi.

Alas, I should have gone too! I too should have been part of that liberating host! But how could I have gone with them when my hump weighed down on me as if it were made of iron and when before making a decision I would spend such a long time caressing the pros and cons, turning the possibilities over on my fingers like a multifaceted stone? I stayed behind, gnawing my bit, with Lucretius, with Catullus, with Messer Pandolfo, and with the anguished old people who commented on the danger that was tightening its grip around our poor land.

The consequences of the expedition for me and for Giulia Farnese—I am not making a mistake: Giulia Farnese I said, not Giulia Gonzaga—were infinitely more serious than anything I had imagined when the column rode off toward the lands of the Colonnas. Always the Colonnas, the hated Colonnas! Historians would later claim that Ippolito's expedition never took place and even that the whole episode of Barbarossa's atrocities in Fondi was invented by overwrought writers of eclogues, by Filonico Alicarnasso, by Mizio Giustinopolitano, by Marino, but I know only too well that the Ariostan tale was as real as that castle in Fondi, which I had come to know during the time I was traveling in search of the letters from Dastyn to Napoleone Orsini, and where all princes and men of arms or letters going from Rome to Naples stopped to see the one considered the most beautiful woman in Italy, among her cedars, her myrtle, and her orange trees. Everything happened exactly that way. Cardinal Ippolito found Giulia Gonzaga in a grove on her way to the Ausonian hills, where she was hiding like Genevieve of Brabant in oleographs. The Turks had disappeared, carrying off on the rumps of their horses the prostrate maidens and the treasure chests. Ippolito de' Medici freed Giulia and gave her castle back to her, but not even with that was he able to arouse love in the inaccessible lady. Giulia Gonzaga was a piece of sculpture, a portrait by Sebastiano del Piombo, a medal by Alfonso Lombardi. Nothing, neither boldness nor sacrifice could melt her ice. And the cardinal consoled himself singing about the locks of Tulia of Aragon the courtesan, just as Filippo Strozzi had sung to her. But my brother had better luck than he—or more misfortune. In Fondi, when the danger was past, the lady entertained her champions with improvised feasts and gatherings, and Maerbale fell in love with Cecilia Colonna. And that love, like everything that came from Maerbale, had an influence on my destiny. But nothing else had such a great influence.

I learned of my brother's passion through a letter from my grandmother. Maerbale had told her of his plan to marry Cecilia and, according to formula, even though no matter what our decision had been he would have gone right on with what he wanted to do, he asked for our authorization of the wedding. He should have written me directly, but he preferred that roundabout way. He was avoiding me; he always avoided me.

Diana Orsini told me that Cecilia was the orphan of Sciarra Colonna, an illegitimate son of the great Fabrizio and as such the half-brother of the distinguished poetess Vittoria Colonna, the Marchioness of Pescara. For anyone who was not one of us the alliance would have had a bright temptation. My grandmother, who sensed my objections, got ahead of me by mentioning to me the Pax Romana that had been signed between Colonnas and Orsinis at the time when I was born; and she hinted at the advantages that would derive from that union for the final attainment of an authentic accord between the two dynastic factions, a union that would be added to other similar ones and which was nothing strange at all now that because of our outstanding position we Orsinis had trouble in finding wives outside of the shadow of the enormous tree that sheltered the enemy line. But I exploded, blind and deaf. The truth was that, much more than by the genealogical reasons, which I kept in mind along with everything else, I was tormented by the idea that Maerbale was marrying so soon and would thereby escape my domination for good. I also grew desperate—and that was the principal cause of my anguish—over the worry that while my marriage remained without succession, Maerbale would soon have a son, a presumptive heir to Bomarzo. There was abundant proof of his capacity to engender one. While still an adolescent he had fathered Fulvio Orsini, whom he refused to recognize and who was being educated, alone and obscure, devouring books with a precocious drive in our palace in Rome.

Needless to say, my answer to Diana Orsini did not let my hidden annoyance show. I declared that if Maerbale wanted to marry the daughter of Sciarra Colonna, he could do so, but that they should not look for my presence at the wedding. And I immediately unfolded the long chapter of the complaints that we were accumulating against that particular branch of the house and which my grandmother knew better than I. Cecilia's father had fought against us alongside Cardinal Pompeo during the sack of Saint Peter's and the Vatican, which had obliged the pope to excommunicate all who bore the hated name of the old Ghibelline leaders. Then he had aided the Bourbon Constable during the assault on Rome. When Giulia's husband, Vespasiano Colonna, died, Clement VII thought that the chance had arrived when a part of their holdings would leave the hands of the family that he detested as much as we. Then Maerbale's future father-in-law unfurled his banners and went to defend what was theirs and he tried to take the castle of Paliano, a famous Colonna bastion. The pope replied by sending one of our people, the cruel Napoleone Orsini, the abbot of Farfa, as pitiless as an executioner—the one who lived closed up in a tower with his concubine and his illegitimate children—who defeated him and put him to flight and killed Rodomonte Gonzaga (what a name for Ariosto!), Giulia's brother and her stepdaughter's husband. We Orsini and Colonnas were linked by the tips of our rival lances and were bathed in blood which was difficult to identify as to which family it belonged. There were too many deaths between us. It was possible for me to have invited to my wedding among the multitude of guests people as hostile, as opposed as the abbot of Farfa and the widow of Vespasiano Colonna; it was possible for Cardinal Pompeo Colonna and Cardinal Franciotto Orsini to be present—and actually there were so many reasons for hatred among great Italian families that if some refused to attend a wedding because others were going, it would have been impossible to count upon a fair number of important people for the ceremonies, for all could find crimes and insults that would justify their absence, and in many cases there would have been no more people present than the bride, the groom, and the priest—but between that case and the fact that my brother was marrying the daughter of Sciarra Colonna there was a grave distance. Diana Orsini did not see it that way. Perhaps her great old age had softened her or had made her more ductile and indulgent as it showed her that anger was vain and ephemeral. According to her, the Colonnas had unanimously approved the match. I had to approve it too so as not to remain behind, so that the contracts would not be signed without my authorization. Maerbale, the rebel, was joined in holy matrimony to Cecilia Colonna in the castle of Fondi, and I holed up in my persistence and did not head the witnesses to the rites as I should have. On the other hand, I did send Orso, Matteo, and Sigismondo to represent me. They were the same ones who presumably had made an attempt on the life of the bridegroom in Venice when I was suspicious of Maerbale's equivocal intentions toward my wife, and that gave a certain secret irony to the embassy that was much to my taste. The three cousins had perhaps forgotten that crime that never came off. They showed a comfortable disinterest in matters of that type. I dressed them like three grandees and surrounded them with servants, so that they might fulfill their mission with the pomp that was worthy of the Duke of Bomarzo. They left, puffed up with pride. I can remember Sigismondo's suit of yellow satin with collar and cuffs of marten. And although my memory was firm and the unexpected attempts at homicide of which I had been the object in my turn, and which probably had been planned by Maerbale, had never been cleared up, I thought that perhaps, if it was certain that Maerbale was so much in love with Cecilia, the marriage would erase his ambiguous pretensions toward my duchess, if such had ever existed, and as a consequence I contrived to find an advantageous side to a wedding that exasperated me. The present-day reader should not be startled. Things happened like that in those days. They were complicated, thorny, and violent. We lived from day to day. It became bothersome to establish strictly with whom and against whom one was at any determined moment. And the most arbitrary and terrible events came about with a fierce naturalness.

Nor did I return to Bomarzo then, even though my administrator was calling for me. I insisted on the pretext of the division of my grandfather's possessions and my investigations in order to prolong my stay in Rome.

The agitated environment of Christ's capital was becoming more and more restless. Francis I had signed a capitulation with Suleiman. In Florence, so tightly linked to Rome by the ties of the Medicis in spite of its hatred for the pontiff, political dissension grew with each new outrage of the duke. Beyond the Faenza gate, on land that had been cleared for the purpose, a fortress was being built that would serve to convert the city into a jail. The cornerstone was laid with a ceremony attended by Duke Alessandro, who would be both the warden of those dungeons and their most important prisoner, because the quarrelsome troops of Charles V would govern from there. Also present was an astrologer, Master Giuliano da Prato, who cast the horoscope required by the circumstances. Since he was a friend of Silvio da Narni, I allowed my secretary, who was so interested in everything concerning the occult sciences, to attend the solemnities, which the Florentines watched with muted rage, and on his return he told me that Alessandro was directing the work personally and was pushing it along without regard to expense, for Filippo Strozzi—with whose money, paradoxically, part of the work was being done—whose friendship with the duke had been broken because of the affront to his daughter Lucia and the assassination of a Salviati by the Strozzi faction, and, accompanied by his fearsome sons, by the Prior of Capua, by Piero, had established himself in Venice. From there the news reached the Tuscan capital that Strozzi and Ippolito de' Medici were conspiring against the duke along with a constantly growing number of exiles.

In September 1534 Clement VII died. He had been a slow and astute man. He knew how to dissimulate like few others. He adored music— and he stood out as an expert in that field—and he would take advantage of instrumental harmony, which he would listen to with his eyes half closed, his hands joined as if in prayer, to ripen his sluggish plans. A Ligurian monk, back from France from where the pope had returned very ill after having capped one of his greatest desires by marrying Catherine to the one who would be Henry II, predicted that he would die that year, and since Clement believed—he was not wrong—in the monk's clairvoyance, the pope himself put the detailed concentration he gave everything into the liturgy and prepared the special vestments for the pontifical wake. His passing was received with joy by Romans and Florentines. Duke Alessandro had to flood the streets of Florence with soldiers in order to squelch it. The joy was multiplied in Rome a month later when the conclave proclaimed the election of Alessandro Farnese, who assumed the title of Paul III. It had been more than a century since we had had a Roman pope, since Martin V Colonna, and the patriotic enthusiasm overflowed, uncontainable. The Colonnas were busy reminding people of the pontiff from their line, of course, but it was the hour of the Farneses. The curious thing was that the champion of the victorious successor to Peter during the arduous days of the voting, the one who persuaded the Sacred College to name him, was Ippolito de' Medici, and as soon as Farnese put on the tiara, the new pontiff, the same as the cardinals created by him, became the implacable enemy of Ippolito. They saw in him, who had fared so badly with Clement VII and who had been despoiled of the Duchy of Florence by his uncle, the shadow of the dead pope. And that shadow, pale as it might have been, made them nervous.

Giulia Farnese traveled from Bomarzo to kiss the foot of her relative who was spreading such glory over his lineage. Accompanying her, in spite of her age and her illnesses and the fact that I had forbidden her to, was my grandmother. She was beside herself with satisfaction. Her clear eyes were glowing; her delicate hands with yellow splotches were trembling. She thought that with such a close relative in the Vatican a new era of splendor would begin for Bomarzo and its people. I received the news with little excitement. As a Guelph prince I was proud of the idea of that alliance with the head of Christianity, which made up in a certain way for what my grandfather Franciotto had never attained, but I was also irritated by the airs that the Farneses immediately began to put on. The worst, of course, was Pier Luigi. The son of the pope, he calculated perhaps that it would be fitting for him through the influence that he exerted on an old father who loved him and feared him to play the role of a second Cesare Borgia. It was soon noticed that Paul III would refuse him nothing. He absolved him for his participation in the sack of Rome; he placed him in charge of the reform of the Church militia, and he awarded him very rich estates, among others that of Montalto, an ancient property of the Farneses that really should have gone to my father-in-law. Then he invested as cardinal the one who would continue his name, Alessandro Farnese, Pier Luigi's son, who was about fourteen years of age at the time, and Guido di Santa Fiora, sixteen, the son of Costanza Farnese. In the following consistory red hats were distributed right and left: du Bellay, Schönberg, Ghinucci, Simonetta, Caracciolo, Fisher, Contarini... For us there was neither a remembrance nor a promise. This was pointed out to me with icy smiles by my cousins from Bracciano and Mugnano and by the abbot of Farfa, as if I were to blame. I told them to calm down, that I would speak to the Holy Father at an opportune moment, but Ippolito, who was quickly disillusioned, told me with a shrug of his shoulders that it was necessary to resign oneself, because everything would be for the rapacious Farneses. And that was how it was. In a short time Alessandro, the boy cardinal, was named governor of Spoleto. Like other universal pastors, Paul III dreamed at the age of sixty-six of establishing the material power of his house, calculating perhaps that the distribution of the peninsula among the great Catholic lines, tied by blood to the heads of the Church, would contribute to the guarantee of that needed Italian unity which would be the only wall against which the ambitions of the emperor and foreign sovereigns would be shattered. If he thought that way, he thought well. It was a pity that he had to use such base individuals as Pier Luigi, people who would weaken the prestige of the Holy See and by their avarice would work in an opposite direction, betraying those high hopes and selling themselves to the people lying in wait across the Alps.

Cardinal de' Medici, offended and disappointed, took refuge in his dreams and intrigues. He would go to Venice to confer with Filippo Strozzi and to Fondi to play the lute beside Giulia Gonzaga. I asked him to write me directly from Venice about Maerbale's prospects of paternity and he told me that there were still no signs. I sighed with relief. My grandmother and my wife returned to Bomarzo. I accompanied them as far as Civita Castellana, where I took leave with great bows. My relations with Giulia Farnese were now impregnated with courtesy, with friendly attentiveness. Such an attitude seemed elegant to me in contrast to that of other princes, who were rude and disagreeable with their wives. I thought that in that way I could compensate for the absence of more tangible testimonies of my consideration, but

I was mistaken. On those opportunities Giulia would look at me with the haughtiness and coolness that she was able to graduate subtly in such a way that her expressions could be interpreted as silent remonstrances, but they could also be held as the expression of an aristocratic race that avoided liberties in public. I avoided her eyes, but her way of acting made my blood boil, because by means of our respective games, she, the Farnese, became the aloof great lady, and I, the Orsini, an actor who was overdoing his flattery. But no matter how much I proposed to act differently when we would come together, I would bow down again. Then, in order to disguise my defeat, I intensified the obsequious clownishness, which disconcerted everyone, and more than one person must have interpreted it, increasing my hidden anger, as the submission of the Duke of Bomarzo to the growing authority of the Farneses. Only my grandmother was not surprised at such games, for from the beginning she had penetrated to the roots of my chronic incapacity and she limited herself to shaking her head with a sad smile in which her invariable indulgence and her loyal tenderness appeared.

In part to defend my personality, which had collapsed before the veiled disdain that flowed from Giulia, and in part also to give way to my sensual propensities, I became involved about that time in sentimental conversations and other more concrete recreations with my cousin Violante Orsini and my brother-in-law Fabio Farnese, both very disposed to any flattering approach. Since it did not go beyond the immediate family circle, it seemed perfectly acceptable to my criterion at the time. My cousin provided me with the testimony of an unfettered virility, and my brother-in-law gave me a victory over the clan in whose bosom I had known, along with Giulia's passive reserve, the humiliating defeat which came from the fixation of a psychological trauma that was impossible to overcome. Violante, who had caused a scandal in Bomarzo after my wedding by her mad behavior with the Duke of Urbino and a halberdier of my guard who was even more handsome than the duke, lightened the sadness of the palace that I had inherited from Cardinal Franciotto with her laughter and gaiety. She brought along a tame bear that the Duchess of Camerino had given to Ippolito de' Medici, who had given it to her in turn, and she, the same as I, awarded it the position of the true patriarch of our line and we gave parties in honor of that common ancestor, whom we crowned with the ancestral roses and before whom Fabio Farnese danced in the role of Orpheus with a golden lyre in his hand to the joy of a group of turbulent guests which included—for if we had not invited him he would have come just the same—Pier Luigi.

Those decorative aberrations distracted me from my bitterness. My marriage had foundered and I had no more hopes of finding the Dastyn letters in which I stubbornly placed so many illusions, as if they held the justification of my useless life. From time to time I would leave Rome to attempt some new vain search or to comply with unavoidable obligations which my position imposed on me.

The victory of Charles V at Tunis, from which Barbarossa escaped, gave him an enviable personal glory. It could be seen, for example, in the accentuation of Aretino's adulatory tone. Imperial arms were enjoying great days: Andrea Doria and Álvaro de Bazán were shining like stars, and the fame of their comrade, the Count of Orgaz, might have been unfading had it not been for the paradox that fifty years later, when El Greco painted an ancestor of his who was not even a count yet, obscure, charitable, and (it seemed) the object of a certain miracle, during his burial ceremonies, the splendor of the painting, located in a chapel in distant Toledo, removed forever the memory of this other and valiant Count of Orgaz. From which it can be observed that a painter can perform a miracle and defeat a fierce warrior in time. Consequently, I now think that perhaps it was for the best that my name became separated from the portrait by Lorenzo Lotto which is admired in the Academy of Venice.

Ippolito de' Medici, always anxious for prestige that would make him shine in the eyes of Giulia Gonzaga, wanted to take advantage of events and engage in a campaign worthy of the "Knight Errant" and to avenge the Lady of the Amaranth. He left, therefore, with his plumes in the wind like a hero out of Romanticism. According to what was said later, his health was declining, for during the summer he had become ill with malaria contracted in the marshes near the beauty's estate, and that was complicated by the ravages of Fracastoro's disease, which he evidently owed to the harlot Zafetta. But that not too honorable version had its origins with his enemies, courtiers of the Duke of Florence. He was accompanied on the trip by some of the most illustrious Florentine exiles such as Piero Strozzi, Bernardino Salviati, and even the poet Francesco Molza, a great friend of Giulia's, who was my friend too, and who, hostile to Alessandro's group, had composed a discourse against Lorenzaccio when he mutilated the statues on the arch of Constantine. At Itri, an estate of his, the cardinal suddenly became worse and could not leave his bed in the Franciscan monastery where they had taken him. His seneschal, Gian Andrea del Borgo San Sepolcro, served him a broth and his end was quickly accelerated. Bernardino Salviati, a prior of Rome, declared that the prince, rolling about, swore between tears and spasms that he had been poisoned.

"Gian Andrea poisoned me," Ippolito managed to stammer.

They called Giulia, who came on the gallop from her nearby castle. In the cloisters the shouts of the afflicted Africans failed to cover over those of the seneschal, whom the lords were submitting to torture. They even put a scribe in his room to take down his declarations. Gian Andrea del Borgo San Sepolcro contradicted himself many times, in accordance with the greater or lesser intensity of the pressures that returned him to his cell bloody and convulsive. He maintained that he was innocent, and then he would assert, when they tightened the cords a little more, that he had put some poison that he had brought from Florence into the broth. Four days later the cardinal's brief life was extinguished. Giulia never left him in his agony. I arrived hours later, advised by the lady herself, for she knew of the sincere affection that I had felt for him ever since childhood. I found a pathetic spectacle there. Ippolito de' Medici was lying livid in his purple robes. Beside him Giulia Gonzaga was praying quietly, and around him, gesticulating, were the exiled noblemen, who saw their dreams of returning victoriously to their homeland falling to pieces with their young leader. And even in those moments, even during the litany of prayers for the member of the Sacred College who had given his troubled soul to God, there was no cease to the cries of the seneschal stretched out on the torture rack.

We went slowly back to Rome. Perhaps Giulia's conscience was finally biting her and her pride was moved at last. The handsome youth who burned with high ambitions had died without ever having obtained anything from her but frivolous words. As for me, I noted with horror how the list of my dead was growing and how the people about me were being reduced. I remembered Florence, I relived the moment of my arrival at the palace of Cosimo the Elder when I discovered in the *cortile* Ippolito de' Medici ready to leave on a hunt. He had been kind and generous to me. Perhaps he had understood me and had penetrated to the deep roots of my troubles. In him, lying for eternity now as rigid as a polychrome figure on a tomb, I was losing a sincere ally, and I needed them so much. I wept in silence frequently as we brought his remains to his titular church, San Lorenzo in Damaso. Summer was ending and the air was quivering, soft and transparent on the Tyrrhenian coast. On the road we stopped at an inn and the servants, on orders from Bernardino Salviati, tortured the seneschal again. When his complaints ceased, the conversation of the servants could be heard again. They attributed his death to Duke Alessandro, of whom Gian Andrea must have been only a creature, and they asserted that the poison had been obtained by a Captain Pignatta, a great coward. One of them lowered his voice, remembering by chance my closeness and relationship to the pontiff, and accused Paul III of the crime, for he had envied Ippolito and had thought that he was too wealthy, and he probably wanted to get rid of the bond of the obligations that came from the debt of the tiara and even benefit Pier Luigi with the prelate's fortune. The tone of Piero Strozzi, hoarse, violent, broken, like a croak, could be heard in the conversation. He was not afraid to be heard.

"Those Farneses," he roared, "are the product of the conspiracy of the Borgias and the Orsinis. Before Alexander Borgia was pope they didn't raise a finger. Everyone knows that our new pope got his red hat the same day as Cesare Borgia, because his sister Giulia was Alexander the Sixth's mistress. She was married to an Orsini, a one-eyed cuckold, that damned lord of Bassanello, the son of a cousin of the Borgias. That's how the circle of influences that brought Alessandro Farnese to the Vatican throne was closed. They used to call Giulia Farnese the 'Bride of Christ.' She lived in the big Orsini palace on Monte Giordano with her cooperative mother-in-law, who forgot about her son's interests in favor of those of her cousin the pope. That was where the Borgia daughter was born who was taken in by the poor Orsini."

"There's still no indication," Prior Salviati added prudently, "that His Holiness is to blame for the murder."

"Whether it was His Holiness Paul the Third or whether His Magnificence Alessandro de' Medici," Piero Strozzi answered mordantly, "what there isn't any doubt about is that the murderer is going to pay for it."

I was listening to them, trembling behind the wall. I should have put in an appearance in the midst of the gossipers to defend the Orsinis at least. Ever since my childhood, that ridiculed Orso Orsini, whom they called "Monocolo," and who hid his troubles in Bassanello, near Civita Castellana, had been the cause of arguments in Bomarzo. My people could not pardon his condescension to the Borgias, particularly at a time when the Orsinis were being persecuted by that line, because the pope was anxious to turn our possessions over to his eldest son, the Duke of Gandía, the one who was murdered by his brother Cesare. Those were very hard times for us, and if we had not defeated the papal forces in the vicinity of Soriano, where Gandía was wounded and Guidobaldo da Montefeltro, his commander, taken prisoner, who knows what fate would have befallen our house. My father and my grandfather, who played epic roles in those struggles and bore themselves like lions at Soriano, would never pronounce Orso's name without spitting to the side in haughty contempt. It should have been my place, therefore, to set things straight before all the curses and show what the fiber of real Orsinis was, but I decided to be silent, until after a while the moans of Ippolito's majordomo could be heard along with the noise of those watching his contortions. Next to me, Fabio Farnese, who had gone with me, as wounded or more than I by the diatribes, had his lean, feline body stretched out and was also silent, squeezing my right hand.

In Rome the matter was not cleared up. The seneschal declared that he had ground the poison between two stones that he had thrown down a well, and then he denied the testimony that he had given under oath. The inquisitors ended by absolving him, arguing that his confession, the product of torture, was not valid. Gian Andrea returned to

Florence, where he craftily wormed his way into the duke's court, but he ended up taking refuge in his village, and there, in Borgo San Sepolcro, months later, the fury of the people did him in and justice was done.

Giulia Gonzaga from then on sought relief more and more in religion. As she was greatly interested in everything that had to do with theological subtleties, she formed a close friendship with the Spaniard Juan de Valdés, concerned about the motives of individual conscience and justification by faith instead of works. Her heterodoxy brought the wrath of other popes down on her, and one of them, Pius V, when the beauty was already dead, pronounced a ringing anathema against her and said that if she had not been dead he would have had her burned alive. It must have been one of those angry phrases cast into the air like arrows under the domination of passion, for neither the Colonnas—although Vittoria Colonna herself was not very tranquil at that time—nor the Gonzagas would have tolerated it. As for me, Cardinal Ippolito's end at the age of twenty-four was something as desolating, as disconcerting, and as impossible as if a demigod had perished. Ippolito de' Medici no longer breathed, and the grove of Pan was silent. The nymphs and fauns were hiding among the rocks chiseled by Benvenuto Cellini, while the astute traitors who were destroying the race of Eros paraded by covered with blood. I loved him from the very first moment, because from the very first moment he loved me, in spite of my hump and my poor fragility. And I also loved him because with his brave frankness, his shining insouciance, and his assurance which conquered men and women and which showed his pride in his smallest movements, in the grace with which he moved an arm, picked up his cloak, jingled his spurs, lifted his lute, kissed a mouth, or tightened his hand on his dagger—even though he was a bastard and an outcast and a sacrilegious priest, all caused by an arbitrary fate that had been imposed on him by an existence of struggling against his ardent vocation of a king and a lover—Ippolito was the jubilant allegory of what I would never be.

# 8. ORAZIO ORSINI

*Homage to Charles V in Naples—My sister-in-law Cecilia Colonna—The marriage of Alessandro de' Medici in Florence—My repulsive and desperate plot—The Aridosia of Lorenzaccio—I gain Giulia—The deaths of Maerbale and my grandmother—The birth of Niccolò Orsini—Cecilia blind—The pleasures of Violante and Fabio—The intellectuals—The assassination of Duke Alessandro—The birth of Orazio Orsini—My strange collections—Silvio da Narni, alchemist—My useless poem—Lorenzaccio in Bomarzo—The skeleton and the manuscripts*

ON NOVEMBER 25, 1535, the emperor disembarked in Naples. Waiting for him there among the many nobles who had come from the various principalities of the peninsula were my wife and I. The pope let us know that he wanted us present at the festivities that would be given to honor the victor of Tunis, and there was nothing to do but bow to his will. Naples was at that time the meeting place of numerous Florentines, partisans and enemies of Alessandro de' Medici, brought together especially by Charles V, who, pestered by one side and the other at a time when he was troubled with very grave problems, proposed to put an end to their complaints. Paul III, for the same reasons that he had been against Cardinal Ippolito, was opposed to Duke Alessandro. Both of them represented the nepotism of the previous pope and as such they troubled him in his wish to establish that of the Farneses. With Ippolito out of the way, he wished to wipe out Alessandro's standing. But they both also embodied two opposite positions. If Ippolito had not been a Medici and the nephew of Clement VII, crowned with privileges that proclaimed that relationship, Paul III would have come to a perfect understanding with him, for the interests of both coincided and complemented each other in certain aspects. The cardinal no longer existed, by the deed of whoever it was, and the pope, quit of a prince who had bothered him personally, while it was convenient for him to share his ideas and those of the group of which he had been the leader, used his influence to support the side of that group even more in the delicate political balance. The emperor supported Alessandro, his future son-in-law, his ally, whom he had set up on the new throne of Tuscany, and who, besides being Duke of Florence, was the imperial lieutenant there. It was logical that Paul III, even though he did it surreptitiously, should back the hopes of the anti-Medici exiles and try by means of that to harass the power of Charles V in Italy, where he yearned to lay his hands on a realm for his son Pier Luigi. In Naples another move in the complex chess game would be played and that explained—even more than the courtly urgency to congratulate the Caesar on his victory over the Muslim—the extraordinary crush of people who hastened to receive him and who remained in the city for the four months during which the sovereign prolonged his stay.

Giulia and I went together from Rome, but, since it was impossible to disobey the Farnese pope, I carried cynicism to such a degree as to include in the coach with the Duchess of Bomarzo her brother Fabio, Violante Orsini, and the latter's husband, the noble Marco Savelli, as famous for the importance of his position in Tuscany as for his ridiculous misfortunes at home. Silvio da Narni followed us on horseback, heading the escort. It was a curious trip, in which the heat obliged us to stop for brief periods to refresh ourselves and rest, and in which the conversation turned about double meanings when the light was dim and Savelli could not read to us from a worn volume in his hands, and with his eyeglasses on the tip of his nose, the sonnets of Petrarch, which we commented on with erudite reflections and ironical sensual allusions as befitted people of so much worldliness and culture. Giulia remained out of the conversation. I would spy on her at times, hiding among the others in the protection of the shadows, and I noticed the beauty of her violet eyes, where the motionless liquid showed no emotion. She had strangely hardened in a short time; she had acquired a contexture that was hard to define, almost mineral. She looked at us without seeing us and it was as if we were carrying in the coach along with the polite laughter a marble statue with mysterious shades. Her presence weighed upon us in such a way that we were suddenly quiet, and then, if Violante or Savelli asked her a question, she would answer modestly after a short pause during which she would blink her eyes and fold her fingers over her skirt as if she were coming out of a dream. But in a short time she would go back to her silence and recover her distance and from it she would observe us, Violante, Fabio, and me, as if she did not understand the reasons for our clownish laughter, or why we stopped to drink the local wine, or what such obvious riddles meant. Silence would overcome the coach again and it was difficult to break it. Then, furious, I would lean out the window and tell them to pull up. She would remain motionless in the coach with Marco Savelli, detached from us, while the rest of us, relieved, would get out with the pretext of taking care of the Duchess of Camerino's bear, which was traveling behind in a cage, nauseous, ill-humored, and which we had added to our retinue on a whim of Violante's.

I can see the emperor's ships once more as if it were yesterday that they anchored in the Bay of Naples and the episode had not happened more than four centuries ago, with their pennants fluttering in the November breeze. On the main galley, which was slowly moving toward the dock, I can see the outline of the Caesar on the poop. I can see the flags of yellow damask about him; his two-headed eagles with the shield on their chests; the pennant of crimson taffeta which showed a cross of gold; the white gonfalon sewn with keys and chalices and crosses of Saint Andrew; and the streamers with the device "*Plus Ultra*" turned about their colonnades. The people fought to get close and some, with sharp eyes, made out the Latin inscriptions of the flags that the learned ones translated: "Take up your arms and shield and come succor me," or "God has sent his angel, may he guard you where you go," or "The law goes before him." And those figures and emblems fluttering in the cold air formed a great multicolored flapping about the victor, as if the ship were an immense glowing birdcage in the center of which a black falcon was lying in wait. Charles disembarked and the princes crushed together to pay him homage. Spanish nobles mingled with Italians:

the Duke of Alba, the Marquis del Vasto, who carried the imperial sword, Antonio de Leiva, the Duke of Ferrara, the Duke of Urbino, the four ambassadors from Venice and the three papal legates: Pier Luigi Farnese, Cardinal Piccolomini, and Cardinal Cesarini. Behind bobbed the heads of every gentleman of title in the Kingdom of Naples, Giulia Gonzaga, whom members of that house had sent to represent them, triumphed with her grace over the other famous beauties, María of Aragon and Isabella Sanseverino. The memory of her recent attack by the pirate whom the emperor had just put to flight and the memory more recent still of the strange death of Cardinal Ippolito, who worshiped her, encircled her with a halo of exceptional prestige. When she curtsied before the Caesar, he raised her up and many thought romantically that the Tunis campaign had really been waged to avenge her against Khair ed-Din Barbarossa. Not far off, Alessandro de' Medici was sharing the commentaries that the widow of Vespasiano Colonna was arousing. He was dressed in mourning for his cousin—he took it off a few days later—and the exiles from Florence, huddled in a corner, muttered about his brazenness. He was flanked by his kinsmen Lorenzino and Cosimo, the future grand duke. In the discussions that developed later between the exiles and Alessandro, who had dragged a paper-bearing horde of jurists and clerks to Naples, the suit was resolved, as expected, in favor of the son of Clement VII, who, crowning his success, gave his engagement ring to Margaret of Austria, but the near-tragic ruin of Alessandro began there, because he was robbed there—robbed by Lorenzino, as was well known—of his fine coat of mail from which he was never separated.

Charles V recognized me among all those gentlemen whose faces were superimposed in his memory as soon as it was my turn to render my homage. There is some advantage at least in bearing an identifying hump about. The sovereign had aged in a short time. Fatigue, like a delicate brush, had painted light lines around his eyes and mouth where one could read, as in a thin script, the depth of his worries. He carried his kindness to the degree of mentioning, with the shadow of a smile, the occasion when the hilt of his sword had come loose while he was knighting me. That brought me a special deference from the Farneses and perhaps the envy of Pier Luigi. For the first time the ironic miracle came about that my hump had aroused envy. That episode gave me such courage that, also making use of the audacity brought on by wine, I tried to force myself on my wife and undertook some nocturnal caresses which might have become concrete in what I yearned for, but Giulia showed that she was not influenced—and in that she differed from the other Farneses—by the official flattery.

"Leave me alone, Your Lordship," she told me. "Violante and my brother Fabio are waiting for you."

With that she proved to me that she knew all about my extramarital activities, obvious, of course, and that perhaps—which brought me a strange joy in the midst of my disorder—she was jealous of me. I left her, therefore, half laughing and half protesting, to give the impression that I was making a joke of her attitude, as if it were not the only one which suited the situation, and during the rest of our stay in Naples I plunged into a whirlwind of pleasures, only beside her when etiquette required it.

We left for Rome with the Caesar's retinue. We spent the night at Fondi as guests of Giulia Gonzaga along with the master of the world, and on that occasion I corroborated the feeling that had been left with the beauty as a consequence of Cardinal de' Medici's death.

"The cardinal had great affection for you," she confided to me as we were getting up from the table. "I loved him too and admired him. But the will of God shows itself in mysterious ways. We must pray for the repose of his soul. There are days when I think he is wandering about here, passing through these rooms, when I feel his breath on my book."

She took a cautious look around, as if the purple shape and livid face might appear from behind the tapestries.

"Love," I answered her, "is a way of surviving."

She looked at me with curiosity. "I have heard people say that Your Lordship will never die."

I understood then that my search for the letters from the alchemist Dastyn and the hope that was spelled out in them had reached the ears of the mistress of Fondi. I shook my head, as if denying the importance of Benedetto's prediction.

"I would prefer," I answered gallantly, "never to die in the heart of Giulia Gonzaga, like Cardinal Ippolito."

But it was not that way: not even he would live long in her mind, for as soon as the distress that he had left her as a vague remorse disappeared, Juan de Valdés absorbed her completely with his spiritual doubts, nor was there anything that interested me quite as much as the immortality (real immortality, without allegories or rhetorical tricks) that had been predicted for me at my birth.

Twenty-two members of the Sacred College were awaiting Charles V at the Saint Sebastian gate when we entered Rome. First went the Marquis del Vasto with more than three thousand infantrymen; then the Duke of Alba on a caparisoned horse, like a bronze statue being pulled along by the troops to be set up in a public square; then the Count of Benavente and the papal family dressed in scarlet. I was one of the Roman noblemen who carried the canopy under which the emperor advanced. Since I was limping and that made me waver, pulling the canopy toward my side, the monarch was watching me out of the corner of his eye, until someone took the pole from my hand. It was Maerbale. I tried to resist, but the emperor raised his brows and gave a brief order. Fabio Farnese took my arm and led me off.

I had not known that my brother was in the holy city. There we met Cecilia Colonna, who was not beautiful, which pleased me, but she made up for it with the grace of youth and a permanent joy. It is not necessary to go into great detail to deduce that she was carrying the promise of an heir in her womb. Giulia kissed her and at the moment when my wife's lips touched Maerbale's I noticed that she was smiling and that smile illuminated her as if the poor dusty lamp inside of her had finally lighted up again.

Maerbale's attitude when he supplanted me in the imperial procession made me furious and eventually would have caused a definitive break between us if it had not been for the intervention and domination, cautioning me with its more serious importance, of the question raised by his obviously approaching fatherhood. Cecilia Colonna, the one with the arched nose, slightly long, the broad black eyebrows, carefully designed, with the innocent mouth, the protruding eyes, always startled, was carefully molding, month after month, the one who, as soon as he saw the light, we would have to consider as my presumptive successor at Bomarzo. And that was more important than anything else, more than protocol, more than vanity. I bit my lips and clenched my fits. It would be necessary to face up to it. It would be necessary to study how to face up to it. Maerbale was not going to despoil me of what was mine, as when we were small and he and Girolamo persecuted me. That thought obsessed me, excluding all other calculations during the days when the Caesar was the guest of the pope, I turned it over and over in my mind every time ceremonial demands obliged me to go to the palace where the emperor was staying and which had sheltered Charles VIII of France in the days of Pope Alexander Borgia. It was known that the sovereign had taken advantage of his meetings with Paul III to complain angrily of King Francis, and had sworn to wage war against him again: a short time before, Francesco Sforza, the Duke of Milan, had died and that death spurred ancient ambitions. But even though the future was so thorny, that prospect gave way for me before the anguish that was shaking me up. I meditated about my problem and my problem had precedence over everything else. I saw the emperor often during the course of Holy Week services. I was at his side on Thursday morning when he washed the feet of twelve poor people with magnificent humility; I followed him on Saturday when he visited seven churches; and I was also in his party on Easter Sunday and I appreciated the elegance with which he took part in the rite celebrated by the old pontiff. Proof of how upset and confused I was over my own conflict could be seen in the fact that when I left the church I did not join the group of agitated noblemen who were grumbling on the steps because in the ceremony Pier Luigi Farnese had carried the globe of the world and Ascanio Colonna the crown, presenting them to Charles V, who had been dressed like a Roman emperor, each time the liturgy called for it. On any other such occasion I would have shouted to high heaven the same as the disgruntled princess. By what right Colonna—by what right? Was it not enough to be constable of the Kingdom of Naples? But at that time I paid no attention, distant and solitary, and I gave my right hand to my wife, taking her off with the poison dart sticking in my chest.

We continued our journey on to Florence behind the Fleming upon whose domains the sun never set. Cecilia and Maerbale went with us and everything happened as if there were the best of family harmony in our grandmother's coach. Giulia, silent until then, did not stop chatting with my brother's wife. They spoke of little things, but suddenly, as if they remembered that they were cultured and that they should raise the level of the conversation, the names of Ariosto, Vittoria Colonna, Castiglione, Bembo, Pliny, Cicero, Seneca, and Lactantius oddly arose in the rocking coach that was lulling the child yet to come, for both of them had been fed on books, like all great ladies of their time, the same as on venison and pheasant. If Giulia had to address Maerbale in the midst of the conversation, she would soften her tone. Violante Orsini, her husband, and Fabio occupied another coach with Pier Luigi Farnese. It no longer interested me to have them by my side. On the contrary, I found them a bother. In Rome, on the other hand, I ordered Silvio and Giambattista Martelli to accompany us. I needed them for the fulfillment of the vague plan that was beginning to take shape in my head. It was such a fantastic, such a tremendous plan that I fondled it and remade it over and over again as we rolled and shook our way along to the wedding of Duke Alessandro and Margaret of Austria.

The emperor only stayed in Florence a week. He left before the wedding in spite of Alessandro's entreaties. He said that he had already been present at the exchange of rings in Naples and that it was urgent for him to reach French territory in order to wage war against Francis I. Since the King of France was the father-in-law of the Princess Catherine, the pride of the Medici family, Alessandro passed over those references as over hot coals. The truth was that what had angered Charles was the coolness of his Florentine reception. The duke did everything in his power to create a cordial atmosphere, but without success. It was in vain that he ordered the San Pietro Gattolini gate— the present-day Roman gate—removed from its hinges and thrown to the ground, showing that wherever Charles V went there was no need for any other defense. It was in vain that he sent the clergy to receive him with tall crosses, the sight of which he thought would be pleasing to the pious soul of his father-in-law; and he sent nobles and magistrates and forty boys dressed in crimson satin and white tights, who, with their well-shaped legs, were a joy to behold as they carried the enormous canopy under which the Caesar marched between the duke and the historian Guicciardini, who was overcome with pride. It was in vain that he ordered placed over the entrance to the palace where I had lived and where the monarch was lodged: "*Ave Magne Hospes Auguste.*" The people hated Charles V and with good reason: what else could he have expected? Jammed behind the tight row of soldiers who prevented their misbehavior, silent, dangerous, the crowd showed the scars on their faces, the missing arms, the crutches, the marks of the fury of that prince and those soldiers whom they now had to honor. The son of the Handsome and the Mad left, therefore, but we remained in Florence. After accompanying His Caesarian Majesty, it was our duty to attend the wedding of Alessandro de' Medici. Neither one thing nor the other pleased Maerbale or me at all, especially me, who since childhood had detested the evil duke with his slave's face, the son of a servant girl of the Orsinis, but the name that we bore obliged us to obey the pontiff, and His Holiness had commanded us to attend the rites.

We stayed in the palace of the Popolani Medicis, located on the Via Larga next to that of Cosimo the Elder, where the ducal family lived. On the second floor lived the widow of Giovanni delle Bande Nere and her son Cosimo; on the third Maria Soderini, with Lorenzaccio and her other descendants. We were all put up in the last part, half settled, but what was certain was that Florence was overflowing with people brought by the wedding. Almost two weeks passed before the ceremony and I used them to bring my project to maturity.

It was an insane, immoral, repulsive idea, but if one looks at it well, less unbearable then than it would have been today. The old Machiavellian formula of the ends justifying the means dominated relationships at that time. Crime and treason were absolved—even applauded—if they had as an object a motive whose benefit was more than enough to overcome the horror, which would be forgotten along with the temporary nausea. I was a man of my time and circumstances had made me worse than average. My defect—my defects—had ended by provoking a kind of blindness in me, without the bonds of religion, without the prejudices of the bourgeois, and before anything else came two preoccupations: the defense of my weak and timid personality, which had been abused by an environment of violence, and the cult of my line, a devotion to that Orsinian glory that was centered and incarnate in Bomarzo, the maintenance of which had the dedication of my soul and energies. At the possibility that Maerbale, as he had supplanted me impulsively in Rome when he carried the emperor's canopy, would supplant me in Bomarzo with a son and the sons of that son, the blood was boiling in my veins. I already had the painful certainty of my incapacity to engender a son in the womb of Giulia. A secret and ironic force forbade me. I had to find a different way of twisting fate, of imposing my will. I could, of course, count on the help of Silvio and Giambattista to kill Cecilia Colonna, but that would only have represented a postponement of the dilemma. Maerbale would marry again and it would not be easy for me to eliminate all of his wives. I did not see myself in the role of an outside Bluebeard. Reason led me to deduce that what was needed was for Giulia to have a child herself, if not mine, someone else's, a child whose paternity would be attributed to me without discussion. The one who would collaborate in my plan would have to be someone on whose discretion I could fully rely. Someone who depended on me. Giambattista? Silvio? Could I give Giulia to them for a single night? Would it not be like giving myself over bound hand and foot to their future whims? And could I resign myself to the fact that my supposed son was an offshoot of our grooms from Narni or a nephew of Porzia Martelli the whore? What would I gain from it except removing Maerbale's line from the succession? Would it not be better, on the contrary, for his branch to succeed, since it was a question of people of our caste? Would not the heir have to be an Orsini? Was that not what Bomarzo required? Then his father would be an Orsini. When I reached the obvious conclusion, I saw clearly, and, as in a game whose players find their places quickly when they see in their midst the one which will serve as a guide to the pattern of the group, I saw that it was the only possible method. My child's father would be an Orsini, an Orsini like me. And it would be Maerbale. Grotesque, was it not? Grotesque and atrocious.

Alas, when I reached the end of the labyrinth through which I had been stumbling I remember that I gave a cry and drew back in horror, for I discovered waiting for me the fateful figure of my younger brother! I was practically alone, looking at the Arno, watching the waves without seeing them, and the palaces softly outlined against the opposite shore. Some passers-by turned to look at the hunchback who had been part of the retinue of Charles V and who was acting so strangely, but I let them do it, indifferent. I had found the key and now that I held it in my hands it was burning me like a hot iron. Maerbale, Maerbale, always Maerbale—surging up on my path with the flexible elegance of his bearing—always waiting for me. At first I cast aside the thought with rage. And then, little by little, astutely, I gained control of myself. It would be very easy for Maerbale, not knowing the hidden and complex motives, to fall into the delicious trap. Did I not know the emotion he had felt for Giulia years back? Could it occur to anyone that his young wife, ugly and made even uglier by pregnancy, would be capable of keeping him away from all temptation, if one kept in mind his excitable lewd proclivities? And as far as Giulia was concerned, had I not sensed for a long time the attraction that she felt for Maerbale? She, who perhaps might have resisted anyone else, would she not give in to him? We were living together in the palace of the cousins of the Duke of Florence. The conditions, the sensual atmosphere were right for the meeting. But, oh, giving her to Maerbale like a prostitute! Was it right? Did the end I sought justify such terrible means?

I fought against the idea, and every morning, every afternoon, in the intimacy of living together, the sight of the bulk that happy Cecilia did not attempt to hide under her clothes convinced me that no other solution existed but that one. The alternatives were either Bomarzo or Giulia, and for me Bomarzo enjoyed the priority. I was shambling about in doubt as if in a cage. Pier Francesco Orsini was shambling about in a cage like a bear, like the Duchess of Camerino's desperate bear. Until one night I found the reasoning I needed to tranquilize myself. As always, my old mental illness needed the saving grace of sophistry to justify me. In a century in which noblemen killed, robbed, and raped simply because they felt like it, without any explanation, when incest flourished in palaces, even between parents and children, and snaked its way up the pontifical steps themselves, I was still more and more in need of justification. It was one of the typical traits of my character—possibly a formula of cowardice—the one that demanded the elaboration of a dialectical excuse. I told myself that what was taking place in my imagination was, after all, a swap: I would do away with the risk that a sprout of Maerbale's would take root in the woods of Bomarzo, and Giulia would have the pleasure that she could not attain because of my partial impotence, and she would get it in the arms of a man who was my equal in blood, in physique, without my deformities, and one whom she may have loved. The humiliation, the spite, the hidden wrath it meant for me to give her up—and to Maerbale!—were the secret and burdensome price that I was paying in exchange for covertly overcoming and destroying the prospects of my brother's son's succession. Another son of Maerbale would succeed me, if anyone would succeed me—and it was strange that things came out in such a way that no matter what happened, my successor would still be a son of his—but that son would be before the world and Giulia and Maerbale themselves, silenced by circumstances, a son of mine, an Orsini of mine. I would arrange it so that at the opportune moment I would proceed in such a way that even Giulia herself, drunk, drugged by me, would be deceived about the paternity, or at least that she would be in a condition to show me, with the appearance of possibility, the pantomime of my paternity, avoiding in that way my having to act as befitted an outraged gentleman and the unavoidable scandal imposed by my vanity of a husband, which would bring the mixup to light and add to my ridiculous position and misfortune.

That was how I went on thinking in my twisted way, bringing up arguments to support my complex machinations as if it were necessary to convince myself when I was already convinced. Can the reader imagine the humpbacked Duke of Bomarzo going through a bedecked Florence, where the mansions were adorned with heraldic trappings to honor the bride of its prince and where the shops showed the dazzling trophies of the best of their cloths, their wools, their silks, their leather, their furs; going along the Via Sant' Agostini and the Via Mazetta to the Piazza San Felice; crossing the Arno on the Santa Trinità bridge; coming out onto the Canto dei Tornaquinci, onto the Piazza del Duomo; greeting people he knew; stopping to chat for an instant with the painter Giorgio Vasari, whom he had known as a boy in the study of Master Piero Valeriano; smiling; buying a jewel; stroking a suit of armor; bowing to the Vicereine of Naples, a guest at the festivities, and introducing his wife, his illustrious Giulia Farnese; answering with a brief gesture the bow of the oil vendor, the cheese vendor, the man selling salt; or pretending to stop to listen to the news of the death of Agrippa, the great necromancer, or that Buonarroti was going back to work on the frescoes in the Sistine Chapel; and all the time ripening that sinuous design, that inconceivable, nauseating immolation of his manhood and his pride on the altars of a rust-colored land with fantastic rocks, a deformed castle, a legend, a family myth born among rupestral bears in the dawn of centuries, and built up by poetic chroniclers, as if he too were carrying under his *lucco* of rich brocade a hidden son who was growing in his insides like a small devouring monster? Can he understand him, can anyone understand him? I no longer can understand him, and yet that was how, with signs of errant logic, the incredible process was developing.

Giulia would give me a son. She would not give me a son, she would give one to Bomarzo. Then Maerbale would have to die. It was inevitable. And this time I would have to make my blow strike home. May God have pity on his soul and on mine.

The first and most urgent thing to do was to acquaint Silvio da Narni with my plans and get his help. I revealed them to him little by little, as if it were some absurd invention of the moment, an original joke (a joke in rather bad taste), the nonsense of a spur-of-the-moment schemer who thought things up as he spoke. I knew my page well. I knew the twists and turns of his mind and I knew that out of ambition he was capable of anything. He had shown me that when he helped me with my ambiguous, lewd inclinations during adolescence, when my father died, and when I gained the hand of Giulia. There was a complicity born of abjection and mystery between us. His rancor, the product of his low status, was similar to that which I felt because of my physique. We both had reasons to hate, we both fed them and were consumed in the flames of their fire. And looking at it closely, none of those reasons was sufficient to give us any authorization or to defend our attitudes toward life, for both of us had the prerogative of unusual forces that were more than enough to compensate for our lacks.

In spite of the distance that separated us, I had shared the most decisive moments of my existence with him during the previous few years and that accentuated our connivance. I had given him a beautiful woman against the wishes of Giambattista, her brother. The possession of the woman he yearned for had seemed to calm him down for a while, as if Porzia had gone beyond his avarice and had replaced it with an ideal of cloistered peace that was centered about his weird studies, but now his true character began showing its claws again. Porzia, ever since she had exchanged a harlot's restlessness for a settled home, seemed to have changed too, until, just like her husband—and perhaps, maybe, as the result of the perfidious remarks of Giambattista, her twin, and the change in Silvio, who after he got her relegated her to an obscure and almost humiliating level—gave in to an unrest that was a prelude to the sourness of spite. A nostalgia for the past, for her sensual diversions, for contact with passionate men of every stripe, not excluding well-placed young noblemen, began to gnaw at her. Silvio neglected her, busy with his books, his alembics, his magical drawings. And he was no Adonis, quite the contrary, which Porzia's beauty flourished more and more. It was inevitable that the girl would slip off the straight path, even if it was to get her revenge. And fall she did. Silvio caught her in the arms of that splendid halberdier who had shared the favors of Violante Orsini with the Duke of Urbino during the time of my wedding. It was the beginning of a series of brutal family scenes, full of recriminations, the echo of which resounded through the servants' quarters, and which the servants and squires at Bomarzo commented on with shameful sarcastic remarks. The halberdier was succeeded by a kitchen scullion who was reputed to be my father's grandson, and he was replaced by the abbot of Farfa, who was followed by my cousin Sigismondo, anxious to give official proof that Pier Luigi Farnese's caresses had not extinguished his virility. The girl finally ran away from Bomarzo. My grandmother found out that another cousin of mine, the Duke of Mugnano, had her with him in his nearby castle, where he gave her gifts and treated her like a princess. I should have claimed her, for it was a question of one of my vassals, and my grandmother considered the case a family affront, but, after all, it was not to my best interests to cross swords with such a fine kinsman. The curious thing was that as soon as Porzia left him, Silvio acted as if he had wanted to be rid of her. He could not have been ignorant of the fact, even when the solitude of his tomes took him away from everyday things, that Giambattista had contributed fundamentally with his advice, with his urgings, to his sister's desertion, and, nevertheless, as soon as she had left Bomarzo, and when the logical thing would have been to think that a bloody conflict would arise between Silvio and Giambattista, the bonds of intimacy between the two that the wedding had loosened were tightened again. Beneath it all they were quite similar and they needed each other. Greed, a desperate craving to thrive at any cost, which had gone to sleep in Silvio's breast during the interval of calm and forgetfulness, woke up hungry again. He had gone through an experience into which he would never fall again. And just as I valued the obvious benefits that obliged me to preserve my alliance with Mugnano and not sacrifice it for a moment of passing pride, so Silvio appreciated those that came from his friendship with Giambattista, who was motivated by aspirations identical to his. The vengeance—if ever there would be vengeance—could wait until later. Vengeance was a luxury which he did not yet enjoy. But despoiled of his wife, in whom his essential resentment of a man who considered himself superior to the circumstances of his origins and his life had taken refuge, Silvio sought new refuge in his old associate: ambition. Because of ambition he would favor my plans. And not just because of ambition, in spite of the fact that as the accomplice in such a grave secret he was awarded privileges over me the likes of which he had never dreamed of: that collaboration with his lord and master, which placed the latter in an even sadder position than his own, worked as a palliative against the bitterness and wrath of the servant, who could feel almost redeemed from his misfortune, for the Duke of Bomarzo, upon whose alms he depended and who played such an outstanding role in the papal court and in haughty Roman aristocracy, had shown himself to be more base than he, much more base.

We understood each other, therefore, and we set to work. It would be up to Silvio da Narni to gain Maerbale's confidence and induce him to fulfill my desires. He would have to do it with extraordinary subtlety, care, and artfulness. He had more than sufficient conditions for it. Not once did he raise objections to my plan. He saw in a flash the advantages that could come to him from it and he excluded any other reflections. Some days later he told me in halting words—because the theme was so thorny and so uncomfortable to deal with, for implicit in it were base and murky aspects of my personality, and he immediately saw the necessity to touch upon it only through terse allusions—about the progress of his relations with Maerbale, whose confidence he had gained on the predictable basis of sour criticism of my way of taking care of the people and the interests of Bomarzo. Things moved rapidly from that point to that of the culmination of the plan. It surprised me that Maerbale did not suspect any intrigue, but the fact that the whole thing was inconceivable, being so rash, escaped his courtly foxiness.

In the meantime, alien to my anxieties, Florence was welcoming Margaret of Austria, fourteen years of age and pretty, blond, with thick red voluptuous lips, and unexpectedly sad eyes under the weight of their lids. I went to San Donato in Polverosa to await her with the nobility. She arrived on horseback on a hot spring midnight with pearls pouring over her under the canopy carried by youths from important families dressed in crimson satin, and we accompanied her to the convent of San Marco and the house of Ottaviano de' Medici, where she would stay. Maerbale, dressed in white the same as I, his chest crossed with a gold chain the same as I, rode next to me, behind Cardinal Cibo. Ironic fate had decided that without consulting each other we had dressed in an identical fashion, or perhaps my brother had had me spied upon and had copied my outfit. When we went down the stairs of the palace of the Popolani Medicis to join the retinue, I noted that similarity and I thought of going back to my room to change and put on some clothes that were different from what Maerbale was wearing, but it was too late. Therefore, we had to pass like that before Giulia Farnese and Cecilia Colonna, who took leave of us at the outside door, as if we were two versions of the same person: one deformed, mistreated, unbalanced, irregular as a rhombus; the other, as thin and graceful as a young sprout, making one think that he was the one who had served as the model for the fascinating youth painted by Lorenzo Lotto.

Giulia's impenetrable look alighted on both of us and I felt the old and well-known prick of jealously in my throat. But wait, was that not by chance what I had wanted, to draw her to Maerbale? Alas, the paradoxical truth was that I wanted her to give me a son by Maerbale but to prefer me—as if that could be possible!

Silvio da Narni informed me three days later that Giulia and Maerbale had spoken in secret. With that piece of news, which I should have expected, and which was minimal compared to the mad thing that I was planning, my reason clouded over and I was ready to tell him to suspend his operations and to make ready for our immediate return to Bomarzo when at that instant, by chance, Cecilia came down the street with one of her ladies—we were looking out of a window in my room—and seeing her was enough to make me reject that impulse. There was nothing left to do but to follow the path that had been laid out.

"Were you there?" I asked him.

"Off to a side."

"Where did it happen?"

"Right here, in the duchess's room."

"Was there anybody else?"

"Nobody else."

"What do you mean? What about her ladies, her servants? Nobody?"

"Nobody."

I understood then how easy it would be for Giulia to deceive me, because if she wanted to, she could get rid of any unwanted witnesses like that.

"Could you hear what they said?"

"I already told Your Lordship that I was off to a side."

"But you could see them."

"Yes, I could see them."

"What were they doing, were they holding hands, were they kissing, were they kissing perhaps?"

"They were talking. They were sitting beside each other and they were talking."

"Will they see each other again?"

"Doesn't Your Lordship want them to?"

I looked at my hands, pale, quite beautiful, the blue veins, the almond-shaped nails, Benvenuto Cellini's ring. Why was not all of me like those hands, like that ring?

"We have to get this business over with and soon. I'll arrange to spend the day after the wedding in Poggio a Caiano. I'll ask Lorenzino to take me. I'll spend the whole afternoon there. You know what to do."

Hesitating, I left. My temples were pounding, my mouth was dry.

On June 13, in San Lorenzo, Margaret and the duke listened to their wedding mass. They left surrounded by flowers. The marriage of Othello and Desdemona must have been like that: he dark, taciturn, lighted by hidden fevers; she fragile, modest, luminous. The voice of Cardinal Antonio Pucci, who sang the office, resounded off the Donatello bronzes so clear, so robust that it was as if a curved musical bridge extended over both of them. We left for the palace of the Medicis behind the newlyweds, Cardinals Pucci and Cibo, the dowager Vicereine of Naples, and Pier Luigi Farnese. On going up to the salon where the reception was held, I passed by the Benozzo Gozzoli chapel and peeped inside. There was a woman kneeling at the altar. When she turned toward me, I recognized in the flickering of the candles that revealed all around, like a slow round of Oriental princes, the procession of the Magi, a masklike face of a woman in her fifties, strong, with broad hips, with the fuzz on her face giving her a harshly masculine touch. It was Nencia. She had been Adriana dalla Roza's companion, the one who ten years before in that same place had possessed me and had abandoned me, undone, on the tiles of serpentine and porphyry, until the pity of Ignacio de Zúñiga had rescued me just when I thought I was unprotected forever, dead perhaps. I jumped back as if I had seen the Devil. Ancient images burst forth all over while, mingling with the noisy procession, shaken by the rustle of the clothing and the pealing of the laughter, I escaped toward the banquet to which violins and flutes were playing a prelude.

After the meal a comedy by Lorenzino de' Medici was presented, the *Aridosia*, but I did not pay much attention to the lusty dialogue that made the ladies blush and brought guffaws from the gentlemen, especially the loud and insolent Pier Luigi. I was thinking about quite different things. I was not in a mood to take part in that ingenious

ORAZIO ORSINI · 443

game, to enjoy that story of avarice and deceit in the plot in which, whenever I paid attention, I could make out for a few instants the obvious traces of Terence and Plautus, and which took place in a setting designed by Bastiano da Sangallo, called the "Aristotle of Perspective," with an imitation marble triumphal arch covered with statues and relief work. I was thinking about myself, isolated among the courtiers. I felt alone, as when I was a very young child and crouched in a corner of our glacial Roman palace under the gloomy tapestries to sob and bite my nails, or as when I was waiting for the dazzling Abul, who was to have killed my page Beppo during the middle of a hunt. Alas, if only I had had Abul by my side, if I had had Ippolito de' Medici, my sense of security would have been quite different, but the ones I had were Giulia Farnese and Violante Orsini! My cousin, annoyed at my distance, moved her body against mine, but I avoided the contact. Nor did I want to touch my wife, whose bright eyes proclaimed her happiness, and who, without doubt, the same as I, was not paying any attention to the wordy comedy and was letting her imagination wander toward the intimate scenes that would follow it. I was alone, completely alone. I was once more, with my sins, with my torments, with my disloyal and repulsive machinations, the little lonely hunchback of the Roman palace who was hiding from Girolamo and Maerbale. What bonds could have linked me to the false joy of the guests?

Lorenzino had gone to extremes in the audacity of his allusions. It was commented afterward that in the first and fourth acts, the scoundrel—whom Alessandro de' Medici's group had jokingly nicknamed the "Philosopher"—had overstressed the theme of nightly visits to convents, for everybody knew that the duke practiced such lewd burglaries in the convents of Saint Dominic and Saint Mary of the Angels, the retreats of noble maidens and that in the third act there had slipped out a malevolent allusion to Charles V, the father of the bride and the political master of his dashing son-in-law; but the music, which Lorenzino himself had chosen with great refinement, cloaked with the clavichord and the organ what was later interpreted as a sharp criticism of the ducal regime, disguised with carnival jokes, and even as an incisive way to stir up the great citizens of Florence against the disdainful and arbitrary behavior of their lord. Lorenzino, whose influence was declining according to many people, because the duke had received several messages from his wary relatives which warned him that his favorite cousin was plotting to assassinate him, was merrily going about the rows of spectators. I stopped him when he leaned on my chair for a moment and I suggested that he take me to Poggio a Caiano the next day, to which he immediately agreed, to leave with a leap for the duke's chair, fling himself down like a lightfooted jester, and kiss the hand of Margaret, who had not smiled a single time during the play. The attitude of the duchess was the object of various interpretations. Some thought that she did not understand the subtleties of the Tuscan tongue sufficiently to grasp the sparks, but several argued that neither her character, inherited from the Caesar, nor the strict upbringing that she had received permitted her to tolerate such boldness. The dowager Vicereine of Naples, fanning herself, shared the severity of her conduct, based on the rigid etiquette of the House of Austria, while the duke, the same as his closest circle, was laughing pleasantly at the brazen impudence of the *Aridosia*, and as a reward for his work, Alessandro gave Lorenzino a fine edition of Plautus, perhaps to indicate to him slyly that everyone was aware of the thefts that he owed to him.

In the afternoon, on the Piazza San Lorenzo, we witnessed a mock assault on a castle. Maerbale took part in the pantomime, with a fine suit of armor that belonged to the Duke of Florence and which had an open-winged dragon on the helmet. It seemed to me that when he galloped like an Ariosto paladin beside Pier Luigi Farnese, accompanied by the shouts of the applauding ladies, he was not going out to assault that scaffolding of poor painted and bedecked wood but the venerable bastions of Bomarzo, whose walls were burning in the red warmth of the sunset. On his steel arm he was wearing, as a touch of medieval Platonic knighthood, a veil, a blue favor. Silvio told me that Giulia had given it to him.


I had never returned to Poggio a Caiano since my childhood. I went back there guided by Lorenzino and accompanied by Fabio Farnese and Giambattista. But just as I could not enjoy the irony of the *Aridosia*, I could not enjoy the charms of the famous villa. In vain Lorenzaccio tried to amuse me by quoting verses in which the Magnificent used mythology to describe the construction of the palace enchanted by the Ombrone and the murmur of its waves. It was useless as he pointed out to me, lighting up with pride, the frescoes that showed the splendor of Cosimo the Elder and his son. Nothing could hold me; nothing could calm my agitation. We looked at the paintings by Andrea del Sarto and his disciple Franciabigio, and other images followed them in my mind. It was as if all of those likenesses had been painted by Sebastiano del Piombo, the one who did Giulia's portrait, for her face, her deep eyes with their mysterious color, and her firm oval face, well modeled like those of ancient statues, were emerging from the secret of the tones as from thick aquatic depths and supplanting the features of the bankers become princes. Lorenzino noticed my preoccupation and stopped in the middle of a line from the *Ambra*, which he was declaiming with feeling.

"What's the matter, Pier Francesco?"

"Nothing. Let's keep going."

Fabio took my hand. I felt the bejeweled pressure of his fingers. He was talking with the little Medici about the festivities of the day before. Every time that Lorenzaccio mentioned the duke, he managed to make his praise sound like a joke and his jokes sound like praise. Could my brother-in-law have suspected what was being done or was about to be done to his sister at my instigation? Who would have suspected?

Lorenzino mentioned my hump. It was not exactly *my* hump, but *a* hump, but it was enough to suggest it in front of me for me to apply the insinuation at once. My restless friend, when we were boys, had managed to do it at other times without arousing my irritation. He was the only one—he had the immunity of a jester—who dared invade such dangerous territory. He was referring to Diane de Poitiers, the mistress of the Dauphin of France, the rival of his kinswoman Catherine de' Medici.

"Do you know that she's twenty years older than Valois?"

I had heard about it. That strange domination of the mature woman, the widow of the great Seneschal of Normandy, over the adolescent future king, timid, melancholy, so different from his haughty father, was rousing disturbing commentaries at the time. Alessandro himself had explained in a roundabout way that Diane de Poitiers and Catherine de' Medici had a good deal of common blood in their veins, for they were the daughters of cousins of the branch of the Tour d'Auvergne. Probably, in spite of the humiliation that the victory of the triumphant favorite meant for the *duchessina*, Alessandro was enjoying the idea of that link that showed how the foliage of the Medici tree was growing over the great houses of Europe.

"What you probably didn't know was that her husband was hunchbacked."

I must have blushed slightly, but I continued the conversation with simulated ease.

"What husband?"

"Madame Diane de Poitiers's."

I had not known. No one would have dared bring up that anomaly in my presence.

"He was a hunchback and a great warrior. Much older than Diane too. And they say that the marriage was exemplary until the beautiful lady was widowed and fell in love with Henry of France, stimulated perhaps by his own father, King Francis. The king hoped that she would arouse his successor. He can't bear for his courtiers not to have mistresses, and much less the heir to the throne, of course."

"Did they have any children? Her husband and she, did they have any children?"

"Yes, why not?"

He was observing me curiously. Why not, after all? I was the only hunchback in the world incapable of having children.

Centuries after that conversation, a short time before the last war, I was going through the cathedral of Rouen and I stopped in front of the famous tomb of that Louis de Brézé, married to Diane, the seductress. Two statues showed him amid the elegance of the decoration. One had him half naked, lying down, with Diane herself on her knees piously praying for his soul; the other, standing, proclaimed the equestrian glory of the soldier. In neither of them was there the slightest trace of his hump. Like Mantegna when he painted the Gonzagas; like Lorenzo Lotto when he painted my image of a hallucinated poet, the artist—perhaps Jean Goujon—had suppressed the deformity. Artists are gods in their fashion; they correct God's mistakes, His tricks. Why project the shadow of a hump into the future?

But evidently as he walked through the castles of Francis I or fought in Italy, Louis de Brézé had not suffered from his hump either. His wife was the most beautiful woman of her time, just as the most beautiful one of mine, Giulia Gonzaga, was the wife of the damaged Colonna, *claudus ac mancus*. Even though she betrayed his memory later, Diane de Poitiers honored it when he was alive. On the other hand I... on the other hand I... I myself was prostituting my noble Giulia Farnese as I chatted with Lorenzaccio about French things and wandered with apparent indolence through the terraces of Poggio a Caiano, going out to look over the smiling countryside toward Florence, toward Prato, toward Pistoia, over hills, fields, and gardens.

My companions let the embarrassing theme drop. They were chatting confusedly about the wedding of Catherine de' Medici, about the cloak with the fleurs-de-lis that the King of France had worn there, about the enormous pearls that had flowed down over our countrywoman. They could not guess that those same pearls would later belong to Mary Stuart and that Elizabeth of England would steal them from her unfortunate rival when she chopped off her head. Those details, if they had known them, would have given some importance to the insipid conversation, but the chat was limited by chronology. Furthermore, I was not in any mood for palace gossip. A terrible anguish was filling my chest. I wanted to go back to Florence, to go back as soon as possible. Without giving any explanations I ran down the steps and jumped onto my horse. I galloped the four long leagues that separated Poggio from the ducal city as if I were being carried by the wings of the wind. Behind, Fabio and Giambattista were spurring their mounts. Lorenzino stayed behind at the portico of the family villa, under the roof decorated by the della Robbias. He was laughing, jumping like a puppet and making wild gestures and expressions at us, as if we were three madmen.

At the door of the palace of the Popolani Medicis, Silvio was waiting for me. From his expression, from the quick wink with which he pointed upstairs to me in the direction of our rooms—for in front of my companions, and especially in front of Giulia's brother, he could not refer to our base plot—I understood that everything was already over. I ran toward my wife's rooms. I pushed open the doors with a brutal shove and slammed them in the faces of my escort, turning the heavy key.

Giulia was still half dressed. She looked at me, startled, for our relations, as I have said, were characterized by a modesty imbued with ceremonious courtesy, and although never at any time—-not then, nor afterward, nor ever—did I allude to what had happened, she understood that I was aware of her betrayal. What she could not have imagined was that I had provoked it in my madness. She got up from the mussed bed and her thin legs shone like swords for a second. Then she drew back, frightened, barefoot, covering her breasts with her hands, toward the back of the shadowy room. She was no doubt afraid that I was going to kill her. But with a push, I laid her down again on the bedstead where my brother had possessed her and there, ferociously, without taking off my dagger and sword, which became entangled in her legs and scratched her about the waist, making her bleed, I attained what I had not attained until then. She had not been mine when she should have been, as a logical consequence to our wedding, but that afternoon she was out of spite. Rancor and jealousy had given me strength, erasing my bonds, my worries, and my hesitant weakness, and had succeeded in what the initial discovery of her hidden beauty, facilitated by blessings and contracts, had not. I did not kill her when I arose, sated at last, desperate, from the covers where the smell of Maerbale was floating, for in spite of my wild alienation, I preserved enough lucidity—lucidity and calculation never left me—to remember the risk that the son of Cecilia Colonna implied for Bomarzo and that he had been the origin of that disaster, of that absurd episode.

Destiny, which never missed a chance to mock me, had once more played a nasty trick on me with serious consequences. In order for me to give Bomarzo an heir, it had been necessary for Maerbale to cross my path and possess my wife before me. And I had to arrange it all with the complicity of a servant. It could have been said that my irresolute sexuality, bound up by strange complexes, had required that atrocious mix-up, that whiplash, in order to show itself. Without the terrible stimulus of rage and disloyalty, it was most probable that Giulia would not have allowed me, and my life would have burned itself out at her side as I watched her decline and her lushness wither. Now we would have a child, of that I was sure, but I would not know whether it was my son or the son of Maerbale.

That thing—the worst thing of all, which would torture my pride most, my dynastic sense, my urge to dominate, my need to find immovable supports to help me continue my wanderings through the morass of life with its dark swamps—would be my punishment for what I had done and what I was getting ready to do, driven inexorably by fate. And the monstrousness of the case, if it is considered carefully, as I look at it now and as I will always look at it, because then, blinded by passion and the prisoner of my miserable structure, I lacked the necessary calm and perspicacity to see it, was that I was the only one to blame for everything that happened to me. My existence could have developed placidly, normally, if the conflicts of my character had not intervened. I was a duke; I was rich; my wife was beautiful and modest; I came from one of the most illustrious houses in Italy, from the one I would have chosen if I could have picked among our ancient crowns; Charles V himself had knighted me; I had inherited an estate and some admirable rocks that were dense with ancient suggestions; many people envied my position, my wealth, my influence, my entree into the pontifical court, my position of equal with important people; I enjoyed art as a refined person should; I wrote poetry that was worthy of being placed alongside that of the poets who surrounded me; I had a handsome face, aristocratic, eyes that reflect majesty and irony and that held the troubled eyes of other people; my sensual capacity, the same as that of so many outstanding people of my time, placed me above prejudice; God, with His miracles and His horrors, did not worry me as yet; I was worshiped by my grandmother, the most extraordinary being that I had ever known; opportune fate had removed those who hindered my progress; if I had been born misshapen, others, a good many others, had been born like that and had overcome it with personalities less prestigious than mine; when I came into the world something magical, something fabulous had been predicted for me which raised me above my contemporaries and which made of me an individual apart, impregnated with vigilant mystery. And yet I amputated and destroyed my life. Of course, in order for me to have acted differently, I would have had to have been essentially different. I would not have been myself.

Maerbale left with Cecilia for Fondi to visit Giulia Gonzaga, their relative, and Silvio left after them. Maerbale took leave of me as if nothing had happened. His cynicism did away with any scruples I might have had left. I avoided any contact between my wife and him by sending her to our castle quickly and suddenly under the pretext that I had heard that my grandmother was gravely ill. I claimed, so as not to go with her, that I had to stay in Florence a few days more to finish some business concerning my Collepiccolo estate with Alessandro de' Medici, but I was really delaying to wait for news from Silvio da Narni.

My secretary was not long in returning. He had run into Maerbale sooner than expected, which was fortunate for the success of our plans, because Maerbale, doubtlessly anxious to see my wife, had changed his direction from Fondi to Bomarzo, running the risk of facing me there. That showed me how much he despised me and how much he wanted Giulia, and it gave me the strength to hear a story whose tragic outcome was obvious without any weakness. His disdain and his desires, the same as his merit, his pride, his elegance, and the love that perhaps he had inspired were of no use to him any more. They were of less use then Paracelsus's lizard, a prisoner in its cage and in the portrait by Lorenzo Lotto, or my grandmother's jester's woman, the prisoner of her own madness.

Silvio told me that my brother had not shown any suspicion when he caught up to him on the way. It was even logical that he should be overtaken, for Silvio told him that I had sent him on to Bomarzo ahead of me. Maerbale replied that he was going there too on some business that only concerned him, and from his expression the false accomplice understood what it was about. What else would he be going for, since he never visited Bomarzo after it had become mine? They stopped together at an inn to have a pitcher of wine and Silvio took advantage of a careless moment of the young condottiere to pour the poison I had given him into his glass. It was all done cleanly and quickly, with more discretion than in the case of Cardinal Ippolito de' Medici. Maerbale died immediately, and, according to Silvio, without any suffering. His escort was rather small and none of those who made it up dared hold the astrologer from Narni, a mysterious and dangerous man, if they possibly suspected him. Silvio himself, whose intimacy with the younger Orsini was known to those servants, for lately he had been seen coming and going to and from his room in the Florentine palace where we were lodged, had taken care to tell them that Maerbale had confided to him that because of his wound in Venice he was suffering from a terrible and mysterious illness that was poisoning his blood and which could put an end to the captain at any moment. They believed him or they did not believe him (I presume that they did not), but deprived of their master, they did not think and they let him leave, for he said with great urgency that he had to inform me at once of a misfortune that was so close to me. Fate had it that among them there was no particularly loyal servant; no companion at arms. They were a few Venetian pages and a squire from Bologna, more concerned about their pay than to show a nonexistent loyalty. They calculated wisely that what was least beneficial for them was to make enemies with someone so close to the Duke of Bomarzo, the only brother of their master, the one on whom their futures would depend, because they must have been aware that they could expect little from the inexperienced Cecilia Colonna. They wrapped the body up and put it in a litter. That was how they continued their trip to Bomarzo, with Cecilia, astonished and despairing, in her sedan chair, pouring out her grief to the deserted highway. Perhaps she would lose her child and that would be all the better. When I reached the castle I would decide what was to be done and how responsibilities would be limited. They thought that I would come right away, but I postponed my return. I did not dare confront the suffering of Giulia, Cecilia, and my grandmother. Cecilia would not attribute a crime whose roots she did not know to me, but Giulia had come rather close to them, and Diana Orsini would soon sense them.

I listened carefully to Silvio without making any comments and then I sent him away. I needed to shut myself up to meditate, although as yet I did not feel any remorse. I had succeeded in what I wanted with perfect comfort, and it would have been hypocritical and useless to deplore it. Now I felt empty, as if I had suddenly cut out all of the bitterness that I had been carrying inside and had not replaced it with anything, neither joy, nor affliction. Maerbale had been wiped out, he had been removed forever from my path, which he had crossed ceaselessly, displaying to me the splendor of his advantages, and that was how it had to be, inevitable, so that I could continue on forward. Days later, when Messer Pandolfo appeared in Florence with teary eyes to tell me that my grandmother had been unable to withstand the shock at her great age and had met death in her room between her white cats, and the pretext that I had invented to get Giulia away from Florence had turned into a dreadful reality—for that is how life avenges itself and mocks our poor machinations—I realized that my last links to the past had been broken. Then I wept at last. I wept for my grandmother, for my father, for Girolamo, for Maerbale, for myself, especially for myself, for the survivor, who was like a dry leaf in the midst of the hurricane, just like one of those yellow leaves that the autumn wind was blowing against the panes of my window. Everyone knew of the feeling that bound me to Diana Orsini, proclaimed in her letters; and my callers, headed by Duke Alessandro, confused my grief with the one I should have felt for Maerbale's death. They surrounded me, consoled me, spoke to me about God, life, resignation, the urgency to pull myself together because of the important duties which awaited me. I let them speak. I embraced Lorenzaccio, Cardinal Pucci, Margaret of Austria, my Orsini cousins without listening to them. The emptiness which filled my insides had become even greater, emerging from within me and enveloping me as if I were inside some immense isolating bell where silence reigned. Until a few dim figures slowly began to be sketched in that isolated immobility. The white silhouette of my grandmother, straight, waiting, at the time when Girolamo was looking at us in horror from the waters of the Tiber as they tugged at his bloody jerkin; that of Girolamo standing by me naked, pushing a pin as long as a dagger through my ear; that of my father, rejecting me, exiling me to Florence without heeding my babbling; that of Maerbale, wrapped around my wife, kissing her, biting her, were all confused in my memory. They passed back and forth like shadows over the sullen view of Bomarzo. But in that succession of images I also saw my grandmother leaning over me, her blue eyes radiant, as on the day she had given me the Etruscan armor, and I saw her consoling me and running her fingers through my fine hair several times, several times, as if I were one of the cats purring on the warmth of her spread. I saw my father stroking my cheek as he told me the story of Michelangelo's David. I saw Girolamo and Maerbale on horseback, quivering with grace and elegance as they returned from a hunt in the midst of torches and the black boars they had killed. And I wept again for all of us.

I returned to Bomarzo after my grandmother and Maerbale had been buried under the slabs in the church. Now I was the only one, the last one, I, the weakest one, the fearful one, the miserable one. I and the creature throbbing inside Cecilia Colonna and the one that had perhaps crept into Giulia Farnese. Now I was alone with Bomarzo; alone with that mass of stone, harsh and adorable, which had cost me so much to conquer for myself.

My grandmother's cats were mewing in the corridors, abandoned, and autumn was saturating the afternoons with melancholy. I locked myself in my room and refused to receive anyone. I did not want them near me, least of all Cecilia, Giulia, and Silvio. Leaning out a window I would observe my wife and my brother's wife as they walked in the garden among the withered roses and leafless trees. Cecilia's stomach was struggling beneath her skirt, enormous. I found out that Giulia was also expecting a child. Bomarzo would have a son. Mine? Maerbale's? I had killed Maerbale, for what? What in the world for? What words of relief could have been said at that time by the religion of Ignacio de Zúñiga, the love of Abul, the friendship of Ippolito de' Medici? Who could have clarified for me why and for what reason life bumped along with only one immutable thing, one lasting thing, one firm and certain thing, the rocks there below in the valley as they emerged from the thorny underbrush, and when I would walk among them in the morning, feeling their shapes warmed by the dew, they seemed to quiver, as if they were colossal human beings, as if they were my people who had broken away from me forever and who nonetheless remained there, inseparable from Bomarzo, rooted in the rich mystery of its land?

Cecilia gave birth to a son two months later. He was christened Niccolò in the church where his father lay buried. Maerbale had chosen the name and Cecilia had respected his decision. It was an old and illustrious name in our family: that of the pope who had dreamed of dividing Italy up among his people; that of the friend of Saint Brigid and Boccaccio; that of the warrior who had protected the see of the popes in Rome, for which he had received important privileges from Gregory XI; that of the famous avenger of his father who had ordered his enemy Ranieri quartered with hot irons and his remains thrown into the Tiber; that of the admirable Count of Pitigliano, the one with the glorious tomb in Venice, the master of the astrologer Benedetto; that of my cousin, the fierce one, the one with the Hebrew concubines. Many Orsinis had been named Niccolò; many would be named that. When the chaplain immersed him in the holy water, the small creature began to cry and Giulia, who was already beginning to show her pregnancy, trembled and kissed his hand. Behind them, between Sigismondo and Matteo Orsini, I presided over the ceremony.

The Duke of Mugnano was also there and he gave me a fragment of a most beautiful marble statue, larger than a normal human body, the torso of a Minotaur, which possibly had been part of a lost group where the statue of Theseus had disappeared and which according to him was a Roman copy of a Greek original from the fifth or sixth century B.C. With that sumptuous gift he calculated that he would be forgiven for the kidnapping of Porzia. The athletic torso, without arms or legs and with the sex organs miraculously saved, was topped by a huge head, the horror of which did not come so much from its bestial features and curly hair covering it between the pointed and broken ears, as from the barbarous mutilation that it had suffered on the face, of which a good part was missing. The contrast between the fascinating voluptuousness of that harmonious body, elegantly supported by one of its nonexistent legs, and that monstrous head horrified me at first, like all anomalous things, and I even began to suspect that my cousin from Mugnano had brought it to me as a joke, perhaps as a cruel allusion to the deformity of my body, but my relations with the neighboring lord were so good and the archeological importance of the piece was such—everyone can see it today in the Pius Clementinus Museum in the Vatican, in the Hall of Animals, after the Muses—that I put aside that outlandish idea and ordered them to set up the monster in the center of the gallery, where it was surrounded by the busts of the Roman emperors from the collection of the patriarchs of Aquileia. There it remained as long as I lived at Bomarzo, as a disconcerting symbol: the fearsome, beautiful, and repulsive myth, and around it the guard of young and old rulers who were watching it with their heads raised or lowered, sometimes overcome by indolence, other times goaded by ambition, sometimes meditative, and who were rendering it homage from the leprosy and pride of their marble as if to a centuries-old secret god.

The unhealthy physiological consequences of a difficult birth, worsened by the upset that came to poor Cecilia from the death of Maerbale, whom she had married purely out of love, were soon observed. Her weakness prevented her from sharing in the work of the ladies which was supervised by my wife, but sitting among them across from the fireplace in the large room where the garland with the initials of Giulia Farnese and mine intertwined, curled about the cornices, she would do some needlework on the clothing for the infant wardrobe that they were preparing together. Until it was noted that her eyesight was failing and she had to give up that minimal participation. Total night finally fell over her eyes. We thought that it was something passing. We consulted the stars, the herbalist in the village, and we brought physicians from Rome, but it was in vain. Cecilia Colonna was blind. And the remorse that I had not felt when Silvio told me of Maerbale's murder grew rapidly and dominated me, overwhelming me with the tortures of the innocent girl. Sometimes when I turned a corner in the garden behind a trimmed hedge I would come upon her and Giulia. Pain had made my sister-in-law's face thin, giving her an enigmatic spiritual beauty which she had lacked before and which accentuated the motionless peace of her eyes. Those deserted eyes would alight on me for a long time, like those of a statue, and next to her, intense, rich with luminous life, those of Giulia would also fasten their mute accusation onto me.

Little Niccolò, rocked by his nurse, was whimpering nearby and I left quickly in order to avoid the scene. Neither she nor Giulia ever mentioned the possibility that there might have been some link between Maerbale's unforeseen death and my fateful intervention. A strange solidarity had grown up between the two since my brother's passing. Both of them had loved him; both of them had lost with him a great deal of their reason for living. What remained for Cecilia in the terrible darkness about her was the consolation of her son, her Niccolò Orsini. Giulia would shortly have a similar relief when the one so prominent in her belly would be born, the one who perhaps would be Maerbale's son. Maerbale was still victorious after his death.

The possession of my wife, attained in such an untimely way, drove me to repeat the experience often. I gave myself illusions by thinking that in that way I was guaranteeing my domination; that every time I was making her more mine; but on every occasion—and she would surrender silently, distantly—when I would leave her, apparently satisfied, I could see that I was not her real master, that either during the culminating moments another form, that of my invisible brother, was being substituted for mine, taking Giulia over, or that she was letting me do what I wished, indifferent, without sharing my excitement. And that circumstance, which made me burn with rage, paradoxically did me much good, for it provided me with one more reason to hate Maerbale and his memory and to give myself the assurance that when I did away with him I had acted in my own defense, as I should have.

Between the spectral Cecilia, who felt her way along the walls with my grandmother's gold cane, and Giulia, whose tight-lipped disdain lashed me with more virulence than the vilest of insults, time passed in a hell which hid its flames inside of me. If I went out at night to wander through the garden, through the woods, with Silvio or Giambattista, the shadowy branches, the fountains, the shapeless rocks would twist themselves and become Maerbale, Girolamo, Beppo. Then I would retreat to my room, where Diana Orsini's unsheltered cats had also taken refuge, and lying on the bed with them beside me, I would imagine that my grandmother was there, just when I was a boy, ready to console me and find some explanation for my misconduct. But I had killed my grandmother just as I had killed Maerbale, and there was no more possibility of protection left for me. Then I fondled the compensatory idea that a sacrifice, a penance, would help me recover my balance, and since my lustful encounters with Giulia meant a suffering and a humiliation for me since their fleeting fire had gone out, I imposed upon myself as punishment the obligation of avoiding all carnal contact that was not with that cold and hostile body. Nevertheless, one night as I was coming down from her room after having enjoyed her, with my sensual hunger still intact, vexed, vilified, I recall that as I went through the gallery with the imperial busts, illuminated by a single flame of dying light, something strange happened. The dancing of the candle was fleetingly revealing the avid faces of the emperors, whose anxiety was mysteriously similar to mine and was evident in the trembling of their lips, the dark rings under their eyes, the greed of their tense profiles, a passion that was bringing life to the stone that had been gnawed at by the centuries and which was animated by the spell cast by the fluttering light. They were all looking at the torso of the Minotaur. I remember that I went over to the statue, that the flame was licking it from time to time, gilding it with a shade of honey, warm and morbid, and that a strange force impelled me to put my arms around that beautiful body which was standing like an altar on its base in the center of the castle; that I leaned by cheek against its muscular stomach, and that, moving my lips up over the long chest, I kissed the mutilated, disfigured, and horrible face.

I had not dreamed for a long time, but that night I dreamed that the Minotaur was Duke of Bomarzo. I myself crowned him with the half crown and dressed him in his ceremonial clothing. Messer Pandolfo gave a long oration in Latin and the Roman emperors rendered him homage. Blood was flowing from the broken marble face of the beast. The scene had the air of an orgy and the rites of some arcane and lewd cult. It was an angry image, worthy of a feverish brain and a period in which ancient works that were recently discovered could assume incomparable importance, and in which priapic themes obsessed princes who were confused by their crimes, by mythology, and by a concupiscence that required delirious incentives.

On the following day I wrote to Violante Orsini and Fabio Farnese, suggesting that they come visit me in Bomarzo and bring some merry company with them. I was so brazen as to tell them that after Maerbale's death I needed to distract myself from the sadness of his memory. In the meantime I went with Giambattista to Mugnano to visit my cousin the duke and his sister Porzia. We returned sweaty, drunken, shouting along the road that was crossed by the moonlit spark of hares. Giambattista was wearing a gold belt with four amethysts which Porzia had given him in the name of her lover. I threw myself onto my bed panting, shaking its posts, and I called for Giulia several times until I fell asleep.

Violante was a good woman in her disorderly way. Her sensuality was more powerful than anything else and it pulled her along into all kinds of frantic episodes, but she was never a hypocrite. From the affair she had with the Duke of Urbino she had a set of topazes and pearls which had enchanted her with their brightness, and from the one she had with the halberdier she had a scar on her throat which she treasured as another jewel. She dismounted at Bomarzo anxious to give me some fun and to have some herself. She had left her husband behind in Rome and Fabio was serving her—not as a real gallant, for obvious reasons—as a cordial companion, always ready to follow her whim. With them they brought several ladies of a life that was scarcely recommendable, pretty, sensuous, among them a cousin of Cecilia's, an eighteen-year-old widow who followed no other direction but that of her changeable pleasure, and a half-dozen intellectuals, some of them rather serious, but like all people who aspired to elegance, ready to follow the path of the nobility so that they would not be considered uncouth or out of style, and always ready, therefore, to catch a crumb in the air, because, after all, one did have to live. That was the nucleus of my future court at Bomarzo, which has inspired comments and a certain amount of literature. Among them in the background there was a prelate, Cristoforo Madruzzo, from a noble family and who was bishop of Trent two years later and some years afterward a cardinal. He was a deep admirer of Giulia Gonzaga. Later on he bought the castles of Galese and Soriano, on the Cimino near Bomarzo, from Duke Caraffa, where he beautified the spring of Papacqua, and that proximity made our relationship very close. Also there was Francesco Molza, the admirable humanist who had been part of the following of Cardinal Ippolito de' Medici and was beside him when my friend died in Itri. The dissolute life that he led in Rome had given him as much fame as his Petrarchan *Canzoniere*, or the stanzas that he had dedicated to the portrait of Giulia Gonzaga by Sebastiano del Piombo, or those of the *Ninfa Tiberina*, which exalted the grace of Faustina Mancini. He had left his wife and children in Modena two years before and had forgotten them completely. He suffered from the same illness as Pier Luigi Farnese, the sickness that Paracelsus had saved me from in Venice, and its inroads were beginning to devastate his thin face, but, the same as Madruzzo, he was grave and solemn in spite of the lordly delicacy of his features and his slightly ironical mouth, which Titian preserved for eternity. Molza was inclined toward mockery, epigrams, and amorous deviations. There was Annibale Caro, the poet, secretary to Monsignor Gaddi, which position he would later hold with Pier Luigi, a numismaticist, archeologist, concerned about stylistic rhetoric, cold and polished. There was Francesco Sansovino, who was only sixteen years old and came from Venice with Claudio Tolomei, the defender of the Tuscan language. There was Betussi, superficial, adulatory, who was already at work on the dialogues of the *Raverta*, and who expressed in verse the praises of my wife, pointing out, as was to be expected, her "angelic and celestial wit" and the beauty that she had received "as a gift of heaven," and who sang (because one day I mentioned to him in passing that truncated idyll of adolescence) of the distant Adriana dalla Roza with the same enthusiasm with which his colleague, the small Sansovino, celebrated me in a biography of praise that would be translated into financial advantages for those who cultivated me. Vicino Orsini appears in the second book of his illustrious men, where he strangely emphasizes my "regal life and appearance" and my no less strange condition as "a lover of arms and letters." They established themselves in the castle and made it merry with their whims, their malice, their witty remarks. Some of them, of course, could be accused of being unscrupulous, the merchants of rhymed praise, envious, sick people with their vanity, but they all outdid one another, with the single exception of Madruzzo, with an outpouring of sparks of multicolored wit which obliged us—the noblemen, much slower, duller, and ankylose when it came to the gymnastics of ingenuity—to keep a constant vigil in order to guide ourselves and not get lost in a labyrinth of puns, allusions, sophistry, and symbols, quotations in Greek and Latin, mentions of Plato, Dante, or León Hebreo, the meanderings of which sparkled with a clash of wits when our guests spoke of love or intrigues or argued about the ambiguities of language. Those continuous acrobatics irritated me a little, because they were above me and my knowledge, in spite of the fact that my new friends at every instant would bring up my lyrical attempts, comparing them to those of Petrarch, but underneath it all that atmosphere of intelligence and respect pleased me and it seemed to me that with the presence of those learned and argumentative people I was paying Bomarzo a tribute that up until then it had not received, as now, for the first time in its history, the ones who were chatting in its salons around the glowing fireplaces or going out, chilly, wrapped in furs which I often had to lend them, to sniff the quiet winter landscape that the snow was whitening and the rain lashing, were not hunters and soldiers, vehement, brutal, who beat with their daggers on the tables to call the servants and rocked the castle with their foul remarks, restless only to tear apart the boar that was roasting on the fire or to find out whether it was better for them to fight under the orders of Milan, Naples, or the pope, but a few fragile and timid men who were striving to compose subtle and complex phrases full of malignant observations and who showed one another papers written with unequal lines, black with crossed-out words and erasures, just as the warriors before them in the days of my father and my grandfather had violently rolled up their sleeves and opened their trousers to show the scars and the marks of swords.

 I listened to them and did very little talking. My decorative prejudice was charmed by merely witnessing their creations. They formed harmonious groups with the frivolous women, with Fabio and my Orsini cousins, having as a chromatic background the paintings by Raphael, Titian, Lotto, Bassano, and Dossi, or turning about during their walks—they did a lot of walking, chatting ceaselessly, when the rigors of the weather would not permit them to leave the castle—to stop by the Minotaur, later to stroll languidly before the busts of the emperors, who contemplated them in turn with disdainful insolence, up to the Etruscan armor, and then to go down between the tapestries to the trophy rooms. We were chatting like that one afternoon when my debtor from Mugnano suddenly appeared. From the intensity of his expression I gathered that he was bearing important news, and I was afraid that Silvio or I had been connected to Maerbale's death, but I immediately rejected that anxiety, because it was a fact that no one—neither the pope nor Cecilia Colonna—was interested in accusing me of that death, but, rather, it was better for them to preserve the friendship of the powerful survivor than to worry about the fruitless dead man. It was indeed a question of death and crime, even though I had nothing to do with them. Lorenzino de' Medici had assassinated Duke Alessandro of Florence. The Renaissance was once more asserting its monotonous obsession which required that none of its important people should die a natural death. We were thunderstruck. Although we had often heard it whispered that Lorenzaccio was a threat to the duke and that he would end up stabbing him, for he had never ceased considering himself alongside the bastard as the legitimate heir of the great Medicis, the character of the little "philosopher" and his constant clowning seemed to exclude the decision and strength that a crime needs. I, who had ordered my brother killed, knew quite well what that meant. I knew the amount of fire that one must carry in his veins to take such a step. Lorenzaccio, the tireless inventor of the duke's pleasures, the organizer of his vices, and the accomplice in his felonies, lacked at first sight the vital impulse which moves such a forceful determination. But immediately, all of us, as happens in such cases, began to search in our memories for some direct trace that would link the author of the *Aridosia* to that new image and in a flash and little by little, as our voices rose in pitch, it was as if one by one we had foreseen it.

Violante Orsini remembered precisely the performance of *Aridosia* which we had attended together during the duke's wedding.

"We had to listen to such terrible things and I'm nobody's modest maiden. But worse than that indecent outpouring was a feeling that behind all those words there was something hidden...something mysterious...some allusion...some incitement..."

"Yes," Cristoforo Madruzzo answered, leaning a hand that emerged from his short lace cuff on the Minotaur's hip, "it was an obvious incitement. That audience of Florentine lords and ladies must have felt something like a lash on their faces red with shame from the repeated mention of nuns attacked in their convents. That was the way the duke carried on, chasing noble girls right into their cells, and that was the thing that got the Florentines most indignant, and Lorenzino, in his mocking way, was simply underlining it."

"Last year, when the emperor gathered the exiles together in Naples after the Tunisian campaign," Annibale Caro argued, "I can remember everybody's saying that Duke Alessandro had lost his coat of mail, which he never let out of his sight, and they said that Lorenzino had stolen it."

"He's a madman, wild, ready for any wild act," Francesco Molza added in turn. "When he mutilated the statues on the arch of Constantine in Rome, I made a speech in Latin to the Academy. Anyone who rereads it can find in the paragraph that I dedicated to the muse Melpomene my prediction of the tragedies that would come later—this one and the one that hit Cardinal Ippolito..."

Fabio Farnese's juvenile voice arose, spoiled, willful. "Lorenzino is a hero. He's a second Marcus Junius Brutus. He's the one who got rid of the tyrant."

"He's a madman," Molza insisted, "and ambitious. Someone who wants people to talk about him at any price. He can't resign himself to a secondary role among his rich cousins. He beheaded the statues to attract attention to his insignificance, and he murdered Duke Alessandro for the same reason, out of resentment. He's a play actor."

"No!" Fabio shouted, and he was backed up by Orso and Matteo Orsini. "He killed because he was a hero! He's another Brutus. He killed to save his homeland, like an ancient Roman."

The connection between the figure of Lorenzino, emaciated and flighty, and that of the eminent Marcus Brutus, who could not be mentioned except in majestic and theatrical terms, fascinated them all right away. They gave in, jubilant, marveling, to the enthusiasm with which the Renaissance regarded august togas and imitated on rundown stages the sculptured immortality of Caesar-like acts. In the midst of the aquiline busts of the emperors, perching like birds of prey on their porphyry bases, the agitated young men were vibrating romantically and predicting Alfred de Musset's *Lorenzaccio*. Molza, who had a bad character and whose illness had intoxicated his soul, told them not to be idiots, and the boys laid their hands on their daggers. Then, to calm them down, to distract their rage, I too evoked the disconcerting atmosphere that had surrounded the relations between the duke and his cousin.

"There were seers and astrologers," I told them, "who, just like our poet Molza, had predicted that death. We all know that a poet is a kind of seer, someone who can predict. In Florence I once met some Poggio from Perugia who had seen the duke murdered in his dreams. And Giuliano del Carmine, the one who took part in the auguries when they began to build the great prison, made no secret of the fact that Lorenzino would murder the prince."

"And I," the Duke of Mugnano added, "I knew of another prophet called the Greek, a Giandomenico dal Bucine, who said the same thing. And I knew the archbishop of Marseilles, the brother of the Marchioness of Massa, who planned to kill Alessandro with a chest filled with gunpowder because he was pursuing his sister, the wife of Lorenzo Cibo. The Archbishop of Marseilles didn't kill him; he was killed by a wild young fellow I had thought incapable of swatting a fly. May God have pity on the soul of the Duke of Florence. I never liked him. He was an abominable person, infamous."

"He had his own mother killed to hide his low beginnings," Sansovino pointed out, but we shushed him up, because it was not proper for a young boy, bright as he was, to converse on equal terms with his elders, and much less, as a commoner, to express himself with such impudence when speaking of the nobility.

My wife and Cecilia, who never formed part of our group and stayed in their rooms with the aggressive young Niccolò, had appeared in the gallery as soon as they had been told of the arrival of our neighbor from Mugnano and they heard the news.

During a pause of silence, the clear tones of Giulia Farnese resounded. "Lorenzino killed the tyrant. He killed the murderer. The murderer was the tyrant and not he. He did well to kill him like that. Kill those who kill... kill those who kill..." She said those words and looked fixedly at me.

Cecilia Colonna came forward hesitantly, touching the bases of the busts with her gold cane, and she shrieked, "Kill those who kill!"

Fabio and the Orsinis applauded. In the setting of the statues through which she advanced with her hand outstretched, the blind princess brought classical figures back to life.

"Lorenzino has lifted the yoke from Florence!" Sigismondo exclaimed, and I was surprised that Fabio and he, effeminate, trivial, worried only about clothes, adornments, tricks and intrigues with men of any station, should take the matter so to heart. The truth was that they had a number of traits in common with Lorenzino; perhaps they recognized in him the best and the purest part of their psychologies.

During the days that followed nothing else was talked about in Bomarzo. Fresh news came from Tuscany with details of the crime and there was being chiseled in our imaginations the figure of the perfumed duke as he chose his leather gloves—his "love-making" gloves as he described them in contrast to his gauntlets of war—and made ready for the adventure that Lorenzo had promised him with his exemplary aunt Caterina Ginori. We saw him leaving his bodyguard behind, even that Hungarian who never left his side; going into the palace where Maerbale and I had stayed during our last visit to Florence and where Lorenzaccio lived; throwing himself down on the bed with his clothes on to await the timid girl who was ready to give in, and receiving, half asleep, the first stab from his cousin who, transfigured, jumped on him like a demon. We saw him defending himself, using a footstool as a shield; jumping, hesitating, twisting, hiding his body in a mortal dance while his blood spattered the walls around like seeds sown in the air; biting Lorenzino's hand in rage until he had almost cut off the index finger; and doubling over under the implacable thrusts, while the shifty Medici and a paid ruffian named Scoroncocolo, whom I had seen in the Popolani palace, chased him like a cornered animal in the bedroom which was dimly lighted by a single candlestick placed on the floor. They finished him off, covered him with the canopy of the bed, and fled.

"Where did Lorenzino go?"

"To Venice, to Filippo Strozzi, who embraced him in tears when he finally believed him, because he didn't believe him at first, and he promised him that his two sons, the two Strozzi great-grandchildren of the Magnificent, handsome as the sun, would marry his sisters, because he'd given Florence back her freedom."

"They want Sansovino to do a statue of him," Betussi said.

"My father will!" The small Francesco Sansovino grew enthusiastic. "I'm sure of it! He's very busy with the construction of a new library in Venice for Cardinal Bessarione's manuscripts, but I'm sure that he'll drop everything to give his time to something like that: a statue of Lorenzino de' Medici."

"Of our brother Lorenzino!" Sigismondo interrupted.

"And they'll strike a medal in his honor," Fabio Farnese said.

"Jacopo Nardi compared him to David the boy defeating Goliath the giant," Orso Orsini said.

"He's the giant today. He'll be the new Duke of Florence!" Matteo exclaimed.

Molza shook his head skeptically. "No, he won't be. The Florentines won't let themselves be ruled by that madman all chewed up by ambition."

"Madman? A hero! A hero and a saint! The glory of Florence!"

It was seen later that Molza was correct. The exiles, with Strozzi at their head, were defeated in Montemurlo, and Strozzi died in that very jail whose walls he had paid for with his money. He translated Polybius and he could not understand how, now that his homeland had shaken off the yoke, he was in prison. They finally poisoned him. And the duke was not Lorenzino, nor Alessandro's natural son, but his cousin Cosimo de' Medici, the astute one, who reaped the benefits of the "philosopher's" audacity and, as payment for his crown, had him pursued through every city in Europe, transformed into a desperate wanderer who saw daggers and more daggers everywhere, as if the shadow of a giant hedgehog were being projected on the wall.

In moments in which the episode aroused spirits and divided opinions, I could not get the memory of the boy out of my mind, but I did not evoke the memory of the tragic murder of Alessandro, whom I had detested so much in my childhood and who had put on my golden spurs, or the young man with whom I had visited Poggio a Caiano on the afternoon when I surrendered Giulia. I was not thinking about the famous tyrannicide or the resentful person anxious for renown. I thought about a dark child, weak and affectionate, who moved with the unreal elegance of people in dreams; a child who could have taken part with a skip in the procession of the Magi by Benozzo Gozzoli and remain forever among their enchanted highnesses; a child who on the night that Adriana dalla Roza died had taken my hand and held it in his and consoled me when, betrayed and abandoned, I was breaking apart in tears beside her cold body. Surrounded by those ghosts of my adolescence, I wandered about alone, since everyone had retired and Bomarzo was asleep. Here and there lights flickered in the small windows, coming from the writers who were jotting down everything that was happening and were taking advantage of the nocturnal calm to compose their rhetorical verses about Pier Francesco Orsini, the perfect prince.

I stopped in front of the Minotaur, who was, like Lorenzaccio, a symbol; I touched his horrible face, from which he was watching me out of the destruction with his one surviving eye, and I murmured, "Do we know why we kill? Do I know, does Lorenzino knows? Can we be sure that we understand anything about anyone when we penetrate the visible layers on the surface and go inside into the lowest depths? Do we understand ourselves? So many subtle elements, delicate, unknown, are at play when we complete every action—that of killing a man or of loving another—that, if we really want to understand any feeling and any attitude, even the most apparently simple, we should dedicate our whole life to taking it apart, piece by piece, the mystery of the accumulated motives that are barely glimpsed; and even then the main part would most likely escape us."


"Now," Cristoforo Madruzzo, who was very wise, observed one morning, "the family of His Holiness [he did not say "the Farneses" right out because of respect for Giulia] will probably want to absorb Alessandro's brand-new widow, Madame Margaret of Austria, in order to strengthen their alliance with the emperor. It would not surprise me if they married her to one of Pier Luigi's sons."

That was how it was and it showed the political perspicacity of the future cardinal, but I must confess that it bothered me considerably when public references were made with such unrestrained ease about matters close to people allied to our line whose machinations should only have been commented on by the high nobility. In any case, I was pleased with the idea of their taking the daughter of the Caesar away from the Medicis and making her a part of our own family, even though it meant new prestige for the voracious Pier Luigi.

Giulia's son was born, and when he was sprinkled with holy water he was christened Orazio. It is strange that of the two of us, Maerbale and me, it was he, the one least preoccupied with such things, who gave his son a name that carried on the Orsini tradition: Niccolò. I planned to give Giulia's son—even now as I write these pages centuries later I do not dare say *my* son—a name even more ancient in the list of the clan. I had planned to call him Rubeus after certain ancestors of ours in the thirteenth century, who had been named in honor of other ancestors even more ancient, the Ildrebrandis. If I did not do it, it was not so much from the oddness of the name as from the fact that Maerbale had chosen a traditional one. I felt that in that way he was invading my realm, forgetting that my brother was just as much of an Orsini as I, and with a violent reaction, I resolved that Giulia's first-born would bear a name that the family had never used and I chose, at random, that of Orazio. And even then dead Maerbale continued to affect my destiny: through his fault (and through my own fault) I did not know, grotesquely, irritatingly, whether my son was mine or his, and foreseeing my reaction, which had doubtlessly suggested to him the name for his son, he was forcing me, the duke, to go against my deepest feelings and give my heir a name that was almost a patent of illegitimacy, that of an intruder in the line.

Whether or not he was my son, I received him, needless to say, as such, with signs of enthusiasm. The same as they say Giovanni delle Bande Nere did when his son was born—that very same Cosimo who had recently succeeded Alessandro de' Medici in the Duchy of Florence, thanks to Lorenzino's involuntary help—I ordered great fires lighted on the towers and hilltops of my various estates in Latium; and the neighbors, learning from those bonfires that something of importance had happened to me, came to Bomarzo, where, along with the writers who had come from Rome and the Orsini and Farnese relatives, they joined in a great celebration for the little prince.

The little prince fascinated and bothered me. Leaning over his cradle I searched in the vagueness of his features, in his still undetermined skull, on his hairy forehead, in his sightless eyes for something, for a sign that would permit me to affirm my paternity or that of Maerbale, but even if I had been able to discern an element which would show it in the small, imprecise face, the truth was that Maerbale and I looked so much alike that any sign that was more or less characteristic would have been shared by both of us. What was really important was that Orazio Orsini was perfectly normal. He had not brought that accursed deviation of his spine to the left or the deformity of his right leg into the world as I had done. If he had had the misfortune to have shared some of those burdens of mine—as a brother of his did years later, the one I named Maerbale—I do not doubt that I would have considered him mine, all mine. Perhaps I would have preferred for him to have been a hunchback. Perhaps ... no ... no ...

I remember that I did something very strange with him three days after his birth. I lifted him from his cradle and went out of the room in spite of the protests of Giulia, who imagined some sort of atrocity perhaps, since I had mentioned Giovanni delle Bande Nere, who, according to what they said, had them toss his Cosimo into his arms from a balcony. I took him with me to the solitary church, before the tomb of Saint Anselm. According to what had been told by my grandmother, and before her by my great-grandmother and my great-great-grandmother, and so on down from the shadows of time, a girl from Bomarzo had accused a deacon of being the father of the child to whom she had given birth, and her father wanted revenge for the outrage and to kill him. They put the case to Bishop Anselm, and the holy man, turning to the newborn child, asked him in the name of Jesus if the deacon was really the guilty one, to which the child replied to everybody's wonder; "This deacon is pure; he is not stained with any sin."

In the same way, placing him over the relics, I asked Giulia's son, "Tell me who your father is." As one can imagine, the little one summed up his impressions in a furious wail, because miracles are not brought about just like that. I am telling about it (perhaps I should have kept quiet) to show with another detail the touch of innocence that helped make up my character, and to what degree it is possible to be a criminal and an innocent at the same time. It probably had crossed my mind that if asked by the Duke of Bomarzo, Saint Anselm, the bishop of that diocese ten centuries before and therefore the vassal of its ruler, would not deny me the homage of a miracle on such a crucial occasion.

Orazio Orsini grew well. The one he most resembled, fat and jovial, was his grandfather Farnese. I was mistaken to think that his presence would ease my relationship with Giulia. My wife had the exasperating trait of never abandoning a line of behavior once she had set it up, no matter what the circumstances. She had obviously resolved what her attitude toward me was going to be and nobody and nothing would ever get her to change it. It was a mixture of courtesy and coldness with exact proportions that created an atmosphere in which neither a vulgar shout nor bitter irony had any effect and in which a touch of hesitant fear could be seen. With Cecilia Colonna she built a limited world about the two children, Orazio and Niccolò, and she would not leave its walled confines. If we had guests, she would speak with them only as long as was necessary and would leave as soon as she could. If the guest was a person of importance, she would stay with our merry group until late, but I would also notice then that her distance was too broad to be bridged and only when she had retired among the pages who went ahead of her with long candles would the company laugh freely, for until that moment it had been as if we had among us a creature made of marble, hard and beautiful, surrounded, like an enchanted castle, by a zone in which all sound died. And if later on, half drunken and raging to conquer once and for all the proud armor with which she humiliated us all, I went into her room and threw myself onto her bed to make her mine, I ended up by leaving her immediately after the carnal spark which did not burn her came, and I would fall onto my own bed pursued by the vision of her imperturbable light eyes, which, like two cruel lamps, were burning in the darkness of my room, lighting up the violence and revulsion of my dreams.

Silvio da Narni cast Orazio's horoscope. According to it his life would not be long but it would be glorious, exactly the opposite of mine. But I lacked faith in Silvio's alliance with the stars. Once before, when he predicted that Pier Luigi Farnese, the son of the pope, born under the sign of Scorpio, was assured of a peaceful death at the age of seventy, I showed my doubts about the authenticity of the augury. In the case of Pier Luigi reason was on my side, but in Orazio's it was on the side of the stargazer, and, in any case, I would not have thought of expressing my skepticism publicly, for ever since he had carried out my orders so meticulously in the case of Maerbale, I treated Silvio with special care.

Both Orazio and his cousin Niccolò were reared in accordance with their position in the world. As time went on they would be seen busying themselves with swords, crossbows, and daggers; riding with skill; growing enthusiastic over the exploits of their falcons—and in that I saw the strength of the blood of my grandfather, Cardinal Franciotto, master of the hunt for the pope—learning the secrets of chess on an admirable set we had in Bomarzo made by Cleofonte Donati from the bone of a black buffalo and which had been given to me by Isabella d'Este; and studying as little as possible. The scenes of my own childhood were reproduced under the same but ever weaker switch of Messer Pandolfo, but, like Girolamo and Maerbale, from the beginning they both resisted any traffic with Latin literature. They got along very well with each other, Niccolò, a bit older, was tall and thin, while Orazio had more delicate features. Both had inherited our dark eyes, our straight chestnut hair, our beautifully formed hands, but in Niccolò the unpleasant haughtiness of the Colonnas was evident, which his mother did not have, of course, and in Orazio the political slyness of the Farneses, all of which, in both of them, together with that basic pride which characterizes the Orsinis and which, along with the similarity of traits, made them so much alike that they could have been brothers. Inseparable, they made their uproar ring through the castle amid the voices of Giulia and Cecilia, who would get up and try to make them settle down. Cecilia especially would tremble whenever she heard the gallop of their ponies. In the prison of her blindness she imagined infinite disasters. Her classical knowledge—for she, unlike her son and Giulia's, had been nourished since childhood by a cultivation of Greek heroes—peopled her darkness with terrible figures. She would imagine little Niccolò hanging from his horse by one stirrup and dragging along in a cloud of dust like Hector's corpse behind the chariot of Achilles. She would suddenly shout in the silence of the afternoon with the equestrian silhouettes of the boys passing by in the background and she would not calm down until Niccolò ran and sank his sweaty brow into her bosom. The cousins were soon joined by my remaining children, who were being born year after year: Scipione, Marzio, Ottavia, Orinzia, Maerbale, Faustina, and Corradino. I think that I chose quite pleasant-sounding names for them. Someone today might think them very extravagant, but if one remembers that Niccolò III d'Este, who had such a passion for chivalric tales, gave his bastard children the names Gurone, Meliaduse, Isotta, and Rinaldo, he would say that I was quite restrained. I do not wish to get ahead of myself, however, and be carried away by the memory of my children as the galleries and terraces of Bomarzo trembled with their fights and their fun. I must proceed chronologically so as not to leave anything out. A person who can recover his lost past from the fabulous distance of time, as I have done, is like a privileged fisherman who has discovered a wonderful bed of pearl oysters in the secret depths of the deep waters and who then proceeds to show them one by one. My children must wait until later, in their proper place, and the truth is that in those days they did not concern me very much. They concern me much more today. I think about them more today than in those days.

What bothered us at that time was the enormous ambitious greed of Pier Luigi Farnese and the obedience with which the pope satisfied it. While a favorable atmosphere for the future Council of Trent—the *Concilium delectorum cardinalium* which was to map out an autonomous reform of the congregation and the ecclesiastical state—was being prepared in Rome, Pier Luigi was accumulating positions and titles: gonfalonier of the Holy Mother Church, Duke of Castro, Count of Pitigliano—the same as the great Niccolò Orsini, instead of the legitimate heir, and that was unbearable!—and was acquiring with money from the Apostolic Treasury on which he drew without scruples, properties like Nepi, or ones he had received from Charles V, like the handsome Marquisate of Novara, and he had even authorized the coining of his own money in Castro. The dazzling and unworthy career was crowned with the rumors that Paul III, pushed by Cardinal Gambara, was thinking of ceding Parma and Piacenza to his son in order to create a dukedom that would make him the equal of the leading feudal lords of Italy, reviving in that way the aspirations of Leo X, who had dreamed of forming a state on the basis of Piacenza and Parma along with Modena and Reggio, under the jurisdiction of his brother, Giuliano de' Medici. And if that exorbitance was not enough, it was learned that Pier Luigi had begun talks with an aim to obtaining Milan for his son Ottavio, the husband of Margaret of Austria, Alessandro de' Medici's widow—as Cristoforo Madruzzo had predicted in Bomarzo following the assassination of the Duke of Florence—and, consequently, the son-in-law of the emperor, but the feelers were a failure. The intrigues produced at the time by the clumsy affair involved the French, infuriated the emperor, and were conducted with such cloaked hypocrisy that not even the poet Annibale Caro, Pier Luigi's secretary, was aware of them. The pressure from Cardinal Gambara was intensified with the help of other cardinals of the Farnese family until the pope gave in and the Consistory took the two cities away from the Church and gave them to the pope's son. Pier Luigi was installed as Duke of Parma and Piacenza. It was nothing for him, therefore, to divest himself of the Duchy of Castro for the benefit of his son Ottavio and to give Nepi and Camerino back to the Vatican.

From the solitude of our castles, we lords who maintained the legacy of the Guelph tradition witnessed with astonishment that devastating progress. Guests or travelers would arrive at times and also urgent messages with news of what was happening in the court of the Vicar of Christ, and we would lift our hands to heaven. I would meet most especially, sometimes in Bomarzo, sometimes in Mugnano, sometimes in Bracciano with the lords of the neighboring lands and there was no end to the complaints and remonstrances of the *editus ursae*.

In the luxury of Bracciano, under the vast fresco that shows Gentile Virginio Orsini assuming the command of the Aragonese troops, one of our people exclaimed, "And are we going to let them push us aside and humiliate us like this? Don't the Orsinis exist any more? Who ever hears any mention of the Orsinis?"

"Valerio Orsini was named governor of Verona a while back," I ventured.

"A while back? Six years at least."

"And then he was appointed governor general of Dalmatia," I continued.

"Those appointments came from the Serene Republic. They had nothing to do with the Holy Father. If they had depended on the Holy Father, the governor would have been a Farnese."

"Besides, Valerio Orsini is dead," Guido della Corbara interrupted.

"Leaving Lorenzo Emo widowed in Venice." The vulgar laugh of the Count of Anguillara burst forth.

I had not known that Maerbale's old master had died. We lived so much apart from one another! News was lost or never arrived. And with Maerbale out of the way I had no more links with Valerio Orsini. I would have to write to Lorenzo Emo. Perhaps he still had that adolescent charm that had fascinated me briefly during my Venetian days.

"But what's going on?" the Duke of Mugnano shouted. "The Farneses have always been aware of the distance that separates them from us and now we're talking about them as if they were our equals, measuring their merits against ours."

They looked at me suspiciously. They could not forget that my wife was a Farnese, a close relative of Pier Luigi. And for my part, even though I shared their distaste for the unjustified rise of the pope's son, I never ceased to weigh the benefits that it could bring my branch of the family.

"Pier Luigi is half an Orsini," I intervened again. "We have to remember that he's married to an Orsini."

The Bracciano people, the most haughty, became justly annoyed: "We renounce the relationship! An evil man, a schemer, a thief!"

The Count of Corbara took advantage of the situation to pronounce the insult that had shaken Europe: "The satyr! the rapist of the bishop of Fano!"

He was referring to an almost incredible event, one of perverse obscenity, which had happened when the gonfalonier of the Church was visiting the pontifical territories on business for his father and the victim of which was an eighteen-year-old prelate, Cosimo Geri, famous for the purity of his ways.

Sigismondo, who until that moment had remained silent, gave free rein to his wrath. "He's a lecher!"

We turned toward him. We had forgotten him in his dark corner, elastic and nervous, inflamed by jealousy, but it was impossible to forget his past relationship with the Duke of Parma. He brought his sharp profile toward the light and his shadow outlined the moving head of a gyrfalcon on the wall. Letting himself go, he came out with the most serious accusation: "Pier Luigi wants to assassinate Emperor Charles!"

"What are you saying?"

It was too late to retreat. He tightened his hands on the thick gold chain that had probably been given to him by Farnese himself, and he said, "He planned the crime with Leonida Malatesta and Matteo Varano. He offered the first one Rimini and Ravenna back and Matteo Varano Camerino."

"Can you swear to that?"

"I swear it."

"How do you know?"

"I know—I heard it from Pier Luigi."

"But why? Why would he want to do it?"

Sigismondo hesitated and his polished ivory cheekbones stood out. "He doesn't want to give back Novara, as the emperor demands, and then too he's going crazy over the influence his son Ottavio has with His Imperial Majesty. He wants everything for himself."

Events were plotting against me again, emphasizing the ambiguous weakness of my position. Matteo Varano was married to Battistina Farnese, my wife's sister, and that had gained him the friendship of Pier Luigi. He was a wrathful bully who had killed the podesta of Camerino, and who, without any doubt, would not think twice about carrying out the audacious plan of doing away with the master of half the world if he could get his poor lands back. As before, my companions watched for my reaction, perhaps with more curiosity than bitterness. I decided to remain silent; after all, in addition to my own problems I was not going to take on those of the despoiled lords of Camerino.

The Duke of Mugnano crossed his fingers over his lips and called for silence. "Not a word of this must get out," he recommended. "We'll make use of it. It's a beautiful weapon. We have to make a solemn promise not to reveal it until the right moment. I'll go see the emperor myself."

A violent argument broke out. Why he? Why was he the one to get the benefit of a piece of news that was worth so much? Why not Bracciano, or the Count of Anguillara, or the Duke of Bomarzo, whom Charles V had knighted? We about, aroused, pecking at each other like falcons.

"We'll settle it when we get together again. In the meantime, let's promise that the secret stays with us."

We held our hands out over the candles. On several fingers there was the glitter of cut stones on thick rings, all with the shield of the rose and the serpent.

The secret was not kept and when it came out the one advised was not Charles V but Pier Luigi, who, fearing in turn the betrayal of Malatesta, imprisoned him in the Rocca di Forlì. But Leonida Malatesta managed to escape and he told Cosimo de' Medici about the plot. From there to the emperor's knowledge was but a step. The one who reaped the advantages of the information was therefore none of us; it was the diligent Cosimo, the lord of Tuscany, who took advantage of the opportunity to hint to Caesar that the pope was involved in the intrigue. Charles of Hapsburg did not seem to give much credence to the monstrous thing they were telling him. The moment would come soon enough for him to get his vengeance, to punish, to grip his thunderbolt. He always got his revenge.

In our circle of provincial conspirators the betrayal left us astonished. Who could have broken the promise? We spied on one another, thick with mistrust. Insults and recriminations abounded. Although suspicions were certainly accumulated over my head, the Duke of Mugnano threatened Sigismondo. But the guilty one was never found out. It could have been Mugnano himself, for he would have given anything to attract the attention and favor of the emperor, and he envied the courtiers of the son of Joan the Mad. It was impossible for us to continue meeting over those embers of burning doubts, for what came out of it was the opposite of what had been proposed. We separated, hating each other, swallowing our suspicions and conjectures. From then on, no one in the group dared ride about the region without an escort. One night, on his way back from a hunting party, Sigismondo fell into an ambush in which four masked men beat him and cut his face. Because of our ties, they were affronting me through him. They did not wish to kill him but to disfigure him, for they were aware of his vanity. From that time on Sigismondo had to wear a black cloth that covered half of his face. I remember that Violante Orsini, during the course of a party that was degenerating into a scandal, snatched off the bandage. We saw with horror his empty socket; they had torn out his right eye. My cousin Violante was more upset than anyone, but conquering her revulsion, she kissed the red cavity.

"You're much more handsome like that, Sigismondo," she said as she tried to console him.

But the young man stood up. With an angry tug he pulled off the tablecloth and the glassware fell with a clatter. The ladies shrieked as the wine spilled out of the pitchers and the golden whippets ran to fight over the leftovers. Sigismondo fled, howling like a wounded animal, followed by Madruzzo, Molza, Orso, and Matteo.

That macabre sight horrified me. The reader is aware, since I have emphasized it so often, of the importance to me of harmony and esthetic balance. I could only tolerate beautiful people and things with a noble rhythm around me. And my court, with a hunchback, a blind woman, and a cyclops, was turning into a sideshow. I used that disagreeable happening to tell Giulia the next morning that Cecilia would have to leave. She had her estates and Maerbale's; it was her duty to take care of them and establish her son on them. It was useless for my wife to argue about the incapacity of my brother's widow, but she begged me not to deprive her of the only companionship she had in the loneliness of the castle, as well as pointing out to me how nice it would be for Orazio and Niccolò to grow up together. My cruelty was obvious and inflexible, and my sister-in-law left without bidding farewell, taking her child, her servants, her many trunks, Maerbale's arms, her birdcages, her favorite dogs, and her immense sadness to Rome, where her aunt, the majestic Vittoria Colonna, had settled in her tiny palace of Monte Cavallo after Paul III, who had established the tribunal of the Holy Roman Inquisition, had dissolved her group in Viterbo, accusing them of heresy, and confiscating their holdings. Cecilia lived there until Vittoria's death a few years later, on intimate terms with Michelangelo. Her august kinswoman had seen the departure, because of fear or obligation, of Cardinal Reginald Pole, the preacher Ochino, Gianantonio Flaminio, Pietro Carnesecchi, friends of Giulia Gonzaga and, like her, disciples of the fascinating Juan de Valdés, the Spaniard who had recently died and whose preachings, saturated with Erasmism, bordered on the dangers of heterodoxy. Vittoria Colonna and Michelangelo generously took in the blind girl. I was worried, of course, about what she might have told them about me and the strange death of Maerbale, but the important thing was for her to leave the castle. Although she had never spoken a harsh word, her mere presence, just the tapping of her gold cane in the galleries, was sufficient to bring back adverse phantoms. If I ever thought about the injustice of my behavior, corroborated by Giulia's silent reproach, I took comfort in the thought that thanks to me Cecilia was enjoying a marvelous privilege which I never had, spending her days in the admirable circle of the master Michelangelo Buonarroti, who like me had been born on the sixth of March, an artist who had a heart with a labyrinth of crisscrossed paths and who wrote ardent love sonnets simultaneously for Vittoria Colonna, the Marchioness of Pescara, the lady "beautiful and cruel," and his inseparable companion Tommaso Cavalieri, whom he painted on the ceiling of the Sistine Chapel, so that in some cases it is difficult to tell to whom they are addressed.

Free of Cecilia and free of the embarrassment brought on by the sterile Orsini conclaves that had as their aim the analysis of the annoying Farnese prosperity, which struck so close to home and which I could not condemn too much, I was able to dedicate myself with relative tranquility to what interested me most at that time: the scholarly classification of my collections and the care of Bomarzo. Also at that time I began to concern myself with what, with the passage of time, would become one of the essential motives of my life: magic.

My collections, my famous collections, had grown in a strange way. They were my faithful image, because they were absurd, intricate, and perhaps monstrous, also they were frivolous. Only a dilettante with strange tastes could have gathered them all together. What they make me think of most now that I recall them—on a much lesser scale, of course, for neither my means nor my relationship with those who provided that baroque merchandise were so remote at the time—are those strange "salons of art and curiosities" maintained by the emperors of Germany, Ferdinand I, the brother of Charles V, his successors Maximilian II and Rudolf II, and the Archduke Ferdinand of the Tyrol. Like them, since childhood I had felt the attraction of the unusual; like them, beyond the great official salons where the family portraits, the fine paintings, the divine statues, and the splendid tapestries were placed on exhibition, I had in Bomarzo my almost secret rooms where time was piling up a most diverse, most disconcerting, and most fascinating accumulation of suggestive creations. They came from the end of Italy, where unexpected persons with whom I maintained a long correspondence dealt in those mysterious and subtle objects which often bespoke, more than a noble esthetic sense, a whim of the imagination. And they came from farther away, from misty Europe, and, through Venice, from the Far East. I bought them without looking too closely, seduced by my agents' fine descriptions, and many spurious items slipped through in that opulent group. But the group was a marvel. When I finally undertook the task of classifying them and putting them in order, now having in Bomarzo the last items that had lain in the attics of my Roman palaces and those which had awaited my decision in other cities of the peninsula, it was as if I had at my disposal a cave of Ali Baba where instead of sacks of gold and jewel-filled chests, hallucinating proofs of human fantasy were being accumulated. That disturbing arsenal, the access to which I had forbidden, was growing in its confused labyrinth as new contributions were added. I could not put off its organization if I did not want the dampness, rats, moths, worms, and filth to endanger its existence. Furthermore, the work would give me something that my anxiety needed at the time, a distraction, a drug to calm my worries. Lost in that forest of objects I could forget the jungle of men.

The chamber covered three rooms on the second floor. Giambattista and Silvio opened up the windows for me, and when the sun came in, in the midst of the musty smell and that of something hidden, old, and dirty—perhaps of my grandmother's cats too, for they got in everywhere, like ghosts, as they had wandered about there—the light embraced the vastness of my treasure. Dark cupboards hung heavily along the walls. Above and next to them paintings climbed up to the ceilings. Many had no frames or had broken ones; many were mediocre and in terrible shape; canvases hung there full of holes, and hungry insects had fed upon their frames; but amid such foggy vagueness, out of so many medieval faces with their cardboard stiffness, there emerged among the oils some few fabulous and light compositions that broadened the perspective until it was a magical world. The whole thing took shape as soon as the doors of the cupboards creaked open. There were the miracles all together. Hanging tightly side by side were the musical instruments; the flat clocks that looked like compasses, as complex as the bells of an abbey; pieces of amber, mother-of-pearl, coral; vases in the shape of mythological figures with enameled relief; dangerous spheres of rock crystal; mosaics made of the feathers of tropical birds; snail shells, conch shells; astrolabes, mathematical instruments; wax figurines; amulets, cabalistic disks with Hebrew letters; ivory horns; cups made of ostrich eggs, gigantic nuts, and monkey skulls; bronze washbasins shaped as centaurs, as lions, as warriors on horseback; fragments of sculptured ceramic and clay; reliquaries; mirrors of many facets; mandrake roots; bezoar stones wired together with gold; automatons; reptile skeletons among which there was one that was supposed to be that of a mermaid; unicorn horns; petrified flowers. A predecessor of the charlatan Tartaglio had sold me some apocryphal monsters that had been skillfully put together from the skin of a ray fish, and the mythical beasts from Pliny that Valeriano had revealed to me in Florence—the basilisk, the Ethiopian sphinx—had been fraudulently added to my collection.

Giambattista, fascinated, entertained himself by placing in motion the mechanisms of the melodic automatons and the clocks; the breeze coming in through the windows shook the hanging bones, which moved like puppets; the cobwebs moved in the thickness of their grayish weave; a troop of rodents fled in sudden fright; the sun brought sparks from the semiprecious stones, the alabaster, porphyry, jasper, aventurine; the geometry of the mirrors glowed, breaking up the images; the rusty metal of old armor was iridescent with the tint of muddy water; and that whole assembly took on a strange life suddenly, as if the hidden wizard who governed its dream had lifted up his unyielding wand. I went from one chest to another, from one cabinet to the next. I dumped out the contents of boxes which were full of green medals, cameos, stamps with inscriptions, rolled-up manuscripts. Yes, it was finally time to put in order the wild confusion that had been growing year after year, hidden and quickly, in the very bowels of Bomarzo, and which was crouching there like that undiscoverable skeleton crowned with roses with whom my father had imprisoned me in his hidden cell, and which, like him, like a cancer, threatened to devour the whole castle, for no sooner did the light and air arouse the arcane beings than I sensed that so great was the hermetic power that they hid and which gave them a most subtle vibration, the fruit of tire accumulated strength of those who had created them, that the moment would arrive when they would invade my house, when they would take power there by means of their secret arts. The superstitions of the place came over me once more and I could feel coming through the paving stones of the floor the breath of the Etruscan earth that was heaving like some huge hidden animal. I looked at the evening sky where the pale light of the constellations was beginning to glow and I remembered what Giordano Bruno had said about the stars, peaceful animals too, with warm blood and regular habits, moved by reason. Everything was alive all about: the land on which the crags of Bomarzo sat, the planets suspended in their dome, the dolls and swaying objects that took refuge in its shadowy heart. In the midst of that universe of fearful correspondences, maintained by the spell of enchanted ties which kept up their inexplicable balance, I was wrapped up in a peace that I never felt except upon exceptional occasions. I lifted up a sphere; with my fingers I raised an amber pendant; I unrolled a manuscript that was decorated with alarming miniatures of naked demons, hermits, and temptresses with no other adornment than their necklaces and diadems; I pushed an automaton that seemed endowed with as much life as the homunculus of Paracelsus, and the hours sped by rapidly, with a miraculous amnesia, while in the distance the cocks gave hoarse crows and the first wagons left for the harvest and the haymows.

Neither Silvio nor Giambattista had the necessary preparation to help me in the task that I had assumed. I was sure that I was up to the decorative part and that of arranging the various elements in a harmonious way, and that Silvio would be useful to me in what concerned magical objects, but the most difficult part would be the classification of the erudite items—the ancient texts, the reading of inscriptions on stones and medals—for that called for the help of an expert. Since my character excluded any outside interference, I set about searching for some young helper who would be so linked to my world that his presence would not be uncomfortable in a place that too much resembled my own complex soul. And I remembered Fulvio Orsini. Fulvio—perhaps the reader has lost him in the remote pages of this voluminous book—was that natural son of Maerbale's whom my brother, while still an adolescent, had refused to recognize, and who, born of a peasant girl in Bomarzo, had been sent by me to Rome to be educated there. At the time he was around fifteen or sixteen years of age and he was already showing that he had the seeds of the learned person that he would be later on. The scholar Gentile Delfini had molded him with enthusiastic patience, and I was aware of the amazement that his precocity had aroused among the most outstanding archeologists of the time. He had lived surrounded by illustrious people who, stimulated by his evident vocation, rivaled one another in the task of contributing to the progress of an investigator who in his physique and his manners showed his illustrious origins. The noble Saragossan Antonio Agustín *doctor utriusque iuris* from the University of Bologna and a judge of the tribunal of the Rota, and the other humanists were charmed by the intelligence shown by the future librarian of the Farneses. Those men versed in ancient letters—Antonio Agustín, Delfini, Ottavio Pantegato, Pirro Ligorio, Basilio Zanchi, Onofrio Panvino, and Carlo

Sigonio—passed on to him their discoveries as they guided his preparation. I learned that, the same as some of his teachers, Fulvio considered that coins, inscriptions, and other engraved works were much more trustworthy than monuments of literature, for in them the stamp of the past remained intact, while successive hands over the centuries had weakened the testimony of classical letters, and beginning with the celebrated antiquarian collection of Petrus Apianus, the *Inscriptiones sacrosantae vetustatis*, published in Ingolstadt in 1534, my nephew had accomplished an arduous task of criticism that went beyond what might have been expected of his young years. I called him to me. It annoyed me, of course, that he was Maerbale's son, that with him again I would have living proof of my brother's superiority, but at the same time it pleased me that someone of our blood should stand out in a specialty that was so different from those that had characterized our line in the world—a specialty singularly close to my own spirit—and it could be that I was even able to tell myself, hypocritically, that if I made him my intimate and protected him, I would atone in part for my crime, for I was taking advantage of an envied opportunity where I could bring to light a boy who—if Maerbale had lived, the one who had denied him as his son—would have been reduced to a miserable and encircling obscurity.

So Fulvio Orsini dismounted at Bomarzo with a gravity that belied his youth, and the effect of his knowledge and his worthy respect conquered me within a week. Did he not represent in addition a political ally against possible gossip, evidence of my innocence as regarded the death of Maerbale? Was it logical that I should have called his son to me if his blood had stained my hands? I left to him the task of plowing through the chests of coins and separating the good from the bad and of translating and interpreting the texts on the marble inscriptions, while for my part, with Silvio and Giambattista, I was working up a plan that fit exactly into the most typical traits of my personality. I brought them both to the secret chamber that I had discovered by chance when I was looking for the hiding place of the hated skeleton, and there I told them what I had in mind. I wanted to take advantage of the secret passage, unknown to everyone, which went down into the valley, and their cooperation was most necessary. Down below, beyond the garden, in the midst of the woods, I would build a great nympheum, with fountains, statues, fruit trees, and excavated rooms like those that adorned other noble estates, and inside of it, which would be in direct and invisible communication with the castle through the passageway, I would locate my collections and have a place of my own, hidden and out of the sight of other people by the conventionally ornamental appearance of the outside, and where I could take refuge whenever I felt like it.

I set to work immediately. The nympheum would be built where the descending tunnel emerged and it would have to be seen to that the workmen were not aware. Silvio and Giambattista, taking turns, saw to it that the passage stayed hidden. Attracted by the strangeness of the idea and by the fact that they were sharing another secret with me, they both took pains to fulfill the part of the work that befell them, and on the other side, the teams of workers, following the sketches of my design, began to put into shape the first of the constructions of my future Sacred Wood. In that way the nympheum of Bomarzo arose, with its outside niches where the innocent figures of the three Graces and the naiads cast water out from their breasts and where crude reliefs done by craftsmen from the region already showed with their wide-mouthed grotesque masks the fantastic creatures that in the future would be spread out through the valley among the streams.

While the construction was being done, hindered by the necessity of flattening out the terrace where it would stand and by the location of the flow of water, Fulvio devoted himself to his learned tasks, and I was calculating in my hidden way how I would distribute my treasures in their hiding place. The months passed as I became involved with the obsession of what I had invented, and during which, even if the intellectuals who made up my little court, and Fabio, Violante, and my cousins, who were still visiting me at Bomarzo, or anything else broke the surface rhythm of my existence as a country prince given over to letters, I lived only to give shape to my mysterious dream. It seemed to me that everything I could obtain from that asylum would bring out great works, and seduced by that illusion, I spared no effort to accomplish it.

Fulvio Orsini and the writers got on well together. Coming together at nightfall, they would talk about the topics that fascinated the period, running through names from antiquity, and even though they were also interested in matters of the day—the emperor, besieged by hunger and illnesses, was decimating his troops, and because of the tenacity of the Lutherans he had signed the Peace of Crépy; in Venice the dome of the Old Library of Jacopo Sansovino had fallen in; Guillaume Postel, the visionary, had been expelled from the Society of Ignatius Loyola and he claimed to have found a woman who would be responsible for the female salvation of the globe, for Jesus had only redeemed men; Lorenzaccio de' Medici, the fugitive, had been spotted in Florence and in Venice, where he was writing his *Apologia*; Orazio Farnese, the son of Pier Luigi, had assumed the title of governor of Rome—what attracted them most was Fulvio's telling them that the reconstruction of the classical monuments under the care of Pirro Ligorio, even if that author was a great antiquarian, suffered from unpardonable excesses where the imagination made up for a lack of knowledge. They rubbed their hands as they listened to him and said right away that he was right.

Finally the building of the nympheum was completed and I inaugurated it with a party at which, instead of water, wine flowed from the breasts of the goddesses. The tables were set in a room where the walls showed mythological and heraldic designs done with painted shells from whose arabesques the spouts emerged. Betussi read a predictable ode and Molza scattered quotes from Catullus over us. Young Orazio Orsini, led by the hand of his mother, appeared dressed as Eros and shot some multicolored arrows into the air.

My pages and I had managed to hide the opening of the secret passageway from the eyes of the masons. A few days later I placed my findings there. I must confess that I was happy, very happy, when I judged the effect of my creation in the light of the candles. I had what I had yearned for, my secret grotto, the walls of which disappeared behind the strange paintings and exceptional objects. The skeletons hung from the ceiling like Pantasilea's deceptive polyhedron, and they were moving slightly. All about, the clocks were watching like the eyes of time, and the automatons were standing guard amid the flashing of mirrors, crystals, and stones. The smell of dampness floated about, impregnating the rugs on the floor. I rewarded Silvio da Narni and Giambattista Martelli with princely generosity. Then I myself, feeling great shame over my clumsiness, placed the lock that would seal the door of the corridor. And for the first time in years I rested, as if the look of God could not follow me down there. No one except my accomplices would enter that redoubt, neither Fabio Farnese, nor Violante, nor Sigismondo. No one, neither Giulia nor her son Orazio. They would not know of the existence of that shelter. There, near the multicolored tombs of the fearful Etruscans, the Duke of Bomarzo was safe, like a beast in his lair. Everything that surrounded him was close by and understood and loved him, with the subtle love that things feel for those they have chosen and which establishes an esoteric union between both. Sometimes, while I was writing, I would get up from my table piled high with books and scratched-out pages to go like a sleepwalker over to a crystal bowl with a faun on the edge, or a lute that reminded me of those of Ippolito de' Medici, or a short gold figure, and because I felt like it, as I had done with the torso of the Minotaur, I kissed it at length.

I was writing a poem of many stanzas. I had written out its title, *Bomarzo*, in tall, ornate letters.

Silvio da Narni brought his astrological instruments down to the nympheum. Upstairs he kept only those used for direct observation of the sky. His annotated books—the Quadripartite of Ptolemy, those of Trithemius and Agrippa, especially the *De occulta philosophia*, and of course the medieval *Tabula Smaragdina*, which was reputed among alchemists to be the most authoritative text—were put in order under the figure of the Agathodaemon, the Egyptian serpent that I had already seen in his room and which had a crown of twelve rays representing the twelve signs of the Zodiac on its lion's head. The new building was a refuge for my secretary, the same as it was for me. Although remorse did not torment him at all, he needed to isolate himself from the past, from the memory of Porzia, whom he vainly pretended to have forgotten, and study offered him a form of forgetfulness. He went back, therefore, with renewed enthusiasm, to his horoscopes and the science of the stars, but soon they were not enough for his despair. It was simply one more step along the path to the secrets of magic, and Silvio set out upon the dark trail. He possessed extraordinary gifts for it. When I took him into my service and began to deal with him when he was a page of my grandfather Cardinal Franciotto—at the time when he was certain that he had imprisoned the demon Amon and when he supported me with black arts—his knowledge, minimal and scattered, proceeded, according to what he told me himself, from an innate propensity to approach the supernatural and unleash dangerous phenomena. Then, as his position in the castle rose, the wisdom of the stars began to dazzle him and he wanted to possess it in order to read the message of fate in the glowing dome. But after Porzia left him, attracted by the opulence of the Duke of Mugnano, his investigations took a more practical and concrete direction. There was revived in him the old dream of the alchemists, that of the Stone that could not be found and which transmuted base metals into gold. He was thinking no doubt that if he found the Stone he would be able to win Porzia back, that with his magic gold he would make her his again and humiliate her.

The search began slowly, alternating with the time he put into charting the movement of the planets and other tasks, but after a few months, the Philosopher's Stone, the Great Elixir, the Quintessence had become an obsession which occupied him completely. Consumed, burning inside, his brow lined with furrows which rose up to his prematurely bald head, his eyes visionary, he would go from the open books to the strange apparatuses that he had set up, one after the other, the three ovens, the *atanor* and the *kerotakis*, talking aloud, it was not known whether to himself or to the devil Amon or to one of those mysterious familiar demons, like Cardano's red rooster, with whom wizards conversed in secrecy. Only I had access to his hiding place, next to my own study; only Giambattista and I knew of its existence, deep in the heart of the frivolous nympheum. Not even Fulvio Orsini, who would often come to the baroque room where I was writing, meditating, or walking back and forth like a caged animal—for the nature of his work obliged me to offer him the hidden intimacy of my refuge—and who would consult me concerning the origins of such and such a bronze or such and such a marble, suspected that behind the wall there was another room—the one, precisely, into which the secret passage opened—and that hidden in it Silvio was repeating the now classic movements of adepts of the Great Art, maneuvering with alembics and bellows, lifting retorts full of distilled liquids, and shaking or pouring, with the broad sleeves of his black robe, the sublimates into the vessels where the *descensum* was taking place, the evaporating dishes, the mortars and pestles, the vials, the cups, the jugs. Glass and metal resounded on the tables, and fire was burning in the ovens. When the smoke escaped through the trees and floated away like a greenish, bluish piece of gauze, the people in the village probably thought that we had lighted one of the fireplaces in the nympheum. They were perhaps surprised by the strangeness of the color that the short column spread out and by its pungent odor. They and those of the castle could think whatever they wanted to. I was not going to be bothered by a few women, poets, children, halberdiers, villagers.

I would frequently leave the room that was filled with my books and strange objects and open the hidden door that went into Silvio's chamber. His investigations were fascinating me more and more, at the same time as my interest in the poem which I had begun with a fervor that was not at all sincere declined. If only I had been frank and honest then, if only I had expressed what I felt in a simple way, alas! Italian literature of the sixteenth century probably would have been enriched by the simplest and deepest of its works. I had before me an opportunity for literary glory and I did not recognize it, I could not grasp it by the hair as it went by. I had no lack of theme or inspiration. I adored Bomarzo, which I knew as no one else did and whose essence was deeply communicated to me in the depths of my blood, and I yearned to praise it in a work that would unite its name and mine for eternity, but two circumstances held me back and hindered me, preventing me from creating an immortal poem, more immortal than the victories of the Count of Pitigliano: On one side, my worldly superficiality made me sacrifice my passion to the tastes of the time and wrap the matter in an allegorical framework that was like painted cardboard, under the emphasis of which it was impossible to capture the greatness of Bomarzo, its incomparable seduction and its anguish made of stone and air; and on the other side, my special status as a great Roman lord bothered me so much that it was, paradoxically, like another hump, and it strangled my free and spontaneous expression, befogging me with stupid prejudices and hinting to me that the Duke of Bomarzo should not deal with a theme like that by using direct simplicity, but by alternating the mythological pomp that characterized the century with an ironic touch that would inform the reader—and especially the courtly reader—that the duke was always the duke, even with pen in his hand, and if he did love, as was logical, the place that he had inherited from his elders, he was not confused by the fact of its possession and he did not intend to use poetry as rhymed propaganda for his dukedom, for he understood quite well that he, as an individual, as a sacred incarnation of the centuries-old primacy of his clan, was far above the curious place which he could praise in a kindly way but without the smile of superiority leaving his illustrious lips and without his considering the task as anything but a palace game, a proof of his facile talents and of the grace which, like everything of his (except, of course, his hump, and who noticed that any more?), reflected a divine predilection.

With such hindrances the poem did not progress well. I wrote a great deal and I tore up a great deal. *Bomarzo* was well constructed, but it was not worth very much. It was imbecilic, inexplicable, that instead of interpreting the mysterious beauty of Bomarzo, its valleys, its hills, its bonfires, its caves, its crags, its fearful tombs, which made me shudder and even moved me to tears, I would use the quite trite pantomimes of Pomona, Ganymede, Flora, and Adonis, the repeated contradance. As was right, I was bored, it was tiring for me to keep repeating that sumptuous masturbation. I was growing desperate over the certainty that I would not reach the glory that I yearned for so much by that route either—in spite of the great praise from my writer friends—and that yet, hanging like a golden fruit a step away from me and in Silvio's room there was what had deserted mine: the warmth of an atmosphere of excitement, of real marvels, whose spurious origins did not diminish the intensity of its vivifying quiver. Also, since inspiration grew weak and no spiritual barrier separated me from my miserable surroundings, accusing shades would visit me in my study, slipping in among the reptile and bat skeletons that trembled above. Maerbale, Girolamo, my grandmother, my father, Beppo, and the blind Cecilia Colonna, as I sat surrounded by the sterility of my manuscript. I was not going to be crushed because of memories; I was not going to be intimidated; a person is or is not a Renaissance man and I was quite a good one; but more than once my going into Silvio's study had the traits of a flight.

In spite of all, I have said on many occasions, magic was suggestive for me. I could breathe fully in its atmosphere. And Silvio da Narni's experiments in search of the Philosopher's Stone, which would give him back Porzia more effectively than his alliance with devils, blended too harmoniously with the tradition of princes obstinate in their search for it, surrounded by alchemists, moving about among explosions, stenches, flames, and bubbling, for it not to make me light up. That way was the one that suited a person who had brought a magical promise into the world. Perhaps there, in the room to which the ovens gave a swaying scarlet light, the Secret was crouching, my Secret.

My children went on being born. The day the hunchback was born, the hunchback Maerbale, I wept, I do not know whether from grief or from joy. He was my son and he was my brother, my true brother. In the meantime, the eldest, Orazio Orsini, was growing handsome. How I looked for myself in him! How I discovered alternately in him myself and my brother Maerbale! His pleasant nature—even though I tried, I was never pleasant—brought him closer to Maerbale's jollity, to the grace that gave amusement as he danced and mimicked, to my grandmother, but it also could have come from my father-in-law Galeazzo Farnese, from Fabio, from my sisters-in-law, who had by now attained eminence with their fine marriages, to a Sanvitale from Parma, to the Duke of Poli, to Matteo Varano, the lord of Camerino, and who, when they came to Bomarzo from time to time would bring to its grim walls a breath of the worldly life of Rome and a laughter whose jingle made the ghosts disappear. Orazio was so handsome that beside him the others withdrew like castoffs. On some mornings, when I found out that he was swimming in the Tiber, I would go and hide in the bushes to watch him sprout up like a small god of Bomarzo with his slim infantile nakedness, and in that way, the same as the laughter of Girolama,

Jolanda, and Battistina conjured the evil spirits away from the castle, the young prince's jumping and splashing drove away the bloody ghost of my older brother from the banks where death had overtaken him. Orazio was a god, an authentic god, and not like the ones I was accumulating, coarse and sententious, tired, like old actors, in the lines of my poem.

Giambattista and Silvio were no longer speaking to each other. Their old dispute had broken out again. Giambattista could not forgive Silvio for the influence he had assumed over me again. He was suspicious, in addition, that all of the smoke, concoctions, and philters in the midst of which he was working from failure to failure, and the hopeful rage of Narni were directed against his twin, Porzia. We learned that she now had an inseparable companion on the estate at Mugnano, Pantasilea. The harlot had spotted my Orsini cousin's mansion as a safe harbor against the inclemency of the years. Between the two marvelous women, the Duke of Mugnano lived for pleasure. His court was one of Dionysiac pleasures, while mine, with so many famous people and parasites, was the court of science and the arts. I admit that on various occasions I felt a longing for an existence like his, infinitely more pleasant than the one I had chosen. But that was how it was. I had chosen it; I had resolved to be the cultured one, the refined Duke of Bomarzo, the esthete with a Florentine education; I had resolved to model that picture of me for the future so that it would triumph over my hump; that of the duke who wrote his melodic poem amid the warmth of his intellectual devotees; the figure of the distant, spiritual, wise duke; and nostalgia was of no use to me. Of course, Violante, Fabio, and Sigismondo continued to be part of my circle, and it was with them that I relaxed, even sensually, taking off the armor that I myself had forged. But I did not love them. I did not love anybody. Silvio was never more than my accomplice; he was not even my friend. I would look at Giulia, remote as she went along the row of poplars and the urns with laurels as if she were made of mist, or as if, like poor Cecilia Colonna, she were blind and could not see me. That was the terrible impression that weighed down on me as soon as I possessed her in the bed where her fear and rancor were disguised as a submissive indifference: that she did not see me, that ever since she had fleetingly put her arms around Maerbale, she had never seen me again. And I did not love her. Her disdain inhibited me too much, it was too clear on the surface of her skin for me to be able to love her. Before, when I had clung to her body, she would avoid my hump; now her hands would alight on it like two tarantulas, reminding me that my hump was still there, and that never, not even in the drunkenness of voluptuous passion would I get rid of its weight. I did not love anybody.

Oh, but I did, I did love someone, I did love someone then with a singular feeling, confused, vaguely incestuous—someone whom Giulia also preferred, because her maternal instinct discerned, perhaps, his essential difference, one which I was unable to pin down—and it was that child who was running about, thin, dancing, through the alleys of the village, toward the valley and the woods, that child who looked so much like me that he was my perfected image, polished, like the poetical projection in the portrait by Lorenzo Lotto. Orazio Orsini. I would hear the gallop of his horse as he left with my cousins, who were teaching him how to train falcons, and my heart pounded. I would go out with a goose quill in my hand onto the terrace of the nympheum and observe from the distance his delicate silhouette which reminded me of Girolamo, agile, graceful, proud. He was already disappearing like a sprite, with a distant glow of the diamonds that glimmered on his sword, on his cap, on Orso's necklace, on Sigismondo's gloves, one of which he was holding to his black patch, as if in the full brightness of day fireflies were lighting up and going out in the bushes.

"Good-bye," I shouted to him, "good-bye!"

And just as Giulia could not see me, Orazio could not hear me. Then, annoyed at the idea of going back to the chore that I had imposed on myself, I went slowly back to the castle. Madruzzo was talking about the marriage of Vittoria Farnese, the daughter of Pier Luigi, to Guidobaldo d'Urbino. The title of Duke of Sanseverino, which would have made Stendhal shudder, had been awarded to Ottavio Farnese and his descendants. Always the Farneses! And how little, how little it all mattered to me! Or if not that, it was about the birth of Alessandro Farnese, the son of Ottavio and Margaret of Austria, the grandson of Pier Luigi and Girolamo Orsini and also of Charles V, the great-grandson of Pope Paul III—how much prestige could have been gathered on one head! I listened to them listlessly. Something had to be done, I had to be shaken up, taken out of my numbness. Standing by the window, taking in the countryside that was being crossed by bats, I waited for the return of Orazio Orsini and the hunters. It was what I had done in Bomarzo ever since I was very small: wait, with my heart pounding, for the return of the hunters.

One night that baronial monotony was broken. I was alone with Silvio by the fireplace in the main room, studying the best way to transfer onto one of the walls the painting of Benedetto's horoscope—there were no guests at the time and Giulia and the children had gone to bed—when we heard noise and voices at the castle gate. Silvio opened a window and looked out into the darkness. Torches were waving in the wind below and the clear sound of Martelli's voice rang out: "It's Messer Lorenzino de' Medici who comes with his mother and asks for Your Lordship's hospitality!"

I ordered that they be brought up at once and I waited for them at the top of the stairs. Maria Soderini came forward slowly, emerging from the shadows of the tapestries like an unreal veiled figure, but Lorenzino sprang up four steps at a time, as agile as always, and he fell into my arms an instant later. They were both wearing masks. In back the servants were struggling with trunks and weapons. My young friend had changed a great deal. When he took off his mask I noticed the aging marks of worry on his dark, thin face. Strange tics were agitating his face, which, when it lost its smile, was difficult to recognize. He looked right and left suspiciously. I calmed him down, assuring him that my affection had not changed, and I kissed Maria Soderini on the cheek and hands. Suffering had eroded her even more than it had her son. She collapsed into a chair and did not say a word. I ordered wine to be brought while their rooms were being prepared, and to give special honor to Lorenzaccio I had them prepare the room where my father had had his study and which had been closed until then. In a short time his mother, worn out with fatigue, left us. She made the sign of the cross over Lorenzino's forehead and we accompanied her to her room where a fire was crackling. Then we went back to the main room and were alone. My friend drank four glasses, one after another. Across from the church we could hear the shouts of the people unhitching the horses from his carriage. And a silence came over us, filled with expectation, for it seemed that the Roman emperors, who were going off into the distance in the gallery toward the twisted shadow of the Minotaur, were also waiting, tense and tight, as the wind rattled the panes and twirled the flames of the fireplace, entwining and unraveling them like red gorgons.

Finally my guest began to speak, stumbling over his words. He told me about his life from the day he had escaped from Florence thanks to a safe conduct pass from Bishop Marzi, a consignatory of the keys to the city, whom he had got out of bed with a ruse. He had traveled a great deal. His story, after the fleeting flash of the crime, was the story of a flight, for Cosimo de' Medici had put a price on his head. First Filippo Strozzi, who had received him as an envoy of Providence, sent him on a mission to the sultan in Constantinople; then, with the defeat of the exiles, he fled, crossing frontiers. He had been in Venice, Bologna, France; he returned to Italy with King Francis, and went back to France once more, to Montpellier, to Paris...

"Did you see Benvenuto Cellini in Paris?"

"I saw him; him and the treasurer Bonaccorsi, and the poet Alamanni. My cousin Catherine too, the future queen, who received me with kindness, and Margaret of Navarre. Catherine and I talked about you many times. But, you know, the others were still with me. They were like two vampires, two wolves; they wouldn't leave me alone."

"What others?"

"The others. Scoroncocolo, Freccia. The ones who had helped me in the Alessandro affair."

"Oh!"

"They dogged my tracks. I can't understand it, but they felt safe beside me. At night I could hear them grinding their teeth and if they moved in bed their daggers would knock against the bedstead. They didn't even take off their boots when they went to sleep. I was finally able to get them off my back. They were worse than Alessandro. Worse than any remorse, if there's such a thing as remorse. I shipped them off on one of Roberto Strozzi's galleys and I was able to breathe."

"Don't you have any remorse? I mean... about Alessandro...?"

"No."

His flight started again soon. His uncle Giuliano Soderini, who had helped him clandestinely with money, had died. Now he went back to Venice, where his existence was spent among those who considered him a hero and those who thought he was a traitor. His means were very limited, for Pietro Strozzi, who had given him a palace, fifteen hundred crowns a year, and some ruffians to protect him, had cut his rations by a thousand scudi.

I vaguely promised to help relieve his financial difficulties, alleging that I had not yet received my tributes, and he thanked me profusely. Fear, which never left him, which buried its teeth and nails deeper than Scoroncocolo's, danced again in his desperate eyes. He looked into the corners, turning his strange, inquisitive rodent's face.

"Are we safe here? Are your people loyal?"

"You're safe. Don't be afraid."

It was startling to think that with those nervous hands he had snuffed out the life of Duke Alessandro. But I, with my thin lips, my poetical eyes, my fragile figure, had I not ordered the death of Maerbale?

He was trembling and laughing at the same time. In order to distract him I spoke to him about his *Aridosia*, but he did not stop trembling. How different he was from Musset's Lorenzaccio, who toyed with death! One of the characters, referring to the assassins who are waiting for him, tells him in the last act of the tragedy, "*Tu te feras tuer dans toutes ces promenades.*" And he replies haughtily, "*Cela m'amuse de les voir.*" When I read the work I did not recognize my unfortunate friend, the one who was trembling in Bomarzo in front of the fireplace, holding out his thin hands toward the sparks, and who kept turning his head to look over his shoulder. But it is well known that poets, and especially romantic poets, make up their own versions of unfortunate individuals. It is well that it is that way.

I took him to his room, carrying the light myself as if I were escorting a king. They had lighted a fire and the dampness was resisting, befogging the panes of glass. No one ever went into that room. Only Silvio and I had been there, because there, as one must remember, was the secret panel that opened into the narrow passageway which connected it to the nympheum, unknown to anyone.

Before I left him, Lorenzino tried the lock several times. He asked me if there was another entrance and I did not reveal the passageway to him. Having pity on his fear, I suggested that Giambattista sleep beside him and he accepted at once. He knew him from Florence, from the time of the duke's wedding. As soon as I got them settled, I went to my room on the top floor, thoughtful. It took me a long time to get to sleep, held back by images of my adolescence in Tuscany, when the small Medici had come to give me his hand while Adriana dalla Roza was breathing her last and thinking about the traitor Beppo.

Two hours later, at dawn, the noise woke me up. Lorenzino and Giambattista were pounding on my door like madmen, half naked, their hair in disarray, their swords glistening in their hands. Maria Soderini, Giulia, Fulvio, and Messer Pandolfo appeared at the doors of their rooms with flickering candles. Grouped behind were the children, and halberdiers and pages were running up and down the stairs, also half dressed, barefoot, buttoning up their baldrics, holding their stilettos, stumbling over their halberds, asking what was going on. Lorenzino was shouting so loud that it was impossible to understand him. He threw himself into his mother's arms and stayed there, quivering like a bird. Then Giambattista explained what had happened.

As soon as they were alone, my restless guest began to insist on the dangers that surrounded him and on the necessity to be alert. He suspected that there was another secret entrance to Gian Corrado Orsini's room, and in spite of the page's denials he set about finding it. He searched the wall inch by inch with the experience he had obtained on many like occasions. I was worried while Giambattista went on that he was going to tell me that they had discovered the panel. But their discovery was even more sensational. Touching the walls, feeling about the fireplace, Lorenzino had touched the spring which I had been unable to find in my careful investigations, the one that my father had put into motion to work the mechanism that opened the way to the skeleton's cell. A small door had slid open quietly, the same as in horror stories, and then, after a brief hesitation, they both slipped in through the black opening. It was not necessary to say anything more to understand what had happened. I too, in my childhood, had experienced a similar horror. The skeleton crowned with mildewed silken roses was still there, his skull resting on his rib cage. The light of the candles, as it fell on the yellow bones and the torn clothing gave the illusion of a flickering life. The period's literary predilection for the macabre, which would culminate in the *Selena* by Gilardi, with its queen and princess holding the skulls of son and husband in their hands for an entire act, and in the *Arcipranda* by Decio, with its famous scene of quartered corpses, had familiarized us with fearsome episodes, but it was one thing to see them on the stage and something else quite different to confront them in reality. Lorenzino stopped for a moment and then he drew back shouting, and he had not stopped shouting from that point. He was babbling confusedly that the Duke of Bomarzo had plotted the nightmare in order to torture him, who could tell with what in mind, perhaps to terrify him with the ghostly memory of Alessandro de' Medici. The idea could not have been more absurd, but in his demented frenzy of a person obsessed, Lorenzino kept on repeating it without listening to any explanations. I vainly tried to clear up his distress and make him understand how much I had searched for that morbid apparition which I considered to be the evil ulcer of Bomarzo. I sent my relatives and servants away and when we were alone I made an effort to make him understand the torture that I had suffered because of that accursed set of bones. He refused to listen to me. He declared that he was going to leave without further ado and with great shouts he ordered his carriage hitched and prepared. I went to Maria Soderini, but from her expression I gathered that when Lorenzino fell into a trance like that it was useless to insist. Possessed by fear, he saw enemies and ambushes everywhere.

The strange thing was that Giambattista told me of his desire to leave with him. Even today I cannot ascertain the motives that impelled him to make such a sudden and thoughtless decision. It was obvious that he was planning to leave my estate because of his differences with Silvio, but the logical thing would have been to have taken refuge in Mugnano, where his sister was taking on the airs of a great lady. His ambition should have pushed him along that road. Nevertheless, he chose the uncertain and risky destiny of Lorenzaccio. Perhaps, even though it seemed strange to me, for he was the one who had driven her into prostitution, he was ashamed to be under the same roof with his sister, a place she had won with her feminine wiles. There was nothing left for me to surmise then but that during the time they were locked in the fateful room, Giambattista had succumbed to the prestigious fascination of Lorenzino. No one will ever know what went on between them during the time preceding the lugubrious discovery. Giambattista was very handsome, and ever since Lorenzino's childhood, since the years of his ambiguous friendship with the insipid Raffaele de' Medici and the predilection which had been commented on by Pope Clement VII—the nature of which I reject—the equivocal inclinations of the young lord had been fully criticized by mockers. Angry, I gave my permission, and without Lorenzino's knowledge, I even gave Giambattista some money to ease the penury of his new and excited master. They left as soon as the coach was ready, in spite of my protests. Clutching his mother, Duke Alessandro's assassin refused to answer my wave. On the other hand, Maria Soderini and Giambattista both kissed me.

The rain was coming down almost painfully. My page galloped away in the midst of the modest escort, and the people of the village, aware that something extraordinary was going on at the castle, gathered together to watch the departure of the creaking vehicle on the doors of which the Medici arms had been scratched out to avoid recognition: the *palle* that had caused so much blood to flow, just as the rain was flowing down over the livid scratched-out scar where they had been.

As soon as they left I went with Silvio into the cell that had been my prison. Nothing had changed there since the day that my father had called me a "son of Sodom" and had flung me into the gloomy darkness. The skeleton, who in open places in his torn garment showed the remains of a defective mummification, was still in his place. The same crown of cloth roses was around his forehead, and from his right arm a withered palm covered with dust was extended. A mysterious grimace, a vague and toothless smile added to the horror of it. Perhaps it was the body of a martyr, but it occurred to me, the same as the first time that I came face to face with the phantom, that an invisible malignant breath emanated from him, an infamous miasma that was poisoning his prison.

"We have to get him out of here at once," I told my secretary. "You have him buried and have some masses said for him. But we have to get him out of here."

Silvio went for help. In the meantime I was alone with the creature, who sometimes looked like a human skeleton to me and at other times a fantastic doll like those that I was collecting in the nympheum. My fear had not disappeared a whit, and added to it was a revulsion that made my flesh tingle. But I wanted to give myself a proof of strength, now that the evidence I gave was invariably that of hesitancy, and to triumph over cowardice. I slowly went over to his structure, holding the candle over my head, and I reached out a hand until I was almost touching the inert body with the tips of my fingers. I tried not to look at him, especially not at his empty sockets and his monstrous jaw, half bone and half dried and cracked skin. In the distance I could hear the footsteps of Silvio as he returned with some servants, and that gave me courage. I reached out my hand a little more and pushed the dead man. The skeleton fell to one side, as if it were falling apart, and the skull rolled to my feet and the fragile fragments that made up the figure broke apart when they hit the stones. The rag petals scattered about him. Then I saw what the skeleton of Bomarzo had kept hidden until then, what he was hiding in his solitude in the bowels of the castle like the guardian of the monster. They were some rolls of parchment tied with a faded green satin ribbon. I scarcely had time to pick them up and put them under my shirt. They scratched my chest. And at that moment the men came in.

I had decided that they would bury the enigmatic custodian of the manuscripts, but I changed my mind. I decided, on the contrary, that they should put the figure back together, as one puts a puppet together, tying and fastening it, and that with his crown and his palm in place, back in his position, he would be placed in the big glass urn that had been built into the base of one of the altars in the church, the one which had in its center the figures of Girolamo and Maerbale receiving rosaries from the Virgin. I decided on that afterward. I decided on it when

I was certain that the folios that I examined in my room were the two letters from the alchemist Dastyn to Cardinal Napoleone Orsini which Paracelsus had told me about and which I had searched for uselessly throughout Italy. Now they were in my possession at last. I finally had my hands on the immortality that was promised in my horoscope. I had looked for those letters in cities and palaces and there they were waiting for me in Bomarzo. It had to be like that for the symbol to be complete. They had to be in Bomarzo and nowhere else.

My father, my grandfather, and the previous lords of Bomarzo, those who knew of the presence of the bones hidden within the thickness of the walls of the castle, were no doubt ignorant of the treasure they were guarding like the legendary sphinx. Or, if they sensed it, they preferred for it to remain there, isolated, powerless, because they feared the consequences that its tremendous secret was capable of unleashing. My grandmother Diana probably was not aware of that secret because of her status as a woman. She would have told me when I questioned her. As master of the place, it was up to me. One might imagine that my father, the day he locked me up with the sinister apparition, was putting me through a cruel experiment. If I found the letters by my own means, overcoming anguish and horror, it would have shown that I was worthy of them. He would not have tested Girolamo that way. He had confidence in Girolamo and it was possible that he had already revealed the disquieting mystery to him. But over the years Dastyn's enigma was waiting for me, the predestined Oedipus. When I opened the folios, a century old twice over, I wept with pride. I could not read them, I could not decipher the dissolved Gothic script, but I wept with pride. Of all the Orsinis I was the one chosen for the miraculous revelation, I, the hunchback, the weakling, the one who had been denied glory was the chosen one, I placed my lips on the crackling sheep skin. In that way I had my revenge for the disdain of Gian Corrado Orsini, the one who had wanted to wipe me out, deprive me of Bomarzo. I was getting my revenge because now I enjoyed the security of being the best of the extensive line which rang with the names of so many illustrious people and of whom none deserved Bomarzo with titles that qualified them to compete with those that destiny had awarded me forever, forever.

And while I looked and looked, passing my grandfather Franciotto's magnifying glass over the pale ocher lines, the text on which the perpetuity of my victory depended, the villagers of Bomarzo were filing through the church and crossing themselves before the remains that the duke was giving them to venerate. Did I know whether those remains might be those of a saint? Was my feeling of evil enough to think the opposite? Could I not have been carrying the evil within myself and projecting it outward? There had been many saints in the region. Saint Anselm, Saint Denis, Saint Hilary, Saint Eustizio, Saint Valentine... Of course, since their holy feet had trod the soil of Bomarzo, ten, twelve, thirteen centuries had passed, and if anything survived of their traces it was only enough to fill a small reliquary. Lords and peasants came from far away, anxious to seek the aid of our new protector. Even my cousin from Mugnano came with Pantasilea—he did not dare bring Porzia with him—and he placed an offering of six thick candles that bore the Orsini shield painted with a jubilant sinople and in bright scarlet on the altar. I spied on them from behind a curtain: the duke in front, dressed in red velvet, a quadruple gold chain about his neck; Pantasilea behind, proud and sparkling like one of her peacocks, pearl lilies in her red curls, kneeling in a prodigious dress of violet damask, with purple flames bursting out of her broad sleeves; and behind, Sigismondo Orsini, whom I had commissioned to receive them, half of his face covered by the dark cloth, his free eye glowing, his turquoise and white outfit making all of him like a precious stone. The three held candles in their hands. What were they asking for, what was each one seeking with fingers clasped in prayer? What could be given them by the skeleton that had been put together piece by piece like a sad pathetic toy grinning there in his urn? When the prayers were over they inspected my room of curios. I was not concerned about their seeing them, but I did not want them to see Silvio's room. Sigismondo started up the automatons and showed off the craftsmanship of the clocks. Unexpectedly, the skeleton had become another oddity among the many at Bomarzo.

Later on the relic was taken from there and moved in its glass box to a small and insignificant altar located on the main floor of the castle, where it still is, changed into a curious object that startles and delights the few travelers who discover it, because no one knows the meaning of that mask of mocking bones or remembers its origins; but when my will imposed its law on Bomarzo, I, Pier Francesco Orsini, sanctified the skeleton which, as an instrument of terror and used with an aim to torture me and terrify me, had been transformed into an allegory of eternal life. Perhaps I was thinking, innocently and proudly, that in the end, among the functions of the duke there was that of creating saints to protect his domains. It was not in vain that there was a surfeit of popes and sainted people in my blood.

# 9. THE ACCURSED WAR

*The study of Dastyn's letter with Fulvio Orsini—Literary discussions—The deaths of Duke Pier Luigi and Giambattista Martelli—Silvio da Narni, mystic, and his wife, mistress of the Duke of Mugnano—The war of Henry II of France against Charles V—My departure for the war—My fine armor—The Guises and Orazio Farnese in Metz—The Picardy campaign: Thérouanne, Hesdin—The false gypsy women and the apocryphal flag— The project for decorating Bomarzo—Michelangelo sends me Jacopo del Duca—His assistants—Fascination for the Sicilian Zanobbi Sartorio— The violet eyes are closed—The serpent—The book of rocks*

I THOUGHT that when I had the alchemist's letters in my power I would soon be master of their secret, but the task of deciphering, translating, and interpreting their contents was quite long. It was hindered from the beginning by two circumstances: the necessity of surrounding the job with the greatest discretion, and the possibility of the help that could be supplied, in spite of his young years and scant experience, by my nephew Fulvio Orsini. At first I had even wanted to exclude him, but I soon understood that if I did not have recourse to his learning at least, my work would not take a single step forward. I locked myself in my room in the nympheum, unrolled the folios, hiding them among the pages of the projected poem to guard against any surprise, and I spent hours looking at those incomprehensible signs.

What I discovered was that Dastyn had used astuteness from the beginning when he wrote the documents: they were written backwards, letter by letter. It was easy to re-establish the text and I dedicated myself to that during the first part of the task. Then I noticed an abundance of capital letters in the construction, chosen to designate the substantial part, and that Dastyn (the pseudo Lully had used the same procedure) had probably used the alphabet at random. Oh, if Fulvio had only been older, if he had only possessed the knowledge that came with experience. The whole process would have gone much faster. But there was nothing for me to do but make use of what I had at hand, trusting in the fate that had brought me to the entrance to the labyrinth. A tenacious certainty drove me on, a certainty that some day I would resolve the enigma, and I thought that there might be applied to me the words an angel spoke in a dream to the distant alchemist Nicolas Flamel as he showed him a book full of magical drawings and about which Silvio da Narni had told me: "Look at this book of which you understand nothing; for many others it will be unintelligible, but one day you shall see in it what no one else shall see."

I would have to trust in one person at least and share my treasure with him. And that person was Fulvio. Above all, Silvio should not even have had a hint of the closeness of the miracle. In order to distract him I helped him as much as possible in his own investigations: the search for the stone. If he found it, so much the better for him. To the previous elements of the laboratory I added several more, some rather costly: the sand oven, the Spanish aludel which was made of vessels of enameled clay, the pelican with two tubes coming out of its belly; and that multitude of objects with mysterious names, all of which designated with frivolous tones (the "philosophical egg," the "prison," the "tomb," the "chicken house," the "bridal chamber," the "matrix," the "mother's womb") everything that was needed to obtain the thing that also changed its name and was called, according to different alchemists: "Philosopher's Stone," "Stone of Egypt," "Power of Projection," "Great Elixir of the Quintessence," "Great Elixir of Gold Tincture," or "Great Teaching."

Fulvio was enthusiastic with the work. He was fascinated by enigmas and all that went beyond learning. Patiently, slowly, he was clearing away the gibberish that filled the four wide folios. In addition to his knowledge of dead languages (there were numerous Hebrew words in the letters), he used a marvelous intuition that later on would astound the readers of his monumental scholarly books and which allowed him to move in an agile way through the midst of the interlocking allegories. Alongside him my help was practically nonexistent. Upset over the slowness of the process—not suspecting that it would take years, decades—despairing that it would even be crowned with success, and taking on hope again with the most minute discovery, the most subtle and weak one, I went back to the desk where the stanzas of *Bomarzo* were waiting for me and added five or six lines to the composition. Behind the wall the fire from Silvio's ovens could be heard crackling.

And in the meantime, up above in the courtly rooms presided over by the portraits by Lotto and Sebastiano del Piombo, the intellectual guests went on with their philosophical arguments, their biting epigrams. None of them could ever have imagined what was going on in the nearby valley below them. No one could have imagined it, least of all, naturally, the peasants, who watched our sophisticated activities from a distance, as if my small court were an unreal world for them, peopled with splendid actors who came and went on an illuminated stage, while they were the only ones who were really alive, because for the peasants the tangible reality of life was plowing fields, milking cows, taking sheep and goats to pasture, heaping up grain, feeding hens and doves, butchering hogs; and everything else belonged to an orbit that went beyond the positive and arose iridescent, unreachable, over the roofs of their huts and barns, sustained perhaps by the multicolored columns of smoke that were coming out of the nympheum; an orbit in which lords and poets spoke enigmatic words and in which existence unfolded without suffering, so similar it was to a strange and exquisite dance.

From Rome, Florence, Milan, Naples, and Venice messengers arrived with mysterious books and rare manuscripts. I acquired the copies of five works attributed to a Benedictine monk who had been dead for a long time, the one who had discovered antimony, Basilius Valentinus (which means, etymologically, "Powerful King"), which were not published until a century later: the *Azoth*, the *Apocalypsis chimica*, the *Manifestatio artificiorum*, the *Haliography*, and the *Twelve Keys*, which were accompanied by disturbing allegorical drawings. And some time later I even got hold of a copy of *The Elixir of the Philosophers* in its Latin version, for it was not translated until 1557, which made reference to Pope John XXII himself, giving it great importance for my investigations, for he was the pope at Avignon who had maintained a correspondence with Dastyn relative to the learned themes that most interested the so-called Sons of Hermes. Fulvio needed them because of the link that existed between the Philosopher's Stone and the Potion of Long Life so that he would not go astray in the fatiguing maze created by the obscure pages he was studying. I was surprised that Fulvio did not abandon the work, but he gave constant testimony of his stubbornness, and the obstacles and difficulties stimulated him. Small, pale, modest, day after day, leaning his high forehead and gray eyes over the volumes, his agile fingers were taking down the copious notes that became familiar sights to me. There was also an abundance of esoteric figures in Dastyn's letters—the three outstretched hands, one of which was black; the ox and the two angels prostrate before the cross; fire and water embracing; the lion devouring the serpent; the cock in the alembic—and Fulvio was copying them down, bringing out the form of their microscopic letters.

From time to time Silvio would ask us what we were doing, closed up in there, and I answered him that we were studying some cameos that had belonged to the patriarchs of Aquileia. He was too preoccupied with his own obsession to be concerned with ours. The missing gold was reflected in his face, which was turning yellow. But we could not prolong the deception. His laboratory was next to our study and the texts that we were using were much too obvious for his specialty. Therefore, grudgingly, although I calculated that I could get some advantage from his cooperation and that Maerbale's death had established between us incomparable links as accomplices, which made the possibility of betrayal remote, I brought him up to date on my project, which was so intimately related to his own. His excitement was great. He pounced upon the works of John XXII and the monk Basilius as upon the food at a banquet, and from then on Fulvio, he, and I worked together. Luckily, immortality did not disturb him as it has agitated the many searchers for the Stone, as much as the above-mentioned Nicolas Flamel and his wife Pernelle, Agrippa of Nettesheim, Ireneo Philalethe, the Count of Saint-Germain, and Cagliostro, part of an extensive list that included emperors of Germany, charlatans, scientists like the Arab ibn-Sina—Avicenna, the prince of physicians—and humble illuminated dreamers. He wanted the gold, only the gold. And, of course, Porzia.

Between Silvio and Fulvio I peered into the atmosphere of magical mystery that ever since childhood, ever since I had sensed in the tense air of Bomarzo the age-old Etruscan presences, had hallucinated me. Everything else withdrew before the urge that brought us together before the *kerotakis*, the oven that had been invented by a woman alchemist, Mary the Jewess. Bundles of herbs hung from the walls like claws, and in the mortars lay the sulphur, mercury, and salt of the combinations while all around we were being watched by the primitive portraits of the divine and human masters who had glimpsed the Great Work—which Silvio had painted with a clumsy hand—Hermes Trismegistus, Agathodaemon, Cheops, Apollonius, Democritus, Alexander the Great, Plato, Aristotle, Heraclitus, Pythagoras, Moses, the Emperor Heraclius, Menos, Pauscris, Prester John, Zosimus, Olympiodorus, Porphyrius, Synesius, Artephius (the one who claimed to have lived for a thousand years), Aeneas of Gaza, Stephanus, Ostanes—surrounded by vague images like the green lion crowned with laurel, the symbol of vitriol; the black raven, who was lead; the white eagle, who was ammonia; the celestial dew, which was mercury; the lepers, the allegory of the base metals. The figures were looking at us, waiting, as we ourselves were waiting. And Silvio, wearing a glass mask on his lean face, which gave him a supernatural look and a kinship with those figures covered with stars and Hebrew and Arabic letters, took the bellows to the oven and pumped them, raising scarlet and blue flames that flashed up about the eternal procession of initiates and lighted up their visionary eyes in the crude paintings.

The children were growing up outside of the secret circle. They were growing up with their mother and Messer Pandolfo. I had no time to give them. The anguish of immortality held me prisoner and prevented me from seeing their play, their quarrels. Immortality was throbbing inside the nympheum, in Dastyn's enigma, if no longer in the pages of my poem. In any case, all of my children were different from me, even the hunchback Maerbale, who was evidently not disturbed by his deformity. Unlike me, the first hunchback of my line, my son Maerbale thought perhaps that his singularity, which made him resemble the duke more than the others, showed his superiority. Yes, they were quite different. They did not have, as I did, a basic feeling for the race. That was evident later, even in their marriages. The blood that they brought into the family through their matches—that of Porzia Vitelli, Marcantonio Marescotti, Nicola Montemellini, the Baron of Paganica, Margarita Savelli, the daughter of the lord of Ariccia—although of noble origin, could not be compared to ours. And they were not really interested in anything that interested me. On some occasions I tried to make them understand, guiding them through the collections in the castle and explaining to them the rarity of the objects accumulated in the nympheum, what those items meant as an index of refined civilization, but they refused to become involved in my game of wonders. They could not understand it. Later on, after years had passed, I learned that among themselves they had criticized the acquisitions that never grew fewer because there was no lessening of my curiosity or temptation concerning the beautiful and the unique, and I knew that they muttered about how those extravagant tastes were compromising their inheritance. But I let them talk. The inheritance would always be mine. As soon as we unraveled the proper formula—and that would inevitably happen, even though many years would have to pass first—my final liberation would come about. They could plot, they could complain, they could say whatever they wanted to. I was going along a different road, surrounded by admirable things and experiences, toward the perpetual light.

Only Orazio shared my likes. He did feel in his veins the proud ancestral warmth. He would question me about our ancestors and listen to me in absorption just as I had listened to my grandmother. But I did not feel comfortable with him. In the depths of his eyes, just as far down as if in deep water, one could see the hidden glow of my brother Maerbale's eyes. He was a trickster like him and unpredictable; dangerous perhaps. He seduced me, of course; he always seduced me. There was something in Orazio Orsini that separated him from the others. My imagination probably added disquieting elements to it that linked him with my guilt over Maerbale's death, but there was no doubt that he had a strong personality that exuded an imponderable charm. I did not wish to follow him into a zone of obvious dangers. Little by little, I entrusted young Sansovino with the task of teaching him everything about the chronicle of our line, and that was the germ of the

*History of the House of Orsini and of the Illustrious Men of the House of Orsini*, the four volumes of which were published in Venice in 1565 by the tenacious courtier. In the end, some time later, Orazio left for Florence. I wanted him, like my grandfather Franciotto, my father, and me to be educated there, for Duke Cosimo—similar to what was done later by his successor Francesco I, married to an archduchess of Austria—followed the rigid protocol of the Spanish court by agreement with his wife, the daughter of the viceroy of Naples, and the children of the important families of Italy and Germany learned in Tuscan palaces the office of page with rigorous ceremony. The Medicis stressed that worldly liturgy more than any other princes on the peninsula, perhaps because they felt the weakness of their position, which was in dispute and artificial, built on quicksand, and they calculated that by instituting a cult with the participation, as reverent and regimented acolytes, of petty noblemen from distant castles where those complex rites were not practiced, they would guarantee their position and they would astutely acquire—at least in its external aspects—the unquestionable prerogatives awarded by the divine right. The Medicis were like gods and their religious service demanded strict attention. The long family contact with popes, the constant advantage of red hats and miters had taught them since long ago about the advantages of solemn pomp and assured them a regimented veneration, and if to it the inflexible traditions of the Spaniards and the Austrians were added, it must be understood that while the turbulent aristocrats learned impeccable manners from them, it did not influence, as was natural, the violence of passion and their terrible outbreaks of it—for few houses have been bloodied by as many crimes as that of Duke Cosimo de' Medici—they did cover their actions with a perfect varnish that rendered so much alike, like brothers, the adolescents painted by Pontormo, Salviati, and Bronzino in the gallery of delicate cheekbones, dreamy eyes, majestic expressions, and clothing that was as alive for its sober original splendor as the boys who wore it. Orazio Orsini went there to be educated and he came back to Bomarzo making me tremble with pride, more handsome, more refined, more lordly, so that next to him my sons looked like rustics dressed up as gentlemen. That was how paradoxical I was: I wanted the best for the one whose paternity I doubted, but mixed in that decision of mine there were ingredients that were difficult to appreciate, among which there was perhaps the idea that by it I was paying in a very small way for the death of Maerbale and that I was giving some pleasure to Giulia Farnese, so bereft of happiness, as well as obeying an inclination that drove me to exalt and polish like an admired diamond a personality that attracted me strongly.

But as great as that attraction was, my preoccupations stopped me from getting close to him. My world was a different one. It was a world that was so subjugating, so forbidden, that since I was reading parts of the difficult Latin *Maccaronea* of Folengo at the time, when I came to the lines that described the palace of Queen Gulfora, the great center of witchcraft, I feared that someday, as had happened to the sorceress, the ruins of my castle would entomb me under their rubble. But for that to happen I would have to die, and that was impossible. The certainty of immortality carried me along like a wing, like a wind. While in the castle the interminable discussions of the writers went on, I would stroll among them as if I were carrying some invisible relic hidden under my clothing over my heart.

We used to stroll at dusk, when the weather permitted, along the terraces of the garden, and it must not have been one of the least curious spectacles that we offered to the peasants who from a distance saw the hunchbacked Duke of Bomarzo as he walked with a tabard over his shoulders, waving his delicate hands in the midst of the poets. Molza left us around that time and he ended up settling down in his native Modena to die in the bosom of his abandoned family. Syphilis was devouring him, but before he left he recited his *Ninfa Tiberina* for us, the eighty-one exquisite octaves that have been compared to Benvenuto's goldwork and which, like it, are complicated and subtle. On hearing its music, as the arabesques unfolded in periods of intertwined parentheses, and in which the evocation of a wooden cup took five stanzas, I understood—for at that time I had sincere praise for the sweet confection, the beautiful dessert with pictures of shepherds and naiads—that I would never be capable of writing anything similar and that my *Bomarzo* was not worth the pens it was written with. But not even with that proof did I decide to put aside the scratched-up manuscript. It was my pretext, my alibi for solitude.

In the meantime, the writers argued tirelessly. They did it with arguments made up of cruel irony, understanding, like Cardinal Bibbiena and according to Castiglione's *Courtier*, that if one should resist crudeness and indecencies, practical jokes were a sign of good taste. And even though Bibbiena condemned them, there was an abundance of obscenities. They fulfilled the culinary function of salt and pepper in the debate, and our laughter would ring out loudly through the peace of the sunset that was being emphasized by the mournful tolling of the bells in the church. I was quite pleased with the tone of the respectful conversations in which pornography was cloaked in urbanity. Rarely was the covenant broken as happened years later when Annibale Caro, the permanent secretary of the Farneses, famous for his translation of the *Aeneid* which roused the jealousy of Messer Pandolfo, evolved his poem in praise of the fleurs-de-lis on the shield of France and those on the Farnese arms, the one that begins, "Come ye into the shade of the great and golden lily." That work provoked a negative reaction in Lodovico Castelvetro and divided the intellectuals of the peninsula into two angry factions, who, abandoning the rhetorical basis of the dispute, did not hesitate to accuse Castelvetro of having murdered Longo, the friend of Caro, and the latter of having ordered Castelvetro's assassination, and the discord grew so hot that the latter had to go into exile to save his skin from the Inquisition. Nevertheless, as I have said, it was exceptional for the controversies to leave the field of literature. Everything consisted of the friendly mocking of one's colleagues or of the recalling with honeyed words of illustrious women, like the harlot Tulia of Aragon, Veronica Gambara, whose house was more like an academy, and Vittoria Colonna, inseparable from the mention of Buonarroti. It pleased them to embroider insolent suspicions about the friendship of the widow of the Marquis of Pescara and the master, for in that way they thought they were eliminating barriers for artists that were considered impassable. I had to bring them back to reality on certain occasions with rough jokes, for I could not forget that, after all, I too had Colonna blood in my veins from one of my grandmothers, and that my sister-in-law Cecilia was the niece of Madonna Vittoria and lived at her side. Downcast, humbled, looking out of the corners of their eyes, my guests went back to enumerating the misfortunes of Bernardo Tasso, the future author of the *Amadigi*, and laughing at the poetry that Alamanni had written in adulation of Francis I of France, as if none of them—not even Betussi or Sansovino, heaven forbid—could have been accused of falling into adulation, that sad and understandable sin of impecunious publicists.

They were also accustomed to go on about theological questions. When Cristoforo Madruzzo, already a cardinal, was visiting me, those conversations became particularly adventurous and attractive. From the time of the opening of the ecumenical Council of Trent, religious themes were in fashion. Professional dialecticians and common people, incited by curiosity, became entangled in arguments that could have ended up with them on the stake. I preferred to avoid them. It bothered me to have them discussed in Bomarzo, where the secret practices of Silvio and the duke were more than sufficient to alert some bureaucratic Torquemada. It had not gone well for the group gathered around Vittoria Colonna in Viterbo, for some of the members were suspected of heresy, like the preacher Ochino and later on the unfortunate Carnesecchi, so much so that the pope ordered Cardinal Reginald Pole, the Englishman, a descendant of the Duke of Clarence, to keep away from his dangerous friends, and I was afraid of something like that happening in Bomarzo. Therefore, as soon as my guests mentioned the session of the council in which the question of the Holy Scriptures was brought up, or the one in which the problem of original sin was debated and its definition was reduced to five points, or the opposing points of view concerning the dilemma of justification by faith, I could smell the dangers and I led the talk back into the field of literature and the bragging of Aretino, who governed timid princes from Venice, although no one dared say anything totally against the pamphleteering dictator, and the dangerous schismatic shoal was left behind.

My eyes would then leave the company and look toward the valley, where a column of smoke with small yellow twirls assured me that Silvio da Narni was still at his desperate task, and on those occasions it was difficult for me to determine which was the authentic truth that was being offered me and which was the absurd fantasy: whether the alchemist who was sunken in the bosom of the earth like a mole, surrounded by the effigies of the supreme wonder-workers and mixing his potions in search of the formula for gold and immortality, or the men of letters who used beautiful and astute words as they exerted themselves to hypnotize one another with metaphors and symbols and practiced a different kind of magic that was precious and sterile.


Pier Luigi Farnese was killed in 1547, on September tenth, as the result of a successful conspiracy in which the nobles of Piacenza were allied with Ferrante Gonzaga, the governor of Milan, who obviously acted in agreement with Charles V. The emperor never pardoned and there had been blood in his eye ever since he had discovered through Cosimo de' Medici that Pier Luigi had planned to assassinate him. That was learned, as the reader will recall, from the revelation made to us at Bomarzo by the jealous Sigismondo and which one of those present betrayed. So that Silvio's horoscope, which had guaranteed long life for the Duke of Parma and Piacenza, was not fulfilled. Pride was also a cause of the loss of the son of Paul III. He had usurped the castles of several noblemen in his domains; he had intervened in the machinations of the Fieschis when Genoa tried to shake off the Spanish yoke, and then he deceived them in favor of Doria, playing two opposing cards at the same time; he had reached an understanding with the shady Piero Strozzi to drive the Medicis off the throne of Florence; and he was involved, with his son Orazio as intermediary, in maneuvers with the French with the aim of their recovering the Milanese. There were too many pitfalls. He himself had become entrapped in the net that he had woven as the strands of it slipped out of the hands that illness had covered with pustules. It was said at the time, for everything concerning him and his father had a magic aura about it, that an elf, guided by a jester—as if specters needed to be guided by jesters—had appeared to him in the middle of the night in the monumental coldness of his fortress and with sibylline certainty warned him to beware of the letters PLAC, but the duke only saw in it the name of the city where he lived and which he considered loyal—"Placentia," as it is engraved on the coins—and it did not penetrate his mind that they corresponded to the initials of the conspirators: Pallavicini, Landi, Anguissola, Confalonieri. His end was horrible. They threw his body into the moat from one of the windows of the citadel after showing it to the terrified multitude, and while some of the conspirators harangued the people, making the withered word freedom flutter in their speeches, and offered the mob, first to calm it down and then to rouse it up, the tempting prospect of sacking the castle, Don Álvaro de Luna occupied the city in the name of Charles of Hapsburg, preceding the entrance of Ferrante Gonzaga with the Piacenzan exiles.

The pope's reaction went beyond imagination. Overwhelmed with grief, he convoked the Consistory—he was almost eighty years old—and declared with tremendous calm, "I have discovered that Gonzaga is to blame for the crime. As his father Alessandro, I will never avenge Pier Luigi Farnese, but as Paul III, the pontiff and head of the Church, I will avenge Pier Luigi, the son and gonfalonier of the Holy Church even if I must suffer martyrdom for it like so many others."

I hastened to kiss his embroidered slipper among the members of the family. He wept as he embraced Giulia. He looked at me as he huddled over, extremely old; he no longer resembled a fox, or, in any case, he resembled a fox who had escaped the huntsmen for a long time but had been wounded by a treacherous crossbow. I never thought that he would react like that, that he had so much love for that vicious offspring whom he also feared. He made us promise—gathered around him were the most important people of his line and the affront involved me not only because of my marriage, but also because Pier Luigi was the husband and grandson of Orsinis—that we would support him in his vengeance. That word "vengeance" sounded harsh in the mouth of the legate of Christ. We naturally promised him everything he asked for. He was trembling on his throne and the robes of the cardinals surrounding him, flaming brilliantly, made the huddled old man look as if he were in the midst of a bonfire. He died two years later without having made the emperor restore Piacenza to his grandson Ottavio. The latter had set himself up in Parma immediately after the murder of his father, and Ferrante invaded a large part of the territory. Taking advantage of a truce, the pope thought that since he ran the risk of losing both cities, he would take Parma back as a papal state, and he commanded Ottavio to turn over its rule to Camillo Orsini, who was acting as governor-general of the Church at that time. The new duke acceded at first, but he soon began to plot with Charles V, who, after all, was his father-in-law, and who, after liquidating his father, owed that much at least to the husband of Margaret of Austria, even if it were only that realm. Paul III's heart spilled over like an overfilled glass and, unable to resist that final blow, he died, shaken by the convulsions of a violent fever.

The idea never crossed my mind to become involved in the bloody politics of my relatives. In the rarefied atmosphere of Bomarzo vigilance followed a different route. We lived as if we were in the midst of an extraordinary dream. The secret laboratory where Silvio was feeding his evaporating dishes, and the room with the wonders, whose hanging automatons and fantastic animal skeletons swayed above the manuscript of my useless poem, were the basic part of my existence, as if, like the stone walls that isolated Ottavio Farnese from his enemies in Parma, invisible bulwarks separated us from the rest of the world.

Early in 1548 Giambattista Martelli sent me a long letter from Venice. His unhappiness showed through the cramped writing. Lorenzaccio was practically holding him prisoner in a big house near the church of San Polo, where he lived with his uncle Alessandro Soderini. Only rarely and in disguise did they leave their imprisonment, with an escort, because they sensed that they were being watched. They would go to visit a lady, Elena Barozzi, married to the patrician Antonio Centani, who lived in the San Tomà section. To be near his beauty, Lorenzino had moved from the palace of Roberto Strozzi to the one in San Polo, and that did not seem to be a good idea to Giambattista, because the protection they had enjoyed in the first palace was incomparably better. The blond Barozzi woman had fallen in love with the Medici as soon as he began courting her, and what was very strange, given his character, Lorenzino had fallen in love with her. He was in love for the first time and he was writing poetry.

As I continued reading I understood the motive that had impelled my friend to throw himself into the arms of that woman whose charms Giambattista was pondering, and who had lighted up in his breast an ardor that he had never known until then. He felt alone. He had no one. And he felt defrauded. The ever-lessening consideration shown him by the Florentine exiles for the death of Duke Alessandro did not modify the situation at all and was not enough to calm his fears or calm the hunger of his pride. Love surged up in him as a need for shelter, as some unknown exalting stimulation. And he gave himself over to love, from which he had fled in his family's court. He had himself called Messer Dario, thinking that the assassins who were doubtless roaming the streets of Venice would not discover him under that peaceful name, as they would not discover him in the strange disguises—that of a gypsy woman, for example—which he used when he decided to leave the palace.

That life had become unbearable for Martelli. He ate little and poorly; he was always fearful; the dangers grew each night, because the urge to see the beautiful Barozzi made her lover go out more often, and although that freed Giambattista from the tedium of his prison, he did not enjoy himself particularly in the residence of the Venetian woman, because there his only task consisted of guarding the door to the bedroom where the couple were dedicating themselves to forgetting their respective woes. Giambattista told me that the husband, the patrician Antonio Centani, was a notable coin collector and a generous patron of the arts, and that, mad about music, he would gather together the nobility of the city for refined concerts. Lorenzino would attend the gatherings in disguise. They called him Messer Dario, but they knew who he was, and the inclusion in the gatherings of that nervous, thin, dark, and ambiguous gentleman (for he could disguise himself as a gypsy woman) who had done away with his cousin, the Duke of Florence—using, which was almost incredible, those thin hands of an author of low comedies on which the glances of the ladies would alight with a sudden shiver—added to the balls in the Centani palace the attraction of a novelty that the mistress of the house exploited skillfully, for even though several of those in attendance had used a steel blade to dispatch some kinsman, there was no one among them who had killed a duke to save his homeland. What Giambattista had not been able to unearth was whether Centani was aware of what was going on between Lorenzino and his wife, although his blindness seemed impossible, because it was taking place right under his nose. The attitude aroused harsh doubts in my former page: on one side the hazards of the amorous plot, on the other the prospects of a knife in the back. The swordsmen hired by Cosimo de' Medici or those that the Venetian hired would end up doing away with Lorenzaccio and his servant. And that anguish and boredom (Giambattista detested serious music as much as it was adored by the music-loving cuckold) produced very slim, almost nonexistent compensations. Everything consisted of wandering through the house in San Polo, chasing the enormous rats through the galleries; waving Lorenzino's hair, something that my page did very well, as I know from experience; sharpening the daggers; slipping through the streets wrapped in a cloak, his hand on the hilt of his sword, never letting his restless master out of his sight; listening for the hundredth time to the cursed violins; standing guard as a custodian of love without enjoying any love. Giambattista stressed the last. His dashing master had assured him when they left Bomarzo that in Venice he would enjoy loves of all kinds, like a sultan's envoy. And there was nothing. Oh, Bomarzo, Bomarzo... When I came to that part of the letter I could feel the heart of Porzia's twin pounding. Bomarzo, where he had been born, where he had been happy. Bomarzo, the afternoons in the garden, the hunts, the fishing parties on the Tiber, the fine words of Messer Betussi, Messer Molza, Messer Pandolfo, the cordial elegance of Signor Sigismondo Orsini... How, from what madness, had it occurred to him to leave it? He added some poignant words: "I look into the dirty water of the canals as they carry off the filth and I think about our green fields. I close my eyes, my Lord, and I can hear the bees on the terraces."

I wrote him to come back whenever he wanted to, that he would always have a home in Bomarzo. But my letter never reached his hands. The two murderers who killed Lorenzaccio and his uncle Soderini as they were on their way once more to a meeting with the blond Barozzi, felled Giambattista with one thrust and threw him into one of those same repugnant canals. Such little importance was given him that in the account that the chief assassin, Cecchino da Bibbona, made of his crime, he did not even mention the end of poor Giambattista. The only thing that interested Cecchino and Bebo da Volterra, his accomplice, was to do away with the killer of Alessandro de' Medici and in that way earn the protection of the new duke. Not only did they obtain that, but they also got that of Charles V himself. They took refuge—their white jerkins stained red, carrying on their crosslets the marks of the swords of their victims—in the house of the Spanish ambassador, Diego Hurtado de Mendoza, the one to whom the *Lazaríllo de Tormes* has been attributed, who rewarded them with lordly splendor, and later on, mingling with his long retinue, they escaped to Florence through the swarms of agents of the doge. The aristocrat Centani had nothing to do with the affair. He went on classifying coins, polishing medals, talking about the young Palestrina, and listening to violins.

The news made me numb. I went down to the chapel and began to pray, as the wicked Cecchino da Bibbona says that he prayed, imploring divine help as he held together the hands that were red with blood. That was not strange. It was not strange that I, my brother's murderer, should pray; nor that the murderer of Lorenzaccio and Giambattista should pray; nor that after he stabbed the Duke of Milan, Girolamo Olgiati should raise his prayers to Saint Ambrose; nor that Benvenuto Cellini, kneeling before Clement VII, should ask for absolution; nor that Paolo Boscoli, the one who plotted an attempt on the lives of the Medicis, should have received communion with fervor before being executed by the headsman. The ones who had killed Pier Luigi probably prayed. We all prayed. One of those, exceptionally, who did not was the unfortunate Lorenzaccio. If he prayed to anyone, for many thought he was religious, it was most likely to Plato. I covered my eyes with my hands and I prayed to God for the souls of the victims. Three of the boys whose adolescence I had shared in the city of the lily—Ippolito, Lorenzino, and Alessandro—had died a bad death. I remembered them lying on the fragrant grass around their cousin Catherine, the *duchessina*, the one who would be Queen of France. Adriana dalla Roza was weaving garlands of jasmines to crown them with and in the background Abul appeared among the pines, like a statue carved of black and turquoise marble. Ippolito was singing, Alessandro was keeping time, and Lorenzino stood up and began to dance by himself, bowing to the air. My eyes filled with tears. And I thought about Giambattista. I saw him floating amid the rubbish that flowed along over the crystal reflections of the palaces, his blond hair spread out like a flower, just as I had seen my brother Girolamo floating in the waters of the Tiber. Once in Venice, the night of the fire at the Cornaro palace, I had pushed Giambattista, out of spite, naked into the waters of the Grand Canal amid the jeering of Pier Luigi Farnese, and I had seen him swim away, mouthing curses, toward the porticoes. But his arms and legs were not moving now. He was floating, stiff, in the nauseating shroud that sparkled with the light of torches. While I was stringing together the threads of a vague Lord's Prayer, I recalled our distant meetings, the time Silvio and I had taken him and Porzia, laughing, playing, anxiously aquiver, to the tomb in Piamiano, where we were surrounded by the equivocal heroes. I could pray and at the same time savor in my memory the images of sin. That double and contradictory possibility was characteristic of the period. We used it like defensive armor. I shall not try to justify it. I am referring to what was going on inside of me, so complex; that pagan and Christian thing that no one would understand today.

I heard some soft footsteps and I sank my face even deeper into my hands. Through my fingers I made out the mysterious skeleton in his case, who was perhaps receiving my confused prayers. Someone had stopped beside me in the uncertainty of the half-light. I turned and drew back in fright, because I thought that coming out of the darkness in which the weak candles were flickering, bathed in tears, was the spectral face of Giambattista. But it was not he. It was his twin sister, Porzia, so identical to her brother that it was frightening. She knelt down beside me and remained there without our exchanging a single word. Her muffled sobs could barely be heard in the solitude of the chapel where the childhood figures of Maerbale and Girolamo were reaching out their painted right arms toward the virgin's rosaries, and where the youthful body of Saint Sebastian glimmered like a white flame. Porzia had been mine too; mine too had been that flesh which time had molded into opulence but from which it had taken away the beauty. I turned my face once more toward hers and through the veil that was wet with tears I kissed her on the lips for a long time. Porzia leaned over, startled; I tried to hold her back, but she left the church. She was going back to Mugnano. When I abandoned the church in turn, I noticed Silvio in the shadows of the doorway, there where the Orsini bear was raising up the Farnese lily.

I do not know if he met his wife, if they had spoken. In any case, that was not important. Silvio—it is interesting to note this other change in his character, for it can be recalled that soon after his marriage he drew away from Porzia and that what drove him along the path of alchemy was the search for the formula for gold that would permit him to get her back—no longer cared about Giambattista's sister. He had renounced her. That psychological change is as difficult to understand by our present-day criteria as the attitude of my contemporaries of the sixteenth century of which I spoke above, the one which mingles pious unction with sinful thoughts and memories. The constant reading of treatises and magical books relating to the Stone had aroused in him a kind of illumination, which was, furthermore, the one sought by *pure* alchemists, those not contaminated by exclusively materialist urges. The Stone, the Great Elixir, ceased to be an end in itself and became a means leading to the perfection of knowledge. Sulphur, Mercury, and Salt were joined together intimately with the persons of the Holy Trinity for those who practiced that strange type of asceticism. The Stone would purify the body and soul in such a way that the one who possessed it, locked up in the darkness of his laboratory, would see the celestial movements of the constellations as in a mirror, and he would understand the influences of the stars without observing the firmament. For those mystics of bellows and alembic, scientific adventure was inseparable from spiritual adventure. Wise alchemists proclaimed it with magical books in which the religious theme always appeared. Phrases such as those of Arnaldus Villanovanus, a famous authority on everything concerning medicine and theology, would put Silvio to dreaming. Here is an example: "Take pure gold and melt it at a time when the Sun enters Aries. Then make a round stamp of it and say at the same time, 'Rise up, Jesus, light of the world, thou art truly the lamb who erases the sins of the world...' Then repeat the psalm '*Domine Dominus noster.*' Put the stamp aside, and when the Moon is in Cancer or in Leo, and the Sun in Aries, engrave on one side the image of a lamb and on the other '*arahel juda v et vii*,' and above that engrave the sacred words 'The Word has been made flesh...,' and in the center 'Alpha and Omega and Saint Peter.'" That text from Villanovanus and so many others that Silvio read and reread cited the Holy Scriptures at every moment, as if the alchemists wished to conjure away with them the reputations of wizards that they enjoyed. The spiritual voyage, the catharsis that had the Stone as its goal and which, once attained and applied would facilitate for the discoverer the privilege of bringing down the great light into the depths of his body and his consciousness, had apparently changed Silvio into a different man. The transmutation of metals had been relegated to a second or third level in his preoccupations, or, rather, it was now only a part of the search for truth which disturbed him and the discovery of which would confer infinite power upon him. The whole process was cloaked in the majesty of a liturgy. There was a reason for his being surrounded by the hermeticism worthy of an initiation. In order to attain the victory, one would have to be almost a demon and also almost a saint. Like his more illustrious colleagues, Silvio had set up an altar in his experimental room before which he would kneel for a few moments before beginning his daily investigations; and a most singular impression was produced by the images of Hermes, Isis, Apollonius, Cheops, by so many deities and philosophers and kings daubed there in a welter of crowns, thyrsi, scepters, croziers, and magical insignia, distributed like a fantastic court about the small cross, with the incense burner perfuming its austere glory.

No, Silvio no longer cared about the one who had been his wife. Nor about Giambattista either. As time went on his hallucinations took him far away from everyday reality and weighed down on him more and more until it assumed the characteristics of a divine madness. But the same thing did not happen to me, even though I shared several hours a day with him in his laboratory and with Fulvio in my study. The death of Giambattista, after that of Pier Luigi, had an effect on me comparable to that of the instant when the curtain falls at the end of a dense act in a tragedy. I was already thirty-six years old. A good part of my life had been spent, on what? On nothing—on organizing poetical games, on piling up rare objects, on pursuing the shadow of an illusion. If I had consolidated my personality in any way at an age when a person who must fulfill himself has already produced the works that will endure or has given evidence of what they will be like, it had been by suppressing without embarrassment those who were in my way. And I could not boast... Everyone else—everyone went through the world pointing out deaths. My memoirs should have had a subtitle that could have been the title of a detective story, something like *Le duc parmi les assassins—The Duke among the Murderers*. But that subtitle, with a change in the name of the character, could have fit the memoirs of any individual of the times.

Giambattista's death obliged me to meditate on my failures, to draw up a balance of my life. What? Would I go on like that vegetating on my estate, waiting to be murdered in turn, for that was the fate of all of my contemporaries of any importance?

I let time keep dripping through its water clock. Pope Paul was replaced by Pope Julius III, who was a Ciocchi del Monte San Savino, wrathful and epicurean. The Farneses were to lose the power they owed to his predecessor. The new pontiff declared himself the protector of the Duchy of Parma, over which Ottavio and Orazio Farnese were fighting, and there were skirmishes in which the French intervened and which were translated into a destruction of crops and pretty country houses until a peace was signed and Orazio had the Duchy of Castro and Ottavio that of Parma. Both had been saved by a hair. Then Ottavio managed to sign a pact with Henry II to defend him against the hostile acts of the emperor, and finally the latter and the pope recognized their dignity and prerogatives. And what else? Lorenzo Lotto, reduced to misery, on his way to becoming an oblate of the Holy House of Loreto, sold the paintings he had left in a financial disaster. I did not buy any of them like a fool; on the other hand, I did buy his cameos, which were worthless, with Sansovino as intermediary. The corsair Dragut, in emulation of Barbarossa, captured Tunis; the Marquis Caracciolo, a member of the most ancient Neapolitan aristocracy, a former minister of Charles V, left the Catholic religion and took refuge among the heretics in Geneva; the Council was dissolved as the barbarians under Maurice of Saxony drew near; in Innsbruck the emperor escaped across the Tyrol on muleback to Carinthia, no one knew how; he almost fell into their hands. War was raging in many places.

I resolved, against my wishes, to go to war. In Bomarzo the familiar feeling that time had stopped was accentuated by heavy indolence. The world was shaking, was on fire beyond the horizon, but in our circle we moved like the automatons in my study. The experiments that

Silvio had begun with such enthusiasm had not progressed a bit. His fervor was intact, even greater, and was growing continuously, but since he had been overcome by foggy mysticism, I had the impression that he was less interested in concrete success than in preserving and deepening that strange state of grace. Sometimes my children would gather around him in the red light of the glowing fireplaces, while the wind howled, and he would tell them mysterious stories of apparitions and dragons, until Giulia intervened, because the children were waking up at night screaming, frightened, and the tales stopped. Fulvio had left. Soon he would be, at the age of twenty-four, a canon of the Lateran, and his existence would develop among books and medals, behind the walls of the basilica of Saint John, where in the sacristy a plaque commemorates him. And my Orsini cousins, men of prey, were growing impatient. They were polishing their arms, mending their coats of mail, currying their horses, and for lack of any other enemy they fought among themselves. They argued about the Caesar's urge for domination and that perhaps he was planning to make the empire hereditary, and about the concessions Charles made to the Protestants in the Augsburg Interim. They spat to one side in disgust, and since there was nothing to do and it irritated him, they would steal Sigismondo's black patch. The people of the village also showed signs of restlessness as well as those of neighboring towns. Their fathers had fought under my father, under my grandfather; some would boastfully display outstanding objects of Venetian or Turkish origin which they kept as mementos of the sacking. War was a good way to die quickly, but it was a way to get rich, to return to the village with some gold plates, a necklace of transparent stones; it was also a way to break the monotony, to flee from the imprisonment of the threshing floor and the silent animals. Late in the day, in the springtime, when I would go to the window to breathe in the warm air, I would hear the noise of the children playing at war and beating drums in the alleys below. My administrator brought me the complaints, the sighs, the whispers, giving them importance. They had none. No opinion of the people did. But Orso, Matteo, and Sigismondo were as restless as angry roosters; and Orazio Orsini wrote me from Florence and in his letters there was the echo of Duke Cosimo's armor. The duke had commissioned Benvenuto Cellini to make his

Perseus, who would hold up over the heads of the people the lopped-off head of the Medusa, like some triumphal symbol of the Renaissance war, beautiful and atrocious. Indecisive, having closed forever the notebook on whose cover the beloved name *Bomarzo* was written, I walked through the deserted rooms and every portrait chided me with the fire of its eyes, its helmet, and its dagger. That one had besieged the Colonnas in the tomb of Augustus and had prevented Frederick of Swabia from taking Rome; that one had fought in San Cesario; that one in Naples, that one on the side of the Most Serene Republic, that one against Cesare Borgia. And that one? That one was I, in the likeness by Lorenzo Lotto, with the roses that had lost their petals, the lizard, the keys, the folio, the beautiful idle hands, the look of slight irony. Irony? Why? And the feudal castle spoke to me with its arcane voice, the savage drive of the Franks, the Lombards, those of Viterbo. The Polimartium, the city of Mars. The bears were in the background with helmets and shields. I could hear their velvet footsteps.

I brought gay women, who twisted like dancers; Pantasilea, who appeared with two gray whippets, for the Duke of Mugnano had strangled her little Maltese dog, out of jealousy, perhaps, so that in his old age he had suffered the same fate as her peacocks. I gathered together boys who were predisposed to traffic pleasantly with their bodies, for it was the only thing they had, and they would flirt with flowers in their mouths. I invited other writers, Roman noblemen. But the noblemen did not come, held by Vatican politics and offers from the great condottieri; the writers spoke about battles, about the cost of a cuirass, about dedicating a poem to Achilles and Patroclus; Pantasilea was growing old rapidly, and she was driving us mad with her whippets, who got under foot and slept on the chairs, the pillows; and as for the rest of them, all the lips had the same taste, and neither Orso, or Sigismondo, nor Matteo wanted to try them any more. They were anxious, they wanted to go to war, to war, to war.

And we went to war.

Sometimes, on the road to Rome, we would come across men who were returning wounded from the distant campaigns. They were begging for alms in God's name, and Messer Pandolfo, who was extremely charitable, had brought some of them to Bomarzo. Blunderbuss shots had destroyed their faces and they were a pity to look at; their arms and legs had been torn off. They made me shudder when we gathered around them in the gallery of the imperial busts. Glancing like hungry cyclopses at the white harlots, showing their stumps, they told horrendous tales. Cardinal Madruzzo and Annibale Caro, quite well informed, also told us about what was happening beyond the Alps. The picture became complete with a letter from Orazio Farnese in France. The son of Pier Luigi had embraced the cause of King Henry II against the emperor and he needed the help of his kinsmen. That letter made me decide to leave, irked, because I had always detested war.

Orazio Farnese was young and witty. Of all of Pier Luigi's children, he was the one with whom I got along best. He was not at all like his father. He had managed to save his Duchy of Castro from the traps set by Julius III, thanks to the intelligence of his good mother, Girolama Orsini, who lived there and was able to absolve her son from his understanding with the French monarch. The pontiff sent Rodolfo Baglioni to occupy the heights of Castro in his name, but Orazio's mother managed to have her son keep governing in name at least and keep his title as prefect of Rome, which he had taken over from his older brother. It was then that Orazio had dealings with Piero Strozzi in light of the news that Ferrante Gonzaga was maneuvering to take over Parma, proposing in exchange the compensation of the Duchy of Sessa for Ottavio Farnese. Orazio was in France at the time, and from there he announced his gallant opposition. His manly attitude brought about a halt in the pope's recognition of him as the real ruler of Castro, and that left him with his hands free to continue fighting under the orders of the Valois. The letter that he sent me and the confidences of Caro and Madruzzo painted the picture without exaggerations.

Henry II, with refined elegance, had received in the ballroom at Fontainebleau an embassy from the German princes who were gathered together in the Diet of Augsburg. It was composed of more than a hundred noblemen with the Count of Nassau at their head. In the midst of the festivities the guests explained the motives for their visit. Charles V aspired to make the succession to the empire hereditary within his family, and he was incorporating the free cities into his domains. The Germans were shouting and showing their fists, while the French kept on bowing, among the paintings by that Giovanni Battista di Jacopo, called "Il Rosso," whose guest Cellini had been when I met him for the first time on the beach at Cerveteri. In the paroxysm of Teutonic shouting, the Count of Nassau suggested to King Henry that if he helped them, he would be authorized to take temporary possession of Metz, Toul, and Verdun. Aroused by the Guises, the king declared war. He left Catherine de' Medici as regent and advanced on Germany. Many cities (among them Metz) fell to the power of the prince, in whose ranks Orazio Farnese was giving constant proofs of gallantry. Others, like Strasbourg, fearful of the excesses of success and calculating that it did not suit them to escape from an old master to give in to a young one, closed their gates and the campaign ended with results that were scarcely complimentary to the forces of France. The Guises, *ceux de* Guyse, made the century ring with the thunder of their name. From petty noblemen of Lorraine, they had become the first lords of the land. Orazio said in his letter that no prelate could be compared to the cardinal, a voluptuous man of a strangely delicate, angry, and superficial spirit, for whom moral barriers did not exist, who had succeeded his uncle, a cardinal like him, in all of his incredible prebends, and was at the same time archbishop of Narvonne, Rheims (he had been from the age of nine), and Lyons, bishop of Valence, Verdun, Luçon, and Dié, abbot of Cluny, Marmoutiers, Saint-Ouen, and Fécamp. His brother François, the great warrior, adored by the Parisians, the famous "Balafré" because of the terrible scar caused by a lance which entered through his right eye and came out between the back of his head and his neck, was governing France with him. They had married a brother to a daughter of Diane de Poitiers, the favorite, to assure the protective intimacy of the royal bedroom for themselves, and a sister to the King of Scotland. The avidity of those descendants of eight lines of sovereigns, among whose ancestors were the monarchs of Anjou, who aspired to the crown of Naples, the memory of which tormented and aroused them, the mad ambition of those turbulent and charming Guises, who had placed the silver eaglets, the "great eagles" of the House of Lorraine over the lilies of France, made Orazio Farnese enthusiastic, for he was not his father's son in vain. He was fascinated by the way they opened their path, elbowing and smiling, up to the foremost positions, leaving behind princes of the blood, even the wrathful Bourbons. They were handsome, witty, unscrupulous, bold, famous for the lightness of their skin and their amatory abilities. François triumphed in battle and Charles in palace intrigues. Between the two of them, the timid king was eclipsed and felt himself safe in the shadow of Diane de Poitiers, who could have been his mother. Orazio Farnese, erect, followed their banners, and under the shelter of those banners, of those bold eaglets, he wrote me, as he had written other relatives, urging me to help him, to aid him with men and money, because the coming campaign demanded it. The King of the Romans, the brother of Charles V, had signed the Treaty of Passau with the Germans in the name of the emperor, which gave them everything they demanded. The Hapsburgs were playing for time; above all they wanted to get back the cities that Henry II, with the title of imperial vicar, had taken under his crown, and it was evident that Charles V would march on Metz. It had to be defended, therefore, saved.

My cousins were burning like torches when I read that letter to them. They shouted, glowed, unsheathed their swords and ran through the gallery of busts as if they were going among the enemy. They were, in reality, the ones who decided upon our departure for the war; they and the noise of the people that resounded all about, and the accusing portraits that were looking at me with clutched swords. They brought me the silver breastplate with the inlaid She-Bear conquering dragons and griffins in the center; and the helmet adorned with the heraldic figures of golden roses and serpents. They were the items that had been beside me during my wedding ceremonies, the day on which I escorted Giulia in her symbolic carriage through the fragrant fields. They put on my spurs, they handed me my dagger, they dressed me in front of a mirror that Sigismondo held. The three of them were jabbering at the same time, adjusting buckles, placing pieces of metal. I let them do it, as if it were the occasion of a masked ball, and I looked at myself closely in the great moon of a mirror, grotesque, tortured, like a Wagnerian singer who was reaching maturity and, surrounded by tailors and theatrical dressmakers, was vainly trying on warlike garments. But those arms were no good. That was what I said to my cousins. It was one thing to parade through the countryside, gaily, majestically, in the midst of butterflies and the shouts of peasants, and something quite different to go to war. Orso, Matteo, and Sigismondo did not cease their efforts. They put ladders up against the walls and brought down ancestral suits of armor from the panoplies. The castle rang with the noise of gauntlets, horns, burgonets, bucklers, coats of mail, standards which fell loudly from their hands onto the stones of the floor, drawing sparks. On top of the chests the pages piled up a rusty confusion of ancient iron objects which they polished and made shine. Nothing was right for me, nothing. My forebears had been giants. I disappeared into their immense pieces of armor as if I were in a diving suit. My cousins looked at each other, bewildered, and they looked at me, half naked in front of the mirror, flanked by useless heroic fragments.

In the meantime a second letter arrived from Orazio Farnese. It was necessary to make haste. The die had been cast and it was impossible to retreat. Therefore I commissioned Matteo to have them make some armor for me in Rome. I told him to speak to Benvenuto Cellini, who was living in the house of Bindo Altoviti, of whom he had made a famous bust that Michelangelo had praised. I told him that he should be careful to tell him that the fame of that piece of sculpture had reached my ears and that then he should ask him for help in finding some armor for me. Matteo returned after a week. He brought the most beautiful armor that I have ever seen, so proud, so unique that I thought that when I was covered by it, even war would become pleasant, because owing to it war would have been transformed into an esthetic pantomime.

It was a jewel of exquisite metals, composed and designed by Guilio Romano, a disciple of Raffaello d'Urbino, which had been bought by a miracle, thanks to the good offices of Benvenuto, for Romano had meant it for a prince who was out of Italy at the time. It was all of bronzed steel, with splendid relief, and with works of damascene gold showing on the burgonet, with the outline of a Boeotian helmet, a visor, and neckpiece which showed Bacchus and Ariadne on one side, and Bacchus and Silenus on the other, with satyrs, centaurs, and undines on the crest; something to stuff the head of the one who wore it with mythological ideas, make him feel part of an enormous triumphant allegory in which the Renaissance and the age of Achilles came together. On the shield, surrounded by a wavy garland of fruits and sprites, the artist had worked out the rape of Helen.

The blacksmith of Bomarzo had to be very skillful to adapt that covering made for a magnificent captain, for a Niccolò Orsini, the Duke of Pitigliano, to my poor frame. He pitilessly cut, mended, smoothed, added, hammered, soldered on the back part, which was changed from something smooth and harmonious into a mountainous terrain of ups and downs. I went to the smithy with Silvio to oversee the operation, and the red glow of the coals lighted up a minute war for me on the reliefs, where fauns were fighting with heroes and where the death of the naked adolescents attained a tragic nobility. Matteo argued that the destruction of the shoulder part, so grotesquely replaced by ugly scars, was not important, because that side would be hidden under my green cape. I finally tried on the chiseled protection and I must confess that it did not give me a bad effect, so bright was its splendor, and when I covered my head with the helmet on which Bacchus, Ariadne, and Silenus were stretching out their happy bodies and which showed the crest of plumes with my colors, and when I lifted up the Homeric shield, I was ready to fall into the trap of adulation from my cousins, Messer Pandolfo, my administrator, Fabio, Violante, the ladies of easy virtue, and the ambitious boys who surrounded me and broke into displays of surprise and applause, assuring me that I was another Hector, an Ajax, an Agamemnon. I was a small hunchbacked Ajax, with such slender hands that their beauty, furrowed by the blue veins, contrasted with the hawks on the long sword as if it were not I who was holding and waving it, but that it had taken my fragile fingers in its rapacious claws.

The Orsini cousins armed themselves as best they could, putting scraps together. They took charge of recruiting people to go with us. Many of the chewed-up boasters that we picked up along the roads and who swore with vile blasphemies that they would never go back to risk their skins on the field of battle joined us. They had been exaggerating before, to move my charity with coughing, wheezing, and sighs; now they were puffing up their chests and casting their fearsome looks about. I ordered their rags replaced as much as possible. I saw some of them dressed in old clothes of Maerbale and Girolamo; there even came to light in a last unexpected remembrance a worn-out jerkin that had belonged to Cardinal Franciotto. When we were ready, I took leave of my children and Giulia and I wrenched myself away from Bomarzo. When I mounted, my stirrup was held by Orazio Orsini, recently back from Florence. He was still too young to take with me. His dark eyes glimmered in the shadows and my heart tightened, because with that frail youth, Bomarzo was saying good-bye to the duke, who, like so many others of his line over the centuries, was giving himself over to the hazards of war.

We crossed Italy. My prestigious armor was on the back of a mule, covered by a thick cloth. As that cloth was torn, at the part where the helmet was hanging down like a shining amphora, people were probably saying that we were guarding a treasure for the most Christian king. The handsome halberdier, the one who had shared the bed of Violante with the Duke of Urbino during the week of my wedding and who had left a mark on her neck, and who later on, when Porzia deserted Silvio da Narni, was her lover too before the Duke of Mugnano, went with us. He went clutching a long lute, as if it were a voluptuous woman, and from time to time he would sing passionate songs to us in which the followers of Mars took off their helmets and armor and enjoyed the panting nymphs among the scattered arms. I listened to him without pleasure, remote. The black and gold armor looked to me like the corpse of a king and we were his poor funeral cortege. What had been left of the prodigious adventures of Ariosto, the pomp of martial parades, the procession of the Magi by Benozzo Gozzoli, the memory of my father, of Ippolito de' Medici, of Abul? Anyone who saw us must have thought of a court of beggars, of jesters, for not even Sigismondo's fierce patch nor Orso's gallant bearing nor the glitter of the halberds and muskets, nor so many flashing eyes could relieve the feeling of melancholy that came from my taciturn presence. Only Giulio Romano's armor and the voice of the halberdier, trembling with portents and fables, reminded us from time to time of an atmosphere of luxury and fantasy. It pained me to leave Bomarzo, my study, Silvio's alembics.

For this, for this indecision, to taste this bitterness in my mouth, had I brought about so many sterile deaths? Would it not have been better for my brothers to have led the troop with their strutting? Where was it, where was my glory hiding, the personal, particular, and special glory of Pier Francesco Orsini, the Duke of Bomarzo, the glory that was rare and mine and would justify me before others and before myself? I had searched for it in an undecipherable manuscript and in a painful poem and now I was looking for it in a sad war toward which no vocation was drawing me. Did it really exist, did that glory really exist?

I half closed my eyes and, drowsy, the reins loose, I listened to the handsome halberdier as he described the naked legs of the nymphs, escaping like white fish in the metallic reflection of the weapons that were glimmering like cold blue water.

I will not go into too great detail concerning the Metz campaign, which holds only painful disappointments for me. Those who may be interested in the story can find it in carefully documented books. Frenchmen, Germans, and Spaniards have all studied the action from opposing points of view.

I reached Metz at a time when the Duke of Guise and Piero Strozzi were finishing its fortification. They had reinforced the walls and bulwarks and were widening the moats. On the outskirts we found nothing but ruins, for the soldiers had demolished anything that could be used in the work, even monasteries. Eight thousand chosen foot soldiers, with three thousand horse, the flower of France, surged through the streets and were making ready in the large houses. It was impossible to walk through the squares without coming across the Prince of Condé, the Duke of Aumale, the Duke of Enghien, the Prince of La Roche-sur-Yon, Monsieur de Nemours, the Marquis of Elbeuf, the Vidame of Chartres. The month of October had unleashed its rains and invigorated its frosts, but all of them, plumed like birds, bejeweled, noisy, had transformed Metz into a great pheasant cage. They amused themselves by gambling and chasing women. Everywhere there was the noise of buildings being built and torn down, the rumble of artillery pieces dragged along, munition wagons, people working in the powder factories, cannons arduously being lifted up into belfries. There was an air of preparation for a duel, a colossal tourney. Messengers were constantly slipping out to the court with the tale of great deeds, and Diane de Poitiers would read them aloud as if she were reading another chapter from a novel of chivalry.

Orazio Farnese received me with enthusiasm. I could see at once that he had not expected me to answer his call for help. More than my weak host, what interested him was the fat purse that I carried. He introduced me to the noblemen, to the Balafré, who was directing the defense for Henry II with the title of "Lieutenant-General of the King in the Three Bishoprics." François de Guise impressed me with his agile energy. He was digging trenches himself along with the soldiers and drinking pitchers of wine with the sergeants. He received me with a show of gracious courtliness, as if we were in the castle of Anet and as complete a man of the world as he was a skillful leader, in a few words he showed me that he was quite aware of what we Orsinis stood for, putting into his voice as he spoke to me a subtle tone that he did not use with Orazio, in spite of his being the Duke of Castro, and the brother of the Duke of Parma. That calmed and relieved me. I was where I was supposed to be and treated as I should have been. In order to match him and his friendliness, I lost money along the way as I gambled with the members of his family, with Aumale, with Elbeuf.

Charles V had wanted to be at the siege in person. Those who knew strategy declared that never had such a powerful army been brought together and he was paying for it all: six thousand Spaniards, four thousand Italians, forty-nine thousand Germans, ten thousand cavalry, besides his court and the hundred thousand men brought later by Albert the Margrave of Brandenburg. The margrave had not allied himself to France because of differences over pay. He was most careful economically. He marauded in the neighborhood of Metz with fifty companies of infantry and five thousand horsemen. One day he took prisoner the Duke of Aumale, Claude of Lorraine, the son-in-law of Diane de Poitiers, whom her brother, the Duke of Guise, had entrusted to get rid of Brandenburg. But Brandenburg was wiser and set a trap for him; later on he presented himself, loaded down with prisoners, in the emperor's camp. But the stubborn Caesar, ravaged by gout, which made him bellow from the torture, had crossed the Rhine with his army, which was under the command of the Marquis of Marignano and the Duke of Alba, and he encamped at Thionville. The roar of our artillery raised echoes more than fifteen miles away. It was raining ceaselessly and the cold was growing stronger when, on November 10, the emperor decided to abandon that shelter and camp outside our walls. Under a leaden sky the plains were so wet that they looked like rivers, and floating on them, half sunken in the frozen mud, were the bodies of men and cattle. The flooding and the rain got into the tents, making them uninhabitable. Epidemics flourished. They say that the imperial forces lost forty thousand men and that the water had been poisoned. My cousin Matteo was saved by the illustrious Ambroise Paré, who has been called the father of modern surgery, and who had managed to slip into the besieged city, sent by the king, and by paying fifteen hundred crowns to an Italian captain.

I, to be sincere, conducted myself neither well nor badly. I did nothing extraordinary, but I stood my post with my roughnecks. I would walk along the fortifications in my splendid armor, which was more dazzling than that of François de Guise, more than that of the Duke of Enghien, more than any other suit of armor worn in Metz, and the water was coming in through my visor and through the joints, chilling me to the bone. Enghien wanted to buy it from me, without noticing the dents on the back at first. But I would not have sold it even if my stomach were grumbling. When I appeared on the defenses, with Orso carrying my sword and gauntlets, the soldiers uncovered themselves. I was almost wounded shortly before the emperor lifted the siege. It was a pity that the bullet did not graze me. That was what I would have liked: for a bullet to have grazed me, ever so slightly...

Charles V decided to leave when he saw that his efforts were useless. His fifteen thousand cannon shots had been of no avail. On December 26, after sixty-eight days of siege, he gave the order that everyone inside and outside Metz had been yearning for. If he had waited another week the people would have run away. We had driven off the danger—or postponed it—but the appearance of Metz, with its first wall knocked down and its rooftops sown with holes through which the eternal gray rain flowed, could not have been more fearsome. Ambroise Paré did not have enough hands to amputate all of the stinking limbs. I took off my armor and put on a black fur cape and shut myself up in a miserable room, shivering like a bear in his den. At a foolish price I got hold of a few pieces of precious furniture that had survived the disaster—a credenza, a table with spiraled legs, a cupboard carved like a great ciborium—and I burned them all in the fireplace to keep warm. Sigismondo was rereading the *Orlando* to me by the light of a candle and I was dreaming of those admirable wars of literature. Maerbale should have been there and not I. Maerbale or Girolamo. I never should have let Girolamo die in the Tiber, nor should I have sent Maerbale to his death after having given him my wife. That life was theirs and not mine. The armor, which was watching over my thoughts from a corner, should have belonged to them. I was living a borrowed life, like an actor. The beggars from Bomarzo who had followed me, hallucinated by extravagant golden promises, were prowling about my hovel like tigers. Many had given their last sigh in the swamps, and their purplish fists emerging from the glacial trenches continued to threaten me from that frosty hell. War was something horrible, repugnant, something that had no relation whatsoever to a helmet on the crest of which Silenus was laughing or to a shield that showed the rape of Helen of Troy. And the Trojan War was probably like that too, with no gods, no handsome, naked chieftains, with rain, and rain, and more rain, and hunger, and cold, and filth, and sores, and boys doubled over vomiting, and surgeons red with blood as they cut off arms and legs. It was small consolation to Sigismondo and me that the emperor, the master of the old world and the new, was running away to his macabre palaces and his heaps of papers and his gloomy signature, mad with rage, both feet tied up with pieces of cloth, twisting with pain, howling with pain. I saw him again clearly, as I always remember him, on the afternoon on which he had knighted me. I breathed in the sour smell of his perspiration, covered by his velvets; I could discern his timid eyes over the distance of time, his anguish, his watchful cruelty. Now they were all being carried off by the wind and the rain and the weeping.

The calm did not last for long. Three months later, in April of 1553, despite the gout that gave him no armistice, Charles V ordered new forces to the northern frontier, in the Picardy sector. We went there, through flooded fields. Although we went on horseback, the water wet out boots, and the foot soldiers were sloshing beside us and complaining that they had never been in a worse situation. And the most boastful among us was Orazio Farnese, for now, to the necessities of glory imposed upon him by his house, there had been added the ones which came from his position as a gallant husband anxious to show up well in his wife's eyes. Taking advantage of the short truce, Henry II had married him to his illegitimate daughter Diane of France, born of Filippa Duci behind the back of Madame de Poitiers, and in that way he carried on the outstanding policy of alliances made through illegitimate children, recalling, without doubt, that Orazio's brother, the Duke of Parma, was the husband of a natural daughter of the emperor. The Farneses, as could be seen, were absorbing the great natural products of the time. Of Filippa Duci I had only heard that Diane de Poitiers had had her disappear into a convent and that since she had given the king no male heir, Madame de Poitiers had decided that the spurious fruit should bear her proud name and be called Diane of France, creating the consequent confusion as to her origins. The wedding, which I attended, was stupendous. Since it took place during carnival time, there was a fantastic masked ball in which we all wore disguises. That made us forget for a moment the difficulties of the war, but in a short time it was necessary to leave over the dangerous flooded roads on our way to Thérouanne. My armor, in spite of the cloth protecting it, was covered with splotches of mud, and the pages spent hours bringing it back to its immaculate splendor.

The campaign on the Flanders frontier could not have been more disastrous. When I remember it my hair stands on end. Duke Antoine of Vendôme, accomplishing a real miracle, had managed to bring his artillery through the hungry swamps to Hesdin. He filled in the town's moat and entered in triumph, which annoyed the emperor tremendously. Charles V had had blood in his eye after the episode at Metz, and he decided that the full force of his realm would fall like a gigantic, squashing hammer upon the disputed region. To subjugate it he sent fifty thousand men under old, experienced captains, men like the Count of Reuss and Martin van der Rosen. We had Robert de La Marek, the Duke of Bouillon, the son-in-law of Diane de Poitiers, and a son of the

Constable of Montmorency. The Duke of Vendôme accomplished one miracle after another. What he had done outside of the town as he guided the artillery from his redoubt became even more of a challenge inside. He was waiting for the promised appearance of Henry II, and the king was taking his time. Emmanuel Philibert of Savoy, on the contrary, was facing us with the waving imperial standards. Mine was unfurled too in Thérouanne alongside the lilies of the Farneses and the personal flag of Orazio, which bore the emblem drawn for him by Annibale Caro at the request of his sister, the Duchess Vittoria of Urbino, and which showed the young Achilles being trained by the centaur Chiron, alluding to the wisdom that Orazio Farnese had received from Francis I, with the motto *"Chirone Magistro."* We had more than enough flags, but we lacked troops. Thérouanne was left behind and erased down to its foundations; the son of the constable was taken prisoner and we fell back on Hesdin with the Duke of Bouillon. An unpardonable mistake of his lost that unfortunate town, so that just as in Metz, where Aumale had been taken prisoner, the sons-in-law of the favorite made nothing but mistakes in Hesdin, but she excused them, as did Henry II, whom she led along by the nose as Hungarians led their tame bears. The one who bore himself with fearful boldness was Orazio Farnese. I, not to do less, did not leave his side, and on more than one occasion he asked me not to expose myself to so many shots. Now I think that what really happened was that I, with my heavy, suffocating armor, which hindered my slightest movement, held him back in his action, for at every instant he was bumping into me as soon as he came back from the loopholes to give orders or ask for reinforcements. Savoy invaded the redoubt and we took refuge in the fortress, until we saw that defense was impossible.

"Get that armor off and get out of here!" Orazio Farnese shouted at me.

His words came too late. A musket shot broke his back. He fell to the ground twitching, and I leaned over with difficulty to raise his head. He was no longer alive. Now he was with the heroes on that Olympus of shining armor where captains take their trophies and mistakes. At that moment a terrible tremor sent me flying through the air as if my cuirass were made of feathers into the open banners that were waving like multicolored wings, and I landed in a trench. The powder that we had accumulated in the castle had caught fire through the fault of Robert de La Marck, and the fury of the fire as it extended out toward the mines which had been dug under us by Emmanuel Philibert of Savoy made shreds of the walls. More than three hundred people perished in the brutal explosion, among them my cousin Orso and my handsome halberdier. I was saved by the trench and perhaps by the armor that had been bothersome until then, as it cushioned the shock. My inseparable Matteo and Sigismondo rose into view crawling, black with earth. Sigismondo had lost his patch and the ugly cavity of his socket was showing. The important thing was to make a ruse, taking advantage of the disorder so they would not capture us as at that very moment they were taking the incapable Bouillon and Ambroise Paré, whom the Duke of Savoy turned over to the governor of Gravelines so that he could cure an ulcer on his leg, because of which he got his freedom back! We were only thinking along those lines; we did not even have time to mourn for Orso. The explosions were coming one after the other in the meantime and the three of us took refuge in an abandoned hut, to which they brought me with great difficulty because of the weight of my ironware, as if they were dragging a great dead crocodile. Heaven came to our rescue. We found some women's clothing in a trunk there, and we decided to disguise ourselves as gypsy women, something that occurred to me when I remembered how Lorenzino de' Medici had used that disguise when he would visit the beautiful Barozzi woman in Venice. It was necessary first of all for me to get my armor off, and that was not easy at all, for it had become terribly dented with the blows and it was as if I were back from a bloody tournament, as it sank into my body and bruised my flesh. They pulled it off me, fighting with the kilt, with the greaves, with the Boeotian helmet that threatened to strangle me. The detached pieces were scattered about on the ground. The helmet, with its three faded plumes, lay like a pompous bird which dogs had stolen from a banquet. We put on the female clothing and tied some kerchiefs about our heads, and we really could have been taken for three gypsy women, for the three of us were dark and slender, and my hump and Sigismondo's missing eye contributed, the same as Matteo's grace, to create the proper aspect of Bohemian women going with their wagons along those paths of God, telling fortunes, stealing chickens, and selling herbs and love potions. Done up like that, we went through the troops, with Matteo being the target of excessive remarks and pinches, and our fulfilling the requirements of the killers as they aspired to know their futures and held out dirty palms to us so that we could interpret the lines, but we got through it all and offered it up to Providence in exchange for our salvation, for otherwise we would have shared the fate of the unlucky Orazio Farnese, the unfortunate Orso, the poor halberdier.

What would the Amazon Princess of Taranto have thought of me then? What would her husband have thought, that Raimondello Orsini del Balzo, who went to win back the Holy Sepulcher, or the Orsini woman married to Andronicus, the Emperor of the East, and the Orsini married to the granddaughter of Charlemagne? Would they have recognized a prince of their blood in that disguised play-actor wearing the garb of a gypsy woman and trembling over the extended hand of a ruffian?

In Paris we got hold of some crowns, bought some adequate clothing, and paid our respects to Catherine de' Medici, my childhood friend, and in short stages we undertook our return to Bomarzo. There were few of those who had followed me on the campaign who returned to the village. No one brought back any gold plates or silver pitchers, just as I did not even bring back my expensive armor. I would have liked to have got it back to place in the gallery of the Caesars near the Etruscan set, by that of my father, that of my grandfather. What could have happened to those fine pieces that I left behind in a hut in Hesdin? Could they be gleaming in other battles, worn by the brave man who deserved them? Three years ago, in the Royal Armory in Madrid, I stopped suddenly, startled, for I thought I saw them in a showcase in the main hall. The helmet, at least, the helmet worthy of Mars, with its golden stripe showing Bacchus, Silenus, and Ariadne, was the same. Still, I am not sure that it was my armor. I had used it so briefly and so long ago!

I kept nothing as a testimony of my military life, but that experience did provide me with the means of being able to speak about war from first hand, and since I had not captured a single standard to add to those collected by my elders, I made an ironic gesture, one that would have amused Aretino and Lorenzaccio de' Medici, and I myself manufactured in secret an imperial standard, with the spread eagle and the pillars of Hercules, using the apocryphal gypsy skirt and some old rags, with the help of Sigismondo, and I had it solemnly hung on the staircase of the castle over some crossed muskets and some doubtful swords in memory of my undertakings in Metz, Thérouanne, and Hesdin, which cured me for a time of the magnificent temptations of war.

In Bomarzo, during the year of my absence, life had gone on without change. On my return, however, I noticed a difference. It was a subtle difference and it came from a kind of intensification of attitudes which the non-initiate would not have been able to evaluate. For example, the distance that separated me from Giulia seemed to have widened for some mysterious reason that had to do with her physical state and her health. As always, she spent time with the children, walked through the garden in the afternoon, cut roses, embroidered, read, but I could sense that she was distant, detached, slower, and although no obvious symptom emphasized the destructive process that could be seen to be within her, she was surrounded by an atmosphere of melancholy over which mortal indications were hovering. My children moved about her as if they sensed secret presences with their delicate infantile intuition, and they too had imposed a new restful and expectant rhythm to their development. When I was in France, Cecilia Colonna had returned to Bomarzo, for rumors of heresy were threatening Giulia Gonzaga and her Valdesian friends and that put the life of Maerbale's widow and little Niccolò in danger. I did not have the heart to send them to their own domains as the time before. The blind princess, paler, thinner, would spend whole afternoons on one of the terraces as if she were listening to hidden voices. She would smile with no apparent motive. She had also changed, as if the grief that bore down on her since the death of Maerbale had descended into darker regions where the thick shadows that had closed over her eyes were establishing themselves in the lowest depths of her soul like thick black minerals, among which there wandered the tremulous light of the memory that made her smile. The two Orsinis who might have been cousins or might have been brothers, Orazio and Niccolò, so much alike, so pleasing in the flourishing of their puberty, walked beside her, listening to her repeated stories, things about Maerbale, about the time when he was fighting with Valerio Orsini for the Most Serene Republic. Lying at her feet, they were isolated in a tremulous and remote world, and when I happened to pass by the whispering would cease. I had the diabolical feeling of being exiled among my own people, for the same thing would happen when I approached my children and Giulia. No exclusion came from their attitude, no repudiation; they never pronounced a hostile word, but it was as if I did not belong to their tight circle of conspirators, as if I were not capable of sharing their furtive feelings. Silvio, in whose study I had thought to find a refuge, had advanced along his fantastic road of magical asceticism that was devoid of earthly worries, and he would quiver like a specter in his floating robe, in the vapor of the alembics, so that one would have taken him for some emanation from the secret mixtures that he was preparing, and it was difficult to tell, as I went into his redoubt, which was the living human being and which were the painted figures floating in the mist of the laboratory. If he was asked something, he barely answered, lost in calculations and dreams like a sleepwalker. And when, fatigued with the oppression that reigned in the castle, and which drove me from one room to the other, I would go out and go through the tightly packed village, I found there a climate that I had trouble defining, composed of unrest and displeasure, perhaps the fruit of the deceptions that the sad Metz campaign had brought with its trail of deaths. I would close myself up, then, along with Matteo and Sigismondo and listen to the lutes. The Duke of Mugnano, Porzia, Fabio, Violante, and Pantasilea would appear from time to time, and even though on those occasions the cold majesty of the Minotaur room would become merry, soon the conversation, as it came to Matteo, Sigismondo, and me in a corner of the gallery would return to the fury and futility of war, and my own image—that of a gold and black tortoise moving slowly through the bastions of Hesdin and Thérouanne, hindering with his shell those avid for glory—would cross once more, weaving grotesquely, the genealogical stage that flanked the imperial busts and come to throw my incapacity up to my face.

I understood that I had reached a crucial moment in my existence, for I was over forty years old, and that it was necessary for me to make haste if I wished to leave my mark on the castle. Then—because for me everything was resolved in decorative solutions—I decided to undertake the task of bringing to the inside walls of my house the scenes, often thought of, that would proclaim the triumphs of my line. Among them, as a central element, there would be a picture that would bring together my people, the closest ones, around the duke, Pier Francesco Orsini, creating in that way the illusion that everything else, the broad forest of age-old deeds, was a projection of the intimacy of my thoughts. It would be a painting similar to the famous fresco of Mantegna in the Wedding Chamber in Mantua. I would be in the middle, with Giulia, with Cecilia, with my children, with Orazio, with Niccolò, and on a second level my Orsini cousins would be seen, my astrologer, Silvio da Narni, my tutor Pandolfo, and those intellectuals, like Madruzzo, Annibale Caro, and Sansovino, who were my guests. The skillful brush would turn us into gods. We would create the Olympus of Bomarzo. My missing armor, which the painter would reconstruct from our lengthy descriptions, would give the appearance of an opulent, plumed, and bearded Mars, without a hump, unhesitant, bolstered by the strength of his shield and lance; Giulia would be Venus; Orazio would be Apollo; the children would be other various symbols of love and fertility with brimming baskets and cornucopias; Cecilia would play the role of Juno; Silvio that of Hermes; my cousins those of Patroclus and Achilles; the writers would be a group of sages, including Ulysses, Nestor, and Calchas. Within the great theater of my forebears, vibrant with victories, there would be inserted my own little personal theater, where everyone would play an admirable mythological role. And there we would remain for eternity, static, stupendous, stronger than Time and Truth, for the wonderment of those who would come after us. But I had to be quick, because the other actors were beginning to flee the scene with their hidden hostility, with their clear aim of not participating in my life, or rather that I should not participate in theirs. I had to bring them together and lock them up in my allegorical stage so that they would not escape me, so that there within the Olympus of Bomarzo, among laurels, helmets, thyrsi, tunics, and naked chests and arms, they would be bewitched for time immemorial.

Since one of my basic traits was one that obliged me to approach everything that had to do with my house in a grand manner, contracting marriage with a lady of the greatest prestige, winning the friendship of Ippolito de' Medici, converting an unknown skeleton into a saint, acquiring the best armor and the most expensive books of alchemy, it occurred to me to go to the first artist of the century and commission him to do that singular work. After serious doubts, and although Madruzzo and Caro tried to dissuade me, I wrote to Michelangelo Buonarroti, proposing the task to him. I should never have done it. It was madness, one more proof of my insane pride. Michelangelo was over eighty years of age and was spending his last energies on the basilica of Saint Peter's, persecuted by calumnies, a lack of understanding, and imbecility. When he received my letter among the immense blocks of marble and the half-carved pilasters piled up in the square, he should have thrown it into the rubble. And yet he answered me with some charming paragraphs in which he spoke of the complexities of his work, his advanced age, and how long a chore like the one I offered him would take. He wrote almost with humility, almost as if he were pained by not being able to accede to my wishes and not being in a position to do so, he who had worked only for pontiffs and the banker princes of Florence, the rulers of art, to come and shut himself up in a vague castle in Latium and adorn its walls with the incomparable splendor of his figures. He ended by telling me that since he now lacked the strength to do it, for he was knocking at death's door and when he looked about he saw only corpses as he realized that everyone he had loved was dead—outside of Messer Tommaso Cavalieri, of course, but there was no reason for his mentioning him to me—perhaps his disciple Jacopo del Duca could do it. He was not a painter, he told me, he was a sculptor and an architect, but he sketched in such a way that he would deserve Your Lordship's approval, and if Your Lordship took him on, you could count on helpers who would fulfill the proposal perfectly. He added that in his judgment it would be proper for the director of a work such as the one I was planning to be someone who knew the laws of architecture because of the necessity of creating a blended harmony, one governed by the proportions of the building, and he insisted that such was his confidence in Jacopo that he had just completed with him the roof of carved wood to the Capitoline palace of the Conservatory. There was a great distance between Michelangelo Buonarroti and Jacopo del Duca, but I did not hesitate and I sent an emissary to the latter, who returned to Bomarzo with the messenger. He brought two assistants along.

Before speaking of Jacopo del Duca, I must speak of his helpers and pupils. Their names were Zanobbi and Andrea Sartorio and they were brothers, of twenty and eighteen years of age respectively, both Sicilians like their master. They had been born in Agrigento, while Jacopo had first seen the light in Cefalù. True Sicilians, their origin, their mixture of very old bloods, Greek, Norman, and Arab, was evident in the sallowness of their skins, with golden reflections, polished like the ancient bronzes of their island, in the neat lines of their features, in the tormented blackness of their hair and eyes, in the feline agility of their bodies, and the Oriental length of their hands. They kept silent and slipped along in the shadow of Jacopo del Duca like two mysterious animals, two Sicilian wildcats, withdrawn and secretive. One of them, the elder, Zanobbi, more handsome than his brother because of a certain indefinable irregularity of his features, impressed me from the very first. I am not being accurate: he did not impress me, he fascinated me, he was very suggestive for me. After a quarter of a century of separation, I felt before him at once the almost painful shudder, the same anguish that I had felt in my adolescence when the Florentine *cortile* of the Medicis appeared before my eyes and I found myself facing Abul and Adriana dalla Roza. After so much time, when I thought that the possibility of those deep feelings had been extinguished for good in my leathery interior, for I was no longer capable of becoming upset, disturbed, there being born in me again was the upsetting heat of youth, the exceptional hidden fire which was burning and blending the other perceptions, leaving me alone, aglow and vibrant as I faced a single object that erased everything surrounding it. I must repeat to the reader to the point of satiety, so that he will understand me correctly, that in the sixteenth century I was a man essentially characteristic of my time, neither better nor worse than the rest. Like the most outstanding personalities of the time, like Michelangelo, like Benvenuto Cellini, like Lorenzo Lotto, like Pietro Aretino, like Lorenzaccio, like the heroic chief of the Bande Nere, I had entered that terrible garden filled with a vegetation of thick, voluptuous sap, with no separation of sexual frontiers. Abul, Adriana dalla Roza, Porzia, Giambattista, Violante, Fabio seduced me equally. I did not distinguish or separate. I burned on the bonfires of souls and bodies, searching beyond differences and oppositions for the passionate glow. But that thing, the one that held me suspended as I observed Zanobbi, was something quite special, something that unhinged and upset me on rare occasions linked to Abul, Adriana, and that happy period of my life during which, without seeing Giulia Farnese, for her father had forbidden it, I dreamed of her without cease. And since the unusual factor of alienation gave me back, suddenly, unexpectedly, and dangerously, the vital flame of my youth, which I thought had gone out forever, instead of reacting against its danger in the defense of my selfish calm, I gave in, on the contrary, to its witchcraft—for with it I was reconquering a region in myself where the desert was beginning to flourish, and forgetting that in that shadowy garden Lorenzo Lotto and Michelangelo Buonarroti, whom I admired and loved so much, had been torn and bled—I went ahead through the garden that was recreating for me, intact and heady, the aroma of dead years toward the unknown person who hid himself beside his master.

Jacopo del Duca, in the meantime, was speaking with fluent ease. He was recalling the triumphs of his collaboration with the greatest artist of all epochs, the time in which, when Michelangelo was working the miracle of Santa Maria degli Angeli in the baths of Diocletian, he had forged a sacramental ciborium for him out of bronze with such refined art that the great sculptor had declared that no one would ever dare to undertake a similar work, and he mentioned his work on the Porta Pia, on the Cornaro palace, on the Villa Mattei on Monte Celio. Other names—that of Daniele da Volterra, that of Antonio da Sangallo, for whose church of Saint Mary of Loreto he had devised a lamp that hung over the audacity of the octagonal cupola—came from his eloquent lips as he made his merits sparkle—for just as the Sartorios belonged to that type of taciturn Sicilian, he was of the garrulous kind, Byzantine, as vibrant as the golden mosaics of his native Cefalù—while I tried to maintain my composure and play before the guests the role of a Roman nobleman of famous lineage who had come back from the wars and was commissioning a job to a distinguished artisan for the greater glory of his immemorial house, accustomed since the dawn of centuries to the homage of creators of esthetic beauty.

I was a weakling. It pains me to confess it—nothing ever pained me as much, because I aspired to that disdainful vigor which had exalted the haughty Orsinis—but what was certain was that I was a poor hunchback, weak, lacking in confidence, to whom destiny had added, to cap his twisted confusion, the noose of a sickly sensibility as it placed him in the radiant coliseum where great men accentuated the haughtiness of their statuesque gestures and their hard, violent, sonorous voices, or made their swords and armor ring against the flaming backdrop of Metz, Thérouanne, and Hesdin, replaying the tourneys of classic splendor. Anyone else in my position would have confronted the nervousness that troubled me with arrogant efficiency. Besides, that nervousness would not have existed for him. He would have limited himself to taking what he wanted, what tempted him, the way one tears off a branch in passing. Not I; I could not. Everything that concerned me became complex, difficult. For that reason I blessed and cursed the day on which Zanobbi Sartorio arrived at Bomarzo with Jacopo del Duca. That night I wandered until late among the kings and wizards, the ovens and the prophets, through Silvio's laboratory, waiting for the right time to say a word to the illuminated alchemist about what was waking up in my intimacy, which made me ashamed and embarrassed, and the deep symptoms of which he knew too well, knowing that I would not be able to put even a sentence together, and that when he finished his daily chores and a single lamp remained in the study flickering on the altar, each of us would go to his room through the secret passage with our different dreams, and knowing that I would not be able to sleep, unsheltered in the absurd tempest that had been unleashed in my soul for no apparent reason, madly and without anything having foretold the rebirth of its fury.

A strange period in my existence began at that time. Already before, during the year in which I wandered through the glacial sites of that

THE ACCURSED WAR · 545

war which I had joined covered by the most beautiful armor in the world, glowing like Perseus, and out of which I had slipped disguised as a gypsy woman, I had pondered, in the very marrow of sinister reality, as if I were outside of reality, because reality for me was the ancestral dream of Bomarzo, within whose walls we floated about, rhythmically, musically, like esoteric allegories, while that other thing, what people called reality, with its explosions, its brutal artillery hauled by hand through swamps, and its dying boys covered with metal scales like so many dragons, belonged, on the contrary, to the world of hallucination. The atmosphere that I found in Bomarzo on my return and which showed me how deep, how authentic my solitude was in the midst of the hazy family figures who avoided me, the vague astrologer and the peasants who hid their faces when I passed, contributed to nourishing the feeling of fictitious life that had haunted me since the marshes of France. And now, the presence of Zanobbi and Jacopo del Duca intensified the impression of fantastic strangeness, because Zanobbi Sartorio, by giving me back in my maturity emotions that I had not felt since adolescence and which made my heart beat faster, had worked the magic of deceiving time, and Jacopo, with his imagination which crackled in the fire of whimsical conversation, was incessantly constructing and tearing down around us, like a quick and extravagant decorator, the fleeting picture of enchantment.

Springtime advanced and I became accustomed to dedicate part of the morning to chatting with the master about the plans that had brought about his residence in the castle. I had a large table set up in a corner of my study and soon it was filled with broad rumpled sheets on which the nervous diversity of the designs was growing. Together, aided by Messer Pandolfo and Sansovino, we consulted the old family texts and the documents kept by my father and my grandmother, from which the future compositions would emerge. For that vast pictorial development I had destined a deserted gallery located in the left wing of Bomarzo, which I had had cleaned, restored, and made ready in a proper way to receive the frescoes that I was planning. It was one of the most ancient parts of the big house, fastened to the rock, and for that very reason, because I considered it most closely joined to the essence of the place, I resolved that the paintings should be spread out on its walls. But before beginning that task of mixing colors and finishing sketches, we had to choose the people for the age-old procession and locate them in their proper atmosphere, which would take months of study and consultation. Jacopo would have preferred to give flight to his imagination, of which he had more than enough, and replace historical exactitude with mythological allusions, and although that did not displease me, for I was always in favor of mingling poetic fiction with rigorous evidence, I determined that we would base our work as much as possible on scrupulous foundations. I must confess that if I proceeded in such a fashion, I did so moved not only by a critical urge, but also because I sensed that in that way the stay of Jacopo and his disciples in Bomarzo would be extended. The latter, in the meantime, inseparable from their master, wandered through my study admiring the curious objects that it contained. They amused themselves copying cameos and sketching the series of engraved items in my collection, which included the profiles of Marcus Aurelius, Faustina, Antoninus Pius and his wife, the heads of Alexander, Scipio, Pompey, Cassius, Tiberius, Nero, Seneca, Ovid, the Medusa, Marcellus the consul, Hercules, and Antiope. Sometimes Jacopo would call them to put an idea down on paper and I was amazed at the intelligence with which they interpreted and linked the traits of my ancestors with the symbols and the decorations. My eyes would then pause on the figure of Zanobbi, on his agile hands, as he bent over the table and ran his pen across the arabesques. I felt like leaving Jacopo del Duca, going over to the disciple, leaning across the table to hear his breathing, to watch his dark cheekbones with their light tint under the carbon of his hanging locks as the sketch swirled and appeared with hesitant designs. I did not ask for anything else; I only asked to look at him, to feel him nearby, and to listen to that unknown voice which was breaking out into distracted humming. But Jacopo del Duca prevented any intimacy. He was a man of thirty-five, robust, bearded, restless. He called me to ask me something or other about the first Orsini popes, about the Boveschis, about the *gente romulea* of the time of Celestine III. The glory of my people untwined from around their pomp. Here Leo IX was handing the golden rose to Ludovico Orsini; there Cardinal Latino was composing the *Dies irae*, farther on Matteo Orso, named chief of the Guelphs by the pontiff, was laying siege to the Colonnas; Nicholas III was dividing Italy, like food at a banquet, among his people; Rinaldo Orsini was sneering at Cola di Rienzo; Romano Orsini was conversing with Saint Thomas; Niccolò Orsini was chatting with Boccaccio; the condottiere Paolo was raising his banners; the Orsini despots of Epirus were advancing in the pride of their imperial alliances with the Comneni and Paleologhi; Napoleone Orsini rose up naked in the church of Aracoeli from a bath of roses like a Homeric hero; Francesco Orsini of Monterotondo galloped over the shields of defeated princes; Lorenzo the Magnificent was bowing to Clarice Orsini, his wife; and the Orsinis of Bomarzo were fighting to defend their beloved fortress. And it was as if all those images, worked into superimposed sketches and scattered about the furniture had no other mission than to give a frame of incomparable luxury to the Sicilian boy who had entered my existence so unexpectedly and who, although he was continuously near me, seemed more remote than those fabulous creatures, than Caius Flavius Orsus, than Mandilla, than the founder of the line who had been suckled by the totemic She-Bear. Once again, as had happened with Abul and Adriana, I was being confused by a mirage. Zanobbi had appeared at the moment in which, abandoned, silently rejected by the others, I needed a presence who would triumph over the remaining repudiation and recenter my emotions, serving my timidity by conjuring away hostile and indifferent people. I do not know even today, over the distance of so much time, whether Zanobbi was as I saw him or whether I had invented him, modeled him, to crown the emptiness that surrounded me and which troubled me with an urgency to be the selfish and imperious axis on which the world turned. The only thing that I do know is that he arrived at the opportune moment and that his golden and essential image blinded me.

The atmosphere of the study, ringing with the victories of my line and with mysterious passion, often became so oppressive that I had to escape from its smothering effect. I would go out with Jacopo del Duca then into the garden, where the plumage of the fountains danced. The master spoke to me about the statues that he had recently carved in the villa of Caprarola, built by Vignola for Cardinal Alessandro Farnese, the son of Pier Luigi, and of the frescoes in that palace which showed the deeds of my wife's family, done in a large part by the Zuccaros. Something like that should be done at Bomarzo. Something like that, but more surprising, more monumental. The sculptor-architect saw the decorations of my castle in accordance with principles dear to the Mannerists, who gave first place to design over color and who exalted the Neo-Platonic concept of the *idea* of the interior image over the bonds of slavish naturalism. His was a wise art, refined, supported by fantastic individual parts and by an unusual linking, almost in jest, of minute realistic details within an environment of unreal essence. His skill had a decadent air, as one which characterized the end of a period and its final and marvelous will-of-the-wisp, and which with its subtle rhetoric seduced what there was in me of the decadent, the culminating, between recherché and capricious, of an illustrious race that was evolving as a result of the demands of circumstance from the splendidly heroic toward the ritualistically courtly. More than a man skilled in the school of Michelangelo, Jacopo del Duca showed himself to be a contemporary of Parmigianino, Pontormo, Rosso, Bronzino, the Zuccaros. He could also have been taken for an artist of the circle of Raphael Sanzio, of those painters who after the discovery of the *grotteschi*, when the subterranean ruins of Nero's Domus Aurea were explored on the slopes of the Monte Esquiline, filled palaces with strange motifs that reproduced the adornment of the Roman grottoes and linked on the walls a disconcerting garland of hippocampi, fauns, harpies, phalli, of monstrous animals put together in an ingenious scheme which filled the small square panels with magical foliage. That skillful and exquisite playfulness was bound to fascinate me, for in addition it was related to basic aspects of my intellectual formation, to Ariosto's world and to what I had learned in Florence with Piero Valeriano as I studied Pliny's mythological zoology and the repeated prodigies of capricious and erudite beauty.

Carpenters and masons raised a web of scaffolding in the gallery of the frescoes and they began to lay out the geometrical divisions that went up the walls and cut the ceiling into audacious polygons, each of which would enclose one of the projected paintings. In a short time, Jacopo, Zanobbi, and Andrea also climbed up onto the platforms and if on one occasion my enthusiasm made me accompany them on the fragile ladders and unsteady planks, I did not repeat the experiment.

I was terrified hanging up there in a web of wobbling wood looking down in horror at the paving stones of the floor, where, minute and as if sketched out, innumerable pails and brushes could be seen. Jacopo and his assistants moved about the fragile and insecure region as if they were on familiar ground which was as much theirs as waving foliage is for birds, and they would go from one plank to another, making the delicate boards quiver, as if they were flying, as if they were light-footed dancers, but I, clinging to one spot, my eyes popping, needed their help to make my ridiculous descent to the safety of the floor, repentant at my having entered a light atmosphere that did not suit me, with my rigid heaviness, just as if I had been wearing the Hesdin armor. Zanobbi took my arm as they lowered my clinging body like a bundle through the jungle of supports, and the only emotion that was stronger than the fear that weighed on me was that of my humiliation in front of the softly smiling boy. From then on I stayed in the lower world of dusty stones, where I came and went in my wide gray-green *lucco*, searching with my eyes up into the labyrinthine branches for the light forms that were chatting and murmuring in the treetops of that forest of beams, like a heavy and deformed toad who was spying in the distant boughs of the trees on the movements of sylphs and flying creatures. From time to time, one of the assistants would slip down to earth, where I was standing stupidly eager, after a piece of paper, a sketch, or some charcoal, and then, leaping, flying up into the midst of the twisted poles, above which I could imagine the clearness of the sky that was hidden from me, he went back into the thickness with the white sheet as if he were taking it to his invisible nest.

On some mornings Giulia and the children would come to watch the work. My wife's health was declining so much that she had herself carried in my grandmother's hand chair, and leaning from it she would consult the designs, pretending to be interested in what she probably considered an absurd dream. Cecilia Colonna also came and I explained to her how scenes that depicted the origins of our family and its early days were being placed on the ceiling, with exotic groups of bears scattered across the dome, following the rhythm of the cornices and the moldings. The broader compositions would extend below, opposite the windows and between them, and in back would be the great fresco that would picture me surrounded by my people, with a border of episodes relating to the Orsinis of Bomarzo and Benedetto's horoscope up above. She was listening to me gravely; she listened to me detail that long and multicolored parade in which the Colonnas invariably came off badly—for such was the history of our house, after all, the rhythm of their alternating fights with the Colonnas—and as I described the decorations of the pictures that were filled with a swarm of pagan inventions, she would turn her blind eyes from time to time to the place where the workers were disappearing into the half-light of that forest of shaking boards, where a laugh, the fleeting stanza of a song, a leap or the gleam of a hammer thrown and caught in flight by a hand prolonged the illusion of a noisy birdcage.

In spite of the protests of Giulia and Cecilia, Orazio and Niccolò scurried up onto the planks like two squirrels and joined the master and his disciples in the imprecise shadows while, next to the blind woman, the solemn Cardinal Madruzzo, and the argumentative Sansovino, who claimed to know the chronicle of my line better than anyone, the impotent hunchback was turning slowly like a toad living in his slime, in the shadow of the foliage of the scaffolding. How much I would have liked to have climbed up there, into that region that was as ephemeral as the mermaids and the unicorns, as the characters from dreams who would soon cap it, and go through the breeze of the tenuous platforms, lightfooted, between Zanobbi and Andrea, in the moments when the first sketches, with graceful foreshortening, would capture my earliest ancestors in the black and ocher net as if they were other birds with proud crests, and make them alight, tremulous, magnificent, with helmets and crowns, in their high golden cages! But that was impossible. I had to stay crawling about beside the red cardinal and the gaunt princess, feigning attitudes of majesty in the sad ooze, and that distance confirmed for me, like a painful metaphor, everything in life that separated me from Zanobbi.

The sickness that was undermining Giulia came to a crisis, and before it was possible to attempt some cure that would have been useless besides, her beautiful violet eyes closed forever. Her death caused me a grief that went beyond the ordinary, like everything of mine, and which was sincere in its strange way. We had lived together for many years. Aside from the doubtful Orazio, she had given me seven children, and when she had sinned it had been I who had set the trap, so that without my intervention, demented, organized, and one calculated to arouse temptation, it was probable that there would have been nothing to accuse her of. I never heard a word of protest or rebellion from her lips. If I drew apart from her it was because I had wanted to. If her coldness froze me, what else could I have expected? Beautiful, aristocratic, generous, a great lady of Bomarzo, venerated by my children and my vassals, she fulfilled her destiny with admirable nobility. Her end, which I should have seen, perhaps, but which, distracted by other troubles, I had put out of my mind as a possibility, took me away from the preoccupations that were weighing on me. Everything retreated and disappeared with her death. The perfect Giulia Farnese had gone and an era for Bomarzo and for my existence had come to an end. Linking myself to her had been a luxury for me; confronting her had been a torture; losing her had been despair; possessing her a burden. Beside her remains, laid out in the ancestral chapel, my tireless imagination, which gave me in fictitious images what life denied me, wove an official grief that I thought was authentic and which moved most of the onlookers. It suggested so much to me that I felt as if my reason for living in the world had expired with her. And all of that was taking place at a time when my spirit was being dominated by Zanobbi Sartorio. But Zanobbi, so recently made a part of my worries, had nothing to do in that process and he was relegated to the background of memory, where his involuntary intrusion could not make me uncomfortable, while the image of Giulia rose up, triumphant, crowning me and plunging me into bitterness. I belonged to her totally, as I never had since the time of our betrothal, while I sat with her lying breathless in the chapel of the castle, and during the days that followed, and thence the anomaly, so very much in keeping with my character, that I loved her deeply in the time before our wedding, when I did not see her, and during the time that followed her death, when I could not see her either. What I loved in her was her status as an august symbol, but the flesh and blood always intimidated me, even on the anguished occasions when I possessed her. Therefore I loved her truly when she had not yet begun to exist for me and when she no longer existed for anybody, that is, when she was only a noble entelechy, with no body, no voice, no smell, no desires, an unalterable and sumptuous archetype. On the other hand, my children wept afflictedly, as did Orazio, Cecilia, Niccolò; the poor women and the poor peasants of the town mourned her daily reality, without rhetorical ornamentation, and at the instant when I went forward and offered my tears, the little ones who were sobbing, consoled by their nursemaids and their tutors in the pew presided over by Messer Pandolfo, rejected my attempts at paternal tenderness with the unconquerable emotional perspicacity that rarely deceives children. We loved and we were weeping for two different people and we could not understand one another. Cardinal Madruzzo, the bishop of Trent, led the response and I answered in a clear and ringing voice. I thought, proud of myself, because as always what was most important to me was the propriety of my public reaction, that I was acting as I ought to have been, that I was feeling what I ought to have felt, and on leaving the church, as the people filed by and embraced me, bowed to me, or kissed my hand, according to their station, Zanobbi Sartorio was for me, as I dislodged from my spirit every other feeling until only the ideal image of Giulia was enthroned there, one of the crowd, just another person, like Jacopo del Duca, like Matteo Orsini, like Fabio, like my administrator Niccoloni, like my head groom, like the boys who cleaned my statues and tapestries, for Giulia Farnese at that moment was mistress of my complete devotion and she shared it with no one.

The death of my wife, whom I considered so inseparable from Bomarzo that there was no prospect of her disappearance in my calculations, as if the promise of immortality had been awarded to her as well, obliged me to meditate on the eventuality of my own death. Sandro Benedetto's horoscope, the poetic figures of which would appear above my projected portrait inside a heavenly sphere in the gallery of family frescoes like an unmovable shield of the many that surrounded the arms of my house, and which had been for me, with its marvelous prediction, the magical force that drove me on, stronger than my weaknesses and my miseries, to face up to the pitfalls of time, could have been a bald illusion, as logic established. Nonetheless I resisted disbelieving it, because my whole life had been built on that base of miracles and because the revelation by Paracelsus contributed to strengthen my privilege as an individual chosen for an exceptional destiny, and my life, reduced to modest sensual traffic, to useless crimes and vague moments of cowardice, would have lacked any meaning. With what merits could I have set myself in the middle of my breed, flanked by its multiple glories if what I brought to it was nothing but sterile musing and thin reproductions? I clung, therefore, to the prediction by Niccolò Orsini's astrologer as I would have to a life raft, but Giulia's death, even though it was connected in no way with my destiny, filled me with uncertainty. In search of relief, of affirmations which would corroborate my hopes, I went back to Silvio's abandoned laboratory. The secret lay there among the impenetrable folios of Dastyn. I had to master them. Impotent, I sank my nails into the manuscript that had been read a hundred times and cast aside a hundred times. Silvio da Narni, in the meantime, went on with his mixtures.

"What is to happen will happen," he answered me mysteriously when I told him of my distress.

I went back to the gallery where Jacopo del Duca's assistants were mixing the multicolored tones in their bowls and turning over the mortar of lime and sand that they would spread upon the wall. One could already make out some sketches in blue and red through the structure of the scaffolding. Suddenly I became aware of the vanity of all of that, of its mad lack of proportion, its pretense, how ridiculous it was.

"Stop! Stop your work!" I shouted from down below, and up above the artists left off what they were doing.

"Come down!" I ordered. "We have to talk!"

Slowly, heavily, rubbing their stained hands and faces, they worked their way down like sailors coming off the rigging. They could not understand what was wrong with me; they did not understand why, after the work had already been planned and undertaken, the lord should interrupt them in the middle of it. They jumped down, one after the other, onto the stones of the floor: Jacopo del Duca, Zanobbi, Andrea, the two masons who were helping them.

"Let it stay the way it is for now," I said briefly.

Jacopo wanted some explanation. What was going on? Was the duke not satisfied with the way in which the work was going? No, no, it was something else. The duke had to think about it for a few days. The duke had an idea, the root of an extraordinary idea. The duke could be very versatile; he was. Was his originality not commented upon in the courts in Rome, Mantua, Naples? The master and his disciples should take a week off. Perhaps Jacopo del Duca could take advantage of it and go to Caprarola, where he had been summoned by Cardinal Alessandro, and which was only a few miles from Bomarzo on the Viterbo road. There was no need for discussion. I eliminated it with a brusque gesture.

The architect-sculptor left that very afternoon. It was true that they needed him in Caprarola. His two disciples stayed in Bomarzo.

A still rudimentary idea was awakening in my mind and beginning its confused flapping. For many years it had been fluttering about in me, waiting for a chance to come out into the light. Since I had been a boy, since I had been obsessed with mysterious dreams it had been struggling to escape. One day, precisely the one on which Nencia took control of my defenseless virginity in the chapel of Benozzo Gozzoli, when I remained lying on the marble, the porphyry, and the serpentine that interwove their geometrical mosaics, empty, naked, I dreamed that I was in a rocky garden with imposing sculptures, and that in the midst of those imposing monsters that were protecting me I felt a great relief. Before that my first night in Florence had given me another dream; I saw myself between the legs of Michelangelo's David, taller than the cypresses that surrounded us in the black garden, like the protection of the dome of a triumphal arch. Ippolito de' Medici, Adriana, and Abul came out of the thickness, and while the young prince looked at us, Adriana and Abul alternately kissed me on the lips. They were two distant dreams, to which stories were related that I had heard from artists and scholars when we spoke about the harmonious David that my father had evoked for me, giving me the only true happiness that I owe him, and as they spoke of the fabulous speculations of Michelangelo himself, of his desire to convert the quarry of Carrara into a cyclopean statue, or about his building the belfry of San Lorenzo as if it were a gigantic piece of sculpture, and of the legends that had disappeared into history, like that of Dinocrates, who had planned to transform Mount Athos into an exorbitant figure of Alexander of Macedonia, holding a city in his left hand. Those titanic fantasies had lighted up my imagination ever since childhood. As I was small and deformed, I yearned for the tremendous, the overwhelming beauty that would triumph over mean and current proportions, and the shadow of which, like that of a great cloud, would wipe out everything else. Among those colossi I could disappear; no one would notice me, because we would all be equal, scattered about in its magnitude: that was what I had dreamed of since my childhood. I wanted to lose myself among them as in a fortress of infinite muscles. And now that I was a man, mature, the anxiety came back to infect me with its fever. Instead of placing myself brandishing the sword that Charles V held in the center of the captains of, my line as their age-old eyes fastened on me, hung on me, as I had conceived it with Jacopo del Duca, I had a deep urge to do the most opposite, the most contrary, for if I did not attain that fleeting and magical immortality, which was obviously getting farther and farther away from my grasping greed, nothing would be able to justify my grotesque stance. Perhaps Giulia's death had accentuated my feeling of loneliness, of abandonment, of failure; perhaps I had suspected that with her, in spite of our separation, there was a break-up of the only thing similar to a maternal protection that I had had in life since my grandmother had gone into the eternal night. And then the remote dream, imprecise, mysterious, came out of the secret of the Etruscan earth, a friend, just like that land that had engendered the supernatural, portentously, in a stony reality. Neither Zanobbi, nor Orazio, nor Silvio, nor Matteo, nor Sigismondo, nor Violante could help me fight hand to hand against life. I had no one. I was just as alone as during the time when Girolamo and Maerbale had chased me angrily through the corridors of Bomarzo. In those years of anguish I had been able at least to rely on Diana Orsini and her white oasis. But now I could rely on no one. Thus I saw what Giulia Farnese had meant for me, and bringing back to life in my breast the restlessness that was growing out of ancient dreams, I wept for her for the first time with desperate consternation. Yes, I had reached the point in my existence where in order for me to live it was necessary for my dreams to live. But first I would have to give Giulia the homage that she deserved.

One time, one single time, I chatted with Zanobbi during the week his master was at Caprarola. At siesta time, since the heat was oppressive and I could not sleep, tormented by that other and more intense heat that came from what was boiling up inside of me and which had never been defined, I left my room, went through the passageway to the nympheum, and from there into the woods. Five years before I had erected in front of the nympheum two obelisks with the inscription *"Sol per sfogare il core, Vicino Orsini nel 1552."* To unburden my heart. I had done it as a whim, a pleasantry to calm my melancholy one afternoon when I was disturbed. I should have sown the park with obelisks like that, with different dates. To unburden my heart. Just to unburden my heart. But now, in order to be unburdened, my heart required much more than a few decorative pillars. I went into the woods that were so overgrown that it was impossible to enter without knowing the hidden paths, climbing up and sliding down according to the way the steep slopes went. Here and there the rocks of Bomarzo emerged from the underbrush like the remnants of a shipwreck rocking on the waves of the turbulent branches. Those gray rocks held the matter of my dreams in their structure. They were what I would have to attack, one by one, as if they were monsters, until I vanquished them. But no, it was not a question of vanquishing; it was not a question of dragons. Each rock represented for me and for my memories an enchanted person. That person was a prisoner underneath the crust. It was necessary to free him and win his friendship. It would be a beautiful and difficult piece of work, this, one which would give back to Bomarzo its strange custodians, Duke Pier Francesco Orsini's private guard. My thin hands had rested time and again upon the roughness of the surfaces that were covered with parasitic plants, over which insects scurried, and my cheeks had also lain against their porous harshness, as if I were trying to listen to the beating of hidden hearts. The stone, sunken into the vegetable dampness, was fresh and comforting. Outside the woods the summer heat was buzzing, but inside the brush that was isolated

THE ACCURSED WAR · 557

by the mass of foliage one could feel a strange delight. More than anywhere else, more even than in the underground tombs, one could feel close to the earth there and to its secret. Lizards ran through the leaves looking for the daggers of sunlight that fell among the leaves; spiders added their transparent weave to the great forest net; and an incalculable world of small creatures was active all about. One could hear above the whispers, the creaking, and the muffled chirps the timid song of the streams as they kept the shadows of the leafy tunnels wet and as they leapt along the stones and broadened out until they were a small river with an iridescent current. Light shadows, those of nymphs and satyrs perhaps, frolicked about in a rapid flash. Everything was becoming much more ancient in that bashful place, as if time had not succeeded in stealing it away from the inhabitants who had owned it since before the coming of the Etruscans, and as if it had given refuge in its wild maze to the first gods, the gods who had governed the region before Charun, Tuchulcha, and other demons, half-man and half-beast, had appeared at funerary feasts.

Suddenly I stopped, fascinated, horrified. Sharp brambles held me on the right and the left as if I were a prisoner, and there in front of me, like a projection of those malignant divinities, a serpent arose, vibrating his forked tongue between his fangs. He was the evil enemy and the timeless, initial, Edenic ally, the Uroboros of the Gnostics, of the Egyptian hermetics, the talisman of Catherine de' Medici, there perhaps to tell me that I should not abandon the road to magic, but also perhaps, with a quick strike, to put an end to my life. He was slowly weaving back and forth, greenish, earthen-colored. A serpent had appeared like that in Bomarzo to Bishop Anselm; it was so tall that it reached up to the ceiling. The saint interrupted his prayers and said to him, "I know that since thy creation thou hast been the scourge of mankind; if thou has power over me, have done and give me my deserts right now." If I had had sufficient wisdom to have spoken to him like that, my existence would have ended right there. And another serpent lay stretched out across my coat of arms, inherited perhaps from the Anguillaras, separating the bars and the rose. My grandmother said that in Pompey's theater, our ancestral house, there had been marble monsters, *fictae ferae*, and that a child of my line, one named Hylas, had put his hand into the mouth of a stone bear and had been bitten by a snake who was hiding in the jaws of the monolith and who put an end to his life. In memory of that episode, which had been sung of by the poet Martial, the reptile had been added to our arms. Therefore, the serpent, who had started out as our enemy, had been transformed into a warlike ally of the Orsinis, because for some reason we had elevated him to heraldic glory, linking him in our shield to our great triumphs. But I had no faith in his thankfulness. I was trembling before him in the brambles, and the reptile was watching me, swaying, his cruel eyes on mine, ready to strike. I squeezed Benvenuto's ring, my amulet. Some bushes moved in back and Zanobbi and Andrea appeared among the leaves. They had probably been swimming in the stream, because all they had on were some cloths about their waists and water was running down across their hair and chests. Dark, lustrous like the snake, they might have been taken for immortal denizens of the woods, and such was their harmony that in spite of the danger that held me paralyzed, I thought that in their tense bodies there remained intact, conquering time, the pure beauty that statues have and which we have been unable to imitate. When they saw the danger they too became motionless. The four of us—the boys, the snake, and the duke—remained like that, motionless, trembling, for a few seconds, as if the day had come to a halt all around, and if it had not been for the fact that somewhere far away, very far away, the whinny of a horse arose and was answered by others in the valley, that static scene would not have been a part of reality but would have been like a bas-relief that illustrated a mythological adventure. Then, slowly, silently, Zanobbi bent down, picked up a stone, and with a well-aimed shot hit the creature on the head. They finished him off with sticks, holding him twisting to the ground. I ran forward and embraced them, still trembling with fright. I could feel their young, damp bodies against mine, their laughter, perhaps their mockery.

That episode quickly removed the barrier that had separated us. Up until then we had gone along on opposite levels: on one side the lord of Bomarzo arose majestically with his lineage, his vassals, his servants, his strange and magnificent objects, giving orders, following his whims, showing his sudden bad moods; on the other side there were the master's assistants, the mixers of clay, the cleaners of pails and brushes, the preparers of pictorial surfaces, very much the artists, of course, and so much so that Jacopo del Duca was incapable of doing what they did, brush in hand, unhesitatingly. My hump and my forty years, my status as a Roman prince, my fortune, my worldly life, and my relative military experience had kept me apart from them for various reasons, their youth, their modesty, their grace, their candor, even their complex Sicilian blood, for I was an Orsini and, if one belabors the point, a Colonna, while they were half-Greek and half-Arab boys. And even the fact that at that very moment the Sartorios were naked while I was wearing a blue and black silk jerkin with thin embroidery and a chain of enamel work and rubies about my neck, made the distance obvious. When they worked at the table in my study, whenever I made an observation—almost always superfluous and attempting to establish an impossible bond—they would both avoid my eyes, especially Zanobbi, as if he had understood, instinctively and confusedly, the oddness of the interest I was showing in him. But now, the destruction of the serpent and the emphasis I put upon the fact that I owed my life to them—something that was quite true, doubtlessly, but which someone else would not have stressed so much—brought about an unexpected link between us that erased frontiers. I discovered that they could be quite different from what they had led me to believe from the relationship imposed by the treatment called for by class distinction. Their timidity and mine gave way at the same time, not only because of the episode I have just spoken about, but also because of the fact that it had taken place outside of the castle, where every portrait and emblem was a reminder of my high position. We were in some woods, some woods in Latium that might have been Sicilian, and the chance that they had no clothes on, which at first had helped to show our inequality, in the end resulted in their favor, for instead of wearing the poor garb that was appropriate to their low station as assistants to Jacopo del Duca, who certainly must have paid them quite poorly, and which would have emphasized my aristocratic superiority, their nakedness conferred on them a dignity with which my deformed structure could not have competed. The whole event worked in favor of the brothers; at the same time they were ascending toward me and I was descending toward them, and we met surprised, at an equidistant point which neither I nor they would have dared to have imagined and which brought us together briefly, reducing us to the basic status of human beings who, beyond prejudices, were helping one another on a forest path.

They began chattering therefore. They knew much more about snakes than I, who had one as a sinople in the division on my coat of arms. I asked them where they had been swimming and they took me to where the stream is broadest. Giambattista and Porzia used to bathe there, Girolamo too when we were children. I would have been quite willing to have taken off my jerkin and joined their enthusiasm, but I did not dare unveil my hump and I sat down on an outcropping of stone that was covered with a cushion of moss. Andrea, more nervous than the older one, more lively, immediately dived in again, but Zanobbi settled down at my feet. We had a long and disjointed conversation in low voices that was broken from time to time by Andrea's shouts. I do not know why it occurred to me to tell the boy about the intimate things of my life, things that I usually did not tell. It was, of course, to win his adhesion by giving him an unusual proof of confidence, for I was aware that there would be no repetition of an opportunity as exceptional as that one, and I had to take wise advantage of it. I spoke to him of my adolescent memories, of my years in Florence, of Abul, Adriana, Nencia, wrapping the story in a mist of implications, of indecision, so that if anything could be drawn from what I was recalling it would depend upon the wisdom of my listener. He listened to me in wonder about the fame of Benvenuto Cellini, the tale of the elephant Annone, the talents of Ippolito de' Medici's Africans, the grace of Adriana dalla Roza, the elastic strength of Abul. But more than that equivocal narration, what made him marvel—and it was obvious—was that the Duke of Bomarzo was treating him with such familiarity and showing him facets of his character that he had not even suspected. For his humility and youth such preference was unheard of. He listened to me seriously, breaking into my monologue with an occasional question, and the splendor of Florence, voluptuous Venice, the solemn stage of Rome, the haughty pride of popes and Charles V, the mystery of Paracelsus and Lorenzo Lotto sparkled before his startled eyes. I decorated the description as much as I could, anxious to show myself in the most favorable light. From time to time I mingled in the richness of illustrious memories the fleeting mention of Pier Luigi Farnese, Giambattista, Sigismondo, their ambiguous attitude toward life, the way the conductor of an orchestra brings out in the middle of an imposing symphony the sound of a delicate instrument like the flute, an arpeggio, and before the note was stressed too much I would return to the harmonious roar of the loud martial trumpets that spoke of my action in Metz, Thérouanne, and Hesdin, or the courtly measures that told of my relationship to the Duke of Urbino, Isabella d'Este, renowned writers, desired beauties. The afternoon was falling down about us, noisy with birds, with distant peasant voices. Andrea had dressed himself and was lying a short distance away on the grass, as if some subtle sense had told him that he should not cut off the bond that was being drawn between us, and Zanobbi kept on listening to me, listening to me as I became intoxicated with words, straightening out lies, telling of prodigious things, mingling the true and the imagined, bringing in and excluding at the same time unexpectedly tightly tuned sensual figures, enchanting him with the skill of an agile magician who was dominating his inexperience and raising an edifice of dazzling fantasy in his honor.

Suddenly he made a curious observation. As if he had conquered the shyness that held him back, he raised his dark eyes to mine and murmured, "Your Lordship's life has been so beautiful, so rich, I would have thought that instead of having us paint the story of your ancestors, you would have had us paint your own life on the castle walls."

I was suspended, like a person who had just witnessed a revelation. The obvious thing had occurred to the boy. Perhaps because it was too obvious, because it was too close to me and I had lacked the perspective with which to appreciate it, I needed someone else to tell me. What had been hovering over me uselessly, striving to be recognized by me, suddenly had come out into the clearness of the afternoon. I stood up as if blinded by the sudden light, and I leaned against a tree. I finally saw what I had to do. My *theme* and I had met and from that second on we formed an indestructible unity. My life, my life transfigured into symbols, preserved for the centuries, eternal, imperishable... That was what I had to tell in Bomarzo, not through the ephemeral frescoes of Jacopo del Duca, the possibility of which remained abandoned forever in the crisscross of the scaffolding, in a deserted gallery of the castle, but by using the age-old rocks in the woods. Those woods would be the Sacred Wood of Bomarzo, the garden of symbols, of monsters. Every stone would have a symbol within it and all together, going up the slope where they had been strewn and settled by age-old cataclysms, they would be the immense and arcane monument of Pier Francesco Orsini. No one, no pontiff, no emperor would have a monument like that. My poor existence would be redeemed in that way, and I would redeem it, transforming it into an example of glory. Even the smallest event would take on the importance of an immortal testimony when generations yet to come interpreted it. Love, art, war, friendship, hope, and despair—everything would burst out of those rocks in which my predecessors had seen nothing but the disorder of nature. Surrounded by them I could not die, I would not die. I would write a book in stone and I would be the matter of that strange book.

The impression was so intense that I forgot about Zanobbi. I walked up toward the fortress, leaving Andrea and him on the bank of the stream. Such a stupendous feeling came over me, and how far away, along with their euphoria, were the esthetic attempts that I had tried until then, the empty rhetorical poem, the paintings that would relate again the deeds of the Orsinis. This would be mine, only mine, unique. It would be my justification, my explanation, the exceptional prowess, the touch of inspired genius that would place Vicino Orsini forever in that long procession of his people who were so difficult to follow, as he dragged his leg and his hump along, and who had humiliated him with their noble violence. A book made out of rock. Good and evil in a book made out of rock. Everything that had shaken me with grief, anxiety, poetry, aberration, love and crime, the grotesque and the exquisite. I. In a book made of rock. Forever. And in Bomarzo, my Bomarzo.

Tears wet my cheeks. I could feel their salty taste on my face. Broad clouds passed by, breaking up and forming sculptures above the castle's ocher mass.

# 10. THE SACRED WOOD OF THE MONSTERS

*The invention of the Sacred Wood—Giulia Farnese's chapel—Ippolito d'Este visits me—The flight of Zanobbi and his return—The Gigantomachia painted in the loggia—Orazio and Niccolò return to Bomarzo—Silvio, lying beside Cerberus—Zanobbi in the secret room—The mad wedding of Sigismondo and the harlot—The demon in the mirror—My marriage to Cleria Clementini—Her commercial wealth—The war against the infidel*

I SENT an emissary to Caprarola urging Jacopo to hasten his return. I was burning with the desire to tell him of my plans and to put them into effect at once. The artist returned in a bad mood because of my change in ideas, disguising as best he could his irritation with my whims. I pretended not to notice his silent reproach and I took him to the nympheum at once. The large table had had the sketches that had covered it, the traces of my previous attempt, removed, and in their place wide, immaculate sheets awaited the materialization of my aspirations. Stumbling over my words, I laid out my program to him, still vague, as it did not go beyond being a general conception, and as I set it forth and answered his successive questions, the idea—which in reality had been hovering in my mind for many years without ever having reached a definition and which Zanobbi had helped me put into concrete form—was becoming clear not only for him but also for me. He was enthusiastic with the new proposal, not so much because he preferred it esthetically, as from the fact that it fitted in much better with his own specialty, for above anything else it was a matter of dropping pictorial ideas and replacing them with a vast scheme in which sculpture and architecture demanded the application of audacious techniques and solutions. We were moving into his domain therefore. He was on firm ground there. And the same as the time before, along with Zanobbi and Andrea, we spent a long time analyzing the multiple possibilities that were presented to us.

The large room in the castle crisscrossed by scaffolding was ambitiously replaced now by the whole woods, the confusion of its underbrush, its groves, its streams, its heights, its rocks. It was necessary first off to uncover the precise shape of that secret landscape hidden by the brush in order to know how we should proceed. With outstanding patience and clarity, measuring, calculating, deducing, guessing, Jacopo del Duca and his helpers made a study of the terrain and its layout, and the hidden disposition of the place, which my predecessors and I had not known until then, began to take shape in the sketches, coming out from under the crusts that had covered it. I saw the beloved and unknown face of Bomarzo appearing day by day in the pictures that were rapidly being sketched by the master and his pupils, and it was as if a very beautiful effigy that had been rescued from the bowels of the earth by skillful archeologists were revealing the soft pattern of its pure lines as it was cleaned, polished, and had old dross and rust removed. The perspectives were spaced and distributed over the paper on neat, graceful levels, beyond my grandmother's garden, beyond the nympheum. Only the immovable rocks, placed arbitrarily, preserved their extravagant characteristics in the midst of the civilized extension, and even they, on being changed into strange pieces of sculpture, would take part in that prodigious rediscovery. I did not want, for nothing would have been more contrary to my imaginative originality, for the woods at Bomarzo to be transformed into a symmetrical park of exact logic, where every piece of construction would respond to calculated correspondences and balances. I would leave that for the parks of other Italian princes. Mine, which would be a reflection of my own life, would also be different from them all, unexpected, disquieting. What there would be of harmonious rigor in it would only serve to stress its fantasy.

The work of cutting and leveling soon began. Forty of my subjects worked for months, smoothing and molding the dark earth into flat terraces on the edge of the isolated rocks and the harsh and shady underbrush. Ancient trees were felled. The roots yielded and were torn out. Going from one window to another on the top floor of the castle, sometimes with Jacopo and his helpers and sometimes alone, watching them as they moved in the distance, microscopic, holding their triangles and compasses as they passed along through the active anthill, and the exhumed landscape reminded me of the warm skin of certain peasant women who had impressed me when I was a boy, and which I had caressed in my young years, and certain armpits suddenly revealed in the smoothness of a woman's body, as in the case, to mention one concrete example which especially aroused me, of those of Fulvio Orsini's mother, the peasant mistress of my brother Maerbale, for the contrast offered by the docile, toasted earth and the cool and tangled brush that was taking refuge in some bend, was similar to the exciting results of those contrasting voluptuous items.

The villagers who were not taking part in the work looked on in stupefaction. They could be seen with their herds of goats watching from nearby heights. They were unable to figure out what the maniacal duke was up to, although they were probably convinced that the basic task of dukes was to organize their whims. The opinions of the inhabitants of Bomarzo, according to what my administrator told me, had been divided into two camps: some, those closest to tradition, the most *Etruscan*, considered the modifications almost as a sacrilege; but there were many others who thought that because of them Bomarzo would join that series of famous villas of Latium and it would help them throw off the hereditary monotony. It was paradoxical that I, the traditionalist, should play the role of a revolutionary. If I had been a politician instead of an artist, the lack of apparent correlation between my principles and my attitude would have been less startling. But I knew that truth was on my side and, besides, I owed explanations to no one. A party from Mugnano would also come from time to time to inspect the work, and Pantasilea's red hair glowed like a torch in the sunset as she slipped along the incipient terraces, smiling at the more muscular peasants. The lord and she examined the designs and they walked about the excavations as she picked up her skirts and he was careful not to get any mud on his jerkin, and my cousin's envy, evident by the insistence with which he classified my work as madness, filled me with jubilation, for in the midst of the workmen I felt like a willful pharaoh confronting harsh nature.

In the background of the perspective, crowning the graduated surfaces, where different levels were marked after a short time with broad flights of stairs that led nowhere, I decided to place the small temple that would be my homage to Giulia. It would be small, like a miniature of Vignola's great constructions—and later on it was attributed to Vignola, for it followed his model so closely—and Jacopo was to take great pains with the sketches. The drawings that he showed me fascinated me. The cupola, rising up behind the short pronaos, was only forty-five feet in height, and its total length another forty-five feet, with twelve free columns and several more surrounding the apse, which suggested very heterodox, very beautiful solutions to the angles. I wanted it, so unusual in its simplicity, to be the initial work, and it was. My contribution consisted of the decoration added to the podium, with reliefs inspired by the Etruscan ornamentation of my collection. But what was most true was that I had no interest in the chapel. I wanted to get to the sculptures as soon as possible, the rocks, the eccentric things. The small temple, perfect in its enchanting rhythm, in its beautiful classical coldness, would represent, in opposition to the monumental strange stones, the same antithesis that Giulia Farnese was to my complex personality. The whole park would culminate there—in that fact and in its noble distinction from the rest of the unusual structures lay the prestige of the homage—but what really concerned me was the rest, the part that was mine, and if I added the Etruscan decoration to its base it was to emphasize in some symbolic way, possession, a link between Giulia and me, one to which I had always aspired and which had not really existed. Jacopo del Duca, imbued with the esthetic prejudices of the villa at Caprarola, put all his effort into that architecture. Unlike me, the basis of my strange dream did not attract him. Because of that I sensed that in order to continue the work I would have to rely solely upon myself, and that abandonment gave me new strength, for the bold work would then be my exclusive creation.

Zanobbi, in the meantime, was showing unexpected aspects of his character. He had become aware of the special attention with which I distinguished him, and sensing his privileged position, he was not afraid to reveal narcissistic and cruel traits. The silent, modest, obscure boy repeated, as the works of the Sacred Wood progressed, proofs of his malice, coquetry, greed. I noticed after a time, through a veil of allusions of false innocence, that he aspired to supplant his chief, and since that was in line with my inner urges, I set about to back him up in his maneuver. Jacopo was not stupid, he smelled the intrigue, but he preferred not to provoke an immediate explosion that would break our relations. He limited himself, therefore, to the construction of the chapel, and left the whole of the park to Zanobbi and me. I spent happy and anguished hours beside Zanobbi. It is worth noting, however, that I, who had decreed the death of my brother in a seizure of rage, was incapable of dominating a young boy whose rise was based on physical attributes that were not at all exceptional. The complication of the feelings that he inspired in me grew, parallel to the building of my masterpiece. Even today, when I recall that period of my life in the sixteenth century, I cannot separate the memory of the arduous growth of the park of the monsters, step by step in the battle with the stones, from that of my latent restlessness because of Zanobbi. My timidity, that famous imbecilic timidity that afflicted me as much as my hump, prevented me from facing up to the matter. I was afraid of losing him—something which at the present time, analyzing things clearly, seems very improbable to me—and I retreated into my shell, affecting an indifference that I was far from feeling and which did not deceive the subtle Sicilian. To take care of my wakeful nights I turned to supplementary wiles and I called to me the faithful Violante and Fabio, those permanent purveyors of sensuality, and, to tell it all in this retrospective confession, I ended up, as at other times, seeking relief in the vice of my adolescence, replacing with serviceable images that I could direct at will what reality had denied me. I proceeded in that way, without knowing it, like many artists, for whom nothing works in the voluptuous domain with as much effect as the obedient and perfect phantoms that one's imagination guides and rules.

It was a strange, shocking, and intense period. I go back to it over the centuries with horror and curiosity. Zanobbi and Andrea, his brother's doubtless accomplice in the objective of gaining power over me, never left my side during the day. As soon as I got up in the morning

I would go with them to see the progress on the chapel, and then I would go into the nympheum with both of them or stop in front of the naked rocks and watch them make drawings according to my indications. I regaled them with gifts, and people whispered, which stimulated me to overdo the presents. Sigismondo's jealousy made me laugh. I declared to him that if he and Matteo did anything to upset them I would not stop until I had cut off their Orsini noses. Dressed like lords, the disciples swelled up with pride, and although I knew that the pages hated them for the way in which they made their familiarity with me felt, I let them play at being princes, dazzled, enchanted. It was a repetition of the case of my fearful enthrallment with Abul, Adriana, and Giulia, the only judges of my weakness, and, to avenge myself, I treated the others with extreme tyranny.

When the chapel was finished, Cardinal Madruzzo consecrated it in a ceremony which was attended by my vassals and for which I gathered together friends and relatives. Monsignor Leone Orsini, Claudio Tolomei, Captain Camillo Caula, Capello, all came at my invitation. Betussi read the lines of poetry that he had composed in honor of Giulia Farnese:

> *Your angelic and celestial wit,*
> *Your lovely soul, your restive thought,*
> *Your immortal and immaculate flame*
> *Are the clearest signs*
> *That your gift of beauty is heaven sent.*

They were obviously vulgar verses, but they received a great deal of praise. Madruzzo, in the middle of the mass, pronounced a florid eulogy of Giulia and added some conceits about the way in which I was exalting her nobility for eternity. My sister-in-law embraced me with deep sobs, and I reached the conclusion that I had paid my debt to the woman who had been my distant companion and whom I had forced into sin. Kneeling among the candles I said to myself that, after all, I had given her the only joys she had: her children and the ephemeral arms of Maerbale. Orazio Orsini, standing behind me, placed his hand on my shoulder. Cecilia Colonna, Niccolò, and my children surrounded me, and I had the ironical impression that I, a man for whom family meant only a part of a genealogical structure of splendid pride, was also a man who loved his hearth.

Jacopo del Duca left that day, and I paid him handsomely. He claimed that the Zuccaros were calling for him in Rome, and I pretended that I believed him. Zanobbi Sartorio's red cheeks indicated to me later that his master had slapped his face, but we never commented on the incident. I thought of sending some ruffians to kill Jacopo and get vengeance for the one who filled my soul so exclusively, but my cowardice advised me not to reveal a doubtful business that might raise comments of ridicule among people in Mantua, Urbino, and Florence. At night Silvio da Narni suggested to me that we dedicate the new temple in our own way. Very late we slipped out toward the chapel, where the cupola was reflecting the light of the moon as it presided over the labyrinth of ditches, stones, and abandoned tools that extended down to the foot of the hill where the castle of Bomarzo stood. The astrologer drew the polygons of the Star of David on the floor under the cupola and placed black candles on its thin angles. In the center he placed some rolled manuscripts and I, kneeling on the pillow embroidered with my arms, in the place where I had been during the religious ceremony in the morning, pale, dark circles under my eyes, the prow of my back sticking out, wearing a smoke-colored outfit (*le ténébreux, le veuf inconsolé*), recognized the dog-eared letters of the alchemist Dastyn. Two angels by Perugino that had belonged to my grandfather Franciotto were watching us astonishedly from the altar. Silvio swung the censer and a smell of musk spread about. The almost forgotten names of Amon, Saracil, Sathiel, and Jana, which I had heard for the first time from the lips of Palingenio on the Via Flaminia, resounded in the magical invocation. But no demon appeared. Only an insect came in, hairy and aggressive, flying about the candles and projecting his insane image against the domes. Perhaps he was some sort of extraordinary ambassador. Silvio did not alter his expression and went on with his prayers. Then he approached the altar, put his hands together and said three Hail Marys. His long dealings with scholars of the beyond had taught him to maintain good relations with both God and the Devil. His rite seemed like a pantomime to me, with no other value except the simply decorative, which so strongly attracted my taste for the exceptional. Just in case, I prayed too, silently, without addressing any unearthly power in particular and including them all in my devotions, for the mystery of the manuscripts to be revealed to me and for me to be awarded an endless life. I was also going to ask that Zanobbi accompany me in the possibilities of that eternal voyage, but it occurred to me that I should not press the difficult request and I stayed motionless, my hands together, as Silvio swung the censer, where the coals were rising and falling among the candles like a red bird. We went out into the muteness of the night. Thick clouds hid the moon and disguised the silhouettes of stones which emerged like strange sails out of the sadness of the valley that had been carved, violated, disemboweled, rough as the waves of a stormy sea. I trembled. I was in a bewitched countryside of Ariosto's, worthy of his heroes, and yet I trembled and sank my head into the hood of the *lucco*.

"Beware of that boy, my Lord Duke," Narni murmured. "Beware of Zanobbi."

I shrugged my shoulders. Nothing mattered very much to me. I wanted to see the Sicilian, have him close to me. That was all I wanted. Fate would arrange the petty details of our relationship. I wanted to see him come forward, grave and delicate, in the shadow of the immense sculptures that told the story of my life. He would remain in the memoirs like another sculpture, small and moving; he would remain in the midst of the quiet colossi like the vibrant summation of my uneasiness, my desperation, my anxiety to survive, to be.

The material realization of the monuments, directed by Zanobbi and Andrea, would be done by the craftsmen of Bomarzo itself. I have referred, many pages back, to the impression I received when I returned from Florence to the castle and began to translate Lucretius, from the fact that some of the workmen who were carrying out the architectural modifications ordained by my father, during their rest periods, would carve stones of the soft local peperino, and I said that they gave them fantastic, rough shapes that brought to the imagination the Etruscan tradition of our soil. Those men would be the ones who would do the

THE SACRED WOOD OF THE MONSTERS · 571

work. Since I wished to bring forth something different, different too would be the ones who did it—not famous or skilled artists or wise technicians—only some men from the place, some ordinary men, raised in those volcanic hollows and with roots in their recalcitrant soil; men like those who would appear in the doors of their huts on summer afternoons as I rode through the street of the village, chatting and carving to pass the time, to occupy their skillful hands, carving fragments of soft stone. If Michelangelo Buonarroti could not carve the rocks of Bomarzo, no other master would carve them. That responsibility would remain for its sons, for those who, like me, had lived in that region since the dawn of time and who felt it as no hired esthete could have ever felt it.

Through the offices of my administrator, I called in those who seemed to be best equipped for the job. They listened to me in surprise and even though I announced tempting remunerations they tried to escape my whims, for they were startled by such an unexpected undertaking, so different from their inherited tasks as herders and plowmen. But I wiped away their answers with a gesture and ordered them served the best wine. With the cups in their hands, dazzled by the majesty of the imperial busts and the horror of the Minotaur—for I had received them with great show in the splendid gallery in order to give the interview an exemplary meaning—they looked at one another. I naturally did not mention the idea that those gigantic monsters symbolized episodes from my existence. I told them, on the contrary, that centuries before, when the Caesarian grandeur of Rome was greater, in the gardens of Pompey's theater, which was later the palace of the Orsinis, there was a collection of *fictae ferae*, of marble images of mythological creatures and ferocious animals, and that what I wanted was to endow Bomarzo with something similar, using for it the very rocks where they lay. I stirred up their local pride, explaining to them that neither in Mugnano, nor Bracciano, nor Caprarola, nor Bagnaia, nor Rome and Florence either would there be anything that could be compared to our colossal statues. Matteo Orsini listened to me skeptically in a corner. For him the only worthy form of fame was military glory, and his eyes turned with nostalgia toward the standard that proclaimed our battle in Hesdin and which, in spite of its having been made out of the skirt of a gypsy woman, was already taking on the attributes of definitive authenticity—which it deserved, furthermore. Sigismondo was also listening to me. His single eye was gleaming beside the blackness of his patch. He was even more skeptical. He ran his bony fingers, as over the beads of a rosary, along the stones of lapis lazuli and the pearls of the necklace which he kept as evidence of his friendship with Pier Luigi Farnese, and he was doubtlessly calculating that an enviable notoriety did not come either from artistic audacity or military victories, for the satisfactions of art and war grew pale alongside those provided by the worldly triumph of lordly elegance in refined courts. And the two Sicilians, Zanobbi and Andrea, as slim as dark angels, went with the pages among the confused peasants, filling their cups and whispering words of enthusiasm.

From then on, along the roads of Latium, the legend began to grow that the Duke of Bomarzo was planning to do something unheard of on his medieval domains. The constant prying brought many noblemen to my lands, anxious to know what exactly I was doing, for the villas that were rising in the outskirts of Rome, in imitation of the classical *deliciae agrestes*, had engendered feuds of pride, rivalry, and rancor. But all they saw were a few ditches, some parapets, some unplanted terraces, and some rocks around which the villagers were busying themselves with chisels and hammers, guided by two inexperienced boys. Not even Cardinal Ippolito d'Este, the son of Lucrezia Borgia and governor of Tivoli, who at that time was busy transforming the old residence of those functionaries, a former convent, into the most marvelous of palaces, subtle as he was, could grasp the singularity of what I was planning. He came to visit me with a retinue of such pomp that, since it was autumn, even the servants were wrapped in furs of silver fox. He was my guest for two days. We spoke of our family ties, of my admiration for Isabella d'Este, of the gout that tormented him, of the buzzing that tortured his ears—and it was curious that he should have chosen such a noisy device as that of aquatic constructions, with their incessant murmuring and echoes, which should have driven him mad—of the daring of his creation. His villa was planned as an architectural offering to exalt the triumph of water, while mine would be the exaltation of stone, so that we did not come to understand each other. He had come to Tivoli from far away, imbued with genealogical stories that had nothing to do with the place, while I was rooted in Bomarzo, spiritually and physically, since the beginning of the centuries. I was an Etruscan and he was a cosmopolitan, half Italian and half Spanish. The water that flowed from a thousand intermingled fountains emphasized in Tivoli, with its prodigious orchestration that broke out in jets, foam, and cold iridescences, the flighty and casual inconsistency of his bond. The statues scattered among the fountains, the steps, the grottoes and the galleries of Tivoli seemed to be made of water too, wrinkled by erosion, covered by the felt of damp moss, appearing amid the plumage and draperies of tremulous freshness that were multiplied afterwards by the successors of the Ferrara Borgia. On the other hand, the rocks of Bomarzo would express, solemnly and strongly, the intimate side of the bonds that united me to them and which, through them, sinking into their opaque matter and passing through it, would reach into the heart of the earth and the ancient tombs. Two concepts were facing each other: the frivolous, courtly, and grandiloquent one of Cardinal Ippolito, which stood out over the noisy background of cascades, and the feudal, esoteric, disquieting, and very personal one of the Duke of Bomarzo, which was outlined against the motionless and mute background of his stone monsters. On one side vaporous arrogance, transparency, the multicolored fountains that mocked time because time disappeared in their bubbles; on the other rooted stubbornness, the static, petrified force of the centuries. And although the disparity did not correspond to the reality of the creators of both plastic arrangements themselves, it had been left for Ippolito d'Este and me to incarnate two divergent feelings toward life and the world; for our works, if they are great, go beyond us and leave us behind in their dynamic evolution. Probably, while we were strolling on the terraces of my property—he leaning on the arm of the hunchback and complaining about his gout—we could both sense the essence of that antagonism that was superior to us, even though certain traits of the cardinal shared the concept stressed by the allegory of Bomarzo, and several of my fundamental characteristics corresponded to what the Villa d'Este represented; but what was certain was that we did not understand each other and that the contrary elements of Water and

Stone, in which the roots of our disparity became concrete, separated us. It was enough for me to hear the prelate say that in my place he would have done away with the rocks completely, replacing them with symmetrical fountains, or that in any case, he would have proceeded in such a way that they would not have ruined the repeated exactness of the design, in order to deduce that we would never understand each other. The garden of his villa was incomparably more vast and sumptuous than the park of my castle, but mine was mine and had always been ours, while his had come down from the bureaucratic governors of Tivoli. He could not interpret me; he could not sense what those rocks meant for me. And he left with his long retinue, laughing, joking, covering his pain with majestic expressions, set to tell people certainly that I was about to ruin a noble site with great carnival figures, with enormous and absurd monsters, which, fortunately, would rise up far from the routes used by travelers, for they would work against the celebrated beauty of the Roman countryside.

When he left, Ippolito d'Este made me a gift of a leopard cub, whom I named Djem, in memory of that unfortunate Muslim, the brother of Bajazet and son of the conqueror of Constantinople, whom his jailer, Pope Alexander Borgia, Cardinal d'Este's grandfather, had had killed with a slow poison. Like him, the feline was a prince and a captive; like him, he was handsome and lithe; and he was dangerous like him, in spite of his apparent submission. For training and care I turned him over to Sigismondo, who took such a liking to the wild beast that they were inseparable from then on. I was annoyed that that great lord should be a prisoner. I had felt something similar with the bear of the Duchess of Camerino, which the other Cardinal Ippolito, my beloved Ippolito de' Medici, had given to my cousin Violante. It upset me to see princes reduced and humiliated. Perhaps, unconsciously, they stirred up in my soul the sad figure that I had been when Girolamo and Maerbale tormented me. But little Djem did not give the impression of a victim. He would cling to the back of Sigismondo's horse on hunts or run behind his master, lunging forward with rhythmical leaps which terrified the peasantry and aroused the haughty blood of the decadent Sigismondo like a sudden goad from the past imperial power of his race. Orazio, Niccolò, and the other children of the family played with him in the rooms of the castle, and on more than one occasion it was necessary to rescue our tapestries from his incipient claws.

The last curious aristocrats left Bomarzo and I turned away those who sporadically followed them. Sometimes, in the midst of the work, I would spot in the distance confused groups who were spying on us, but the work went on as if we had not noticed their presence, until those curious tourists ceased to come. Finally Bomarzo and I were alone. Finally, in that withdrawal that had unthought-of mystical aspects, I gave myself over fully to the spell of inspiration as if I had wiped out every other prod of my will.

Every rock had an enigma hidden in its structure, and every one of those enigmas was also a secret of my past and my character. I had to uncover them. I had to remove the crust that covered the essential image in each rock. For a long time, along with Zanobbi, I would walk among the rocks like an illuminate, like a madman, observing and touching them. Andrea, meanwhile, was copying the figures of my horoscope on one of the walls of the gallery with the imperial busts.

For the present I resolved that the rock located behind the nympheum, at one side of the broad upper level, would show Abul and his elephant Annone. I set to work at once, and Zanobbi did a drawing which showed the slave sitting on the head of the pachyderm, who had a castle on his back. Directed by the boy, the craftsmen began their work, and the stone, aghast, under attack, and broken for the first time, flew into splinters. It did not yield easily. The work was not as simple as it had seemed at first, and the improvised sculptors assaulted it with a fervor that showed the glow of their obedience to an unknown but certain vocation, one which emanated from shadowy ancestral urges and from the fact that they were doing something that rescued them from their status as rustics, lighting up their vigor and their sweat with its flame—so beloved by Renaissance men—one which belonged to artists. Spring was already creeping into the valley, the hills, with its buds and odors, with its soft languor. As the rough lines of the design were glimpsed on the monumental effigy, the thought occurred to me that the stony mass which rose up in front of the beast's huge head could be the figure of a defeated warrior held by the powerful trunk. That warrior would be Beppo, slain by Abul. Enormous, the elephant was outlined against the twisted background of the park of Bomarzo. It was my first work. After having satisfied my obligation to Giulia Farnese in the tiny building whose severe elegance and whose columns recalled the ceremonious elegance of my wife, my thoughts turned toward Abul. It had to be that way. The strange figure of Abul had governed a period of my life.

I refused to undertake any work before I finished the one that called for the limits of our capacity. But as the statue was being created, ideas kept boiling up in my mind. Week after week, the park, the Sacred Wood of Bomarzo, was taking shape in my spirit. It was inside of me, carved with obsessive neatness, even when the first of the bold structures had not yet been finished. And the morning when I saw that the figure of Abul, Beppo, and Annone was ready, and when I could see that it was exactly what I had wished for, because its design had a tone that was different from everything else I had seen until then, rougher and stronger, more elemental and candid, in spite of the sumptuous proportions of the shapes—something which, like the structures that grew up beside it in that refuge on Monte Cimino, among primroses and ferns, can only be compared to certain masterly and exotic carvings in India, the existence of which I did not even presume at that time—I understood that I had succeeded with a unique plastic vocabulary that was so tightly allied to the place and its soul, even though the figure was foreign, that I leaned my forehead against the wrinkled flank of the stone in order to hide my emotion.

From then on the vast effort grew. I had in me an ardent certainty that drew me along with its impulse. I showed all of my ideas to Zanobbi at once, and what I planned to see converted into quick reality was so important that Andrea abandoned the sumptuous fringes and courtly gods of the horoscope, summoned to add his hand to a task that demanded our greatest effort. As summer and autumn advanced and winter turned things pale, the valley was filled with the strange sound of hammers, crowbars, chunks torn out. Above the green grass, the golden leaves, the hard ground, the snow, frightening off snakes and lizards, weasels and moles, beetles and birds, there rose up a mysterious world of exorbitant phantoms. My children walked about startled, going from one group to another, asking questions of the teams of workmen, shouting and pointing as if they were children of today and were in some fabulous amusement park, in some strange Luna Park of stone—which was the impression that Bomarzo suggested to the writer Moravia not so long ago—and their chattering only stopped when at the turn of a rock or as they went down a terrace they suddenly ran into the duke, into the little hunchback who went by without seeing them, the long tufts on his temples gray, moving his chiseled hands in his monologue, captured by the miracle and joy of his creation.

The tallest rock was transformed into a huge Neptune leaning his naked torso against a cyclopean wall. With his long beard and hair flowing down over his shoulders and chest, he was the powerful allegory of the sea, of oceanic infinity, of eternity, of immortality, of the great dream that was born when I opened my eyes to life. A horrible monster on whose great brow a sphere decorated with the bars of the Orsini shield stood was my own figuration, that of the deformed person who was holding up the heraldic weight of family glory. Up above I had a fortress designed, the fortress of Bomarzo. The Orsinis and Bomarzo were bearing down on me, but I sustained them in my terror, almost sinking into the mother earth. Then there was the tortoise topped by a musical figure from which an ingenious mechanism run by water drew out soft sounds and which signified the defeat and anguish of my poetry. Scholars of today have declared that the statue was inspired by a story of Pausanias about a statue by Phidias, an Aphrodite who was resting her foot upon a tortoise, and by a fresco by Vasari in the Hall of the Elements in the Old Palace in Florence, where Fortune is carrying a tortoise under her arm, but that is not how it is. That was as far away from me as the Hindu creations. Then came the colossal whale, carved crudely in honor of the divine Ariosto, commemorating the scene in which Astolfo—that Astolfo whom in my adolescence I sensed to be reincarnated in Benvenuto Cellini—took refuge on an island that in reality was a cetacean. Portentous stories, heard in Rome, Florence, and France from ancient mariners also influenced me to include the whale in my bestiary, because in them I heard the echo of Ariosto's prodigious fantasy, which became reality in the passion-arousing New

World. To Adriana I dedicated a sphinx, for that was what she had been to the erotic awakening of my years, an equivocal and adorable sphinx. I gave Pantasilea the features of an abandoned nymph, because the first time that she had put her arms around me I had left her without having possessed her; Nencia that of an opulent naked woman, so enormous that the craftsmen climbed up over the globes of her breasts, hoisting themselves up as if they were scaling a mountain, until they reached the huge jar that gleamed on the top of her head and in which a whole tree was growing, as I tried to express in that way the fact that Nencia had covered me with her immense shadow, a shadow that seemed as wide to me as the palace of the Medicis where she overpowered me. And the frightful skeleton that was proof of my father's hatred was outlined with its skull and tibias on a pilaster with a triangular pedestal, while my persecution by my brothers had its allegory in the two winged persons that I hid at the base of the giantess and who were holding the strong figure of a young boy face down. The battle between a dragon and two dogs was my military action put into one stone. The dragon was Charles V and the bulldogs my campaigns in Metz and Picardy. The death of Maerbale was expressed, on the other hand, by the struggle between two identical titans, one of whom was quartering the other. Some people have tried to recognize in that ferocious group the episode of Hercules and Cacus, or have brought in Polyphemus as he tore the companions of Ulysses limb from limb. Only I knew what it represented, as only I knew that a nymph with a broad lap and no feet, for they disappeared into the blackness of the earth, represented my grandmother Orsini as she rose out of the maternal soil of Bomarzo. And lastly, nobody, not even Zanobbi, who carved that double head guessed that the two-faced Janus, showing a feminine and masculine side, inseparable, meant for me the dual emblem of Eros, which ever since I opened my eyes had stalked me and worried me with its opposing and complementary faces.

A world of images and unknown people—my fantastic biography—sprang from the bowels of my ancestral lands. I have had to use over and over again in order to describe it such words as enormous, immense, gigantic, colossal, using synonyms to the point of satiety. Everything was formidable in the Sacred Wood, and many more figures were added to those mentioned, ones like the old tritons and the young tritons of the fountain, like the fork-tongued serpent, like the harpy with the tail of a snake, and the series of ornamental vases standing more than fifteen feet tall, the stately pines and the bears who held up our shield, and the infernal Cerberus. The maze of calm or violent poses there was intermingled and connected to the inscriptions that I myself had written to disturb visitors to the labyrinth, as for example:

> *Voi che pel mondo gite errando, vaghi*
> *di veder meraviglie alte e stupende,*
> *venite qua, dove son faccie horrende,*
> *elefanti, leoni, orsi, orchi et draghi.*

or:

> *Cedan et Memphi e ogni altra meraviglia*
> *ch' ebbe già il mondo in pregio, al Sacro Bosco*
> *che sol se stesso e null' altro somiglia.*

or even:

> *Chi con ciglia inarcate*
> *e labbra strette*
> *non va per questo loco,*
> *manco ammira*
> *le famose del mondo*
> *moli sette.*

or:

> *Tu ch' entri qud pon mente*
> *parte a parte,*
> *e dimmi poi se tante*
> *maraviglie*
> *sien fatte per inganno*
> *o pur per arte.*

or this one that I placed at the base of the mortal duel between the two brothers:

> *Se Rodi altier fu del suo colosso,*
> *pur di questo il mio Bosco anche si gloria,*
> *e per più non poter fo quant' io posso.*

My pride sparkled in those texts that I added as the work progressed. I sincerely thought that I was accomplishing something great, and I could barely hide my vanity under an ironic veil.

I decided to include a special homage—a singularly caustic one—to my intellectual friends when the work had advanced enough so that even if the end could not be seen, at least the final arrangement could and I imagined instead of a piece of sculpture, a building of reduced proportions, exquisitely harmonious, but at a slant, built at an oblique angle from the ground, so that it would be difficult to walk through its small rooms, and there I placed a plaque in praise of the good Cristoforo Madruzzo, Principe Tridentino, and I filled the place with small paintings relating to the exercise of letters.

Actually, the ordering and the work of the garden of monsters lasted for the rest of my life at Bomarzo. The valley was continuously echoing with the distant ring of hammers; from then on there were also groups of people or solitary silhouettes making an effort as they leaned over a rock to extract its secret. Time went on indifferently. Orazio Orsini, along with Niccolò, received his baptism of blood in the last war of Pope Paul IV, which took place in the Roman countryside; Charles V died; a little before him the bothersome Ferrante Gonzaga had died; Henry II died at a tourney; they all died and their crowns rolled at their feet onto the tattered robes that other princes hastened to put on; the Duchess Margaret of Austria assumed the governorship of the Low Countries; Giulia Gonzaga had to defend herself against the fangs of the Inquisition; a daughter of Duke Cosimo married my cousin from Bracciano; the Amadigi was printed, which Bernardo Tasso read before the court of Urbino and in which there were allusions to Vicino Orsini and his Sacred Wood, for my fame and that of my creation was growing with time; Paolo Orsini, of disagreeable memory, was created

Duke of Bracciano; a book by Pietro Crescenzio Bolognese, dedicated to the Roman villas and translated by Sansovino, was published and it left me cold, for nothing deserved to be compared to my garden; Cardinal Madruzzo, in order to be closer to me, acquired the height of Soriano, behind the Cimini mountains; Orazio Orsini left for Florence, where Duke Cosimo de' Medici had founded the Order of Saint Stephen, and the boy was made a knight in it, something which gave him great joy (and me too, in spite of my grumbling that for a person of our house an honor awarded by a Medici was nothing but claptrap), for becoming widespread in Italy—and it has never diminished—was a passion for titles and decorations which made the grandsons of bankers and merchants lose their heads, as was quite natural. And in Bomarzo the work went ahead. The incomparable monuments rose up toward the votive chapel of my wife, where the Franciscans celebrated daily masses for the repose of her soul and in which, on sabbath nights, in secret, Silvio da Narni, wearing a black chasuble, would officiate at his heterodox rites, which I attended, mistrusting, kneeling on my cushion.

Messer Pandolfo also died, at a very old age. We buried him with his Virgil under his head. Before that he had asked my permission to be carried through the magical park in my grandmother's chair.

"The Orsinis," he told me on his return, "are the enemies of stone. The condottiere Bertoldo, of the Pitigliano branch, died in the East, where he was commanding the forces of the Most Serene Republic against the Turks, from having been stoned by a woman during the assault on a stronghold, and another Bertoldo, a senator of Rome with Luca Savelli, was massacred and buried under stones by a hungry mob on Capitol hill."

I laughed and replied that those misfortunes had happened to Bertoldo Orsinis, that I was immune.

"Those stones," he murmured, "those stones..."

Zanobbi and his brother had left. They had sneaked away, taking advantage of one of my visits to Bracciano, taking with them my large gold chain and the sword that Charles V had held, and my astrologer's prediction had come true. I sent soldiers to look for them, but to no avail. That betrayal left a bitter taste on my lips, and I shut myself up in my study in the nympheum and in Silvio's laboratory. I would leave those rooms to walk through the park, where I chatted with the workmen and the guests who had come from Rome. Everything was beautiful and sad at the same time. In the main hall my horoscope entwined its promissory signs with the allegories of the gods and the stars, the round of Venus, Mars, Saturn, the Moon, the Sun. I thought that now nothing could happen to me, nothing, nothing, that my history was written in indelible letters of stone. My daughter Ottavia married; my daughter Orinzia married. Their husbands were frivolous and fatuous, and I found out that they criticized me among themselves, that they thought I was a bit demented. On several occasions I surprised them looking very closely at my paintings, my marbles, my alabasters, my cameos, and my clocks, as if they were estimating their worth. That Marcantonio Marescotti and that Count of Montegualandro—bah! The only one of my children who interested me was the fragile Maerbale, the little hunchback. I tried to get close to him, reach an understanding, but in vain. Fate brought us together in the garden one afternoon; I took him by the arm, using my lameness as an excuse, and led him through the works as if I were a critic or an archivist and we were going through an exhibit of historical objects. I revealed to him— I disguised my intention with jokes, mentioning false individuals to whom I attributed my own adventures and reactions—the salient events of my life and the twisting of my temperament and conduct. In front of the monster that represented me with his cruel monolithic metaphor, the one holding up the shield of the Orsinis, and in front of the double face of love on the bust of the god Janus, I tried to awaken an echo, perhaps a gesture of solidarity brought out by the words with which I was confusedly revealing obscure intimacies to him. He listened to me attentively, opening wide his eyes, which were just like mine and those of my brother Maerbale, but nothing indicated to me that he understood me, that he shared my restlessness, that he forgave me. Perhaps he was too young for me to try an experiment like that on him. Perhaps the similarity that twisted our backs was only external and did not reach into the roots of our consciousness. I never tried to get close to him again, and as a consequence of that fruitless plumbing I felt even more lonely.

One day—the day I reached the age of fifty-two—they awoke me with a strange tale. They had seen pass along the Tiber a boat filled with demons wearing green armor. Others had seen a second vessel, the crew of which was made up of saints from Bomarzo, with Saint Anselm in the prow, his miter gleaming. I called for the presumptive witnesses of the apparition and they turned out to be some quivering, senile old women who were guided and counseled by the Franciscans who took care of Giulia's chapel. The grannies spoke in a singsong, rolling their rheumy eyes and raising them up to heaven. I gave each one of them a silver coin as alms and the chronicle of miracles became enriched with successive stories. A peasant woman, when she was going through the park at dusk, had suddenly come upon the skeleton from the church, whom she recognized from his crown of withered flowers. He was riding a reddish donkey, carrying a horrible bundle, and she described it so minutely that I thought of the one that Michelangelo had painted in his house in Monte Cavallo a short time before his death, which was carrying his coffin on his shoulders. Then the daughter of one of the jesters swore that the deity supported by the colossal tortoise would spin about slowly at dawn and that the monument of the naked combatants, the allegory of Maerbale's destruction, would vibrate and sway at certain times as if the struggle were still going on.

I proclaimed that I would have the next spreader of tales lashed, and that if the stories did not stop, I would have the leopard Djem unchained and turned loose in the park as soon as the first star came out. The people calmed down, but the few times that Silvio went down to the village, the inhabitants would make the cabalistic sign of the horns and the fig and flee into their houses. The multicolored column of smoke that floated above his laboratory paralyzed them with fear. The monks of the *Poverello* calculated that the time had come to intervene, but I cut off their timid discourses with a dry swat of riding crop. I informed them categorically that if they would not let me govern my estates as I saw fit, I would send them to Cardinal Franciotto's palace in Rome, where in the cells there they would have plenty of time to meditate upon their imprudent audacity until the end of their days. On the lips of the oldest I thought I saw the glimmer of the word "Inquisition," and, liquidating the whole matter, I reminded them of how close was the friendship and alliance that had linked popes and

Orsinis since the beginning of time. Then, calming down, I sent a chalice that had belonged to Diana Orsini to the church of Saint Francis in Assisi.

It was around that time that Zanobbi Sartorio returned to Bomarzo.

Zanobbi brought the sword with him. Perhaps he had not dared sell it because it would have put people on the trail of the robbery. Prostrating himself before me, he embraced my legs—the right one, the defective one too, which made me shudder with anguish and obliged me to disengage him with feigned indignation—and he sobbed that Andrea had been to blame for the theft, and that he had fled to Sicily, to his native Agrigento, or to Cefalù, or even farther into the heart of the island, to the mountainous regions of Enna, where it would be impossible to hunt him down.

"But I'll find him someday!" he swore, making a cross of his fingers and kissing it noisily. "I promise Your Lordship! And I'll get my vengeance that day! I'll make him sweat for every diamond and every gold link!"

I pretended to believe him. I felt so happy at finding him again that I would have forgiven him in any case, even if he had not hidden from me the fact that he had been the instigator of the theft, being much stronger and more dominant than his brother. Beyond all of that, it was evident that time had left its marks on him. Little by little during the days that followed, because, as must be understood, I aimed to take advantage of the superior position that circumstances offered me and play the role of the aggrieved and despoiled master, I learned what had happened during his absence. According to him Andrea had taken flight, abandoning him as soon as they reached Rome. For one instant the idea of coming back and prostrating himself at my feet crossed his mind, but he did not dare. He hid the sword, which he was anxious to return to me, and went to Florence. There the future Grand Duke of Tuscany employed him at various tasks, but the wave of crimes that came over the city of the Lily obliged him to flee again. Lucrezia, the daughter of Cosimo de' Medici, had been poisoned by her husband, the Duke of Ferrara, who had accused her of infidelity. Her brothers,

## THE SACRED WOOD OF THE MONSTERS · 585

Garzia and Cardinal Giovanni, had also died, and it was rumored that the first had been stabbed by the second during a hunt in the marshes of Pisa, and that Duke Cosimo himself, blind with rage, had killed his son Garzia. As can be seen, people did not feel very secure in the most beautiful city of Italy. And even then there were crimes that were not mentioned: the murder of Leonor of Toledo at the hands of her husband, the libertine Pietro de' Medici, and that of Isabella de' Medici, strangled by her mate, my cousin Paolo Giordano Orsini, the Duke of Bracciano, who then married Vittoria Accoramboni, who, in order to be eligible, had barbarously done away with her first husband, a nephew of Pope Sixtus V. Missing too were the mysterious deaths of the Grand Duke Francesco and his wife, Bianca Capello, who had authorized the homicide of her previous husband, and perhaps also that of the Archduchess Joan of Austria, who was a hunchback like me. Zanobbi trembled as he added up the atrocities that had taken place in Florence. He gave the impression of really having been terrified, and later on he even hinted that he had had something to do with them, for otherwise there was no cause for his insane fear. The truth is that although I may have said that I had let my brother Girolamo drown and had ordered the death of my brother Maerbale, those deeds would have seemed tolerable, as ones that took place in the bosom of great families, in comparison to the passionate cataclysm that destroyed the Medicis, as we have seen, and which stained with blood all the branches of that upstart line which was in a hurry (it could be said) to give itself the tone of the time-honored families that had spaced their respective and unavoidable tragedies over the centuries.

I heard the popular and palace versions of the ferocious crimes from his lips as if I were listening to one of the violent tales that the *cantastorie* of Sicily tell. Those luxurious and important people, whom I had known since they were very young and to whom I was related, appeared in my imagination gripping daggers and clutching throats like wax figures in a horror museum, irreconcilable with reality. Reality for me at that time was found exclusively in the salons and the garden of Bomarzo, in a hermetic world which had as its boundaries the laboratory of an alchemist, the study of a collector of odd items, a chapel where magical liturgies took place, and a garden on the terraces of which the stones of the gigantic monsters gleamed among the trees. In the midst of those originalities I was lost, I faded away, hidden by the sculptured myths and by the enigmatic ceremonies, and my hump and my thoughts vanished into the air that smelled of musk, sulphur, of the attempted and rejected mixtures of the Great Elixir, of roses, jasmine trees. Everything else, what was crowded beyond the Cimini mountains, belonged to the realm of the invented, the hypothetical. The scarlet story of the Medicis, which Orazio Orsini had also told me in detail in a letter, startled me, as was natural, but it did not surprise me any more than many of the legends that Messer Pandolfo used to tell, stressing the fateful names of my clan and those of the heroes of literature. On the other hand, Zanobbi, who had lived in that climate of unrest, had brought from Florence, along with my sword, the stigmas of a new fright.

I said before that his absence had left deep marks on him. He was no longer the graceful adolescent who had accompanied Jacopo del Duca with a brush or a triangle in his hand. The rings under his eyes had deepened and his eyes had a different glow. But he still had that secret fascination with which he had bewitched me when I saw him for the first time. One could even say that his power of seduction had grown as he matured. As before, without confessing it, for we never spoke of that, I was his prisoner. Always, ever since the days of my grandmother, of Adriana, I had been burdened with the necessity of being dependent on somebody, of *belonging*. I, so rebellious, so proud, was the slave of my feelings. My weakness took refuge in that implicit subjection as in a bastion.

In order to occupy Zanobbi and keep him at a distance, for I resisted showing him at once how far his domination over me went, I planned a great painting to be done in the loggia beside the Room of the Horoscope and which would have for a theme the battle of the Giants. I was obsessed with that matter, the same that I had dealt with in the monument representing the death of Maerbale. I wanted something similar to the Gigantomachia that Perino del Vaga had done for Andrea Doria in Genoa, and the one that Giulio Romano did in the Te palace in Mantua, but more complex, more like Ariosto, closer to the prodigious conceptions of Briareus, with his thousand arms, of Typhon, with his three bodies, a mixed-up mythological anatomy that would bring the fantastic concept of the park into the castle and would stress the esthetic unity of my creation. I wrote about that to Annibale Caro, who was in Frascati at the time, lying awake at night planning his Tuscan villa, and a brief correspondence followed in which the secretary of the Farneses had the audacity to point out to me that in his judgment, the giants symbolized the evil lords, who, since they were greater and had more advantages than others on earth, were setting out to challenge their peers and God. He suggested to me that since I planned to dedicate one of the walls of Bomarzo to describe the eternal war of mortals with immortality, I should assign the sketches to Taddeo Zuccaro. But I had my own painter and I sent him to Rome to talk to Caro. The impression (I rejected it) that Sartorio made on him could not have been better. I can imagine the tricks that Zanobbi must have used to charm him, the eccentricities, the false timidity, the adulation. Without mentioning it—because of that distraction the name of Zanobbi does not figure in the chronicles that speak of me— Annibale told me that the young man was very wise and that probably he would be able to bring off the difficult task.

Those letters have suffered a fate that leads one to reflection. Of the uncountable ones that I received during the length of my long life, they are the only ones that have survived, and every time a historian or commentator refers to Pier Francesco Orsini, he reproduces them and comments on them. The other letters that Annibale Caro sent to me on various occasions have been lost, and they were of much greater importance, the same as those from my two grandparents, those from Giulia Farnese, Ippolito de' Medici, Lorenzino, Pier Luigi, Giulia Gonzaga, Michelangelo, Madruzzo, Molza, Lorenzo Lotto, Sansovino, Aretino, Betussi, Ippolito d'Este, Benvenuto, Paracelsus, Messer Pandolfo, Piero Valeriano, Giambattista Martelli, Orazio Orsini, the Duke of Mugnano, Pantasilea; those I sent to Giulia during our betrothal and which, in my opinion, were quite admirable, have been lost. During that time we wrote a great deal to one another, and everything that concerns me has been lost. I, who was such a collector and classifier of objects, was not an archivist like my father. I tore up, I lost. When Bomarzo was sold to the Lante della Roveres, they made bonfires of the papers that were there, yellowed in the oblivion of chests, without even looking at the fame of those who had signed them. There have only survived, ironically, of that treasure, two letters from Annibale Caro. It can be deduced from that how difficult it is to judge a man after he is dead from the few documents that drift about, absurd, disconnected, arbitrary, in the disorder of his wake. The biographer sets up his puzzle conscientiously, taking advantage of the incoherent, shredded pieces of written testimony that the whim of fate has preserved, and the rest, the intimacy of the person and quite often his essential characteristics and the knowledge about him are lost. He thinks that he has caught in the net of scholarship and exegesis someone to whom he is related by some incalculable affinity, dead for many years, and all he is doing is collecting the irregular fragments of a shipwreck. If the subject of that study were able to examine the results of the investigation, stupefied, he would not recognize them. I am the proof of it. Caro's letters have persecuted me. People say that no one else was ever interested in me. And the interest that they show is quote modest. Happily, I have enjoyed the supernatural prerogative of putting these memoirs together, for otherwise—and in spite of the immense effort I have taken to protect my memory of what has been forgotten—no one would have known anything about me except for certain genealogical information and certain genealogical details, which are generally mistaken. But—the reader must ask—is it worth the effort to write such a long book about such an unimportant life? I must answer him that for me it is not unimportant, that no one's own life is unimportant to himself, but unique and marvelous, and that no one is obliged to read it. And I must answer him and tell him to observe my existence carefully and then he will be unable to say that it was not a marvel. For some reason, after all, I have been given the possibility of telling it detail by detail.

The scaffolding that had been erected in the other distant gallery when Jacopo del Duca began his interrupted work was set up in the loggia and Zanobbi hid himself there with his colors. He was afraid to run into me, and for my part, I preferred at first not to see him. Although I concealed it when it happened, the news of the robbery together with that of the quick departure of the Sicilians had doubtless spread, and nothing irritated me as much as gossip based on my weaknesses, so that I attempted to treat him as just another servant, and I made the sacrifice of eliminating any conversation. Standing on the terrace of the nympheum, I would look at the cage of the loggia, the cage of thin columns conceived by my father, inside of which the dark bird was jumping from perch to perch. He worked in his aerial cage all day long, and as soon as the shadows of dusk fell, the remote glimmer of lights told that Zanobbi was still at his tasks. But sometimes I could not resist the temptation, and fortified by the pretext that I should oversee the progress of the painting, I would go into the artist's redoubt. Up on the ladder Zanobbi was looking at his sketch and wetting his brushes. He would smile at me from on high, looking for my approval, and we would scarcely say a word to each other.

"That struggle of the giants," he said to me one morning, "is my struggle."

And I thought of the war that passions were waging on his youth, ambition, the urge to be somebody, the urge to accomplish something beautiful, outstanding, which would raise up his name like a flag, and the urge to make up for his mistakes and attain complete forgiveness for his perfidy.

"It's my struggle too," I answered him.

I thought, in good faith, that by expressing myself in that way I was referring only to my struggle for immortality, similar to that of the titans to take over heaven, but underneath that splendid idea, which lighted up my life with a glorious glow, struggling there, vulgarly, creeping in, was the miserable idea of the struggle that my deformed desperation had turned loose—then as always—against disdainful beauty.

Behind the scaffolding, the Gigantomachia of Zanobbi Sartorio spread over the walls with the impetus and fire of its convulsions. The sketch was far from perfect and yet, out of that baroque mingling, out of those ardent tentacular connections, entwined and curled about the confident disdain of the gods, there arose a brutal feeling of strength, which gave the loggia a kind of cruel vibration, the product of the meeting of two angers. It seemed impossible that a boy so weak and flighty, all eyes and tousled hair, could have been capable of such a complicated enterprise. Perhaps the Sicilian had put his own wrath into it, his peasant hatred, that of a poor dependent artist against the lords to whom circumstance had submitted him, but what was certain was that even if he thought of it, the gods, the princes, carried victory in their makeup, not only because it was imposed by the demands of the theme, but also because on his part there was the firm certainty that grew out of a divine privilege. Seeing that gave me new peace, as whenever my anguish ran into the confirmation that victory would be mine in the end, for that privilege, in order to be justified, had to have a sense of the supreme and then, beyond the resentment that separated us, I began to feel toward him an indulgence freed from the bonds of passing and sad sensuality.

Orazio and Niccolò returned to Bomarzo between campaigns. They came from Venice, where the senate had entrusted sixty galleys to Girolamo Zane. Christendom was watching the movements of the Turks with growing anxiety. Chios and Naxos had fallen to the power of the sultan, and all that Venice had left in the Levant were Cyprus and Candia. The two Orsinis were full of fresh news. As I listened to them I saw how narrow my selfish enclosure was. Names that I had not heard of until then, those of Ottoman troops, echoed in the halls of Bomarzo: the Janissaries, founded by Murad I in imitation of Alexander's phalanxes; their leader, the Grand Aga, who commanded twelve thousand men and was the son-in-law of his master; the *bolucbassi*, captains of a hundred Janissaries; the *deli*, the picturesque and fierce *wild* Turks, wrapped in leopard skins, rising up on horses covered with lion skins and covered all over with feathers, even to their shields, which looked like open wings over which lances and scimitars gleamed. The strange and dangerous Orient invaded my refuge, surrounding the young soldiers with its diabolical air. Both of them were so handsome and so chastely virile that the splendid items of my study retreated before their glow. They spoke of exotic women who depilated themselves with vampire blood, ivy sap, and goat gall, and who washed their mouths with wine of cinnamon and corn. They described their bodies as if they were embracing them, tightening their hands. They made one think of the ancient heroes about whom the rhapsodes sang; they recalled the primitive days, brusque and simple, in which our refined complications were unknown and in which responsible men made a strict distinction between good and evil, placing them justly into opposing camps.

I led them to the loggia so that they could appreciate the progress of the painting, and I heard them criticize the Gigantomachia, not as artists but as soldiers. Zanobbi came down from his ladder, and when he bowed before the princes, he seemed base to me, vile, without substance: a monkey between two tiger cubs, jumping about, playing with pots of color. We went out onto the parapet to look down at the Sacred Wood. Sunset was dragging a heavy cloak of thick reds and yellows over the sculptures. The workmen were returning to the village, and in the solitude of the valley where the streams were having their dialogue, the sculptured rocks seemed to be asking questions, raising emphatic arms, twisting great rough heads. Soon the moon began to float over the mountains, and the great stage took on a religious majesty. The screeching of the owls and the bats mingled with the tremulous voices of the water.

The boys laughed when I told them that the peasants had been startled by specters in the thickets and that on the Tiber they had seen a boat with a crew of demons.

"The demons are in the Adriatic and the Aegean," Niccolò said.

"They're coming from the Sublime Door to kill us," Orazio Orsini added.

We remained silent. The mist was drifting in over the distant river. The stone monsters became silvery.

"It's like a theater," Niccolò murmured.

"It's very beautiful," Orazio said. "It's as if we were outside of the world."

Zanobbi, who was beside me, brushed me with his elbow, but the rub was not casual. I remembered, over years and years of distance, a similar feeling in Florence. Adriana and I had softly touched each other on the palace stairway when Ippolito's huntsmen were leaving. I turned toward the painter and looked at him sternly. Then I took the two boys by the arms and went with them into the salon of the emperors.

"We'll have to have a big party," I told them, "to celebrate your return."

Orazio's eyes lighted up. "In the park—and with torches..."

"And with costumes," Niccolò added, "a wonder—the disguises, the masks—among the monsters."

I promised them I would do it, even though my work was not ready yet. We would send invitations to our illustrious relatives, to Rome, everywhere. A ball by the light of torches with people disguised as satyrs, nymphs; with scenes of the war against the Turks on the archipelago; with bears and rare birds and Djem decorated with purple garlands, led by Sigismondo, who would be dressed as a Persian prince, half of his face under a bandage sprinkled with rubies; Violante showing her naked breasts anointed with hemlock, camphor, incense, and vinegar, like those of Friné; and the ancient empresses and queens of the House of Orsini coming in on horseback behind pages who carried smoking torches, and fireworks, and all around the monsters, the tortoise, the whale, the mermaids, the wrestlers, the hermaphrodite, the giants, the triumphal arches covered with flowers and emblems...

The warriors quickly became courtiers. They copied lists of names. We must not forget the daughters of the Duchess of Poli, the nieces of Giulia Farnese, whose bodies were so rhythmical that when they walked it seemed as if they were dancing; or Cardinal Ippolito d'Este—we had to dazzle him—but he would not come because he had a buzzing in his ears; or the Duke of Bracciano, who claimed, with no basis at all, to be the head of the Orsinis; or the wealthy Leone Orsini, the one who had ended up by avidly collecting all of the estates of his branch; or the sisters of the Count of Montegualandro, who were languishing in Perugia among fabulous tapestries and goldwork.

I let them go ahead. I suddenly had the feeling that they did not have long to live and it was as if a metal fist clutched at my chest. They laughed, they rubbed together their young hands that were more accustomed to gripping swords than running pens across paper. Through the crack in the door that led to the loggia, Zanobbi was spying on us. For five days our happy enthusiasm grew. We would go down into the park and calculate where things should go. Here Zanobbi Sartorio would place a wooden obelisk covered with Latin inscriptions referring to the triumphs of love, there Silvio da Narni would put some mysterious symbols. On the sixth day a letter came from the Signoria of

Venice. They were summoned. Four Muslim galleys had arrived along the coast near Fortore, and from Fiume and Trieste they had sighted the eternal enemy, the flags with the crescent moon. Orazio and Niccolò left at once. They scarcely waited for their horses to be shod. I gave Orazio my sword, the one with the sheath of pearls, the one that had been held by Charles V. The ball at Bomarzo would never take place. The castle and the garden were deserted.

Some time later Silvio foretold the death of the Grand Master of the Order of Malta, Jean de La Valette. It was learned afterward that several astrologers had foreseen it when they learned that the falcon that the King of France had given him, his red parrot from the Moluccas, and the tame lioness that slept in his bedroom had all died a short time before. What was strange was that on the shield of the Provençal commander who accompanied him during his last moments, there were a silver falcon and a gold lion. It was also learned that the day on which he gave up his soul to God, the noblemen gathered together in his bedchamber heard a fearful discharge of musketry, so violent that it shook the walls. La Valette sent one of his aides to find out what it was. Nothing exceptional was going on in the calm sky where the sudden thunderclap had evidently rumbled. Fishes were fleeing from the sea. There were many larger than dolphins who crowded into the bay of Marsa Scirocco. Silvio knew nothing of those omens and yet he announced the prince's death. From then on I decided to pay more attention to his oracles and my faith in his arcane knowledge, which had been broken when he had been so rudely mistaken in the case of Pier Luigi, the Duke of Parma, was reborn.

But I could not take advantage of his wisdom. Silvio da Narni died in November of that same year, 1568. He had seen with startling clarity the final agony of the Grand Master of Malta, which had occurred many miles away from his laboratory on an island washed by the waves of the Mediterranean, and he had not foreseen that his own existence would be over shortly. They found him with a broken neck in one of the ditches near the votive chapel where he used to celebrate his nocturnal rites, a step away from the infernal three-headed Cerberus. They told me that a thick, fetid stench was floating about the body, one which could not be attributed to any known beast. They took Dastyn's manuscripts from his stiff hands. For months, in spite of perfumes, I could not get rid of that odor, which would rise up like a nauseating breath every time I unrolled the parchments.

The death of Silvio, the departure of Orazio and Niccolò, and my married children's leaving—Faustina had in the meantime contracted matrimony with the Baron of Paganica, and Marzio with the daughter of Vincenzo Vitelli—left the castle depopulated. Only the youngest of my descendants, Corradino and Maerbale were left with me. A few grandchildren began to be born from time to time, in Perugia and in Bologna. They would bring them to Bomarzo, but they would not stay very long. My children's spouses and I did not get along. They felt more comfortable on their own estates. They disapproved of my park, my collections, my eccentricity, what they had learned of my life. They especially disapproved of my spending. They would appear in the castle with their noses in the air as if they were sniffing something. Actually, the indifference I had, since I received my inheritance, for the government of my finances, the embezzlement and greed of my administrators, the costly purchases that I incessantly made, the work done at Bomarzo, and the dowries of my daughters had sapped a fortune whose limits I had never felt and which my father and grandparents had seriously compromised. I lacked the pay and booty that enriched the condottieri, with which my forebears had repaired the leaks, and the administration of my properties was characterized by its incongruence. On various occasions, like other princes, I had to pawn jewels, and I even sold some paintings that I never got back. But then I would acquire some new pictures—like an admirable Giorgione and a series of portraits by Titian—and the delivery by my administrator, Bernardino Niccoloni, of inexplicable receipts continued maintaining the fiction of an ease that did not exist, but which permitted me to continue my ostentatious appearance of a great Roman lord who could satisfy his tastes with no problems.

Those problems did not upset me. I did not regard them as important, accustomed as I was to imposing my whim. On the other hand, my solitude did upset me. Silvio's laboratory, the only key to which was

## THE SACRED WOOD OF THE MONSTERS · 595

in my possession, filled up with dust. When I went into it from time to time, the cold mixing dishes, the empty alembics, and the thick, incomprehensible texts would depress me. Nor was I attracted to the study in the nympheum where, since I was no longer writing my poem, I had nothing to do. I would walk among my collected rarities, brushing against the skeletons hanging like strange marble lamps as I passed, or stopping to lift up and look at some delicate work of gold which had lost its shine, since I would not allow it to be touched.

I would see Zanobbi at mealtime. We would come together in the big room, among greenish drapes and transparent crystal and we would not say very much. Several items had disappeared from the nympheum, unimportant things, more strange than valuable, and I deduced obviously that he, having access to that locked place, was the author of the thefts, but I did not reproach him or try to get the things back. Boredom, ill humor, an ambiguous fatigue all held me fast. Perhaps if I had been able to get to him, to make him mine, my attitude might have changed. I knew that it was impossible. A cruel curse impeded me even physically from winning those people who really mattered to me and my irresolute hesitation felt well served by the equivocal prize of his presence, watching him go through the rooms, chatting with the servant girls and pages. I guessed and had proof that others had obtained what I did not dare attempt, and a first moment of fury was followed by the weakness of depression. Let them do whatever they wanted to. In order to get that small victory I dedicated my leisure to spying on him, keeping watch over him, going with him when the goad of boredom obliged him to seek pallid distractions in Mugnano or Bagnaia. He had finished the work on the Gigantomachia and I proposed a second fresco to him, a scene of centaurs, which was nothing but a few confused sketches. He was repeatedly asking me for money, clothing, and jewels. He did it without hiding his disdain, certain that I would not deny him anything. My occasional guests, headed by Madruzzo, warned me of the absurdity of that humiliating situation and they preferred not visiting me any more.

One night I went from my bedroom down to the library in search of a book. I was unable to sleep. The heat made my shirt stick to my chest. Unexpectedly, I met Zanobbi in the gallery of busts, which was barely lighted up by the indecisive moon. Somebody was hiding in back, in the shadow of the Minotaur. It was a girl, who ran off, hiding her pearly nudity in the pantomime of the marble statues. I went over to scold the painter, having had too much, annoyed, but he gave me a push and a foul insult came from his lips. The blood ran impetuously through my veins and I felt a strange, forgotten delight, for suddenly I felt as if I were being reborn, as if my old stiff limbs were recovering their agility. With a quick movement I drew my dagger without giving him time to get his and I put the tip on his stomach. He looked at me, astonished, his dark eyes wide, for it had evidently never occurred to him that I would react like that. He was perspiring from the fire of the summer night, from the amorous exercise in which I had surprised him. His terror did me a great deal of good. I was breathing from the depths of my lungs and I know that I began to laugh. Hot flashes came to my face. The dagger shook in my right hand, it was tearing the fine linen that I had given him and some drops of blood stained the whiteness. I pressed a little harder and he cried out. I also cried out, with joy.

"It's all over," I told him. "We've reached the bottom."

With the point of the dagger I led him to my father's room. Zanobbi retreated, stumbling, giving terrified looks around, babbling. No, I was not going to kill him like that. My stiletto was barely red with some crimson tears, nothing important. I pushed the spring to the secret cell, the cell where my father had locked me up with the skeleton, and I pushed him into the dark interior. But first I kissed him on the cheek, which was moist with sweat and ran my fingers through his damp hair. Then I closed the panel, abandoning him forever in his prison, and I stayed for a few minutes in the deserted room that had sheltered Lorenzaccio de' Medici. Not a sound could be heard. The walls of Bomarzo were thick and faithful. I went slowly down into the park. The monuments stood out menacingly in a light that was almost celestial, like a sapphire, and which was cut by the buzz of mosquitoes. I went into the woods as when I was a child. The brambles scratched my cheeks, my arms as I went along the gloomy path alongside which frogs were croaking. I finally reached the stream and, without taking off my clothes, with a grotesque leap that profiled my hump and showed the wrinkled maturity of my face in the broken lunar mirrors, I dove into the cold water. I joined my hands together as they were bathed in the blessing of the water that came from the bosom, from the bowels of Bomarzo, and I began to pray. Please do not ask for any explanation. I can only tell you what I did.

Bomarzo, so depopulated, was peopled with nightmares. Where there had been men before, there were specters. In the middle of the night I woke up moaning, and I ordered two halberdiers to sleep across my door and two pages to take turns on the platform beside my bed. Sometimes I would open my eyes, after the anxiety of a horrible dream, and I could make out through the wavering of the dying candles the hazy silhouettes of the pages lying there as they watched over the sleep of their master. But the master was not resting. The master, when he passed by Cecilia Colonna as she felt her way along the statues, would be shaken with ungovernable chills. He felt that the castle was poisoned. A new carrion had replaced the old skeleton in the heart of the stone and its poison was impregnating the walls with a pestilence that only I was capable of perceiving and which reminded me of the evil vapors that had clung to Dastyn's manuscripts after the death of Silvio da Narni.

Beppo, Abul, Girolamo, Maerbale, Silvio, Zanobbi rose up in my delirium. The intensity of the hallucinations grew as dusk came on and they inexorably dominated the night. I decided that all the rooms in the castle, even those where no one ever entered, would be lighted at dusk with candles and torches. The rooms looked like great altars, and since I was obsessed by the looks coming from the paintings, I ordered the pictures of my ancestors taken down from the walls or turned over, and I had the Gigantomachia covered with long drapes. The only thing I kept in place was my portrait by Lorenzo Lotto, with the childish illusion that its youth would give me spirit. I also had them light bonfires in the park as soon as the shadows came on, and the result was worse than anything I could have imagined, for the frenzy of the wind, twisting the bonfires, made the shadows insane and gave an atrocious life to the fearful colossi which, when I spied on them through the half-opened gate, would move about heavily like great sinister and bewitched dolls toward the walls of the big house.

Why did I not escape? What dark force held me back in Bomarzo? In the morning I would go to the masses sung by the Franciscans in Giulia's chapel, and I would run away from the ceremony, watched suspiciously by the monks, for behind the altar, rising up, I had seen the rigid form of Maerbale or Zanobbi. Nor did I find any relief during the day among the rocks of the Sacred Wood, molded precisely in order that my anxiety could take refuge in their shadow. The rocks changed into those I wanted to forget most. Little by little I noticed that the immense Neptune was changing into Girolamo, and that the figure hanging from the trunk of the elephant who symbolized Beppo looked too much like him.

As on other occasions I found relief with Violante and Fabio. I needed to fill the castle, flood it with people, conjure away the phantoms with happy chatter, with drunken singing, with music, with the muffled shouts and the sound of unbridled love. They brought along a new adolescent following.

The pope, the lean Pius V, a saint who suffered from his gall bladder and ate only boiled chicory, mallow, sage, and aromatic Saint John grass, had replaced the previous pomp with the severity of a hermit. In the Vatican the splendid ceremonies and triumphal costumes had come to an end; His Holiness girded his thin body with rough clothing and he brought down his wrath on the freedom of his domains. The high-class harlots had to leave Rome, and the *modest* ones were shut up in the Trastevere and from there to the section by the tomb of Augustus. In vain did the ambassadors of Spain, France, and Florence intervene, dismayed at the departure of the beautiful women, who had transformed the face of the city. The theater of the Cortile del Belvedere was shut down; it was prohibited for people with a home of their own to frequent public taverns. As for the love "that one did not dare call by name"— they even burned in effigy a prince who had dared to show signs of it. So that the young people, aroused by the tales of their elders about life in the Vatican in the days of Leo X and Clement VII, and even those of the recent Pius IV, who had been a Medici from Milan, a false Medici, intent on establishing his nonexistent kinship with the Magnificent and Cosimo, took advantage of every opportunity that was offered to loosen the monkish yoke.

Boys and girls poured hungrily into Bomarzo. Violante and Fabio, mature now, were at their head. At night I slept between the two of them in the bedchamber with the ceramics, my nuptial chamber, their bodies clinging to mine, and I would sink into a doze which was broken, when my insomnia came back, by the ratlike sounds of the running of naked feet and the muffled whispering that shook the castle. My hands would then search for those of Fabio Farnese and Violante Orsini, who were breathing, coughing, and huddled against me, and if in the shadows of the room there began to appear the ghost of Zanobbi, livid as a demon, the supernatural twin of the skeleton in the chapel, my shouts and trembling would terrify my companions and they would cover my frightened mouth with theirs until I was calm again, and, exhausted, perspiring, I would fall back into my black gloom.

Sigismondo Orsini announced something to me during those days that was so mad that at first I refused to believe it and thought that it was one of his jokes. But Sigismondo was no longer a jokester. Of the graceful, witty, agile, and slim young man who had fascinated Pier Luigi Farnese, there scarcely remained any trace in that serious gentleman who hid half of his face under a black cloth and who, very poor, covered up and veiled his penury with the old clothing that I would give him when I noticed his need. He would go through the valley with the leopard on a hunt and sometimes we would not see him for a week or more, because my cousin in Mugnano had taken a liking to him and with Porzia and Pantasilea they would play endless games of cards and chat about the things that the limited intelligence of my relative and squire could grasp: the luxury of Pier Luigi, the Duke of Parma, his great friend; the campaign at Hesdin. The handsome Matteo Orsini, the other survivor of the three comrades I had inherited from Girolamo, had married a great lady from Naples, related to the Caraffas, and had disappeared from Bomarzo. On the other hand, Sigismondo continued on as a bachelor courtier, preoccupied with the customs, manners, and privileges of aristocratic society, not interested in traffic with women, for his inclinations led him in the opposite direction.

I was extremely surprised, therefore, by what he transmitted to me through timid circumlocutions. He now wanted to get married. The years were beginning to weigh upon him and he felt lonely in his stone house near the castle. The bride—the bride would not be very young, nor would she belong to a line that could be compared to ours, but her beauty had been famous and, as the result of a life in which it was prudent to look to the future, she had put aside sufficient money to assure the comfort of both and even a certain ease that deserved consideration. Next to him, the Duke of Mugnano—I was puzzled that he was with him for the interview, but then I thought that in that way Sigismondo was attempting to give it greater solemnity—was silent, and without our cousin's noticing it, he was making faces at me and opening and closing his hands and shrugging his shoulders, as if to indicate to me that he had nothing to do with the request. Finally, with great difficulty, the name of the presumptive fiancée came from the lips of Sigismondo. It was Pantasilea. My first reaction was one of rage, rejection. What? Had we sunk so low? A noble Orsini of the Bomarzo branch, and that archnotorious and archhandled prostitute, whose charms, when I had possessed them, had been used and paid for by a whole generation of Italian nobility, in Rome, Florence, Bologna, everywhere? The remote anger caused by the memory of my first meeting with Benvenuto Cellini's former mistress, plotted by my grandfather Franciotto, and my damage in the palace of the peacocks, made me boil, as if no time had passed since then and as if Sigismondo were still the adolescent prince who had decorated the prows of gondolas in Venice like some rare and precious object of refined luxury. Mugnano squeezed my arm and that pressure calmed me down. Our cousin was looking straight at us, shamefaced, feigning a calmness that he did not feel. What did it matter to me, after all? Was I the guardian of the race? Could my own life be exhibited as a model? But in the midst of my mistakes and evil deeds I had kept intact the anxiety to exalt our house, to support, even if superficially and for the eyes of the masses, its august position, and the prospect of giving our name to that retired whore, with no background—for if she had belonged to a family of relative standing, it is likely that my instinctive reaction would have been quite different—wounded and revolted my pride. In any case, what could I do? Oppose it? Did I, by any chance, have jurisdiction over Sigismondo Orsini's freedom? I told him to follow his own judgment, and that he was more than old enough for that, and that, besides, the age of the betrothed couple and—I could not help the cruel remark—the well-known tastes of the groom were a guarantee to us that the alliance would be lacking in succession. Sigismondo embraced me with feeling, and I even promised him, along with Mugnano, that between the two of us we would find some way so that he would not come to the wedding with his hands completely empty.

The news, which spread fast, stirred up the castle, the village, and the region around. Sigismondo enjoyed popularity with Violante's group and the people liked him in spite of the past adventures that had taken place in the area. He was, without doubt, a pleasant man, anxious to amuse himself and consequently to amuse others. The years had made him more and more humane and tolerant. And the idea that he was going to marry Pantasilea, which displeased the old villagers, clinging to tradition, attracted the younger ones, perhaps because it showed them a chink in the age-old coat of mail that isolated and affirmed our haughty strength.

Fabio had always been jealous of him. They had been rivals for my favoritism. It was Fabio who invented the farce, who convinced Violante and her friends that the wedding offered them an opportunity to add one more distraction to those of Bomarzo. We would have to plan the splendid caricature and follow it through like a work of art. The others grew enthusiastic. Anything, as long as it broke the daily monotony of repeated pleasure, anything. Sigismondo and Pantasilea—could anything more absurd, more unnatural, more bizarre be imagined? We would confront that madness with something logical, and the contrast would give us a delight we could never have dreamed of. It would be necessary, therefore, to celebrate the ceremony with magnificent pomp. Pantasilea would come from Mugnano as if she were the Duchess of Mantua, or Giulia Gonzaga, or Giulia Farnese at the time of her marriage to me. Fabio's pitiless ferocity whetted his ingenuity. Pantasilea would make the triumphal journey in the same allegorical cart that my wife had used to enter Bomarzo as its mistress. She would come covered with jewels, with Sigismondo, her paladin, at her side. And we would amuse ourselves on the terraces with the sight of the mad procession. No one thought about anything else. Even I put aside my fears, my frights, my cowardice, and I became infected with the frivolous and sadistic virus that plagued the castle.

Out of the stables, they took the broken-down carriage that had sheltered innumerable hens since it had been stored there and which, as it came out on its rusty wheels, imitated, provoking the merriment of the company, the clucking that had been heard so much inside of it. At the rear there still stood the large gilded wooden bear holding up the Farnese lily, which I had had carved on the occasion of our ritual entrance. I had the idea, in order to stress the irony—and, in reality, I did not share it with the other witnesses because the secret behind it was best kept hidden—to replace the lily with the apocryphal banner from Hesdin that had been made out of the skirt of a gypsy woman and some pieces of cloth, and which showed the eagle of Charles V, stretching it over a stiff framework that was held up by the claws of the Orsini bear.

When everything was ready, I sent the carriage to Mugnano. A dozen halberdiers escorted it. We made ourselves comfortable on the terraces, in the loggia, and we prepared to laugh. Thanks to those preparations and that madness I felt as if a heavy weight had been lifted from me, as if I had become the same happy boy who was preparing to present Giulia to his vassals on the day of his marriage and, dimly, it seemed to me that with that grotesque liturgy I was getting my revenge for remote humiliations, for the arrival of Pantasilea and Sigismondo, ridiculous and antithetical, would put in relief the high lordly position of the hunchback, the one who was the victor, with the majesty of his tone, of his following, and of his world, over arbitrary nature and also over poor parodies.

It was a long wait. We enjoyed it with music, with the coming and going of pages who offered drinks and pastries, with Fabio's epigrams. Until we saw the cortege advancing along the road beyond the attentive sculptures that the sun was turning bronze. It was very small, unlike mine, which had stretched out, winding back with long family groups

## THE SACRED WOOD OF THE MONSTERS · 603

on horseback, among whom was Sigismondo himself, and the coaches of the ladies of the House of Farnese, and the wagons loaded with gifts and baggage. Pantasilea was in the carriage, which was drawn by six white mules. Her dyed red hair and her ample dress, yellow and violet, embroidered with rubies, glowed scandalously in the sunlight under the banner of the gypsy woman, so that from a distance one might have thought that a bonfire was burning in the vehicle. To one side the armor of Sigismondo sparkled as he rode a black horse. They were followed by the Duke of Mugnano and Porzia, also on horseback. The men with their halberds brought up the rear. As they approached, the chuckling on the battlements increased. I mounted in turn when they were sufficiently close, and at the head of eight servants I went to wait for them, according to plan, at the entrance to the Sacred Wood of Monsters. From there, with a sweeping gesture, I saluted the accomplices who stayed behind in the castle.

I was able to see the couple from close by before the others. And instead of facing a spectacle of comedians, what came before my eyes disconcerted me with its wonder. The elements that might have aggravated the buffoonery of the scene—Pantasilea's excessive makeup as she sat up very straight, stouter now, on the swaying seat as if on a throne; the jewels that Sigismondo had shining on his breastplate and which testified to the erotic generosity of Pier Luigi Farnese; the complicated hair style of the bridegroom, whose bald spot had been disguised by the arts of Porzia with a subtle weaving of his surviving hairs; the fabricated flag; the very presence of Porzia, the widow of my astrologer and the mistress of the Duke of Mugnano—instead of taking brilliance away from the group, gave it a kind of undefinable magic. A page was leading Djem, who was tugging on his leash; another held a hooded falcon of my cousin's on his fist as it flapped its wings. The Duke of Mugnano, the precious stones on his blue jerkin flashing with his slightest movement, was holding Sigismondo's sword, just as my brother Maerbale had held up mine. Porzia's beauty, in her maturity, was like a fine ripe fruit, and the traces of Pantasilea's were enriched by the singularity of her clothing, the fire of her red braids, and her eyelids shaded with green, by the Olympian air that she had received from her intense dealings with men of quality. Sigismondo, erect, terribly aristocratic, governed his mount with one hand and with the other held the foliage of his military helmet in the crook of his arm. He was like a knight-errant, like a character from a legend, a novel, Amadis or Orlando, whose mere presence proclaimed the dignity of his lady. His hair combed forward in Caesarian style, over his brow, and the black patch made one think of gray laurels. I joined the group, alongside Mugnano, and in that way, with a creaking of harnesses, we made our way up the steep hill.

The ceremony took place in the hall of imperial busts. People crowded on the stairways, for many had come from the neighboring estates. There were people in doorways, on balconies, and pages balancing on banisters and ladies half hidden behind handkerchiefs and fans. Even before we dismounted we could hear the giggles and the whispering. The uproar stopped when we entered and went in a procession up the stairs. Sigismondo, holding out three fingers, escorted Pantasilea, carrying his exquisite attention to extremes. She was walking like a goddess, as she had learned to do after years and years of satisfying exigent people with her supple bearing. Behind them Mugnano was leading Porzia. There was no reason for laughter. The lords of Bomarzo, the Orsinis, were returning to their palace with slaves and guests. One of my cousin the duke's Negro boys knelt down to spread out an Oriental rug on the stones. There was no reason for laughter and a dazzled disappointment could be read on all the faces. Even Fabio's laughter froze in his throat. If anyone might have provoked sad mockery it was the hunchback, the brother-in-law of that same Fabio Farnese who was tasting the sour disappointment in his mouth, who was swaying along behind, dragging his sword on the carpet. Violante came forward, curtsied, and kissed Pantasilea on the lips. They smiled at each other. They were not so different after all. And the smell of incense rose in zigzag columns, enveloping the Minotaur and the emperors, while the Latin of the Franciscans mingled strangely with the ill-humored growls of Djem.

The distraction that came from the wedding was passing. I was very mistaken—as were the comrades in Violante's group—when I thought that Sigismondo's marriage would offer us a delightful theme that we could develop over a long time, always discovering new motives for humor in it. Quite the contrary. We did not even talk about the ceremony. We were ashamed of our lack of awareness. We were ashamed at not knowing that Sigismondo would be a prince, no matter what the circumstances, and that Pantasilea was supreme in matters of courtly respect. We sensed that what there was of the grotesque in their twilight union was worthy of tenderness and endowed with a different kind of nobility, and a different, pathetic, disturbing beauty.

The ghosts came back to haunt me. My malignant attitude as regarded my cousin had only stressed my meanness, my perversity, my baseness. I felt alone again, even more alone than before, alone as I deserved to be. The avid band unconsciously drew apart from me. That fearful situation reached its climax near the end of summer. Once more the guests tried to cheer me up and cheer themselves up with a special spectacle. The Pantasilea scene had not come off, but this one would not fail. The idea of a masked ball had enchanted Fabio when I mentioned it. Although we did not have the great party that I had planned with Orazio and Niccolò, and we did not invite the illustrious guests that I had thought to gather to show my Sacred Wood to, why not take advantage of the presence in Bomarzo of so many young and handsome people to see what magnificent fun it could be? And the same as when they found out about Sigismondo's projected wedding, the news spread among the idle people, stirring them up. They put together costumes and adornments and again, for a week the ghosts deserted the castle. There was no room for them with so much activity. I let the company do it their way. I saw them place garlands on the monsters; fix torches on the terraces; ask about the stocks of vernaccia, Trebbiano, Sicilian and Greek wines, sweet malmsey and muscatel from Candia, white wine from Gallipoli, red wines from Asia Minor.

Four days before the one chosen for the carnival, I gave in to Fabio's requests and took him to the attic. I had never been back there since Girolamo and Maerbale had humiliated me with the female attire, and the presumptive heir to Bomarzo had pierced my ear lobe with a pin. It was still much the same as we had left it then, more than forty years before. The pages managed to pry open the musty windows and the light came in hesitatingly over the scattered cobwebs that contributed to the fantastic look of the place. Mice and moths had been at work on the velvets and brocades that peeped out of the chests and covered the dusty floor. The Romans shouted with joy as they pulled out the ancient clothing and jewelry, and clouds of dust and filth rose up around, with ancient odors that nauseated the women and brought on coughing, tears, and sneezing. I watched them, reliving the fateful scene of my childhood, but they left me no time for the panic brought on by the memory. Pale and trembling, I went from one chest to another, and the boys pulled at my *lucco*, showing me some wide breeches from the beginning of the century, a tabard of hairy fur, a flat hat with feathers that hung down, eaten and faded. They would declaim passages from comic poems, raising up like the folds of a chlamys the strange weasel and ferret wraps. And Fabio organized the sack and directed the flow of the ill-smelling remains toward the spiral staircase, where it jumped from step to step, dragged along, stepped on. That gothic glory, the splendor of the first Renaissance was thus transformed, like any fashion out of style, into a cause of mockery. I went down with them, squeezed in among the doubtful wave that was pouring down around us in a cascade of cloth, trimming, braids, and ancient glories. I unconsciously raised my hand to my ear and felt the opened lobe.

The following mornings and afternoons, Bomarzo offered the strange look of a castle preparing for an exceptional festival, using for it, however, its worst items. From all of the windows of the loggia, from the parapets, instead of noble tapestries, there were hanging torn and trampled pieces that were being aired in the sunlight. Pins and scissors sparkled. Masks were made, *bautte*, extravagances of velvet, lace, silk, metal decorations. Every one of the girls who would have considered manual work a burden in Rome, shut herself up in her room with her servants in order to conceive and execute the secret of her fantastic costume. It was rumored that Pantasilea was going to dress as the Queen of the Amazons. Violante presented me with an orange-colored robe with puffy sleeves and a helmet adorned with fruits and pearls, along with a mask that was prolonged into a thin nose, as if it were logical that I too, with my imposing birthmark, unable to be hidden, could disguise myself.

The very night of the party an episode happened, the recollection of which, even after so many years have accumulated in my memory,

## THE SACRED WOOD OF THE MONSTERS · 607

makes my blood run cold. I was in the room of the ceramics getting dressed. I was being helped by the funny little Negro boy, about thirteen years of age, called Antonello, the one who had unrolled the carpet on the stairway for the nuptial party to walk on during Sigismondo's wedding. His master, the Duke of Mugnano, had made me a present of the little slave, and since he had entered my service he kept fluttering about, trying hard, bringing and removing useless things with a thousand bows and attentions, looking at me all the time with his jet-black eyes, which gleamed like two insects, like beetles round my hump. So there was no one else in the room except for the leopard Djem, who was dozing, chained to one of the bedposts. Sitting in front of a mirror, I was trying to find a way to adjust the mask, which was too large. Through the open window the sounds from the park came up to us, laughter, the discord of instruments being tuned. The air was so calm that not a leaf was stirring. I went to the terrace and watched the torches that were beginning to be lighted about the monsters. The dancing fountains could be seen in their light, the tables covered with pyramids of things to eat, the coming and going of the servants as they carried more lights, the activity of two or three masked figures—Violante and Fabio perhaps—who were going among the servants and musicians making gestures, arranging some garlands about the trunk of the enormous elephant and, enclosing the scene like the backdrops of a stage set, the encircling trees and hills, where the wings of night had alighted on top of the twisted confusion.

I went back to the mirror to put my helmet on, aided by Antonello, the helmet with fruits and strings of pearls, difficult to adjust. Finally everything was ready. Over the song of the fountains, the fragile song of the violas could be heard as they wrapped it about like another garland in a wavy cadence, answering one another, picking up the theme, raising it up, complicating it, and then reducing it to the scheme of a neat design, so soft, so softly beautiful, so moving that I stopped for an instant in front of the mirror as if waiting. In the octagonal shape I saw my unknown face under the strange adornment which raised its interwoven multicolored diadem above my forehead. How old, how old I had become! Deep wrinkles furrowed my cheeks and came down alongside my mouth. The only things that remained intact in all that devastation of the boy Lorenzo Lotto had painted were the intense feverish eyes, the always avid lips that had begun to grow pale. Antonello handed me my mask. I lifted my eyes again and in the mirror I distinguished another face behind mine, one that did not belong to the little page. Djem woke up, stretched, and growled softly. I thought that someone had probably come into the room without knocking, but when I turned toward the inside of the room there was no one. The leopard, his hair on end, was sniffing and pulling at his chain. Surprised, calculating that perhaps I had been the object of one of the hallucinations that persecuted me, I spun slowly around toward the mirror. In the still water the alarming face was waiting, somewhere behind me, it seemed, in the shadows of the room. I began to tremble, but I tried to calm myself, and I clenched my fists. I could not distinguish its features because it was wrapped in some inexplicable vagueness, like a greenish mist, or as if it were enveloped in very thin cobwebs. Nor could I have told whether it was the face of a man or a woman. What I was sure of was that I had never seen it before. It did not belong to any of my ghosts. A ferocious roar from Djem shook the room, and Antonello, startled, clung to me and wrapped his arms around one of mine. In the mirror, the face, motionless until then and apparently not belonging to any body, became distorted in a grimace, and the cobweb fell into shreds which hung like pieces of skin about the hollow of its mouth. I would have liked to have fled, but I was fastened to the stool. I could only manage to point into the mirror and ask, in a voice that sounded hoarse, foreign, unreal, more unusual particularly in the midst of the concert that was coming up from the park with the perfect order of its enchanted strings.

"There...there...that face..."

Antonello clung even tighter to me, trembling with fear, and he scrutinized the mirror. "Where?" he asked. "Where?"

And his eyes, his beetles, jumped about the mirror as if they were trying to penetrate the opaque surface.

"There..."

Nothing. He saw nothing. And the face, meanwhile, was coming toward me very slowly, as if it were coming up from the secret depths of some well, crossing through the haze. It was horrible. Its horror did not come from the features, veiled by the curious gray-green matter that kept them wrapped as if in a floating secretion, but from the expression, from the incomparable evil, which beneath the thin weave of humors, the ooze, which was not really that, but something like the moss that clings to mummies, came from its eyes, imagined underneath the putrefaction or whatever it was, like two shinning and dark holes, and from the atrocious sensuality that came from its lips, from its thick lips that had much of the animal or vegetable about them, of the beyond-human, and which showed their leprosy as something apart from the rest, like the pale meat of a crustacean that has been imprisoned in a trap of dirty nets. I looked behind again and just as the first time, I saw no one there. There was no one and the room quivered in the half-light. No one but Antonello. Djem, standing on his hind legs, struggling against his collar of iron and turquoises, was scratching at the air and roaring. His efforts moved the immense, heavy bed, which was rocking like a boat, along with its drapes. An irresistible force, a tremendous fascination, obliged me to turn again and look into the glass. The face was beside mine now, almost rubbing the absurd helmet, the crest, its lambrequins of fruit and jewels. Antonello began to cry. It was not, I insist, it was not a face with frightful features, hairy ears, wolfish teeth. It lacked features and it was, quite simply, horrible. The wide-open mouth, disproportionate, was as deep as the entrance to a grotto. In the gardens fireworks were bursting forth with fans of stars, and applause echoed through the paleness of the night. The repulsive odor that had impregnated the corpse of my astrologer and the Dastyn manuscripts was floating in the air and even the page trembled when he smelled it. I had already guessed at that moment of my overwhelming experience who it was that was visiting me like that in the intimacy of my chamber. My education, typical of the time, attained alongside Messer Pandolfo and Piero Valeriano, which made me mingle everything that happened to me with literary memories, brought dancing up in my mind at that singular, fearsome moment one so unlikely for intellectual references, a mocking line from Niccolò Machiavelli, from his *Song of the Hermits*, the one that I had heard the students singing when I was on my way to Venice with Silvio da Narni: "One who really sees the Devil does not see him with so many horns and not so black..."

I got up, still looking at the mirror, my eyes boring into the sockets of the apparition, and I took the first thing within reach and smashed the mirror. Then Djem, with an enraged bound, pulled on his chain and leaped on me. His claws sank into my shoulder, into my hump; I felt his sharp teeth in my arm. Bleeding, shouting, I ran toward the stairs after Antonello, who had grown wings on his feet with panic. We reached the gallery of the busts from the patriarchs of Aquileia, where the masked people were waiting for me, preceded by the musicians and the Duke of Mugnano's jesters, and I fell beneath the Minotaur, turning the stones red. My helmet rolled off and the pearls scattered about. The last vision I have of that scene is the startled face of Pantasilea, celestial so pale it was, her naked breasts and her sinewy legs swollen with varicose veins. She ran up the hallway screaming that I had been murdered, and dancing behind her were the quiver and the panther skin of the Queen of the Amazons.

There was no party at Bomarzo that night, nor was there ever another. Djem had his throat cut by Sigismondo, who adored him, with his Spanish dagger. The guests left at dawn. I hovered between life and death for a long time. When I recovered my senses I recognized, faint, transparent, Violante, Fabio, Antonello, the Franciscans, Cardinal Madruzzo, who had come from his castle at Gallese, and some of my children, who wavered and vacillated around my bed. And that smell... They had put me into a different room, next to the loggia with the Gigantomachia, and still its fetid odor poisoned everything. I recognized Orazio and Niccolò, their agile elegance, their brusque virility, their incessant questions, but I could not speak to them. Those moments of reason lasted but a short time: the family figures faded away and in a short time Pier Francesco Orsini went back to his Hell like a convict, to his monsters, to his worms, to his demons, to that great gloomy mouth, to his unshared terror.

The convalescence was long. The wounds healed, but I took a long time in regaining my full strength. They put me in the loggia when the weather was good and spring came up through the valley, with some recent books that they thought would distract me. But the treatise of my nephew Fulvio Orsini, his collection of images of illustrious men of antiquity, tired me as I thumbed through the thick folios of Latin inscriptions engraved on medals and reliefs, and as for the texts of Andrea Palladio on architecture, even though Vasari himself declared that there was no palace in existence more worthy of a prince than that of the Colleoni Portos which Palladio had built in Vicenza, they irritated me because of their obsession with symmetry, so opposed to the baroque spirit of the Roman school of Michelangelo, Vignola, and Fontana, was also the most opposite to my own character. What did I care about those studies anyway? I moved and operated a thousand miles away from them. Sometimes I would take a few steps on the terrace and lean over the railing to contemplate my strange work in the park. What had I done, after all, violating nature like that, distorting it until I had reduced those magnificent rocks to monstrous objects? What sin was I guilty of? What could justify that act of pride, impelled by the presumption of perpetuating the deeds of my hateful life? What did I have to be proud of that was worth its eternal proclamation? There were the great accusing witnesses, I had put them there myself, I had turned my rule over to them. Now I was their vassal. And they would be there forever. I went back to the bed they had set up under the shrouded Gigantomachia and I lay down to forget. That was what I yearned for most: to forget, to dissolve, to turn into dust; and the monsters, the huge stone guards forbade me to. I had heard that the cabalists of Safed in Galilee, in order to keep away the Angel of Death, who was stalking a brother of the mysterious Duke of Naxos, had changed his name, calculating that by those means they were tricking the inexorable, and I too would have liked to have changed mine and stopped being the Duke of Bomarzo if it would get me away from my memories.

In the meantime, all about, my relatives were speaking of the worries of Europe. The arsenal of Venice had blown up and it was claimed that the fleet had been destroyed. During those days the Sultan Selim II—the successor to Suleiman the Magnificent—Selim the drunkard, the licentious, the one who ruled from his seraglio, had sent an ultimatum to the Most Serene Republic demanding the surrender of

Cyprus, and the world prepared for war. The Jews had been expelled from the lesser centers of the Papal States because it was supposed that they were conniving with the Turks, their protectors. Orazio and Niccolò left Bomarzo. They leaned their chests of steel against my chest; they clasped my fragile hands in their gauntlets. Until later, until their troop evaporated behind the mountains, I kept on hearing the brutish neighing of their mounts in the courtyard. The knights of the Order of Saint Stephen were to join those of Malta in battle. Orazio wrote me afterward, telling me how the Maltese squadron, to which he belonged, had halted a group of refugees from Pesaro on the high seas as they fled to Palestine, and that they had made slaves of them. "I have for Your Lordship," he said to me with an idea to amuse me, "a wonderful slave, a sculptor. Perhaps you can put him to work on the rock that remained untouched beside the elephant." But I was no longer interested in that rock, which I was saving for one last prodigy. I was thinking vaguely about the risks of war. Italy had been a real paradise for the Jews until then, where the wise men of the dangerous race shared with Christians the grave and secret studies that were being done in Tiberias and Safed, and where the majority of rulers employed Jewish physicians. It was rumored that the Duke of Naxos in question, the marrano Joseph Nasi, to whom the sultan had given the title after expelling from his domains Prince Giacomo IV, of a Verona family, aspired to be King of Cyprus and bring the children of Israel there.

Exotic figures with turbans like the domes of mosques and scepters and swords like minarets passed through my mind, which would be excited by fever at dusk. I had known some of the Italian lords of the Aegean: the Querinis, the Gozzadinis, the Sommaripas, the d'Argentas, and that same Giacomo IV Crespi whose line had succeeded to that of the Sanudos in the rule of Naxos, those who had governed there three centuries before. I had seen them in Rome, where they attracted attention, almost like mythological figures, thanks to their archipelagos peopled with fables, vineyards, and famous marbles. In Venice, when the Duke of Naxos disembarked from his ship, four noblemen dressed in scarlet escorted him to the Hall of Hearings preceded by six trumpeters, and the doge would stand up to embrace him and made him sit beside his throne. And the medieval Mediterranean, heroic and poetic, was being lost. Lost for us were the Cyclades, where Theseus had abandoned Ariadne, where the giants destroyed by Hercules lie, where Apollo was born, the possessions of the Duke of Naxos, the Count of Andros and Paros, the Lord of Melos and the Isles, whose palace, the historic castrum of Marino Sanudo rose up over the ancient acropolis. Cyprus was being lost, where a parvenu, a Portuguese banker, the friend of viziers, was perhaps to put on the crown of King of the Jews, that crown which, according to what voyagers said, Joseph Nasi kept in his house in the Belvedere of Constantinople alongside a standard embroidered with the arms of the dynasty of Lusignan, which had ruled Cyprus for almost three hundred years.

No, the books on current art and on ancient art could not distract me. To the restlessness that remorse caused me was added that of the knowledge that Orazio's life was in danger. I also felt a new specter floating about me, one more material than those that had haunted me until then. My children were huddling with the administrator of my lands, with the notaries, with attorneys, and they were shaking their heads in desperation. The ruin that had been postponed was closing in on us. Giulia's inheritance, the remains of which were being pecked at by my children in the midst of the disorder, was not enough to hold off the disaster. The wild idea occurred to Fabio Farnese that a second marriage of mine would shore up the creaking structure, and although I guessed what they were plotting, I did not get involved in their conversations. To hell with them; they could do whatever they thought best. I no longer had any will. Getting married close to the age of sixty, haunted, sick—bah! I would squint my eyes and spy on them in the distance.

My health came back little by little. Sigismondo kept me company. My father had been painted by Lorenzo Lotto in the polyptych in Recanati as Saint Sigmund in a portrait that I had never managed to decipher, and now, thanks to this other Sigmund, it was as if my father were walking beside me on the short strolls through the gardens, a kind, understanding father, with half of his face hidden behind a dark cloth, a father whom I had never known. We would chat quietly like two monks about old things, our things, things which the others could not understand, and everything else—war, bankruptcy, the incoherent wedding—would recede and be erased the same as the goblins disappeared, the dead loves, the dead hatreds, and even the horrible face in the mirror. Antonello, like a smaller version of Abul, would walk in front, with Pantasilea's favorite monkey on his shoulder, pulling on his bright red leash. From time to time he would turn around and smile at us. I did not notice that Sigismondo, out of friendship, had been plotting with our cousin Violante; that if he had not left me it was because he was thinking too—perhaps incited by the strong homebound spirit of Pantasilea, of Pantasilea Orsini—that the presence of a rich woman by my side would not only help to straighten out my sad finances, but would also give me back the peace that had been corrupted. It was he who finally told me of the results of the investigations made by Fabio and Violante, it was he who undertook to propose to me the name of the one who would be Duchess of Bomarzo, the savior of the Sacred Wood. Her name was Cleria Clementini.

They would not have dared raise the question under different circumstances. I really had to be in bad shape, weakened, and my eroded estate had to show its decay for them to have gone so far. The origins of the Clementinis—why hide it, since it would do no good?—could not have been more doubtful and obscure. Although they boasted of being descended from the Clementinis of Rimini (and even that was not certain), and that their house had many rather famous people, like Pietro, a condottiere with a thousand men under the command of Boemondo of Taranto; Giordano, who went to the Near East with Frederick Barbarossa; and Giovanni, secretary of state to Sigismondo Pandolfo Malatesta the Great; and although they boasted that their name came from their kinship with the pope Saint Clement—or with Clement II or III, it does not matter—and my cousin showed me, half serious and half in jest, a mad family tree that authenticated it all, this last wild pretension only managed to accentuate the absurdity of their aspirations. What was certain, on the other hand, was that they had prospered enormously, working with the banker Mariano Chigi, the father of Agostino the Magnificent. In the shadow of the wealthy Chigis, who had accelerated the ruin of my grandfather Franciotto, from transaction to transaction, the Clementinis had reached a high point that was complicated by enterprises of all kinds. That same protective shadow that had facilitated their material progress had relegated the old men of the family to a fortunate background, vaguer than the condottieri of Rimini, defended by bales of merchandise and tall numerical columns, to which the only ones who had access were merchants and moneylenders of Genoa, Venice, Antwerp, and Lisbon, far from the luxurious scenes where the great lords fought against poverty at times when war did not give them an opportunity to recoup their expenses.

Cleria Clementini claimed that she was forty-seven years old. Strangely, she was still unmarried. She was outstanding, according to what Violante told me, for her stainless piety and for a pride which obliged her to reject the offers of marriage which were presented, some of them quite acceptable, because she judged them inferior to her merits. In reality, if she had not contracted marriage, it was because in the beginning, when she had still not received her fortune, an orphan among her astute uncles, she had planned to enter a convent, something that she kept postponing as she was tempted by other prospects perhaps that would match the vain traits that made up her character, and because the candidates who came along were too mediocre for her presumption. The substantial fortune reached her hands quite some time later, after a succession of deaths gave her the position she had dreamed of. She was unquestionably opulent. Violante had met her in Rome through the relationship of those merchants with her husband Savelli, and she had spoken to her of me, a lonely widower in Bomarzo. My cousin said that the mention that she let drop of a possible alliance had lighted up her imagination. The Duchess of Bomarzo, she! Joined to a line which abounded in popes (authentic ones), saints (also authentic), holy men, martyrs, cardinals, archbishops, knights of Saint John of Jerusalem, Templars, everything there was to attract her devout bent, and where there was already great progress on the golden list that would give eleven Orsini queens to a like number of thrones and twelve Orsinis wedded to the daughters of kings and emperors, which pleased, titillated, delighted, and made her haughty pride light up marvelously! Such glory! Such a prospect for attaining at last, at the age of forty-seven, the supreme victorious peace that her turbulent soul required, solicited in contradictory directions by the splendors of heaven and earth! The fact that I was hunchbacked, sickly, difficult, in my fifties, loaded down with children and debts did not seem to matter much to her. Without doubt she had forged a special image of me, something like the equestrian statue that crowns the tomb of Niccolò Orsini in Venice like a Saint George, all plumes and steel, a prince by antonomasia. A person whose first ancestor was a hero who had been suckled by a bear, to whom the Empress Pulcheria had given castles and towers eleven centuries ago, could not in the eyes of the bedazzled Clementini woman be anything but an admirable lord. The image of her that I was forming from Violante's descriptions did not emerge with such beautiful attributes. When Sigismondo spoke of the majesty of her bearing, I imagined, from the distance of my weakness, an appearance befitting a compact, sturdy, and strong-willed female. I was not mistaken. My cousins and Fabio avoided concrete allusions to her looks and personality, and they abounded in details about her fortune. On that theme they really did go on without euphemisms. Cleria Clementini was rich, rich, rich. The list of her properties could be compared to that of our saints and kings. The Lord be praised! And how they persecuted me during the defenseless period of my convalescence! How they stressed the advantages of a serene and dignified companion, the nearness of someone who, aware of my immense superiority, would live in perpetual submission! And everything else—the river of gold! She had no relatives, only two vague nephews; the advantage of new lines was that there were few kinsmen.

I listened to them, huddling up, absorbed. But had not Sigismondo Orsini married Pantasilea? Alas, I remembered that at the time of my marriage to Giulia Farnese, some people—including myself—thought that the alliance was terribly out of balance, and that the Farneses ... I was young then and Bomarzo was flourishing. Now all I had left from my youth were my eyes and my hands, and as for Bomarzo, the Devil had entered Bomarzo, it no longer belonged to me. A prayer-chanting, miracle-chasing, ambitious big woman; and ever so much money; a chance to put my children's future in order—who knows!—to attain one final moment of balance, to repair myself, to rest.

The wedding was performed in Bomarzo two months later by Cardinal Madruzzo, who had turned over the Tridentine diocese to his nephew Ludovico and was living in Rome. Cleria did not turn out to be exactly as I had predicted. She was physically and intellectually along the lines of Nencia, the one who had conquered my virtue in the court of Florence. That was because of her stiff and heavy body, the fuzz that was visible, the inquisitive blue-eyed look, the passion with which she looked upon anything that concerned the Orsinis, a certain masculine efficiency. She treated me ceremoniously from the first moment, and I returned her attitude. We would meet in the galleries, in the park, in the chapel, and we would bow deeply, and the only thing she expected of me was for me to tell her about my ancestors, to mention some great deed, something outstanding, and to incorporate her, as if it were logical, into the illustrious framework of our house. I had the strange feeling that I was going back through time, returning to the palace on the Via Larga, once more the little boy whom the strong woman worshiped because of everything that had accumulated around him over the centuries. Of course, contrary to what had happened that time, the sensual element, which had played such a powerful role, such a decisive one for my adolescence, was excluded from our relationship. Since I did not attempt any contact at all, Cleria did not demand it either. Most likely, when the plans for our marriage began to be laid, she calculated that things would happen that way. Nor was I, in my fifties, hunchbacked, thin, in declining health, with a gray beard that I had let grow, and thinning hair, in a position to bewitch anyone.

My second wife spent a good part of the day in the church and in Giulia's chapel. The respectful fervor that she dedicated to me was shared with the memory of Giulia Farnese, for the life of Cleria Clementini was fueled by the delight of having succeeded in the duchy to a niece of Paul III. In the evening she would dress splendidly and preside at the table of guests who, attracted by the rich ease that had come to the castle, came from distant cities. I saw my children more often. Marzio and his wife, Porzia Vitelli, made great but useless efforts to conquer me with my oldest grandchildren, Orazio, who was a pontifical captain, Trifonia, a future nun. The most significant thing, however, was that I stopped seeing my ghosts. Cleria imposed a rhythm on Bomarzo that it had not known before. On going from one room to another, she would have herself escorted by a pair or two of ladies, like an Austrian archduchess. She would move about in a retinue of ladies in waiting, pages, and genuflections. She excluded Pantasilea from her immediate circle, but she did not cut her off completely for fear of making a wrong move, for she knew of my intimacy with Sigismondo and how much he had contributed to the arrangement of my new wedding. Pantasilea was bothersome to her. She was, like her, an exotic Orsini, and that placed the duchess, in spite of her fortune and her strict chastity, on the same upstart fringe as the ex-harlot. But Pantasilea, from her intensive dealings with the great, had unconsciously (or consciously) acquired a familiarity with our customs, our tone, our tics over many years, while Cleria had a great deal to learn, and the ritual exaggeration of her pomp and etiquette, which would have startled Giulia, served to disguise her hesitancy. She flattered my sister-in-law, Cecilia Colonna, until she won her over. The poor blind woman, startled, came out of her retreat once more and was in the center of the worldly circle. After meals Cleria would withdraw with Maerbale's widow, the Duke of Mugnano, and Cardinal Madruzzo. They would chat quietly, slowly. My wife—it is difficult for me to call her that because of the indifferent weakness of our bonds—radiated satisfaction. Antonello would fling himself at her feet along with the dogs, the parrots, and some dwarf belonging to my cousin the duke. Until then I had prohibited their bringing those miserable, noisy creatures, covered with bells, whose presence embarrassed me, but Cleria understood that they were inseparable from courtly show, and I gave in to her wishes. It was whispered that in Mugnano, as in ancient Greece— where they had a term to designate those torture devices: *glootokoma*— there were special chests where very small children were placed so as to impede their growth, but since I had never seen any proof, I think that it was mostly an invention of the villagers, whose imagination, when it came to describing our lives, went far beyond that of their princes, because our pleasures, our extravagances, and our excesses never seemed sufficient for their calculations. Cardinal Vitelli, the uncle of my daughter-in-law, had a banquet served for thirty-four dwarfs around that time. Cleria was possibly aspiring to something similar. In the meantime she limited herself to observing the duke's jesters with haughty decorum, listening and learning. Although she said few words and reduced her show of agreement to solemn gestures, barely making her powdered face of an astute banker move, her blue eyes shone with joy. She was happy and I let her be so, but I did not mix into her liturgical and aristocratic circle.

Months afterward tedium, the most atrocious tedium, took hold of me and I realized that I was beginning to detest the intruder who was playing roles that did not befit her, playing with great effort, in different ways, that of abbess and that of duchess, and talking ceaselessly about the condottieri of Rimini and the pope Saint Clement. Nothing deep united us, nothing genuine. In reality, I never became adjusted to the anomalous, humiliating situation that Fabio and Violante had set up, taking advantage of my weakness. I perceived—Cleria would not have risked showing it to me openly—that the Clementini lady hated my Sacred Wood, its creatures and its monsters. She was unable to discern the enthusiasm that its originality aroused among our more subtle guests. She would have preferred an imbecilic and luxurious garden, one of those works of conventional design where it was impossible to make a mistake because everything was so obvious, with cascading waterfalls, a small caricature of the villa of Ippolito d'Este. She did not understand me. She did not understand anything about me, neither the good nor the bad. She was smothered by snobbery and piety—which in her was another form of snobbery, her liking for pomp, vestments, incense, and rank—and she would turn from her conversations with the Franciscans to her dialogues with Sigismondo (because she noticed my rejection and she prudently took refuge with my cousin) to satisfy her double hunger in which her vague mysticism was mingled with the recently acquired heraldry, and she even loosened the knots that had eliminated Pantasilea from her noble group, with the object of softening the frivolous cyclops. Sigismondo, who valued the benefits that derived from the friendship with someone so powerful, for, beginning with the sentimental intrusion of Pier Luigi Farnese in his uncertain life, he sincerely thought that his passage on earth should be paid for by others, and that after his nuptials with the redheaded Pantasilea he was in no position to look askance on any parvenu, overwhelmed her with his attentions and perhaps obtained some morsel as the fruit of it as he unrolled for Cleria the tapestry of our senators, our prefects, our gonfaloniers of Rome, making mistakes, of course, for he had never been able to master the difficult material of our complex dynasty. I especially detested Cleria, I can deduce now, because—so painfully, as the poet Géraldy explains with exceptional wisdom in his poem about fools—of what I discovered in myself that resembled her. Yes, Cleria and I, while being the most opposite of people, possessed points of contact that embarrassed me, they were so degrading. She had come to annoy me in such a way that I even thought of suggesting that she go to Rome and that there, on a much broader stage, a more fitting one, she could give herself over entirely to savoring, like an intoxicating wine, the awesome privilege of being Cleria Orsini, the Duchess of Bomarzo.

Orazio wrote to me around that time, enumerating the events that foretold the imminent war against the infidel. In the middle of June the papal contingent would embark from Civitavecchia on the twelve galleys under the command of Marcantonio Colonna, a general of the Church, to join the allied forces, Venetian and Spanish, in Messina. Niccolò and he would make the trip on the *Serena*, under the command of Ettore Caraffa, the Duke of Mondragone.

I spent a week with the letter in my purse, turning over the ideas that were besieging me. The sea, the broad sea, Constantinople... Other members of my family had left on similar expeditions to regain the Holy Sepulcher, to twist the pride of the Ottoman. Why not I? Why should I not go? Since immortality was being denied me along the path of alchemy, why should I not attain it, like so many others, by means of an epic deed? In Metz, in Thérouanne, in Hesdin I had not borne myself too badly. Here I would do better. After all, what did I have to lose?

Cleria herself made me decide. One morning, after her three masses, I ran into her in the loggia. It was very hot, the June heat that fells animals and withers crops. The previous winter had been very harsh. And there was no rain. The thirsty sheep were bleating in the yellow of the fields. In some part of the mountains, through the reverberating atmosphere that gave a slight oscillation to the countryside, making it vibrate, as if we were looking through a torrid mist, one could hear the agonized and plaintive call of the horns, the occasional shouts of the crossbowmen, and the angry barking of the hounds. From time to time a falcon would take flight and glide off, high and secure. My son Marzio was hunting with the sons of Leone Orsini. Dead birds fell among the cypresses and the hawks brought back others in their talons. It was necessary to be very young to risk one's life like that under the sun that was burning up the dry estate.

Cleria had put on lighter clothing, but the stiffness of her rigid skirts and her shawl oppressed her with their suffocation. She curtsied (always, for no reason, she would make exaggerated curtsies to me), and Violante, who was by her side, smiled slightly.

"I have a favor to ask of you," my wife said to me.

She never asked for anything. She had more than enough money for her slightest desire to be fulfilled immediately. She had everything, everything. Perspiration had placed a tremulous ridge of dew along her lips. I arched a brow and waited.

"It's something very small. Your Lordship can judge..."

And she also smiled as she held out her hand to me. I felt her fingers between mine, hers chubby but firm, which her sweat was moistening, and I felt a shiver of unbearable repugnance. Now the falcons, two falcons, were holding their wings open against the lead of the sky. They were burning up there, stock still.

"Our arms"—Cleria went on, lowering her voice, searching with her hard blue eyes for mine, but I avoided them—"Your Lordship knows them—the three stars, the shield of the Clementinis...of our pontiff..."

My right eyebrow rose even more.

"I should like—I should like for you to have them placed on the walls of the castle, or in one of the rooms."

I remained silent and that seemed to relieve her. I was stunned, blinded by the heat, her stupidity, her pretensions. I hated her; I really hated her.

"That of the Farneses is there," Cleria continued, "and I think that it would only be fair...in the church, above the door..."

I took my hand away from the one that oppressed me, sticky.

"I thought that a good craftsman could be brought from Rome—with no thought of the expense—the bear...the rose...the silver stars..."

I took a deep breath. The white hot air came into my nose, the air of Bomarzo. It was as if I were breathing in Bomarzo, my Etruscan Bomarzo, infinitely old, the fields, the hills, the rocks. I was covered with Bomarzo, it was thick within me. I spoke crisply, stressing the words. "No. It won't be done. It cannot be done."

I turned to leave, but first I saw the extra flame of an insult on the face which had been reddened by the heat of summer. Violante took my arm and we left. We did not say anything. She kissed me on the cheek when we went into my room. That very afternoon I wrote to Marcantonio telling him of my proposal to join his forces. I did not need his approval; an Orsini did not need the authorization of a Colonna in a matter of defending Christendom, Saint Clement, Pius V, and the popes we had given over the centuries, the Holy See. Immediately, with Sigismondo, with Antonello, with ten busy pages, opening and closing chests, testing swords, beating on breastplates and coats of mail, happy at last after a long, long time, I began the preparations. I was going to war. The Duke of Bomarzo was going to war one more time, perhaps to die. And the strange thing, the stupendous thing was that I did not feel any fear at all.

## 11. MY LEPANTO

*My departure with the page Antonello—The papal ships in Civitavecchia—The Jew Samuel Luna, slave and sculptor—The Duke of Naxos—Cervantes rescues me in Messina—Reading Garcilaso—Don John of Austria—The Battle of Lepanto—The glory of Orazio Orsini—The cabalist rabbi from Tiberias—Cleria Clementini, disappointed and vengeful—The carving of the Mouth of Hell—The explanation of Dastyn's enigmas—The hermit duke—The chalice of immortality—The prophecy of the visionary nun of Murano*

SIGISMONDO did not go along with me on that undertaking as he had on the one to France. He stayed behind in Bomarzo with my wife and his, certainly torn by remorse over not facing fate alongside me. Pantasilea opposed his leaving with all the weight of her tenacity, for, having won such a noble husband, late and unexpectedly, she was not about to risk him in the macabre and splendid game. Furthermore, Sigismondo's attacks of illness were making him more of a burden than a help. Distant pleasures, ulcers and rheumatism were demanding their returns for ancient accounts and keeping him in bed from time to time, making him huddle beside the fire like an old man, replacing bandages and drinking infusions. Nor was I any model of gallantry and ferocity, but the precise reasons that might have tempted Sigismondo not to leave our lands—the peace of the hearth, the wise caresses, his pillows, bland meals, memories, feeling himself more the lord during my absence, consulted and flattered, a book (for Sigismondo had discovered reading in the melancholy twilight of his existence, when we avid and veteran readers, surfeited, tend to put it off or abandon it)—were for me the very reasons that had induced me to flee that slough, where the obsessions of Cleria Clementini and sinister memories joined together to show me that good health would be found away from Bomarzo. And, in addition, the question of immortality was also involved, that of glory, that of the debt I took on with my name. And there was the prospect of meeting Orazio, of finally winning him over, for at that time of life, as I felt my way along through the shadows, with anguish, burdens, and grief, sick to death of the mean remnants left about after so many unjust deaths, Orazio was for me the one last light in a desolate landscape.

Cleria did not try to hold me back. She lacked the influence or arguments for it, and she probably liked the idea that her husband, whose nearness bothered her, was joining the heroes who at that very moment were readying their swords and souls for the great action. I took leave of her gravely, in a ceremony in which, before my gathered vassals, I kissed her moist hand, from which there always hung, between her index finger and her thumb, a long floating handkerchief. And I departed, followed by six harquebusiers, four pages, and Antonello, who proudly carried, hanging from his saddle horn, his virgin sword. The broad summer breeze was blowing all around. I looked at the overheated monsters and we left in the direction of the sea. Pale bonfires were smoking in the dawn.

Marcantonio Colonna, the Duke of Paliano, received me cordially in Civitavecchia, but my touchy spirit told me that he was not paying as much attention to me as he should have. Three times he interrupted the conversation, which vaguely concerned Cecilia's condition and the work at Bomarzo, which he could not understand and which he thought of as a horrible pageant with giants and big-headed monsters, to deal with officers who came in bearing dispatches and to bark his insolent commands. He was twenty years younger than I and was famous for his military experience. Nevertheless, it was rumored that he knew nothing at all about naval warfare, for he belonged to a line that was rich in famous captains but which had not given Rome a single admiral. He despised us, even though he was married to an Orsini, the sister of the Duke of Bracciano; at least to me, always mistrustful, it seemed, even if I could not see it, that he hated us, and yet my reception, I repeat, was cordial. There were still enough reasons left for his wrath. During Paul IV's campaign, in which Orazio and Niccolò Orsini took part on the side of the pontiff, Marcantonio had fought against the pope, serving under the Duke of Alba, and after that he had assumed the responsibility for the conduct of the war and made a prisoner of Giulio Orsini, one of the outstanding members of our clan, and had treated him quite badly. Paul IV had already excommunicated him during that period along with his father, the patriarch Ascanio Colonna, confiscating his estates, and now another pope, a saint, Pius V, was naming him a general of the Church and turning over to him the banner of the League. That shows how contradictory the world is. Bah! he could think whatever he wanted about us. I did not care a whit. We gave it back to him a thousandfold. What was certain was that at the moment of my arrival, he was burdened with an immense responsibility. Civitavecchia was boiling over with people. And he offered me a place, along with my men, on his galley, the *Capitana*, which had as commander (as was natural) another Colonna, his cousin and lieutenant Pompeo, who had been at his side during the heretical challenge of the above-mentioned Roman campaign, and before that had murdered his mother-in-law, another Colonna, for profit. Orazio and my nephew had been transferred to that ship. On board I found old friends and enemies: Pier Francesco Colonna (there was a surfeit of Colonnas), the defender of Malta; the Duke of Mondragone, Marcantonio's son-in-law (he was a Caraffa, and Paul IV had confiscated Marcantonio's goods for the benefit of the Caraffas, his relatives, for everything was cooked *en famille* in those days); Michele Bonelli, the cardinal's brother and the Holy Father's nephew; the valiant Pirro Malvezzi, Pompeo Gentile, Lelio de' Massimi, some knights of Malta, Camillo Malaspina—but there was no surprise comparable to the joy of embracing Orazio and Niccolò.

There were no better captains in the fleet. Tanned and leathery, they were dazzling. Especially Orazio. He tried to give me back Charles V's sword, but I refused. He would wield it with greater skill than I. He should keep it, therefore, bright as a jewel, and unsheathe it for the terror of the Turk and the renown of the *editus ursae*. They were surprised that I was with them, that I was going to face the risks of the expedition.

Did I not still bear the wounds left by Djem? Would it not have been better for me to have stayed at Bomarzo, involved in my own affairs, in my artist's studio, my park, my stone fantasies, enjoying the caresses of my new wife? When I heard them ask that last question, I began to laugh, and I made an effort to have my laugh sound hoarse, harsh, and military. Come, come now—Cleria Clementini! Just among ourselves, united by blood and comradeship, there could be no secrets. Cleria meant absolutely nothing. She did not exist. Only we existed, the Orsinis. And I clapped them on the back as they doubtlessly exchanged glances of amused surprise.

In order to accentuate the complicity that I was yearning to establish between the young heroes and the hunchbacked old man who was playing the part of an improvised recruit, I asked them to help me hide Antonello. Pius V had solemnly prohibited two things to Marcantonio Colonna and Onorato Caetani, the general of his infantry in the army of the League: that they let beardless young men embark and that they tolerate blasphemies. And Antonello, my little Negro boy, did not have a single hair on his chin. They agreed, quite pleased. He was so small that he would fit anywhere. We put him inside a basket and hid him in the narrow cabin that I shared with them. At night, under the shelter of darkness, while we were still anchored at Civitavecchia, he would go ashore down a rope ladder, leaping like a monkey. And the four of us lived together for a few days that shine in my memory among the most beautiful of my existence, as we awaited the order to weigh anchor.

Soon a fifth person joined us, recently come from Rome, Samuel Luna, the Jew from Pesaro whose lot had fallen to Orazio during the distribution of slaves when the Maltese squadron had seized the ship on which many Sephardic refugees were escaping to Palestine to settle in Tiberias, attracted by the propaganda of Joseph Nasi, the *soi-disant* Duke of Naxos, the sultan's favorite. I remembered that Orazio had told me that Samuel was a sculptor, and that he had even proposed that I assign him the carving of the rock that was still intact across from the figure of the elephant Annone. He was a man with the characteristics of Jacopo del Duca, strong, muscular, and circumspect, around forty years of age, and he expressed himself in a slow way. I mentioned in his presence the possibility of his doing that work and his gray eyes lighted up, shaded by his thick eyebrows, but at once he recovered the taciturn expression that only gave way at times when Samuel was facing something—a building, an object—that moved his sensitive and deeply hidden fibers, which would quiver at the spectacle of beauty.

We were an odd group—the hunchbacked duke; the two knights of Saint Stephen, agile, with their great red crosses on their chests; the little black boy who showed his teeth and shook the beads on his turban as he danced; and the Jewish slave, robust and silent, who brought up the rear with the imposing equipment of crossed daggers on his stomach—and people would turn to look at us whenever we went into Trajan's port in search of taverns and houses of prostitution. My role, although I seemed to be the central figure of the company, was merely secondary. I would sit down to drink, served by Samuel Luna and Antonello, as the tavern keepers gave them pitchers with a special deference, and as the two knights, who had not, of course, taken the vow of chastity—for the order founded by the Grand Duke of Tuscany was strictly for the pursuit of pirates, the rescue of Christians, and the spread of the Catholic faith—held the white breasts of dockside prostitutes against their red crosses, I was filled with the contentment of not being alone, of having established a real intimacy with both boys. Only much later, when drunkenness broke down my defenses and brought me helplessly back to the world of my sins, would I feel in my confusion that even during those privileged hours the weight of anxiety hovered over my deformed back. Then, isolated words, incomprehensible for the Orsinis, would tremble on my lips. The memory of the betrayal of Giulia Farnese, the fruit of which I most likely had before my eyes in the shape of that beloved son whom I did not consider such, and the death of Maerbale, whose offspring affectionately pressed my hand between his, alternated with the memory of Zanobbi Sartorio, who also appeared, impossible to suppress, in the gathering of my tormented recollections. Zanobbi had been handsome, as handsome as Abul, and an artist and an exotic person. He had stirred my emotions, bewitched them at times, and I had paid him for it by burying him alive. When they saw me like that, decrepit, babbling, half drunk,

Orazio and Niccolò would leave the women and we would go back to the ship. Samuel would carry me in his arms as if I were a child as we went up the gangplank, followed by Pompeo Malaspina, Lelio de' Massimi, or the Duke of Mondragone, who would be returning at the same time, smelling of wine and boasting of their presumptive conquests, and by Antonello, who hid like a cat in the capes of the knights of the cross.

On June twenty-first we set sail from Civitavecchia. Before that we passed in review. Imposing ladies, my cousin, the wife of Marcantonio Colonna, and Anna Borromeo, came to see us off. The papal soldiers had been recruited from every city in Italy, and they had brought their own arms, their harquebuses, their halberds, their helmets, which contributed to the variety seen there. It was rather cold at sea. I did not own, as at Metz, a fine suit of armor. Sigismondo had put one together for me with the blacksmith of Bomarzo by adjusting and refitting ancient pieces. I threw over it an oversized and smothering bearskin cloak. The old bear of the Orsinis was also going along with the squadron to fight against the Turk. When the fur parted a little as the cool breeze moved the hair, the skin of bronzed steel could be glimpsed on the chest. Marcantonio told me the following day, as we were preparing to anchor in Gaeta, to be careful, for the air of the Tyrrhenian Sea was quite treacherous. He added, putting a hand on my shoulder, that he knew I was taking a Negro boy along with me, one of Mugnano's little pages, and that in spite of the Holy Father's order he would let me keep him, bearing in mind my age, my illness, and the good will that I showed for the cause of Christ. All of that made me particularly angry, and I shook off his protective pressure like a bear. On the twenty-fourth we reached the harbor of Naples, where we spent almost a month. Operations in those days took place with an incredible slowness. I was itching to get into combat, and Orazio and Niccolò would laugh at my impatience. Cardinal Granvelle, the Viceroy of Naples, invited us to dine with him on several occasions. He was of French origin, from Besançon, a bit younger than I, the grandson of a forger or locksmith, extremely courteous, and he had succeeded the Duke of Alcala to the post two months before. His gallantry had not stopped him from sending some women to prison as heretics about that same time. In

Messina we joined the Venetian fleet of Sebastiano Veniero, and we spent our time waiting for the Spaniards, who were coming from Barcelona with Don John of Austria.

The news that the people from Venice brought us could not have been worse. Cyprus was aflame on all sides. Famagusta was still resisting, and from the walls the women were flinging small bags filled with gunpowder at the Turkish fires. The sultan's forces had sacked, close to the Greek mainland, the island of Zante, and they had gone on to Cephalonia, with an aim to make the Gulf of Patras indefensible. But there in Messina, to assure us, were the vessels of the Most Serene Republic: fifty-seven galleys and eleven galleasses. There were still eleven galleys missing, which, under the command of Canale and Quirini, were preparing to leave Candia and come under Veniero's flag.

The daughter of Marcantonio, Donna Giovanna, the wife of the Duke of Mondragone, died around that time, and the general ordered his military staff and his guards to dress in mourning, and that a coat of black funereal color be stretched over the red paint of his ships. It was, in a very short time, the second evil omen that had worried us, for a few days before, the Marquis of Pescara, the Viceroy of Sicily, had died. He had been a great swordsman, the inventor of famous thrusts. In the house of his father, the Marquis of Guasto, I had seen him make five opponents kneel one afternoon.

The Spaniards took another month in arriving. They joined us on the twenty-third of August of that glorious and troublesome year of 1571. I can never forget the dates. In Genoa, Gian Andrea Doria, Philip II's admiral, who from his earliest years had taken part in all of the campaigns of the great Andrea, his famous uncle, offered a masked ball in honor of Don John. Don John was twenty-three years old. His handsome appearance glowed like that of an archangel. He danced admirably, holding in his right hand, instead of a scepter, his useless mask. The echoes of that ball had preceded him to Messina along with those of the Neapolitan reception during which Cardinal Granvelle turned over to him the standard that had been blessed by Pius V, as the noblemen from there grumbled because the Dukes of Urbino and

Parma, also both very young, accompanied the bastard son of Charles V during the ceremonies, for in reality that honor belonged to the barons of the kingdom. The sumptuous news made the Roman youths, bored in their Sicilian port, quiver with nostalgia. Orazio and Niccolò, in a brothel, danced a mad pavan with the harlots, arching, puffing up, with such grace that Don John of Austria could not have done better. Antonello gravely mimicked them.

The arrival of the Spaniards flooded Messina with princes. The one from Parma, Alessandro Farnese, paid me a visit because of our kinship. I received him with my cousin, the Duke of Bracciano. He spoke to me of Don John as if he were a god, an Apollo, a Mars. They all spoke about him that way, the Marquis Cibo, the Count of Santa Fiora, the Count of Procena and his brother, who mingled the blood of the Sforzas with that of the Farneses. Surrounded by so many kinsmen, more than anyone, I lived a few moments of singular prestige. My age also had its advantages. I enjoyed those Italian aristocrats, so vehement, so proper, plumed like fighting cocks, the same as I enjoyed those of Iberia, the gallant, legendary Don Álvaro de Bazán, Don Juan de Cardona, Don Luis de Requeséns, the Grand Commander of Castile; as I had enjoyed in Metz the Duke of Guise, the Duke of Aumale, the Duke of Enghien, the Prince of La Roche-sur-Yon. But of all of them (I never revealed that to anyone) I preferred the Spaniards, dressed in black, jet-black from head to toe, with no more glow on their dress than a gold chain and an abbreviated ruff, taciturn, somber, their looks aflame, as if it could have been said that they were on fire inside, in contrast to the multicolored luxury of the Italians and the French, like eaglets in a cage of pheasants. And above the rest, Don John made me marvel when I went to pay my homage on board his ship. There was good reason to call the mainsail of a galley, the one that carried the most wind, the "bastard." A child of love—and God knows how much I detested bastards in a period when, however, the offspring of popes founded dynastic lines—the spurious son of Charles V lighted up ships and salons like a beacon with his presence.

During my stay in Messina I renewed my acquaintance with the exiled Duke of Naxos, Giacomo IV Crispi, an intelligent and superficial gentleman, a tirelessly worldly man, whose tiny court had equaled in libertinage, the same as that of his father, the episodes described by ancient Roman historians. He was a traditionalist in that sense. He had governed (without governing) his duchy under the dominion of the Turks for only two years. Then, bereft of it, he would be seen in the antechambers of Pius IV, telling the cardinals a thousand times over about his flight from Constantinople, where he had gone intending to bribe the functionaries of the Sublime Door. His sister, the mistress of the isle of Andros, married to Gian Francesco Sommaripa, escaped with him to the Venetian possessions in the south of Greece and thence, via Ragusa, to the capital of Christendom. The pope received him with pomp and gave him a pension; as did the Signoria of Venice. He even headed a group of followers and went to the island of Tenos in an attempt to recover his lost possessions, but the sultan had declared himself firmly in favor of the Jew Nasi—and now the duke was marching under the pontifical banners to get his vengeance on the Turk. All of that misfortune had not undermined his good humor. He was extremely witty. When he spoke about his lost properties, about his castle on its acropolis, about his beloved archipelago, which stretched out in the sun amid the foam of the transparent Aegean like a gathering of lazy mermaids, Giacomo would suddenly become medieval. Even his face would take on an expression of other times, a patrician rigidity, as if painted on some archaic piece of board, and those of us who listened to him had the impression that in his eyes there were appearing, as on veiled balconies, with a flashing of swords, his heroic forebears. But at once, judging, no doubt, that his appearance was not very elegant, out of step with his delicate irony, and fearing that we would take him for a bumptious provincial—the cardinals had hinted at something like that—he would come out with some unexpected joke, recite an epigram from Aretino, mock the Ottoman officials and the sultan himself, full of alarming details about the eunuchs of the harem, break into laughter and propose to us that we go out and assuage those memories among comfortable and obedient women, the memories of Melos, Thera, Syros, Ios, Anaphe, and of their vagabond duke, who as an amulet kept in a precious piece of jewelry hanging over his chest a chunk of marble from his island of Paros, with which he ceaselessly played. It could be seen, however, no matter how much the ruin of their most famous crags, which had belonged to the Crispis of Verona since the fourteenth century, pained him, that in our war he conducted himself at the head of his five hundred men with an unexpectedly exemplary fierceness for someone of such frivolous appearance. Nevertheless, he never got his Naxos back.

One night I was returning to the harbor with Giacomo Crispi and Antonello. The anchored ships were a magical spectacle as they rocked softly with lanterns on their masts. The sea disappeared under a crisscross of figureheads, masts, rigging, and sails under the twinkling of flames that mingled with the twinkling light of the stars, so that it was impossible to tell where the nocturnal firmament began and ended. There were three hundred vessels there, all alight, all glimmering, like great birds, those of the pope, from Spain, Venice, Naples, Savoy, Genoa, Sicily, Malta ... Almost eighty thousand soldiers were crowded on the docks, in the taverns, and in the cheap eating places, in brothels and in the streets that echoed with the noise. One ran into them everywhere. And they did not hide their restlessness. They would quarrel over the smallest trifles, in spite of the severe prohibitions and the stern punishment.

Around where the statue of Don John of Austria stands today, across from the Norman church of the Annunziata dei Catalani, we ran into a group of drunken Genoese who were involved in an incoherent dispute with several Sicilians. The Duke of Naxos tried to intervene and separate them. He never should have done it. The frantic quarrelers, under the influence of wine, did not recognize our status. Nor was there time for us to declare who we were. They fell upon us with sudden solidarity, forgetting about the initial dispute, and before we could unsheathe our swords, they had laid out Crispi with a thrust and they had clubbed me on the shoulder at the precise spot where the leopard had torn me with his sharp claws. The wound reopened and I fainted, while Antonello shrieked like a madman, and the wretches, staggering off, left the scene of their crime.

When I came to my senses I was in my cabin, with Naxos, already recovered, for his wound had been superficial, thanks to the protection of his coat of mail, the two Orsinis, Antonello, who was still moaning, and Samuel Luna, who was guarding the door, firm and solid, against the entry of any intruders. I moved a little and it was as if someone had struck a dagger into my left shoulder. I gave a cry.

"Easy, easy, old friend," Giacomo Crispi said softly. "It'll go away. We've been quite lucky with everything that happened to us. We owe it to this gentleman."

In the shadow of the room there emerged the thin aquiline face of a young man whose name was spoken by the duke without my catching it in my suffering upset, because it came wrapped up in a flow of words that described the opportune intervention of the foreigner and the way in which, drawn by the cries of Antonello and Crispi himself, who had come to, he had picked me up and carried me to the ship in his arms. He was a Spaniard, a page of Cardinal Giulio Aquaviva. I made an effort to express my thanks to him, but the boy would not hear it as, with a lively tone, he answered the questions that were being asked by those around me. I heard him in confusion, I was so drowsy from the long faint. He was speaking of how he had met the cardinal in Madrid, during the mission he had headed to Philip II to express the grief of Pius V over the death of his son Don Carlos, and of how he had gone with him to Rome in his retinue. The cardinal—I had met him in the house of his father, the Duke of Atri, and I had spoken to him afterward in the house of my father-in-law Farnese—was well known for his culture, and the page (he smiled as he confessed it to us) had also made a few attempts at poetry and had even written an elegy for the death of Elizabeth of Valois, the third wife of the king. Then, attracted by the profession of arms, more in accord with his spirit than palace business, he had joined the company of Captain Diego de Urbina, which was garrisoned in Italy and separated from its corps, which it soon rejoined. He sailed with them on board the *Marquesa*.

The presence of my unknown savior gave me new spirit. From his eyes, his gestures, his personality there flowed a powerful influence. At the mention of his lyrical inclinations I told him, without losing my condescending air, that I too was a poet, and I told Antonello to fetch the copy of Ariosto, which never left my side. I gave it to Aquaviva's page and asked him to keep it as a memento of my gratitude. He took it with respect and said something about how much he admired the *Furioso*.

"If Your Lordship will permit," he said, "I should like in turn to leave with you the book of a fine writer, a poet of Castile."

He took a dog-eared book out of his pouch, and Orazio read in the dim light that it was the works of Garcilaso de la Vega, published the year before. The visitor added that I would be especially interested in the influence on him of Petrarch and Sannazaro, which had been stimulated by Andrea Navagero, the ambassador of the Signoria of Venice, when he had suggested to Garcilaso in Granada the possibility of using Italian meters in his own language.

The Duke of Naxos was listening to us with the posture of someone who knew—for he really knew very little about such things, and he knew very much about women, falcons, and feasts—and I, even though my senses were not very clear, did not want to pass as a layman in such matters either, and I answered that in Bologna, forty years ago, during the celebration of the papal coronation of Charles V, I had heard mention of the beauty of the eclogues of Garcilaso, who had been there among the young men closest to His Imperial Majesty. Cardinal Bembo had been strong in his praise, and Bernardo Tasso had been his friend in Naples.

"Garcilaso," the young man added, "was a poet and a warrior, the same as Your Lordship. He died in France during the siege of a fortress on the road to Fréjus. He was crushed by an enormous stone; he fell into the moat. He was thirty-three years old."

I, involved with myself, instead of encouraging him to go on speaking about events in the life of the hero, began to talk about my own literary creations. I mentioned the *Bomarzo*, my nonexistent poem, put aside in the end, as if I had really written it. He listened to me with courteous solicitude. I have kept a clear image of him in mind: his high forehead, his dark eyes under the precisely sketched brows, the sculptured cheekbones, the strong and sensitive nose, the smiles that would make him light up, the long fingers that caressed the binding of the Ariosto.

Marcantonio Colonna's physician came in to change the bandages. They all left except Antonello, who, proud of his responsibility, stayed behind to hand the doctor the clean cloths and the bowl, but he would twist his face and avoid the sight of the bloody bandages. Before he left, I asked Cardinal Aquaviva's page to come visit me. He promised to do so, but on the following day he did not appear on the *Capitana*, and on the next, the eighth of September, the fleet passed in review in Messina. I never saw him again and I finally forgot about him. Centuries later I have thought about him ever so many times in desperation. For the rest of the voyage I read the poems of Garcilaso. Only then did I notice on the second page of the book the signature of the person who had given it to me. It was done in two lines, joined together by the design of the flourish, and into it was squeezed a name that I had never heard on the lips of anyone: Miguel de Cervantes Saavedra.

Alas, if I had only known, if I had only guessed! But I was in no position to know about the publication of *Don Quixote*, for which thirty-four years still remained, or about anything, anything... Cervantes was reduced to all of that for me: a page, a servant of Cardinal Aquaviva of Aragon; a soldier of Captain Diego de Urbina in the corps of Don Miguel de Moncada, who had carried me in his arms from the square of the Annunziata dei Catalani to the galley of the Duke of Paliano, just as Samuel Luna had carried me on other occasions; a poet, a boy to whom I had given my copy of Ariosto and who had given me his of Garcilaso de la Vega, a pair of dark eyes, a slight smile... My blood had no doubt stained his jerkin as he held me, embraced me. The heart of Cervantes had been alongside mine—and I, imbecile that I was, lied to him about my rhetorical *Bomarzo*, in forty ghostly cantos, a rain of invisible stanzas, while he was silent and approved of my poor phrases that were loaded with vanity. If I had only known! I would have brought him to my castle; I would have treated him like a monarch, better than Cardinal d'Este, better than the Duke of Urbino, better than the Marchioness of Mantua, better than any of them. But he disappeared from my side, fearful, perhaps, of annoying me, of bothering the great Roman nobleman who was writing a poem destined for immortal triumphs. And the Garcilaso was lost. It was probably lost by my children, or my grandchildren, or by the Lante della Roveres. Who would pay any attention to a greasy book? Who would notice him if not I, or the Duke of Naxos, or Orazio, or Niccolò Orsini—or anyone, absolutely anyone, in an army of eighty thousand men—at moments when the only thing that stirred us up was finding out what Don John was going to decide, whom Marcantonio would favor, what was afoot with Alessandro Farnese, the Marquis of Santa Cruz, the knights of Saint Stephen, the Maltese? No one sensed what there was among us, hiding obscurely, embodied in a boy from Alcalá who would lose a hand in the undertaking, the painful glory. But now, as I think that my blood spattered his jerkin, perhaps his fingers and his face, during the assault in Messina, my veins grow warm and I start to tremble.

Don John of Austria's ship, the *Real*, weighed anchor first. Sixty rowers moved it with the rhythm of their oars. The nuncio of His Holiness, from a brigantine at the harbor mouth, blessed the fleet as it left for the seas of Greece. One by one the galleys, the galleasses, and the frigates paraded by. Some of them were very beautiful, with golden decorations on poops and prows, sculptured like the façades of palaces. On Gian Andrea Doria's ship a large mappemonde of transparent crystal served as a beacon, the gift of his wife. Waving in the breeze were the flags that would distinguish the various divisions of the fleet: for the main body, led by Don John, blue; for the right flank, under Doria, triangles of green taffeta; for those of the left, under the quartermaster general, the Venetian Agostino Barbarigo, yellow; white for the reserves under the Marquis of Santa Cruz; but on the *Real* and on the capital ships, like mine, instead of pennants, thin streamers waved from the masts as they received the breeze.

There were still twenty days left before the battle. The news that reached us from Corfu was not encouraging. We were rowing at first without any help from the wind, towing the heavy galleasses, pausing to send out boats when we learned that waiting for us on shore were some new Spanish contingents from the jails of Naples, coming to bolster the oarsmen, and some militia from Puglia. The incessant sound of the oars could be heard, the shouts and lashes of the boatswains, the calls that commanders exchanged between bridges, the creaking of the masts, the chant of the cabin boys as they announced the time. An entire city was being moved along over the waves, passing by the tip of Italy. The leaders, gathered in council, were arguing, although each captain on leaving Messina had received a lengthy memorandum which showed his position and his course. In the calm sky, a night that was silver with stars, with a north wind blowing, a blinding light broke out that crossed the space with its whip of flames. A great clamor arose from the lookouts in the crow's nests. God was giving us the sign of victory. And I witnessed that white-hot sign. I was sitting in my chair next to the mainmast, wrapped in my bearskins. My torn flesh hurt. I would have liked to have had Silvio da Narni beside me to talk to about the celestial omen, but Silvio was dead, like Maerbale, like Girolamo, like Ippolito de' Medici. Everybody was dead and we were sailing toward the death that was awaiting us in the seas of Greece, surrounded by miraculous omens.

I spent a good part of the long days in that chair. Marcantonio Colonna had urged me to stay in Messina, because prudence advised it, but I refused. The admonitions of the Duke of Bracciano, Orazio, and Niccolò were also futile. And Colonna, who was continually worried by graver problems, washed his hands of the matter. He was not going to waste his time getting angry over a stubborn hunchback who had already been allowed to bring along his Negro page. So, with Antonello by my side, ready to fulfill any whim that my illness might have aroused, wrapped in the warm furs, I let the weeks go by. I was reading Garcilaso de la Vega in the copy that Cervantes had given me, as years before I had reread Ariosto in Metz, and I was doing a great deal of thinking. Since I would be unable to fight, I would watch Orazio fight, I would fight by means of him, through him.

The memory of that voyage is confused in my mind with Garcilaso. Even today, as I recall it, it is impossible for me to separate in my mind three images that became superimposed and which blend until they are one alone: that of Garcilaso, that of Orazio Orsini, and my own. The Duke of Naxos, in order to keep me happy and also to forget about his own worries, had looked into the facts about the Spanish poet, of whom I really knew very little. On board the *Capitana* there were some people who had known him in Naples during the years of his exile in the court of the Viceroy Villafranca; or at the emperor's conquest of Tunis; or during the siege of Florence; or during his embassies to Andrea Doria and Don Antonio de' Leiva. Those references filled in what his verses suggested to me. Married to Doña Elena de Zúñiga, he had loved another woman all his life, Isabel de Freyre. He had elevated her in his poems to an ideal of perfection, pursuing her, beseeching her, and when, finally, exhausted, he possessed her—one single time—he resolved never to see her again. Isabel lived again for eternity in his eclogues. The lament, the sweet lament of the shepherds who told of the deceptions of love, was only an attempt at expression by the disconsolate Garcilaso as he burned in Isabel's flames. A love like that, one so strong, was like the wind that drove our ships. The poetry swelled up from it like a sail. Was it possible that I did not love Bomarzo as I should have? Was that why my poem lacked vigor and fell apart? No, I loved Bomarzo above all else; I thought about it continuously; my eyes alighted on the tight, round sails and in them I saw the shapes of the rocks in my ancestral park. What, then? If I had dedicated my poem to Abul, to Giulia, to the disturbing Zanobbi, if I had investigated my feelings... But when I wrote my love poetry to Adriana dalla Roza it was no good either. It fell apart into ashes, hollow, useless. It lacked the passionate anguish that moved that of Garcilaso, which raised it up like the majestic flight of a hawk among clouds of gold. Had I not loved Adriana, Abul? For whom had I bled myself with weeping? For whom had I forgotten about myself, about the Duke of Bomarzo, the rhetorical esthete, his exigent immortality? Had I never really loved anyone except myself? My love for Bomarzo, could it have been a love for the air around me, which I loved simply because it was impregnated with me? I, who hated myself so much, who fled from my image in the mirror, where the grimace of the Devil had appeared (who could have been *the* Devil and could have been *a* devil), who despised my hump, my legs, the caricature that I was, could I have been the sole object of my selfish love, and, like a horrified Narcissus, could I have been begging in other people, in men and women, what my mirror refused to show me, always looking for myself, for the perfect Pier Francesco that I adored?

I read the eclogues, the sonnets, and I also thought about Orazio's love, because that reading invited meditation love, demanded meditation on it, as the fleet of Don John of Austria sailed on, its pennants and multicolored streamers unfurled, and the eighty thousand men of the expedition, from princes to oarsmen, moved about in the midst of a fire of flags and thought about the loved ones left behind in villages and in palaces, their eyes foggy with tears. Whom did Orazio Orsini love? Did he love someone perhaps? Who could his Isabel have been? The time for his marriage had already arrived. With Niccolò he would burst into a brothel and the women would drop everything to kiss them; they were so handsome. And in the courts too, in Venice, in Parma, in the drawing rooms of Milan. Whom did Orazio love? For whom was he sighing at that very moment, his eyes fixed on the horizon, beyond the masts that made their canvases sway along with the figures of saints, virgins, and winged lions. He had lived alongside Niccolò, his cousin, perhaps his brother, ever since childhood. They shared their arms and women. They were joined together perhaps by some terrible and ingenuous oaths, like the young heroes who, thousands of years ago on the same sea where our prows were heading, had fought and loved with incomparable splendor. I felt a sudden violent jealousy for their friendship. The resentment was very old: it had already disturbed me during the time when, still scarcely more than children, they would run away from me in the woods of Bomarzo and hide in the caves, unreachable, secret. It was becoming mature now, miles and miles away from Bomarzo, in a hostile environment to which I, a man of the earth, a man of the rocks of the Cimini mountains, of Etruscan immobility, of inherited security, could not become accustomed, for nothing belonged to anyone here, everything shook and vibrated with a mad, fleeting indecision, and even our lives had the ephemeral worth of inconstant water. Orazio and Niccolò had something that I had never possessed: a bond, the strong chain of friendship. They had forged it, link by link, through childhood, through adolescence, and it was useless to try to separate them. Love would not release its bond, which had the strength of love, which showed another form of love. Women came and went in their world without disturbing it. The heroes would enjoy them and let them go. Then they would go back to their intimate pact. Alongside them, what did I mean? Did they think about me? Did they see me? Did they see the old duke who was wetting his index finger with his lips to turn the pages of Garcilaso de la Vega, and who, his eyes lost on the waves, was reviewing the legions of his ghosts? They would look at each other; they would exchange helmets, armor plate, daggers, their shields with reliefs of Venus, Mars, Hercules, and Jupiter.

Around my weak chair their iron clothing made them sound like giants. And I would raise my eyes from the dialogues of Salicio and Nemoroso, which the poet sang in his noble Spanish, and I would suddenly feel the slap of jealousy across my face.

But Garcilaso succeeded in the miracle of calming me, in channeling my anxiety along different paths. He and I were one single person, with Orazio Orsini; a single being, exalted, yearning, dense with love. Magically, by means of a few inflamed lines—for, as always, literature gave me what greedy life denied me—just as I told myself I would fight through Orazio, I told myself I would love through him. I was no longer myself. I shook loose from my isolated mirror. And a strange jubilation came over me and succeeded my feverish sadness as I watched military preparations of Giulia Farnese's son and listened to the banter between him and Niccolò. From then on I would live through him, I would redeem myself through him.

In the meantime the squadron went on its slow way. Don Jerónimo Manrique, of the illustrious House of Lara, whose magnificence rings through the ballads, sang the mass of the Holy Spirit on the stern of the *Real*, using as a backdrop the mythological characters carved by Juan Bautista Vásquez of Valladolid. I prayed for the first time in many years. I prayed for Orazio, for Niccolò, for Don John, for our fleet. I prayed to God to give me the gift of repentance, to remove my crust of sin, but I was still too deeply enmeshed in the brambles of old passions. I knelt down beside my chair, supported by Antonello, even though the pain was torturing me; and the Duke of Urbino, who was the nephew of Orazio Farnese and therefore showed me special consideration, knowing that his uncle had died in my arms in Hesdin, chided me softly for my madness, warning me to conserve my strength, because the hour of battle was drawing near.

Corfu... Don John and the main leaders inspected it and came back on board with sadness. Orazio Orsini told me that they had found the signs of sacking and rapine everywhere. His rage was aflame. As soon as we sailed from Gomenitza, on the coast of Albania, he told me about the dissensions that were upsetting our people. The Venetians were against taking orders from Doria, a Genoese admiral, because of the bad feelings between the two naval republics; Veniero ordered the hanging of a Spanish captain who had downed one of his officers with a harquebus, and things became tense; we were ready to lay hands on one another, forgetting about the Turks who were lying in wait, or about the Dominicans, Franciscans, Capuchins, and Jesuits, who had given every soldier a rosary that had been blessed, and an *Agnus Dei* made of consecrated wax; Marcantonio Colonna was called three times in the middle of the night to attend turbulent meetings of the high command; Don John's anger was such that if Marcantonio had not calmed him down, who knows what might have happened; we would have attacked each other, the Venetians on one side and the Spaniards and pontifical forces on the other; but Sebastiano Veniero, whose seventy irascible years stood up to the supreme authority of the expedition, the Holy Father's "dear son," would no longer participate in meetings of the staff; in his place he sent Agostino Barbarigo, who passed on his instructions.

Spies told us that the enemy was at Lepanto, and we sailed for Lepanto in the mist. The galley slaves rowed, wet with perspiration in spite of the coldness of the dawn. Their acrid odor of caged beasts rose up to my cabin, where I was shivering underneath the furs. The Duke of Naxos showed me through a porthole the island of Ithaca, the island of Ulysses, looking like a shipwreck in the vagueness of the fog. I remembered Messer Pandolfo, the teacher Piero Valeriano, my remote books, Ippolito and Alessandro de' Medici, as we translated word by word the text of Homer, stumbling along, as the insects flew about in the rays of the Florentine sun, and princes, schoolboys, we calculated the time left before we could leave the prison of study for the happiness of the hunt, and I thought of Catherine de' Medici, Adriana, the smiling daughters of the Marchioness Cibo, so small and so courtly, Lorenzaccio's uproar, Giorgino Vasari, Abul...


A brigantine coming from Candia brought us more bad news. Famagusta, the last bastion of Cyprus, had fallen and Marcantonio Bragadino, the captain of the city, after he had capitulated conditionally, had been betrayed by Lala Mustafa, the cruel Turkish leader, who had ordered him skinned alive before his eyes and his skin stuffed with straw, and that they exhibit that grotesque tragic puppet before sending it to Constantinople. The reader can imagine the effect that the news had among us, particularly our own Bragadino and our own Marcantonio. Years later the victim's brother acquired the remains for a large sum and he put them in a marble urn in the church of San Giovanni e Paolo in Venice, where my uncle the Count of Pitigliano lies.

It was what was needed to stir us up at last. The members of the council considered the possibilities of besieging Sopoto, Castelnuovo, Santa Maura. Against those temporizers and because the stormy season was close and threatened to make the colossal enterprise useless, there prevailed the inspired audacity of Don John. We would continue on, in order to prevent the enemy from taking refuge in the Bosporus. We were already very close to the Turks. When the figures were revealed after the battle, it was seen that the forces were evenly matched: two hundred eight Ottoman galleys; two hundred nine galleys and galleasses of Christendom. Ours had protective parapets, while the sultan's prows were open; our soldiers wore helmets, breastplates, shields; the enemy bound their heads with turbans, with an occasional sumptuous helmet, like the sallet of Ali Pasha, which was adorned with thirty-six rubies, which came down over the ears with a mixture of diamonds and turquoises; and they also wore armor of damascene steel with raised religious inscriptions. But until the noisy encounter, no one, neither they nor we, had an exact notion of the power he was facing.

On Sunday, October 7th, very early in the morning, both fleets came in sight of each other. At first we could not tell, the enemy sails looked so small in the mist, whether or not they were just some fishing boats. I saw the first enemy ships—they were two—through the lens of Niccolò Orsini's telescope as if I were observing some curious miniature framed in a bronze hoop, but soon the scene was capped with white spots, as if a flock of albatrosses had taken flight in the distance. The whole infidel fleet was waiting for us in Lepanto. Then Don John of Austria put on a stupendous spectacle for us, one of those displays that the Renaissance was rich in when the necessary moment arose, with its incomparable sense of theatrical beauty, something that moved us to the marrow, that flooded us, even the thick-skinned, sinful skeptics, with a radiant mystical fervor, because we recognized in the young leader not only the son of the Caesar's passion, a small, thin Mars with long legs that had been carved by divine craftsmen, as perfect as one of Benvenuto's jewels, but also the messenger of Christ, the chosen one who had brought out of the pope the famous cry: "There was a man sent by God, whose name was John."

In a frigate he inspected the right wing of the fleet. The Grand Commander of Castile was inspecting the left side at the same time. Don John was not carrying arms but had an ivory cross in his hand. He passed before Veniero, who stood at fierce attention, and he gave him a short, friendly salute that showed his forgiveness. He passed before Spinola's galley, where the Duke of Parma, the grandson of Charles V and Pier Luigi Farnese, was aboard; past that of Gil de Andrada, that of the Duke of Bracciano. Like a warrior monk he was carrying scapulars, rosaries, and medals. He was throwing them to the generals and sailors pressed together on the prows. He even had to give away his hat and gloves. On his way back I saw him from very close by, for Samuel Luna had carried me in my chair to the railing. Don John's twenty-three years were inflamed, thickening, as if he were suddenly much older than any of us. A mournful, responsible gravity weighed on his eyes, which grew wide, as if he already knew who was going to die and who was going to live to mourn the dead. He looked at us for a second and it could have been said that he was choosing us, assigning us to life or death like some mysterious judge. His pale hands blended with the ivory of the image. He said words of encouragement, sonorous and virile, but one could see that he was trembling with emotion. He said to us, "Remember that you fight for the Faith; no coward shall gain Heaven." The Duke of Naxos gave me one of the rosaries, black and rough. I curled it around my wrist on the same hand where ever since childhood I always wore Cellini's ring. I wore it there ever since then, like a bracelet. With every one of my movements its cross would shine in the air or knock against tables and walls. Then the prince put on his armor and appeared on the *Real*, aglow. They raised the flag of the League. The silk cloth stretched out the whole papal mythology as if it were getting up, and it showed the design of the crucifix between the apostles Peter and Paul. Underneath, the Holy Christ, who miraculously lowered his chest as a shot was about to sink into it, held out his arms of multicolored wood. Don John of Austria knelt and prayed. Everyone did the same. I too, as my wound pained me. At that instant in Rome, Pius V stood up and declared to his treasurer, "Go give thanks to God, for our fleet is about to enter combat with the Turks and God will give him victory." From convents and from churches in that vast and wakeful Europe they were praying for us. Perhaps they were praying in Giulia Farnese's chapel at Bomarzo, and Cleria Clementini was responding to the Hail Marys of the Franciscans, pompous and frowning. The flag of the Prophet was raised on Ali Pasha's ship, white and embroidered with green verses from the Koran, while all through the infidel fleet there broke out a babbling among the Muslims as they sang and danced on their bridges. On our side there was an enormous silence. The priests were giving their blessing and absolution on the various ships. Someone called to me, lost in the midst of the thick spars lined up for battle.

"Duke! My Lord Duke of Bomarzo!"

The one who was calling me in that way—it was hard for me to find him—was a Jesuit, on whose face there fell the light of one of the lanterns of the *Real*. Leaning on Antonello's shoulder, I stood up to have a better look. Between us there was a confused webbing of agitated people, for the first cannon volleys that Don John had shot off to provoke the enemy into battle had sounded and the soldiers were in their places preparing for defense. Suddenly I recognized the priest. It was Ignacio de Zúñiga, who had accompanied me as a page with Beppo when they sent me as a child to Florence, and who, at times when Beppo was chasing girls, would give himself over to solitary meditation, scrutinizing the sky. In the growing bustle I was able to make out his gesture of blessing, and it was as if the past, with the imminence of the crucial moment, was pardoning me. At least I, without deserving it, tried to think of it in that way, because the intensity of the mystical atmosphere that I was breathing was so acute that it made one become part of it and arbitrary miraculous deeds became logical. I tried to speak to the Jesuit, so that I could be sure of the pardon, but a flash of oars moved the ships and along with them the image that had come out of the depths of time, so that I was unable to know whether or not it was a case of hallucination. Years and years of sins, of crimes, of indifference, of fatal pride floated over me for an instant with the blowing of the wind and despair, as the masts spun like heraldic birds, with infinite paintings and banners, showing me and hiding from me the blue dome that was being cut into shining symbols like the windows in a cathedral. I told myself that perhaps I too had received my sign, as probably each one of the men in the fleet had received his, amid so many supreme premonitions, and without renouncing my pagan roots, but impelled by a new and neophyte anxiety, I kissed the cross of Don John's rosary and the loop of Benvenuto's ring.

Orazio Orsini came by my chair, wearing the sculptured armor of Greco-Roman style, whose steel was modeled after the muscles of the torso, like that worn by the ancient Caesars, and which, in the gallery at Bomarzo, decorated some of the busts that had belonged to the patriarchs of Aquileia. He seemed to be naked and made of silver. His slightest movement lighted him up with flashes that made one close his wounded eyes. Heads of satyrs were on the short pants, and on the shield a decoration inspired by the *Triumph of Love*, by Petrarch. He shone, flashed, catching and returning the light, as in a sparkling duel, thanks to the play of the iridescent steel, and suddenly I needed from my memory, like the appearance of Ignacio, something very remote, which I was unable to locate and which disturbed and distracted me at that grave moment, until I finally located it, and it turned out to be, through a fantastic association, Pantasilea's polyhedron of perfect crystals that I had destroyed in her palace in Bologna. Niccolò, so much like his friend, reproduced his fireless image as he moved about, black and plumed, like a shadow of dark steel.

Painters have embellished the victory of Lepanto with broad allegories. As in Homeric combats, the action took place on two levels with them, and as men were being torn to pieces below, up above in that same heaven that was hidden by the sails, holy warriors, angels, and Muslim demons fought hand to hand, under the eyes of the immutable Trinity, certain of victory, and watched by the great people of the earth—the pope, King Philip, the doge—who from a comfortable invisible boat were present at the angry fight. I only saw the atrocious human battle, although I can understand how the magnificent baroque versions were meant to give comfort. There were no winged horses or cherubim for me. My archangels were Orazio, Niccolò, Marcantonio Colonna, the Duke of Urbino, the Duke of Naxos, the Duke of Bracciano, the Duke of Mondragone, Alessandro Farnese, the Marquis of Santa Cruz, the Jew Samuel Luna, the page Antonello; my wrathful celestial messenger was Don John of Austria.

Orazio had ordered Samuel to keep me in my cabin to avoid risks, but when the slave from Pesaro tried, I resisted so fiercely that he gave up and stayed beside my chair protecting me. Antonello was also there with his virgin sword.

The hand-to-hand combat assumed horrible proportions. Even today, as I write in the quiet of my study, there resound in my ears the savage cries of the Turks, the cries of pain, the commands, the noise of galleys ramming one another, of oars that flew into a thousand pieces like gigantic insects. The left flank made contact with the Mohammedans and the first of our leaders to fall was Barbarigo, his skull pierced by an arrow. He was immediately replaced by his nephew Contarini. And the Turks gave way. I saw them dive into the water and swim toward the shore. The Viceroy of Alexandria, who was directing that part of the operation, railed at them with tremendous curses, while Don John and Ali Pasha, the two admirals, faced each other. The spur of Ali's galley bit so deeply into the Spanish *Real* that it penetrated to the fourth bank of oarsmen. They were stuck together and musket shots were heard everywhere. The ships, battered, shaken, were a single mass under the tattered sails. The whole immense succession of ships that in pictures are lined up jauntily as if on review or in a theatrical naval scene, clung together in groups where flames leaped from bridge to bridge and from canvas to canvas. If the saints were watching our battle, it must have looked to them like a giant dragon with darts sticking out of its skin throwing flames from its glowing scales and twisting in the gulf, making boiling smoke hang over the clear air. The mercenaries of the Sardinia regiment, on Don John's command ship, faced Ali's Janissaries and archers. His Highness was at the bow, standing under his banner, covering the prow with his body.

On our galley one deed followed another. Passing a few feet from my chair, like lightning, were Marcantonio Colonna, Pompeo, Mondragone, Bonelli, Gentile, Lelio de' Massimi, Count Castelar, Malaspina... Orazio stood out in the battle because of the glow of his armor, the cross of Saint Stephen that waved about on his cape, the shadow of Niccolò Orsini as he danced madly around him. We took the ship of the Bey of Negroponto and went to the aid of Don John. Our capital ship rubbed against his, creaking, and against that of Ali Pasha and that of Mehemet Bey. In a short time the flag of the Prophet was hauled down on Ali's galley and his defeat was so obvious that the pasha, in order to avoid capture, sank his dagger into his throat. They cut off his head and fixed it on a pike to give to Don John, who was revolted by it and told them to throw it into the waters of the Gulf of Corinth. But all was not yet over. The battle began at noon and ended at dusk. All that remained was for Uluch-Ali, the famous strategist, to retreat, weeping with remorse and carrying the standard of Malta, which the sultan placed in the dome of the mosque of Saint Sophia. There were still a few hours of honor left. The sound of trumpets and the furious beating of drums joined the noise from the huge prow-heads as they crashed during the boarding action. The galley slaves were shouting; the heroic Venetians of Veniero's fleet were dying, even that fascinating Giambattista Benedetti of Cyprus, with whom I had tested the wines of Asia Minor in Messina. Kara Yusuf, the son of terror, was cut down by the guard of Onorato Gaetani, the general of the papal troops; Monseigneur de Ligny, a captain of Savoy, was trembling in convulsions from his wounds; Paolo Ghislieri, the nephew of Pius V, faced the corsair Karabaivel, the intimate friend of a rais whose slave had been Ghislieri himself, and his days were ended by a musket shot; Don Juan de Cardona owed his life to the cuirass that had been given to him by the Grand Duke of Tuscany, so that the munificence of princes does have some value; my cousin from Bracciano, Paolo Orsini, was permanently lamed by an arrow he received as he leaped, waving his sword, onto the galley of Pertev Pasha; Don Quixote was almost, almost never written...Why go on making a list when wherever one looked there was nothing but inseparable torsos and legs, arm guards and breastplates and leg protectors all mixed in, as if all that metal and those limbs had been thrown into some gigantic mixing bowl? Alas, as in Hesdin, as in Thérouanne, the decorative beauty of the wars of epic poets and courtly painters, with great esthetic poses, with famous phrases, with splendid captains carrying their swords like votive candles, gave way to a consternating hodgepodge, a repugnant slaughter with entrails strewn about among crossbows and broken swords, in which it was difficult to recognize friend and foe, and in which monsters of metal and froth devoured everything in their path, vomiting fragments of embossed silver, enamel, gold, ivory stained scarlet with blood, obsessively alive in the midst of death rattles, until it too ended, blending in with the serene purple of the sunset!

Our deck was swarming with enemies. They came from Ali's ship and that of the sanjak of Negroponto, waving their scimitars. Several surrounded my refuge and were exterminated by Samuel's mace. Even Antonello drew his sword, taking shelter, fearful, behind the huge Jew. And I myself stood up, radiant with joy, as the white flag of the Prophet was taken down and unfurled in its place were the bright colors of the League. A clamor that ran through the vessels like another fire proclaimed the victory. I was taking part in it, sharing in it, at last I was a part of the tradition of the illustrious Orsinis. I was redeeming myself and I was shouting absurd things. I thought that I would have the statue of Orazio Orsini dressed in his imperial armor carved, and that statue would be my monument too. The last rock left intact at Bomarzo would be reserved for it. We would hold our councils, as the primitive lords did, in the shelter of the intrepid figure. At that instant an imposing Janissary, dripping with blood, came toward Samuel. The battle was lost, but he doubtless calculated that if he killed one more man, that determined foe before him, the paradise of the houris would be his. I raised my sword to help the slave. Orazio saw it and came to our aid. The engulfing armor slowed him down, and the Janissary, caught between two forces, spun around quickly and with an accurate thrust, broke the visor, making Orazio fall to his knees. Blinded, Orazio was slashing about uselessly. When Samuel reacted it was too late. The Turk had raised his scimitar with both hands, like an axe, and had lowered it with all his strength against the helmet. I remember that the Janissary fell in turn, killed by Niccolò; I remember that I dragged myself over to the body of the infidel and stuck my sword into him, twisting it, feeling the flesh part under its edge; I remember that Antonello managed to get Orazio's helmet off and that his handsome face appeared, red with blood, his open eyes like opaque glass; I remember that when I got up, aided by Samuel, I saw adrift, abandoned to the rocking of the waves, a Christian galley with broken oars that bore the insignia of Doria on the mainmast and was swaying with its macabre cargo of motionless bodies like a ghost ship; I remember that my eyes clouded over, my legs grew weak, and I stumbled, moaning, over to the tragic shape of Orazio; I remember the clash of our armor, as the patches that the blacksmith at Bomarzo had put on my shoulder piece because of the hump stood out in the light of the sunset; I remember the taste of the hot blood that wet my mouth.

The end of the enterprise is engulfed in my memory in a grayish cloud. It was as if Orazio, when he died, took away with him all of the color and the glow. The arms and the clothing, the sails and the bunting, the golden prows—everything that until then had contributed to surround us with a miraculous halo—paled as if some subtle cancer had begun to gnaw at the very essence of what had been our splendor. I never knew until that moment that Orazio had meant so much to me. Or perhaps he began to mean so much from that moment on. The death of the hero, of the youthful and glorious incarnation of Garcilaso, appeared before my eyes as the death of something very much mine, of something that was dying inside of me. My hopes for redemption through him, of salvation from the uselessness and injustice of my life through his—because his life, beginning with the crowning glory of Lepanto, in the joy of pure sentiments and the sparkle of calm, virile beauty, could have been the one that I had dreamed of for myself in distant adolescence—my hopes tumbled down and left me alone once more with my own reality and without consolation. I no longer had anyone to lean on to help me along the way. They had died, one by one, those who had risen up in my path, dazzling me with their souls or their bodies and helping me forget myself along the way, or at least to tolerate myself, substituting their images for mine. Love, to my eternal anguish, had not been the discovery of another, but the forgetting of myself. And now, when I was alone with myself, totally unprotected, the first symptom of that evidence was summed up physically in the strange paleness that came over my surroundings, giving me the impression that I was moving about among transparent specters. The luminous warrior had vanished, and in his place there remained his double, the warrior made of shadows. Niccolò, as he reproduced the traits of his cousin, taking the color out of them, even in the trivial matter of his dress, symbolized better than funeral rhetoric the fundamental change of my loss. I had not lost Orazio Orsini; Orazio had lost me at Lepanto. And the feeling of emptiness that came over me and caused a permanent nausea condemned me to look within myself, to see my interior like the depths of a cavern inhabited by fierce and sad monsters. It was a desolating feeling. Until then the hard crust of my egotism, my mistrust had protected me from it, but Orazio's death brought down my bulwarks. I was old; I was tired. The weight of other losses, other deaths, far away or close in time, those of Adriana, Abul, Maerbale, Giulia, Zanobbi were heaped up together on my shoulders. It crushed me and I felt suddenly what I had never felt deeply when those periods had passed, for on each occasion I had looked ahead. There was no longer any way to look. And everything—arms and clothing, sails and bunting, the golden prows, the victorious celebration of life—fell apart into ashes.

The words of Don John, of Marcantonio, of the Duke of Naxos, of Ignacio de Zúñiga were in vain. They could not sense the depth of my depression, because they could not know that with Orazio more than a son had left me, more than one last goad to my always restless emotion which made me tremble with confused anxieties. He had been the last possibility of giving my existence a course and a justification. Besides, they had no time to worry about me. They were busy with too many other concerns.

Many people had died at Lepanto. They say that seven thousand five hundred Christians and twenty-five thousand Turks entered into fame and oblivion at that time. Venice alone saw the death of seventeen captains and twelve lords; Malta sixty knights; the Italian and Spanish dead were more numerous. For the nobility, that is. As for the others, almost all of the sailors and galley slaves of the Order of Malta perished; for example, of the five hundred Spaniards of the regiment of Sicily only fifty returned. But even though the lists stretched out endlessly, as the leaders learned of new losses, the only death for me at Lepanto was that of Orazio Orsini. Another Orsini, Virginio, of the Vicovaro branch, also paid for his audacity, and Niccolò brought me to pay my respects to his remains as the oldest member of the clan. I went as if I were walking in my sleep, with the Duke of Bracciano. We were both limping. Each corpse with its armor as a shroud before which I had to bow—Barbarigo, Quirini, Malipiero, the Marquis of Santo Eremo, Francis of Savoy—became transformed in my eyes into Orazio Orsini. The cuirasses repeated from one bier to the next the muscular shape of Orazio's breastplate, but perhaps because I was looking at them through my tears, perhaps because, as I noted before, everything had turned dull and had taken on a ghostly paleness, instead of the work of goldsmiths there appeared the work of glass blowers. The glass paladins, fragile and breakable, were lying in the half-destroyed ships. And over them floated a mist that hid the sun. It was a damp and tenacious mist, built out of my inconsolable grief which, in the same way, impregnated those of us around the table at a banquet on Gian Andrea Doria's capital ship, the only one intact, as it did those that weighed anchor with Pompeo Colonna to announce the victory to the pope, who already miraculously knew about it; and the one hundred forty captured vessels that we had in tow, bulging with captives and liberated Christians; and the task of getting what artillery could be saved off the flooded ships, under the command of the Marquis of Santa Cruz; and even the rich booty that we divided up in Santa Maura immediately after the battle, and which caused so many complaints, because it was rumored that the lot assigned to each Spanish soldier was larger than that received by the admiral of the Most Serene Republic. Don John received six galleys and seven hundred twenty slaves. The sultan sent him many presents afterward, clothing lined with sable and lynx, marten capes, rugs, two dozen scimitars from Damascus covered with precious stones, six saddles covered with gold, bows and arrows, stirrups... I received, including Orazio's lot, three Turkish slaves. Only two were given to the Marquis of Avila, the Duke of Mondragone, and Diego de Mendoza; but Alessandro Farnese got thirty and Bracciano twenty-five. There were, as I have mentioned, angry protests. No one was satisfied. I simply kept still, even when Niccolò and the Duke of Naxos stirred me up and urged me to complain. A leaden, melancholy fog hung over the landscape and the people and I did not have enough strength left even to speak.

Slowly, dragging behind us on strong chains the evidence of the Ottoman disaster, we returned to Messina. The two sons of Ali Pasha were crying like females. One of them was thirteen years old and Don John would give him to the pope. The ships went forward with difficulty in the midst of the corpses. There were, doubtless, floating all about over the remnants of the shipwrecks, many wounded and dying, but who could stop to pick them up? At the rail of Colonna's capital ship, leaning on Samuel and Antonello, I saw their desperate eyes turned toward us, their hands twisted by atrocious grips. We picked up a few, as if we were casually fishing with harpoons and nets. In Corfu the noblemen drifted away. The Duke of Urbino went back to his lands on the Abruzzi road; also leaving were the Count of Santa Fiora and the Duke of Parma. I learned afterward that in Venice the festivities had been incomparable; that the vessel of Giustiniano, the bearer of the news, had arrived at the docks by Saint Mark's like a great elegant lady, dragging the infidel flags through the water like a multicolored train embroidered with crescent moons and golden stars; and that when the doge tried to reach the church to give thanks to God he was almost unable to make his way with the Signoria in the crush of the shouting crowd.

I was to change ships in Messina and continue on aboard the one that would bear the remains of the knights of Saint Stephen to Pisa, where the tomb of the order was located. I ordered them to take Orazio's shield that was decorated with a scene from the *Triumphs of Love* of Petrarch, for I wanted to keep it in Bomarzo, but I left him his splendid armor. I did it in an automatic way and I listened to my own words as if they were coming from other lips remote in the shadows that darkened the fleet and that only my eyes could see. From time to time, although it was not cold, I would tremble in my bearskin cloak. The songs and laughter of the sailors rose up the masts along with the rhythmic strokes of the oars, as I touched the wrinkles over my thin cheekbones, final old age.

In Messina Samuel's father joined my small entourage. He could have been his grandfather, that old man whose racial characteristics were evident in his traits more clearly than in those of his son and which showed the traditional type of hook-nosed Jew with a skimpy beard, dark inquiring eyes, and veiny hands; the dark garment that flowed about his spare body. His name was Solomon Luna and he came from Tiberias, where he had learned by chance of the misfortune of his offspring after having waited for him in vain. He had left there in search of him, for he loved him above all else. As soon as I met him, in spite of the circumstances that veiled my understanding and kept me apart from everything going on around me, I understood that I had before me a man of exceptional awareness. He spoke little, stroking his beard as if he were milking it. Samuel told me that among the scholars of the Holy Cabala, those initiated in the wisdom of the *Zohar*, of the *Book of Splendor* by Rabbi Simeon ben Yohai, his father was outstanding, along with Elias of Chelm, who with the help of the book *Yetzirah* had put together the Golem, the artificial man, and Isaac Luria, and his disciples Moses Cordovero, Hagiz, Vital, and Joseph Caro, the author of *Shulhan Aruk,* the ritual code of mysterious visions. From Safed, the center of the cabalists, he had moved to Tiberias, attracted by the false Duke of Naxos. He lived there, surrounded by manuscripts, meditating, praying, and waiting for Samuel. When the latter fell into the hands of Orazio after the ship that was carrying him to Palestine was sunk by the knights of Malta, Rabbi Solomon did not stop until he found out what had happened to him, and in spite of the risks that surrounded the voyage through a sea infested with Barbary pirates, he returned to Italy after his son. If his God had disposed that Samuel was to be a slave, he would also be one. He would always follow him, begging, if that was what the Lord demanded. That strange and moving tale left me indifferent at first. I allowed the old man to come on board and accompany us to Pisa and go with us eventually to Bomarzo, but no new worry could distract me from the one that was bearing down on me. During the trip I chatted with him on two occasions. Numbers and letters held no secrets for his magical clairvoyance. Any word, any sign enclosed for him in the hermeticism of its context another word and another sign. It was then that I sensed that perhaps

Solomon Luna would be the only one capable of solving the enigma of the letters from Dastyn to Cardinal Orsini. Samuel, meanwhile, was modeling a small statue of Orazio dressed in his Greco-Roman armor. It was beautiful and simple, quite distinct in its popular simplicity from the sumptuous taste that was an inseparable part of the sculpture of the time. I thought that I would dedicate the last rock of Bomarzo to reproduce the effigy, but then I became convinced that I would not, that the stone had been saved for the image of the Devil, the image that I had seen in the mirror and which could not be missing in my biographical gallery.

God and Devil plagued me together. I kept coming back to them during my unseemly speculations, while the galley slaves drove us along to the docks of Pisa, where Orazio would lie forever under the mantle of the red cross, among his brothers of the Order of Saint Stephen. The apparition of the terrible head in the mirror; the picture of Don John of Austria kneeling on the *Real* like a divine messenger whose saintliness was passed on to those around; the unexpected blessing from Ignacio de Zúñiga as he rose up out of the depths of years and years; and the death of Orazio Orsini, the sum of the great deaths that I had caused, the allegory of my own death and condemnation, were added together in the same way as other indications that exhorted me to prepare myself. The harm that I had caused on the altars of my pride came before my eyes in deep relief, fully, as if a bandage had been taken off my eyes. The medieval man, the old essential Orsini, Christian, loaded down with guilt, was replacing the Renaissance man and his proud pagan indifference. The centuries where my power had been affirmed and which had nourished my haughtiness, recovered for me at last the debt of privilege. In order to be a proper Renaissance man it was necessary to go through the world with no other riches but one's own will. My riches, on the other hand, belonged to those who had gone before me. I tried to rebel against them without having to stop making use of them, which was impossible. The inventor of symbolic monsters in the park of Bomarzo, I did not see that I myself had been changed into a monster, as I tried to bring forth the astute synthesis of contradictions. And now life was escaping from my lips and I did not have the time necessary to redeem myself and arrive at my authentic expression. Nor did I myself know in that crucial instant what it was, what it meant, as I was being pulled by opposing forces. When they promised me that my life would be eternal, I had trembled with mad arrogance, as if they were offering me an incomparable instrument for my passion for victory, for imposing my mediocre extravagance, tyrannical and absurd, and which did not retreat before the blood of others, because my poor shape was nourished on blood in order to forget its poor construction, and because my soul was just as mean as my body and had become infected by my body, had become twisted like it; and at that moment of decomposition, already inhaling the miasma of death, I understood that if there was reason to prolong my passage through the world and sink into the shadows of an endless future it was because it was required by the penance for my sins. Duke Orsini was not supposed to do things halfway. Everything that concerned him—and when I reflected in that way I did not notice how intact the curse of my pride still was—demanded extreme, unique solutions. I was wandering with hallucinations, ill. I was acting, surrounded by sinners, sniffing the murky air of sin that impregnated my epoch, as if I were the only guilty one, the one chosen to pay for all guilt. The complexes that I thought I had destroyed were overwhelming me in my loneliness. Basic fear was sinking its nails into me and I saw my exact symbol in the incessant beating of the waves against the swaying vessel. I ran my fingers over the beads of Don John's rosary and I prayed to the saints of my line, to the Boveschi popes. My future and my eternal health suddenly depended on two Jews: Solomon Luna would have to give me the formula of immortality, and Samuel Luna would have to build for me, hollowing out the rock, the hermitage that would evoke the horror of Hell and serve me as a refuge. I would give the castle to Marzio, to the Baron of Paganica, to Vitelli, to him who wanted it, and I would shut myself up, erased from everybody's memory, in sackcloth and with a rosary, in that earthly Hell to win back, hour by hour and day by day, my lost grace. Romantically, with princely exaggeration, I planned my esthetic future in that way as I returned to Bomarzo over the roads through gentle Tuscany. Of all the fears that attacked me, the most intense was that of loneliness. And now I felt irremediably alone, among ghosts. I even assured Solomon that if he could decipher the letters from Dastyn, I would give his son his freedom back. The rabbi replied that neither he nor any other cabalist gave credence to the legend of immortal man on earth, that those things were—and he smiled slightly in the tremor of his goatlike beard—for Theophrastus Paracelsus, but that, in any case, he would study the texts and try to interpret them.

Cleria Clementini had taken advantage of my absence to establish herself in the rule of Bomarzo. The command that she exercised over my vassals, based on constant donations, was not at all similar to what Giulia Farnese had gained with her goodness. It was superficial; it worked on convention and advantages. The ridiculous situation of the lady of the castle bordered on the intolerable. Fatter, heavier, covered with more jewels, constantly changing her adornment and dress, she was taking on the airs of a queen. Not even the condescending abnegation of Cecilia Colonna could go on tolerating it. The blind princess had finally shut herself up in her rooms, remaining in that way an important element for the small court invented by my wife. In order to show off her fruitless pomp, Cleria could only count on the Duke of Mugnano, who was extraordinarily amused by the theater, Porzia, Sigismondo, Pantasilea, Fabio, and some occasional visitor as witnesses. From time to time, Cardinal Madruzzo, who would die five years later, would get out of his coach at the gate and elevate with his presence the level of the modest gatherings, in which mimes and minstrels from Mugnano played the main role. Cleria had imposed her Clementini presumptions to the point of fatigue. Pope Saint Clement and the condottieri from Rimini were always on her lips. In the main room, alongside the Sandro Benedetto horoscope painted by Andrea Sartorio, she had had placed the shield of the gold chevron and the three silver stars, with a horned lion in the crest, and I did not have the spirit to tell them to remove it. She could go to the devil. She doubtlessly misinterpreted my attitude, thinking that I was giving in, that I approved, that I was also playing the laughable game, because, having feared at first that I would take down the intruding arms, she was now all puffed up with satisfaction. But my indifference, which was not the result of disdain, but rather of my new distant position toward everything, shocked her more in the end than my past ironies and prohibitions. She had calculated that when I returned to Bomarzo, there would be a radical change in the rhythm of life. She imagined that, with her wealth and my position, Bomarzo would be changed—as soon as the period of mourning for the first-born Orazio was over—into the great mundane center that she had always dreamed of. She had put together guest lists, aided by my cousin the duke and those around him, and my declaration that I was planning to spend the rest of my life in retreat upset her at first and then it offended and deeply irritated her. Incapable of grasping the spiritual crisis through which I was passing, repeating to herself in order to remain calm and to quiet the nasty comments from Fabio, she thought it was only due to the grief brought on by the death of my dear son, and that time would soon heal the wounds. She would scratch her forehead and when she was convinced that I was inexorably serious in my plans, a boiling fury replaced her first enthusiasm. What? Was the duke returning from the Gulf of Lepanto, anointed by glory, and thinking of disappearing, of turning off the lights of the palace festival? Did not the duke know that everywhere they were celebrating the heroes of the great undertaking; that the triumph of Marcantonio Colonna, when he entered Rome covered with gold brocade, dragging along five hundred Turk slaves with ropes around their necks, had outdone Scipio's and that the banquet in his honor had been served in the Capitol? He was aware of it. He knew of the wagons loaded with arms, with spoils from the sultan's ships; he knew about the reception given by Pius V in the basilica of Saint Peter's, where awaiting the conqueror were twenty-four cardinals and part of the nobility, shining like rubies; he knew about the silver column—the column of the Colonnas—that the general had given to the church of Aracoeli, where the head of the Colonnas and the head of the Orsinis had purified themselves two centuries before in a bath strewn with rose petals. And so why had I not gone to Rome to take part in the memorable parade? Why had I not brought her there as the parades passed through the imperial forum and deep voices rose up in the *Te Deum* over the lances and the banners to enjoy the fame that they deserved? Had not the Duke of Bomarzo and his nephew Niccolò

Orsini taken part in the most famous naval operation that history remembers, more famous than Actium? Would my only reward after a tiring campaign in which I had lost my son be the hanging of Orazio's shield among the trophies of my house and, like a foreman of masons, directing a group of infidel slaves as they worked on rocks in the park?

She was angrily spying on my activities with the two Jews among the monsters of the Sacred Wood. When I would shut myself up with Solomon Luna in Silvio da Narni's study, which Samuel and Antonello had cleared of useless objects, Cleria would talk about it with Porzia. A strange relationship had grown up between the two of them. Giambattista's twin, the former harlot of Bologna, was enjoying herself in that friendship as she would with a new perfume. Accustomed, in spite of her beauty, to be held in low esteem if she left the protection of the walls of Mugnano, and made to feel the irregularity of her situation from small, cruel insinuations, she was pleased by Cleria's affectionate courtesy, not noticing that the latter was in great need of making allies, and not being aware that the best path for Cleria to follow in order to gain the good will of my cousin was to flatter his mistress. Porzia also suffered disappointment from the results of my conduct. As she was awaiting my return along with Cleria, she was sharing her ambitions. She told herself that things would change for her when I returned to Bomarzo; that bolstered by the immunity that was assured her by her strange link to the mistress of the place, she would play an important role in the new life of the castle; and now, along with Cleria's hopes, her confidence was suddenly breaking down. What did it mean to them, the two of them, with their multicolored jewels, rich dresses, the disagreeable nocturnal operations that they followed to preserve the freshness of their skin, things like wrapping their faces in tight bandages that held slices of raw veal soaked in milk? What did it mean also to Pantasilea, who added her own frustrated appetite as a fiery member of the Orsini family to that of the duchess and that of the Duke of Mugnano's wanton, married to a poor one-eyed country gentleman whose only wealth was a necklace of pearls and lapis lazuli, the gift of a vice-ridden prince, as she aspired to replace the weakness of home finances with the compensation of elegant flattery? The three women conspired, surrounded by the noise of Mugnano's jesters and acrobats, who went through their overworked tricks. They would appear in the loggia of the Gigantomachia and watch me from a distance as I limped along, leaning on my cane and Antonello's shoulder, from the rabbi's laboratory to where Samuel Luna was working.

The work was coming along with difficulty. The Jew had drawn, following my instructions, the design of a great head with a flat nose, round eyes, arched eyebrows, and a great open mouth, a reproduction of the features that had frightened me in my mirror. The most difficult part of the task, left to the Turkish slaves, was to transfer the sketch onto the stone and to hollow out the interior like that of a cave in order to convert the great rock into the eventual abode of the hermit. From dawn, as when I had carried out the other works, the park resounded with the hammering of the sharp instruments, and the villagers, who did not contribute to the work this time, exchanged surprised looks when they saw the nightmare of the infernal head rising up among the wonders of the Wood. I ceaselessly encouraged the workers so that they would speed up their labor, promising them better rewards, and I did the same with Rabbi Solomon, who, shut up night and day in the laboratory, was taking apart, word by word, the writings of Dastyn according to a method completely different from that of Fulvio and Silvio—whose lack of experience in arcane matters I was now aware of—and he was looking into each word that he took apart, as if it were a machine, for the reluctant thread of the message. Opposite his skeptical doubts about the usefulness of what he would find, my certainty was growing that there, in those kneaded parchments, the secret of immortality was hidden. Trembling with impatience, I had no time to give to my own intimate anguish—it would have, later on, measureless time to torment and calm me alternately in a kind of utopian masochism—nor to the bizarre group at the castle, who, in their urge to find out unknown details of the battle of Lepanto that they could exploit in improbable future conversations, had to rely on the facts supplied by the circumspect Niccolò. On occasional afternoons I would pause in the main room, attracted by the voices of Violante, Madruzzo, and the poet Betussi, and listen to them arguing over the results of the naval encounter. As always, those who had not taken part in the campaign rose up as its critics, complaining that we should have taken advantage of the victory to take over the Peloponnesus, the neighboring islands, perhaps Constantinople. When Niccolò argued that we had been low in rations, they answered that we could have had them sent from Sicily and from the Ottoman warehouses in Patras; when he said that we lacked galley slaves, they showed that there were more than enough on enemy galleys; when he said that the number of our dead was very high, they objected by saying that there were many more survivors. They had answers for everything, those quiet stay-at-homes, especially the Duke of Mugnano and Sigismondo, who could not console themselves for not having taken part in the great event. Comfortable in my chair, I would listen to them distantly, as if they were the captains of the League and Niccolò and I their submissive audience. My eyes would turn to the small statue of Orazio Orsini placed on one of the tables among the figures surrounded by pearls given me by Pope Clement VII on the day of my first marriage. More than ever then the urge to get away once and for all, to bottle myself up in the analysis of my anguish, unwinding the confused braid of my life, shook me. And while Cleria, Violante, Pantasilea, and Porzia made a border for Madruzzo's purple with the flashy shine of their clothes, and Sigismondo, before the marble of the fireplace, was striking warlike poses, his nervous hand on the dagger in his belt, I would withdraw, taciturn and heavy like the bears on my shield, hoping that my silence would be enough to counteract their haughty allusions to the lack of consideration that was shown by the Duke of Bomarzo by not approving the commemorative festival that had been planned for our return.

Her links to the Chigi bankers had taught Cleria since childhood to pretend and temporize in order to get what she wanted; and even though, when faced with my resolution to abstain from collaborating in her greedy plans for rising in the world, she had governed herself with relative wisdom, keeping behind herself the opportunity to knock down my defenses with her tenacity, the moment arrived with her obvious impotence obliged her to play the card that Porzia had given her. I must confess that it upset me at first and that I almost fell before her extortion. She informed me one morning that she wanted to talk to me, sending a page to the terrace of the Sacred Wood from which I was watching the progress on the Mouth of Hell that Samuel was carving with strong blows from his hammer, aided by the Turks.

When she began her conversation, Cleria told me that Porzia had learned, through a letter from Silvio da Narni, who, tortured by remorse, had sent it to her a short time before his strange death, about my part in the death of Maerbale. The queer thing was that Cleria did not criticize my procedure; she used my crime to make me the victim of a piece of blackmail whose motives were so frivolous that the lack of proportion was absurd. Instead of terrifying me with the fratricide, she and Porzia were using their guilty secret in exchange for my opening wide the gates of Bomarzo to their prospects of a superficial brilliance. I must say that I hesitated at first. After all, what they demanded of me was foolish, almost childish, but I could see that without being aware of it, Cleria was working like an instrument of Providence and was giving me a chance to take another step along the road to salvation. I did not deny the authenticity of what Silvio had confessed, supporting, therefore, his revelation, and I told her that she could use the letter as she saw fit. The surprise, which she had not counted on, left her pensive. I added that I would soon disappear and that Bomarzo would be hers and that the duchess would be in a position, with more than enough means, to give the castle the fate that she thought best. That—my disappearance—was precisely what she most feared. Without me Bomarzo would lose its principal attraction, for I was the real Orsini, the creator of the original monsters that were spoken about in all of the courts, a hero of Lepanto too, and on the other side, Cleria did not get along well with my children and their balky spouses, and she had no doubt that my successor would suppress whatever attempt she might have made to have her influence felt. She begged, she undermined, she insinuated. It was in vain. It would have cost me nothing, really, to accede to her grotesque entreaties and supply her greedy vanity with the food that it had been hungering for ever since Madruzzo had blessed our unequal union, but Cleria was not aware that with her act of intimidation she had pointed out the precise direction of the possibilities of my liberation. I left her overwhelmed by shame and wrath, mumbling menaces, and when I went to the laboratory where the rabbi was meditating over the horoscope and Sandro Benedetto's prediction, I breathed in the air of relief for the first time in years.

My relationship to Niccolò Orsini had never been very close. When he was a child I saw in Maerbale's heir a prolongation of his inseparable Orazio, and when he was an adolescent that impression was still the same, but the mistrust caused by his friendship, which framed the distance between generations and emphasized the bonds that should have joined me to my first-born child could never have been so strong as those that linked him to his companion at arms, prevented me from getting close to the son of Maerbale and Cecilia. The death of Orazio sank Niccolò into a stupor that took a long time for him to shake off. An invariable companion in love and war, accustomed to a permanent dialogue in which common urges accentuated their solidarity, he was going about now as if he had suffered an amputation. He would hang about me like a sad dog, and he became accustomed to accompany me, barely exchanging a word, when I would visit Solomon Luna and when I inspected the work that Samuel was directing. Sometimes he would ask me about the people in the family portraits and about the meaning of the sculptures in the Wood. In spite of his resemblance to Orazio, which made of him an exaltation of my own image, beautified and perfected, I never managed to love him. Perhaps I could not pardon him, refusing to confess it to myself, for his having been the survivor and Orazio the victim. But the way in which I excluded him from my affection (telling myself, perhaps to calm myself, that I was doing it because the course that I was driven to follow denied me the grace of new affection) did not succeed in dominating my attention to such a degree that I did not notice a difference in Niccolò. That change in his attitude toward me, so subtle that only my alert antennae could have perceived it, came about months after our return to Bomarzo and it was not translated into any obvious reaction but into something indefinable that floated in the atmosphere that surrounded him. Furthermore, the preoccupation with speeding up my two complementary projects prevented me from assuming new worries.

The clarification of the alchemist Dastyn's enigma and the completion of the work on the Mouth of Hell came about almost simultaneously. Like his predecessor, Rabbi Luna lighted the old ovens and covered his face with the crystal mask in order to manipulate the secret materials, until, using the formula that was hidden in the letters sent to Cardinal Napoleone Orsini, he produced the desired brew that would seek my presumptive immortality. That happened on the first of May of 1572, the date of the death of Saint Pius V.

Those who have had the patience to read these pages from their distant beginning will understand the emotion that came over me when the Jew told me that his efforts had been rewarded. My whole life, ever since the moment when Sandro Benedetto told my disbelieving father about my prodigious destiny, had been governed by the mystery of that announcement. Like a magic lamp of blinding light the promise had hung over my head wherever I was. It was something so much mine that the light seemed to rise up from inside of me. Nor during moments of greatest delirium, when the whirlwind of passion dragged me along like a fragment did I doubt the truth of the prophecy that had served me as an impulse. Now at last I understood its reason, which I had not penetrated in my young years, as I imagined that the extraordinary privilege that isolated me from my fellow men had as its single goal the eternal consecration of my pride as the offspring of an Olympian race and my triumph over the deformed flesh that fate had assigned to me, for the imminence of an infinite life had been produced with my learning that I would have to use it for purging my sins. The cruel deaths, the selfish dark loves, the subjection of everything that surrounded me to my will of a deformed Narcissus, the diabolical dealings, and, especially, the proud dismissal of God, whom I removed (as if that were possible) from my existence, having recourse to Him only on the few occasions on which I imagined that I was imposing as between equals my status as a Guelph prince, conceited because of his alliance with innumerable saints, required an important payment. Even then—I insist that even then—the perfidious arrogance which I could not get rid of, not even during the supreme hour in which I thought I had found the path of divine pardon, stuck its claws into my chest, for I did not notice, or did not wish to notice, that on proclaiming that the magnitude of my sins corresponded to the magnitude of the prerogative of expiatory immortality, I was acting as if I myself were God, endowing myself with a unique right. The proof of it was in the three inscriptions that I had them chisel at the time on the terrace that looks toward the east, where with Silvio I had invoked the demons a short time before the death of my father at the siege of Florence, the night on which we heard the ominous cries of the invisible peacock in the park and when the Etruscan armor had fallen down. Samuel himself carved over the words "SIC ERIS FELIX" the admonitions "NOSCE TE IPSUM; VINCE TE IPSUM; VIVE TIBI IPSUM—in this way wilt thou be happy: know thyself; conquer thyself; live for thyself." I, myself, always myself, knowing myself, conquering myself, and living for myself, and I would attain happiness.

During the few days that separated the discovery of the alchemist's key by the scholar from Safed and the culmination of the sculpture of the Orcus, an episode occurred which under other circumstances would have made me despair, but which at a time when I was making ready to renounce everything that belonged to me, only worked as a stimulant for my avidity to detach myself from the world. There was a terrible fire in Bomarzo. In front of the nympheum, taking advantage of the shadows, someone had piled up some of the most valued treasures that I kept there: astrolabes, clocks, crystal spheres, reliquaries, mirrors, automatons, enamelwork, books and manuscripts, and had set fire to them. He added several items that he found in the study of Silvio da Narni to the fire, the annotated texts that I remembered, the *Tabula Smaragdina*, the Quadripartite of Ptolemy, the painting of the Egyptian Agathodaemon with its zodiacal diadem of twelve rays, the broken alembics, the mixing pots, the *kerotakis*. It all burned, along with the triumphal coach that had been used at my wedding to Giulia Farnese and at that of Sigismondo and Pantasilea, and which had been left on the decorative terrace. They also burned the letters from Dastyn to Cardinal Napoleone Orsini. But it was too late. The formula had been found and was in my power, with the glass that contained the smoky liquid.

The nearby villagers and the servants of my neighbor Sigismondo ran to fight the flames in a useless effort. The white-hot tongues were growing about the golden bear on the coach, and it was as if my past were burning on the pyre that brought to mind the autos-da-fé that the Preachers of Repentance, the followers of Savonarola, had repeated in Tuscan cities to the sound of trumpets as they burned portraits of harlots, books of pagan poetry, carnival costumes, combs, harps, lutes, perfumes, which Venetian merchants tried in vain to ransom, offering many gold florins for those objects. The pieces in my collection that were lost were worth considerably more, worthy of that of the holy emperors, but the despoilment did not upset me. In the red, green, and yellow light of the fire as it twisted about with acrid odors and quick outbursts, showing me in carbon forms the strange figures that had made difficult trips to reach my hands, sometimes from the frontiers of barbarian lands, I noticed on the upper level, dominated by Giulia's distant chapel and where there rose up in their strange way the elephant with Abul and Beppo, the colossal Neptune who represented my immortality, the opulent woman who symbolized Nencia, and the fight between the dragon and the dogs which alluded to my war experiences in Metz and Picardy, the enormous mask of Hell, with the inscription inspired by Dante about the open mouth: "*Lasciate ogni speranza, voi ch'entrate.*" That was my hermitage, my cell, my ultimate truth. I told my son Marzio that it was his duty to investigate the attack, because very shortly, perhaps in two or three days, Bomarzo would be his. Although he was aware of my intentions to retire, which everyone knew about, the news surprised him. The fire had deprived him of magnificent possessions, but I sensed his shock, his shudder of pleasure. Cleria, who was to the side and in back, and who even on that occasion had not abandoned the stiffness of etiquette, had heard me. Her eyes were shining in the darkness. Accompanied by Sigismondo, Niccolò, the rabbi, his son Samuel, and Antonello, I climbed slowly up the hill to the castle.

Before climbing up the nine steps to the entrance to the Mouth of Hell, which, according to what I thought, would exile me forever from Bomarzo, in the very heart of Bomarzo, in the Polimartium, I decided to make a general confession. That was handled by the oldest of the Franciscan monks who took care of Giulia's chapel, who listened to me with alternating expressions of Christian horror and those of worldly indulgence for the aberrations of the grandson of Cardinal Franciotto, his protector. I would have preferred having received absolution from Ignacio de Zúñiga, but the Jesuit hidalgo was far away and we would never see each other again. I received communion afterward in the church, kneeling before the skeleton adorned with gray flowers that I had placed there in a glass casket, and which I decided not to remove from its place so as not to provoke a scandal among the people, for it enjoyed widespread admiration in the region, and peasant women would pray to it, especially on the eve of giving birth. I was also on the eve of a birth, so that more than once, as the mass went on, I would raise my eyes toward the mysterious toothless figure. Looking at it, I remembered my father, the sadness of his cruelty. For the ceremony, in order to give it maximum importance, I had put on the ducal clothes that they had dressed me in for the festivities when the pope anointed Charles V, the old-fashioned red cloak with a fur collar, which hid my hump, and the half crown. Neither Cleria nor Pantasilea nor Porzia was present at the service; nor was Cecilia, who was keeping to her sickbed. Between Sigismondo and Marzio, with my remaining children and their spouses and Niccolò Orsini behind, I fingered the beads of Don John of Austria's rosary. After the benediction I took leave of all of them. They kissed my cheek and Sigismondo embraced me tenderly. I stayed alone in my room until dusk, meditating. My children were doubtless calculating that my intentions of an anchorite would not last very long, that I would soon return to the castle with demands and the lawsuits would begin. Gathered in the loggia of Zanobbi's Gigantomachia, they were arguing, lowering their voices until they were nothing but vehement whispers above which there arose the treble tone of the Baron of Paganica. I knew that there would be no lawsuits on my part, that the die had been cast conclusively and that if my resolution brought on differences and litigation, they would be produced, because of my abstention, among my heirs. The buzzing increased, as if the castle had been transformed into some gigantic beehive and the drones were quarreling over the disputed honey that was being watched over by a queen bee who could not be bribed, Cleria Clementini. I smiled, in spite of my wishes for contrition.

When night fell I opened the door. Waiting for me, in accordance with my instructions, were Rabbi Solomon, Niccolò—whom I included in memory of Orazio—and Antonello. The rabbi took the goblet and gave it to Niccolò, who represented my line for the occasion, and we went down to the Sacred Wood. I could imagine curious heads in the twinkling windows of the castle. Cleria's window was dark. Since the cloak was uncomfortable, and I would soon change it for sackcloth, taking off the crown too then, Antonello held the end of its scarlet velvet like a train bearer. To the very end the innate baroque taste for solemn ritual accompanied me. The fantastic hermitage itself that I had chosen shared those characteristics. Everything of mine had to be exceptional.

Several torches that Sigismondo had had lighted in the perfumed May night illuminated the park. Moving in their light, like vague, slow dancers out of dreams were the Roman statues that I had distributed among the roses and laurels of my grandmother's garden. We advanced through the sound of the fountains. When I turned to look at my small retinue, I saw the crystal goblet shining in Niccolò's hands, the silver star that hung down from the neck of the Jew, Antonello's white teeth, the tremulous jets from the fountains, the smoky torches that hid the cypresses, and, behind, up high, the yellow windows of the fortress of Bomarzo.

"Night is more beautiful than day," Niccolò said.

"At night," Solomon Luna answered, "we are closer to God."

The familiar chorus of the frogs and owls was going through its lyrical responses. The architecture of the terrace of the nympheum, where incendiary traces still remained, the shape of the obelisks and the small slanting house that I had dedicated to Cardinal Madruzzo stood out in the light of the stars. We reached the upper level along one of those graceful stairways that left behind that nympheum that had sheltered so many extravagant illusions. The rosary wrapped around my wrist added a weak jingle to the murmurs as it struck against the banisters, and I had the impression that I was dragging along a chain, the soft sound of which, as it measured my ascent, was the same as that of manacles, for I too, like the galley slaves at Lepanto, was a captive. Up above, the monsters were awaiting us. We made a fabulous picture, an illustration from one of those magical books entitled *Musaeum Hermeticum* or *Amphitheatrum Aeternae Sapientiae*: the hunchbacked king; his Negro page with the feathers shaking on his turban; the old bearded Hebrew with his funereal robe, his metal star; the prince with shining hair and violet jerkin, his thin legs clad in tights, who was bearing a chalice as if it were a present for another king; the stone elephant, the infernal head lying in wait to devour me. And if one keeps in mind what the goblet contained, he must conclude that the simile is not exaggerated.

A thin voice joined in the gabble of the batrachians as they seemed to be conscientiously counting coins. I recognized it at once: it was that of a grandson of Fulvio Orsini's mother, a shepherd child who was playing the harp. In the quiet of the night his song rose up, hesitant, and the notes of the instrument were cut out one by one. I felt then that a nostalgia was taking possession of me and tearing me apart: a nostalgia for my youth, for my remote adolescence, a nostalgia for the simple life that I had lost, something similar to the melancholy, incomprehensible for many, of Sigismondo on the day when he told me that never, never again would he dance beautiful courtly steps or make great bows as when he was young to the rhythm of the music in the salons that were aflame with the virginal ardor of those who had no past and who held their hands out to one another, scarcely touching the tips of their fingers and enjoying that unimportant moment until they could no longer bear its sweetness, and then they would close their eyes and go on with the cadence of the dance. The notes of the harp vibrated and awakened ancient echoes. The countryside knew that tone quite well, for it was that of Etruscan harps. I sighed, I took the chalice that Niccolò offered me and I went up the steps to the Orcus. I did not turn my head to say good-bye. I was praying mechanically, slipping over the beads of the rosary without thinking about what I was doing, perhaps without thinking about anything—*lasciate ogni speranza*— about anything except the voice of that shepherd boy whom I had scarcely ever seen who was playing the harp and singing like an Etruscan shepherd.

The colossal head was a broad, expanded reproduction of the one that had appeared to me in the mirror, so I clenched my fists when I went inside, but I did not feel any anguish, but rather an incomparable feeling of well-being. A psychoanalyst would probably have explained that it was due to the fact that in the half-shadows I found myself again in the happiness of the maternal cloister, the refuge of that mother whom I could not remember, or perhaps the protection of my grandmother's lap, that of the marvelous Diana Orsini. A bronze door closed the mouth of the great mask and I shut it. Sketched before me like an allegorical painting by Botticelli was the scene from the *Orlando furioso* in which Astolfo closes up the entrance to Hell with pepper trees and amomum plants so that the harpies cannot escape from their prison before he is received in Paradise by Saint John. The difference was that I would be staying inside with the harpies.

A stone bench set against the wall ran about the room, around the table in the center that looked like a catafalque. They are still there. Antonello had improvised a bed for me on the side and had put a pitcher of water and some food next to it. A single candle was flickering on the table and I set the goblet down beside it. I took off the cloak and the crown and I sat down on the bench. The wavering of the flame moved the shape of my hump about on the nakedness of the rough walls. Placed in the middle of the cave, as if I were in the throat of the Devil, I opened the door and from my enclosure I contemplated the moonlit night. Standing out in the cavity of the mouth underneath the two great stalactite fangs were the shadows of the woods and through the hollows of the eyes the sky of old silver was shining. Bomarzo was letting go of me, and I loved it so much, as it stressed its painful beauty.

Antonello had followed my orders. He had put several devotional books within my reach. I picked them up, distracted, and I saw that he had added Miguel de Cervantes's *Garcilaso*. But I did not want to read or reflect yet. I was approaching the climax of my weary existence, the one toward which I had been sent, willingly or unconsciously, by all of my discordant aspirations. The chalice was tall and thick, and it had been fashioned like an immense piece of jewelry. The milky liquid that filled it to the brim was moving and trembling, stirred by secret forces that brought out a slight bubbling, and it seemed to be giving off an opal light, as if another lamp were illuminating the rock of my enclosure. I raised the chalice slowly, as is done in rituals of consecration, and I drank it. A long shudder shook me. I lay down on the cot, and the hermitage was being lighted by aquatic colors, frothy greens, vacillating indigos and cobalts. Uncertain figures—those of Maerbale, Girolamo, my father, my grandmother, Giulia, Orazio, Zanobbi, Sigismondo, Abul, Pantasilea, Silvio da Narni, Adriana, Beppo, Pier Luigi Farnese, Lorenzino de' Medici, Cecilia Colonna, Cleria Clementini, Giambattista Martelli—were being sketched in a hesitating way on the wall that was shining like a Venetian mosaic.

"My God!" I murmured. "My God!"

I still had enough lucidity to observe the shape of the silhouette of Don John of Austria at his misty prow, and that of Charles V with the broken sword in his right hand, and everything grew hazy. The sharp tingle of yearnings and the shepherd's harp crept up into the buzzing of my ears. Time no longer existed. Other images, strange and terrible, began to climb up out of their secrets. But time did not exist. From very far away came some desperate shouts. Cecilia Colonna had appeared at the window of her room in the castle and, her blind eyes knifing through the darkness, she was repeating my name: "Vicino, Vicino, Pier Francesco...Vicino!"

Then I understood that I was going to die; I understood that I was not going to live forever, but that I would die right there; I understood that Cleria, out of spite, had told Niccolò about the essential role that I had played in the death of his father, and that the boy, as we were going to the Orcus, had mixed poison into the same chalice into which Solomon Luna had poured the potion that was to seek for me the eternity announced by Benedetto. My end would be so paradoxical, so worthy of the contradiction of my life, so perfect, so proper, in its exact structure, for the fascination of the poet that I had dreamed of being, that in spite of my horror, I smiled. I stood up with difficulty.

"My God!" I murmured again. "My God!"

I went over to the table that was like a catafalque and fell face down on its surface. Vibrating about was the phrase that my father had written under my horoscope with his insolent and aristocratic hand: "Monsters never die." Yes, they do die; monsters die too; we all die; immortality—my grandfather the cardinal had told me on his death-bed—is the will of God; the only one; one day the monsters of stone that my pride had erected would die.

Centuries later I enjoyed the inscrutable privilege—and by it Sandro Benedetto's promise was subtly fulfilled, because one who remembers is not dead—of bringing back the distant life of Vicino Orsini in my memory when a short time ago, three years ago, I went to Bomarzo in the company of a poet and a painter, and the bewilderment brought the images and emotions that had been lost trooping back. In a vast and noisy city in the other hemisphere, a city that could not be more different from the village of Bomarzo, so different that I could be on another planet, I rescued my story as I unraveled its rough and ancient braid, and I brought back, day by day, detail by detail, my past life, the life that was still alive in me. In that way came the realization of what had been augured for me in Venice, through the intervention of Pier Luigi Farnese, by a visionary nun from Murano, to whom I owe the prophecy that none of us understood at the time and which we attributed to her mystical madness: "Within more time than human kind can measure, the duke shall look at himself..." The duke died; Duke Pier Francesco Orsini, who would later be startled as he looked at himself, died from poison, unoriginally, like any other Renaissance prince, at the precise moment in which he thought that he was going to be a complete medieval ascetic prince, the emulation of the great saints of his family. But even there, in that tragic irony of being poisoned by the potion that was to assure his perpetual existence, the Duke of Bomarzo was different from the numerous dukes of his time who had been poisoned, just as his famous park was different from all others, for everything related to him was different from the rest. He died that May night of 1572 in which I, lying on the table in the Mouth of Hell, could feel the coldness of the stone against my face.

A more intense cold began to invade my legs and waist and freeze my heart, and the only thing that I could feel, for I could barely move, was my hands, the long fingers in the portrait by Lorenzo Lotto. I stretched out, moaning. I wanted to kiss Don John's rosary, the rosary blessed by Saint Pius V, which hung from my stiff wrist, and my lips were motionless halfway there, between the string of black beads and Benvenuto Cellini's ring, the one made of pure steel, the last thing, in my clenched fist, that my eyes saw before implacable night blinded them and dragged me off, poor Bomarzo monster, poor little monster, anxious for love and glory, poor sad man, toward the woods of real monsters and toward the last, invincible, and pacifying light.

# OTHER NEW YORK REVIEW CLASSICS

*For a complete list of titles, visit www.nyrb.com.*

**DANTE ALIGHIERI** Purgatorio; translated by D. M. Black
**OĞUZ ATAY** Waiting for the Fear
**HONORÉ DE BALZAC** The Lily in the Valley
**ROSALIND BELBEN** The Limit
**ANDRÉ BRETON** Nadja
**DINO BUZZATI** The Betwitched Bourgeois: Fifty Stories
**CRISTINA CAMPO** The Unforgivable and Other Writings
**CAMILO JOSÉ CELA** The Hive
**AMIT CHAUDHURI** A Strange and Sublime Address
**LUCILLE CLIFTON** Generations: A Memoir
**COLETTE** Chéri *and* The End of Chéri
**E. E. CUMMINGS** The Enormous Room
**ANTONIO DI BENEDETTO** The Suicides
**JEAN ECHENOZ** Command Performance
**FERIT EDGÜ** The Wounded Age *and* Eastern Tales
**MICHAEL EDWARDS** The Bible and Poetry
**GUSTAVE FLAUBERT** The Letters of Gustave Flaubert
**BENITO PÉREZ GÁLDOS** Miaow
**MAVIS GALLANT** The Uncollected Stories of Mavis Gallant
**JEAN GIONO** The Open Road
**ELIZABETH HARDWICK** The Uncollected Essays of Elizabeth Hardwick
**HENRY JAMES** On Writers and Writing
**PAUL LAFARGUE** The Right to Be Lazy
**JEAN-PATRICK MANCHETTE** The N'Gustro Affair
**THOMAS MANN** Reflections of a Nonpolitical Man
**JOHN McGAHERN** The Pornographer
**EUGENIO MONTALE** Butterfly of Dinard
**AUGUSTO MONTERROSO** The Rest is Silence
**ELSA MORANTE** Lies and Sorcery
**PIER PAOLO PASOLINI** Theorem
**DOUGLAS J. PENICK** The Oceans of Cruelty: Twenty-Five Tales of a Corpse-Spirit, a Retelling
**HENRIK PONTOPPIDAN** A Fortunate Man
**RAYMOND QUENEAU** The Skin of Dreams
**RUMI** Water; translated by Haleh Liza Gafori
**JOAN SALES** Winds of the Night
**JONATHAN SCHELL** The Village of Ben Suc
**ELIZABETH SEWELL** The Orphic Voice
**ANTON SHAMMAS** Arabesques
**WILLIAM GARDNER SMITH** The Stone Face
**VLADIMIR SOROKIN** Blue Lard
**GEORGE R. STEWART** Fire
**GEORGE R. STEWART** Storm
**MAGDA SZABÓ** The Fawn
**SUSAN TAUBES** Lament for Julia
**YŪKO TSUSHIMA** Woman Running in the Mountains
**LISA TUTTLE** My Death
**KONSTANTIN VAGINOV** Goat Song
**PAUL VALÉRY** Monsieur Teste
**MARKUS WERNER** The Frog in the Throat
**XI XI** Mourning a Breast